LEGENDS OF THE WAAAGH!

AN ORK OMNIBUS

Other great Warhammer 40,000 fiction featuring the orks

BRUTAL KUNNIN
by Mike Brooks

DA BIG DAKKA
by Mike Brooks

WARBOSS
by Mike Brooks

GHAZGHKULL THRAKA: PROPHET OF THE WAAAGH!
by Nate Crowley

GHAZGHKULL THRAKA: WARLORD OF WARLORDS
by Denny Flowers

GROTSNIK: DA MAD DOK
by Denny Flowers

DA RED GOBBO COLLECTION
A collection featuring the novellas *Da Gobbo's Revenge, Da Gobbo's Demise* and *Da Gobbo Rides Again* plus two short stories
by various authors

THE GREEN TIDE
An omnibus featuring the novels *Warboss* and *Catachan Devil,* the novellas *Iron Resolve* and *Prisoners of Waaagh!* plus four short stories by various authors

THE BEAST ARISES: VOLUME 1
An omnibus edition of the novels *I Am Slaughter, Predator, Prey, The Emperor Expects* and *The Last Wall*
by various authors

THE BEAST ARISES: VOLUME 2
An omnibus edition of the novels *Throneworld, Echoes of the Long War, The Hunt for Vulkan* and *The Beast Must Die*
by various authors

THE BEAST ARISES: VOLUME 3
An omnibus edition of the novels *Watchers in Death, The Last Son of Dorn, Shadow of Ullanor* and *The Beheading*
by various authors

LEGENDS OF THE WAAAGH!

AN ORK OMNIBUS

DAN ABNETT | SANDY MITCHELL
AARON DEMBSKI-BOWDEN

BLACK LIBRARY

A BLACK LIBRARY PUBLICATION

'Ork Hunter' first published in 2002.
Caves of Ice first published in 2004.
'One Hate' first published digitally in *Heroes of the Space Marines* in 2009.
Helsreach first published in 2010.
I am Slaughter first published in 2015.
'The Only Good Ork' first published digitally in 2022.
This edition published in Great Britain in 2026 by
Black Library, Games Workshop Ltd., Willow Road,
Nottingham, NG7 2WS, UK.

Represented by: Games Workshop Limited – Irish branch,
Unit 3, Lower Liffey Street, Dublin 1,
D01 K199, Ireland.

10 9 8 7 6 5 4 3 2 1

Produced by Games Workshop in Nottingham.

A CIP record for this book is available from the British Library.

ISBN 13: 978-1-83609-304-6

See Black Library on the internet at

blacklibrary.com

Find out more about Games Workshop
and the worlds of Warhammer at

warhammer.com

Printed and bound in the UK.

For more than a hundred centuries the Emperor has sat immobile on the Golden Throne of Earth. He is the Master of Mankind. By the might of his inexhaustible armies a million worlds stand against the dark.

Yet, he is a rotting carcass, the Carrion Lord of the Imperium held in life by marvels from the Dark Age of Technology and the thousand souls sacrificed each day so his may continue to burn.

To be a man in such times is to be one amongst untold billions. It is to live in the cruelest and most bloody regime imaginable. It is to suffer an eternity of carnage and slaughter. It is to have cries of anguish and sorrow drowned by the thirsting laughter of dark gods.

This is a dark and terrible era where you will find little comfort or hope. Forget the power of technology and science. Forget the promise of progress and advancement. Forget any notion of common humanity or compassion.

There is no peace amongst the stars, for in the grim darkness of the far future, there is only war.

CONTENTS

I AM SLAUGHTER

DAN ABNETT

ONE

ARDAMANTUA, 544.M32

The Chromes were relatively easy to kill, but they came in ferocious numbers.

Eight walls of Imperial Fists boxed one of their primary family groups into a scrub-sided valley east of the blisternest, and reduced them to burned shells and spattered meat.

Smoke rose off the hill of dead. It was a yellowish air-stain composed of atomised organic particulates and the backwash of fyceline smoke. According to the magos biologis sent to assist the undertaking, sustained bolter and las-fire, together with the chronic impact trauma of blade and close-combat weapons, had effectively aerosolised about seven per cent of the enemy's collective biomass. The yellow smoke, a cloud twenty kilometres wide and sixty long, drained down the valley like a dawn fog.

The magos biologis told Koorland this as if the fact had some practical application. Koorland, second captain of Daylight Wall Company, shrugged. It was a non-fact to him, like someone saying the shape of a pool of spilled blood resembled a map of Arcturus or Great-Uncle Janier's profile. Koorland had been sent to Throne-forsaken Ardamantua to kill Chromes. He was used to killing things. He was good at it, like all his company brothers and like every brother of the shield-corps. He was also used to the fact that when things were killed in colossal numbers, it left a mess. Sometimes the mess was smoke, sometimes it was liquid, sometimes it was grease, sometimes it was embers. He didn't need some Terra-spire expert telling him that he and his brothers had pounded the Chromes so hard and so explosively that they had vaporised part of them.

The magos biologis had a retinue of three hundred acolytes and servitors. They were hooded and diligent, and had decorated the hillside with portable detection equipment and analysis engines. Tubes sniffed the air (this, Koorland understood, was how the magos biologis had arrived at his seven per cent revelation). Picting and imaging devices recorded the anatomies of dead and living Chrome specimens alike. Dissections were underway.

'The Chromes are not a high-factor hostile species,' the magos told Koorland.

'Really?' Koorland replied through his visor speakers, obliged to listen to the report.

'Not at all,' the human said, shaking his head, apparently under the impression that Koorland's obligation was in fact interest. 'See for yourself,' he said, gesturing to a half-flayed specimen spread-eagled on a dissection stand. 'They are armoured, of course, around the head, neck and back, and their forelimbs are well formed into digital blades–'

'Or "claws",' said Koorland.

'Just so,' the magos went on, 'especially in sub-adult and adult males. They are not harmless, but they are not a naturally aggressive species.'

Koorland thought about that. The Chromes – so called because of the silvery metallic finish of their chitin armour – were xenosbreed, human-sized bugs with long forelimbs and impressive speed. He thought about the eighteen million of them that had swarmed the valley that afternoon, the sea of silver gleaming in the sunlight, the swish of their bladed limbs, the *tek-tek-tek* noise they made with their mouthparts, like broken cogitators. He thought of the three brothers he'd lost from his wall during the initial overwhelm, the four taken from Hemispheric Wall, the three from Anterior Six Gate Wall.

Go tell them *not naturally aggressive*.

The Chromes had numbers, vast numbers. The more they had killed, the more there were to kill. Sustained slaughter was the only operational tactic: keep killing them until they were all dead. The rate at which the Imperial Fists had been required to hit them, the duration, the frenzy – no damn wonder they aerosolised seven per cent of their biomass.

'Chromes have been encountered on sixty-six other worlds in this sector alone,' said the magos biologis. 'Twenty-four of those encounters took place during compliance expeditions at the time of the Great Crusade, the rest since. Chromes have been encountered in large numbers, and have often defended themselves. They have never been known to behave with such proactive hostility before.'

The magos thought about this.

'They remind me of rats,' he said. 'Rad-rats. I remember there was a terrible plague of them down in the basements and sub-basements under the archive block of the Biologis Sanctum at Numis. They were destroying valuable specimens and records, but they were not, individually, in any way harmful or dangerous. We sent in environmental purge teams with flame guns and toxin sprays. We began to exterminate them. They swarmed. Fear, I suppose. They came flooding out of the place and we lost three men and a dozen servitors in the deluge. Unstoppable. Like the sub-hive rats, the Chromes have never behaved this way before.'

'And they won't again,' said Koorland, 'because when we're finished here they'll all be dead.'

'This is just one of a possible nineteen primary family groups,' said the magos biologis. He paused. Koorland knew that the magos intended to address him by name, but, like so many humans, he found it difficult to differentiate between the giant, transhuman warriors in their yellow armour. He had to rely on rank pins, insignia and the unit markings on shoulderplates, and that information always took a moment to process.

The magos biologis nodded slightly, as if to apologise for the hesitation.

'–Captain Koorland of the Second Daylight Wall–'

'I'm second captain of the Daylight Wall Company,' Koorland corrected.

'Ah, of course.'

'Forget about rank, just try to remember us by our wall-names.'

'Your what?'

Koorland sighed. This man knew more than seemed healthy about xenos-breeds, but he knew nothing about the warriors built to guard against them.

'Our wall-names,' he said. 'When we are inducted, we forget our given names, our pre-breed names. Our brothers bestow upon each of us a name that suits our bearing or character: a wall-name.'

The magos nodded, politely interested.

Koorland gestured to a Space Marine trudging past them.

'That's Firefight,' he said. 'That brother over there? He's Dolorous. Him there? Killshot.'

'I see,' said the magos biologis. 'These are earned names, names within the brotherhood.'

Koorland nodded. He knew that, at some point, he'd been told the magos biologis' name. He hadn't forgotten because it was complicated, he just hadn't cared enough about the human to remember it.

'What is your name, captain?' the magos asked brightly. 'Your wall-name?'

'My name?' Koorland replied. 'I am Slaughter.'

TWO

ARDAMANTUA

In less than six solar hours, they were back in combat.

A filthy dusk had settled over the landscape. In the reddish haze of the sky, the low-anchored bulks of their barges hung like oblong, tusk-prowed moons. The Chapter Master had ordered over ninety per cent of the Fists' strength out on this undertaking. It was a huge show of force. Too much, in Slaughter's opinion. But it was political too. The Adeptus Astartes were very good at prosecuting and finishing wars. Whenever extended periods of peace broke out, especially in the exalted systems and holdings around the Terran Core, it became harder to justify the sheer might of a standing army like the Imperial Fists. It was good to get them out, to give them purpose, to chalk up a staggering victory that the core system populations could celebrate. The extermination of a xenosbreed threat like the Chromes was ample justification for such lethal institutions as the Imperial Fists.

Strategic surveys put the Chrome numbers at something in the order of eighty-eight billion, and migratory scans showed a pronounced in-curve diaspora towards the core worlds. Besides, Ardamantua, Throne-forsaken Ardamantua, was just six warp-weeks from Solar Approach.

Since the very earliest ages of the Imperium, the Imperial Fists had been the primary defenders of Terra. Other Chapters – Legions, as they had been known, until the Great Heresy and the instigation of the Codex – might crusade, explore or take war to the furthest corners of Imperial space. But the Imperial Fists were the primary guardians of Terra and the core. This was what they had always done. This was the duty their beloved Primarch-Progenitor had charged them with when he had left them.

It was their legacy.

Surface scans had shown another Chrome family group of significant size moving around the blisternest. Daylight Wall had led the way across the river, with two walls at their heels and another crossing further up. The river was broad but slow and heavy, no more than waist-deep, and muddy. The brackish water fumed with insects.

The Chromes started to resist when they saw the Imperial Fists wading out to the nest side. Some plunged into the water and attempted to attack. Shooting began, brothers firing from the soupy water, pushing the foe back, driving the Chromes up the claggy banks even as the xenos gathered in greater numbers to plunge in. The enemy became agitated. The slow tide was soon full of Chrome corpses, spinning end to end as they drifted downstream. The Imperial Fists advance seemed almost sullen; they came slowly, trudging through the stinking water, firing because they had to at targets too ridiculously easy to hit.

Slaughter roused his men. If they were going to engage, they were going to do it with dignity. They were coming up the bank, approaching the huge, septic shape of the blisternest rim.

'Daylight Wall stands forever,' he voxed. 'No wall stands against it. Bring them down.'

The men of the company clashed their boltguns and their broadswords against their combat shields and chanted the refrain back. The advance began to accelerate.

A wall of men. A wall of supermen.

Slaughter reached the bank. It was a steep, slick mire threaded with coarse vegetation. Glinting in the smoky light, Chromes bounded down onto the ridges, rising up into threat postures and challenging him. He came out of the water, oily green moisture trailing off his yellow armour. Frenzy was at his left hand, Heartshot was at his right.

The first of the Chromes came at him.

Slaughter's broadsword was a two-handed power blade with a silver cross-hilt and a black pommel. It had fought at Terra, during the Siege, in the hands of a Fist called Emetris, who had fallen there. It was as broad as a standard human male's thigh. He brought it up and it described an arc in the air as the first Chrome leapt. It split the xenos through its gleaming bio-armour and cut it in two. Ichor showered in all directions. A second sprang, and he smashed it aside, slashed open. A third met the blade, impaled itself, and thrashed wildly until he ripped the sword back out.

It was just the beginning. They started to rush. A dozen, two dozen, all at once. Slaughter liked sword-work. It was economical. It saved munitions for more significant moments. The broadsword was a finely balanced instrument in his huge hands. The two-handed grip could turn and shear each swing in a surprisingly subtle number of ways.

Slaughter began to slaughter.

He left a trail of dead behind him: ruptured silver husks weeping ichor into the matted, trampled vegetation. Each step was an impact as another two or three Chromes came at him and were met by the brute, full-stop force of his blade. Organic debris flew from each killstroke. Ichor and other xenos fluids squirted high into the air and dappled his armour like dew, like rain.

Frenzy tore through the stand of dry weeds to his left, swinging an axe that had been the proud possession of a series of Fists since before the Great Crusade. The curve of its bite had been notched by the skull of a green warboss during the Malla Vajjl compliance. Frenzy, a big-hearted generous man, possessed particularly acute hand-eye coordination. His movements were so fast and precise, they seemed almost random. He had earned his wall-name through his grace on the field, the constant motion, the changing grips, the reversals, the back-steps, the aggression. His axe moved from grip to grip like a baton or a staff whirled by some ceremonial parade-ground officer. It seemed to fly from his hand many times as he turned and changed position, but it never left him. Like Slaughter, he had eschewed his bolter for the clearance work.

Slaughter wished he could stop and admire the battle-craft of his friend and brother, but there was no opportunity. The enemy's numbers were increasing.

To Slaughter's right, tearing through the reed beds and the dried mucus walls of the blisternest edges, came Heartshot and Chokehold. Heartshot's rotary cannon made a metallic din like a stamp-press forge at full production. Chokehold's bolter exploded two or sometimes three charging Chromes with each shell.

Slaughter barked orders, kept the line firm. He didn't want over-step. He didn't want the Chromes to find a way in through any gap in their line. Heartshot and Chokehold moved ahead fast, cutting their path with firepower. He had to keep them leashed.

He called out wall-names – Cleaver, Arm's Length, Coldeye, Lifetaker, Bleedout – and urged them in at the back, ordering them through the reed beds to fill and cover.

His head snapped around from a sideways blow. He smelled blood in his nose, blood that clotted instantly. A screamer alert sang in his helm and his visor display blinked up mottled damage patterns.

He recovered. This took less than a second. One of the big adults had raked his head with a forelimb claw. He'd taken his eye off the fight for a micro-moment to check the line.

His sword killed the thing for its insult and for the scratch it left in the yellow surface of his helm. But there was another at its heels, an even bigger adult. It was two-thirds his size. He hadn't seen Chromes this big before. Its appearance was different too. It was not chrome or silvery. Its chitin and armour, and its claws, seemed resiny black and brown, as if made from a horny bark that was still growing.

It ripped his chestplate. Slaughter got his shield in the way, took off its limb mid-forearm, and then reversed his blade and killed it.

Two strokes for one kill. Inefficient.

The thing had been big. It had required the extra effort.

Another large, dark form appeared, and then two more. What were they? A sub-species? A larger, more aggressive form of the basic Chrome xenotype?

Slaughter's helm was alive with vox-chatter reports from across the offensive, all describing the same new type: larger, darker, bigger, stronger, harder to kill.

Tactical re-evaluation. Slaughter started to issue advisories even as he met the next of the new kind. Two strokes to kill one, three to finish the next. More gouges down to bare metal on his armour.

Why would any force, any species, keep its largest and strongest warrior-forms in reserve? Why would they not send them out into open combat? They might have halted or driven back the Adeptus Astartes' attack long before they had cut their way to the blisternest.

The *tek-tek-tek* noise the Chromes made with their mouthparts, that malfunctioning data-engine clatter, was changing. The bigger, darker warrior-forms made a lower, duller noise, a *clack-clack-clack*. Two brothers in the line had already fallen to their superior power and savagery.

'Do we fall back?' Frenzy voxed. 'Slaughter, do we break and regroup? This is new. This is–'

'Hold the line,' Slaughter replied. 'No regroup. No fall back. Hold the line. Daylight Wall stands forever. No wall stands against it. Bring them down.'

'Understood.'

Frenzy's unquestioning *understood* was instantly echoed by a hundred voxed voices.

Slaughter ducked a slashing brown claw the size of Frenzy's axe-head. He was smiling.

He had made a realisation. He knew what this was.

They are us. They are Daylight Wall.

The blisternest was the Chromes' Palace of Terra. They had kept their bravest and best and mightiest warriors in reserve to defend it, in case an enemy ever got through.

This was their last ditch. Their last stand. This was their final wall, their do or die.

The Imperial Fists were just hours away from completing their undertaking to Ardamantua and adding another proud tally to their glory roll.

This was the bloody endgame, and it would be a battle to relish.

'Hold the line,' Slaughter ordered. Then, as a practical afterthought, he added, 'Use your bolters.'

THREE

TERRA – THE IMPERIAL PALACE

The air was smoke.

In preparation for the midday Senatorum meeting, servitors had lit the burners in the upper galleries and the approach halls, and in the alcoves along the Walk of Heroes, whose great leaded windows, miraculously spared by the pounding overpressure of the Siege, had looked out onto the stately yards behind Eternity Gate for two dozen centuries.

The burners fumed with camphor and septrewood, rose-ash and parvum, the sacred incense of the Saviour Emperor, thought to smell exactly like the incorruptible sanctity of His Eternal Form.

Vangorich couldn't attest to this. Given his office as a Grand Master, he might have requested, and even been granted, the chance to show observance at the foot of the Golden Throne. He had never bothered. The dead did not interest him, not even the divine dead. What interested him – obsessed him – were the mechanisms by which things *became* dead, and the opportunities those deaths afforded the living.

He had entered the Inner Palace that morning through West Watch, and then followed the hallway walks behind the High Gardens and Daylight Wall before pausing in the chapel ordinary behind the cloister wall to make a small devotion at the basin font.

Vangorich was not a pious man. He was a man of faith, but it was not a spiritual faith. He made his devotion because he knew – or at least could be fairly certain – that agents from a dozen or more ministries and factions were watching him at all hours of the day and night. It was easier to make sure he was seen to be doing what he was supposed to do, than it was to waste manpower eradicating those spies on a daily basis.

Let his rivals do the hard work. It was no great effort to act a part.

Drakan Vangorich had been doing it all his life.

So he did what was expected of him. As a Grand Master – albeit of an Officio that had once been powerful and was now regarded as an atavistic throwback to a more brutal age – he was expected to attend all meetings, formal and discretionary. He was supposed to show humility and dignity. He was supposed not to express any cruel or bloodthirsty appetites, the sort of appetites his rivals assumed that a Grand Master of the Officio Assassinorum must harbour. He was supposed to show respect to the Creed.

All Senatorum members took a blessing or expressed some devotion before taking their seats at meetings, so that the will of the God-Emperor might guide their thoughts and wisdom. Some, like the odious Lansung, made a great show of doing so, in full dress uniform, usually in the chapel-vault of one of his battlefleet vessels in orbit. Mesring was the same, leading a train of gowned, gold-helmed savant-priests into the rotunda church below Hemispheric Wall. Pompous idiots!

Vangorich, dressed in simple, ascetic black, opted for a less showy effect. The chapel ordinary was used by Palace servants and householders for their daily observances. It was not a public place, just a very plain cell with frugal appointments. Vangorich was aware that using it made him look dutiful, restrained, and very humble. It made him look more admirably spiritual than the lords who made their observances for show. It spoke of simplicity and a lack of arrogance.

It made him look trustworthy and noble. It made him look good. He liked his rivals' spies to see that. He knew it irked them beyond measure to hear that he had stopped for a few minutes in a private, unostentatious servants' chapel to make a discreet act of faith. How it bothered them that he was so unimpeachably wholesome.

The truth was, he probably thought more about how he looked at all times, and what his image said about him, than the likes of Mesring and Lansung. Their activities were conducted publicly, to win popular support; Vangorich's were conducted simply for the benefit of the ever-circling spies. He performed for his rivals, playing the part he wanted them to see.

How would they see him now, coming to the meeting? As a man of medium height and medium build, dressed in black, with black hair oiled back like a clerk's across his narrow skull. His skin was pale from the constant twilight of life in the Palace, and he had precious little in the way of distinguishing features, except for his dark, wide-set eyes and the duelling scar that canyoned the left part of his mouth and chin.

Vangorich never spoke of the duel, except to say that it had happened when he was a youth, before he took office, and he regretted it in as much as the matter should not have been resolved face-to-face with rapiers, but rather with him placed behind his adversary, dagger in hand, and his adversary unaware of his presence.

Drakan Vangorich liked to kill things. He liked to kill things as efficiently as possible, with the least possible effort, and he only ever killed things if there was a reason: a good reason, a persuasive reason. Death was the pure solution to life's greatest and most confounding problems.

This was what so many of the offices and agencies seemed not to understand about the ancient Officio Assassinorum. It was not an archaic killing machine, lurking to spread disorder and mayhem at the whim of some mercurial Grand Master, poisoning here and stabbing there. It was not a thirsty sword hung in a rack, aching to shed blood.

It was a necessary and purifying fire. It was the last resort, the end of arguments. It was hope and it was salvation. It was the noblest and truest of all the Offices of Terra.

The Emperor had understood this, which was why He had instigated the office and allowed it to function during His lifetime. He had understood the necessity for ultimate sanction. He had, after all, permitted the VI Legion of the Adeptus Astartes to exist simply to function in that role as it applied to primarchs and other Legions. Grand Master Vangorich's office existed to perform that function at a court level.

That was why the other lords were afraid of him. They all presumed he might stab them in the spine. They always forgot that he was their instrument. *They* got to vote on who he killed. *They* should spend more time worrying about each other.

'Good day, Daylight,' he said as he stepped out of the chapel ordinary to continue his walk to the Great Chamber.

The Imperial Fist, his armour polished and perfect, turned slowly and offered Vangorich a shallow tip of the head.

'Good day, Grand Master,' the Space Marine replied, his voice welling up as a volcanic rumble through helm-speakers. He towered over the human lord, ornamental spear in his left fist, litany-inscribed shield in his right. Vangorich felt sorry for the wall-brothers of the VII. They were reputed to be the very finest of all, the most excellent and capable of their Chapter. Yet, because of ritual and ceremony and honour, they were fated to remain here for their entire service lives; the best of the best, one for each of the Palace walls that the Fists had protected, wasting their immense potential, serving out their time in the one place in the galaxy that war would never visit again.

They didn't even have names. They simply wore the names of the walls they patrolled, every day and night, in perfectly polished armour.

'I'm probably late for the meeting,' Vangorich remarked.

'You have six minutes and thirteen seconds remaining, sir,' replied the Space Marine. 'However, I suggest you take Gilded Walk to the traverse behind Anterior Six Gate.'

'Because they're not meeting in the Great Chamber?'

The Space Marine nodded.

'They are not, sir.'

'They keep doing that,' said Vangorich, peeved. 'I think it is unseemly. The Great Chamber was good enough for our ancestors. It was built as our parliament.'

'Times change, sir,' said the warrior Daylight.

Vangorich paused and looked up at the grim and unfathomable visor. Light glowed like coals behind the optic lenses.

'Do they?' he asked. 'Do you wish for that, Daylight? Do you wish for the chance to kill?'

'With every fibre of my soul, and every second of my life, sir,' the Imperial Fist replied. 'But this is the duty I have been given and I will perform it with my entire heart and will.'

Vangorich felt he ought to say something, but he could not think of anything adequate, so he nodded, turned, and walked away down the gloomy hallway.

FOUR

TERRA – THE IMPERIAL PALACE

The Great Chamber had been the seat of power on Terra since the Palace had been established. It was a formidable stadium, a veritable colosseum, with a central dais and seats for the High Lords, and then vast tiers of seats for the more minor officials and lords, lesser functionaries, petitioners and so forth. At full capacity, it could hold half a million people. It had been damaged during the Siege, but it had been restored and repaired in a sympathetic fashion. A huge statue of Rogal Dorn had been erected at the east end, commemorating his superhuman efforts of defence in general, and his extraordinary running battle in the hallways just outside that very place.

It had not been Dorn's choice. Guilliman had ordered the statue raised.

'My brother watched over the Palace during our darkest hour,' he had said. 'He should watch over the council evermore.'

Of late, in the last few decades, the Senatorum Imperialis had taken to meeting in other places. The Great Chamber was too big for anything except full meetings, many claimed: too noisy, too formal. Favour was placed on more closed sessions, in smaller chambers, for intimacy and immediacy. The Clanium Library was often used, almost as a private cabinet. Sometimes, the High Lords convened in the Anesidoran Chapel.

Most preferred was the Cerebrium, a comparatively small, wood-panelled room near the top of the Widdershins Tower. It was said that the Emperor had favoured the rooms of the tower for meditation and mindfulness, and the Cerebrium in particular. 'It makes us feel closer to His thoughts to convene here,' Udo had once exclaimed, defending the regular use of the room.

Vangorich knew perfectly well why they did it.

The Cerebrium had a large, figured wooden table at its centre, and the table was big enough to take twelve chairs.

Only the twelve members of the High Senatorum could sit in session together. Secondary officials, like Vangorich, were obliged to lurk in the shadows, or take seats along the wall.

It was power play. It was infantile.

The Cerebrium was a fine room, well-appointed and quite atmospheric. Opening the casement shutters afforded the room an extraordinary view across the Palace roofscape and down over the ring-gates and the armoured flanks of the world. Vangorich had often thought it would make an excellent private study or office.

However, it was hardly a place to run the Imperium from. It was too small, too insubstantial, too amateurish. It was a back-room, fit only for private thoughts and back-room deals. It was not a place of government.

Vangorich entered, his attendance solemnly noted by the servitor of record. The High Lords were taking their seats. He nodded a greeting with Lord Militant Heth, his only true ally among the High Twelve, and then found a place in the flip-down wooden pews under the east windows, where other lesser lords and functionaries were seating themselves. They greeted him as if he was one of them.

He was not.

Less than a century before, one of the permanent seats among the High Twelve had belonged to the Grand Master of the Officio Assassinorum. The office was one of the 'Old Twelve' that had sat in governance of the Imperium since the Senatorum's inception.

Times, as Brother Daylight had said, were changing. Some offices, and none more than the Office of Assassins, were now seen as obsolete at best, or archaic and primitive at worst. They had been edged out of the inner twelve, and either dispensed with altogether, or relegated to the lesser seats outside the High Circle. Other, newer, stations had advanced in their place.

This was ignominious. Vangorich accepted that some of the Imperium's newer institutions absolutely deserved a seat at the table. Both the agents of the Inquisition and the ecclesiarchs of the Ministorum required representation among the High Lords since the Heresy War. They were fundamental parts of the modern Imperium. Vangorich would not argue that. What he would argue was that the council should have been expanded to admit them rather than culled to find them places.

He watched them take their seats at the table, talking together, some laughing. Wienand, the Inquisitorial Representative, was the only one not talking to anybody. She was quiet and reserved and surprisingly young, with sharp cheekbones and very short, steel-grey hair. Technically, she was his replacement. Technically, the Inquisitorial Representative had taken the permanent seat that had traditionally belonged to the Grand Master of the Officio Assassinorum.

Vangorich held no grudge. He quite liked Wienand, and he'd admired her predecessor. He believed in the near-autonomous function of the Inquisition, because it reflected, in spirit, the same safety-catch mechanism as the Assassinorum. He often met with Wienand and others of her kind, in private of course, to discuss operational techniques, methodology of detection and research, jurisdiction, and also to share inter-agency intelligence. He found that the inquisitors were often astonished at the level of intelligence his office was able to gather, and they often turned to him, clandestinely, for favours.

It was all part of the give and take.

Heth was the Lord Commander Militant of the Astra Militarum, an old, maimed veteran. Though the Guard was the largest military body in the Imperium, Heth felt it to be very much the junior third service to the Adeptus Astartes and the Navy. It was probably why he sought out unlikely allies with voting rights, such as Vangorich.

Lansung was certainly ignoring him. Lansung, broad, red of face and booming of voice, was the Lord High Admiral of the Imperial Navy. His corpulent form was encased in a uniform of oceanic blue threaded with silver braid. He took a while to be seated, engaging Tobris Ekharth, the Master of the Administratum, in some convoluted piece of scandal-mongering while Vernor Zeck looked on with patient indulgence. Zeck, the giant among them, was the Grand Provost Marshal of the Adeptus Arbitrators. He was one of the two most heavily augmented humans among the High Twelve. He was not particularly amused or even diverted by Lansung's outrageous gossip, but he was forcing himself to at least feign a show of interest. Vangorich was aware that Zeck's mind was a billion light years away, processing the layers of administrative and forensic data, the ceaseless work of keeping Terra's gargantuan hives ordered and policed. The look of wry amusement on his leonine face was a simulation for Lansung's benefit.

Similarly, Lansung wasn't at all interested in speaking to Ekharth, other than to cultivate the loyalties between Navy and Administratum. He was telling a story at Ekharth so he could get Zeck's attention, and be seen to be the close and genuine confidant of the Provost Marshal.

Maybe I should draw up a map, thought Vangorich. A map or chart, some kind of visual aid, a diagram of the basic interpersonal relations of the High Twelve. It could be colour-coded to reveal areas of contempt, deceit, insincerity, political expediency and outright rancour. Yes, I might do that and present it to the Senatorum one day under 'any other business', he thought.

At the other end of the table, Kubik, the Fabricator General of the Adeptus Mechanicus, was conducting a dialogue with Mesring, the Ecclesiarch of the Adeptus Ministorum, and Helad Gibran, the Paternoval Envoy of the Navigators. Kubik was, of course, the other extensively augmented person present, but his alterations had been elective and had begun at an early age, rather than being the result of repair and injury like Zeck's. Vangorich watched Kubik's actions and movements with great interest. He had only limited experience of killing servants of the Mechanicus, and it was a skill he felt he ought to develop given the vast political and materiel power of Mars. He thought, instinctively, they would be hard to kill. The Navigators, equally inhuman, at least seemed physically frail and vulnerable.

Vangorich had already prepared methodologies on some of the other 'sub-species' at the table. The haunted, spectral servants of the Astronomican, represented in the High Twelve by Volquan Sark, the Master of the Astronomican, were still human enough for conventional processes. The telepaths... Ah, the telepaths were a different order of things. Abdulias Anwar, the Master of the Adeptus Astra Telepathica, was typical of their malevolent and discomforting kind. To deal with telepaths, with the Imperium's most powerful sanctioned telepaths... Well, that was why Vangorich had brokered such close ties with Wienand and her ilk.

Juskina Tull, the Speaker for the Chartist Captains, was the eleventh of the High Twelve. A magnificent woman in an almost theatrically ostentatious gown, she occupied a role that many thought was the most trivial of all the seats. On the other hand, the Merchant Fleets represented nearly ninety per cent of the Imperium's interstellar capability. In times of crisis, the Speaker wielded power greater than the Lord High Admiral.

A bell sounded. The delegates moved to their places, even the most exalted of them. Cherub servitors and vox-recorder drones buzzed around the Cerebrium as though it were an aviary.

Lord Guilliman entered the crowded, panelled chamber and took his seat. He bowed his head to his eleven senior fellows. He was the Lord Commander of the Imperium, the commander-in-chief of all Imperial military assets. His head was shaved, and the huge old scar traversing his scalp and neck was very visible. Though beyond any single discipline or arm of the Imperial war machine, he wore a braided uniform that was, in style at least, an echo of the grand admiral's uniform he had worn during his illustrious pre-Senatorum career.

His name was Udin Macht Udo. He was not the first human to hold the chair of the Senatorum Imperialis, but like all his predecessors, human and transhuman alike, he used the formal, honorary title of his office, the name of the first Lord Commander: Guilliman of Macragge.

Udo glanced around the chamber. His eyes, the left one glazed and milky under the lip of the long scar, fixed upon Ekharth, the Master of the Administratum.

'Bring us to order, sir,' Lord Guilliman said.

Ekharth nodded, activated the cogitator-recorder that was crouching on the table in front of him, and began to type on the quivering spindle keys that unfurled from it like the wings of a giant moth.

'High Lords, we are now in session,' Ekharth began.

FIVE

ARDAMANTUA

The loops and coils of the tunnels ahead resonated with the dull *clack-clack-clack* noise that told Slaughter what was waiting for them.

More fierce resistance. More of the new, more powerful warrior-forms. Many more.

The Imperial Fists had smashed and torn their way into the outer layers of the Chromes' huge blisternest. Daylight Wall had made the first entry, an honour mark for their company, and then Hemispheric Wall had punched through about ten minutes later on the far side of the vast edifice's sloping sides. Brothers of the shield-corps were now pouring into the alien nightmare of the Chromes' nest through two dozen breaches.

The blisternest was an organic structure the size of a large Terran hive. Its walls, compartments, chambers and linking tunnels were curved and organic, and seemed to have been formed or grown from some greyish, semi-transparent material that had been extruded and then woven, hardening in the air. From the outside, it looked like a swollen blister. Inside, it was like venturing through the chambers of some alien heart. There was a general dampness and humidity, and sections of the structure throbbed and pulsed wetly, heaving with pus-like fluids that pumped and writhed through the building's skin. The compartments and chambers inside were more like valves and organic voids, the spaces inside living structures. There was mould and fungal growth, and pockets of vapour. The echoing tubes throbbed with the *tek-tek-tek* sound, and the deeper agitation of the more powerful warrior-forms.

At regular intervals the interior sounds generated by the nation of Chromes were drowned out as airstrike support howled in overhead. Low-flying attack runs left blossoming trails of firestorm fury in their wake, engulfing the upper levels of the blisternest. Flights of Caestus rams, specialist vehicles designed for ship-boarding actions, had been unleashed too, driving their armoured prows into the skin of the vast nest to deliver assault squads of shield-corps brothers.

Slaughter waged his own war through the dank, miasmal chambers. The muzzle-flash of his bolter, jumping and sun-bright, lit up the green twilight of the nest. He kept his sword drawn. The big warrior-forms tended to get the bolter rounds. The regular Chromes met his blade's edge. In places, the dipping, curved floor of the nest tunnels was ankle-deep in swilling Chrome ichor. The standing fluid reflected the crackling light of multiple fires, and crimped with ripple patterns every time an airstrike shook the ground.

A pack of Chromes rushed him down the flue of a tunnel. Slaughter stood his ground and set in with sword and boltgun. Severed or exploded aliens peeled away on either side of his resolute form, or were hurled backwards into their kin. Slaughter bellowed the battle cry of Daylight Wall, and urged his brothers up the ducts and grimy arterial conduits that the nest used as corridors.

His yellow armour was flecked with soot and slime. He smashed a charging Chrome away from him with the back of his fist. The thing broke as it hit the nest wall and left a spatter of juice as it slid down. One of the bigger, darker things attacked. With a grim smile, Slaughter realised he was thinking of these things as 'veterans'. They were the old guard. He admired their skill and their power. They had fought wars for their benighted race out among the stars. He could see that in them. They had protected their own and perhaps conquered territory. He wondered which xenos species they had battled that he had also fought.

The first thing a good warrior always did was respect his enemy. He evaluated and assessed his foe, and woe betide him if he failed to appreciate what his opponent brought to the field. Slaughter had nothing but appropriate respect for the 'veterans'. He'd seen them gut and dice enough of his shield-brothers that day already. The losses were going to be high. At least, he reflected, the damn lordlings and politicos would be pleased. The war against the Chrome advance was proving that serious threats still remained, and that military forces like the Imperial Fists were not expensive luxuries.

The second captain met the veteran's approach with his blade, deflecting the scything claws of the upper limbs. The veteran was strong, and managed to smash the sword out of Slaughter's grip.

He cursed and shot it through the brain case with his bolter. The entire front of his armour was sprayed an instant grey. Another lumbered towards him and he shot that too, blowing out its midsection and snapping its spinal membranes. Frenzy finished the next with his axe.

'Getting tired, captain?' Heartshot asked Slaughter.

Slaughter told him what he could do with his rotor cannon, and then retrieved his sword.

'Anterior Six and Ballad Gateway are now in the nest with us,' reported Frenzy, his voice a vox-buzz.

'That's good enough,' said Slaughter. 'Four walls should bring this place down.'

'There are assault squads from Zarathustra in the upper levels too,' said Coldeye.

'We can close the book,' said Slaughter. 'By the next time the wretched local star rises, we–'

His words were drowned out. A sudden and deep noise boiled out of the guts of somewhere, out of space itself. It was brief, but it was immense. It shook the nest. It overloaded the frequencies of their vox-systems for a moment. It hurt their ears.

Slaughter's visor display took a moment to reboot.

'What in Throne's name was that?' he asked.

'Contacting the fleet,' reported Frenzy. 'Checking.'

'Some kind of transmission,' said Chokehold. 'Ultra-high frequency. Gross intensity. Duration six point six seconds. A new weapon, perhaps?'

'Perhaps,' said Slaughter grudgingly.

They resumed their advance. After a few minutes, fleet tactical reported back that they hadn't been able to identify the sound either. It had been picked up by Imperial forces all across the planet, and in orbit too.

'A new weapon,' muttered Chokehold. 'I told you...'

There was another burst about half an hour later, duration seven point nine seconds. By then, Slaughter's force was locked in a furious hand-to-hand war with dozens of veterans. The noise took them all by surprise.

When it ended, the Chrome veterans were slightly stunned, and then recommitted to the fight with renewed fury. As though they were afraid, and starting to panic.

SIX
ARDAMANTUA

The magos biologis' name was Phaeton Laurentis. When the first noise burst occurred he was preparing to enter the blisternest behind the shield-corps advance. The blast of sound terminally damaged two of his six sensitive, audio-specialised servitors. Like Slaughter, he immediately contacted fleet tactical, and also sent direct vox-burst communiques to the staff of his own vessel, the survey barge *Priam*, which was in the vanguard of the Imperial Fists fleet.

'Tell them I need at least a dozen more audio-drones shipped to the surface,' he told his communication servitor. The servitor, a grinning bronze skull mounted on a cloak-swathed wire anatomy, chattered its teeth mechanically as its brainstem fired processed vox data-packets into the aether. Laurentis reeled off a list of other complex devices he would need: techno-linguistic engines, parsing cogitators, vocalisation monitors, trans-aetheric responder coils.

'Permission denied for surface drop of requested material,' the communication servitor replied after a minute. Its voice, which emanated from a mesh speaker cone fused into its verdigrised collarbone, was oddly that of a young woman. As the voice spoke, the bronzed skull clacked its teeth aimlessly and uselessly.

'On what authority?' asked Laurentis, offended.

'Undertaking Command,' the servitor replied.

'Open me a direct link with the Chapter Master,' said Laurentis.

'Pending.'

'Of course, he will be busy. Inform me when the link is open,' Laurentis said, and strode off to mount one of the motorised carts that would convey, on their heavy, clattering treads, the magos' survey staff into the alien habitat.

Smoke from the nest clambered into the sky as if trying to flee the warzone. The heavens above were black with filth, and embers rained down. Around the edges of the nest, which were cracked and splintered like the shell of an egg, the soil and vegetation were awash with draining bio-fluids from ruptured nest organics and the ichor of slain Chromes. There was a pervasive stink of rotten fruit.

Such a sight, such a vivid display of an alien ecology, even one so damaged and desecrated, should have filled Magos Biologis Laurentis with total fascination. His life had been dedicated to the study of xenoforms, and it was very rare, even for a man as distinguished and respected as he was, to see such a spectacle first hand. Usually, the only traces of hostile xenoforms and their habitats that magi biologis got to inspect were burned scraps and fused tissue residues brought back by undertaking fleets.

However, his enthusiasm for his research, and the alien specimens spread out before him awaiting his probes and scalpels, was muted. The sound had bothered him, and he knew exactly why.

A total of four noise bursts, each of progressively longer duration, occurred in the following ninety minutes. After the fourth, Chapter Master Cassus Mirhen walked slowly and thoughtfully across the gleaming bridge space of the battle-barge *Lanxium*, took his seat on the great steel throne, and gestured to the vox-servitor that had been waiting patiently for almost two hours.

The command crew and the bridge officers watched the Chapter Master anxiously. He was a great man, arguably the greatest warrior alive in the Imperium. His deeds and achievements were recognised on an honour roll that was the envy of all other Chapter Masters. He was commander of the Imperial Fists, and the living embodiment of Dorn himself.

But he had a temper, oh yes indeed...

Since the latest phase of the attack had begun in the early part of the day, Mirhen had been on his feet in the ship's strategium, watching every last scrap of data as it came through from air and ground forces, and taking personal control of every tactical nuance. Defence was the Imperial Fists' greatest skill, and even in attack, the Chapter's strategy was reflective and complex. Nothing was left to chance. Nothing was over-extended or risked. Leave the headlong insanity of assault to the likes of the Fenrisian Wolves or the White Scars. The Imperial Fists were the Imperium's finest military technicians, and even the most fluid plans of assault were made with the same precision reserved for indefatigable defence. It was often repeated that the Lion had once scoffed at Dorn's precision thinking, remarking that 'no plan ever survives contact with the enemy,' to which Dorn had retorted, 'Then you're not making the right plans.'

Indeed, Imperial Fists methodology, the methodology that had saved Terra in its darkest hour, the methodology espoused by Rogal Dorn and inherited by Mirhen, seldom used the word 'plan.' Mirhen prided himself on 'schemes of attack,' whereby layers of careful, preconsidered variables could be stripped back as necessary. Every step of combat – that most chaotic and mercurial of all circumstances in the galaxy – gave way to multiple possibilities. Some warriors, especially the noble Ultramarines, reacted intuitively to such possibilities as they occurred.

An Imperial Fist identified and prepared for all of them, and simply diverted to the part of the scheme that was most appropriate.

Most believed that Mirhen's presence in the strategium, and his hands-on approach to the Ardamantua Undertaking, was typical of this obsessive precision thinking. In truth, Mirhen liked the challenge. War did not come often enough for him. It was a test, a game, an exercise, a trial. He wanted to be involved, entirely involved; he wanted to push himself.

War was fading away in the Imperium of Mankind. The purposes for which the likes of the Adeptus Astartes had been engineered were dying out. They had done their job. Peace prevailed across a billion worlds. Only distant skirmishes and half-hearted wars boiled along the hem of the frontier, most of them the endless campaigns of suppression against the ubiquitous greenskins. The orks never went away. They menaced and harried the edges of the Imperium like packs of feral dogs, and every now and then broke in through the metaphorical fence and got at the metaphorical livestock. Once or twice every few centuries, a new and potent bestial warboss arose, their numbers multiplied in response, and another of their mass onslaughts was unleashed. Mirhen knew from intelligence briefings that the greenskins were currently enjoying one of these periodic revivals, and that for the last few decades some of the frontier wars had been especially hot. But even so, they were exactly that – *frontier* wars. They were very far away, far too far to act as effective demonstrations of Imperial might to the population of the Terran Core. And the orks had not been a serious, palpable threat since they had been stopped at Ullanor by the beloved Emperor Himself.

Ardamantua was different. It wasn't the frontier, it was close. It was a genuine xenos threat without being a critical one. It was also an opportunity to live-test the capabilities of his Chapter and his own mind, and to demonstrate the enduring worth of the Adeptus Astartes. Opportunities on the scale of Ardamantua were all too rare.

Mirhen's temper was famous. It manifested, more often than not, when those around him failed to keep pace with his tactical thought process. He'd even been known to rage at cogitators and data-engines. His anger showed when the rest of the universe failed to stay in step with his brilliance.

First Captain Algerin had privately remarked that Mirhen had become Chapter Master *because* of his anger. Yes, his tactical genius was astonishing, but it was equalled by three dozen of the senior ranking Fists. What Mirhen had was a tactical genius tempered by passion and the unpredictability of gut feeling. Some said there was more of Sigismund in him than Dorn.

When Mirhen retired to his throne during the pitch of the assault, all of the bridge crew expected his anger to emerge. The noise bursts had confounded them and there was a tense feeling that they represented something that had not been factored into a precondition.

'Connect me,' the Chapter Master told the vox-servitor.

The servitor extended its vox-speakers and opened its mouth. A beam of light projected out of it and formed a hololithic image on the deck at the Chapter Master's feet.

A jumping, inconstant pict image of the magos biologis appeared, cut and broken by atmospherics and data-feed. Laurentis was in profile and appeared to be riding on some kind of open vehicle, and the light conditions were poor.

'Magos,' said Mirhen.

'Sir,' the magos crackled back over the speakers. He turned to look at his pict unit, his face turning full on in the image.

'You sent a signal?'

'Over two hours ago, sir. I need to transport equipment to the surface from my vessel, and permission has been denied.'

'There is an assault underway, magos. I was not in a position to grant orbit to surface passage for any non-military transport.'

'Are you now in a position to authorise my request?' asked the magos. 'If I can explain, I need the items so I can–'

'You don't need to explain, magos,' said Mirhen.

'I don't?'

'It concerns these bursts of noise, doesn't it?' asked the Chapter Master. 'Your comm-request came through very shortly after the first one. You have not got in my way before, magos. It was slow-witted of me not to realise that you would only request a surface drop in the middle of an action like this if it was both urgent and pertinent.'

'I appreciate the compliment, sir. You are quite correct.'

'Tell me what you know,' said Mirhen.

'I believe the sound is organic in origin.'

'Organic?' asked the Chapter Master. 'On this scale? Magos, it was a global detection–'

'Organic, though it may have been synthesised and boosted,' Laurentis replied. 'I cannot explain why I feel this to be the case. I hope you will trust my experience and judgement. Both of those things tell me it is organic.'

'A bio-weapon? Something the Chromes have that we haven't predicted?'

The holo-image of Laurentis shook its head.

'I think it is communication, sir,' he said. 'We just have to work out what it is saying. Hence my request for additional equipment.'

'Your transport is already underway at my order,' said Mirhen.

'Thank you, sir.'

'Are you suggesting the Chromes are trying to communicate with us? Since mankind first encountered them, they have not shown any propensity for sentient communication.'

'This attack may have pushed them to a level where they feel communication is necessary, sir,' replied Laurentis. 'Perhaps they have broken their long silence because they are desperate to sue for peace or surrender. I cannot answer that yet, but I believe it's clear that *something* is trying to communicate.'

'Stay on this link, magos,' Mirhen said. 'I want to hear more about this, and I want to be apprised as soon as–'

He broke off as the pict image of Laurentis became choppy. The magos appeared to be agitated. There were flashes of light, and a great deal of background noise and interference. The image started to jump and wink out.

Then it shut off altogether.

'Reconnect!' Mirhen roared. 'Reconnect that link!'

'Transmission disrupted at source, sir,' the servitor reported.

'I think the magos' party has come under attack,' said Third Captain Akilios, awaiting his master's orders.

'I can damn well see that,' said Mirhen. 'Route the nearest available ground forces to him immediately. Pull his fat out of the fire. I need him alive.'

SEVEN

ARDAMANTUA

Claws. They were definitely claws. They weren't 'digital blades affixed to or articulated from forelimbs,' which was a phrase Laurentis was pretty sure he'd used several times in the genotype description he'd composed for the Chromes.

They were claws.

It was perfectly straightforward to see them as such when they were swinging at you.

The Chrome was massive. It was one of the darker-hued forms, one of the new ones that Laurentis had overheard a great deal of vox-traffic about once the Adeptus Astartes had entered the blisternest.

He'd been dying to see one.

How ironic.

It must have weighed about five hundred kilos. Its hard-shelled back was ridged, with a pronounced, sclerotic-looking hump. The shoulder portions and upper joints were bound with layers of muscle and sinew, like a great simian. The face... The face was not a face. It was a knot of ocular organs on the snout of the armoured head-crest, surmounting a powerful set of chattering mouthparts. The sound it made – *clack-clack-clack* – was like some funereal march, like a death-drum, like rot-beetles clicking away in wood.

The Chrome warrior-form had come out of a side aperture in the nest tunnel and attacked the leading carts in the magos biologis' convoy. One cart was already mangled, and the curving tunnel walls were spattered with blood and lubricant fluid from three servitors that had been dismembered in the first strike.

'Warrior-form' was the word the Imperial Fists were using. It was a perfectly apt term, simple and technically appropriate. The creature was combat adapted. It was built for fighting. It was not, like the regular Chromes, a worker or drone obliged to defend the nest.

Gun servitors in Laurentis' retinue had already opened fire, but their lasweapons were not sufficiently powerful to wound the armoured hulk. It came forwards, wrenching a second cart into the air, spilling its occupants, tipping it.

The confines of the tunnel were so tight. There was nowhere to run, to move to, no air to breathe. The light was poor and gunfire was causing intense visual disturbance. Everyone was shouting. Las-shots howled. Laurentis could hear the voice of the comm-servitor as it tried to reconnect his link with the Chapter Master.

He was caught up in it. It was exactly where he didn't want to be, exactly where he'd spent his career trying not to be. He was caught in the untameable insanity of combat.

'Save yourself, magos,' the pilot servitor beside him said in a flat and oddly sad tone. Hardwired and bone-bonded into the cart's driving position, the servitor itself could hardly escape. Even so, Laurentis wanted to snarl in outrage. Save himself? How? Where could he run to? Up the tunnel, away from the survey convoy? Into the nest, alone?

There was a sharp bang. The warrior-form had ploughed into one of the gun servitors, its claws ripping open the plated bio-organic torso like chisels. Power cables shredded and the servitor's power plant exploded, showering sparks and sizzling fragments and releasing a stink of ozone.

Brain-dead, transfixed by the claws, the gun servitor went into a death-shock spasm, its autonomic systems reacting mindlessly, ungoverned by any programmed control protocols.

The double lasguns mounted onto each of its twitching wrists began to fire, the blue barrels pumping to and fro in their pneumatic sleeves as they spat out bolt after bolt of lethal, shaped light.

The first flurry ripped through three servitors and a biologis assistant standing on the stern of the nearest cart, killing them and making them tumble like skittles. Another wild burst blew out the port-side motivators of the same cart, and then killed two servitors on the ground beside it.

Laurentis flinched as another stray shot whined past, blowing out the head of his cart's pilot servitor. The servitor didn't even slump. The braced and bonded figure remained rigid in its driving socket, smoke streaming from the burned-out bowl of its skull.

Laurentis leapt over the side of the cart, and started to run up the narrow space between the cart and the tunnel wall. He could hear his comm-servitor, wired to its dedicated function, single-mindedly trying to reconnect his link with the Chapter Master in orbit.

Laurentis found his robes tangled in his feet. He was aware of a hot prickling in his lungs and chest, in his throat. Terror. Panic. He was going to die. He was going to die. Fleeing was the only possible option, but it was pointless. He was going to die.

Behind him, the warrior-form shook the dead gun servitor off its claws and sent the servitor's corpse crashing away, bouncing off the tunnel roof and then the fairing of another cart.

Laurentis ran. He realised he wasn't very good at it. The tunnel floor underneath his feet was spongy and thick with slime or mucus, and his boots weren't in any way the right sort of footgear for these conditions. He banged his elbow on the vector cowling of the cart, and it really hurt. He could feel sweat streaming down his spine. He was hyperventilating. He was about to throw up.

A body flew over his head, hit the tunnel wall with a twig-snap of fracturing bones, went limp and fell at his feet. It was Overseer Finks, the convoy manager. Laurentis recoiled and felt the hot acid of reflux in his throat. He wanted to stop and help his colleague, though the overseer was clearly past helping. He didn't need a Laudex Honorium in Advanced Biologis to know that any human missing quite that much torso probably wasn't alive any more.

It felt squalid, however, squalid and shameful to just step over the man's body. It felt improper to pass by and keep running. But the alternatives, stopping or turning back, seemed even more unfortunate.

Laurentis realised, with a scientist's detached precision, that he had frozen. Fright had conquered flight. He was shutting down.

The cart he had dismounted from, the cart he had been in the process of running past, suddenly overturned and slammed into the side of the tunnel. It deformed and buckled, metal plating and machine components shredding and scattering. It had been half-sheltering him, but now he was alone, a man standing beside a corpse with a curved, slimy wall behind him.

The cart compressed further as the advancing warrior-form pounded it and mashed its structure into the wall. The heavy throb of *clack-clack-clack* welled out of the dark beast's oesophagus. Blood and oil drooled off its claws.

'Golden Throne preserve me,' Laurentis muttered, his voice as quiet as a sub-vox echo.

EIGHT

ARDAMANTUA – ORBITAL

Captain Sauber, known as Severance, commander of Lotus Gate Company, cocked his head to one side.

'This isn't the noise bursts?' he asked.

'No, sir,' replied the adept. 'Though they are recurring.'

'We have compiled a list of timings and durations, sir,' added another adept. 'Would you like to review it?'

'No,' said Severance. He kept staring at the cogitator screen, processing the data. 'You're saying this *isn't* the noise bursts?'

'No, sir, a separate phenomenon,' replied the first adept.

'Gravitational?' asked Severance.

'Yes,' said the adept.

'It reminds me of the mass-gravity curve of a Mandeville point,' said Severance.

At his side, Shipmistress Aquilinia clucked her tongue, impressed.

'What?' asked Severance, turning to look at her.

'You recognised a Mandeville curve from a schematic profile,' said the shipmistress, looking up at him. 'I thought you were just a soldier. That's impressive.'

'The mass-gravity curve is similar to a Mandeville point,' said the adept, 'though of far, far less magnitude–'

'Which makes it all the more impressive that the captain recognised it,' Aquilinia snapped at him.

'Yes, mistress.'

'Can we get to the point?' asked Severance. 'Are we detecting gravitational instabilities in the Ardamantua orbital zone?'

'Slight ones, yes, sir,' said the adept.

'The whole zone was surveyed as we approached,' said Severance.

'These are new,' said the adept.

'Like the noise bursts?' asked Severance.

The adept nodded. 'We noticed the first approximately two minutes after the initial noise burst occurrence. And only then because of a slight drift in our orbital anchor point. Analysis showed that a tiny gravitic anomaly had occurred eighty-eight point seven two units off the portside drive assembly, causing the anchor-slide. We corrected. Then we scanned, and saw that sixteen other anomalies of similar profile had occurred during the period.'

Severance turned and crossed the long, narrow bridge of the strike cruiser *Amkulon*. It was like the nave of an ancient cathedral, with various function-specific crew departments working in lit galleries stacked on either side above him. Aquilinia hurried after the massive armoured warrior.

'Open a channel to the flagship!' she cried. 'The captain wants voice to voice with the Chapter Master!'

'You read my mind,' said Severance.

'I grasp the significance,' she replied. 'If there's genuine, previously undetected gravitational instability in the orbital zone, we will have to back the fleet out. That would seriously compromise the ground assault.'

Severance nodded. He felt cheated. His wall wasn't even deployed yet. His men were prepped and ready in the drop holds of the *Amkulon*.

'Did you see them?' he growled at Aquilinia. 'The gravity blips, popping up like blisters, and then closing again. Have you seen that before?'

She shook her head.

'I've seen gravity fraying close to major mass giants,' she said. 'And you get that kind of peppering, blistering effect on the fringes during translation in and out of the empyrean.'

'Hence the similarity to a Mandeville profile?'

'Exactly. Throne's sake, captain, I've seen plenty of non-Euclidian gravity effects on the rip-curve of the translation interface. Daemon space does not behave itself, as my mentors used to say.'

'But you think this is natural?'

She shrugged. A brass-framed optic slid down from her crested headdress, spearing data-light into her left eye so she could review the adept's findings again.

'I believe so. Yes, yes. It has to be. There's no patterning. We have to accept we've entered a gravitationally unstable zone.'

'I'll inform the Chapter Master,' said Severance.

He took the proffered speaker horn in his huge left hand and waited a moment for the vox-servitor to cue him that connection was established.

'Speak,' said Mirhen's voice over the link.

'Severance, Lotus Gate, *Amkulon*,' said Severance. 'We're plotting increasing gravitational instability in the upper and outer orbital zone, sir. Routing all data to your bridge.'

He looked at Aquilinia, who nodded and began issuing orders to her data-adepts.

'You should be receiving data now, sir,' Severance began.

The deck shuddered. There was a dull, heavy sound of something vast and leaden colliding with something of equal mass. Hot, acrid smoke gusted across the bridge.

Alarms started to sound.

'What was that?' Severance asked.

The shipmistress was already yelling commands and requesting clarification. Bridge personnel dashed to their stations.

'*Amkulon*? Severance, report.' Mirhen's voice scratched out of the vox-speakers.

'Stand by,' Severance replied. He looked at the shipmistress.

'A gravity pocket spontaneously opened in our starboard reactor core,' she said. 'We're ruptured and venting. I don't know if we can contain the damage and maintain our position.'

'There must be–' Severance began.

'Captain, please get your company and all auxiliaries off this ship now,' said Aquilinia, 'before we suffer catastrophic anchor-point failure and nose-dive into that planet.'

NiNE

TERRA – THE IMPERIAL PALACE

The Senatorum session had lasted for almost seven hours. Tedium had been etched on some faces by the time it drew to a close, and few had been able to disguise their dissatisfaction when Ekharth had announced that they would resume after a three-hour interval as there were still eighty-seven items remaining on the agenda.

Vangorich withdrew to his private suite to rest his mind. The problem as he saw it, and he believed he saw it very clearly, was that the instrument of governance was not as sharp as it had once been. The Old Twelve had met regularly, and had dealt specifically with high-order matters. Everything else had been delegated to the lower tiers of government and the Administratum. Any review of the parliamentary records showed how economically and concisely the Senatorum had dealt with state affairs in previous, greater ages. Greater ages, populated by greater men.

Now the Senatorum was bloated and fat, over-stuffed with hangers-on and minor officials, and it met on a whim, whenever Udo or any of the other core members felt that it should. Business piled up, most of it far too trivial to bother the dignity of a proper Senatorum. And as for the actual process! These people weren't politicians. Procedure trudged along. No one knew how to debate properly. The most mindless committee vote took forever. At every touch and turn, the in-fighting and rivalries between the High Twelve spewed out and gnawed like acid into the gears of government, slowing everything down.

The decision taken on isotope shipments, for example. Utterly ridiculous. They had actually voted through a policy that would actively harm the Imperium by retarding the efficiency of shipbuilding in the Uranic shipyards. Did anyone dare see it that way? Of course not! Mesring had wanted the vote swayed to protect his family's huge commercial interests in the Tang Sector, and he had called in favours from those in his power bloc. House Mesring had benefited. The Imperium had not.

Vangorich's suite was quiet. His signet ring deactivated the pain door and rested the alarm systems. He went inside. The outer room was panelled in dark oak, and lined with couches dressed in gleaming black leather upholstery. On a lit display stand ancient fragments of pottery, pre-dating the Golden Age of Technology, hung in suspension fields.

Vangorich put down his data-slate and a sheaf of documents, and walked to the sideboard to pour an amasec. The drinks, a modest collection of fine marks, were kept in special, tamper-proof bottles. He sniffed the empty glass for residue before he poured. Old habits.

Before he took his first sip, he used his thumb ring to deactivate a secret drawer in the top of the sideboard cabinet, slid it open, and took out the elegant, long-barrelled plasma pistol cushioned inside.

Without looking around, he said, 'The left-hand armoire, beside the De Mauving landscape.'

Then he turned and aimed the weapon at the item of furniture he had just described.

A small but powerfully built man in a black bodyglove stepped out from behind the armoire and nodded sheepishly to Vangorich.

'Nice try,' said Vangorich, and lowered the weapon.

'Every time, sir,' said the man. 'What was it on this occasion?'

'Body-heat sensors,' said Vangorich, taking a sip of his drink.

'I deactivated them.'

Vangorich nodded.

'And, therefore,' he said, 'I got no body-heat notifications from the security overwatch when I entered the suite, not even my own.'

'Ah,' said the man, slightly ashamed.

'Also, you managed to throw a slight side-shadow under the foot of the armoire. You didn't take into account the glow-globes to your left.'

The man nodded, chastened.

'Where is she?' asked Vangorich.

'The atrium, sir,' said the man.

Vangorich poured a second amasec and carried both drinks through to the small inner courtyard. Wienand was sitting on the bench beside the thermal pool, watching the luminous fish dart in the steaming shallows.

'All done humiliating my bodyguard?' she asked, not getting up.

'A visit from you wouldn't be the same without an opportunity to humiliate your man,' he replied, handing her one of the glasses.

'Kalthro is very good,' she said, 'the best we have. You're the only person who ever catches him out.'

'I consider it to be part of his education, a gift from the Officio Assassinorum to the Inquisition.'

He sat down next to her and crossed one knee over the other, rocking his glass.

'Your visits are less frequent these days, Wienand,' he said. 'I was beginning to think you didn't like me. To what do I owe this pleasure?'

'Agenda item 346,' she said.

'346?' He paused and thought for a second, running through the day's fearsome data-load in his eidetic memory. 'The Imperial Fists' undertaking to Ardamantua?'

'Yes,' she said.

'It was the quickest item of the day. It was raised and covered in about two minutes. Pending, awaiting reports from the Chapter Master.'

Wienand nodded. Her cheekbones were as sharp as glacial cliffs. Her hair was silver in the light.

'What of it, Wienand?'

She pursed her lips.

'A threat is developing,' she said.

'A threat?'

'In the opinion of the Inquisition, yes.'

'A xenos threat?'

She nodded.

'They're called... Chromes, aren't they?' asked Vangorich. 'I did see the briefing paper.'

'The Imperial Fists have undertaken the mission to Ardamantua to suppress a xenoform outbreak. The xenoforms are known as Chromes.'

He raised his eyebrows.

'What am I missing?' he asked.

'You tell me.'

Vangorich shrugged. 'I don't know. As I understand it, these Chromes are like vermin. Nothing out of the ordinary. They have to be dealt with. I gather their numbers are greater than usual. The Fists have mobilised in prodigious numbers, almost full force. I understood that was a political gesture, to show them being useful in peacetime.'

He hesitated.

'Wienand, if it's a threat that seriously jeopardises an almost full-strength Chapter, you're starting to worry me.'

She cleared her throat.

'No, the politics should worry you,' she said.

'Go on.'

'Mirhen's taken pretty much his entire Chapter to Ardamantua to deal with the xenos threat. He's the only one taking it seriously.'

'And why is he taking it seriously? Who alerted him to it?'

'We did,' she said.

'Of course you did.'

'The Fists are more than capable of dealing with the Chrome problem,' Wienand said. 'The point is, they shouldn't have to. The Imperium should be meeting the challenge. Ardamantua should have been a joint undertaking between the Astra Militarum and the Navy, with a backbone of Fists as its cutting edge. Deploying the whole Chapter was ungainly and clumsy.'

'Heth should–'

'Heth can't commit Guard forces without the cooperation of the Navy, and Lansung is more interested in the glory wars against the pathetic greenskins on the frontier. That's where he's sending his fleets. He's fighting border wars and claiming territory practically in his own name. And with Udo backing him, he's pretty much got a free hand to do that.'

'Like too many seats on the council, Lansung places his own interests above those of the Imperium,' said Vangorich.

She nodded again.

'Ardamantua is just six warp-weeks from Solar Approach. It's not a frontier war. It's on our doorstep.'

'And?'

'We've been intercepting comm-traffic between the undertaking fleet and the Chapter House. In the last ten hours, relative, problems have begun to arise. We anticipate that Mirhen will be forced to request support and reinforcement inside a week.'

'Against a xenos threat? Against... *vermin*?'

She held up a hand.

'He will need it. And Lansung won't give it. We must make sure we apply pressure today.'

'Pressure?'

Wienand's soft smile tightened.

'Mirhen may have underestimated the nature of the xenos threat.'

'Since when did the Imperial Fists underestimate anything?' asked Vangorich.

'Since, I think, they were forced to act without the combined support of the Senatorum,' she replied. 'I believe – that is to say that the strategic planners at the Inquisition, and my immediate superiors, believe – that the Imperial Fists will require direct fleet support within the next three months in order to complete the undertaking.'

'Or?'

'Or the xenos threat could actually threaten the Terran Core.'

Vangorich thought about that.

'There hasn't been a threat inside the Core for... centuries,' he said lightly, much more lightly than he was feeling. 'Xenos or otherwise. It's unthinkable.'

'Politics could make it happen. Power play.'

He considered her carefully.

'These... *Chrome* things? Really? That dangerous?'

'We believe there is a palpable and credible xenos threat. We brought it to the attention of Udo, Lansung, Kubik and Mirhen as a Critical Situation Packet. Only Mirhen agreed on its credibility.'

'What aren't you telling me, Wienand?'

'Nothing, Drakan. Nothing at all.'

She fixed him with eyes as chilly as starlight.

'It's the principle of this matter. Personal ambition is allowing the Senatorum to become weak and inefficient. This is a matter we have discussed before. Now it threatens to become more than a theoretical annoyance. I will not stand by and see a core world burned or overrun just to demonstrate the fatal inadequacies of the Senatorum.'

'What are you proposing?' he asked.

'We bring the issue into special business. Lansung, Mesring and Udo are too strong, and too many look to them, even if we swing Heth with us. Zeck too, perhaps, because the reputation of the Adeptus Astartes is at stake and he holds them in especial regard. The point is, we don't try to change the world overnight. All we want is the Senatorum to recognise the problem, and get Heth to propose a fifty-regiment reinforcement expedition to back up the undertaking. We basically shame Lansung into approving fleet support. The Lord High Admiral does not want to go down on the parliamentary record as the man who refused support and left the core worlds wide open.'

'Can he commit what we need? If we embarrass the man, we could corner him.'

'I've reviewed it,' she replied, 'carefully. There are three Segmentum quarter-fleets he could mobilise easily enough, or two vanguard attack squadrons standing off Mars. He has the resources. Thank Throne, he hasn't sent them all to the frontier.'

Vangorich sat back and watched the fish dart about.

'Let's not make it a hard vote,' he said.

'How so?'

'Let's not push him or humiliate him into compliance. Let's make the case and give Lansung the opportunity to look magnanimous.'

'You let him be the hero of the hour?'

'Does that matter if the Terran Core is protected? Let's give him the opportunity to look good in the eyes of the Senatorum and the populace. Let him take it as a win. Wienand, you get much more out of people if you let them feel good about doing what you want them to do.'

She laughed.

'And if he does not?'

'Then we apply pressure. Then we threaten him with shame. You have my vote. I have a little sway with Zeck, and I believe I can call in a favour owed by Gibran if necessary.'

'Good,' she said.

'Good,' he replied, smiling. 'I like our little talks.'

She rose to her feet and handed him her empty glass.

'This xenos threat, Wienand,' he asked. 'Really, what aren't you telling me?'

'I'm telling you everything,' she said.

'I see.' He shrugged. 'When will you allow me to know your forename, Wienand?'

'My dear Drakan, what makes you think you even know my surname? Killing is your business, sir. Secrets are ours.'

TEN

ARDAMANTUA

The warrior-form came at Laurentis, jaws open, ropes of saliva stretched out between the points of laterally extended biting parts.

A force knocked it aside. The creature was smashed to the magos biologis' right, splashing into the muddy slime that drooled along the tunnel floor. The impact that felled it was like the concussion of a demolition tool-bit working rockcrete.

The huge beast couldn't get up. Something had it pinned. A humanoid form in yellow: an Imperial Fist.

A captain. Laurentis could see the rank marks, despite the wash of gore and mud plastering the Space Marine's armour.

Slaughter. It was Slaughter.

Slaughter had brought the Chrome down, floored it and pinned it by the throat with his left fist. The Space Marine's right fist was a piston, ramming a huge combat knife into the Chrome's distended belly over and over again. Something burst. Brown liquid sprayed out across the tunnel. Laurentis recoiled from the vented reek of formic acid and rancid milk.

The warrior-form went slack. Slaughter got off it, but his combat knife was wedged between the integuments of its armour. A second large xenos thundered down the tunnel on the heels of the first, trailing the semi-articulated pieces of a driving servitor from one of its limbs.

Slaughter abandoned his combat knife. Leaving it embedded in the torso of his first kill, he threw himself over the corpse and into the face of the second warrior-form. He drew his broadsword as he leapt, sweeping the powered blade out of its over-shoulder scabbard and forwards, so that its cutting edge led the way.

Space Marine and Chrome warrior-form met. The clash made an air-slap that hurt Laurentis' ears. The Chrome smacked Slaughter hard, twice, its claws drawing sparks off his armour. The Space Marine rocked, reeled back from the blows, and then renewed his efforts, hefting the blade into the Chrome's shoulder with both hands.

It was the Chrome's turn to reel. It staggered sideways. Taking a better grip on his gore-slick sword, Slaughter delivered a second blow that did significantly more damage. Split open, the Chrome tilted and fell backwards.

Laurentis hadn't even seen the third enemy. Slaughter had. The warrior-form was very dark, the colour of a bruise. It came down the tunnel from the other direction, moving with extraordinary speed, claw-limbs hinged out to rain lethal downstrokes on the Imperial Fist.

Slaughter switched around to meet it, hacked with his sword, and took off one forelimb. The creature milled at him, claws glinting in the noxious light. Slaughter ducked aside, letting the blow go long over his shoulder guard, stooping his back into a turn that took him under the Chrome's guard and into its chest. He stabbed his sword in, tip-first, cracking the organic armour, and then shoulder-barged the clacking alien backwards, freeing his blade so he could thrust it again. The second time it went clean through the creature.

He ripped the sword out, and the warrior-form went down.

'Magos?' Slaughter called out, checking up and down the tunnel, sword ready.

'Yes, captain?'

'Are you alive there?'

'I am, captain.'

'Get ready to move with me when I tell you. The Chapter Master has sent Daylight Wall to get you out of this.'

'It is very much appreciated,' said Laurentis. 'I thought I was d–'

'Shhhh!' Slaughter warned him.

From the distance, Laurentis could hear the sound of bolt-weapons firing.

'There's a lot of opposition in this zone,' Slaughter said. 'A lot.'

Laurentis began to wonder where the rest of Daylight Wall Company had got to.

'Let's move,' said Slaughter, and beckoned the magos biologis after him. The captain had made some kind of assessment presumably based on the data his armour was feeding him and incoming vox-signals, neither of which Laurentis was privy to.

They began to work their way back down the nest tunnel, picking their way through the ruins of the magos biologis's convoy. The carriages were all shredded and crushed. His servitors and juniors were dead or fled. Blood-smoke wafted in the gloom of the tunnel. *Now our matter is vaporised,* Laurentis thought unhappily.

'They have shown unexpected resolve within the perimeters of their nest,' he said.

Slaughter grunted in reply.

'We don't much like the unexpected,' the captain said.

'Because?'

'Because nothing should be unexpected.'

'I see.'

'I didn't expect to run out of bolt-rounds today, for example,' Slaughter said. Laurentis saw that the Space Marine captain's massive firearm was clamped to his belt. He'd exhausted its munition supply. The fight must have been extraordinarily intense.

Slaughter glanced down at Laurentis.

'There are supposed to be munition trains moving into the nest, at least one near here,' he added.

'Ah, so that's what I owe my salvation to,' Laurentis replied, trying to sound brave. 'You were looking for the ammunition.'

'I had an order,' snapped Slaughter, 'from the Chapter Master.'

'Of course. I apologise.'

'The fact that you were near a munition train was simply a bonus.'

Laurentis managed a laugh. Then he realised something that chilled him. Just as Laurentis had done, the Space Marine captain was trying to make light of the situation.

They really were in the most terrible trouble.

ELEVEN

ARDAMANTUA – ORBITAL

Chapter Master Cassus Mirhen watched the stricken *Amkulon* begin to fall out of fleet formation. There was something significantly wrong with the strike cruiser's engines. It was venting radioactive clouds and all contact had been lost in a blizzard of vox-interference.

'Did Lotus Gate get clear?' he asked.

Akilios shook his head.

'We don't know yet, sir.'

'Find out as soon as you can. I don't see any drop-pods or escape boats.'

The truth was, it was hard to see much of anything. The incoming feed to the main viewers and the repeater and image-booster screens was fogged by the radiation backwash and some kind of gravimetric distortion. That was what Severance had been trying to warn them about. Mirhen had most of the *Lanxium*'s tech-staff working on the issue, analysing the data sent over from the *Amkulon*. Initial reports were bad. Pockets of gravity distortion were being detected in a range of orbital locations. No one could explain it, and no one could adequately explain why there had been no sign of the phenomenon before the fleet moved into its assault anchor.

Now there was the *Amkulon* itself. A whole ship, a good ship, and a whole wall of shield-corps brothers, potentially lost.

Mirhen watched the flickering, jumping screen image. The majestic strike cruiser was making a slow, pitching descent into Ardamantua's gravity field, unable to support its mass. How long? An hour? Two? Four? The crippled drives would probably blow out because of the stress before that.

'Can we get relief boats out to them?' he asked.

'We're trying now, sir,' replied Akilios.

'We must be able to fetch some of them off it.'

'Yes, sir.'

Mirhen turned to the ranks of the technicians and science adepts.

'I want this explained,' he said. 'I want this accounted for and explained.'

The adepts nodded, but Mirhen felt no confidence in their response. They were as mystified as he was.

He was about to add further encouragement – at least, what he felt was encouragement – when the bank of screens behind him lit up brightly for a moment.

'What was that?' he asked, turning. 'Was that the *Amkulon*?'

The airwaves were filled with vox-static and ugly distortion.

'No, sir,' replied a detection officer. 'That wasn't the *Amkulon*. Sir, the battle-barge *Antorax* just... just exploded, sir.'

TWELVE

ARDAMANTUA

The sky was weeping light.

Slaughter kicked his way through a half-collapsed section of tunnel wall and hauled himself onto the softly curving upper surface of the blisternest.

It was raining some kind of liquid that wasn't water through an ugly squall that blew sidelong and made every surface slick and sticky. The nest was a huge sprawl, like some mass of offal oozing on a slab, magnified to titanic proportions. There were loops of tunnel that looked like intestinal knots, there were renal lumps and lobed chambers. Some sections of the vast, organic city were patterned coils like the fossil imprint of ancient seashells. Other sections were crushed to pulp by orbital bombardment and airstrikes. Smoke bled up from the blisternest in a thousand places, mixed with the wind, and washed into the squalling storm. Slaughter heard the downpour tick and tap on his helm and armour.

'Come up,' he called.

Cutthroat climbed after him, and then reached down to haul the dishevelled magos biologis up out of the tunnel. After them came Stab and Woundmaker. Slaughter had left the rest of Daylight Wall inside the nest under Frenzy's command. The Chapter Master's express orders had been to get Laurentis to the contact point. Well, four of them could do that. There was no sense pulling a whole company out. He'd voxed that decision to the *Lanxium*, but he hadn't had a reply. Something was chopping vox and pict to hell. Atmospherics. It was like Karodan Monument all over again. They'd been deaf and blind there.

And they'd still won.

The magos biologis was looking around, blinking at the daylight. The rain ran off his face and plastered his robes to his body.

'What's that?' he asked, pointing at the sky.

'We haven't got time for sight-seeing,' snapped Woundmaker. Woundmaker was a sergeant, a good man. In the last stretch of tunnel, they'd come upon one of the automated munition trains sent in to support them. It had been mangled beyond recognition by Chrome warrior-forms, and the servitors slain, but Woundmaker and Stab had managed to drive the enemy off and recover some reloads for their bolters. He was sorting and distributing them.

'No, look,' said Laurentis.

Slaughter took the four clips Woundmaker handed him and turned to look where the magos biologis was pointing. There was a light in the sky. It was a broad, diffuse light, weeping out of the ugly cloud cover, but there was a malicious little glowing coal at the heart of it, small and red, like the ember-fragment of a star.

'That's a ship death,' said Cutthroat bluntly.

Slaughter heard Woundmaker curse. He'd been too ready to dismiss the magos biologis' comment, but he could see that Cutthroat was right. They could all see he was right. They'd all seen a ship die from planetside. It was a heartbreaking thing.

'When in Throne's name did these vermin get orbital weapons?' asked Woundmaker. 'When did they get ship-to-ship capability?'

'We still don't know precisely how the Chromes distribute themselves across space,' said Laurentis. 'It is presumed they employ some form of pod or seed dispersal via fluctuations in the warp, but a full scale migration of the magnitude that would explain their population density here has never been witnessed or described. We don't believe they have what we would consider to be ships or a fleet, no vessels at all, but–'

He fell silent. Four angular visors glared at him, rain beading off their beaked jaws.

'I... I'm just saying,' Laurentis managed. 'I don't know how the Chromes could have taken out one of our ships. Perhaps it is an unhappy coincidence, or an accident.'

'There are no coincidences!' Stab told him.

Cutthroat began to say something about accidents and defaming the ability of the fleet.

'Well, something's happened,' said Slaughter, cutting them both off. 'That's a dead ship up there, and a big one too. The magos is right. If the Chromes couldn't hit it, that leaves accident, or coincidence. And coincidence means–'

'What?' asked Laurentis.

'Someone else,' said Slaughter.

A noise burst filled the air. Outdoors, in the stinking open air, it was like the booming of a warhorn, the braying of some daemonic voice. The air seemed to shudder. All four Imperial Fists winced as it stripped through their helmet vox-systems and assaulted their ears. Laurentis felt it prickle his skin. The hairs on his arm rose, despite the rain. Static. Ozone. Around the distant, broken steeples at the blisternest heart, chain lightning flickered and crackled in a sickly yellow display. Two more noise bursts followed. Laurentis felt the actual structure of the blisternest beneath them resonate with the plangent sound.

'The Chromes are capable of a great deal more than we realise,' Laurentis told his guardians. 'These noises... these bursts of noise... They are why your Chapter Master has charged you to protect me. I have a theory–'

'Tell us,' said Slaughter bluntly.

Laurentis nodded and shrugged.

'I will, sir. I think it's communication. I think the Chromes are trying to communicate with us. We understood them to be non-sapient animals, but we may have been very wrong about that. I wish to test the communication theory, and that is why I need to get to the drop-point to access specialist equipment.'

Slaughter nodded. He checked the auspex mounted across his left forearm.

'Tracking the drop. It'll be down at DZ 457 in the next twenty minutes. Let's move.'

They started off, crossing the oddly ridged humps and rain-slick gullies of the blisternest's upper surface. The Fists, with their strength, long stride and armoured feet, had no trouble negotiating the unpleasant material. Laurentis kept slipping and slithering. He was wet, and cold to the bone. Woundmaker kept picking him up by the scruff of his robes and setting him back on his feet as if he were some clumsy toddler.

'The point of the communication,' said Laurentis, out of breath and struggling to keep up. 'I mean, the point I was making was that if the Chromes are capable of communication, if they are capable of language, then they may be capable of much else besides. They can clearly cross between worlds and star systems in ways we cannot divine. Maybe they can take out ships. Maybe they have potent weapons for void fights.'

'Ships of their own, after all,' said Slaughter.

'Perhaps.'

'If they are capable of communication,' said Slaughter, pausing for a moment to look at the magos biologis. 'If you prove your theory...'

'Yes?'

'What are they trying to say?'

Laurentis paused.

'I first presumed, captain, that they might be trying to negotiate surrender. That was when they seemed to be at our mercy, when their nest seemed to be toppling under assault.'

'And now?'

'Now, I wonder if it might not be a warning. A cry of defiance. A challenge. Now I wonder if they might not be demanding our surrender.'

'Because they are hurting us?'

Laurentis sighed.

'They are, it seems, taking out our starships. They are harrying our ground assault. The successful outcome of this undertaking is not as clear-cut as we first imagined.'

They followed the rim of the nest down, along to the ugly, chordate ridges that pressed like giant finger-bones into the mud of the river's edge. The noise bursts continued to bark across the smoke-wrapped distances, causing the rain to squall and billow. Laurentis tried to keep a basic log of observable details on his data-slate as he struggled to keep up with his transhuman bodyguards. Fountains of ash and light vomited into the air from regions on the far side of the central blisternest, and the concussive booms reached them a moment later.

'Major munitions,' said Slaughter.

'Orbital strike?' asked Cutthroat.

Woundmaker shook his head.

'Looked like... subterranean.'

'So... our enemy has further weapons we don't know about?' asked Stab.

'That they destroy their own nest with?' asked Cutthroat.

'Don't argue. Don't debate,' Slaughter snapped. 'Get moving.'

Another blast rocked the ground and a huge plume sheeted into the dismal sky six or seven kilometres away. The Fists of Daylight Wall stoically and obediently ignored it and started moving onwards. Laurentis hurried with them.

'It *could* be a new weapon,' conjectured the magos biologis, a little out of breath. 'They might, I suppose... They might destroy their own nest if there was nothing left to be gained from protecting it. It might be... uhm, intended to create confusion and disarray, to take as many of us with them as possible.'

'For what purpose?' asked Slaughter, getting his hand under Laurentis' armpit and frog-marching him over a stretch of mud so slick it was like quicksand.

'If they had a final asset to protect?' Laurentis ventured. 'A queen, or the equivalent? A dominant reproductive female? The egg source? I am just hypothesising, but if the nest was lost, they might destroy it as cover for an evacuation of the queen.'

There was another blast. This one came from much closer at hand. The force of it knocked all five of them over and slapped out a wall of mud and steam. Debris pattered down, and the rain ran brown. The Imperial Fists struggled to their feet. Laurentis coughed and shivered, trying to clear his head.

'My gravitics are shot,' reported Stab, checking his visor display.

'Mine too,' said Cutthroat. 'No, correction. Gravitic register *is* working. It's just showing very irregular patterning.'

'Agreed,' said Stab, 'rechecking. Local gravity just looped for ten milliseconds, and that blast focus was gravitically strong.'

'These weapons... these new weapons...' Slaughter asked. 'They're what? Gravity weapons? Gravity bombs?'

Laurentis struggled to reply. He tried to formulate a reasonable-sounding explanation for why the Chromes should have mastery over gravity, one of the universe's most notoriously uncooperative forces. Maybe their intersystem travel relied on some gravitic drive?

'Watch your heels!' Cutthroat yelled.

Chromes were rushing them from the nest pods behind them. They were standard forms, their silvery shells glinting in the stained light, spattered with mud and liquid, but there were a lot of them. Cutthroat and Stab met the first of them, side-by-side, driving strokes and slices with their hefty blade weapons that sent the xenos tumbling and bouncing backwards, slamming into the ranks behind, slit and spraying. The stink of ichor filled the rain.

Slaughter and Woundmaker got Laurentis back, and began to struggle down the reed-choked slope towards the waterline. The ground, wet as a marsh, was littered with dead xenos from the first phase. Moving backwards, Stab and Cutthroat came after them. Laurentis, gasping with anxiety, marvelled at their bladework. The speed of it. The relentless fury. The precision.

Severed pieces of Chromes flew up into the air, spinning. Ichor jetted. The pushing ranks of assaulting xenos stumbled and clambered over the bodies of their dead.

Laurentis had seen ants do that. Forest ants, at the edge of a stream, the first ones drowning and dying so that those behind could use their corpses as a bridge, as a growing bridge.

The ants always got across the stream.

Ants never mourned their dead. They used them.

Another wave of Chromes scurried towards them along the bank to their right, clacking and sounding out the *tek-tek-tek* noise they made with their mouthparts.

Slaughter, positioned on the right, turned to meet them, his broadsword coming out. None of the Space Marines had resorted to bolters. Conservation of munition supplies.

Slaughter's blade met the first Chrome, half-impaled it, then hurled it bodily across the river. It arced and hit the water with a dirty splash. His sword swung back and decapitated the next, and then cleaved the third down the middle through the head.

'Protect the principal!' Slaughter roared.

Laurentis cowered on the mud flats. The four Fists closed in around him, at compass points, each one meeting the assault as it swirled around them from the two lines of attack. There was so much ichor spray in the air that the rain tasted of it. They were all dappled with it. The Chromes threw themselves against the four-point defence, finding only death and dismemberment as a reward for their efforts. *There is nothing,* Laurentis remembered the old saying, *as deadly as an Imperial Fist standing his ground.*

Laurentis wondered how much scrutiny the Masters of the Chapters and other senior minds of the Imperial military, and even the beloved and exalted Emperor Himself when He had set to devising the Legiones Astartes, formulating their minds and bodies... How much scrutiny had they given to natural history, to the behaviour of cooperative animals and insects, to their selfless and almost mechanical efforts? The individual was never important, only the group effect. One quick glance at a magos biologis' notebook or cyclopedia would reveal a thousand examples in nature of selfless cooperation, postlogical stratagems, and ensured survival.

A huge, armoured beetle could easily kill a tiny, lone ant.

But the ants always got across the stream.

THIRTEEN

TERRA – TASHKENT HIVE

'You look unhappy,' remarked Esad Wire.

'Do I?' replied Vangorich. 'Do I really? You can tell that?'

Wire shook his head.

'No, you can't read that in a face. Not for certain,' he admitted. 'You can't read anything in a face for certain.'

He stared at Vangorich for a moment, Vangorich just standing there in the doorway of the monitor station control room like a shadow brought in by the dusk, and considered him carefully.

'Been a very long time, besides,' Wire added. 'A long time not seeing your face. I'm no longer familiar with its nuances. I wouldn't know what sadness looked like anyway, even if I could read it for sure.'

Wire rose from his worn leather seat, brushing imaginary lint from his double-breasted arbiter jacket.

'A long time,' he said, an echo, spoken only to himself.

Vangorich was still in the doorway. Wire beckoned him.

'You can come in, sir,' he said. 'Come right in. Or do you have to be invited over the threshold like a night ghoul?'

Vangorich stepped inside the control room. It was brightly lit, too brightly lit, the hard shine of the lamp-globes and spots revealing every fatigued edge and scuffed fascia of the control suite: the dials and levers worn by centuries of hands, the milky read-outs, the chattering banks of antiquated switches, the electric noticeboards with their mechanical letters and series lights that stated the day's crimes and actions and, every few minutes, reshuffled and revised, like the journey monitors at transit stations.

Monitor Station KVF (Division 134) Sub 12 (Arbitrator). It had taken Vangorich four hours to get there. An hour's flight east from the Palace by suborbital, then a three-hour descent into the underhives of Tashkent Spire, a journey of rattling lift cages, suspension platforms and dank hallways.

It had taken Esad Wire a great deal longer to reach Monitor Station KVF. After his past life was laundered and washed clean, three years at Adeptus Arbitrator incept training, two more at the Procedural Division in the Asiatic Domes, and then eight years with Tashkent Major Case and another six as a jurisdiction subcommander. Then he got the Sector Overseer star to pin on his jacket, and a monitor control room full of antiquated switches.

Everything was processed, everything formalised. Every crime had to be catalogued and filed, described and posted, and redirected to the appropriate division. It was a ritualised system that had never really coped with the actuality of real life and real crime in the vast hive, but it was considered the optimal solution and thus persevered with. Running the data-switching station was also considered a task of great responsibility, and thus always awarded to a man of significance or ability, as a mark of promotion. Esad Wire was not a law enforcer. He did not fight crime. He simply filed it.

The room was essentially automated. Wire made a gesture, and two junior arbiters, the only other living people present, went off to find duties in adjacent chambers.

'"You look unhappy"', said Vangorich. 'After all this time, that's the beginning of your conversation?'

Wire shrugged.

'It struck me as so,' he said.

'How has life treated you since you left the Officio?' Vangorich asked. He did not look at Wire. He studied the chattering, updating lines of tile-type that were rattling up and down the displays.

'One never really leaves the Officio, sir,' Wire replied, with a half-smile.

'No need for the sir,' said Vangorich.

Wire shook his head.

'I think so. You are a man of a certain position in life and the world, and I am another, of another position. The inequality of our states seems to indicate I should call you that.'

'It's good to see you, Beast,' said Vangorich.

'And you, sir.' Wire grinned. 'Damn, I haven't been called that in a long time.'

He walked to the side cupboards and poured two mugs of thick, black caffeine from a jug. He handed one to the Grand Master.

'Social call, is it? Been a couple of decades, about time I visited Esad?'

'I've wanted to before, many times,' said Vangorich with surprising directness. 'Never been appropriate.'

'Is it now?'

'No, but I did it anyway. I needed to get out. I needed to... converse with someone who wasn't anything to do with anything at the Palace.'

'Find a priest,' suggested Wire. 'A confessor.'

'The priests all have agendas,' replied Vangorich.

'So... you're here. Go on.'

'Little men,' said Vangorich, taking a seat at one of the monitor stations and sipping his caffeine. 'Little men, playing at being High Lords. Personal ambition is in danger of costing the Imperium very dearly. I tried to block it, but the Officio doesn't have the clout it once wielded, and I got played.'

'Lansung. Udo. Mesring,' said Wire quietly.

Vangorich smiled.

'Well informed.'

'There's little to do here, sir,' said Wire. 'I fill my time with the data-slates and the court reports. I do like to keep up with the reported business of the legislature and the Senatorum. Politics has always been an interest of mine.

My old dad used to say that politics is what determines who lives and who dies, so though the business of parliaments sounds dull, it pays to keep an eye on what those idiots are up to.'

'Published Senatorum records don't show the half of it,' said Vangorich.

'They show enough to see that Lansung's after Lord Commander, and Udo's happy to facilitate that succession. Mesring and Ekharth will go along for the ride and lend their weight, if they get rewarded on the other side. Or is that read too simplistic? Am I just an armchair amateur?'

'Good enough,' said Vangorich. 'It's the usual power play.'

'But?'

'They're so busy playing, they've taken their eyes off the board. The Fists have gone to address the situation, but they'll probably need support. Navy support.'

'The Fists will need support–?' Wire began.

'Let's skip that for now. It's a threat. The Inquisition says so.'

Wire whistled.

'How far out?'

'Far too close. We need the Navy, and we need the Guard, and if we need the Guard, we need the Navy anyway. But Lansung doesn't want to get his toys broken.'

'So make him look good.'

'I tried that,' said Vangorich. 'We brokered a little persuasive block vote to make him commit his fleets, but which allowed him to look like the hero of the hour. And he took it, but he played us. He said that if the Fists needed full support, they should be allowed to commit their entire reserve. He made ships available. Even the wall-brothers have gone from their eternal posts. For the first time ever. The whole Chapter. There isn't an Imperial Fist left on Terra or on the *Phalanx*. It's as if he's handing them glory, as if it's his to give. Of course, by making it possible for the entire Chapter to deploy, he's reduced the commitment of fleet and Guard forces he needs to field.'

'That's not right,' said Esad Wire. 'You don't commit a whole Chapter in one go. That's basic.'

'You do if you're an idiot with dreams of a de facto throne. You do if you put yourself above the needs of mankind. And you do if you've become so complacent after decades of peace that you think nothing can ever harm us again. Beasts arise.'

Wire laughed, though his face was troubled.

'They do,' he agreed. 'When you least expect. First lesson they ever taught us.'

'And the reason for your nickname,' said Vangorich.

'That belonged to someone else,' said Wire, losing the smile. 'I'm a respectable civil servant now.'

He looked at Vangorich.

'When did this happen?'

'Six weeks ago. It wasn't publicly announced. A matter of security. The reinforcements should reach the main force very soon.'

'*That* close?'

'Oh yes.'

Wire shrugged.

'So, may I ask, sir,' he said, 'what was this visit? An opportunity to vent to a sympathetic ear? Or did you think that I could somehow offer a solution to help an entire Chapter of Adeptus Astartes in trouble?'

Vangorich smiled.

'Back in the day, I would not have put such a task beyond the powers of Beast Krule.'

'Beast Krule's long gone,' said Wire.

Vangorich stood up.

'Anyway, no. Not at all,' he said. 'I don't expect you to have a solution, and we don't need one. It's the entire Chapter of Imperial Fists, plus support, Beast. They will quash this threat very quickly. Very quickly. Then no one will notice or remember how close we came to being stupid.'

He faced Wire.

'That's the real crisis. That's why I came to ask your opinion. It's not what's happening now. What's happening now is an act of strategic idiocy sanctioned by men who are too busy chasing the highest office. It's ugly and ham-fisted, but it will resolve itself, and all will be safe. We can trust the Fists. But in the long term, we are left with men who made it happen, let it happen, and thought it was absolutely fine that it happened. And that presents us with the possibility of what might happen next time, and the time after, and the time after that, until such acts of idiocy really start to cost. These men are not fit, Beast. But they represent a seamless power bloc at the heart of the Twelve that cannot be unshaken or dislodged, even with the most radical tactical voting from the rest of us. The Senatorum Imperialis is theirs and will remain theirs.'

Wire nodded ruefully.

'I came, old friend,' said Vangorich, 'because there is a possibility, with all other options exhausted, that one day soon I might have to ask you to go back to your old job.'

'Glory,' Wire whispered. He took a deep breath. 'I can't go back, sir. Not after all this time... I mean, that's not me any more. I left the Officio...'

Drakan Vangorich looked at him without pity or humour.

'Beasts arise, Esad,' he said. 'And besides, one never really leaves the Officio.'

FOURTEEN

ARDAMANTUA – OUTER SYSTEM APPROACHES

The translation bells were sounding along the quarterdeck of the *Azimuth*.

Daylight rose to his feet from the arming block, took his helm off the rack, and lowered it over his head. The neck seals hissed and whirred into place.

An attendant approached, dressed in a yellow gown.

'I heard,' said Daylight before the man could speak.

The Imperial Fist methodically placed his bolter in its clamp, selected a gladius and sheathed it, and mag-locked a combat knife to his chestplate. Then he finally adorned his head with the laurel wreath that marked him as the senior Imperial Fist in the reinforcement detachment. The laurel symbol had already been painted on his shoulderplates.

He turned and walked from the arming chamber, out onto the quarter-deck space. Hundreds of attendants in yellow robes stopped and watched him as he strode forwards. It was a moment, a singular moment. Daylight was going to war.

Daylight was aware of the significance. He had longed for war, and felt guilty for doing so. Only the best were ever given the reward of wall-brother status, but it amounted to a punishment, because it took them from the zones of glory and made them live out their lives on ceremonial sentry duty in the draughty halls of the Palace of Terra.

This had been his dream since he had won the status. Going back to war had been his dream.

Yes, the significance was not lost on him. It was a day full of significance. It was the first time ever that wall-brethren had been allowed to leave Terra and the *Phalanx* and go to war in support of their kind, the first time that the entire Chapter had been committed at one stroke since the days of the Siege, when they had been a Legion still. The first time since then that a capital threat had come inside fifty warp-weeks of the Terran Core.

Though he was a creature bred for war, Daylight was not blind to the political significance either. Attending the Palace as he had done for so many years, he had watched the activities of the Senatorum and knew power play and counter-agendas when he saw them. Daylight's glorious return to war, and the wielding of the Imperial Fists as one unified weapon at this time of crisis, were merely by-products of Lord High Admiral Lansung's ascension. He had made himself look quite imperial by moving his forces in support of the Fists, and even more imperial by magnanimously suggesting that the Fists support and preserve their reputation. He had, in effect, facilitated everything that was happening. The fact that he had effectively sent an entire Chapter of Adeptus Astartes to war left a great deal more unsaid about his power.

Attendants swept up on either side of Daylight and attached a long cloak to his shoulders, a cloak of blue silk that trailed out behind him. Armed footmen fell in step around him, an honour guard supplied by Heth. Just like politics, the cloak was an encumbrance that Daylight would dispense with in combat.

They moved up the quarterdeck, and under the valveway arches. The burnished deck throbbed beneath them as the warship bled out power. The warp had just spat out the *Azimuth* after six and a half weeks of travel, and now, translated into the realm of real space, they and the rest of the reinforcement squadron were slicing in across the outer banks and belts of the Ardamantua System into the compliance zone.

As he walked, Daylight processed. Data-feeds were inflowing to his visor mount, and had been since the trip began. He processed the latest intercepts and battle reports from the line formation, archived data on the planet and the blisternest site, force composition and a rolling track of action-by-action detail from the very first moment of deployment onwards. From the outside, Daylight looked like a ceremonial figure walking in a grand state parade. On the inside, he was a strategium in war mode.

Most of the data he could process was archived, however. It came from the early part of the compliance, and from intercepts received before the reinforcement squadron had left the Terran Core. They had spent weeks in the empyrean, and nothing viable or reliable had entered the data-streams of astropathic communication links during the voyage.

Now they were back in real space, the vast leap of their extra-universal transit achieved, communication could resume.

Except, Daylight could see from the feeds, nothing was coming from the world called Ardamantua.

Nothing human.

He entered the warship's state bridge. Navy officers turned to acknowledge him with formal stiffness, but a gesture sent them back to their vast consoles, set in tiers up the mountainside flanks of the chamber. On high platforms with gilded handrails, strategy officers plotted courses and operated the vast hololithic displays of the central strategium. Lines of Navy armsmen in formal uniforms, in ranks forty long and seven wide, stood facing each other on the central, mirror-polished steel floorspace of the bridge, forming an avenue down which Daylight could proceed to the command dais. They came to attention, their silver lascarbines raised.

Daylight walked the line, still processing.

Nothing human, nothing human...

Admiral Kiran stepped off the dais to meet him, escorted by General Maskar and a small army of aides, subalterns and autoclerks. Kiran was Lansung's appointed proxy, a slender and unfriendly-looking man in late middle age with a permanently cunning expression on his face. He wore silver and blue, and a broad bicorn hat. He carried the ship's command wand in his left hand. The wand was a jewel-encrusted device the size of a sceptre or battle-mace, and it hummed soft songs of deep space and the warpways to itself.

Maskar was Lord Commander Militant Heth's proxy on the command warship, though Heth travelled with the squadron aboard the grand carrier *Dubrovnic*. Unlike Lansung, who had seen the Ardamantua crisis in purely political terms and had instructed his officers to conduct it on his behalf, Heth was a more selfless individual. He appreciated the potential scale of the crisis and had elected to join the reinforcements in person. He led sixty-eight brigades of the Astra Militarum, the biggest deployment from the core seen in years, and he was not about to place that in the hands of his juniors. Heth wanted to show that unlike Lansung and, indeed, the other High Lords, he was prepared to get his hands dirty. The Imperial Fists required the assistance of his Astra Militarum, and he intended to deliver that in person.

It had caused a stir when Heth had announced his intention of joining the squadron. There was nothing Lansung could say about it that wouldn't look petty, but Lansung's thunder had been stolen a little. Heth was positioning himself as a willing man of the people, a leader who *did* rather than *told*. It was clear that Heth saw this moment as an opportunity to show that the Astra Militarum, vast and reliable, was the most important service standing in the Imperium's defence, the truest and most doughty.

It was also an opportunity for Heth to ease himself out of the shadow cast across the Senatorium High Twelve by Lansung, Mesring and Udo.

As per protocol, not all the squadron's senior officers travelled on the same vessel. Vox-officers set up a real-time link to Heth so he could coordinate with them.

Maskar was a useful officer, short and bullish, with an excellent track record. He had not long returned from service in a frontier campaign, the 'blood fresh on his tunic' as the phrase went. Daylight had read Maskar's file. He liked the man, liked him for what he could do.

None of that data was pertinent now: not Maskar's file, not the politics on Terra.

'Sir,' said Kiran.

'Anything?' asked Daylight. 'Anything from the surface?'

'No,' replied the admiral.

'Nothing human,' Maskar added with a growl.

'I have reviewed the incoming data,' said Daylight. 'It's very noisy down there.'

Kiran nodded to one of his analysis officers, who projected a small holo-lithic display between his tech-engraved hands as though he was opening a book for them to look at.

'Since our last data from Ardamantua,' the analysis officer said, 'the surface and atmospheric situations have degenerated catastrophically. The planet seems to have been plunged into some kind of stellar crisis. It's almost primordial down there. We presumed at first that it might have been struck by another body, a large meteor, but there is no trace of that very distinctive damage pattern.'

Daylight watched the man's shifting display, staying one step ahead of everything he said.

'Ardamantua has been rendered unstable in the six weeks since we last saw it,' the analysis officer continued. 'It is unstable atmospherically, geologically and orbitally. There are gross levels of surface radiation, and significant signs of massive gravitic instability.'

'There were never any indications of gravitic weaknesses in the early planetary surveys,' said Admiral Kiran.

'However,' said Maskar, 'some of the last few intercepts we received from the expedition force before we departed spoke of what appeared to be gravitational anomalies.'

'That data was never substantiated,' said the analysis officer. 'We have been attempting to contact Terra astropathically to see what they may have heard from the expedition fleet while we were in transit.'

'The answer is precious little, it seems,' said Kiran. He looked directly at the towering Space Marine. 'All effective contact with your Chapter Master and the expedition fleet was lost over six weeks ago, two days after we entered the warp.'

'So they are gone?' asked Daylight. 'Dead?'

'There is no sign of the fleet or of any surface deployment,' said Maskar. 'But that isn't to say they aren't there.'

'The planet and its orbital environs are a mess of interference patterns and disruption,' said the analysis officer. 'It is quite possible that the fleet is there, as well as surface forces, but our scanners can't detect them and we can't hear their vox.'

'So what are we hearing?' asked Daylight.

'Massive amounts of sonic and infrasonic noise bursts,' said the analysis officer, 'similar to the kind of noise bursts reported by the surface forces before comms went down, but of greater intensity, duration and regularity. It's as though the planet is howling in agony.'

Kiran shot the man a scolding look. The analysis officer stepped back, ashamed of his colourful description.

'What's making the noise?' asked Daylight.

'I think it's some kind of stellar effect,' said Kiran. 'A solar storm, perhaps, or a transmitted by-product of the gravitational mayhem.'

'Except,' said Maskar.

'Except?' asked Daylight.

'It reads as organic,' said Lord Commander Militant Heth's proxy. He said it hesitantly, as though he didn't quite believe it himself.

'How can it be organic?' asked Daylight.

'A voice,' murmured the analysis officer. 'It's like a voice...'

'It's something amplified and broadcast,' said Maskar.

'A weapon of some description?' suggested Kiran.

'What action do we take?' asked Maskar.

'We deploy, of course,' said the unmistakable tones of the Lord Commander Militant.

They turned. The vox and pict link had been established to the Lord Commander Militant's vessel, and his face, slightly crackled by interference patterns, had appeared in the ruddy field of a large hololithic projector unit.

'Is that not rash, my lord?' asked Admiral Kiran. 'We don't even know how close we can get and maintain the safety of the squadron.'

'We travelled six weeks to face a problem and perhaps save the lives of some honoured friends,' said Heth, his voice signal distorting slightly. 'We are also investigating a potential capital threat to the Terran Core. I don't think this is the time to be prissy. How long until we're inside a decent deployment distance, admiral?'

'Four hours and seventeen minutes,' replied Kiran.

'Are the men ready for planetary landing, general?' Heth asked.

'All infantry and armour support will be boarded on the drop-ships and surface landers within the hour, sir,' replied Maskar. 'I can commit a full force drop as soon as we are in range.'

'And the Imperial Fists?' asked Heth. 'The wall-brethren?'

'We are ready,' replied Daylight.

'Then the only thing that appears rash,' said Heth, 'is the notion of me making this decision rather than waiting to hear it from the nominated and honoured commander of this expedition. Forgive me, sir. The call is yours.'

There was a pause.

'Thank you, my lord,' said Daylight. 'Given the extremity of the conditions, I believe it would be prudent to arrange an advance recon, fast and powerful, to penetrate the zone and report back before we risk the bulk of our forces. I will lead this. Have a ship prepared.'

Daylight looked at Heth.

'The main force should be held at readiness. As soon as we have data, and as soon as an enemy or objective is identified, the fleet elements and the Imperial Guard will take it with the fury of the Emperor Himself. Does that seem like a plan to you, my lord?'

'I couldn't have put it better myself,' replied Heth.

'Then let us begin,' said Daylight.

'The Emperor protects,' nodded Maskar and Kiran, making the sign of the aquila.

'And we, in our turn,' replied Daylight, 'protect Him.'

FIFTEEN

ARDAMANTUA

Like stooping raptors, pinions swept back for the long dive, the Stormbirds plunged into the swirling atmospheric halo surrounding stricken Ardamantua.

The planet was swathed by a bright, visible corona of agitated energy, a sensor-opaque aura that shrouded the orb to almost the depth of its own radius. It resembled a solar storm, a swirling, luminous ocean of gas, dust and radiation that flickered in blues, golds, ambers and reds. The planet itself was just a dark globe, silhouetted within the maelstrom.

Just as the wall-brothers had been drawn out of traditional service and allowed to roam away from Terra, so the Stormbird war machines, the fastest and most honoured of all the drop-craft in the arsenal of the Adeptus Astartes, had been selected for the reinforcement mission. Stormbirds, sleek, powerful and large-capacity, had been born in the earliest years of the Great Crusade, developed from the almost mythical Skylance drop-ships that had served during the final days of the Unification Wars splitting open the hives of Ceylonia and Ind. Stormbirds had been the inter-orbital weapon of choice throughout the Crusade, and through the dark, treacherous time that had been the unexpected sequel to that bright glory.

The Heresy had consumed them in great numbers, however, just as it had consumed men and brothers and Legions, and the forces of the Imperium had been obliged to resort to more utilitarian vehicles that were cheaper and easier to mass produce. These replacement craft were now ubiquitous in all Chapters, and had proved worthy of service through their simple functionality and durability.

Still, for those with long memories, there was nothing like a Stormbird to stir the heart. The symbol of the Emperor's wrath, wings hooked back like an aquila – one only saw them in ceremonial flypasts these days, or in the Hall of Weapons, or as escorts for High Lords, warmasters and sector governors.

Daylight had ordered six of them to be raised from the Fists' Chapter House hangars and stowed aboard the reinforcement fleet. No one had argued. Heth's presence on the campaign mission had helped. He was a High Lord, after all.

Firing from the capital ships like missiles, the Stormbirds formed a formation spread and scream-dived into the unholy vortex surrounding the planet. Ardamantua lay beneath them, a vast curve of grey mottled with orange and crackled with veins of fire. Cloud banks and storm patterns of vast magnitude curdled and swirled across the boiling surface. Magnetics, radiation and the pop of gravity blisters rendered the nearspace realm a lethal soup.

'We have substantial vulcanism around the equatorial belt,' reported the lead Stormbird's tech-adept. 'The crust there is faulting and splitting.'

The Stormbird was shaking. Daylight keyed up the data on his overhead monitor and swung it down on its gimbal arm. On the flickering pict, strung with overlays, the planet seemed to have a burning, white-hot girdle around its waist.

'Something's happening to the magnetic poles,' said the adept. 'The planet is deforming. I–'

His voice cut out briefly as another noise burst ripped through the vox-links, squalling and deafening. The screech was painful, but Daylight's ears could endure it. He had a concern for the human component of his task-force, however. The unmodified, unaugmented humans of the Imperial Guard formed the greatest proportion of his strikeforce. They would suffer, either through mortal injury from the noise bursts, or through lack of coordination if vox-comm proved unviable. What were the implications if he was unable to deploy any of his Guard strength to the surface? Could the wall-brothers complete the mission unassisted? Could they find and rescue the shield-corps?

Rescue was a word he certainly did not like.

The Stormbird began to shake more furiously as they entered the outer radiation bands of the high atmosphere. Plumes of what looked like flame flashed past the small, semi-shuttered cabin ports. The tongues were blue, mauve and green, like noxious gases burning in a lab. For a moment, Daylight wondered if they were some trace of the warp, some daemonic lightning. All along there had been quiet rumours that the silent hand of Chaos, whose actions had been absent from the galactic theatre for a troublingly long time, might be playing a part in the Ardamantuan misadventure.

But it was not false fire or warp-scald. It was a geomagnetic display, auroras of charged particles ripping through the maddened thermosphere.

'Any indication of vessels in nearspace?' asked Daylight.

'Negative,' replied the tech-adept.

Another hope dashed. There was a fleet here, somewhere, the best part of the entire Imperial Fists battlefleet, unless it had been utterly reduced and annihilated already. Where was it? It could be directly in front of them, but veiled from them by the tumult.

The descent turbulence became progressively worse. The Stormbird was shaking like a sistrum at a fervent ritual. Lines of red alert lights were flashing into life along the pilot's enclosing consoles, filling entire rows. Deftly, with great calm, the pilot took one black-leather-gloved hand off the helm and muted the alarms.

Daylight began to flick through the meagre and imperfect surface scan readings they were finally obtaining, as they got closer and their auspex systems penetrated the atmosphere a little more deeply. They were on a pre-selected dive towards the location of the blisternest, working on the tactical assumption that the site was the last place their forces had been reported. But there was no clear sign of the structure, and little of the surrounding landmass matched, in relief or topographical schemata form at least, the geography logged by the survey teams that had accompanied the original assault.

'Is this just bad luck?' asked Zarathustra.

Daylight turned and looked at the wall-brother strapped in beside him. Zarathustra's war-spear was mounted like a harpoon on the weapon rack above his grim-helmed head. He was the oldest of all the wall-brothers and had been the most reluctant to abandon the old tradition and leave the walls of the Palace behind.

'Bad luck?' replied Daylight. He noted that Zarathustra had selected the discretion of a helm-to-helm link. There were other wall-brothers in the craft alongside them, not to mention forty atmospherically-armoured shock troops of the Astra Militarum Asmodai Seventieth, Heth's finest. The Guardsmen and their leader, Major Nyman, seemed to Daylight to be about the finest and most resolute warriors that unmodified human flesh could compose, but he did not want them overhearing dissent from an Adeptus Astartes warrior as they fell headlong into Hades. Through the dark and slightly breath-fogged visor lenses of their faceplates, he could see pale, drawn, anxious faces that winced at every violent buck and lurch the Stormbird threw.

'Bad luck happens even to good men, Daylight,' said Zarathustra, his voice chopped and frayed by the interference patterns even on the short-range dedicated link. 'Sometimes the forces of light prevail, sometimes the forces of darkness take the upper hand. Sometimes, as history teaches us, fate itself intervenes.'

He turned his impassive visor to look directly at Daylight. There was a gouge of raw metal across the otherwise perfectly polished faceplate, a gouge that had been left by the blade of one of the Sons of Horus during the fight at Zarathustra Wall. Heresy wounds were never patched, though the brother who had taken that stroke no longer dwelt inside the armour.

'Think of Coldblood and his wall, at Orphan Mons,' said Zarathustra. 'They took that day against the eldar raiders, full of glory. Then the star went nova and took Coldblood, his wall and the surviving eldar. Victor and defeated alike, levelled by the whim of the conscienceless cosmos.'

'They say the eldar corsairs engineered that stellar bomb to effect a pyrrhic victory,' said Daylight.

'They say... they say... Don't spoil my story,' grumbled Zarathustra. 'My point is sound. Sometimes you kill the enemy, sometimes the enemy kills you, and sometimes the universe kills you both. This may have been a very conventional fight against these xenoforms, these Chrome things. Mirhen was probably wiping the floor with them, soaking the dust with their blood, or whatever they have that passes for blood...'

Zarathustra's eye-slits were milky pale, and back-lit by a faint green glow, but Daylight could feel the intensity of his old friend's gaze upon him.

'Then the planet dies. Solar storm. Gravity anomaly. Tachyon event. Whatever. Doesn't matter who's winning then. We end up with a mess like this.'

Daylight glanced at his overhead again. The only time he had ever seen data footage of a planet as catastrophically mangled and tortured as Ardamantua was in feeds of unstable worlds to be avoided as 'not supportive.' Six weeks earlier, the cream of his Chapter, the majority of his kin, the shield-corps itself, had been down there, dug in and on a solid footing, burning out the last vestiges of a numerous but outclassed enemy.

'Are you suggesting we turn back and give them up as lost?' he asked.

'Of course not.'

'Then what?'

'I'm suggesting that we prepare ourselves for the worst,' said Zarathustra. 'If this mudball has up and died under Master Mirhen and our brothers, then...'

'We will make a great mourning like never before, greater even than we did for our Primarch-Progenitor,' said Daylight, simply.

'It would be the worst loss imaginable,' agreed Zarathustra. 'For the Imperial Fists, the Old Seventh, greatest of all the Adeptus Astartes, and the most loyal of all defenders of Terra, to be reduced to... to nothing, to nothing but the last fifty wall-brothers stationed at the Palace. To lose all but five per cent, to be diminished to a twentieth... How would we ever recover from that?'

Daylight had no answer. Zarathustra was right. It was unthinkable. Even a force of transhuman warriors dedicated to dying in the service of the Imperium did not like to consider what might happen if they *all* died. The gene-seed loss alone would be an atrocity. Could they ever rebuild, even turning to Successor Chapters for support and bloodline? No loyal First Founding Chapter had ever been entirely swept away, not in the history of the Imperium, not even in the Heresy War.

Would the Imperial Fists be the first to pass into legend?

Some said, quietly and very informally, that it was inevitable. The Adeptus Astartes were a dying breed. Bloodlines and gene-seeds were gradually failing over time. The vigour had waned, and long gone was the time, pre-Heresy, when thousands upon thousands of Space Marines marshalled under the stars. The bitter gall of the Heresy had cut them down, halved their Legions, decimated the surviving loyalists, and tragically reduced the Chapters' ability to produce new Space Marines in anything like the numbers of old. With the possible exception of the Ultramarines – and even there, there was the contention that the same plight ultimately afflicted them too – the Adeptus Astartes were diminishing. They were a finite resource, used only for the most elite missions and efforts. They were slowly, very slowly, dying out. Senior men in the Chapter predicted that within four or five hundred years, unless effective new methods of gene-seed synthesis could be developed and a new Golden Age brought about, the Space Marine would be a thing of myth.

In his early life, before the honour of wall-brother had been granted him, before he had become Daylight, Daylight had fought the eldar. In fact, it was his deeds in the face of the eldar that had led to the wall-brother honour being bestowed upon him.

Daylight had admired the eldar immensely. They were truly worthy opponents, and he had always thought them sad, tragic, like figures in an ancient play. He had thought about them often as he paced the ritual patrol routes in the cold hallways of Daylight Wall. They were great warriors, the greatest their species could produce, and in their time, in older ages, they had been peerless among the infinite stars.

Their time had passed, however, and their glory with it. Their suns were setting, and they were but ghosts of their old selves, unimpeachable warriors with great stories, proud histories, old glories and fine hearts, who were simply fighting their end-day wars as they waited for extinction to overwhelm them. When Daylight had slain the crest-helmed master of Sethoywan Craftworld, there had been tears in the alien's eyes, and tears in Daylight's too. When great eras end, all should mark them, even the champions of the next epoch. And no great heroes should ever pass unto shadow unmourned.

For a long time, Daylight had felt that the Space Marines were facing a similar long decline. They were more like the worthy eldar than they cared to admit: giants from another age who were simply living out their twilight amongst mortals, incapable of fending off the gathering darkness, and unable to recapture their halcyon greatness.

Daylight had not expected to see that end approach so fast inside his own lifespan. If the Imperial Fists were as lost as Zarathustra feared, perhaps the age of the Adeptus Astartes was coming to a close faster than anyone imagined.

Zarathustra's words had troubled him in another way. He had spoken of the terrain turning against friend and foe alike, of Ardamantua and its geological mayhem being the true enemy.

That was a bleak prospect. The pride of the Imperial Fists was their ability to defend anywhere from anything. How could they hope to excel if anywhere and everywhere, the very ground itself turned on them?

The Stormbird bucked again, more violently than ever. More warning lights lit and a klaxon sounded. The pilot and his co-pilot were too busy controlling the breakneck descent to be able to cancel it this time. The lurching turned into a protracted bout of shuddering vibrations.

'Atmospherics worse than cogitator prediction,' said the tech-adept, a flutter in his tone. 'Crosswinds... also, ash in the upper airbands.'

'Ash?'

'Volcanic ash, also particulate matter. Aerosolised mud. Organic residue.'

'Hold on!' the pilot yelled suddenly.

The Stormbird started to bank along its centre line. The exterior light beaming into the gloom of the cabin through the slit ports began to rapidly creep up the cabin walls, over the ceiling and back down the other side, illuminating the struggling, desperate faces of the Asmodai troopers behind their visor plates, cheeks and chins tugged by the inverting gravity.

The banking turned into a full rotation, then another, and then another, faster. Daylight knew that the humans aboard weren't built to withstand that kind of flight trauma. The Stormbird crew members were modified enough to withstand it, with their reinforced bones and muscle sheaths, their inner ears and proprioception senses replaced by augmetics, and their stomachs and regurgitative mechanisms removed and regrafted with fluid ingesters.

But the Imperial Guardsmen would be disorientated, panicked, distressed, vomiting inside their helmets, choking.

'Stabilise!' Daylight ordered.

'Negative! Negative!' the pilot yelled back. 'We've hit some kind of gravitational–'

He didn't finish the word. The turbulence became too great and too noisy for voice contact. The unpredictable gravitational anomalies that plagued Ardamantua were regarded as the greatest threat of all because they couldn't be mapped and thus avoided.

And they couldn't be explained.

Daylight heard the pilot yell something again.

On the ground, a broad plain of mud and boiling pools lay beneath the angry sky. Ragged grasses blew in the hot crosswinds. In the distance, the broken horizon coughed and smoked, and spat sparks into the sky.

The sky was low, a rotting mass of swirling cloud striped by lightning. The clouds were running swiftly across it, like a pict-feed playing fast. Far away, six bright raptors punched out of the clouds, diving, catching the sun. They stayed in formation for a second, but they were fluttering, beset by both savage crosswinds and a gravitational pocket that refused to obey the reality around it.

One burst into flames, like a flower blooming, scattering its shredded fuselage. A second failed to recover from its dive, and plunged like a stone into the distant hills. A third tried to bank, but then spun away like a leaf on the wind, out of sight.

The other three stayed true, pulled up, cut low, but their trajectories were not stable either.

Gravity stammered again, bubbling the sky and slamming them hard.

They fell into darkness and black cloud, and were lost.

SIXTEEN

ARDAMANTUA

Anterior Six was dead. They carried him from the crash site and laid him next to the nine Asmodai fatalities. Daylight waited for Nyman to tell him the extent of the other injuries.

Zarathustra clambered back into the wreck to recover his spear. Daylight knew he was also going to mercifully finish off the valiant pilot and co-pilot who had brought them down as intact as they were, and now lay mashed and bleeding out in the Stormbird's compressed nosecone. They were plugged into the drop-craft's systems anyway, nerves and neural links. They had burned their minds out sharing the Stormbird's impact agonies. Even without their limbs and torsos irrecoverably sandwiched in ruptured metal, they could never have been disconnected to walk away.

It was a duty Daylight would have preferred to do, but he had command, and there were too many duties to deal with. He appreciated Zarathustra taking that sad burden from him.

He looked down at Anterior Six's body. On impact, a fracturing spar had sheared the wall-brother's head off.

'I never thought I'd see him dead,' said Tranquility, at Daylight's side.

The plain they had come down on was a broad one surrounded by low, smoke-dark hills. It was grassy, and peppered with curiously pretty blue flowers. Some of the petals, torn up by the crash and scattered by the wind, had fallen across Anterior Six's yellow armour, as if laid there by mourners.

'No time for sentiment,' said Daylight. 'Give me a situation report, brother.'

Tranquility cleared his throat.

'Flight crew dead, Daylight,' he said. 'Transport destroyed, vox-link down. No bearing from our instrumentation and portable auspex is flatlined. Last known location was forty kilometres short of the blisternest site.'

Daylight nodded.

'No contact with the other birds,' said Tranquility.

'I saw one blow out.'

'I think at least one other crashed before we hit,' Tranquility agreed. 'Gravity was just shot. We probably all fell out of the sky.'

'So we're all that we can count on,' said Daylight.

'There might be others nearby who survived the landing and–' Tranquility began.

'This is not a place where we can deal in "mights" ,' replied Daylight.

'Even the laws of the universe are playing tricks. We can only count on what we know.'

'I understand,' replied Tranquility. 'Then we have you, and we have me. We have Zarathustra and we have Bastion Ledge. We have decent resources of ammunition and our close-combat weapons. We have no ground transport. We have Major Nyman, a brain-damaged tech-adept, and twenty-six Imperial Guardsmen with kit.'

'I thought there were nine fatalities amongst the Asmodai?'

'There were, outright. But there are another five more of them are too torn up to walk away. Out here, they'll all be dead in an hour, less perhaps. Even with express evacuation to a medicae frigate, they probably wouldn't make it.'

'We move out,' said Daylight. 'Find high vantage. Assess the landscape and consider our next action.'

Tranquility nodded.

Daylight strode back through the flowering grasses towards the Stormbird wreck. Zarathustra was just emerging, spear in hand. He reminded Daylight of one of the ancient, pre-Unity demigods, born alive from the belly of a fallen eagle. He liked the old myths. Paintings and tapestries of them filled the galleries and halls of the Imperial Palace, their meanings, names and symbolism lost forever, except perhaps in the memories and dreams of the Emperor.

'Bad?' asked Zarathustra.

'And getting worse,' Daylight replied. 'We're heading for those hills. You and I will move ahead with Bastion. Tranquility can escort the Guardsmen.'

'We should stay together.'

'They'll slow us down. They'll never cover the ground like we can. Besides, they're in shock.'

'What of their wounded? They'll make them even slower.'

'I know. I'll do it.'

They walked back to the gathered survivors. A few of the Asmodai were carrying munitions and equipment crates from the opened stowage cavities of the Stormbird. Others crouched beside their injured brethren. Daylight noted that a few had formed a perimeter, lasweapons ready. Not in *such* shock, then. They remembered their duty.

The sun came out suddenly, covering the ragged plain and its sea of straw-coloured grasses and nodding flowers in a hot golden light. The roiling black clouds had parted briefly. The Stormbird had torn a two-kilometre scar across the ground, a long gouge like the one that the Horusian blade had left on Zarathustra's faceplate. The Stormbird's impact had ripped up grasses and soil and bedrock, and scattered silvered shreds of its bodywork, wings and undercarriage. The fragments of metal caught the sudden sunlight like pieces of mirror or broken glass scattered in the swishing grasses, or like the cut jewels of a broad cloak spread out behind the noble craft.

'We're moving for those hills,' Daylight told Major Nyman.

'I've activated a beacon, sir,' said Nyman. His voice was a reedy croak issuing through the speaker grille of his orbital armour. Through the tint of the man's visor, Daylight could see an abrasion head wound that was starting to clot.

'Good. At least any who follow can trace our landing point.'

'Will any follow?' asked Nyman.

Daylight was turning away, but he stopped to look back down at the human soldier.

'I told them not to, but Lord Commander Militant Heth will send others,' he said. 'He will not give up. I would not in his place.'

Nyman followed Daylight over to the Asmodai casualties.

'Some of us will scout ahead,' Daylight told him, 'but even allowing for your rate of advance, we cannot be encumbered. You know what I have to do.'

Nyman's mouth opened in horror, but he had no words.

'They will all be dead in an hour, less perhaps,' put in Tranquility, repeating the summation he'd made to Daylight. 'Even with express evacuation to a medicae frigate, they probably wouldn't make it.'

There was a moment's pause. The sunlight blazed. Radiation made their built-in meters crackle like crickets at dusk. Thunder, wind and volcanics rumbled in the distance and made the ground fidget.

'Is there going to be an issue here?' Daylight asked Major Nyman.

'No issue, sir,' Nyman replied with great effort. He turned his back, and signalled his men to do the same. In slow realisation and horror, they stepped back and looked towards the bleak edges of the horizon bowl. One hesitated, a hand on the grip of his sidearm. Bastion looked at him, and that was enough.

Zarathustra came to stand with Nyman and his men, and gazed at the distant hills and the sky filled with smoke. He began to declare the Litany of the Fallen, as it was said in chapels and templums and sacristies across the loving Imperium, the words set down by Malcador himself during the bloodiest months of the Heresy. His voice was clear and strong, and carried from the speaker of his battle-helm. Bastion and Tranquility joined him in his declaration, a mark of honour to the fallen Guard and the sacrifice of the Asmodai. Nyman made the sign of the aquila.

The three wall-brothers boosted the amplification of their speakers as they intoned the Litany, partly to add power to their statement of respect, and partly to mask the sound of bones snapping.

Daylight drew a breath and then, quickly and gently, broke five human necks in quick succession.

SEVENTEEN

ARDAMANTUA

The sunlight seemed to be at odds with them. It followed them across the grassy plain, away from the crash site. From underfoot came the thump and shake of a planet in convulsion, and great sprays of burning ash lit up the sky far away, volcanic plumes thousands of kilometres wide.

The sunlight followed them still, as if their world were a tranquil place.

Daylight, Zarathustra and Bastion moved ahead, covering the grasses with clean, strong, bounding strides, outpacing the sturdy efforts of Nyman's fighting pack. Daylight wondered if he ought to have finished the tech-adept too. The man had been cortex-plugged to the Stormbird's cogitator system when they crashed. He had suffered neural feedback, and the impact had torn his plug out and mangled the primary socket in the back of his neck. He was stumbling along at the back of the secondary group, escorted by one of the Guardsmen. Daylight thought he would give him an hour or so to see if his head cleared and reset. If it did, the adept might usefully operate some of their portable equipment. If it didn't, Daylight would revise his decision.

Plumes of ash smoke and white streamers of steam were borne across the plain on the wind, residue of distant cataclysms. They left the crash site far behind, the wreck and the heresy-scar of its death across a foreign field, and moved towards the nearest hills.

Noise bursts continued to beset them, coming from both near at hand and far away, as if wilderness spirits, the genius loci of Ardamantua, were howling at them and taunting them for their efforts. Daylight wished the tech-adept could set up and examine the audio patterns, but the man was incapable. The noise bursts, some of them long and tortured, were overwhelming their limited-range vox too, and causing discomfort to the Asmodai. Daylight instructed Nyman and his men to switch off their suit comms. Thus, the only communication between the two moving groups was the vox-link between Daylight's party and Tranquility who was escorting the Guard. It was not ideal.

Daylight also possessed enough imagination to know that it was not ideal for the individual Guardsmen either. Each one of them was alone in his stifling and cumbersome orbital drop-suit, the armour heavy and rubbing, with fear and disorientation in his heart, and trauma and grief in his bones. They were trudging along in the strange and sickly sunlight, hearing the distant roar of the noise bursts as contact vibrations transmitted by their atmospheric armour-helms, with no voices and no vox-chatter, only the inexorable sound of their own breathing inside their suits for company.

The three Space Marines, advancing away from the beleaguered troopers, were approaching the foothill slopes of the ragged outcrops that edged the plain. Now the sun was going in and out as clouds gathered and spilled across the sky. Something had detonated on the horizon and the sky was filling up with blackness, the smoke trying to erase every corner of light.

Zarathustra led the way, using the haft of his war-spear as a climbing staff, leaping up slumped boulders and ridges of displaced stone. Bastion and Daylight followed, almost amused by the old veteran's vitality.

They reached the peak. Beyond them, a thousand kilometres away, the next ridge of mountains was on fire, a ring of active volcanos. Darkness seemed to have gathered above the next rift valley like a threat. Jagged and almost magical explosions rippled across the valley floor as spontaneous and random gravitational anomalies, like the one that had downed the Stormbirds, chewed up the ground and blew sub-crust magma into the air. Impact patterns of disruption on a seismic level travelled through the ground away from the explosions. At this sight, Daylight's mind turned to other images stored in the books and paintings of the Imperial Palace: visions of the apocalypse, of the circles of the Inferno described by Dantey, of the imagined hell once thought to exist beneath the Earth.

The rift valley was a vast plain of smouldering rubble that shifted and flexed, exploded and shivered. Mountains had both been raised and had fallen, overnight. Valleys had uplifted into hills, fracturing the surface, and summits had plunged like avalanches into the bowels of the ground. Flames leapt up from the mangled earth in burning geysers, like signs or portents. Flammable noxious gases released from deep in the planet were burning with strange colours: purple, blue, green, yellow, as varied as the magnetic auroras that had wreathed their wings on their descent.

In places, the flames were black, and a mile high.

'Has the Archenemy touched this place?' asked Bastion Ledge cautiously. 'Is that warpcraft?'

'No,' said Daylight. 'This is just a planet dying. Strange phenomena manifest when a planet dies.'

Four or five kilometres from them, beyond the initial spill of rubble and rocks, there was a broad lake, silty and muddy, its surface stirred and chopped by wind and vibration. Daylight selected data from his helm memory and began to patch and re-patch quick overlays.

'That's the river,' he said.

'The river?' asked Bastion Ledge.

'The blisternest was sited beside a large river. The geography has been traumatically altered, but that is the river, I'm sure of it. There are just enough comparatives to make the connection. The river has broken its banks and overspilled, and then been dammed into the lake formation by the collapsing outcrops *here* and *here*. The blisternest will be partly submerged and, I think, partly covered by geological debris, but it should be in this position.'

He marked the proposed site on his optics and then copy-bursted the overlay to the visor displays of his two wall-brothers.

'An objective, then?' asked Bastion Ledge.

'The blisternest was the last reported location of our shield-corps ground forces,' said Daylight.

'Ardamantua was the last reported location,' growled Zarathustra. 'I don't think we can say anything more specific than that.'

'We'll head for it anyway,' said Daylight. 'It's a place to start.'

He clambered back across the ragged top of the peak to vox-link to Tranquility and inform the secondary group what the new intention was.

Below, he saw the flash of lasweapons discharging. In the sunlit grassland, under an alien storm of ash, Tranquility and Nyman's Asmodai Guardsmen were under attack.

EIGHTEEN

ARDAMANTUA

It was a Chrome. Major Nyman knew this because he'd thoroughly reviewed the briefing packet that had been circulated among the officers of the reinforcement taskforce, and the packet had included helm pict-captures of the Chromes in action.

It came at him through the grass, claws raised and mouthparts snapping, making a most peculiar noise that he could only half-hear in the claustrophobic isolation of his atmospheric armour.

He shouted an order that he instantly realised no one except him could actually hear, brought his laspistol up and shot two bolts at the charging xenos.

It slowed it down, but didn't kill it. Nyman had to snap off four more shots before it dropped a few metres short of where he was standing.

He looked around, having to turn his whole body to maximise the view through his narrow visor port. He could hear his own rapid respiration, as if he was in a box. He could smell the rancid bitterness of his sweat and breath, laced with adrenaline. Muffled noises came to him, as though through water. The dull bangs of weapons. Shouts. Sunlight shone into his visor. Glare.

There were Chromes all around them, most of them the glossy silver xenotype. He wasn't sure where they had come from, but the odds were they were burrowers and had come up through the soil, clawing their way out. His men, without orders to give them structure, had nevertheless obeyed essential combat drill and were forming a box, firing out at the things rushing them from all sides. The Asmodai were fine soldiers, trained by the very best in the gun schools of the old Panpacific. Their proud boast to be the best in the Astra Militarum was not without merit.

Lasrifles flashed and snapped in disciplined volleys, the searing las-bolts ripping open organic armour and mutilating limbs. Puffs and squirts of ichor drizzled into the bright air.

One of the Chromes, a very large, dark variant form, survived the rifle-fire barrage and made it to their line. It got Corporal Vladen in its claws and tore him in half, the way a man would rip a sheet of paper when he was done reading the message written on it. Ribbons of bright red blood shivered into the air and covered the grass. Vladen's armoured suborbital drop-suit split like overheated plastek wrapping.

Tranquility, the massive Imperial Fist, waded in, and drove the dark creature back, striking it twice with his power hammer. Leaking fluids through crush-splits in its shell, the Chrome reared back and launched itself at the Space Marine. There was no time or space for a defensive swing. Tranquility met the heavily built animal and grappled with it, gripping its chattering mouthparts with his left hand and tearing, while he tried to stave off its claws. As they broke again, Tranquility came away with part of a mandible in his hand. Ichor spurted down the Chrome's throat and chest. Tranquility knocked it down with a hammerblow and then swung his power hammer down in both hands and finished it with a devastating overhead strike.

More Chromes tore up out of the ground, flinging soil and uprooted grasses in all directions. Some of them were big and dark like the thing that had murdered Vladen. The Asmodai redoubled their fire rate, snapping off shots to keep the creatures at maximum distance. Nyman kept shooting, directing fire by means of gestures.

There was no way of knowing how many more of the things lay under the ground.

Tranquility closed with another of the more massive forms, despatched it with two clean blows of his hammer, and then found himself beset by two more of the dark beasts. They clawed at him, fending off his attempts to swing at them. With a curse, he drew his boltgun and shot each one point-blank, exploding their carcasses in showers of meat, gristle and body fluid.

He'd cut them a path. Nyman could see that, and he could plainly see the Space Marine's emphatic gestures. They had a path towards the hill slopes. In the distance, he could see the other Imperial Fists wall-brothers bounding down the hill to join them.

The hill slopes offered the protection of boulders and rocks for cover, and a small hope of staying alive until the other Space Marines reached them. Nyman knew his men would have to double time, and shoot as they ran.

He sent the signal, and most of them started to move, but visibility in the suits was so poor that some missed the gesture and found themselves caught out, alone. Nyman ran to them, grabbing them so he could look in through their visor plates and press his head against theirs, yelling so that the touching helms would transmit the sound.

'Get moving! The hills! Move it, man!'

They started running. Nyman and Trooper Fernis scurried the poor tech-adept along. The damaged man had little clue what was going on. Trooper Galvet had been slow to recognise the intended effort, and once he did, ran the wrong way. Nyman, dismayed, believed that Galvet had suffered some concussion during the crash, and was not thinking clearly.

His fuzziness cost him his life. Two silver-shelled Chromes ran him down and fell upon him, shredding him with their claws.

Nyman didn't watch. He ran, dragging the tech-adept by the arm with one hand, firing at the Chromes that menaced them with his weapon in the other.

As soon as the Asmodai were moving towards the hill slopes, Tranquility fell in behind them, his back to them, retreating and fending off the Chromes that gave chase. He whirled his hammer and struck them down as they came at him, knocking them over onto their backs, splitting their shells, breaking their limbs and their spines. His power hammer was a long-hafted, weaponised version of a stonemason's mallet, the sort of tool that had been used to raise the bulwark walls and defences of the Palace of Terra. Its design was symbolic. Its effect was not.

Nyman, still moving with Trooper Fernis and their befuddled charge, was suddenly aware of yellow shapes racing past them from the direction of the slope. Daylight, Bastion Ledge and Zarathustra had joined the fight.

Daylight had his gladius raised. Zarathustra was lifting his war-spear. Bastion Ledge hefted a power mace. They reached the line where Tranquility was single-handedly stopping the Chromes and crashed into the mass of them, rending and slicing, smashing and tearing.

Nyman reached the lowest of the heaped boulders at the foot of the slope, and pushed the tech-adept into cover, with a gesture to Fernis to look after him. His men were taking up positions among the tufted rocks and outcrops, slithering up the scree and loose pebbles and sighting their rifles as they found good firing places.

They looked back at the fight.

Several hundred Chromes, most of them silver-shelled, had broken out of the soil of the plain and were assaulting the line. Dozens of them already lay dead, generally split or sliced open. Steam from hot fluids clouded the cool air of the grassy plain. Overhead, a looming volcanic darkness threatened to close down the light.

The four Imperial Fists, wall-brothers, battle-kin, shield-corps, fought side by side. It was diligent work, dutiful work, holding ground so that the Guardsmen could find cover and in turn support them with directed fire. It was a blocking action, it was a defensive stance, it was *holding ground*, it was everything that the Imperial Fists did best.

Daylight knew that none of them, none of the four of them, would or could ever admit that joy was filling them at that moment. Despite the crisis, the predicament, the threat, and the possibility that their Chapter was lost and dead, they secretly felt joy.

Their greatest and darkest prayer to the God-Emperor of Mankind, and to the Primarch-Progenitor who sired them, had been answered.

After years of silence, ritually patrolling the walls of the Imperial Palace, they had been granted the right to fight again, perhaps for one last time.

War, for which they had been wrought, had finally admitted them back into its secret, dark and savage mystery. They were whole again. They would make the most of it.

Nyman and his men watched in awe as the four wall-brothers fought back the tide. Imperial Fists chosen as wall-brothers were the greatest of their kind, and had excelled at feats of arms. It was for their very excellence that they were selected as the embodiment of the Chapter's creed, and set to stand guard on the walls where they had mounted their greatest defence and paid in blood.

He could see why these men had been chosen.

He could also see how many more Chromes, hulking and dark-bodied, were splitting the soil of the plain and clawing their way into the sunlight.

NINETEEN

ARDAMANTUA – ORBITAL

'Any signal from the surface?' asked Admiral Kiran.

The vox-officer shook his head.

Kiran slowly crossed the bridge of the *Azimuth* to meet Maskar and Lord Commander Militant Heth. Heth had joined them from his warship as the reinforcement fleet decelerated to the drop-point.

'We've lost them, then,' said Maskar. 'Sheer madness going down into that murk and mayhem blind.'

Heth looked at him.

'I suggest you get your men ready, Maskar, because you'll be following soon enough. We're not going to leave the Imperial Fists to rot down there.'

'And what makes you suspect they are anything except dead already, sir?' asked Maskar. 'With respect, look at the screens. Look at the dataflow. This is a fool's errand. Nothing has survived the fate that has befallen Ardamantua. Not even their damned fleet survived.'

'We give them another five hours,' said Heth. 'That's my word on it. Five hours, then we send in more scouts. The first thing Daylight will do is set up a workable uplink or send some kind of signal.'

Maskar looked at Kiran. There was no love lost between the Navy man and the Guard commander, but they were thinking the same thing. Heth, a High Lord, was painfully out of touch. He clearly thought the Adeptus Astartes immortal. There were certain situations, certain conditions, certain environments, that nothing could survive. They were both working men, fighting men, and they had seen how bad it could actually get, not how bad it could be imagined from a throne in the Palace.

'Move the picket ships in closer,' Admiral Kiran told his deck officers. 'Have them despatch more long-range probes.'

'Probes will be obliterated, just like the last spread,' said Maskar.

'Some may survive,' replied Kiran curtly. 'Even if one of them survives to send back a millisecond of data, it will help. Besides, with the picket ships closer to the atmospheric rim, we can try penetrating deeper with auspex and primary sensors.'

Heth nodded. The deck officers hurried to their stations and began to relay instructions.

They watched the strategium display as the reinforcement fleet began to move into its new spread, circling the stricken planet. Indicator lights and icons drifted like sunlight dapples across the topographic grid. In the lower portion of the strategium's vast hololithic array, columns of data spread, jumbled and reassembled, processing the energetic flux and signature of the planet. Kiran had never seen a planetary body generate so much wild and contradictory data so rapidly.

'Wait!' he said, suddenly.

He crossed to one of the observation consoles and shoved two sensor-adepts out of his way. He began to manipulate the controls himself.

'What are you doing?' asked Heth.

Kiran didn't reply immediately. Most of the crew in the huge bridge space were watching him. Kiran irritably yanked off his gloves so he could better manipulate the control surfaces. His fingers wound back the brass dials and adjusted the ivory sliders until he had recaptured the data-stream information from a few moments before.

'There,' he said.

'I don't know what I'm supposed to be looking at,' Maskar ventured.

'Admiral, please elucidate,' said Heth.

'I know what I'm seeing,' said Kiran, 'and I'm sure my senior officers do too.' In truth, many of them hadn't immediately recognised it. Few had Kiran's years of experience, and few had seen as much cosmological data speed by them as the admiral had, but given a few seconds, with the data-stream artificially suspended and frozen, they could pick it up.

'A ghost,' said the primary auspex supervisor.

'A ghost,' agreed Kiran with a grin.

'It could just be an imaging artifact,' said the gunnery officer.

'Or the echo of a piece of debris blown out by the surface disruption?' suggested the oldest of the navigation adepts, running the same data through his own, handheld quantifier.

'I don't believe it is,' said Kiran. 'I think that's a ghost, the ghost of a friend.'

Heth and Maskar moved closer to the vast display, trying to work out what everyone seemed to be seeing.

'This blip?' asked the Lord Commander Militant. 'This shadow here against the relative lower hemisphere of the planet?'

'Yes, my lord,' said Kiran. 'Sensorus! Have the advancing picket ships direct their full-gain auspex and detector grids at that shadow. And the fleet too, for what it's worth. Address all our scanning arrays, passive and active, at what the Lord Commander calls "that blip" and have the data streamed to my console.'

'But what is it?' asked Maskar.

'It's a ship, my dear general,' said Kiran. 'One of ours.'

TWENTY

ARDAMANTUA – ORBITAL

The ship emerged from the elemental fury surrounding Ardamantua, rising out of the radioactive soup and lashing ocean of charged particles like a wreck brought up from the seabed. Streams of energy and magnetic backwash, lurid and phosphorescent, spilled back into the pulsing blister of gravitational madness encasing the planet.

The ship rose, powered by its own half-failing engines, summoned by the frantic hails from Kiran's ships, voices that gave it a direction to head in. It was ailing and damaged, they could see that. Many decks were blown out and the hull was ruptured as though titanic battles had been waged on every level. At least one of its main engines was dead and bleeding clouds of lethal atomic blood into the vacuum.

Two of Kiran's most powerful cruisers, at the admiral's direction, moved in closer to the struggling revenant and secured tractor beams, slowly hauling back and assisting its desperate ascent from the cauldron of seething cosmological destruction.

'Identity?' asked Lord Commander Militant Heth.

'It's Aggressor-class, my lord,' said Kiran, 'which means it has to be either the *Amkulon* or the *Ambraxas*. They were the two Aggressor-class cruisers assigned to the Chapter Master's undertaking.'

'Keel number and auto-broadcast codes confirm it is the *Amkulon*, sir,' a sensory officer announced.

'Let's raise her now she's clear of the backwash,' said Kiran. He walked over to the main communication station, where plugged-in operators and servitors worked at the steep banks of titanium keys. They looked as though they were attempting to play some nightmarishly complex cathedral pipe organ, out of which only the clacks and taps of their keys would issue.

'Connect me,' said Kiran.

Eerie squeals and screams suddenly blew up out of the vox-speakers, the ambient sound of space being tortured by radiation and gravity. Beeping and pulsing signals resolved out of the screams. Hololithic energies crackled around the cable-fed and rack-mounted hoop of the station's projector array, and then an image began to shimmer into place, suspended inside the rim of the hoop like soapy water inside a child's bubble-blower.

There was a great deal of distortion. They could see a face, but it seemed like a face as seen through a white veil of mourning, or some cerecloth for funereal binding.

'This is Admiral Kiran, commanding the reinforcement squadron. I am speaking from the bridge of my vessel, the *Azimuth*. *Amkulon*, can you hear me?'

Static. The moaning of vacuum ghosts.

'*Amkulon*, *Amkulon*, this is *Azimuth*. Can you hear me?'

'It is my pleasure to confirm that I can, admiral,' a broken voice said from the projector and the speakers. 'We thought we were lost. Lost forever. This is *Amkulon*. This is *Amkulon*. Shipmistress Aquilinia speaking.'

'Aquilinia! By the Throne, it's good to hear your voice,' said Kiran.

'Have you come to save us all, admiral? That will be quite a feat. The brave fleet is gone. Ardamantua is dying and it is taking the last of our best along with it.'

'Shipmistress,' Heth said, stepping up beside Kiran. 'Forgive me, this is Lord Commander Militant Heth. I am commanding this taskforce that has come to reinforce and assist the Imperial Fists effort here.'

'My most honoured lord,' the pale, half-seen phantom replied. 'I never expected that a man so great would come for us.'

'Can you, shipmistress, account for the situation as you understand it? We have precious little data. Can you give any report?'

'I have maintained my mission log since these events began,' Aquilinia replied, the edges of her words shaved off by static. 'I will link the data directly to your cogitators, so you may inload and review the information in full detail. To summarise – we were close to victory. The blisternest was under assault and due to fall. Ground forces had been despatched, and others were preparing to drop. Then the noise bursts began. You will have heard those. First the noise bursts, then the gravitational anomalies. There were not supposed to be any hazards of that sort in this system, but they ripped through the planet's nearspace like a plague infection. One of them opened in my starboard drive and crippled us. Saved us, too.'

'Explain, please, *Amkulon*,' instructed the Lord Commander Militant.

'It nearly brought us down. We had to drop our personnel and troop strengths by boat and teleport. But I managed to arrest our descent by ejecting the damaged core, and we were able to withdraw to a safer high anchor point above the planet where we began repairs. As a result, we were the only vessel a great deal further out when the full gravitational storm erupted. It destroyed the fleet, my lord. I saw ships torn apart, and others fall on fire into the planet. I saw the *Lanxium* die.'

'Great God-Emperor!' Heth whispered.

'We were far enough out to survive the worst of it, but we were caught inside the wash of the storm, and blinded. All directional input was lost, sir. I could not move for fear of running directly into Ardamantua. I could not move until the sound of your voices showed me which direction was *out*.'

The battered *Amkulon* was still pulling clear of the worst spatial distortion. Debris trailed out behind it, whipping back into the gravity well like silver dust. Resolution on the communication image was improving, and the vox quality had got cleaner.

'The *Amkulon* was transporting Lotus Gate Company,' said Maskar to the Lord Commander.

'Shipmistress?' called Heth. 'Did Lotus Gate Company get clear, or are they still with you?'

'At my instruction,' she replied, 'they teleported to the surface. I personally gave Captain Severance the teleport locator wand so that I could recall them if the situation improved. But I lost all contact with the surface. Sir, I did not even know where the surface was. I have kept the locator's transmission signal on automatic recall, but I fear the captain and his wall are lost to us.'

They could see her on the hololith now. Her bridge was a charred ruin behind her. The image distortion had cleared somewhat, but part of what they had first taken as distortion remained. Shipmistress Aquilinia, and those members of her command crew who were in view, were all swathed head-to-foot in white cloth. It was stained in patches, as if pink fluid was gradually seeping out from within.

'Radiation burns,' muttered Kiran. 'Sweet Throne, I've never seen such extensive... They've shrouded themselves in protective veils, but they are burned, burned so badly...'

'Shipmistress,' Heth announced. 'We are sending rescue boats to you. Medicae teams will–'

'Negative,' she said. Her voice was quiet but firm. 'We are thoroughly and lethally irradiated, my lord. All of us, poisoned and scorched. We will not survive long. My entire ship is contaminated by the drive damage and utterly deadly. No one must come aboard. To board us is a death sentence.'

'But–' Heth protested.

'You have dragged us from the flames, sir, but we do not have long to live. Stay away. All I can do for you now is present my testament of events and convey all the information I have.'

'I won't accept that, shipmistress!' cried Heth.

'You must, my lord. A great disaster has overtaken the Imperial Fists here at Ardamantua.'

'We can plainly see,' said Kiran, 'a cosmic event, a gravitational hazard that–'

'It is not natural, admiral,' said the shipmistress through the vox-link.

'Say again?'

'It is not a natural phenomenon. Ardamantua has not killed us all because of some whim of the universe. This effect is artificial. This location is under direct attack.'

'Attack?' echoed Maskar.

'By what? By the Chromes? The xenoforms?' asked Heth.

'I do not believe so, sir,' answered Aquilinia. 'There are alien voices in the noise bursts. Listen to them. And watch the rising moon.'

'Ardamantua has no moon,' said Kiran.

'It does now,' said the shipmistress.

TWENTY-ONE

ARDAMANTUA – ORBITAL

'That simply cannot be a moon,' said the *Azimuth*'s First Navigator, studying the large printout that had been unfolded on the silver display tables of the charting room. 'It is far, far too close to the planet itself. Look, it is within the very aura of the nearspace disruption. That close, its gravitational effects would split Ardamantua in two.'

'Am I honestly hearing this?' asked Heth. 'We have what appears to be best described as a full-blown gravity storm besetting this planet and coring out the heart of the system, gravitational anomalies all around the near-space region, and you say–'

'My lord,' said the First Navigator. 'I am quite precise. The gravitational incidents, the disruptions that we are seeing, are considerable. But it is random and it seems to be manufactured by distortions in space. If a planetoid appeared in such close proximity to the world, it would be a much more focused and significant effect. Ardamantua would have shifted in its orbit, perhaps even been knocked headlong. The hazard we are encountering is like sustained damage from a shotgun. A moon... that would be a blow from a power hammer.'

'But still,' said Maskar, tapping his finger on the oddly shaded part of the printout. 'This... What is this?'

'An imaging artifact,' said the First Navigator.

'It's of considerable size,' said Maskar.

'It's a considerably sized imaging artifact, then, sir.'

'The *Amkulon* was an imaging artifact too,' Heth reminded them quietly. 'Then it turned out to be a ship.'

'The physical laws of the universe would simply not permit a moon or other satellite body to move so close to a planet, nor could such a body appear–'

'I've seen daemons,' Heth growled. 'Up close. Don't talk to me about the physical laws of the universe.'

They stood in silence and stared down at the huge printout. The chart room was cool and well-lit, arranged for the study of cosmological documents. The air circulator stirred the edges of the vast vellum sheet that hung over the edges of the silver table.

None of the ships in Kiran's fleet had been able to detect or resolve anything resembling a moon in the gravitational and radioactive maelstrom surrounding Ardamantua. The printout image had come from the mission log data transmitted to them from the *Amkulon*. Aquilinia had recorded and stored the auspex scan as she dragged her ship out of its death-dive. This had been shortly before the tumult increased, swallowed her up, and blinded her.

'We have examined the resolution,' said one of the several tech-adepts assembled in the chamber. 'The so-called "moon image" is indeed a ghost. Verifiable data is hard to find, of course, but that object seems to be only partly material, as if it is an echo of something not quite there.'

'An imaging artifact!' the First Navigator declared.

'No, sir,' said the tech-adept. 'It is like something trying to emerge. To pass through. To translate. As if through a warp gate.'

'Hellsteeth!' cried Heth. 'Then who or what are we dealing with?'

'I don't know,' said Admiral Kiran, 'but I place my full-throated support behind your efforts to pursue this, sir, rather than giving it up as a dismal and lost cause. We must find out what is happening here, and who has wrought it. Because if they can move a planetary body here, then they can pretty much move one anywhere, and do *anything*.'

TWENTY-TWO

TERRA – THE IMPERIAL PALACE

The meeting done, Wienand dismissed the four interrogators. They rose from their seats, bowed to her, raised their hoods, and left the tower-top chamber.

The Inquisitorial Representative sat alone with her thoughts for a while. There were documents and advisories to review, and her rubricator had been urging her to annotate the latest watch list.

Time enough for all of that later. The morning's news had been grim – pretty much exactly what she had been anticipating, but grim. Her masters in the three sub-divisions of the Inquisition expected much of her, and they had set her in place among the Twelve to accomplish a great deal, but it was a complicated dance, a matter of balance and timing. The Inquisition was an instrument of the Imperium. It did not set Imperial policy.

Unless it knew best, in which case it could not be *seen* to set Imperial policy.

Wienand's quarters were an eight-level suite in the armoured crown of a tower overlooking Bastion Ledge and the Water Gardens. There was not much of a view because of the tower's ample fortification. Agents of the Inquisition had added defences of a more specialised nature when the tower was acquired for the Representative's use. The very walls and the armourglass of the windows were threaded with protective wards woven from molecular silver fibres, and potent runes had been discreetly worked into the patterns of decorative ornamentation on the carpets and ceilings. Automatic weapon arrays and intruder denial systems had been retrofitted into every staircase, doorway and floorspace, and most of the servitors were wired for weapon activation at a moment's notice. The suite was cloaked, in addition, by multiple counter-surveillance fields, and several more exotic effects derived from the esoteric arts that the Inquisition both practised and guarded against. A cone of silence, psychically generated yet psychically opaque, covered the uppermost storeys, and there was even a Mars-built, engine-rated void shield in the tower core that could be activated by voice command.

Wienand rose to her feet. She was dressed in a simple, full-length gown of pale grey wool. Her rosette adorned her wrist, as a bracelet. She felt she should summon her rubricator and begin the day's correspondence, but she was enjoying the solitude, the calm emptiness of the room.

She walked to the side table beside her desk and poured herself a glass of water from the fluted crystal jug, wishing her mind were as clear as the cool water. She raised the glass to her lips.

'There really could be anything in that, you know.'

Wienand tried not to react. She maintained her composure with an extraordinary, invisible effort. Without sipping, she set the glass down again and returned to her seat at the desk without making any eye contact, or any outward show that there should be anything troubling in the fact that Drakan Vangorich was suddenly sitting in one of the seats vacated by the interrogators.

'Such as?' she asked, moving some papers.

'Oh, toxins,' said Vangorich. 'I hear toxins are very popular. Untraceable, of course. Not necessarily lethal, but certainly mood-altering, or behaviour-modifying. Toxins that make you compliant and suggestible. Toxins that render you open to autohypnotic implanting. All sorts of things.'

'I see.'

'Don't you have a taster? An official taster? I thought you would have. A person like you.'

'I'll recruit one if it makes you happy,' she said.

'I'm only concerned for you. For a friend.'

She looked at him, directly. He was smiling, and the smile did not sit well with his scar.

'Why? Did you place a toxin in my water, Drakan?'

He shook his head.

'Throne, no. No, no. Why would I? What an awful thought.'

He paused, and looked her in the eyes.

'But I could have done. Anyone could have done, that's my point.'

'No one could have, Drakan.'

'Why is that?' he asked sweetly.

'Because no one–'

She broke off.

'Because no one can get in here?' he asked. 'Well, I seem to put the lie to that.'

He rose to his feet.

'You really are the most composed person, Wienand. Applause for that. Not even the courtesy of mild surprise at finding me here.'

'I should not be surprised,' she said.

'Even though your security advisor told you that this suite had a triple-aquila secure rating that nothing short of a primarch could get past?'

She didn't blink.

'I was quoting directly from his written report submitted for your approval nine months ago.'

'I know.'

'Page eighteen, line twenty-four.'

'If you say so.'

'Quite a colourful turn of phrase... "Nothing short of a primarch..." though not terribly technical.'

'I agree.'

'And not terribly accurate,' he said.

'I noticed.'

'I'd sack him, if I were you.'

'Drakan,' she said, done with his games, 'I'm impressed. All right? Does that satisfy you? I'm impressed that you got in here without setting off any alarm or countermeasure. It is almost inhumanly chilling that you were able to do so.'

'Thank you,' he replied. 'For what it's worth, when it comes to the private Palace apartments of the High Twelve, this is by far the hardest to get into.'

He looked at her and affected an expression of innocence.

'So I'm told,' he said.

'I presume you came here for a purpose,' she said.

He sat down again, leaned back and crossed his legs.

'I *presume*,' he echoed, 'that you read the transcripts this morning?'

'In particular?' she asked.

He sighed.

'You're really going to make me work for it, aren't you?' he asked. 'The first intercepts are back from Heth's valiant rescue mission. Ardamantua is a mess. Worse than could be imagined. The sheer scale of the loss isn't yet reckoned, nor is the true nature of the threat. But... it's bad news.'

'Yes, I saw that,' Wienand replied.

'You're very calm about it,' he observed.

'There's no point panicking,' she answered. 'There's every point making a considered and rational response. It is a threat. A severe threat.'

'Just as you originally suggested,' he said. 'That's why I thought I'd come and have a little word with you. You used me slightly, Wienand. You used me to move against Lansung in the Senatorum. That's fine. I quite enjoyed it. It's nice to feel wanted. You were concerned about the threat, because no one seemed to be taking it particularly seriously, but you were far more concerned with Lansung and his power bloc of allies, and the way the threat – and others like it – might be mishandled by them. It was a political manoeuvre to realign the High Lords. That's how you sold it to me.'

'Agreed. So?'

'The threat's very, very real, Wienand. It's not a valid excuse for brokering, it's a palpable problem. And I think you knew it was when you co-opted me. What does the Inquisition know that the rest of us don't?'

'I was concerned with Lansung's high-handed attitude towards–'

Vangorich raised a hand.

'There is a threat to the Imperium that is of far greater magnitude than anyone imagines, but the Inquisition is reluctant to disclose it. Instead, the Inquisition attempts to use political subterfuge to alter Imperial doctrine and policy.'

'Not so,' she said.

'One would hope not, or that might be regarded very badly. The Inquisition taking over effective control of Imperial policy? There's a word for that.'

'A word?'

'The word is "coup".'

'Drakan,' she said, 'you're beginning to frustrate me with your paranoia.

The Inquisition is not attempting to mount a political coup from within the Senatorum.'

'Well,' he replied, 'it would seem to be one thing or the other. Either the Inquisition is trying to take control because it knows something the rest of us don't, or you really are very concerned at the fitness of Lansung and his kind to sit at the high table.'

She said nothing.

'What is the threat, Wienand?'

'It is what it is.'

'What is the nature of the threat?'

'You know as much as I do, Grand Master. It is a xenos threat that requires attention.'

He rose again.

'So you're sticking to your story. This is all about your concern about power balance and the fitness of Lansung, Udo and the others to rule?'

She nodded.

'Well, that rather makes it my problem, then, doesn't it? An issue for my Officio?'

'What do you mean?' she asked, with a slight note of anxiety.

'Well, if any High Lord is deemed by his peers to be unfit or unworthy, the ultimate sanction has always been the Officio Assassinorum. It's why we exist. It is our purview. Political subterfuge is entirely a waste of time when you have the Officio to clean house.'

'Vangorich, don't be medieval.'

He leaned on her desk and stared into her face.

'Then I suggest you start trusting me,' he said. 'Tell me the nature of this threat. Share it with all of us. Tell me what is so terrible. What scares the Inquisition so much it needs to take control of Imperial policy? What do you know?'

She stared back at him, and hesitated.

Then she said, 'There's nothing. Nothing to tell.'

He stood up straight.

'I see,' he said. 'I see. If that's all you'll say, I see I must take you at your word. I suppose I had better get about my business.'

'What does that mean?' she asked. 'Drakan, what are you suggesting?'

He walked to her side table, picked up the glass of water she had poured, and drank it down.

'I'm not suggesting anything,' he said. 'I am going about my business and performing the duties entrusted to me.'

He walked towards the door.

'Drakan,' she called after him. 'Don't do anything. Don't do anything foolish. Please. This situation is very sensitive. This moment... You mustn't act rashly.'

'I'll try not to,' he replied. 'But if no one tells me where the sensitivities lie, I cannot help but step on them, can I?'

The door opened, and Wienand's bodyguard Kalthro strode in, a pistol raised. He halted when he saw Vangorich.

'Far too little,' Vangorich told him as he strode past, 'far too late.'

TWENTY-THREE

ARDAMANTUA

Daylight led the way over the broken ridge and down into the rubble-strewn valley where the lake spread out under a black sky. His armour, and the plate armour of the other three Imperial Fists, was spattered with ichor. No one had made any attempt to clean it off. They had left the field on the other side of the ridge strewn with dead xenos, piled high. It had plainly astonished Major Nyman and the Asmodai troopers, who had moved in towards the end and helped to slay the last few dozen with targeted fire.

Gravity, shifting and flexing like an invisible serpent through earth and air, shattered a distant row of hills with a noise like thunder. The clouds boiled past overhead, on fast-play. Flames of red, green and yellow danced around the ridges of broken rock and upturned, split earth.

'Once we reach the lake, then what?' asked Bastion Ledge.

'From the lake, the nest,' replied Daylight.

'Then?' Bastion Ledge asked.

'Then we look for survivors,' replied Daylight. 'For signs.'

'And if we find none?'

'We look elsewhere.'

'And if more of those things appear?' Bastion Ledge asked.

'Then we kill more of those things,' said Daylight.

They skirted a series of murky pools and crooked ponds that were offshoots of the lake, their trudging figures reflected in the water, the running sky behind them. The wind blew. The noise bursts continued to break the air, howling barks that came from everywhere and nowhere.

The gravity blister popped without any warning except a slight shrug of physical matter. A random anomaly, it opened on the edge of one of the pools about fifty metres from their procession. The physicality of the world, the rocks, the air and the pool altered instantaneously. It went off like a bomb, hurling tonnes of stone and soil into the air sideways, like a blizzard. The ground broke open and water turned to steam. The main volume of the pool surged in the opposite direction in a spontaneous tidal wave three metres tall, and broke across the next ridge with enough force to shatter rock.

Flying rocks and debris, along with mud and water, ripped along the line of Daylight's party. The Guardsmen were knocked off their feet. One died, his head crushed by a boulder. Only the frail, mind-addled tech-adept, bewildered and confused, remained upright.

Rocks and stones rained off the Imperial Fists, pelting their armour. In that instant, Daylight once again felt the uneasy fear. The Imperial Fists excelled at holding ground, but how did a warrior do that when the ground itself couldn't be trusted?

The thought barely had time to form before another blister ripped the world open. It was smaller than the first, a gravitic aftershock, but it was right under them. Two of the Asmodai simply atomised, turning into clouds of blood and whizzing armour shreds, their forms lost in the explosive upchuck of rock and bludgeoning concussion.

Bastion Ledge died too.

As the smoke and steam cleared, and the last of the rock debris rained down and skittered around them, as the ground stopped shaking, Daylight saw his wall-brother. Half of Bastion Ledge, most of the left-hand side of his body, was missing. It was folded and compressed in on itself, flesh, bone and armour alike. He looked as though he had been snatched up by a giant and squeezed until he was crushed like a tin cup. Black blood drenched his buckled, ruined wargear.

Zarathustra knelt beside him to check for vitals, but they all knew it was in vain. Bastion was gone, killed by the world, killed by the ground, killed by the forces of nature they ought to have been able to trust.

For a second, Daylight felt hopelessness, but there was no time to consider such luxuries as emotions.

A third gravity blister blew out on the far side of the valley, and the *boom* rolled around the outcrops. It hardly mattered. There was a more immediate threat.

Major Nyman was shouting. He'd ripped his helmet off so he could be heard and he was yelling, gasping in the thin air.

Daylight turned.

Chromes were coming out of the stretch of lake behind them, scrambling towards the shore. They were all large, dark, mature and powerful. Flying rocks hurled by the third gravity detonation hammered across the lake, killing several of them and sending up spouts of water, as though heavy-calibre gunfire were peppering the surface. The Chromes churned on regardless, bounding up the stony shore to attack the Imperial party.

Nyman and his men began to fire, though some of the Asmodai were still dazed from the triple hammerblow of the gravity blisters. Zarathustra sprang up and charged down the slope into the water, impaling first one and then a second dark Chrome with his war-spear. He felled a third with a savage back-thrust of the spear's haft, and then threw himself full-length to tackle a Chrome in the shallows that was bearing down on Major Nyman. Nyman's repeated shots were not slowing it down. Zarathustra knocked the creature sideways, and then tangled into a wrestling brawl with it, kicking up sprays of froth and water.

Tranquility used his boltgun as he moved down the shore, picking off two more of the Chromes that had come too close to the Asmodai line. His mass-reactive shells stopped them dead in a way that the poor Guardsmen's las-rounds could not. It took sustained, saturating fire to stop a warrior-form with a lasrifle. Having bought enough time with his shots to get at the Chromes close-quarters, Tranquility holstered his bolter and unslung the power hammer from his backplate. He crushed one Chrome's skull down into its shoulders and then struck another sideways, into the shallows. Its cranium split and ichor sprayed out. A third, attacking the Imperial Fist furiously, was knocked back with the butt of the haft, leaving it open for a downward smash of the head that ruptured it like a well-cooked piece of shellfish.

Ichor stained the frothing surface of the lake at the shallows.

Daylight met the attack with his gladius in his right hand and his combat knife in his left. He stabbed his sword through a sternum plate, and then slashed a mouth and throat open with his knife. As his second kill fell back, Daylight used the combat knife to block the striking claws of a third Chrome warrior-form, shoved the creature's limbs up and aside, and ripped his sword through its exposed midriff with a sideways slash.

A fourth Chrome closed. Daylight outstepped its charge and hacked his sword edge into its spine as it passed him, dropping it on its face into the pool. A fifth beast ran onto his extended knife. A sixth died from a cross cut, a double slash of both weapons that ran from shoulders to hips.

A particularly large Chrome seized Daylight from behind, sawing into his armour with its claws, gnawing into his backplate with its mouthparts. It hoisted him off his feet, backwards, tilting.

Daylight inverted his grip on both blades, letting them fall out of his hands so he could catch them again reversed, and then stabbed past either side of his hips with the sword and the knife, impaling the torso that was braced against his. The Chrome burst at the wound points and sprayed ichor. It collapsed, pulling Daylight down with it into the water in a thrashing commotion.

Others rushed at him, trying to rip into the Imperial Fists wall-brother before he could regain his footing. Zarathustra and some of the Asmodai saw this and moved to support. The Guardsmen fired at the thrashing Chromes, and Zarathustra charged them, spear raised.

Gunfire raked the surface of the pool, cutting down dozens of the Chromes. It resembled the fury of spume and spouts that had been kicked up by the rock debris, but it was real gunfire.

Rotor cannons.

Tranquility turned.

Zarathustra reached Daylight and hauled him upright, stabbing at the Chromes that tried to mob and menace them.

Figures moved down the stony shore towards them, a squad of men. Two in the lead carried rotor cannons, firing bursts into the pool as they approached to drive back the xenoforms.

They were Imperial Fists.

Daylight crunched up the shoreline out of the water to meet them, Zarathustra at his heels.

The squad commander faced them, and removed his helm.

'Severance, captain, Lotus Gate Wall,' he said. 'Where did you come from?'

TWENTY-FOUR

ARDAMANTUA

'We've been on the surface six weeks,' said Severance. 'At least, I presume it's about that long. Gravity distortion is so prolific planetside, I feel we can't trust any other laws. Several suit chronometers are showing significant time variances. This world is not aligned with the natural flow of the cosmos.'

'Increasingly so,' Daylight agreed. 'Six weeks is a reasonable estimate. We've been in transit roughly that long, from Terra.'

'Who's with you?' asked Severance.

'Everything that was left. The *Phalanx* is emptied and the walls of the Palace are bare. We've got a decent fleet support, and a substantial Guard cohort.'

Severance shook his head.

'I can't believe we've left the walls bare. I can't. If Mirhen...'

'Does the beloved Chapter Master still live?' asked Daylight.

Severance shrugged.

'My wall made an emergency drop to the surface via teleport when the *Amkulon* was holed. It was an extreme measure, and I would rather not have abandoned the vessel.'

Daylight saw that Captain Severance carried a battered teleport locator on his harness. A power light showed that it was still, futilely, activated.

'By the time we were down, we were blind,' Severance continued. 'The gravity storm had closed in. We've been scouring the surface for survivors or contacts ever since. We saw drop-ships. Stormbirds? That's what brought us this way.'

'You must have been in the vicinity already,' said Zarathustra.

'Yes,' said Severance. 'We managed to identify this zone, despite the geological upheavals, as the site of the original blisternest, so my wall has been section-searching the area to look for survivors.'

'And ammunition,' remarked Severance's second-in-command, Merciful. His tone was mordant.

Daylight smiled. He was amused that both he and Severance had independently lighted on the same strategy. It reassured him that the core training of the Chapter was both profound and reliable.

'Have you found anything?' asked Zarathustra.

'A few pitiful dead,' replied Merciful. 'Crushed by the tormented planet or overthrown by the Chromes.'

'They're not the real enemy,' said Severance.

'What do you mean?' asked Tranquility.

'The Chromes are just a hazard, and the cause of our undertaking here,' Severance replied. 'But there's something else. Something that wasn't here before. You can feel it. You can hear its voice on the wind.'

As if to underscore his remark, noise bursts echoed across the valley.

'Substantiate that,' said Daylight very directly.

'I cannot,' Severance replied. 'It's a gut feeling.'

'The walls do not deal in gut feelings,' said Daylight. 'The shield-corps relies on what is verifiable.'

He looked at Severance uneasily. Perhaps the brother had been here too long, subjected to the extremities of the environment. Perhaps gravity, or one of the other natural or even unnatural forces being twisted and convoluted on Ardamantua, had affected his personality or his brain chemistry. Where Daylight had felt reassured by the overlap of their tactical decisions, he now felt a distance, as if the bond of the shield and wall did not connect them at all.

'Have you seen the shape in the sky?' Severance asked.

'What? No,' said Daylight.

'Some things cannot be substantiated,' said Severance. He rose from where he had been sitting on the boulders scattered at the shore and gestured Daylight to follow him. Daylight did so reluctantly. The pair clambered up an outcrop overlooking the dark mirror of the lake.'

'Wait,' said Severance. 'Look.'

'At what? What am I looking at? The sky?'

'No, look at the lake.'

'You asked if I had seen the thing in the sky–'

'Be patient, Daylight. It comes and goes.'

They waited. Daylight felt he was wasting valuable time.

'Look,' said Severance.

The scudding, racing cloud-cover, moving across the heavens like a black lava flow, parted briefly, riven by the wind and orbital disruption. Sunlight speared through in a pale beam. The sky beyond the cloud was white and blank, like static. There was nothing to be seen.

But in the lake...

Daylight started. It was there and gone in an instant, but he had seen it. He reset his visor recorder for immediate playback, and then froze the image.

Therein, the clouds were parted, drawn like drapes to show a colourless sky where nothing resided. In the reflection below, however, trapped in the surface of the lake, the patch of bright sky did contain something.

Something large and ominous, an orb that seemed to press down on the wounded planet.

It was a moon. A black, ungodly, hideous moon.

TWENTY-FIVE

ARDAMANTUA

They had been walking around the lake edge in the company of Severance's squad for several hours when they spotted the flare.

It lofted up in the distance, an incandescently bright pin-prick, then shivered as it hung in place, before fading and falling away, all effort spent.

'One of mine!' Severance cried. 'Move!'

They began to make the best pace possible. As the leaders ran ahead, Captain Severance told Daylight that his subdivided wall had agreed to use basic flares and visual signals to stay in contact, given that everything up to and including short-range helm-to-helm vox was useless.

The ragged Asmodai troopers couldn't keep up. Major Nyman had put his helmet back on, exhausted by the impure air, but rather more troubled by the constant noise bursts. Even those Asmodai who had kept the visors of their orbital drop-suits firmly sealed since planetfall were feeling the effects. The noise bursts echoed into the cavities of their helmets and armour, unsettling them. It was psychologically hammering them.

Severance pointed to four of his men and told them to stay with the Guardsmen and bring them along behind. Then he set out at full pace.

It took them half an hour to reach the origin of the signal flare. Daylight was beside Severance as they slowed to approach.

It was a second search party from Lotus Gate Wall, commanded by a sergeant called Diligent.

'Good to see you, sir,' the sergeant called out. He hesitated as he saw Daylight and the other Space Marines new to him.

'I see you've made discoveries of your own,' he remarked.

'What did you find?' asked Severance.

'The blisternest, or what's left of it,' said Diligent. 'And survivors.'

The survivors of the original undertaking assault had taken shelter in the ruins of the blisternest, using its structure to weather out the worst the gravity storms threw at them. They had, in the weeks since, constructed a makeshift stockade from boulders, wreckage and parts of the nest structure.

Inside the jagged walls, there were men from Ballad Gateway, Hemispheric, Anterior Six Gate and Daylight walls, about one hundred and thirty of them all told, together with a few, fragile servitors. There was no substantial equipment, no heavy weapons or vehicles with them, and precious little munitions supply.

First Captain Algerin of Hemispheric had command.

'Well met in bad days,' he said to Severance and Daylight. He looked at Daylight, and at Tranquility and Zarathustra nearby.

'You left the walls unguarded to come for us? I'm not sure I approve.'

'You're not the first person to express that thought, captain,' said Daylight. 'We made our choice. The Chapter was beset.'

'Worse than beset,' said Algerin. His voice dropped. 'Worse than beset.'

He looked at the ground. His armour was almost black with filth, and it showed hundreds of nicks and gouges from Chrome claws.

'The Chapter Master is dead,' he said, aiming each word like a las-bolt at the ground. 'He reached the surface by teleport before the flagship was lost. He came to us. He was with us for three weeks. Chromes took him. Rent him. There were three hundred of us then. They wear us down. There are so many of them. Attrition, the coward's tactic.'

Algerin looked at them.

'He was so angry,' he said. 'Mirhen, such a great man, but so *angry*. He railed at the gods, at the stars, to see his fleet wrecked and his Chapter shredded, and the honour that has carried us through at the forefront of all Chapters, since the very start, shredded away... by animals. By vermin and a crooked planet.'

He took a breath.

'They killed him because of his anger, you know,' he said. 'He wanted to kill them. He wanted to kill them all, but there were too many. I tried to pull him back. He–'

Algerin stopped. He looked at Daylight.

'You have brought ships to take us off here, wall-brother?' he asked.

'I have,' replied Daylight. 'But conditions are still bad. We have to devise a way for them to get close enough to effect evac.'

'I don't think conditions will improve,' said Algerin. 'Not any time soon.'

He looked up as Severance's men brought the Asmodai stragglers into the makeshift fortification.

'Men,' he said, unimpressed. 'They will not last long. We had about fifty auxiliaries with us at the start. The noises drove them mad in the first week. We had to... It wasn't a good situation. Only one of them survived. I suspect it's because he was scatter-brained to begin with. He's determined though, I'll give him that. Determined to puzzle it out.'

'What do you mean?' asked Daylight.

'See for yourself,' Algerin invited. 'He's with one of yours.'

'I am Slaughter,' said the second captain of Daylight Wall Company.

'I am... Daylight,' said Daylight.

'I'm glad of the sight of you,' said Slaughter. 'You came for us. That won't be forgotten.'

Daylight nodded. 'I am heartened to hear that sentiment from one mouth at least. Who is your charge here?' he asked. A bedraggled and filthy human in ragged robes was hunkered in the corner of the nest chamber, working at various pieces of Imperial apparatus. The devices, stacked and piled against the chamber wall, many of them damaged, were running off battery power. Several of them had clearly been customised, refitted, or repurposed.

'He is the magos biologis sent to accompany our mission,' Slaughter explained. The chamber was gloomy and dank, part of the surviving underground burrows of the blisternest. Water dripped from the organic arch of the roof.

'He was supposed to study the xenoforms while we killed them. I was set to guard him when our fortunes changed. I've been doing that ever since, pretty much.'

They approached the scientist. He was intent on his work, muttering to himself. He was in need of a decent shave. His hair, dirty and unruly, had been clipped back in a bunch using the bent clasp of an ammunition pack.

'His name is Laurentis,' said Slaughter.

'Magos,' said Daylight, crouching beside the magos biologis. 'Magos? I am Daylight.'

Laurentis looked at him for a moment.

'Oh, a new one,' he said. 'You're new. He's new, Slaughter. See? See, there? I'm beginning to tell you apart.'

He smiled.

Noise bursts echoed outside the chamber, and Laurentis winced and rubbed his ears roughly with begrimed knuckles.

'The wavelength is changing. It's changing. Today, and these last few days. Greater intensity. Yes, greater intensity.'

The magos biologis looked at them as if they might understand.

'I had specialist equipment,' he said. 'I was sent it by the Chapter Master himself...'

He paused, and thought, his eyes darkening.

'He's dead now, isn't he?'

'Yes,' said Slaughter.

'Well, yes. Sad. Anyway, before that happened, him, dying, he sent me equipment. I asked him for it. Specialist equipment. I asked for it, you see? But so much of it was damaged before I could use it. Everything went a bit crazy. Yes, a bit crazy.'

'The magos believed from the very outset,' Slaughter said to Daylight, 'that the noise bursts were a form of communication. He wanted to decipher them. A drop of specialist equipment to allow him to do that was arranged, but it had been overrun by Chromes and half-scrapped by the time we got to it.'

'Communication,' said Daylight. 'From the Chromes?'

'I thought so at first,' said Laurentis, jumping up suddenly to stretch his cramping legs. 'Yes, yes, I did. At first. I thought we had underestimated the technical abilities of the Chromes. I thought we had underestimated their sapience. They migrate from world to world. That suggested a great capacity for... for, uhm...'

Another noise burst, a longer one, had just echoed though the darkness of the stockade and the ruined nest, and it had rather distracted him.

'What was I saying?' he asked them, digging his knuckles into his ears again and jiggling his head.

'Communication?' prompted Daylight. He remembered very clearly what had been spoken of on the bridge of the *Azimuth*. The noises coming from Ardamantua read as organic – boosted and amplified for broadcast, but organic. Like a voice. 'You believe it's communication?' he pressed.

'Yes! Yes! That's what I thought! That was my theory, and it seemed a valid one. I thought the Chromes were trying to surrender, or negotiate peace, that's what I thought at first. Do you remember me saying that, Slaughter?'

'I do, magos,' said Slaughter.

'Then I thought they might be trying to compose a challenge. Then I thought they might be warning us, you know, *warning* us not to mess with them. Then, then I thought they might be trying to warn us about something else.'

'Like what?' asked Daylight.

'Well,' said Laurentis, 'it doesn't much matter, because I don't believe it is them at all any more. Do I, Slaughter?'

'You don't,' said Slaughter.

'I think it's someone else. Yes, that's what I think. Someone *else*.'

The magos biologis looked at them both.

'What do you think?' he asked.

'I think I'd like you to explain more,' said Daylight. 'Who do you think this someone else is?'

Laurentis shrugged.

'Someone very advanced,' he said. 'Very advanced. Take gravity, for example. They are very, very advanced in that field. Gravitic engineering! Imagine! They're shifting something. And this world, it's just the delivery point.'

'What are they shifting?'

'Something very big,' said Laurentis.

'A moon?' asked Daylight. Slaughter looked at him sharply.

'It could be a moon. Yes, it could be,' said Laurentis. 'You've seen the reflection in the lake, have you?'

'I have,' said Daylight.

'Whatever it is, it's still in transition. If it's a moon or a planetoid... well, Throne save us all. That's a different class of everything. I mean, we can terraform, we can even realign small planetoids in-system. But shifting planetary bodies on an interstellar range? That's... *god-like*. There are rumours, of course. Stories. Myths. They say that the ancients, the precursor races, they say they had power of that magnitude. Even the eldar once, at the very peak of their culture. But not any more. No one can do that any more. Not on that scale.'

'Except... whoever the voice belongs to?' asked Daylight.

'Yes, well, perhaps,' said Laurentis.

'And who does the voice belong to?' asked Daylight.

Noises boomed and howled. Laurentis scrabbled at his ears again like a man with headlice, and pulled a pained face.

'That's the real trick, isn't it?' he agreed. 'Knowing that. Knowing that thing. We'd have to translate the words first, and find out what they were saying. Maybe... maybe they're introducing themselves to us? Maybe this is a contact message. A hello. I've spent six weeks trying to figure that out...'

He made a sweeping gesture that encompassed his makeshift pile of devices and equipment.

'...six weeks, working with these items, which are hardly ideal. It's so hard to jury-rig what I'm missing. The parsing cogitators are a particular loss. And the vocalisation monitors. I've made do with quite a lot, actually, quite a lot, but Throne alive! What I wouldn't give for a decent grade tech-servitor, or a vox-servitor... or... or an augmetic receiver. Cranial! Cranial implants! I never took them myself, you see?'

'If this is contact,' asked Daylight, 'it's surely hostile?'

Laurentis nodded, blinking away another noise burst with a shake of his head. 'I mean, definitely. Definitely. But it would still be worth hearing what it had to say for itself.'

'You would confirm a hostile intent, then?'

'I don't have to!' Laurentis exclaimed. 'Look at the rats!'

'The rats?' asked Daylight.

'No, not rats. The Chromes. That's what I mean. The Chromes. *Like* rats. You can gather so much data by observing the behaviour patterns and habits of animals. Rats. Remember when I first called them rats, Slaughter? Remember that?'

'I do, magos,' said Slaughter.

'I said it as a joke, at first,' said Laurentis. 'I said it because their behaviour reminded me of rat behaviour. Rats suddenly turning hostile and flooding into a new area with great and uncharacteristic aggression. It can be very scary. Very dangerous. They're not a threat. They live under the floorboards and in the walls for years, never harming anyone, and then they are turned into a threat. *Turned into* one!'

'How?' asked Daylight.

'Because *they* are threatened, by a greater natural predator. Something they fear. Yes, fear enough to make them attack things they would not normally attack. In this case, the Imperium. And Space Marines! Goodness me, the Chromes are just animals. They are just vermin! They're rats, rats, you see? We're fighting them because they've been driven into our zones of space by something they do not want to be around. They are fleeing, fleeing for their lives, and it's made them desperate enough to battle us.'

He looked at them both.

'It makes sense, doesn't it?' he asked, pleased with himself. He grinned. Daylight noticed that, at some point, several of the magos biologis' teeth had been knocked out. The gappy smile made him look more like an eager child than a credible expert.

'If they're animals, how are they travelling between worlds?' asked Daylight. 'How are they effecting interstellar and void transport?'

Laurentis clapped his hands and did a little jig.

'That's another thing, you see? You see? That's sort of what clinches it because it neatly answers the other mystery! How do the Chromes get from world to world? How do they migrate? What explains their diaspora? Nothing! They can't do it! They're animals! QED something is bringing them here! They're moving through the tunnels!'

'The... tunnels?' asked Daylight.

'Yes. Tunnels. There's probably a better word for it. I haven't really worked this material up into a presentation form yet. Tunnels will have to do. The tunnels built by whoever the voice belongs to.'

He looked at Slaughter, and then Daylight, then back to Slaughter.

'Whoever owns the voice,' he said quietly, as though someone might overhear, 'is equipped with a highly superior tech level. They can manipulate, at a fundamental level, gravity and other primary forces of the universe. They can, so it would appear, reposition planetary bodies over interstellar distances. They do this by constructing tunnels – let's use that word – tunnels through space. Perhaps through the warp itself, as we understand it – not that we *really* understand it, mind – or through some closely associated stratum of subspace. Perhaps a gravitational sublayer, or even a teleportational vector. I can't really be sure yet, so let's simply settle on the term "subspace tunnel", shall we? Now the Chromes, they're vermin, you see? Pests? They live in that subspace realm we're talking about. Like rats live in an attic or a sewer. The subspace realm is an attic of the universe we don't ever see. A cosmic sewer. And as the owner of the voice moves through that attic... subspace realm... you still with me? As the owner of the voice does that, it drives them ahead of it.'

'The Chromes are spread indirectly,' said Daylight, 'via the transportational rifts constructed by this... unknown xenoform.'

'Very well put!' Laurentis exclaimed. 'Can I write that down? Like rats in an attic that's on fire, the Chromes are being driven out ahead of the flames, fighting anything that gets in their way. Or like rats in a sewer, where there are big lizards of some sort, and the big lizards are trying to eat them, so they're afraid and they're running away from the big lizards and–'

'I get it,' said Daylight. 'Calm yourself, magos.'

He looked over at Slaughter.

'We very much need to find out what's coming, captain,' he said.

Slaughter nodded.

'It's not going to be pretty when it arrives,' said Laurentis, quieter now. 'It's an immense threat. The Chromes may be pests, and essentially non-sentient, but they are durable, and resilient and highly numerous, and their entire population – whole nests, whole family communities, millions strong – is being forced to flee for parsecs across the galaxy, through the cellars and chimneys of space.'

He paused.

'Just like rats.'

Daylight was thinking.

'Did you say,' he asked the magos biologis suddenly, 'that you needed a servitor? What about a tech-adept? Would a tech-adept do?'

TWENTY-SIX

ARDAMANTUA

'But his primary socket's ripped out!' Laurentis complained.

'He was hurt during the crash,' Major Nyman explained patiently. He had opened the faceplate of his atmospheric suit so he could be heard. The major clearly didn't trust the filthy, matted magos biologis at all. He was wary of his manic, agitated behaviour. 'He's been hurt. Stop manhandling him.'

'Please be calm, major,' said Daylight. 'Magos, perhaps you could be a little more gentle with the adept? He is injured and hardly in the best shape.'

'Yes, yes, of course,' Laurentis said.

Nyman and two of his Asmodai had brought the tech-adept into the magos biologis's chamber, and were helping him settle on a seat made of a munition crate beside Laurentis's repurposed workstation.

The humans had all been fed from some of the rations in the stockade's supplies. They'd been given purified water too. First Captain Algerin didn't think much of their survival odds. Humans, in his experience, had about four or five days' tolerance for the conditions of Ardamantua. Algerin also didn't seem to think much of Daylight's interest in the magos biologis' theories. To Algerin, Laurentis was an eccentric who had been driven half-mad by his prolonged exposure to the environment, and was probably fairly deranged and obsessive in the first place. 'It's a miracle he's survived this long,' Algerin had remarked, and Daylight wasn't clear if that meant Algerin was surprised that Laurentis had outlasted the other human survivors, or if he thought it was a miracle he hadn't silenced the magos long since.

The tech-adept seemed a little calmer for food and water, and also to be out of the open, in a place where the noise bursts were more muffled. Nevertheless, his eyes were still dead and wandering, and his movements jerky. The sudden attention and manic eagerness of the tattered magos made him shrink back, timid and alarmed.

The magos made soothing, cooing noises, and began to examine the ruined primary plug in the back of the tech-adept's neck. The touch of his fingers on the blood-crusted injury made the adept wince. Laurentis made a tutting sound and looked elsewhere.

'Secondary plugs,' he said, with some relief. 'Here in the sternum, and under the arms. Also the spine. Not as clean and direct as a primary cortex, but it should do the trick. Yes, very good, under the circumstances.'

He looked sidelong at Daylight and whispered, 'The fellow looks a little ropey, though, sir. A little wobbly.'

'He's been injured,' said Daylight. 'In the crash. So he might be a limited resource. He's not strong or mentally robust.'

'Crash. Right. Yes, I remember you saying that,' said Laurentis. 'I'll just have to use whatever I can.'

He began fiddling with the dirty brass dials and levers of his machinery. Oscilloscopes flashed and pulsed, and small hololithic monitors lit up, displaying angry storms of ambient noise. The relayed echoes of noise bursts and other background sonics, most of them from the upper atmosphere and nearspace, fluttered out of the speakers at low volume.

The tech-adept shivered as a series of long, low, booming noise bursts filled the air outside. He shivered again as Laurentis began to connect jack leads to his implant sockets. His eyes rolled back as the last lead plugged into his spinal augmetic and linked to his damaged cortex.

'I've had the basic parsing program complete for over a week,' Laurentis explained as he worked. 'I mean, it was relatively simple. Relatively. The problem was the lack of a decent vocalisation monitor. I basically made the translation, but I couldn't read it, you see? I couldn't read it. To read or hear the translation, you need to pass the translated data-stream through the language centres of a live cortex. The language centres sort of do the work for you. They get the signal and interpret it.'

He looked at Daylight as he adjusted some settings on the devices, and then tweaked the fit of the adept's sternum plug.

'I thought of using my own language centres,' he said pleasantly. 'That would work. Except I don't have the cranial plug. No cranial plug. There are ways around that, I suppose, but I couldn't find a knife clean enough.'

The adept suddenly stiffened. His spine went rigid. His head started to twitch.

'That's good,' said Laurentis, adjusting some dials.

'Is it really?' asked Nyman doubtfully.

'Very good,' Laurentis insisted.

He turned a gain knob, and then gently dialled up a feed source.

The tech-adept began to twitch more violently. His head rocked and jiggled, and his eyes rolled back. His mouth began to move. Saliva flecked his lips as they ground and churned, as though they were trying to form words.

'Stop it,' said Nyman.

'It's all going very well,' said Laurentis.

'I said stop it,' Nyman warned.

'Back off or get out, Major Nyman,' Daylight said.

There was a sound. A soft sound. A tiny blurt of noise. They all looked. It had come from the adept. His chewing, churning mouth, with spittle roping from it, was forming words. He was speaking.

'What was that?' asked Nyman.

'Listen to him!' Laurentis insisted.

The adept began to make louder noises. He gurgled and choked on the amorphous sound-forms and half-words bubbling out of his voicebox. The sound was coming from his throat, across his palate, as if he was enunciating something primordial, something from the dark, hindbrain portions of his mind.

It grew louder still, deeper, more brutal. It was an ugly sound, an animal sound, atavistic.

Finally, there were words.

'Did you hear that?' Laurentis cried.

'What did he say?' asked Nyman.

'Did you hear that?' Laurentis repeated, excitedly.

The tech-adept, blind, rigid and drooling, was repeating one phrase, over and over, in a deep, bass voice.

'I am Slaughter,' he was saying. 'I am Slaughter.'

'Oh, that's not right,' said the magos, suddenly disappointed. 'That's you.'

He looked at Slaughter.

'That's what you say,' said Laurentis. 'That's the thing you say. He's overheard you and he's just repeating it. Poor, mindless fool. I said he was no good. Too damaged, you see? Too damaged. Just repeating what he heard. What a pity. I had such high hopes. The whole thing's a failure.'

Slaughter looked at the tech-adept, who was still in rigour, grunting out the crude phrase.

'He's never met me,' he said. 'He's never heard me say that. He's never met me.'

TWENTY-SEVEN

ARDAMANTUA – ORBITAL

Something was happening to the nearspace shadow around Ardamantua. The gravity storm was intensifying. All the sensors and auspex arrays on the bridge of the *Azimuth* went into the red scale, and then the vermillion, and then went to white-out. Glass dials cracked and blew out of their brass mounts. Sensor servitors squealed and clutched at their aug-plugged eyes and ears, or wrenched out their cortical jacks in sprays of blood and amniotic fluid. The main strategium flickered and then died in a ribboned flurry of collapsing hololithic composition streams.

Admiral Kiran, who had been closely observing the attempts to steer the wounded *Amkulon* towards the flank of a recovery tender, leapt out of his high-backed throne. The cosmological event had accelerated so suddenly, so violently. The seething, simmering storm surrounding the target planet had, in the space of twenty or thirty seconds, turned into something else entirely. The cream of his sensory and detection bridge crew were crippled and blinded, and most of his primary range-finding and scanning apparatus was annihilated. He was quite sure that the planet was about to die. From the energetic signature dynamic, as he had briefly glimpsed it before the screens went dead, the gravity anomaly was expanding, spiking. The planet would never survive a trauma like that. Tectonic rending and seismic disruption would husk the world like a ripe crop, and squirt the molten core of Ardamantua into space in a super-cooling jet of matter.

'Shields! Shields!' he yelled, though his experienced deck crew were already enabling the *Azimuth*'s potent forward shields. Kiran hoped that the commanders of his fleet components closest to the nearspace rim would have the wit to initiate emergency evasive manoeuvres and pull back from the planet zone as rapidly as their real space drives would allow.

If the planet died, his fleet would die with it.

'What's happening?' Heth yelled, running onto the bridge in his breeches and undershirt, braces around his hips, shaving cream covering half of his chin. His aides and attendants rushed after him as if they could somehow complete his ablutions while he yelled at Kiran.

Maskar also appeared, emerging from the chart room with data-slates in his hand, a bemused expression on his face.

'We have a situation,' Kiran said, trying to pull data up onto his repeater screens. 'We have a very serious situation. Something is happening to the planet.'

He turned and yelled at the strategium officers.

'Get that thing re-lit! Get a data-feed up! I don't care if you have to act as live connectors and hold the power couplers together with your bare hands!'

They rushed to obey him, though there seemed to be little hope of restoring the feed. Sparks and filaments of shredded and burned-out cable showered from the cavernous roof of the *Azimuth*'s bridge. Several of the gleaming silver consoles had burst into flames and two large monitor plates had cracked with gunshot bangs and exploded. Servitor crews rushed forwards to extinguish the conflagrations and haul the injured crewmen away, burned and peppered with glass chippings.

Kiran's bridge crew were some of the best in the Imperial Navy. Whatever could be said about Lord High Admiral Lansung, he insisted on the highest degree of schooling for the first-line and primary battlefleet candidates. Working with the tools they had to hand, the sensorium techs managed to reconnect the strategium main display and re-engage it to half-power.

An image blinked into view, fuzzy and indistinct, flaring with distortion and interference.

'What is it? What are we looking at–' Heth began.

'Shut up!' Kiran said, flapping a hand at him and peering at the display.

'How dare you speak to the Lord Commander Militant in that–' Maskar exclaimed.

'You shut up too!' Kiran bellowed, his eyes never leaving the strategium display. 'Look! Look at the damned display!'

In the hololith, the orb of Ardamantua was buckling and shuddering, surrounded by a vast halo of sickly, bright radiance. Overlay schematics told Kiran that two of his vessels closest to the planet had already been overwhelmed and immolated by the outrushing energies ripping from the planetary sphere. He waited, braced, knowing that he was about to see the planet blow apart.

But it did not.

A second planet had appeared beside it instead, smaller, like a conjoined twin, so closely nestled against the larger globe of Ardamantua that it looked like a swollen, cancerous growth extending from the target world.

It was the phantom, the auspex phantom, the so-called imaging artifact.

It was the ghost moon. And it had finally manifested, solid and real.

'I don't understand what I'm seeing,' murmured Lord Commander Militant Heth.

'I do,' said Kiran. Alert overlays, bright red, zoomed in on the display to triangulate and identify hundreds of tiny shapes that rushed from the new moon like missiles.

He didn't need the overlays. He had already seen them.

They were ships. They were warships.

They powered out of the gravity storm of nearspace towards his fleet in attack formation.

'Gunnery! Gunnery!' he bellowed. 'Weapons to bear! Now!'

TWENTY-EIGHT

ARDAMANTUA

A blast of stunning sound and pressure swept across the stockade.

The force shredded parts of the fabricated structure and spilled over many of the stone blocks and boulders that Algerin's survivors had expertly stacked into protective walls. It was an overpressure burst, the sort of concussion that might have accompanied a multi-megaton detonation on a neighbouring landmass. The wall of the blast travelled through the anguished atmosphere of Ardamantua like a sonic tidal wave, crossing continents, swirling seas, lifting soil, stripping vegetation and levelling forests.

It was accompanied by the longest, loudest noise burst of all, a burst that every living thing on Ardamantua could feel in its guts and in its diaphragm. It shook internal organs, even those encased in the transhumanly reinforced and plate-armoured bodies of the Adeptus Astartes. It made eardrums burst and noses bleed. It burrowed into brains like iron spikes.

In the blisternest chamber, the tech-adept had risen triumphantly to his feet, the jack cables straining at his sockets, his arms outstretched as he howled the words aloud.

'I am Slaughter! *I am Slaughter!*'

The magos biologis' makeshift apparatus was beginning to malfunction. Connections were shorting out and monitor screens were rolling, blanking or dissolving into squares of hissing white noise.

Laurentis and Nyman had fallen, clutching their ears in agony. The ground shook. The walls reverberated and cracked at the huge atmospheric disturbance passing over the stockade. Fragments of the blisternest material, translucent and grey, dropped out of the deforming walls and the curve of the fracturing ceiling. Daylight and Slaughter began to move up the tunnel to the surface to learn the nature of the crisis, but the rushing, concussive force of the wind drove them back.

Then the wind and the noise were gone, abruptly gone, and the vibration began to ease. The tech-adept stopped speaking forever and collapsed, snapping out the last of his plugs with the slack motion of his body.

Daylight and Slaughter rushed to the surface, their steel-cased boots thundering along the xenos-woven flooring.

Threads of vapour hung in a twilight world. The stockade was ruined. The brothers on the surface had been more grievously mauled by the overpressure than those, like Daylight and Slaughter, who had benefited from the comparative shelter of the nest tunnels.

The sky was a sickly, blotchy colour, like bruised flesh. All cloud cover seemed to have disappeared, and the wind had dropped. It was hard to think where all the clouds could have gone to. There was an odd, loud buzzing sound in the air, and a thin, pitiless rain fell straight down, hard and cold.

The moon hung above them, filling the sky. It was vast and black. It seemed so close that it must be resting on the rim of Ardamantua, propped up on the planet's mountain peaks. That was just an illusion, of course, but no heavenly body could ever be so close to another without some form of technical suspension or energetic holding field far beyond the capabilities of Imperial humanity.

Daylight and Slaughter could see the surface of the moon, gnarled and interwoven, a vast pattern of fused wreckage and interconnected metal plates. It looked like a giant clockwork mechanism, half-rusted, or some intricate toy planet whose brightly painted cover had been removed to expose the inner workings.

Daylight saw the ships, tiny by comparison, that flooded out of the moon's interior into the sky. They looked like insects swarming in their masses, coming out of their colony mound on the one hot day of the year to take wing and migrate.

Thousands. There were thousands of them.

They were too far away to identify with any confidence, but Daylight had enough of a grasp of comparative scale to know that some of them were smaller atmospheric aircraft, and some were vast void-capable warships.

They were seeing an attack formation, a multi-strand attack designed to hit surface and nearspace targets simultaneously.

A rapid-deployment raid of huge magnitude.

An attack on a planetary level.

An invasion force.

Daylight heard the whistle of high-altitude munitions auguring in. The first blasts ripped through the hills above the stockade, turning them into steam and light. Monumental cannons, vast missile arrays and planet-slicing beam weapons were being fired at the surface from the invading moon and the fleets of attack ships it was disgorging.

Bombs rained down, chewing their way across the valley in mushrooms of smoke, or hurling water from the lake in towering columns. Stabbing beams of light raked in from high above, vaporising ground targets and scoring deep canyons of blackened, fused glass in the rock.

'Rally! Rally!' Daylight yelled. He couldn't see First Captain Algerin anywhere, but what little force the Imperial Fists had left needed to be focused and directed.

Projectiles smashed into the countryside around them like meteors. They fell like giant bombs, but they didn't detonate on impact. Thunderclap concussions blasted out from each strike.

'Landers! Troop landers!' Slaughter cried.

Daylight didn't argue. The enemy, this brand new enemy, was deploying in unimaginable strength. Daylight saw the first of them appear, flooding from the impact crater of one of their lander projectiles.

Smoke washed the air, but he could see their ground forces distinctly. He could see what kind of creatures they were. The face of the enemy, revealed at last.

It either made no sense, or it made the worst sense of all. Daylight *knew* this enemy. Every brother of the shield-corps knew this enemy. Warriors of the Adeptus Astartes might almost regard such a foe contemptuously due to over-familiarity.

Except this particular foe never operated in this *particular* manner. It simply didn't. It *couldn't.*

There was no more time for questions. The roaring enemy was upon them, and all that remained was war.

Daylight drew his sword.

'Daylight Wall stands forever,' he voxed. 'No wall stands against it. Bring them down.'

TWENTY-NINE

TERRA – THE IMPERIAL PALACE

An individual was more vulnerable when he or she was alone. That was basic.

The Officio taught its agents and operatives to watch the behaviour patterns of a target patiently and methodically, learn their routines, and then carry out the play when the individual was most vulnerable.

Alone. In a bath, perhaps, or a bedchamber. On a retreat to a country property, or in transit in a small craft. When at his ease or relaxing, his guard down. Eating, that was a good moment.

Approaching a target when he or she was accompanied by other people made things much more difficult. The play might be compromised. A definitive killing action might not be possible. The individual might be surrounded by bodyguards, retainers or a security retinue. Whoever they turned out to be, and whatever their level of expertise, vigilance and reaction, they were witnesses. The presence of others increased the agent's vulnerability. It reduced the chances of success, or anonymity. It reduced the chances of finishing the play and withdrawing alive.

There were eighty-four thousand, two hundred and forty-seven people with Lord High Admiral Lansung when Vangorich approached him. Vangorich knew the figure precisely because he had swept the immense domed chamber with a miniature sensor drone.

He knew exactly what he was doing.

Lansung, dressed in the gold and scarlet robes of the Winter Harvest Battlefleet, had just finished delivering the commencement speech at the Imperial College of Fleet Strategy, and the vast audience of immaculate cadets and staffers was still applauding. Golden cherub servitors flew overhead among the banners and streamers, clashing cymbals and playing fanfares on long silver trumpets. Lansung was coming off-stage with his armsmen around him: twelve bodyguards from the Navy's *Royal Barque* division. The *Royal Barque* was the name of a mythical, or rather conceptual, ship of the fleet. It was not an actual, physical vessel, though it had a serial code, a keel number and a registration mark, as well as its own sombre ensign design. When a man was selected to join the crew of the *Royal Barque*, he was being recruited into the Navy's elite protection squad. Such individuals were all highly trained and experienced killers, who were then further trained and honed, and appointed as bodyguards to the high-ranking admirals and fleet officers.

They were all tall, stone-faced men in black uniforms with red piping and frogging. Each carried a sheathed cutlass and wore a pair of red dress gloves. One of them, the chief protection officer, carried the admiral's fur shako.

The armsmen tensed slightly when they noticed Vangorich approaching through the crowd of cheering cadets, and the beaming tutors and executives hurrying to congratulate the admiral on his perceptive and inspiring remarks.

'Step back,' one of them snarled quietly, hoping to avoid a scene. Lansung was busy shaking hands with the Head of the Bombard School. Vangorich simply smiled at the armsman.

Lansung, alert as ever, saw Vangorich, and saw he was being challenged. He expertly detached himself from the Head of the Bombard School and swept in.

'Really, Romano,' he said to his armsman, 'you must learn not to obstruct a member of the Imperial Senatorum.'

'My apologies, lord,' the bodyguard said to Vangorich. He clearly didn't mean it. He had not recognised the modest and unostentatious man in black when he had approached, and he did not know him any better now.

'Do you often come to hear me talk, Drakan?' Lansung asked.

'Almost never, my lord,' said Vangorich. 'But I must do so more often.'

They started to walk together through the huge chamber into the mobbing crowd, followed by the men from the *Royal Barque* detachment. Trumpeting cherubs and psyber-eagles flocked after them through the air. Lansung smiled and nodded to those he passed, shaking hands with some. He barely looked at Vangorich as they continued their conversation. Vangorich, for his part, paid more attention to the finely painted ceiling fresco visible through the flags and banners high above, great images of battlefleet ships at full motive, gunports open, crushing enemies.

'Why have you come, Drakan?' asked Lansung. 'Surely not to kill me, or you'd have chosen a less public moment.'

'Oh, you don't realise how good I am at my work, my lord,' Vangorich replied.

Lansung shot him a look. He'd made his comment in jest. There hadn't been a sanctioned Senatorum assassination in a very long time.

'My lord, I'm joking,' said Vangorich. 'Rest assured. Indeed, I chose this moment precisely because it *was* public. I'd have hated you to get the wrong idea if I'd shown up suddenly, unannounced, in a more private place. Things can get so complicated. *Messy*. I don't know what it is. People just get jumpy around me. Must be my face.'

'I'm busy, Drakan,' said Lansung, energetically shaking hands with Lord Voros of Deneb.

'Then I'll cut right to it, my lord,' said Vangorich. 'We need to become allies.'

'What?'

'Political allies, my lord.'

'Why?'

Vangorich smiled.

'I know. It sounds insane. We've never been allies before, and I absolutely know why. I'm not important enough to cultivate. And you, my dear lord, *you* are about as important as it gets.'

'Where is this going, Drakan, my good friend?' asked Lansung, trying to glad-hand others.

'Now *there's* an encouraging phrase,' said Vangorich. 'Indeed. "My good friend." I know you don't mean it in any *literal* way, but it shows me you're willing to make a decent show of civility, and put a good face on a public encounter. That does encourage me. So, let me press this. We need to become allies.'

'Explain to me why before I lose patience,' Lansung said, smiling a fake smile at two august fleet commanders.

'You are a very important man, my lord,' Vangorich said. 'One day, perhaps one day soon, you may be the *most* important man of all. The balance of power you hold in the High Twelve is very solid. You, Lord Guilliman, his excellency the Ecclesiarch. You draw the others around you. None can stand against you.'

Vangorich wasn't blind to the fact that he was standing in the middle of a vivid demonstration of Lansung's personal power and influence, the cult of his personality. The Imperial College of Fleet Strategy, the Navy's most elite academy, was on its way to becoming Lansung's private youth movement. Lansung had been a graduate, and he favoured it unstintingly. All the best fleet promotions went to graduates from the College. In return, the cadets showed the Lord High Admiral a form of blind support that bordered on adoration. Many proudly referred to themselves as 'Lansungites,' and modelled their tactical theories after Lansung's career actions.

'The trouble is,' said Vangorich, 'though none can stand against you, some might *try*.'

'What do you mean?'

'It would be foolish. Divisive. But there are some parties, my lord, who might try to oppose you even if it was futile. And that could harm the Imperium at this time.'

Lansung looked at Vangorich directly for the first time, and held his gaze for a moment.

'Who are you talking about?' he asked.

'It would be inappropriate to betray a confidence, sir,' Vangorich replied, still smiling. 'The point, sir, the *real* point, is Ardamantua.'

'Ardamantua? Drakan, that's an entirely military issue. Why is a political outsider like you even slightly interested in–'

'We should *all* be interested in it, sir. All of us. Ardamantua is turning into a debacle. An extraordinary military calamity actually, and we don't yet know what the consequences will be. But let's imagine for a moment that they are the worst *possible* consequences.'

Lansung murmured an agreement, turning to shake more hands and mouth more small talk. He was still listening.

'If Ardamantua turns into a disaster, sir, as you may suspect it might, it may well have long term effects on the security of the Terran Core.'

'We can deal with anything–'

'Sir, the problem as I perceive it... and, of course, I am only a mere *political outsider*... but the problem as I see it is a disagreement *about* how we deal with it. Certain... parties, certain quarters... they see things in different ways. When push comes to shove, they may well disagree with your proposals as to how to handle the matter. They may wish to employ *alternative* policies. They would *fight* you over the correct way to deal with Ardamantua and its fallout.'

Vangorich leaned closer so he could whisper, while Lansung shook hands. 'That might be fatal. Your power bloc in the Twelve is unassailable, but others might be so desperate they would fight it *anyway*. Then what? Stagnation. Impasse. Brutal, political, internecine war amongst the High Lords. *Paralysis*. An inability for the Senatorum to act, to make policy of any sort... just when the Imperium is under threat? In short, my dear lord, my dear *friend*, the fact is if Ardamantua develops into the threat that it really could be, then it is not the right time for the High Lords of Terra to become locked in a pointless, hopeless battle with themselves, with each other. The Imperium must not be left so vulnerable, nor can such a vulnerability even be risked.'

Lansung looked at Vangorich again.

'I may be a political outsider, my lord,' said Vangorich, 'and my seat and Officio may carry very little weight compared to the influence they used to bear. But I will not stand by and see the Imperium under such jeopardy of political paralysis. After all, if my Officio ever had any purpose, it is as the final safeguard against precisely that danger. And that, sir, is one of the two important reasons you need me as an ally.'

The audience around them was clapping more enthusiastically again. Lansung raised his hand to acknowledge them. His armsmen steered him towards the stage steps.

'Oh, they love you,' said Vangorich. 'I'm not surprised. They're stamping and shouting. They want you back on the podium for an encore.'

Lansung turned at the foot of the steps and looked back at Vangorich, who had stopped walking with him.

'We'll talk again, at your convenience,' said Vangorich. 'Soon. Now, go! Go on! Shoo! They want you up there!'

'What is the second reason?' asked Lansung.

'My lord?'

'You said there were two important reasons why I needed you as an ally,' Lansung called out over the rising roar of the crowd. 'What is the second reason?'

'Very simple, my lord,' said Vangorich. 'You may not much want me as an ally. But you definitely do not want me as an enemy.'

THIRTY

ARDAMANTUA

Laurentis regained consciousness. He knew at once he was pitifully injured. His neck, throat and chin were wet with the torrents of blood that were leaking from his ears and nose. There was pain in his joints and organs that he was sure would be crippling him into immobility if his nerves weren't so dulled.

He hauled himself to his feet. The tech-adept was dead, and most of Laurentis' apparatus flickered empty with equivalent lifelessness. Major Nyman lay sprawled on the chamber floor nearby, twitching and moaning.

A terrible noise rumbled from above ground. The whole structure shook from repeated detonations and impacts. Laurentis had lived through fearful events in the previous six weeks, and that had included the most appalling climatic upheavals and gravitation storms.

They had been nothing compared to this tumult.

Leaning on the oozing wall of the blisternest tunnel for support, he dragged his way towards the surface to see for himself what new ordeal had been visited upon them. Noise bursts continued to reverberate though the ruined nest. He could hear what seemed like gargantuan warhorns too, warhorns sounding out long, braying, raucous, apocalyptic notes.

The end of the world. The end of this world. It was about time. They had suffered enough.

Laurentis came out onto the surface, into the dank twilight and the rain, and cowered in the mouth of the tunnel. He gazed in wonder at the stockade and the world beyond. The moon filled the sky. The stockade was on fire and overrun. Around him, in the smoke and lashing rain, he could see figures in yellow, Imperial Fists, locked in furious battle, grossly outnumbered.

The place was swarming with orks.

Laurentis had never seen a living one close up. He had only examined preserved specimens brought back from the frontier. He didn't really understand what he was looking at. Where had the orks come from? What part did they play in the disaster overwhelming Ardamantua? Were they another by-product threat that had spilled onto the planet because of the subspace realm, like the Chromes?

Laurentis struggled. He knew he was hurt, and that his mind wasn't clear enough for reasoned consideration. The noises hurt so much. He wished he could make sense of it. Orks? *Orks*?

Slowly but surely, terror began to permeate his numbed body. The intellectual issues ebbed away. For the first time since he had faced down the Chrome warrior-form in the tunnel, he felt true mortal jeopardy.

In life, in the stinking flesh, the orks were colossal. Every single one of them was as big as a Space Marine. They simply radiated weight and power, from the huge knotted masses of their shoulders to their treelike forearms and wrecking-ball fists. Laurentis had never seen creatures express such manifest strength and density by simply existing. They were muscle and power, they were fury and rage, they were raw noise and brute strength. They were truly monsters.

They were armoured in metals and hides, but the armour was nothing like as crude as he had imagined it would be. Hauberks and shoulder guards were expertly woven from steel wire and reinforced animal skin or synthetic fibre fabrics. Seams were precise. The level of ornamentation was marvellous. Shields were studded and curved for impact resilience, and some of them smoked with heat and ozone, revealing they were self-powered with built-in kinetic fields. The weapons, clamped in prodigious fists, were the immense, burnished cleavers and swords of frost giants, not the crude blades of ogres. The huge-calibre firearms were of eccentric design yet superb craftsmanship.

The orks had dyed and painted their green flesh with powders and inks, making intricate tribal designs and motifs. Laurentis wished he could understand what each of the marks and stripes and hand-prints signified. There was something primevally shocking about an ork head dusted in white or pale blue powder, its eyes glistening, its mouth splitting open to expose splintered yellow tusks and rotting molars, its maw shocking pink and covered in spittle. It was an atavistic thing. The ork was the primordial predator that man had fled from when he had lived in caves. It was the beast, the uber-myth behind all other monsters. It was the murderous face of man's oldest, purest terror.

The monsters barked, roared and bellowed as they attacked, their tusked, open jaws as massive as those of grox. They hacked and slammed their blades into the warriors of the shield-corps, ripping Adeptus Astartes ceramite plate asunder. Every blow resounded like a thunderclap, like a slap to the face. The rain sprayed off everything, bouncing off armour, helms and blades, mixing with blood, flooding the ground, splashing underfoot.

Dazed, Laurentis stepped backwards. He trembled. He knew there had been long ages in Imperial history when the greenskin tribes had posed the greatest of all threats to the security, the continued existence, of the Imperium of Mankind. He'd always presumed this was simply a result of their sheer numbers, their ubiquity. He'd never considered the orks to have any potency as a species. They were little more than animals, mindless and unskilled, mobbing in the fringes of the stars, an endless supply of cannon-fodder for Imperial guns in the frontier wars. They were not a genuine threat, not like the malevolent forces of the Archenemy, or the threat of heretical civil war, or even the genius machinations of the eldar. Those were dangers to be taken seriously. The orks were a joke, an annoyance, a bothersome chore. They were an infestation that had to be managed, cut back, and kept down. They were not a critical hazard. They were not... They were not...

They were not *this.*

He understood now. Laurentis understood. He understood why past eras of mankind had lived in fear of the greenskins for centuries, why the frontier wars had raged forever, why the periodic Waaagh!s had been threats that had caused the entire populations of colonised systems to evacuate and flee, why the prospect of a credible warboss and his horde was something that could make a sector governor or a warmaster quake. He understood why, more than any other accomplishment of the Great Crusade, the God-Emperor had been so determined to stop the greenskin threat dead at Ullanor.

He understood why the orks were an eternal menace that could never be ignored.

He just didn't understand how they could be six warp-weeks from the Terran Core.

He looked up. The rain hit his face, washing blood out of his beard. He stared at the manifested moon. Its machined, pock-marked, plated surface was ork technology. He could see that. How? How had they done this?

The moon whirred. Surface features moved and adjusted. Vast armour plating structures re-aligned. Shutters the size of inland seas opened and folded. A huge maw appeared. The stylised image of a vast and monstrous ork face manifested on the surface of the rogue moon. Its eyes burned with magmatic light from the moon's core. Its titanic, tusked mouth stretched open wide, and it bellowed at the world below, the loudest and biggest noise burst of all. It was like a pagan god screaming at a sacrificial offering.

I am Slaughter.

Laurentis shuddered. He was having difficulty standing up. A hand grabbed at his arm.

It was Nyman.

'What are you doing?' Nyman yelled. 'Get into cover!'

At least one of the rampaging beasts nearby had spotted the magos biologis. It was coming for him through the rain, shield and cleaver raised. Nyman fired several shots at it with his pistol and then began to drag Laurentis back into the tunnels. The ork came after them. As it entered the confines of the blisternest duct, its roaring screams began to echo and resound.

Nyman stopped and fired at it again. The ork advanced. Laurentis could smell it. It seemed to fill the tunnel, head down, shoulders hunched. The rasping tone of its voice was deep, deeper than any human voice.

'Run!' Nyman told the magos biologis. Laurentis tried to obey, but he wasn't very good at it. Nyman had pulled a grenade from his battledress pouch. He primed it and hurled it at the advancing monster.

The blast brought a section of tunnel down, either burying the ork or driving it back. Nyman and Laurentis picked themselves up and struggled back towards the magos's chamber.

'We're finished,' Nyman said. 'Did you see their numbers?'

Laurentis realised he could hear the major quite clearly, because the major had opened the faceplate of his orbital armour.

Laurentis could hear something else, something tinny and thin crackling out of the man's helmet set.

'Your vox is working,' Laurentis said.

'What?'

'Your vox!'

Nyman noticed the noise.

'I... Yes, I suppose it is. The signal's live again.'

Laurentis thought feverishly. He sank to his knees in front of his bank of devices and instruments, and began to reset and adjust them. White-noise screens flickered back into life. He had resolution on several of them, and dataflows. Some of them had burned out entirely, but many were functioning better than they had done in weeks.

'There's still gross interference from the noise bursts,' Laurentis said as he worked, 'but the gravitational storm has eased. Yes, look. Look.'

Nyman crouched beside him.

'We've got vox-banding again,' he said. 'And data sequences.'

'Exactly,' said Laurentis. 'All the while the moon was in transition from... from wherever it came from... there were colossal levels of gravitational disruption. The storm itself. The whole of Ardamantua was stricken with it. Most tech was as good as useless.'

The magos biologis glanced at Nyman.

'But now the moon is here, now it is fully manifested, the gravitational flare has subsided. We have a little technology back on our side. Major, can you contact your fleet?'

Nyman had already pulled his helmet's vox-jack out of his armour and was connecting it to the battered vox-caster unit that formed part of Laurentis's equipment stack. He plugged it through to use as a range booster. Static fizzled from the speakers.

'*Azimuth, Azimuth*,' he called. '*Azimuth* taskforce control, this is Nyman. Repeat this is Nyman, surface drop. Do you read me?'

'This is *Azimuth*,' the vox crackled out.

'The command ship,' Nyman told Laurentis.

'*Azimuth*,' he said into the vox, 'We've found survivors from the original undertaking, but none of us are going to live long. There are orks everywhere. Full invasion force. Unimaginable numbers.'

'Reading you, Nyman. Ork threat identified orbitally already. Extraction of your personnel not viable at this time–'

'*Azimuth*? *Azimuth*?'

There was a pause.

'Stand by, surface,' the vox hissed. 'I have the Lord Commander for you, vox to vox.'

A different voice suddenly came over the speakers.

'Nyman? It's Heth. Great Throne, man, you're alive?'

'Just about, sir. It's not looking good.'

'What strengths have you got down there?'

'Virtually nothing, sir. The Imperial Fists are decimated. We're overrun and being murdered. Sir, do not drop or try to reinforce us. You could put every scrap of the ground forces at our disposal planetside and you would still never take this world back. I've never seen greenskins in these numbers.'

'Understood, Nyman,' Heth replied. 'To be brutally honest, a surface assault was not a likely possibility. We're in the middle of a void fight. Assault drop not an option.'

Laurentis pulled at Nyman's arm.

'Let me talk to him,' he said.

Nyman hesitated.

'Sir,' he said into the vox, 'I have the magos biologis from Chapter Master Mirhen's original undertaking mission here. He wants to speak to you.'

'Put him on, Nyman.'

Nyman threw a switch on the caster and handed Laurentis the handset.

'My lord, my name is Laurentis, magos biologis.'

'I hear you, Laurentis.'

'Sir, if I may be so bold,' said Laurentis, 'you need to do two things. You need, as an absolute priority, to communicate this emergency to Terra. This is just the beginning. Ardamantua is not a high priority target. Whatever mechanism the greenskins have used to bring their attack moon through subspace, Ardamantua is simply a convenient stepping stone, a rest point. Maybe it's a matter of range limit, or power generation. Whatever. They will mass again from here. They will perhaps bring other planetoids through.'

'Throne! How do you know, magos?'

'I don't, sir. I am speculating. But we have to prepare for the worst contingency. Yesterday, we did not know they could do this. Tomorrow, we will learn what *else* they can do, and it will be too late. Sir, you have to transmit a full disclosure warning to Terra. I have some equipment here. I have been trying for weeks to translate the noise bursts. Now we have confirmed the identity of the xenos threat, I can narrow my linguistic programs to include what data we have on record of ork syntax and vocabulary values. Sir, I need to open a direct data-link between your primary codifiers and my resources here. If we work fast, you may be able to include, in your urgent warning to Terra, some actual detail regarding the greenskin intention and operation.'

'How so, magos?' Heth asked.

'By learning, sir, what they are telling us.'

THiRTY-ONE

ARDAMANTUA – ORBITAL

Admiral Kiran had drawn his sabre. He'd done it subconsciously, his mind on the fight. The light on the bridge gleamed off its exposed blade. It was a habit of his during a void fight. The sword would play no part in a battle between behemoth warships, but Kiran always felt better with a weapon in his hand.

He had even admitted to his officers, just between them, over dinner in his stateroom, that he had a fear and a shame of dying unarmed.

'When death comes for me, I won't go quietly,' he had said.

The bridge officers manning the stations and consoles around him, diligent and determined, saw the sword come out of its scabbard and knew what it meant.

They were going to deliver death to the best of their considerable ability, but they were awaiting death too.

The bridge of the *Azimuth* was a place of pandemonium. Alarms sounded, most of them notifications of damage to other decks, some of them target or proximity alerts triggered by the attacking warships. The air was rank with smoke from artifice deck fires. Crewmen rushed in all directions, delivering data, or attempting frantic repairs on crashed bridge systems. For now, the strategium was working again. On it, Kiran could see the ships of his line, a curve of green icons hooked like a claw into the nearspace region of Ardamantua. He could see the enemy too, a blizzard of red icons spilling from the hazard marker of the rogue moon.

The taskforce fleet was outnumbered thirty or forty ships to one. A bridge officer did not need years of training at the Imperial College of Fleet Strategy to know how this was going to end.

'The odds are too great,' said Maskar. 'We run. Obviously, we run.'

Kiran shook his head.

'No time, sir. They'd bring us down stone dead before we ever made it to translation.'

'Then what?' asked Maskar, horrified.

'Tell the Lord Commander to make a full statement of the events as we know them, and send it via astropathic link as fast as possible. I will buy him as much time as I can, but it won't be long. We will take as many of them with us as we can, general.'

Maskar looked at him.

'Quickly,' Kiran said, tightening his grip on his sword.

Maskar saluted him. Kiran saluted back. The Astra Militarum commander turned and hurried towards Heth, who was at the vox-station across the bridge.

'Gunnery!' Kiran yelled.

'Gunnery, aye!'

'Status?'

'Status effective!'

'Target selection is now at my station. Primary batteries live.'

'Primary live, aye!'

'Secondary batteries may fire at will.' Kiran drew his free hand across the touch-sensitive hololithic plate of his console, aligning targets in order of priority.

'Autoloaders live!' a sub-commander called out.

'Gunports open!' yelled another.

'Let's kill them,' said Admiral Kiran. He stabbed his finger at the glass to activate the first pre-programmed firing sequence.

The *Azimuth*'s main forward batteries and spinal mount fired. The recoil stresses made the vast ship's superstructure groan. Beams of energy lashed out from the ship, followed by slower-moving shoals of missiles and void torpedoes.

An ork warship died in a ball of light, like a sun going nova. A second ship ripped open, spilling its mechanical guts into the void in a cloud of oil and gas and flame, tumbling end over end, inertial stability lost.

Kiran tapped the second sequence. He was already loading a third, a fourth, a fifth, a sixth, his eyes never leaving the complex mapping of the strategium display. Two more kills. Then another two. The *Azimuth*'s shields began to reach saturation.

He ordered them forwards on their coursing plasma engines. The real space drive swept them in to meet the rising enemy swarm. To port, one of his frigates was engulfed and annihilated. A second later, the fleet tender suffered a shield failure, and was lost in a puff of superhot gas and vapour. To starboard, the grand cruiser *Dubrovnic* fended off swarms of ork boarding ships as it targeted and slew three bulk warships with its main batteries. It took the third with a passing broadside that shredded the monstrous attacker.

Kiran saw the massive ork cruiser hoving in on an attack vector.

'Focus shield strength!' he yelled. 'Starboard bearing!'

The cruiser began shelling and lacing the void with beam-fire. The *Azimuth* shook, shields flaring, straining.

Maskar crossed the shuddering deck to join Lord Commander Militant Heth.

'Summon the astropaths,' Heth told him without looking up from the communication console. 'We have to make this good. There will be data to send. As much as we can code and packet.'

'Yes, sir,' said Maskar. He signalled to aides to prepare the astropath chamber.

'Look,' said Heth, gesturing to the comms console. 'Look at this.' Various images were displayed on adjacent pict monitors. One was of the rogue moon, showing the macabre ork visage that had been mechanically created to glare out at them. Maskar could hear both coded transmission signals and noise bursts running through the vox-caster station.

'Help from the surface,' Heth explained. 'The magos biologis. We're unravelling some of the ork transmissions. It's all bloodthirsty threat, I think.

Nothing of substance. Just declarations of hatred and pronouncements of destruction. And this began about three minutes ago.'

He indicated one image in particular, and then enlarged it onto a console's main overhead screen. The image made Maskar blench. It was a pict feed, streamed through some exotic form of image capture system, that was being broadcast directly to them. It was a transmission for their benefit, for the benefit of any victims the orks came upon.

There was little sense of scale, but Maskar appeared to be looking into the eyes of the most immense ork warboss. The creature was so mature, so vast and bloated, its features were distorted. Broken tusks like tree trunks jutted from the cliff edge of its lower jaw. It was staring right out of the screen with tiny, gleaming yellow eyes, its jaw moving.

'That bastard thing is aboard the moon,' Heth said. 'It's their leader. I think he's the size of a damn hab-block, Maskar. Saints of Terra, there hasn't been an ork boss that massive since Ullanor. I mean, they just don't develop to that size any more. Look, look. In the foreground? Those are greenskin warriors. They look like children.'

'Save us,' Maskar murmured.

'Too late, my friend,' said Heth. 'Look at the bastard. Look at him. Those noises we can hear? The noise bursts? It's him. His voice. He's talking to us.'

Heth pointed to another display, one that showed the glaring face on the surface of the moon.

'Look. See how the mechanical face moves? It's working in sync with that bastard thing. Look, the lips part and close at the same time. That's amplifying his voice, turning his vocalisation into that infrasonic signal.'

Maskar felt the ship jolt hard as its shields took more hits.

'Oh, hellsteeth!' Heth moaned suddenly. He spotted something new.

Other portals had opened in the surface of the attack moon: three large circles like giant crater rims or the red storm spot on Jupiter. From them, vast, glowing beams of energy were projecting down onto the surface of Ardamantua. Within seconds, they could see something dark and blotchy flowing up the beams into the attack moon.

Heth ramped up the magnification.

It was rock. Planetary matter. The attack moon was aiming immense gravity beams at Ardamantua and harvesting its mass, sucking billions of tonnes of physical matter and mineral content from the crust and mantle.

'What the hell is it doing?' asked Heth.

'I think...,' Maskar began. 'I think it might be refuelling.'

The attack moon clearly didn't require all the material it was swallowing to replenish its mass ratios. Huge chunks of impacted mineral deposits began spitting out of the moon's spaceward surface. The moon was manufacturing meteors and firing them at the Imperial ship positions using immense gravitic railguns. The *Agincourt* was blown in two by a direct strike from a rock projectile half its size. A huge chunk of quartz and iron travelling at six times the speed of sound raked the portside flank of the grand cruiser *Dubrovnic* and ripped away half its active shields.

Heth was lost for words.

'We've... We've beaten them before, sir,' Maskar said. It was all he could find to say.

'What?'

'The greens, sir. We've always beaten them before. Even at Ullanor...'

'The Emperor was with us, then, Maskar,' Heth replied darkly. 'And the damned primarchs. It was a different time, a different age. An age of gods. Damn right we stopped them then. But they've grown strong again, stronger than ever, and we've grown weak. The Emperor's gone, His beloved sons too. But the greenskins... Throne! They've come just six damned weeks shy of Terra. No warning! No damned warning at all! They've never been this close! They've got technological adaptations we've never seen before, not even on bloody Ullanor.... gravitation manipulation! Subspace tunnelling! Gross teleportation... whole *planetary bodies*, man! And they've all but exterminated one of the most able Chapters of Space Marines in one strike!'

'The Emperor protects,' Maskar said.

'He used to,' said Heth. 'But we're the only ones here today.'

THIRTY-TWO

ARDAMANTUA

There would be no glory. Daylight knew that now. He had been foolish to expect it and wrong to crave it. A warrior of the Adeptus Astartes did not go to war for glory. War was duty. Only duty.

He had yearned for reinstatement for such a long time. Like all the wall-brethren, passing their silent and lonely years of vigil on the Palace walls, embodying the notion of Imperial Fists resilience, he had secretly and bitterly mourned the deprivation. He had yearned for so long, even to the point, on some dark days, when he had almost wished for a threat to come to Terra, or another civil strife to ignite, just so he could defend his wall and test his mettle again.

When the call had finally and unbelievably come, he had armoured himself without hesitation and left his station on Daylight Wall to go to the side of his Chapter.

Making that journey, he hadn't been able to help himself. He hadn't thought of duty.

He had thought of glory.

Instead, he had found this. A slaughter, a final, miserable slaughter. In the twilight shadow of a nightmare moon-that-should-not-be, in the freezing, pitiless rain, on the blood-soaked soil of a broken, unimportant backwater world, his ancient Chapter was being cut down to the very last man. The venerable order, the illustrious heritage, the bloodline of the Primarch-Progenitor, it was all about to be lost forever. It could never be brought back.

Terra's greatest champions were about to be rendered extinct, and the gates and walls of Eternal Terra were to be left unguarded. The enemy was already inside, terrifyingly close to the core.

Stupidity had led to this. Strategic carelessness, the vain ambitions of High Lords and the complacency of veteran warriors who should have known better and had led to this. A calamity had been mistaken for a minor crisis. An ancient and so frequently dismissed enemy had been woefully, *woefully* underestimated.

What's more, no one would learn from this dire mistake, because no one would live. Terra would burn.

There would be no glory.

* * *

The orks were upon them, bestial, roaring faces in the streaming rain. They swarmed across the lakeside in their thousands, raging and howling, blowing their dismal warhorns, slamming their weapons against their shields to beat out the final heartbeats of the last few human lives. Above, low and impossible, the face on the clockwork moon howled threats at the world it was killing.

Rainwater and blood streamed off the visor of Daylight's helm. He tightened his grip on his gladius. His ammo was spent, so he had clamped his combat shield to his left forearm to meet the foe up close and force them to pay a bitter tithe for his lifeblood.

The orks rushed in, tusks bared, spit flying from snarling lips. Daylight met them, drove his sword blade through a head, severed a limb, gutted an armoured torso. Algerin was already gone, a butchered, headless corpse on the blood-black ground. The rain was a curtain, a veil of silver, like fine chainmail. Tranquility was at his left hand, Zarathustra at his right. Together, they formed as much of a wall as they were able, stabbing and hacking, ripping green flesh and brute armour. Zarathustra's war-spear punched through plate and leather, flesh, bone and blood. Broken mail rings and shreds of leather flew up into the rain from the blows of Tranquility's hammer. Blood squirted, jetted.

Daylight put the edge of his gladius through a jaw and a tusk. He backswung to open a throat, blocked an axe with his shield and stepped in to kill the owner. Too many, now. Too many. Too many to strike at. Too many to fend off. Relentless, unending, like the noise bursts, the gut-shaking roars. Daylight felt the first of the wounds, blades reaching in under his defences, around his shield, from behind. Waistline. Hip. Lower back. Nape of the neck. Upper arm. Thigh. Armour splitting. Warning alarms in his helm. Pain in his limbs. Blood in his mouth. Red lights on his visor display. Teeth clenched, he turned in time to see Tranquility fall, head all but severed by a jagged cleaver, the greenskin whooping its triumph, drenched in Space Marine blood. He heard Zarathustra roar in rage and pain. Daylight staggered. He fought. He swung his sword, even though it was broken.

He said, 'Daylight Wall stands forever. Daylight Wall stands forever. No wall stands against it. Bring them down.'

He said it as though it still meant something. He said it as though there was anyone other than the orks left alive to hear it.

He kept on saying it until the pack of beasts tore him apart.

THIRTY-THREE

ARDAMANTUA

Ship deaths lit the sky. Bright fires flared across the face of the attack moon. Some were pale green ovals of expanding light, some messier smudges of flame, drive fuel and torched munitions. A few were massive detonations that spat out expanding hoops of burning gas.

Slaughter hoped that some of them were greenskin ships, slain by the batteries of the reinforcement fleet, but he had a grim suspicion that most were the grave-pyres of valiant, outnumbered Imperial warships.

The stockade was lost. Slaughter had lost sight of Woundmaker when the west wall caved under the ork body crush. Missiles hammered in from the sky.

He swung the ancient sword of Emetris, put it through two charging greenskins, and then headed for the nearest fractured outlets of the ruined blisternest, which jutted like broken drain pipes from the mire. The rain was still heavy. Every surface shone almost phosphorescently with rebounding rain splashes.

Another ork, its face dyed crimson, swung at him. Slaughter ducked the blow, got his sword in, and cut the creature wide open. It fell back into the wet, sheeting water up as it landed.

The Imperial Fist reached the blisternest outlets. He saw a man just inside, lying where he had fallen, cut through the spine and the hip.

'Brother!'

The dying Fist looked up. Severance, of Lotus Gate Wall.

'Slaughter,' he wheezed.

Slaughter tried to lift him, to patch him, but there was far too much damage, far more than even the accelerated biology of a transhuman could repair.

'All gone,' murmured Severance. 'All gone.'

'Stay with me!' Slaughter growled.

Severance shook his head.

'Too late for me,' he said. He unfixed the battered teleport locator from his harness. The power light was still on.

'Take this.'

'It doesn't work,' said Slaughter.

'Not for me. No use to me. But take it. All the while there's hope.'

Slaughter took the locator and clipped it to his belt.

'Thank you for the thought, brother,' he said, 'but I fear we are all past saving.'

Severance didn't reply. Death had taken him.

Slaughter could hear more of the greenskins closing in. He moved on down the tunnel. Two found him there in the alien darkness, and he killed them both with his sword. Then he heard las-shots and a terrible scream.

A human scream.

The chamber used by the magos biologis was awash with blood. Major Nyman was dead, split in half by an ork's sword. Laurentis, stabbed in the gut but not yet dead, had fallen across the precious apparatus, smashing most of it.

The ork warrior turned as Slaughter entered. It swung its sword, but Slaughter parried, deflected, and sliced the greenskin's face off. It pitched forwards, issuing a ghastly, frothing squeal, and Slaughter finished it with a beheading cut.

Laurentis had only a few sucking breaths left in him.

'Finished now,' he whispered. 'The vox just went dead and the link failed. That means the *Azimuth* has gone. The flagship. Lord Heth. All of them.'

'Just us,' said Slaughter.

'Just you, really,' replied the magos biologis. His breathing was very shallow.

'We can still get out, if...'

Laurentis laughed.

'Still trying to make light of it?' he asked weakly. 'We really are in trouble.'

Slaughter nodded.

Laurentis managed a half-smile. Then he closed his eyes and died.

Slaughter rose to his feet and turned, his broadsword in his fist. Orks loomed in the doorway, sniffing and growling... two of them, four, six, more...

'Who's first?' asked Slaughter. 'There's enough for all of you bastards.'

THIRTY-FOUR

TERRA – THE IMPERIAL PALACE

'This statement must necessarily be brief,' the recording continued. The pict quality was not sharp. It had been subjected to extreme astrotelepathic transfer and encryption, and there was a lot of distortion. It was just possible to make out the face of Lord Commander Militant Heth. There were other figures around him, though they were indistinct, and behind them, what appeared to be the bridge of a starship. The recording source kept jarring and vibrating.

'The ork "attack moon" that I described has immense capabilities and possibly almost limitless resources. As we have no hope of outrunning the greenskin fleet, Admiral Kiran, whom I commend utterly, has taken this ship in close. We have attempted to damage the so-called attack moon with primary weapons, to no avail. It is both armoured and shielded, possibly by some form of gravitically manipulated field. It is bombarding us with crude but effective rock-mass projectiles. Our scans reveal that the moon is partly hollow, and – internally – not a sphere at all. The attack moon is simply the physical end in this location of the orks' subspace tunnel. It is the mouth of a corridor, a conduit through which they can transport potentially unlimited reinforcements and vessels.'

On screen, Heth looked up briefly as the ship he was aboard shook wildly. The pict image blinked off for a second and then restored.

'With the very little time and limited resources available to us, we have attempted a rapid transliteration of the broadcasts being made by the attack moon. Magos Biologis Laurentis, whom I also commend without reservation, has devised some translations which seem reliable. They are all statements issued by the apparent warboss of the ork horde. All recorded transmissions from the ork vessel, along with all of Magos Laurentis's notes and ciphers, are attached to this communication in compressed data form. We have deduced that the orks refer to their subspace tunnel as a *Waaagh! Gate*. That is a reasonably close translation. The warboss refers to himself by a name that is harder to find a single, specific translation for. Depending on nuance, it seems to be "beast" or "slaughter", or "lord that will make great slaughter". I don't think it matters. His intent is obvious and–'

The image blanked again. This time it took longer to return.

'Time's almost gone,' said Heth when he reappeared. He had been cut by something, probably flying glass. He looked straight into the recorder source. 'Study the files I've sent. Study the damned data. For the love of Terra. You need to understand. You need to be ready. The Imperial Fists are gone. They've wiped them out. The entire damned Chapter. We are finished here and unless you prepare yourselves you–'

The screen went blank.

'The communique ends there, sir,' said the aide.

Lansung nodded. He sat back and thought for a long while.

'Send a message directly to Lord Udo. Tell him we require an emergency sitting of the High Lords immediately. *Immediately*.'

'Yes, sir. Is that the whole of the Senatorum, my lord?'

'No,' said Lansung. 'Just the High Lords. *Just* the rest of the Twelve. No others.'

'Study the files I've sent,' the uneven image of Heth was saying. 'Study the damned data. For the love of Terra. You need to understand. You need to be ready. The Imperial Fists are gone. They've wiped them out. The entire damned Chapter. We are finished here and unless you prepare yourselves you–'

The screen went blank.

'Lights up,' Wienand said. She rose from her seat as the light levels in her private chamber intensified. She looked at her silent circle of interrogators. Despite their novitiate robes, some were far more senior than they appeared.

'That was the latest intercept,' she said. 'It went directly to the Admiralty via a secure beacon, but we extracted the data-copy thanks to well-placed friends in the Adeptus Astra Telepathica. Lansung will present it, or redacted highlights of it at least, to the High Twelve in the next hour.'

She paused.

'I think three things are self evident. One, we must act and act now, without hesitation. The crisis is as bad as anything we feared and predicted. Two, the public must not be informed of the extinction of the Imperial Fists. That is a priority matter of morale. Three, we must raise our game. There is no more time for subtlety. We knew what was coming in more detail than the Navy or any other body. We did not share that knowledge with the High Twelve because we knew that Lansung's power bloc would make it impossible for us to direct the correct and appropriate policy. Traditional and hidebound military dogmas would have hamstrung us and delayed our ability to react. We must determine policy from this point on. We must be the actual and real root of power during this crisis and beyond, or the Imperium will not survive.'

There was silence. One of the hooded figures raised his hand.

'What, mistress, of the rogue elements?' he asked. 'What of them? There are more pieces involved in this game than the main and obvious players.'

'This is a crisis of unparalleled proportions,' replied Wienand, 'not a game. As for the minor pieces, they will be brought to terms, or contained. Or they will be silenced.'

'What, mistress, of the rogue elements?' asked the hooded interrogator sitting at the back of the chamber. 'What of them? There are more pieces involved in this game than the main and obvious players.'

Wienand looked at her questioner carefully.

'This is a crisis of unparalelled proportions,' she replied, 'not a game. As for the minor pieces, they will be brought to terms, or contained. Or they will be silenced.'

Vangorich pressed a key on his data-slate and the screen image of the Inquisitorial Representative's private suite froze, paused.

Vangorich sat back in his chair, put the slate down, and steepled his fingers.

'Beasts arise,' he murmured to himself. 'And as they arise, so must they fall.'

THIRTY-FIVE

TERRA – TASHKENT HIVE

It was a snowy night. Out of the steel-cold blackness, blizzards drove in and coated the spires of the vast hive as if they were a range of mountain peaks. Lights twinkled in the vertical city, numerous as the stars.

The routines of Adeptus Arbitrator Sector Overseer Esad Wire had been carefully observed for some time. His work at Monitor Station KVF usually ended at around three in the pre-dawn shift, and he would return to his habitation on Spire 33456 via an eating house in the Uchtepa District, which served food after hours.

On this particular day, there were variations. Two hours into his shift, Wire received a personal transmission via encrypted vox, a call that lasted only eight seconds, and which Wire did not contribute to. He merely listened. The nature and content of what he listened to was not possible to ascertain.

Presumably as a result of this transmission, Wire reported to his superintendent that he was ill, the unfortunate flare-up of some chronic condition. He requested, and was granted, permission to leave work early and visit the district medicae before returning to his hab.

He left the station three hours before the scheduled end of his shift, as soon as the relief overseer arrived to cover him, but he did not travel to the district medicae's office, nor did he travel home. Instead, dressed in his long, brown leather storm coat, and carrying a small but apparently heavy bag, he went west through the Commercia District towards the Mirobod Transit Terminal. The Mirobod Terminal served the Trans-Altai maglev lines.

Approaching the terminal, Wire did not seem to be aware he was under observation or being shadowed. The exterior rail shutters had been opened, and snow was blowing in under the canopy, dusting the concourse.

Wire went down two levels and then, oddly, walked into the seedy basement section of the terminal where derelicts and low-life individuals congregated. Wire vanished briefly into the dank, concrete underlevel of support pillars, garbage and oil drum fires.

Uneasy, Kalthro decided it was necessary to act before Wire began to suspect anything. He left his vantage point, dropped down the east wall of the terminal on a micro-filament cable, and waited for Wire to emerge from the north end colonnade of the underlevel.

When the man in the long brown storm coat reappeared, Kalthro pounced. He brought the man down cleanly, broke his back, and snapped his neck.

The corpse was face down on the filthy rockcrete floor. Kalthro got up and rolled the body over.

'You don't need to pay a poor man to wear a thick coat on a night like this,' said Esad Wire from behind Wienand's agent.

Kalthro turned. He was very fast indeed. The snub-las was already in his hand. He was, as Wienand had boasted, a superlative operative, the best in the Inquisition's employ.

But, as he turned, he was no longer facing Esad Wire, Sector Overseer, Monitor Station KVF (Arbitrator).

Beast Krule met him with a smile. He touched Kalthro's right forearm and shattered the bones there. The snub-las dropped out of a useless hand. Then Krule put his right fist in Kalthro's face.

It went through. Clean through. The knuckle points fractured out through the back of Kalthro's skull, jetting tissue and blood with them under considerable pressure. The operative's body hung off the fist, twitching. Krule jerked his hand back, and it came out gore-slick and steaming.

Kalthro crumpled onto the floor beside the dead vagrant in the brown coat. More steam rose. Blood pooled, dark and glossy. Then it began to clot and then freeze in the desperate temperatures.

Krule looked down at the body.

'Not bad,' he allowed. He wiped his bloody hand clean on Kalthro's jacket, recovered his coat, and picked up his bag.

Then he walked away into the frozen night towards the maglev terminal entrance, whistling an oddly cheerful refrain.

CAVES OF ICE

SANDY MITCHELL

Editorial Note:

This, the second extract from the Cain archive which I have prepared and annotated for those of my fellow inquisitors who may care to peruse it, is in much the same format as the first. The astute among you will realise that it follows my previous selection, Cain's account of the Gravalax incident, quite closely chronologically although with his usual disregard for such niceties it was actually recorded at an earlier point in the archive itself. I have chosen this section of his memoirs not only because it is relatively self-contained, requiring little background knowledge of his earlier exploits to appreciate, but also because the records of the Ordo Xenos contain quite a bit of detail about events on Simia Orichalcae that year and anyone with cause to consult them is certain to find the only complete eyewitness account of considerable interest. (Not least because it confirms the suspicions many of us have long harboured about the part played by certain members of the Adeptus Mechanicus in the affair, which may be useful in future dealings with them.)

It may be argued that Cain is not the most reliable chronicler of events, but I am inclined to accept his version of events as absolutely true. Here, as throughout the whole archive, he rarely gives himself credit for what, to any unbiased observer, appear to be acts of genuine courage and resourcefulness (however few and far between).

As before I have been largely content to let Cain tell his story in his own words, confining myself to annotating the original text to clarify occasional points and expand upon the wider background to the events he describes since typically he tends to concentrate almost exclusively on things that affected him personally without much regard for the bigger picture. I have also, as before, taken the liberty of breaking his account down into chapters to facilitate reading, although Cain himself didn't seem particularly bothered by such stylistic niceties. Where I've drawn on other sources they are credited appropriately; all other footnotes and interpolations are mine alone.

Amberley Vail, Ordo Xenos

ONE

Warp knows I've seen more than my fair share of Emperor-forsaken hell-holes in more than a century of occasionally faithful and dedicated service to the Imperium, but the iceworld of Simia Orichalcae[1] stands out in my memory as one of exceptional unpleasantness. And when you bear in mind that over the years I've seen the inside of an eldar reaver citadel and a necron tomb world, just to pick out a couple of the highlights (so to speak), you can be sure that my experiences there rank among the most terrifying and life-threatening in a career positively littered wixth hairs'-breadth escapes from almost certain death.

Not that it seemed that way when our regiment got its orders to deploy. I'd been serving with the Valhallan 597th for a little over a year by that point, and had managed to settle into a fairly comfortable routine. I got on well with both Colonel Kasteen and her second-in-command Major Broklaw; they appeared to consider me as much of a friend as it was possible to be with the regimental commissar, and the kudos I'd earned as a result of our adventures on Gravalax stood me in good stead with the men and women of the lower ranks as well. Indeed most of them seemed to credit me, not entirely wrongly, with having provided the inspirational leadership which had allowed them to prevail against the vile conspiracy that had unleashed so much bloodshed on that unhappy world and provided them with an initial battle honour to which they could all point with pride.

At the risk of seeming a little full of myself, I did have some cause for satisfaction on that score at least; I'd inherited responsibility for a divided, not to say mutually hostile, regiment, cobbled together from the combat-depleted remnants of two previously single-sex units who had disliked and distrusted one another from the beginning. Now, if anything, I was faced with the opposite problem: I was charged with maintaining discipline as they became comfortable working together and the new personnel assignments started bedding in. (Quite literally in some cases, which only made matters worse of course, particularly when acceptable fraternisation spilled over into lovers' tiffs, acrimonious partings, or the jealousy of others. I was

1 Despite my best efforts to track it down, the origin of this name remains obscure. It seems fairly safe to conjecture that the world in question was famed for the presence of some statue or effigy in a past epoch, but why anyone should have chosen to commemorate this particular animal in such a way remains a mystery.

beginning to see why the vast majority of regiments in the Imperial Guard were segregated by gender.) Fortunately, there were very few occasions when anything harsher than a stiff talking-to, a quick rotation of the protagonists to different squads, and a rapid palming off of the problem to the chaplain were called for, so I was able to maintain my carefully-constructed facade of concern for the troopers without undue difficulty.

Being iceworlders themselves, of course, the Valhallans were overjoyed to hear we were being sent to Simia Orichalcae. Even before we made orbit the viewing ports were crowded with off-duty troopers eager for a first sight of our new home for the next few months and a chatter of excited voices had followed Kasteen, Broklaw and myself through the corridors towards the bridge. My enthusiasm, needless to say, was rather more muted.

'Beautiful, isn't it?' Broklaw said, his grey eyes fixed on the main hololith display. The flickering image of the planet appeared to be suspended in the middle of the cavernous chamber full of shadows and arcane mechanisms, surrounded by officers, deckhands and servitors doing the incomprehensible things starship crewmen usually did. There must have been a dozen at least of them buzzing about, waving data-slates at one another, or manipulating the switches inlaid into the age-darkened wood of the control lecterns which littered the main deck below us. Captain Durant, the officer in charge of the old freighter that had been hastily pressed into service to transport us from our staging area on Coronus Prime,[2] shook his head.

'If you like planets I suppose it's all right,' he said dismissively, his optical implants not even flickering in that direction. Of indeterminate age, he was so patched with augmetics that if it hadn't been for his uniform and the deference with which his crew treated him I might have mistaken him for a servitor. It had been courteous of him to invite the three of us to the bridge though, so I was prepared to overlook his lack of social graces. It wasn't until some time later that I realised that doing so was probably the only way he would ever meet his passengers, as he showed every sign of being as much a part of the ship's internal systems as the helm controls or the Navigator (whose quarters were presumably behind the heavily shielded bulkhead which loomed ominously over where we stood.)

Cynical as I was about such things, I had to concede that Broklaw had a point. From this altitude, as we slipped into orbit, the world below us shone like an exotic pearl, rippled with a thousand subtle shades of grey, blue and white. Thin veils of cloud drifted across it, obscuring the outlines of mountain ranges and deep shadowed valleys which could have swallowed a fair sized city. Despite the poor resolution, I couldn't help searching for some sign of the impact crater where a crudely hollowed-out fragment of asteroid had ploughed into the surface of this pristine world, vomiting its cargo of orks out to sully it.

'Breathtaking,' Kasteen murmured, oblivious to the exchange. Her eyes

---

2 Coronus Prime was a major Imperial base on the fringes of the Damocles Gulf where the Imperial forces withdrawn from Gravalax were sent for reassignment. Presumably the Munitorum decided it wasn't worth diverting a fully-fitted troopship to deploy just a single regiment, and commandeered a suitable civilian vessel for the job.

were wide like a child's, the blue of the iris reflecting the projected snowscape in front of us. The clear light struck vivid highlights in her red hair, and like her subordinate she seemed lost in a haze of nostalgia. I could readily understand why: the Guard sent its regiments wherever they were needed, and the Valhallans rarely got the chance to fight in an environment where they felt completely at home. Simia Orichalcae was probably the closest thing to their homeworld either officer had seen since they joined up, and I could sense their impatience to get down there and feel the permafrost beneath their boot soles. I was rather less eager, as you can imagine. I've never been agoraphobic like some hivers, and quite enjoy being outdoors in a comfortable climate, but where iceworlds are concerned I've never seen the point of having weather, as we used to say back home.[3]

'We'll get you down as soon as possible,' Durant said, barely able to hide his enthusiasm for getting nearly a thousand Guardsmen and women off his ship. I can't say I altogether blame him; the *Pure of Heart* wasn't exactly a luxury liner, and the opportunities for recreational activities had been few and far between. The crew clearly resented their facilities being swamped by bored and boisterous soldiers, and the training drills we'd devised to keep our people busy in the few cargo holds that weren't stuffed with vehicles, stores, and hastily-installed bunks hadn't been enough to let them blow off steam completely and there had been some friction.

Luckily the few brawls which had broken out had been swiftly dealt with, Kasteen being in no mood for a repeat of our experiences aboard the *Righteous Wrath*,[4] so I'd had relatively little to do beyond telling the freshly-separated combatants that they were a disgrace to the Emperor's uniform and dish out the appropriate penalties. And of course when you have several hundred healthy young men and women cooped up in a confined space for weeks on end many of them will find their own ways of amusing themselves which raised the whole range of other problems I've already alluded to.

Despite the constant irritation of dealing with a host of minor infractions, I wasn't particularly eager for our voyage to end. I'd fought orks before – many times – and despite their brutishness and stupidity I knew they weren't to be underestimated. With numbers on their side, and the orks always had superior numbers in my experience, they could be formidably difficult to dislodge once they'd gained a foothold anywhere. And by luck or base cunning they had found a prize on Simia Orichalcae worth fighting for.

'Can we see the refinery from here?' Kasteen asked, reluctantly tearing her eyes from the hololith. Broklaw followed her lead, his dark hair flicking against the collar of his greatcoat as he turned. Durant nodded, and apparently obedient to his will a section of the gently-flickering planet in

3 Despite his frequent references throughout the archive to his being native to a hive world, Cain never specifies which one; and most of the (few) details he gives about his origins are inconsistent. The folk saying he quotes here isn't recorded in any of the anthropological databases, but that doesn't necessarily mean much; it could easily have been common in one small section of his home hive, such as a particular hab level or underhive settlement.

4 A serious disturbance broke out on board this troopship shortly after Cain joined the regiment, and several troopers and Naval provosts died. For further details see his account of the Gravalax incident.

front of us expanded vertiginously as though we were plummeting down towards it in a ballistic re-entry.

Despite knowing that it was only a projection my stomach lurched instinctively for a second before habit and discipline reasserted themselves and I found myself assessing the tactical situation before us. The slightly narrowed eyes of my companions told me that they were doing the same, no doubt bringing their intimate knowledge of the environment below us into play in a fashion that I never could. Within seconds we were presented with an aerial view of the installation we'd been sent to protect.

'That valley looks reasonably defensible,' Broklaw mused aloud, nodding in satisfaction. The sprawling collection of buildings and storage tanks was nestled at one end of a narrow defile, which would be a natural choke point to an enemy advance. Kasteen evidently concurred.

'Place a few dugouts along the ridgeline there and we can hold it until hell thaws out,' she agreed. I was a little less sanguine, but felt it best to appear supportive.

'What about the mountain approaches?' I asked, nodding in apparent agreement. The two officers looked mildly incredulous.

'The terrain's far too broken,' Broklaw said. 'You'd have to be insane to try coming over the peaks.'

'Or very tough and determined,' I pointed out. Orks weren't the most subtle tacticians the forces of the Emperor ever faced, but their straightforward approach to problem solving was often surprisingly effective. Kasteen nodded.

'Good point,' she said. 'We'll set up a few surprises for them just in case.'

'A minefield or two ought to do it,' Broklaw nodded thoughtfully. 'Cover the obvious approaches, and lay one here, on the most difficult route. If they meet that they'll assume we've fortified everywhere.'

They might not care, of course. Orks are like that. Casualties simply don't matter to them. They'll just press on regardless, especially if there are enough of them surviving to boost each other's confidence. But it was a good point, and worth trying.

'How far have they got?' I asked. Durant swept the hololith display round to the west, skimming us across the surface of the barren world with breathtaking speed. The broken landscape of the mountain range swept past, the higher peaks dotted with scrub, lichen, and a few insanely tenacious trees – apparently the only vegetation which could survive here. Just as well too, or there wouldn't be an atmosphere you could breathe. Beyond the foothills was a broad plain, crisp with snow, and for a moment I could understand the affection my colleagues had for this desolate but majestic landscape.

Abruptly the purity of the scene changed, revealing a wide swathe of churned-up, blackened snow, befouled with the detritus and leavings of the savage horde which had surged across it. A couple of kloms[5] wide at least, it resembled a filthy dagger-thrust into the heart of this strangely peaceful world. The resolution of the hololith wasn't good enough to make out the individual members of this barbaric warband, but we could see clumps of

5 Kilometres: a Valhallan colloquialism Cain acquired from his long association with the natives of that world.

movement within the main mass, like bacteria under a microscope. The analogy was an apt one, I thought. Simia Orichalcae was infected by a disease, and we were the cure.

'Seems like we got here just in time,' Kasteen said, putting all our thoughts into words. I extrapolated the speed of the ork advance, and nodded thoughtfully; we should have the regiment down and deployed roughly a day before they reached the valley where the precious promethium plant lay open and defenceless. It was cutting it fine, but I was just thankful we'd get there ahead of them at all. Fortunately they'd crashed in the opposite hemisphere, and that had given us just enough time to make the journey through the warp to oppose them.

'I'll get everyone moving,' Broklaw offered. 'If we get the first wave embarked now we can launch the shuttles as soon as we make orbit.'

'Please yourselves.' Durant somehow managed to make his immobile shoulders convey the impression of a shrug. 'We'll be at station-keeping in about an hour.'

'Are the datafeeds set up?' I asked, while I still had some measure of his attention. He repeated the gesture.

'Not my department.' He inflated his lungs, or whatever he used instead of them. 'Mazarin! Get up here!'

The top half of a woman almost as encrusted with augmetics as the captain rose on a humming suspensor field to join us on the command dias. The cogwheel icon of a tech-priest hung from a chain around her neck. As we spoke she hovering roughly at my head height, the tunic she wore stirring unnervingly in the faint current from the air recirculators at what would have been level with her knees if she'd had any. 'The one in the fancy hat wants to know if you've wired up his gadgets.'

'The Omnissiah has blessed their activation,' she confirmed, in a mellifluous voice. Her hard stare at the captain told me his irreverence was an old and minor annoyance. 'They are all functioning within acceptable parameters.'

'Good.' Kasteen, to my mild surprise, was looking distinctly uneasy, her eyes flickering away from the tech-priest whenever she thought she could politely do so. 'We'll have full sensor coverage of the planet's surface then.'

'As long as this old blasphemer remembers how to keep his collection of scrap in orbit,' she agreed. Once again the two of them exchanged a look that confirmed my initial suspicion that their bickering was a sign of an easy familiarity rather than any genuine friction. A waving mechadendrite reached forward across Mazarin's shoulder, clutching a data-slate, which she thrust towards the colonel. Kasteen took it with every sign of reluctance, all but shying away from the mechanical limb. 'The appropriate rituals of data retrieval are on this.'

'Thank you.' She handed the slate to Broklaw as though it were contaminated. The major took it without comment, and began scanning the files.

'Waste of a perfectly good starship if you ask me,' Durant grumbled. 'But the money's good.'

'We're most grateful for your co-operation,' I assured him. A troopship would have been equipped to deploy a proper orbital sensor net, which would have been infinitely preferable, but the battered old freighter's navigational array would just have to do. Our deployment was a hurried one, made in response to a frantic astropathic message from the staff of the installation below us, so we had to make do with what we could grab instead of waiting around for the right equipment.

'You've got the easy job,' Broklaw assured him. This much was true: the *Pure of Heart* only had to stay in orbit over the refinery, feeding her sensor data into our tactical net, so we could keep an eye on our enemies from above. Given the size of the horde we'd seen, that was a comfort. It looked even larger and more formidable than my most pessimistic imaginings, outnumbering us by at least three to one. On the other hand we'd be on the defensive, which would be to our advantage. And they'd want to take the place intact, so we wouldn't have to worry too much about incoming artillery fire. The extra intelligence our orbital eye would give us would help immeasurably in deploying our defences to frustrate their attacks.

'You call this easy?' Durant asked rhetorically. A sweep of his arm took in the humming activity of the bridge. 'Having half my systems rewired, trying to hold it all together...' His voice trailed off as Mazarin floated away with a faint *tchah!* of disapproval, and something a little softer entered his body language.

'Your tech-priest seems efficient enough,' I said, trying to sound encouraging. He nodded.

'Oh, she is. Far too good to waste her time on a tub like this really, but you know. Family ties.' He sighed, some old regrets surfacing in spite of himself, and shook his head. 'Would have made a good deck officer if she hadn't got religion. Too much of her mother in her, I suppose.' Startled, I tried to make out traces of a family resemblance, but the main feature they had in common seemed to be an abundance of augmetics rather than anything genetic.

I took the first shuttle down, of course, as befitted my entirely unwarranted reputation for preferring to lead from the front. I'd be well under cover before the orks arrived and should have my pick of the quarters planet-side; I wasn't expecting much in the way of comfort in an industrial facility, but whatever there was I meant to find it. In this I had a valuable ally, my aide Jurgen who had an almost preternatural talent for scrounging, which had made my life (and no doubt his own, although I was careful not to enquire about that) considerably more comfortable than it might otherwise have been in our decade and a half together. He dropped into the seat next to me, preceded as always by his spectacular body odour, and fastened his restraint harness.

'Everything's in order, sir,' he assured me, raising his voice a little so that it carried over the chatter of the troopers surrounding us, meaning that our personal effects had been stowed in the cargo bay to the rear with his usual efficiency. Despite his unprepossessing exterior, and his apparent conviction that personal hygiene was something that only happened to other people, he possessed a number of positive qualities which few people apart from me were ever able to appreciate.

From my point of view, the most important was his complete lack of imagination, which he more than made up for with his dogged deference to authority and an unquestioning acceptance of whatever orders he was given. As you can imagine, having someone like this as a buffer between me and some of the more onerous aspects of my job pretty much amounted to a gift from the Emperor. Add to that the innumerable perils we'd faced and bested together, and I can honestly say that he was the only person I ever fully trusted – apart from myself.

The familiar kick of the shuttle engine igniting cut our conversation short. It went without saying that rather than military dropships, the *Pure of Heart* was equipped with heavy-duty cargo haulers which had been hurriedly converted to meet our needs as far as possible. The end result was better than I could have reasonably expected, but was far from ideal. The front third of the cargo space had been partitioned off with a hastily welded bulkhead, and then subdivided into half a dozen decks with metal mesh flooring. Somehow Mazarin and her acolytes had managed to cram some five score seats with their associated crash webbing into this space so that we were able to disembark a couple of platoons at a time. The rest of the hold had been left open, to take our Chimeras, Sentinels, and other vehicles, along with a small mountain of ammo packs, rations, medicae supplies, and all the other stuff necessary to keep an Imperial Guard regiment running at peak efficiency.

Looking around I could see men and women hugging their kitbags, holding lasrifles across their knees, their faces half hidden by the thick fur caps worn in anticipation of the bone-biting cold on the planet's surface. Most had fastened their uniform greatcoats too. These were mottled with the blues and whites of iceworld camouflage, and I was suddenly acutely aware of what an obvious target my dark uniform and scarlet sash would make me out in that icy waste. No point worrying about it now though, so I gritted my teeth and forced a relaxed smile as the first faint tremors of the hull announced that we'd started to enter the upper atmosphere.

'Pilot's making the most of it,' I said, half joking, and raising a few grins from the troopers around me. 'Must have been watching *Attack Run*[6] in the mess hall.' Jurgen grunted something. He too was swathed in a greatcoat, but, like everything else he ever wore, it contrived to look as though it were intended for someone of a slightly different shape. He suffered from motion sickness on almost every combat drop, but that never seemed to affect his fighting ability once he was back on terra firma. I suspected he was so relieved to be back on solid ground he'd take on the enemy with a sharpened stick rather than have to face the possibility of retreat and being airborne again.

This time though, he wasn't the only one. The overloaded shuttle was being buffeted by the thickening atmosphere, bouncing around like a stone

6 A popular holodrama of the time, about a squadron of Lightning pilots who shoot down an unfeasible number of enemy fighters during the Gothic War. I quite enjoyed it, although Mott, my savant, claims to have counted four hundred and thirty-seven historical and technical inaccuracies in the first episode alone.

on a lake, and pale, sweating faces were everywhere I looked. Even my own stomach revolted on a couple of occasions, threatening to spray the narrow compartment with the remains of my lunch. I swallowed convulsively; I wasn't going to compromise the dignity of my office, not to mention become a laughing stock among the troopers, by throwing up. Not where anyone could see, at any rate.

'What the hell does he think he's playing at?' Lieutenant Sulla, commander of third platoon, and a sight too over-eager for my liking, scowled, which made her look even more like a petulant pony than usual.[7] Nevertheless the distraction from my somersaulting stomach was a welcome one, so I invoked my commissarial privileges and retuned the comm-bead in my ear to the frequency of the cockpit communicator to find out.

'Say again, shuttle one.' The voice was calm and methodical, undoubtedly the ground controller at the refinery landing field. The answering voice was anything but: a civilian suddenly in the middle of a war zone without a clue as to how to survive, and clearly not expecting to. Our pilot, without a doubt.

'We're taking ground fire!' The edge of hysteria in his voice was unmistakable. Any moment now he was going to panic, and if he did we were all likely to die. I doubted that our overloaded engines had any tolerance left for evasive manoeuvres, and if he tried, the chances were that he'd lose control completely. As if to emphasise the point we hit another air pocket, and dropped vertiginously for a handful of metres.

There was nothing else for it: I unbuckled my seat restraints and lurched to my feet, conscious of Sulla's eyes on me. I grabbed the nearest stanchion for support. It was embossed with an Imperial aquila, which I found reassuring, and with its support I was able to take a couple of halting steps towards the cockpit.

'Is that wise, commissar?' she asked, a faint puzzled frown appearing on her face.

'No,' I snapped, not having time to waste on courtesy. 'But it's necessary.' Before I could say any more another lurch slammed my body weight into the narrow door to the flight deck, propelling it open, and I staggered inside. My overriding impression was one of flashing lights and control lecterns, uncannily like miniature versions of the ones on the starship bridge, and the bleak white snowscape passing below us at an alarming speed. The pilot stared up at me, his knuckles white on the control yoke, while his navigational servitor continued regulating the routine functions of the ship with single-minded fixity of purpose. 'What's the problem?' I asked, trying to project an air of calm.

'We're under attack!' the man shouted, raw panic edging into his voice. 'We have to pull back to orbit!'

---

7 This is the celebrated General Jenit Sulla, at a very early stage in her career. Despite the illustrious reputation she was later to achieve, Cain tends to regard her with, at best, mild antipathy throughout the archive; we can only speculate as to why. My own feeling is that he considered her tendency to decisive action unnecessarily reckless, since it put the lives of the troopers under her command (and by extension Cain's) at risk. Ironically it's clear from her own (almost unreadable) memoirs that she regarded Cain very highly, and as something of a mentor.

'That wouldn't be wise,' I said, keeping my voice level, and grabbing the servitor's shoulder to steady myself as the shuttle lurched again. It just kept on adjusting controls with a complete lack of concern. Beyond the thick vision port the bleak and frozen landscape hurtled past as serenely as before. I could see no sign of enemy activity anywhere. 'We'd take hours to rendezvous with the ship if we abort on this trajectory, and we only have limited life support. You'd probably suffocate along with everyone else.'

'We have a safety margin,' the pilot urged. I shook my head.

'The rest of us do. You don't.' I let my right hand brush the butt of my las-pistol, and he turned even paler. 'And I don't see any immediate danger, do you?'

'What do you call that?' He pointed off to starboard, where a single puff of smoke burst briefly. A moment later a small constellation of bright flashes sparkled for an instant some distance below and to the left. Bolter shells detonating against the ground, after some trigger-happy greenskin took a hopeless potshot in our direction.

'Nothing to worry about,' I said, almost amused. 'That's small arms fire.' The analytical part of my mind noted that the main bulk of the ork advance was still some distance away, which meant we ought to be on alert for a small scout force attempting to infiltrate the refinery (which was now looming reassuringly in the viewport), or reconnoitre our lines. 'The chances of anything actually hitting us at this range are astronomical.'

One day I'm going to learn to stop saying things like that. No sooner had the words left my mouth than the shuttle shuddered even more violently than before, and pitched sharply to port. Red icons began to appear on the data-slates, and the servitor began punching controls with greater speed and abhuman dexterity.

'Pressure loss in number two engine,' it chanted. 'Combustion efficiency dropping by sixteen per cent.'

'Astronomical, eh?' Strangely the pilot seemed calmer now his fears had been realised. 'Better strap in, commissar. It's going to be a rough landing.'

'Can you make it to the pad?' I asked. He looked tense, his lips tight.

'I'm going to try. Now get the hell off my flight deck and let me do my job.'

'I've no doubt you will,' I said, boosting his confidence as best I could, and staggered back to my seat.

'What's going on?' Sulla asked as I buckled in and tensed for the impact.

'The greenskins put a dent in us. There's going to be a bump,' I said. I felt strangely calm; there was nothing I could do now except trust in the Emperor and hope the pilot was as competent as he sounded. I considered saying something to reassure the troopers, but I'd never be heard over the noise of the crash alarms anyway, so I decided to save my breath.

The waiting seemed to take forever, but could only have lasted a minute or two. I listened to the chatter in my comm-bead while the pilot read off a number of datum points which meant nothing to me but sounded pretty ominous, fighting down the growing conviction that we weren't going to make it as far as the pad. In fact, the traffic controller seemed pretty insistent that we avoid the installation altogether, which I could well understand, as dropping an unguided shuttle into the middle of the promethium tanks would end our mission pretty effectively before it had even begun. The pilot responded with a couple of terse phrases which managed to impress me even after fifteen years of exposure to the most imaginative profanity of the barrack room, and I began to think we were in safe hands after all, and might just make it.

This impression lasted all of a dozen seconds. Then a violent impact jarred my spine up into the roof of my skull, driving the breath from my lungs. A sound uncannily reminiscent of an ammunition dump exploding echoed through the hull. I gasped some air back into my aching lungs, and tried to clear my blurring vision as the screech of tortured metal set my rattling teeth on edge. I became gradually aware, through the ringing in my ears, that Jurgen was trying to say something.

'Well, that wasn't so...' he began, before the whole ghastly cycle repeated itself another couple of times.

At last the noise and vibration ceased, and I gradually became aware of the fact that we'd stopped moving and I was still alive. I struggled free of the seat restraints, and wobbled to my feet.

'Everybody out!' I bawled. 'By squads. Carry the wounded with you!' In the back of my mind a lurid picture of overheated engines exploding into flame tried to ignite a little beacon of panic, but I fought it down. I turned to Sulla, who was trying to stem a nosebleed. For that matter I suppose we all looked a bit the worse for wear, except possibly Jurgen, as with him it was hard to tell. 'I want casualty figures ASAP.'

'Yes, sir.' She turned to the nearest NCO, Sergeant Lustig, a solid and competent soldier I had a lot of time for, and started snapping out orders in her usual brisk fashion.

The door to the cockpit burst open, and the pilot staggered out, looking as bad as I felt.

'Told you we'd make it,' he said, and threw up on my boots.

TWO

The freezing air outside was worse than even my most pessimistic anticipation, and I'd been on enough iceworlds before to have had a pretty good idea of what to expect. In truth, I suppose, it was no colder than Valhalla or Nusquam Fundumentibus, but it had been some time since I'd trodden the snows of either, and my memory had obviously skipped over the worst of those experiences. The bone-numbing wind seemed to flay me alive the moment I set foot on the ramp, despite the extra layers of insulation I'd put on before leaving my quarters aboard the *Pure of Heart*.

As I staggered down the metal incline, already treacherously slippery from the thin coating of snow which had settled on it, needles of ice seemed to penetrate my temples, replacing the residual headache from the crash with one a thousand times worse. I buried my face in the muffler at my throat, being careful to breathe through it in case my lungs froze, but even so the air rasped in my chest like acid fumes.

A broad plain of ice spread out before me, hazed with wind-driven snowflakes which reduced visibility to a few tens of metres, although the flurries cleared occasionally to reveal the low, grey ramparts of the encircling mountains. They stood out clearly against the lighter grey of the sky, and a moment later I realised that what I'd at first taken for some unusually regular outcrops were the towers and storage tanks of the refinery, still too distant to make out any detail.

'Seventeen injured, fourteen of them walking.' Sulla bounced up to me, the trickle of blood from her nose now frozen to her face, and saluted eagerly. 'Eight of those are ours.' The others would be from first platoon then. I nodded, not trusting myself to talk yet. It would have been a wasted effort anyway, as behind us an engine roared into life and the first of our Chimeras rumbled down the exit ramp, filling the air with the noise of its passage and the rank smell of burned promethium. Thank the Emperor for that, I thought, at least I wouldn't have to slog all the way to the refinery on foot. Sulla noticed the direction of my gaze. 'Lieutenant Voss is assessing the condition of the vehicles now.'

Her opposite number glanced up from a huddle of troopers near the ramp, a data-slate in his hand, and waved a cheery acknowledgement. That came as little surprise, as Voss tended to be cheerful about everything. He was clearly in his element now, grinning widely as the churning tracks bit into the snow, and, dear Emperor, his greatcoat was still unfastened. I immediately felt another ten degrees colder just looking at him.

'We got off lightly,' he told us, his voice crackling over the comm-beads. 'Minor damage only. Nothing we can't get fixed.'

'Should be easy enough,' Sulla agreed. 'A place like this must be crawling with tech-priests.'

'Maybe they can do something with this heap of junk too,' I said sourly, kicking a lump of snow at our downed transportation and deciding to risk talking despite the rush of razor blade air to my lungs. If they couldn't, the loss of one of our shuttles would be a major blow, severely delaying the deployment of our forces, perhaps to the point where we wouldn't be fully prepared by the time the orks arrived.

'We're in the right place at least.' Jurgen had materialised at my elbow. I was mildly disconcerted not to have noticed his approach, feeling that something was inexplicably wrong, before I realised the cold had effectively neutralised his body odour. Either that, or my nose had frozen off.

He was right about that at any rate. The pilot, who I was beginning to forgive for having soiled my footwear, had been as good as his word, bringing us down on the main landing pad after all. Not being entirely reckless he'd aimed for the outer edge though, leaving us with a kilometre or so of packed snow and ice to trudge across before reaching the shelter of the storage tanks I'd noticed before. The faint scar of melted and refrozen ice that marked where we had bounced and skidded our way to a stop was already beginning to disappear under the drifting snow.

'It looks more like a starport than a landing pad,' Sulla observed. I nodded, quite impressed by the scale of things myself, but determined not to show it.

'The shuttles from the tankers are over five hundred metres long,' I said, dredging up a half-digested fact from the largely ignored briefing slate.[8] 'And they land up to twelve at a time.' Sulla looked suitably impressed. Certainly the thought of a swarm of shuttles almost half the size of the starship we'd arrived in filling the air above where we stood was an awe-inspiring one – or it would have been if I hadn't been freezing my gonads off at the time.

Any further thoughts I might have had on the subject were quickly driven from my head at that point, however, by the rather more urgent matter of a bolter shell exploding against the ceramite hull less than a metre from where we were standing.

'Orks!' Sulla shouted, rather unnecessarily under the circumstances I thought. I whirled around to look in the direction she was pointing. At least she had the common sense to do it with her lasgun, though, and opened fire on a small knot of greenskins that was closing fast, slogging through the snow with implacable ferocity.

'Are they mad?' Voss's voice crackled in my ear. 'We must have them outnumbered about ten to one!'

That did strike me as pretty stupid behaviour, even for orks, and I was just

---

8 A quirk of behaviour Cain repeatedly alludes to in the archive. His habit of neglecting to read the background information provided to senior officers prior to deployment on a new planet is rather odd, given his caution in most other respects. (Although given the density and dryness of most Munitorum documentation, it's probable that he'd developed the ability to extricate anything relevant with a quick skim of the contents, and felt little would be served by wading through it page by page.)

casting about desperately for the main force which must surely be flanking us when the explanation suddenly hit me. I was the only human they could see; the Valhallans' camouflage uniforms were blending them into the snowscape, as they were supposed to, and with my commissar's black and scarlet making me stand out like an ogryn in a beauty pageant, they hadn't bothered looking for anyone else. I breathed silent thanks to the Emperor for the flakes of drifting snow which obscured the others from their sight.

'Cease fire!' I snapped, seeing the opportunity for the perfect ambush. A quick glance around me made out at least three squads fully disembarked. They were lying flat in the snow which they'd scraped out into small hollows. A tactic, I vaguely recalled, which had worked well for their forefathers when an ork horde had had the temerity to attack their homeworld. 'Let's draw them in.' Far better to cut them down at short range than engage at a distance, where we would run the risk of a survivor or two escaping to report our arrival back to the warboss.

'Good plan,' Sulla said, as though it were up for debate, and I suddenly realised that it left me the only one in immediate danger. Ork marksmanship wasn't much to worry about most of the time but even greenskins got lucky occasionally, as the downing of our shuttle had proved, so I dropped suddenly with a dramatically out flung arm and a theatrical scream. It was a performance which wouldn't have fooled a five-year-old, but I heard a whoop of triumph from the leading ork, who was carrying what looked like a crudely-fashioned bolter. The others began remonstrating in harsh gutturals, and I was able to hear enough to gather that they were arguing about who should get the credit for killing me.[9] But then if I had a coin for every time that's happened...

'Hold your fire,' I broadcast over the comm-net. Hardly necessary of course, these troopers knew what to do, but I didn't want any mistakes. The orks came on regardless, running apparently tirelessly despite the treacherous footing and the biting wind which would have sapped the strength from an unprotected man in seconds. I began mentally counting off the distance. Two hundred metres, one hundred and fifty...

The closer they got, the more detail I could make out, and the less I wished I could see. There were ten of them in all, about half carrying the bolters I'd noticed before. The others held heavy close combat blades and pistols which looked as deceptively ramshackle as the bolters. I'd seen enough examples in previous encounters not to be fooled, though. Crude as they appeared, the firearms were perfectly functional, and quite lethal if they should happen to hit anything. The same went for the axes, which, with the power of an ork's muscles behind them, were capable of shearing through even Astartes armour.

On they came, snarling and bickering, crude icons decorating their sleeveless vests, which alone spoke volumes for their inhuman robustness in this killing climate. Oddly, I noticed, they were all dressed alike, in dark grey,

---

9 Cain wasn't exactly fluent in orkish, but had managed to pick up a few phrases in the course of his adventures. Mostly insults and obscenities, of course, but it could be argued that they make up the whole language.

which blended better into the winter landscape than the more vivid hues I generally associated with greenskins. Then I realised the last ork in the group wasn't armed like the others. A huge calibre barrel was slung across his shoulder, the bulk of the weapon hidden behind his body. What it was I had no idea, but I was pretty sure I wouldn't like the answer.

The mystery was solved a few seconds later as they caught sight of the idling Chimera, which had been hidden from them by the bulk of the downed shuttle. Evidently intent on looting it, and arrogantly sure they could slaughter any surviving defenders, the sudden appearance of a military vehicle threw them into momentary disarray. After a quick exchange of snarls, during which the leader, who I was able to identify with a fair degree of certainty thanks to his habit of emphasising instructions with blows to the head (not unlike one of the less popular tutors during my time at the Schola Progenium) pointed to the Chimera. The ork with the bulky weapon swung it round to reveal a crude rocket launcher. This at least explained how they'd managed to damage the shuttle, albeit with an incredibly lucky shot. Before I could vox a warning the ork fired, a streak of smoke marking the vector of the warhead, which detonated a few metres to the left of the Chimera.

No point expecting the crew to delay their retaliation, I realised, as the next shot might get them. And sure enough the heavy bolter in the turret swung round to bracket the orks. Puffs of snow and ice were thrown up around them as the explosive projectiles detonated thunderously, tearing a couple of them apart. One of them, to my intense relief, was the rocketeer.

It was then that we saw what makes these creatures so dangerous on the battlefield. Where other, more sensible foes would have taken cover or retreated to regroup, these savages felt no urge stronger than to close quickly and neutralise the threat. With a bone-shaking cry of '*Waaaaarghhhh!*' they ran forward as one, charging headlong into a hail of withering fire.

Well, there was no point hesitating after that, particularly as one foul-smelling foot missed my head by centimetres as it passed, so I rolled to my feet and issued a general order to fire at will.

I don't suppose they even knew what hit them: suddenly struck by the concentrated fire of a couple of score lasguns, not to mention the unrelenting hail of heavy bolter fire, there was nothing much left of them apart from some unpleasant stains on the snow within seconds. Sulla ambled over to inspect the mess, and spat a small gobbet of ice into it.

'So those were orks,' she said. 'They don't look so tough.' I bit down on the sharp rejoinder that rose to my lips, suppressing it. She might as well feel confident for as long as possible. I knew from bitter experience that when the main force got here the next day it would be a different story.

'First blood to you, then, commissar.' Kasteen grinned at me, her red curls falling free as she took off her heavy fur cap, and glanced around the conference room in the heart of the refinery. The smile faltered a bit as her eyes flickered past the little group of tech-priests at one end of the heavy wooden table, but re-established itself as she took in the other people present: a mixed bunch of Administratum functionaries seated in strict order of precedence, and a group of men and women whose hard hands and lined faces indicated that they did most of the actual work around here.

'Luck rather than judgement, I can assure you,' I said. Kasteen had come down on the second shuttle, about twenty minutes after our advance party had made it to the shelter of the refinery hab units, and I was still feeling like a freezy stick.[10] I tightened my fingers around the mug of recaff Jurgen had found for me, feeling the warmth spread through the real ones (the augmetics felt the same as they always did, of course.) I could have done without the transparent wall at the end of the conference suite, beyond which the snow was falling steadily – a visual reminder of the chill which still had me in its grip. Nevertheless the view of the processing plant with its huge structures and belching flames was undeniably spectacular. The sheer size of it struck me for the first time, and I began to understand why it took hundreds of people to extract the raw materials from the ice beneath our feet and process it into the precious fuel.

'You call that luck?' Mazarin hummed into the room behind us, making Kasteen start. 'Bending a perfectly good shuttle?'

Perhaps there was a family resemblance to her father after all, I thought. She'd come down on the same drop as Kasteen to assess the damage, and had just returned from the landing field, thick flakes of snow beginning to melt across her head and shoulders. 'Nothing I can't fix though, praise the Omnissiah.' That was a relief, at least our deployment wouldn't be as delayed as I'd feared. She levitated across to the little group of tech-priests we'd noticed before, and began to converse with them in a weird twittering language that set my teeth on edge.

'She's asking for the use of their facilities to repair the shuttle,' one of the Administratum adepts said, evidently noticing our confusion. He was a youngish man, with thinning blond hair and the pasty complexion of someone who spends too much time with a data-slate.

'You understand that gibberish?' I asked, impressed in spite of myself. He grinned.

'Dear Emperor, no. If I did they'd have to kill me.' He smiled as he said it, although for all I knew he wasn't joking.[11] 'She's just filed a request with the main depository for the spare parts.' He stuck out a hand, and Kasteen shook it formally. 'I'm Scrivener Quintus, by the way. If you need anything, come to me. If I can't get my hands on it, I'll know who can.'

'Thank you.' Kasteen smiled warmly. 'Colonel Kasteen, Valhallan 597th. This is our regimental commissar, Ciaphas Cain.'

'An honour.' His handshake was firm and direct. 'I've seen your statue in Liberation Square on Talethorn. I must say it doesn't really do you justice.'

'That'll be the pigeon droppings,' I said dryly. 'Tends to erode my natural

---

10 A popular snack on many worlds with a temperate or tropical climate, particularly among juves; fruit juices are frozen solid, with a stick embedded in it to facilitate eating. It sounds bizarre, I know, but is really very refreshing.

11 Almost certainly not. 'Binary,' as the tech-priests refer to their secret language, is one of their most sacred mysteries. Cracking it has long been a priority of the Inquisition, but so far even the most rudimentary syntax has yet to be established.

dignity.' He laughed, with every sign of good humour, and I decided I liked him.

'Let me introduce you to a few people,' he said. He waved at the group of tech-priests, singling out a man of about his own age who was talking to Mazarin with every sign of rapt attention. 'That's Cogitator Logash. My opposite number, so to speak.' His voice dropped slightly. 'You'll get more done if you go to him first instead of wasting your time with anyone higher up in the Mechanicus, if you get my drift.'

'Not unlike you and the Administratum,' I suggested, and he smiled.

'I didn't say that,' he pointed out. 'But Logash and I aren't quite so rigid in our thinking as some of the higher ranks in our respective orders.'

'You can say that again.' The man I took to be the leader of the workers joined our conversation. 'How many more of us are going to have to die down there before they sit up and take notice?' He had the hard eyes of a man used to physical toil, and his hair was grey; nonetheless he burned with a passion which seemed at odds with the coldness that permeated everything else around here.

'Technically, no one has died,' Quintus said.

The man snorted.

'Disappeared, then. Five people in as many weeks.' Quintus shrugged. 'I've done my best to get them to investigate, you know that.' The man nodded reluctantly. 'But they just argue that accidents happen. Icefalls, gas pockets...'

'I've been working here for over twenty years,' the man said. 'I know all about icefalls, and a dozen other hazards you quill-pushers haven't even heard of. And they all leave bodies.'

'But officially, without a body there's nothing to investigate.'

'That's insane,' Kasteen said. The man smiled for the first time.

'That's what I keep telling them. But the lad here's the only one with a functioning brain, apparently.' He stuck out a hand. 'I'm Artur Morel, by the way. Guild of miners.' His grip was firm.

I have to admit, all this talk of death and mysterious disappearances had me spooked. If we were going to fight a battle I didn't want to be looking over my shoulder the whole time, and I resolved to have a longer talk with him at the earliest opportunity. We'd already encountered one ork scouting party after all, and if there was another one already lurking in the mine we'd have to clear them out as a matter of priority.

But first things first: we had a war to plan. Mazarin left the room with Logash trotting along behind her, evidently detailed to sort out her requirements, and the highest ranking Administratum adept, a white-haired woman called Pryke, called the meeting to order with every sign of enthusiasm.

Needless to say, it turned out to be interminable. The facility seemed to be equally dependent on the three factions present to keep functioning, or at least that's what Pryke fondly imagined, although I'd have laid a small wager that putting the Administratum drones out in the snow to keep the orks amused while we prepared our defences would have had a negligible effect on the promethium output. Every point she raised was politely challenged by Magos Ernulph, the senior tech-priest, who would remind everyone that without his people to perform the appropriate rituals the plant would simply grind to a halt. Of course without Morel's miners to provide the raw materials it would do so anyway, but the guildsman was tactful enough not to drag things out even further by pointing this out, for which I was extremely grateful, especially since my stomach had started to realise how empty it was.

Fortunately Kasteen had a much lower level of tolerance for idiots than I did, so it was with some relief that I saw her stand to interrupt the ageing bureaucrat in mid flow.

'Thank you all for your input,' she said crisply. 'It's clear that you all have particular insights to offer, which we will be calling upon as and when we see the need.'

'I think my colleagues will require a little more than that,' Pryke rejoined. 'May I suggest you provide us with daily progress reports?' Ernulph nodded in agreement, his blank metal eyes turning on the colonel. She ignored him, with an effort only I knew well enough to discern.

'You may not. We're here to fight a war, not push files around.' There was an edge to Kasteen's voice now which every officer in the regiment had learned to be wary of. Pryke bristled.

'That's just not good enough. There are procedures to be followed...'

'Then let me relieve you of them,' Kasteen snapped. 'This facility is now under martial law.' The result was hugely enjoyable, I have to admit. Pryke went scarlet, then white, then scarlet again. Ernulph probably would have done too, if he'd had enough organic bits left to manage it. Both stood at once, shouting excitably.

'You can't do that!' Ernulph boomed, his voice apparently magnified by some implanted amplivox unit. It was a cheap trick, and one which remained resolutely un-terrifying to anyone who'd been shouted at by a daemon as I had.

'Yes she can,' I confirmed quietly, my voice carrying all the more effectively for not being raised like all the others. 'A field commander has the right to declare martial law at any time with the approval of the highest ranking member of the Commissariat present. Which is me. And I do.' I stood, and gestured to the plant outside, and the barren snowscape beyond. 'By this time tomorrow all you'll see out there is orks. We're your only hope of not ending up dead or worse. So shut up, keep out of our way, and let us do our job.' Morel and Quintus, I noticed, were openly enjoying their colleagues' discomfiture.

'This is unacceptable,' Pryke said, her voice tight with outrage.

'Live with it,' Kasteen said. 'Unless you prefer the alternative.'

'I most certainly do.' Pryke glared at both of us.

'Fine.' I drew my laspistol, and dropped it on the table from just the right height to produce a nicely resonant thud. 'Under the powers bestowed upon me by the commissariat in the name of His Divine Majesty, I serve notice that any civilian obstructing His forces in the defence of His realm will be subject to summary execution under article seventeen of the rules of military justice.' I raised an interrogative eyebrow at Pryke and the tech-priest. 'You were saying?'

'I withdraw my objections,' she said tightly. Ernulph nodded too.

'On reflection, the colonel's assumption of authority seems entirely the best course of action,' he conceded.

'Good,' I said, leaving the gun where it was – no harm in concentrating their minds a little further. 'Colonel. You have the floor.'

Editorial Note:

There can be very few readers who will be unaware of the enormous importance of the promethium production facility which Cain describes, both strategically and economically. Since its retention or seizure was so vital an objective for the contending armies, I felt a little extra information on this amazing substance wouldn't come amiss. Unfortunately I haven't been able to lay my hands on very much, as such things remain the jealously-guarded province of the Adeptus Mechanicus, so this is the best I could do.

From *Our Friend Promethium*, Imperial Educational Press, 238th edition, 897 M41

From the Emperor-blessed fighting machines of the Astartes to the most humble spaceport cargo-hauler, it can truly be said that the Imperium runs on promethium. This might seem amazing enough on its own, but this miraculous substance gives us so much more than just the power to feed the animating spirits of our vehicles. The alchemical by-products of its production provide the raw materials to create a vast array of everyday necessities, from dyes, plastics and pharmacopoeia to the synthetic protein bars which make up the bulk of the proletarian diet on some of the drearier forge worlds.

But it's the combustibility of promethium which allows its most holy use. From the flamers which scourge the unholy with the purifying fire of the righteous to the alchemical constituents of the explosives which blast them into oblivion, it's this most blessed of substances which keeps us safe and preserves our homes from the depredations of the alien, the mutant, and the heretic.

Promethium itself can be produced in a variety of ways, and from an astonishing number of sources. Among the most common are the atmospheres of gas giant planets, subterranean deposits of ancient organic materials, and certain kinds of rare ices found only on the coldest of worlds...

[Of course it's the illustrations which are the real charm of this little book, particularly those of its narrator, Pyrus the Flame. Even now I can't help smiling at the expressions on the faces of the heretics he's burning on page twenty-eight, just as I did as a child all those years ago.]

THREE

'Sieur Morel. I'd like a quick word with you if you can spare the time.' I judged my movement precisely, so that to the casual observer it would look as though we'd reached the door of the conference room together purely by chance. The grizzled miner turned in my direction, assessed the situation with keen intelligence, and nodded, dismissing his staff with a casual wave. They filed out along with the tech-priests and the quill-pushers, Ernulph and Pryke, still simmering nicely leaving us alone with Kasteen and Broklaw.

The major had joined the conference shortly after Kasteen dropped her little bombshell, taking over the tactical debriefing of the refinery staff. Now the two of them were huddled over data-slates refining their strategy for the defence of the plant. Ernulph, Pryke, and their respective hangers-on had turned out to be quite helpful after the sight of my sidearm had cleared the air, no doubt reflecting that the orks might very well get them if they didn't do all they could to help, and if the greenies didn't I most certainly would.

A handful of troopers were bustling in and out of the conference suite, setting up map boards and a large urn of tanna leaf tea. It looked as though this was going to be our command post, at least for the time being. (Kasteen claimed it was an excellent vantage point from which to direct the troops, but I suspected she just liked the view from the window.) I found the gradual transformation from civilian decadence to the purposeful military atmosphere quietly reassuring; how the miner viewed it I had no idea, or interest, come to that.

'Of course. How can I help?' Morel asked. I poured myself a bowl of tanna tea, and offered him one. After a moment he took it, sipped cautiously, and appeared to approve, although the Valhallan brew isn't to everyone's taste.

'Earlier you mentioned some of your miners had disappeared in mysterious circumstances. Would you care to elaborate?' An expression of mild surprise crossed his grizzled features. I suppose after being stonewalled by the other factions here for so long our interest was unexpected.

'Five people, in just over a month. It might not sound much out of a workforce of six hundred, but believe me it matters to us.' He shrugged. 'Of course the Administratum and the Mechanicus don't give a damn. Just trot out the same old line about the losses being within acceptable statistical parameters.'

'What's your opinion?' I asked. Morel sipped his tea, formulating a response, and I forestalled him. 'I want your gut reaction. Don't feel you have to be polite.' He laughed, and looked at me with renewed respect.

'Just as well. Diplomacy isn't exactly my strong point.' He sipped again. 'Something's definitely wrong down there. Don't ask me what, though.'

'Then we need to find out,' I said. Kasteen broke off from her conversation with Broklaw long enough to nod.

'Quite,' she said. Broklaw nodded too.

'Absolutely. No point in fortifying the place if the trouble's already inside with us.'

'You think we've got orks in the tunnels?' Morel paled at the thought. Whatever he'd thought the problem might be, this clearly wasn't it. I shook my head doubtfully.

'It's possible. Although sneaking around picking people off one at a time isn't exactly their style.'

'And I don't see how they could have got here that soon,' Kasteen added, with a glance at the hemisphere map pinned to the wall close to her seat. 'It's taken them over six weeks to get here from the crash site. If an advance party was taking your miners they'd have had to have got halfway round the planet within a few days of their arrival, and we've seen no sign of any rapid deployment capability.'

'Unless they teleported,' I suggested. 'It has been known.'[12]

'We're not jumping to conclusions are we?' Broklaw mused. 'Could it just be an unfortunate series of accidents after all?'

'That hardly seems likely.' Morel stared at the plan on the opposite wall. The straggling and meandering lines looked like nothing so much as a detailed diagram of a plate full of noodles. A map of the tunnels beneath us, I realised, where the precious veins of ice which could be transmuted into promethium had been hauled out for countless generations.[13]

'Can you show us where the missing miners vanished from?' I asked. That might give us some kind of clue. Morel nodded, picking up a stylus from the desk, and marked the points in rapidly; I realised he must have done this before, no doubt hoping to find some connection himself. I stared at the rumpled sheet of paper, translating the lines in my mind into a three dimensional image, and trying to get a feel for the space.[14] If there was a pattern to be discerned, however, it eluded me.

'Have you spotted something?' Kasteen asked hopefully, aware of my tunnel rat's instincts from my reports on the Gravalax incident. I shook my head.

'There's no obvious connection between these points,' I said. I tapped one with a fingernail. 'This gallery's a dead end, for instance. An assailant would have to get past an entire shift of workers unobserved.'

'And that's just not possible,' Morel confirmed. Which begged another question that Broklaw was obliging enough to ask.

'Unless one of the refinery staff is responsible...' he began, but trailed off as Morel's face darkened.

---

12 Ork units were deployed by teleporter on several occasions during the Armageddon campaign, for instance.

13 Only about half a dozen, in actual fact. The processing plant on Simia Orichalcae was relatively new.

14 As I've noted elsewhere, Cain had an uncanny affinity for the layout of underground passageways, probably as a result of his early upbringing on a hive world.

'If you're planning to accuse any of my people of murder, you'd better have some damn good evidence.'

'No one's accusing anyone of anything,' I soothed, biting back the unspoken *yet*. 'You've brought a potentially serious security breach to our attention, and we're trying to get to the bottom of it, that's all.'

'If it saves any more of my people I'm glad to help,' the miner said, somewhat mollified.

'I'm glad to hear it.' I gazed at the map of the mine workings again, as though deep in thought. 'But I don't think we'll solve the problem talking about it over a bowl of tea.'

'Then what do you suggest?' Kasteen asked. I sighed with every appearance of reluctance and shook my head.

'I'll just have to go down there and take a look around,' I said.

Now if you've been reading my memoirs with any degree of attention it's probably struck you that this apparent willingness to put myself in harm's way is somewhat uncharacteristic, to say the least. But try to see things from my point of view. For one thing, if I hung around here while the defences were being prepared there was a pretty good chance I'd end up in that bone-chilling cold again, and I was most reluctant to do so. Not to mention the fact that there was a horde of greenskins on the way. True, they weren't expected to arrive in force for another twenty-four hours or so, but that hadn't held back the advance party we'd encountered already, and who knew how many more of them might be lurking out there waiting for an unwary target to show itself?

Tunnels, on the other hand, were an environment I felt right at home in, and I could match my fighting skills in a dark confined space with anything we might find down there. And it wasn't as if I was going in alone either; anything used to taking on solitary unarmed civilians was in for a big surprise if it tried jumping a squad of troopers with lasguns. So all in all I was pretty confident that whatever might be lurking in the dark lower levels, it wouldn't pose nearly as much of a threat to my continued well-being as hanging around outside like a chunk of deep-frozen ork bait. (In this assumption I was, as it turned out, both quite correct and catastrophically wrong. Of course I had no reason to suspect at that point what our investigation would ultimately lead to.)

I've seen some sights in my time, and it takes a lot to impress me, but I have to admit that even today, after more than a century, the ice caves of Simia Orichalcae stand out in my memory as a sight to behold. I don't know what the troopers made of them, but to a born and bred tunnel rat like me they were quite spectacular. Though broad mining galleries ran off into the distance beyond the reach of our luminators, it was never quite dark, as the ice surrounding us reflected the light back so that it rippled away in a faint blue sheen as far as the eye could see.

And the walls glittered, every single irregularity in the surface reflecting and refracting the beams, so we moved through an ever-scintillating constellation of ephemeral stars. Our boots crunched gently on frost-packed floor, and our breath puffed visibly with every exhalation, but down here, away from the flensing wind, I found the temperatures tolerable enough. They were certainly no worse than those in the average Valhallan billet when they could get the air conditioning to work, and I was used to that. It was even warm enough for Jurgen's characteristic odour to have returned, albeit in a slightly muted fashion, for which we were all grateful. I'd requested Lustig's squad for backup, as after our adventures on Gravalax I was confident in their abilities, and I found the familiar faces and the sergeant's taciturn presence a welcome boost to my spirits. I'd declined the offer of a guide from among the miners as I was confident in my own tunnel sense, and if there really were orks down here the last thing I wanted was some hysterical civilian getting in the way in the middle of a fire fight.

The early stages of our descent had been through the bustle of the upper workings, where miners and servitors hurried through broad, well-lit thoroughfares reminiscent of the streets of a Valhallan cavern city, and mobile ore bins full of shimmering ice shoved everything else unceremoniously out of the way. But as we penetrated further into the complex, into the lesser-used passages, they grew narrower and less well lit, until the only illumination was what we carried with us. From time to time we heard sounds of activity from the main galleries, where Morel's colleagues were still hacking the precious ice away with the aid of tools which looked alarmingly like the meltas we used as weapons, but after an hour or so of steady descent even this had faded away.

'What are we looking for, exactly, sir?' Sergeant Lustig asked. I shrugged.

'Emperor knows,' I said. 'Just something unusual.' His squad was spread out in a standard search pattern, with everyone in visual range of at least two other troopers. I wasn't going to have any more mysterious disappearances if I could help it, particularly if one of them was likely to be me. The sergeant's broad face creased in a grin.

'Well that narrows it down,' he said, glancing round at our surroundings. Coming from an iceworld as he did, I suppose he found them bordering on the mundane. In a way, that's what I was counting on; between the Valhallans' feeling for ice and my hive boy's affinity for enclosed spaces, whatever was down here was bound to have left some traces which would strike one or another of us as odd.

'Penlan here.' The voice of one of the troopers hissed in my comm-bead, followed a moment later by the attenuated sound of her actual speech overlapping the transmission like a distorted echo. She could only be a hundred metres or so away. 'I've got something. Looks like tracks.'

'Hold your position,' I ordered, and worked my way towards her silhouette. She was backlit by the luminator she'd taped to the barrel of her lasgun. Jurgen trotted at my heels, his own weapon levelled and ready for use. Experience had taught both of us you could never be too cautious in circumstances like this.

'What do you make of it, sir?' Penlan asked, turning towards us. As she did so, she brought the patch of discoloured skin on her left cheek where she'd taken a glancing las hit on Gravalax into the beam of Jurgen's luminator. Her expression was as puzzled as her voice, brown hair falling into her grey eyes from around the rim of her hat.

'Damned if I know,' I said, not relishing the doubt. She shone her light directly on the marks she'd found, deep gouges in the frozen floor, which indeed looked uncomfortably like claw marks. After more than a decade and a half in Imperial service, during which time I thought I'd encountered pretty much every malevolent life form in the galaxy, I should have been able to recognise them. The fact that I couldn't was deeply disconcerting. Even the mark of ork boots, which I'd been half expecting, would have been preferable.

'They look a bit like genestealer tracks,' Jurgen said uncertainly. He was partially right: they'd been gouged out by what looked like powerful talons, but the spacing was all wrong to be the work of a 'stealer. 'Or 'nids, maybe?'

'I don't think so,' I said. 'The weight distribution's all wrong.' Which given the hive fleets' ability to conjure new and unpleasant creatures out of thin air wasn't exactly a certainty, but if there was a bio-ship or two in the sector the chances of them getting this far into Imperial space undetected were negligible. I pointed that out too, and pretended I hadn't seen the momentary flicker of visible relief on Penlan's face. The two original regiments which now made up the 597th had fought the tyranids shortly before I joined them, and both had been all but annihilated. Come to that, I'd seen more than enough of the 'nids to last me more than a lifetime by this point too.

'We'd best press on,' I decided after a few moments' reflection. Somehow the confirmation that there was something down there made it easier to do that than go back, however strong the impulse to retreat I now felt. I knew from experience that an unknown enemy is always a bigger threat than one you've identified, and, in truth, nothing much had changed. I still had a crack squad of veteran troopers between me and anything malevolent lurking up ahead. Not to mention Jurgen, whose peculiar gifts had saved my hide on more than one occasion, even though neither of us had been aware of their existence until our encounter with Amberley and her entourage on Gravalax.[15] Lustig nodded, and gave the order to move on.

The mood was, if anything, even more sombre after that. The occasional outbreaks of joking and banter between the troopers sounded hollow now, uncomfortable, and soon petered out into silence punctuated only by the terse monosyllables of report and response. The trooper on point, Penlan still I think, began communicating by hand signals wherever possible, and resorted to the comm-net only when absolutely necessary. Almost without thought we'd slipped into the assumption that we were now in hostile territory.

I found that comforting. A healthy dose of paranoia goes with my job, of course, but it was nice to know that everyone else was as jumpy as me for once, with the possible exception of Jurgen, who never seemed particularly put out by anything which didn't involve aerodynamics. Almost without thought my hands went to my weapons, loosening the chainsword in its scabbard and drawing the laspistol. No point in not being prepared, I thought.

15 Very early on in my association with Cain and his aide, it became obvious that Jurgen was a blank: a staggeringly rare attribute which made him immune to daemonic possession or psychic attack.

'If there's anything down here we must be right on top of it,' Lustig muttered. I nodded. We were only a few dozen metres from the end of the gallery by now, and the dead end I'd spotted on the map. The chances of whatever had left those tracks staying behind to be bottled up by our advance were remote in the extreme, I knew, but still my mouth went dry, my stomach cramping with the anticipation of combat, my imagination running wild with images of rampant Chaos spawn.

'That's it. Dead end.' Penlan's voice had an unmistakable edge of relief, which rippled around the rest of the squad like a breeze through summer grass. I exhaled, feeling my muscles relax, unaware until then of how tense I'd become.

'Take a look round,' I said, starting forward to join her. Jurgen stayed at my shoulder as always, and behind me I heard Lustig issuing orders with his usual calm efficiency. He was deploying the rest of the squad to secure our perimeter. Good. That meant no unpleasant surprises while we were poking around.

'Frak all that I can see.' Penlan moved carefully, sweeping her luminator ahead of her. The beam picked out a blank wall, where the tunnel had simply been abandoned when the seam of refinable material had run out. Then it swept on to pick out a jumble of ice boulders over to the right. The palms of my hands started to tingle as they always did when my subconscious alerted me to something untoward. Penlan started towards the heap of rubble.

'Be careful,' I started to say, as the realisation began to seep through to my forebrain. The tumbled pattern of ice blocks looked familiar, scattered like the debris from an underhive roof fall. I swept my own luminator beam towards the ceiling, where a crack began, no thicker than a hair, before widening to the width of my fist as it reached the wall. From there the fissure grew exponentially, terminating in the pile of frozen rubble.

It still didn't feel right to me. For the debris to have fallen in that pattern, the wall itself must have been undermined. A faint, but ominous cracking sound echoed through the chamber.

'Penlan!' I shouted. 'Get back!' But I was too late. She was half-turning towards me, an expression of puzzlement on her face, when the floor gave way beneath her and she vanished from sight with a single startled shriek.

'Penlan!' Lustig started forward, until I restrained him with an arm across the chest; there was no knowing how far the treacherous deadfall extended. 'Penlan, report!' Static hissed in our comm-beads.

'Watch that first step, sarge.' Her voice sounded winded, but if she could crack jokes she couldn't be that badly hurt. 'It's steeper than it looks.'

'Better move carefully,' I counselled the sergeant. 'No telling how unstable the rest of the floor is.' I inched forward cautiously, Jurgen at my side, just enough to shine the beam from our luminators down into the hole. It seemed sufficiently solid. From here I could see that a thin crust of ice had formed across the gap where the roof fall had breached the ceiling of a chamber below us. A chamber, I suddenly realised, which didn't appear anywhere on the map.

'That froze over recently,' Jurgen said, with the certainty of an iceworlder. I edged a little closer to the hole, from where I could see Penlan. She'd fallen about five or six metres, but most of that, thank the Emperor, had been down a steep slope rather than a sheer drop. A friction-gouged channel in the ice showed where she'd slid most of the way. Seeing my face appear in the gap, she waved.

'Sorry about that, sir,' she said. 'My foot slipped.'

'So I see.' I got Jurgen to direct his luminator around the chamber she was in. It was roughly circular, no more than a few metres wide, and I began to suspect that it might have been a natural ice pocket. It was easy to imagine a solitary miner falling the way Penlan had, and being less lucky about landing. The gap they'd left behind them could have frozen over before the search party arrived. Perhaps Morel's mysterious disappearances had been accidents after all. 'Does that hollow look natural to you?'

'Maybe.' Penlan shone her own beam around, then stiffened, aiming the lasgun. 'There's another tunnel here. I can't tell how far it goes.'

'Sit tight.' Lustig appeared at my elbow, a coil of climbing rope in his hands. He began looping it round himself, and threw the end down to Penlan. She grabbed it, slung her lasgun, and began to swarm up the rope. After a second she hesitated.

'Sarge. There's something down here. I can hear movement.' After a second or so I heard it too. The scrape of claw against ice, moving fast, and the loud panting of a predator which has caught a fresh scent. I joined Lustig, grabbing the rope, and hauled until the muscles in my back cracked.

'Get her up!' I shouted. Jurgen ran to help too, and between us we dragged Penlan a good three metres up the ice face. From there her boot soles caught some purchase, and she was able to scramble her way up the wall. I dropped to my knees, feeling the cold bite through the fabric of my trousers, and extended a hand down into the darkness. 'Grab it!'

Penlan did so, a firm grip clamping round my wrist, and I tightened my grip on hers. We'd nearly made it, when something seized the dangling rope below her and jerked it hard.

'Frak!' Lustig and Jurgen dropped suddenly, pulled off balance, and Penlan's weight dragged me down. For a moment I thought we'd make it, but the ice beneath me had too little traction, and for a long, agonised moment I felt myself slipping. My hand tightened reflexively around her wrist, instead of letting go which would have been far more sensible, and before I knew it I was plunging forwards into the shadowy pit.

I landed hard, the breath driven from my lungs, a dozen small pains flaring across my body where I'd bounced on the way down. Penlan groaned beside me, face down and winded. Just as well, a small analytical part of my mind told me, or the slung lasgun might have broken her back.

'Commissar!' Bright light shone down on us, the luminator taped to Jurgen's lasgun, and I heard the distant echo of running feet as the rest of the squad responded to our plight. They wouldn't be quick enough, I thought, as the creature – whatever it was – rushed out of the darkness. I had a brief, panic-stricken image of claws and jaws too large and terrifying to be real, and as I scrabbled frantically backwards. My hand fell against the lasgun on Penlan's back. Without thinking I twisted it round, finding just enough play in the sling, and fired without even aiming properly.

Either luck or the Emperor was with me, because she'd left it on full auto. As my panic-spasmed hand locked on the trigger a hail of las-bolts sprayed the chamber, blowing chunks of ice from the walls and deafening us with the roar of ionising air and ice flashing into steam. The creature screamed and fled, even more terrified than I was, and as the power cell died and relative silence descended on our ringing ears, Penlan stirred.

'I've got to stop doing that...'

'I'd appreciate it,' I agreed. A degree of understanding returned to her eyes. 'What happened?'

'The commissar saved your hide,' Lustig said. I was suddenly aware of the ring of faces around the hole over our heads. No point mentioning that it was purely by accident, of course, so I made a show of mild embarrassment, and patted the frost from my greatcoat.

'Better get the medic to check you over,' I said, just to reinforce my caring image.

I took a glance around the chamber. It looked bigger from down here, and the hail of las-bolts had melted a number of small pits into the walls. Something seemed to be embedded in one, and I tried to focus on it, to stop my head spinning. Then my brain finally interpreted what I was seeing, and I regretted my curiosity at once.

'Looks like we found our missing miner,' Penlan said, with what I felt was rather unseemly relish.

'Almost,' I agreed. It was a human hand, severed at the wrist, the stump scored with vicious bite marks.

'What was that thing?' Jurgen asked, his habitual phlegmatic tone a welcome calming influence.

'I haven't a clue,' I admitted, scooping my laspistol up from the floor where it had fallen. As I did so I noticed a thick smear of ichor on the ice. The sight cheered me remarkably, not least because if I'd managed to wound the creature it was unlikely to come back for a while. 'But it bleeds.' I thrust the sidearm back into the holster on my belt with a sense of grim satisfaction. 'And that means we can kill it.'

FOUR

'And you don't have a clue what it was?' Broklaw asked. I shook my head. In the three or four hours since we'd returned from the depths of the mine I'd been asked that question often.

'None. But you wouldn't want one as a house pet, believe me.' A few of those present in the command centre chuckled dutifully. Besides myself and the major, Kasteen was the only other person seated on what I couldn't help thinking of as the military side of the conference table. Facing us was Morel, whose interest in the situation was undeniable and whose reaction had fallen somewhere between shock at the news that his worst fears were founded and grim satisfaction that his forebodings had been vindicated. Alongside him sat representatives from the Administratum and the Adeptus Mechanicus. Around us the rest of our senior officers continued to monitor troop positions and intelligence reports, ignoring the little knot of civilians in our midst as best they could as they bustled in and out with data-slates and mugs of tanna.

Remembering Quintus's advice I'd requested that he and Logash be our liaisons with their respective orders, and was pleased that this decision had proven to be wise. The young scrivener was as affable as I remembered, and Logash had turned out to have a quick wit and a courteous manner at marked odds with the defensiveness of his superior. To Kasteen's evident relief he had few visible marks of augmentation as well, beyond a pair of faceted metal eyes, which caught the light as his head moved, and although the Emperor alone knew what his robes concealed, she was able to keep her revulsion in check. (When I asked her why she found the tech-priests so disturbing she just shrugged, and said, 'They're weird, that's all.' She never reacted that way towards me, or anyone else in the regiment with augmetic replacements, so I guess it was just the sense she got from them of having voluntarily, if not eagerly, surrended part of their humanity.)[16]

'I've taken a look through the Codex Ferae,' Logash volunteered, 'based on the commissar's description of the beast. I'm pretty sure whatever it is, it isn't native to Simia Orichalcae.'

'Then how the hell did it get here?' Morel asked. Logash shrugged.

---

16 A common reaction to members of the Adeptus Mechanicus. Personally it's their air of smugness I find most off-putting. And isn't it about time the Ordo Hereticus started asking some pointed questions about this Omnissiah cult of theirs?

'Maybe the orks brought it with them.'

'That's highly unlikely,' Kasteen said, taking a little too much satisfaction in contradicting the tech-priest. But he took it in his stride and gave way to her greater expertise.

'You'd be a better judge of that than me.' He shrugged again. 'Maybe it stowed away on one of the tanker shuttles then.' Quintus nodded in agreement.

'They're certainly big enough for something to hide in undetected. I remember a couple of years back a few of the miners thought it would be funny to smuggle in some...'

'Who cares how it got here?' Morel broke in. 'The question is, what are we going to do about it?'

'Go back down there and kill it,' I said. Morel nodded with grim satisfaction, but Quintus's eyes narrowed a little.

'I don't want to sound as though I'm doubting your sense of priorities, but surely the orks are the real threat. Can't this thing wait until you've seen them off?'

'It's not the creature we're worried about,' Kasteen said. 'It's the unmarked tunnels the commissar found down there.'

'Probably burrowed by the beast,' Logash said. He pulled a data-slate from the recesses of his robes, and started scribbling notes with a luxpen embedded in the tip of a finger. 'That might account for the size of the claws the commissar saw...'

'It doesn't matter who dug them,' I pointed out. 'What matters is that they're a potential hole in our defences.' As if to underline my words a bright flash cut through the flurrying snow outside the window, followed almost at once by the concussive thud of explosive detonation. The orks had obligingly arrived on schedule and were busily throwing themselves (or more probably their gretchin cannon fodder) against our outer defensive line with a gratifying lack of success so far. Luckily, Mazarin and her acolytes had managed to get the damaged shuttle flying again in a matter of hours, and the rest of our deployment had gone without a hitch, so we'd been more than ready to meet them despite my fears.

'I take your point,' Quintus said. 'What do you suggest?'

'I'm going back down there,' I said. 'With a squad of troopers. We'll map the tunnels as we go, and kill the creature when we find it.'

'You're leading the group personally?' Logash asked. I nodded.

'Commissar Cain is by far the best man for the job,' Kasteen explained. 'He has more experience of tunnel fighting than anyone else in the regiment.' Not from choice, I might add, but if it kept me out of the cold and away from the orks, I wasn't about to object.

'I'd like to come too, if I may,' Logash said. I think I'm hardly exaggerating when I say the rest of us simply stared at him in blank astonishment. 'Xenology's a bit of a hobby of mine. I might be able to identify what we're looking for.'

'This is a search and destroy mission, not a stroll around the zoo,' Kasteen said irritably. Logash looked a little crestfallen, I thought she was being unnecessarily hard on the boy. At least he was trying to help, which was more than his superiors were willing to do, and it didn't seem too good an idea to squash that enthusiasm. Besides, I had no objection to presenting the beast with another potential meal,to stand between me and it. (Of course if I'd known just how much trouble he was going to turn out to be I'd have left him behind, or even shot him on the spot, but regrets are a waste of good drinking time, as my old friend Divas used to say.)

'It would be at your own risk,' I told him. 'And you'd be under military authority. That means you do what you're told at all times. All right?'

'Fine.' He nodded eagerly. 'Do I get a gun?'

'Absolutely not,' Kasteen and I said simultaneously.

After seeing the civilians out, Kasteen, Broklaw and I returned to the business of fighting the war. Our strategy seemed to be working, at least for now, keeping the main line of the ork advance bottled up in the neck of the valley quite nicely. The peculiar nature of an iceworld, and the Valhallans' understanding of how to exploit it, were paying handsome dividends, as the latest sensor downloads from the *Pure of Heart* were making abundantly clear. I gazed at the blurry image in the tactical hololith. It looked like someone had dropped it on the journey up here from the landing pad, as the three-dimensional representation of the battlefield would occasionally jump a few centimetres to the left, blank out, and reset itself. I reflected ruefully that perhaps we shouldn't have been quite so eager to get rid of Logash. (Who had practically skipped out of there, eager to be off, and prattling about various unpleasant life forms our intruder probably wasn't.)

'Never a tech-priest around when you need one,' Broklaw murmured, obviously thinking the same thing. He cast a sidelong glance at the colonel who pretended not to have heard.

Thanks to the frozen landscape we'd been able to fortify in depth with an ease which would have been impossible practically anywhere else. I was looking (when the blasted hololith would let me) at an extensive network of trenches and firing pits which would have taken weeks to dig in more normal terrain, but which had been hollowed out in mere hours by adroit use of our heavy flamers and multilasers. Of course half the troops manning them would have frozen to death by now if they'd been anyone else, but these were Valhallans, and the bone-chilling temperatures outside were just like a holiday resort so far as they were concerned. I'd even had to break up a couple of snowball fights before the orks turned up to spoil the party.[17]

'So far so good,' I said, quietly satisfied with the conduct of our troopers. The line was holding nicely, and the view from orbit showed that the ork advance had pretty much ground to a halt in the face of this unexpected resistance. So far as I could tell, the topography of the valley was working to our advantage as well as we'd hoped, with the broad front of the ork advance funnelling into the mouth of it and running right into our killing zone. Of course being orks this didn't diminish their enthusiasm, quite the

---

17 From which we can infer that, despite his reluctance to step outside, Cain had visited the front line at least once by this point, probably after his return to the surface.

reverse. Some flashes of gunfire on the outer fringes of the mob indicated that fratricidal firefights had broken out as the groups farthest from the fighting had run out of patience and had started blasting their way through their own comrades to get to us. Well that was fine with me, the more of them who killed each other the better I liked it, but there were still plenty left where they'd come from.

'What's that?' Broklaw asked, pointing at a blip some way behind the bulk of the ork army. Whatever it was it was massive, and moving slowly but inexorably towards us. A heavy sense of foreboding sank into my stomach as I stared at it. I had a horrible suspicion as to what it might be, but prayed fervently to the Emperor that I was wrong. (Not that I thought for a moment that He might actually be listening, but you never know, and it relieved the stress.)

'According to this, it's huge,' Kasteen said, a hint of confusion in her voice. Rather than verbalise my fears, which would somehow make them more concrete, I voxed Mazarin aboard the orbiting starship to request a more detailed analysis. That way I could continue to cling to the hope that I might be wrong for a few more precious minutes.

'Single contact, about two hundred kloms... kilometres to the west,' I said. 'Can you give us a little more detail?'

'If the Omnissiah wills it,' the tech-priest said cheerfully, and busied herself for a few moments with the appropriate rituals. After a short pause her voice returned, with a slightly harder edge to it. 'It's a single artefact, approximately eighty metres in height. Self-propelled, with a high thermal signature which indicates combustion processes of some kind. Metallic shell, mainly ferric in composition.' Her voice faltered. 'I'm sorry, commissar, I don't have a clue what it is. I can meditate on it, but...'

'There's no need, thank you,' I said. 'You've just confirmed what I suspected. It's a gargant.' Kasteen and Broklaw stared at one another in horror. The orkish equivalent of a Battle Titan, the approaching construct might be crude but it would certainly have enough firepower aboard to punch through our defensive lines without even so much as slowing down. 'Any suggestions you might have about vulnerabilities we can exploit would be gratefully received.'

'I'll analyse the data and see what I can find,' she promised.

'We can't ask for more,' I said, and turned back to the other officers. We studied the hololith together, brows furrowed. 'I reckon we've got less than a day before it gets here...' I began, then Mazarin's voice interrupted me again.

'Sorry to break in, commissar, but the captain would like a word.'

'This isn't exactly a good time,' I said, then changed my mind. If things went horribly wrong, which they looked very like doing at the moment, the *Pure of Heart* was my best chance of getting out of the system with my hide intact. And annoying Durant would be a seriously bad idea. 'No, put him on.'

'Why's my ship crawling with groundlings?' the captain asked, his voice tinged with an asperity which didn't seem entirely affected. 'I've just got rid of your troopers and now you're shuttling up half the population of this miserable iceball.'

'We're sending up rather more than half,' I said, trying to sound reasonable. 'I thought the Administratum here had cleared it with you.'

'You mean Pryke?' A phlegmy sound of disgust rattled the speakers of the vox unit. 'Impossible woman, doesn't listen to a word you say. How in the Emperor's name did you manage to get her to co-operate with you?'

'It was surprisingly easy after the commissar threatened to shoot her,' Kasteen said, with a hint of a smile. Durant seemed speechless for a moment.

'Harrumph. Worth a try I suppose.' A faint tinge of amusement entered his tone. 'But that still doesn't answer my question.'

'We're evacuating as many of the civilians as we can,' Broklaw explained. 'Especially the workers' families. They'll be a lot safer with you than they are down here.'

'And we can fight more effectively if we're sure they won't be getting underfoot,' Kasteen added, a little more candidly.

'Under your feet, you mean.' The captain sounded mollified. 'I suppose we can stick them in a couple of the cargo holds now they're not cluttered up with your military junk.'

'That would be appreciated,' I said.

'No problem. I'm sure the Administratum can afford their fares.' He broke the connection abruptly.

Of course there was another, unspoken reason for evacuating the workers from the plant, although none of us wanted to think about it. If we were unable to hold the place, and I was a lot less sanguine about that now than I had been twenty minutes ago, the orks would want to make use of it. No point in leaving them a pool of highly skilled slave labour which would maintain promethium output at the current high levels. Their own meks would figure out the process eventually, of course, but they wouldn't be nearly so efficient. And with any luck we'd have had time to launch a counter attack or call the Astartes in to sterilise the place before they got the plant up and running again.

I stared at the hololith, and the almost imperceptibly moving blip of the gargant. We had nothing in our inventory capable of fighting something like that: no tanks, no artillery, and most especially no Titans of our own. Broklaw noticed the direction of my gaze.

'Cheer up,' he said. 'We'll think of something.'

'Better make it quick,' Kasteen said.

Editorial Note:

It is with profound apologies that I append the following excerpt, but feel that some wider perspective on the tactical situation than Cain's typically self-centred one may prove of interest. I just wish I'd been able to find something a little more readable. If you find the prose style (or more accurately, lack of one) as painful as I do, feel free to skip it.

Extracted from *Like a Phoenix From the Flames: The Founding of the 597th*, by General Jenit Sulla (retired), 097.M42

The green tide broke against the bulwark of our defences as surely as an ocean wave against a harbour wall. For such we were, protecting the little islet of civilisation at our backs from the monstrous sea of barbarity which threatened to wash it clean. To the pride of all, it was us, Third Platoon, Second Company, which had been given the all-important task of holding a hastily-constructed redoubt at the very centre of our forward line, and not a woman or man of us shirked that responsibility. Crouched below the parapet of a rampart of ice I scanned my tactical data-slate, heedless of the bolter shells bursting against it to shower me with a refreshing powdering of frozen dust, noting with satisfaction the disposition of the squads under my command. As I'd come to expect, all were positioned with perfect precision, and I permitted myself a moment of pride in the level of battle-readiness they showed.

'Here they come!' someone shouted, a voice shaded, to my great satisfaction, by exultation rather than fear, and a quick glance over the frozen rampart confirmed it. A horde of orks was running towards us, yelling in their barbarous tongue, and I gave the order to hold fire. On they came, trampling the corpses of the dead we'd already left strewn across the virginal icefields, kicking up powdered snow as they came, so that it seemed as if the front ranks were wading waist-deep in mist. Like the wave that had assaulted us before they seemed scrawny specimens, quite unlike the heavily-muscled monstrosities which

Commissar Cain had so resourcefully defeated after our shuttle was grounded,[18] but they died no less easily as I divined when they came within close range of our lasguns. 'Fire!' I ordered, and a devastating wave of las-bolts tore into the front ranks. Dozens fell, and more behind them as the casualties tripped those who followed after: forthwith the emplaced lascannons and multi-lasers we'd carefully sited finished the job, putting out a withering crossfire which ripped them to pieces. After a moment of indecision the survivors broke and fled in all directions, leaving a few more normal-sized specimens who seemed to have been directing them cruelly exposed to our sight and firepower; and this was to prove their death warrant, as they were summarily cut down by a second barrage.

'Like shooting rats in a box,' the young corporal next to me remarked. I reproved her, but could scarce keep the satisfaction from my own voice.

'I doubt they'll give up that easily,' I said, and of course I was right. The frontal attack, as I had half suspected, was a diversion, and the roar of engines heralded a flank attack by a squadron of curious vehicles which resembled motorcycles with tracks replacing the rear wheels. Heavy weapons, bolters I assumed, were slung from them on outriggers, and opened up with a roar which almost drowned the noise of their engines.

'Fire at will,' I ordered, and the snow around them erupted with the concentrated firepower of our doughty host. 'Death to the enemies of the Emperor!'

I must confess my heart swelled at the answering cheers of the heroes under my command, and the conviction of our inevitable victory buoyed my spirits to such an extent that, despite our peril, a smile forced its way onto my face.

---

18 Almost certainly the weaker subspecies known as 'gretchin,' a distinction Cain was well aware of, as his earlier remark makes clear.

FIVE

Of all the experiences which have befallen me in a century or more of service to the Golden Throne, creeping through a network of darkened tunnels in search of a foe which could be lurking almost anywhere is one I could very well have done without becoming so familiar with. I don't know why, but show me an enemy of the Emperor and chances are I can point to the nearest hole in the ground with the near certainty of finding their lair festering away down there. Chaos cults, genestealer swarms, mutants, you name it, they all seem to scurry for the darkest corners they can find; and then, of course, someone has to go in after them and winkle them out.[19]

And, far more frequently than I'd like, that someone turns out to be me. Partly, I suppose, that's due to my inflated reputation (when something dangerous needs doing who better than a hero of the Imperium to get stuck with it?), but in truth I suspect that, as Kasteen told Logash, in most cases I really am the best man for the job. (In theory at any rate, my old hiver's tunnel sense brings a definite advantage, but in practice enthusiasm for the job is most definitely absent, you may take my word for that.)

In this case, though, while not exactly pleased to be back in the network of tunnels, it was rather more attractive than the alternative. True, there was our mysterious beast to worry about, but I'd already wounded it once and didn't anticipate it putting up much of a fight, not with a full squad of troopers to back me up, and the indispensable Jurgen, who'd managed to scrounge a melta from somewhere. He'd done the same on Gravalax, and we'd both found cause to be thankful for his foresight. Indeed, after that little incident he'd become quite partial to that particular item of equipment, and tended to bring it along whenever we might meet heavier resistance than we anticipated. As it turned out I was to have occasion to be even more grateful than usual for this little habit of his. But in all honesty if I'd known what we were going to find down there I would have charged the orks, even the gargant, with a broken chair leg rather than set foot in those caverns again.

As it was though, I remained in blissful ignorance, and even felt relaxed

19 Cain is exaggerating a little here, but it's certainly the case that a significant proportion of the heretical and unclean gravitate naturally to undercities and similar habitats. Then again, given the hostile nature of many worlds, both Imperial and xeno, the population may have had little option but to burrow underground to survive, which at least partially explains the prevalence of such labyrinths throughout inhabited space.

enough to joke with my aide as he fell in at my shoulder, preceded as always by his distinctive bouquet.

'Did you remember the marshmallows this time?' I asked, echoing Amberley's jest when she caught sight of the melta he was carrying on Gravalax. He smiled sheepishly.

'Must have slipped my mind, sir.'

'No problem. We'll just have to find something else for you to toast,' I said.

'I'm not sure that would be wise,' Logash said, hurrying to join us, and looking somewhat askance at the heavy thermal weapon. 'That would pretty much vaporise the creature.'

'Along with a fair sized chunk of the wall behind it,' I agreed. Meltas are designed to punch through tank armour, and using one to eradicate a single creature might seem like overkill to most people, but so far as I was concerned there was no such thing. Especially when you were dealing with something the size of the beast I'd glimpsed before.

'Then we might never know what it was,' Logash objected. I shrugged.

'That's a disappointment I could learn to live with,' I said, then took pity on his crestfallen expression. 'But I'm sure it won't come to that. Jurgen's choice of weapon is purely for worst-case contingencies.'

'I see,' he said, nodding, and clearly trying to imagine what those contingencies might be. Well, he was going to find out soon enough.

'We're here,' the pointman said, his voice tinny in my comm-bead. The squad sergeant, a stocky young woman called Grifen, called a halt, and Logash shut up, eager for a sight of our quarry. I would have preferred to be accompanied by Lustig and his team, as they'd been down here before, but Penlan was too stiff from her healing injuries to tackle any more ice faces and I didn't want to be backed up by an under-strength squad. Besides which, as veterans, they were needed at the front line, especially with the approaching menace of the gargant.

Grifen's squad had seen little combat so far, and the sergeant herself was newly promoted, so this little errand had seemed like an ideal chance to break her into command without too much pressure (ironic, as things turned out.) Her troopers seemed competent enough, and had got over their impulse to gawp at the ice formations and the sparkling reflections in the first few minutes, settling into the routine of a xeno hunt with reassuring efficiency.

I looked down the tunnel to where the beams of our luminators reflected back from the tumbled heap of ice shards which marked the boundary of the hole I'd fallen into before. It was as eerily beautiful as ever, and despite the grimness of our errand I found myself savouring the sight as I turned to speak to Grifen.

'This is it,' I said. 'The end of the map. Once we pass this point we're in unknown territory.'

'Understood, sir.' She saluted crisply, without betraying her nervousness to anyone less skilled than I was at reading body language. She began to issue orders to her squad. 'Vorhees, on point. Drere and Karta, cover him. Hail, Simla, watch our backs. We're moving as soon as the commissar gives the word, so look alive, people.' Despite her inexperience she was a good motivator, and I began to feel a little easier about our travelling companions – most of them, anyway...

'Are there any tracks?' Logash asked eagerly. Grifen looked at him with an air of vague surprise, as though it had slipped her mind for a moment that we were being accompanied by a civilian. She shrugged.

'You're the expert. You tell us.' Anyone else, I suppose, would have had the sense to realise he was being snubbed, but Logash, like most of the tech-priests I've come across, had the social skills of a bath mat.[20] Instead of subsiding like any normal person he nodded eagerly, and started waving an auspex around as though it were an incense burner.

'There are some interesting striations in the ice layer,' he said, 'which could be frozen-over claw marks. Still too vague to make a clear determination, though...'

I caught the sergeant's eye, and raised my own brows in a pantomime of tolerant exasperation. She smiled back a little nervously, not quite sure how to respond to a commissar with a sense of humour, and no doubt in awe of my reputation.

'I think if your people are ready we might as well move on,' I said, already sure they would be, and she gave the order with alacrity.

'Vorhees, front and centre. Let's get ourselves a new trophy for the mess room wall.' Logash shot me an unhappy look, which I ignored, and the pointman dropped nimbly through the hole in the floor.

'I'm down,' he said, his voice still attenuated in the comm-bead. 'No sign of life.' The rest of his fireteam[21] followed him, rappelling into the darkness below. The glow of their luminators was visible now, diffusing through the ice floor like the first faint echo of the dawn breaking somewhere a klom or two over our heads,[22] rippling like an aurora borealis.

'Our turn,' I said, with a cheerfulness I hoped no one would realise was forced, and stepped confidently up to the gap, trying to suppress the memory of my vertiginous plunge into the unknown the previous day. I bounced down the slope, the support of the rope more of a comfort than I'd realised, and found my boot heels crunching against the hard-packed scattering of ice crystals on the floor before I even knew it. The chamber was just as I'd remembered it: featureless save for the tunnel mouth we'd come to investigate. But it was crowded with troopers this time. A moment later Jurgen slithered down next to me. The heavy melta slung across his shoulders pulled him over to one side, but he regained his balance and hefted it properly back into position. The small knot of troopers around us took a step or two away.

Logash came next, clinging too tightly to the rope so that he descended in a series of jerks and wild parabolas. The Guardsmen and women watched his progress with unconcealed amusement and the expectation of an ignominious

20 Probably something to do with all those augmetics. It must be difficult to interact with mere humans when you feel you've got more in common with a beverage dispenser.

21 The Valhallan 597th divided its squads into two fireteams of five troopers each, a common, though unofficial, practice in regiments experienced in urban warfare.

22 In fact, according to the schematics, the lowest level of the mines was almost three kilometres below the surface at this point.

tumble to come. To his credit he made it though, letting out his breath in a wild rush as he reached the floor of the cavern.

'Are you all right?' I asked, reaching out a hand to steady him. He nodded.

'Yes. Fine. I'm just not very good with heights, to be honest.' He caught sight of the splash of ichor from where I'd shot our quarry and went scuttling off to examine it without another word. Soon I heard him muttering in disappointment at the way our boot prints had disturbed any tracks the thing might have left.

I looked up to check the progress of Grifen and the remaining four troopers, who were all descending without any problems. When I looked back the little tech-priest was arguing furiously with private Vorhees. I strode over to investigate, wondering once more whether bringing him was turning out to be more trouble than it was worth.

'What's going on?' I asked, trying to sound reasonable. Vorhees had the young tech-priest held firmly by the upper arm, evidently restraining him. The trooper jerked an irritable head at the mouth of the tunnel down which the creature had disappeared.

'He tried to get past me,' he said. I shone my luminator into the darkness, the beam catching a thousand glittering highlights from the irregular walls. Then I turned to glare at Logash.

'I thought I made it clear you were to stay close to Jurgen,' I said. My aide had accepted the ad hoc bodyguarding assignment as phlegmatically as he did every other order, and I suppose Logash could be forgiven for being less than enthusiastic about it. That wasn't his main concern at the moment though. He jerked his arm free of Vorhees's restraining grasp with a degree of petulance which reminded me of a sulky juve, and pointed at the tunnel floor in the pool of light from my luminator.

'I was looking for tracks,' he said, clearly wanting to say a great deal more. 'The ground in here's too trampled to tell anything from.'

'Right. Fine,' I said. I turned back to Vorhees. 'Keep him in sight. He goes no further than five metres.' I returned my gaze to Logash. 'That should be enough for you, right?'

'Oh yes, indeed.' He trotted a couple of paces into the tunnel, spot lit by the beam of the luminator Vorhees had taped to the barrel of his lasgun, and squatted down to wave the bloody auspex around. Sure he could still hear me, I turned to grin at Vorhees.

'Maybe we'll catch it quicker if we leave some bait out.'

'Worth a try,' he agreed, with a smile of his own. Logash ignored us, already wrapped up in his data-divining rituals. After a few moments he walked back to join us, still muttering under his breath as he studied the display of the little machine.

'Well?' Grifen demanded. 'Can you tell what it is yet?' Logash looked confused.

'Well, there are indications. If we were anywhere else I might take a guess. But the habitat's all wrong...'

'Then just give us what you can,' I encouraged gently. Grifen nodded, flicking her black hair out of her eyes as she tried to make out the runes on the screen, but they were all tech-priest gibberish and none of the rest of us could make head or tail of it. Logash shrugged.

'It definitely burrowed these tunnels,' he said. 'There are claw marks on the walls and ceiling as well as the floor.' A flicker of apprehension rippled around most of the troopers. The narrow passage was high enough to stand up in without stooping, even for me,[23] and if not quite wide enough for two abreast had at least enough room for us to be able to see past the man in front (and shoot, too, which was more to the point.) The creature must have a considerable reach – that much was obvious.

'Well, we're not going to find it by standing here,' I pointed out, more to steady the troops than anything else. 'And we still have to map these tunnels.' So we set off into the dark, our nerves taut with fearful anticipation.

I was more at ease down here than any of my companions with the possible exception of Jurgen, who simply accepted the situation as he did everything else, with taciturn stoicism. These tunnels were different from the ones I was used to, however. They turned and meandered apparently at random, with innumerable branching corridors which came to a dead end or turned back on themselves to rejoin the one we'd just left, or split into further radial passageways. I had several occasions to thank the Emperor for my sense of direction, without it I'd have been disorientated within moments, but the subconscious instinct which lets me know roughly where I am and how far I've come in an underground environment proved as reliable as ever.

'It's a frakking maze down here,' one of the troopers, Drere I think, muttered under her breath. Grifen silenced her with a few well-chosen words, in the manner of sergeants the length and breadth of the galaxy. Logash was travelling in the middle of the group next to me, as I hoped to keep a respectable number of heavily-armed troopers between me and the creature whichever direction it approached from. Logash agreed, heedless of the sergeant's admonishment.

'Surprisingly extensive for so recent an excavation,' he added. Just then the palms of my hands started tingling, in the way they do when my subconscious warns me of something my forebrain has yet to grasp.

'How recent?' I asked. Logash pointed out something on the screen of the auspex, which I couldn't see clearly.

'A few weeks,' he said. 'A couple of months at the most.' In other words, about the same time the orks turned up, and that was just too much of a coincidence. Not that I believed for a moment it was some kind of squig[24] we were after. The chances of that were extremely remote, as anything the greenskins had brought with them would have arrived at the same co-ordinates. But the space hulk which had brought them to the system

23 Cain was just under two metres in height, and was generally among the tallest in any given group.

24 A generic term for a bewildering variety of organisms apparently associated with orks. Opinion in the Ordo Xenos remains divided as to whether they represent true symbiosis, or are simply an entire genus of unpleasant creatures sufficiently close to the greenskins' peculiar metabolic processes to flourish in close proximity to them. It is undeniable that they do seem to accompany most orkish infestations, however. Where Cain picked up the word is conjectural, presumably from the same source as the rest of his smattering of orkish.

(and, to my intense relief, dropped back into the warp again within hours) could have carried any number of other horrors in its bowels, and if that were so it wasn't unlikely that something else had seized the opportunity to make planetfall at the same time.

I made a mental note to ask Quintus to look through the sensor logs of the refinery's orbital traffic control system when we got back. The chances were the blaze of warp energy emitted by the hulk's emergence, a thousand times stronger than that of a starship, would have swamped them, but there might be a clue there we could disentangle given time.

Any further opportunity I might have had to muse on the matter was abruptly curtailed as I felt a faint tremor through the soles of my boots. My palms tingled again, foreboding flooding through me. The narrow passageway seemed even more claustrophobic than before, although that's not a sensation I'm normally familiar with either. The faint tremor intensified, and I stopped trying to identify it. I felt a yielding impact against my shoulder blades as Grifen walked into me, and halted in her turn.

'Commissar? What is it?' she asked.

'Quiet!' I looked back and forth down the tunnel, craning my neck to see as best I could past the troopers on either side of me. The light from our luminators receded in both directions, still striking dazzling highlights from the deep blue surface of the ice around us. 'Something's coming!'

'Nothing here,' Vorhees said, his voice crackling over the comm-net from a hundred metres or so up the tunnel.

'Nothing back here either,' Private Hail chipped in, her voice tense. I can't say I blame her for that, the rearguard is the second most vulnerable position in the column. Everyone stared at me, probably wondering whether the commissar had gone bonkers. Except for Jurgen of course, who had doubtlessly made up his mind on that score years before. But all my hiver's instincts insisted I was right, something was coming, even if we hadn't seen it yet...

Sudden understanding punched me in the gut. The creature we were hunting was a burrower! It didn't need to come at us along an existing passageway. No doubt it had detected our presence in some way, probably picking up the vibrations of our footfalls, and was heading straight towards us by the most direct route.

'Jurgen,' I shouted. 'Give us some elbow room!' Divining my intentions the troopers nearest to us scattered back along the passageway. Logash was hauled away protesting by Grifen, who couldn't be bothered trying to explain. His voice was drowned out abruptly by the hiss of the melta as Jurgen fired at the wall, instantly flashing a dozen cubic metres of ice into steam, which condensed almost instantly in the subzero temperatures, filling the narrow passageway with mist.

He was just in time, too. An instant later the newly frozen wall burst in on us in a hail of glittering ice shards, and the living nightmare I'd encountered before was among us.

By sheer foul luck I was the closest to it, and I barely had time to draw a weapon before it was upon me. This close up a gun would have been all but useless, so I drew my chainsword almost without thinking, and made a block with the instinctive lack of thought that comes from assiduous practice. It was lucky I had. An impossibly long arm, tipped with the talons I'd glimpsed before, swung at me as I thumbed the selector to maximum speed. It would probably have disembowelled me if I hadn't deflected the blow. The blade whined, cutting deep through plates of chitin which wouldn't have seemed out of place on a tyranid, and the thing howled with rage and pain.

I was vaguely aware of Jurgen standing aside to make room for some of the other troopers, whose barrel-mounted luminators spot-lit the confrontation. They were hoping they could get in a shot which wouldn't vaporise me along with the monster I fought, but the hope was a vain one. We were locked in too close, and circling too fast, for anyone to have a hope of getting a clear line of fire.

(It's moments like this, incidentally, which point up the wisdom of fostering the illusion that I cared about the common troopers. I have no doubt at all that, were I the type of commissar who relies on intimidation rather than respect to get the job done, and there are all too many of those around, most of the grunts would have taken the shot anyway and cheerfully reported that the creature got me first. It's a lesson I try to pass on to my cadets, in the hope that the less bone-headed among them might actually get to enjoy a reasonably lengthy career, but it's probably a wasted effort.)

I drove in under the thing's barrel chest, which barely came up to my chin, and tried to avoid the huge mandibles which snapped at my face as I ducked. Bizarrely the thing's unnaturally long arms were jointed about two-thirds of the way up its length, so the closer in to it I remained the harder it would be for it to reach me. Well that suited me fine. I swung the humming blade at its thorax, feeling the teeth bite home, and was rewarded with a spray of ichor and foul-smelling viscera. It screamed again, opening the mandibles impossibly widely, and bringing its head down to snap at me.

That was precisely what I'd been hoping for. The tactic worked well on some of the larger tyranid bio-forms, so I was ready and waiting, thrusting the tip of my trusty chainsword up through the open maw to chew its way contentedly through what passed for the creature's brain. I snatched my hand away quickly, fearing the reflex closing of those terrible jaws, and opening up a wide gash which split the side of its head open from the inside. A jet of blood and cerebral fluid sprayed the wall, which hardened to ice within seconds.

That was enough; the creature fell, making me scramble backwards in an undignified fashion to get out of the way, crashing into the ice at my feet. Thin flakes of powdered ice, condensed from the steam, rose into the air, and fluoresced like miniature galaxies in the light from our luminators.

'That was amazing,' Grifen said, clearly torn between protocol and the urge to pat me on the back. The murmur of voices among the troopers told me that she wasn't the only one to be impressed. Only Logash was looking at the creature rather than me, his face an almost comical mask of confusion.

'There's your specimen,' I told him, returning my trusty chainsword to its scabbard. 'Do you think you can identify it?'

'It's an ambull' he said, shaking his head in bafflement. 'But it can't be. They're native to Luther Macintyre IX...'

'Never heard of it,' I said. 'But it wouldn't be the first time a species jumped planets.'

'That's not the point. Ambull colonies are already known on dozens of worlds.' The young tech-priest looked completely bewildered. 'But they're all desert-dwellers, like their native stock. This creature shouldn't be on an iceworld at all.'

'Maybe it got lost,' one of the troopers suggested. His comment was accompanied by derisive laughter from his squad mates. I didn't join in. Something was badly wrong here, that much was evident, even without my tingling palms to underline the fact. And as I looked at the creature I'd slain, I noticed something else that wasn't quite right.

'Where are the lasgun wounds?' Jurgen asked, putting my thought into words an instant before I could. 'I definitely saw you hit it the last time...'

'It's a different one,' I said, looking to Logash for confirmation. 'That means there must be another one of these things down here with us.'

'More likely several,' he confirmed eagerly. 'Ambulls tend to form extended social groups.'

Better and better, I thought sourly. But if only I'd known, there was far worse still to come.

Editorial Note:

Thanks to the obsessive record-keeping of the Administratum it's possible to extricate practically any piece of information you may desire, however trivial, from the depths of the Imperial archives. That is, if you can actually find what you're looking for among the impenetrable thickets of worthless verbiage surrounding it. Suffice it to say that locating the minutes of the meeting between Kasteen and the officials in charge of the refinery complex was frustrating, to say the least, but on balance it was probably worth the effort, especially as the transcript provides some vital background information without which Cain's account of later events can seem a little confusing.

The minutes were taken by Scrivener Quintus, whose somewhat idiosyncratic recording style leads me to suspect that he never expected anyone to actually read them.

Minutes of the meeting of the Committee for the Defence and Preservation of Simia Orichalcae From the Orkish Incursion (by the Grace of His Majesty), convened this day 648.932 M41 (just too early for a decent breakfast.)

Those Present:

Colonel Regina Kasteen of the 597th Valhallan, a fair and gallant warrior, acting military governor of the Simia Orichalcae system.

Major Ruput Broklaw, her second in command, equally gallant but not remotely as fair.

Artur Morel, professional hole-grubber.

Magos Vinkel Ernulph, senior tech-priest, with too much metal where his brain should be.

Codicier Marum Pryke, the Emperor's gift to the Administratum, at least in her own mind.

Me.

Assorted sycophants and hangers-on.

Order of Business:
Defence of the refinery (actually the only thing we discussed.)

Proceedings:
Colonel Kasteen called the meeting to order. Then she called it to order again. Major Broklaw fired his bolt pistol into the ceiling, and the meeting came to order.

Colonel Kasteen put forward a plan for disabling the gargant, and hopefully eliminating a significant number of the besieging orks into the bargain. This relied on the fact that the mining tunnels extended some way beyond the perimeter of the refinery proper; given the immense weight of the thing it should be possible to collapse the galleries underneath it with sufficient quantities of explosive.

Magos Ernulph wanted to know just how close to the refinery the explosion would be, pointing out that the promethium tanks were almost full, and that if things went wrong the entire refinery could be reduced to a smoking crater.

Major Broklaw pointed out helpfully that in that case none of us would be around to complain about it.

Codicier Pryke raised the point that a significant credit value was attached to this installation, and that its destruction would result in a 0.017 per cent fluctuation in the mean commerce averages of the sector. She went on to suggest that an alternative strategy should be found. Colonel Kasteen said she was welcome to go outside and ask the orks to go away if she thought that would help.

Morel offered the assistance of his miners in determining the optimum placement of the explosive charges, citing their expertise with the local geology, which the colonel appreciated (she has a very nice smile.)

As no one had any other suggestions for disabling the gargant, Ernulph conceded that we might as well blow the place up ourselves before the orks do it.

I raised the matter of Commissar Cain and his scouting party, asking how they were likely to fare if they were still underground when the mine was blown up. Kasteen and Broklaw evinced a degree of concern on this point, admitting that their chances of survival under those circumstances would be slim. Broklaw added that he was sure they'd be back by then, as the commissar had something of a knack for avoiding such difficulties. I suggested voxing them with a warning, but apparently they were too deep underground now to get a message through.

No doubt wherever he was, though, he'd be having a better time of it than we are.

SIX

I'm sure I wasn't alone in brooding over Logash's off-hand announcement as we penetrated deeper into the maze of passages that made up the ambull den. The thought that we shared these tunnels with an indeterminate number of heavily-armoured predators wasn't exactly comforting, and we pressed on with renewed caution. The labyrinth was remarkably extensive, as the tech-priest had noted; if we'd had to walk every metre of it we'd still have been down there when the Emperor stepped off the throne,[25] but fortunately that wasn't going to be necessary. Between my hiver's instincts, Logash's knowledge of xenology, and the readings of his auspex we were beginning to get a pretty good idea of the layout of the place.

'Any idea how many more of those things there are down here?' I asked him, once I was sure we were out of earshot of any of the troopers (except Jurgen, of course, whose discretion I knew I could rely on absolutely). No point in spooking them any further if the answer was as bad as I feared. Logash looked pensive for a moment, as though communing with some inner voice. (Which he may well have been, I've known plenty of tech-priests with augmetic data stores plugged into what's left of their brains. But he may just have had indigestion.)

'Judging by the extent of the tunnel system, and assuming that your guess they arrived on the same space hulk as the orks is correct...' he began. (Which it wasn't, as we were shortly to find out, but the timing was the same so it didn't make any practical difference in the end.) He was interrupted by a fusillade of lasgun fire further down the tunnel, and a babble of shouting voices that overlapped into nothing but multitudinous echoes in the confined and twisting tunnels. I activated my comm-bead.

'Grifen. What's going on?' I asked.

'Contact. Another creature.' Her voice was crisp and steady, so the situation seemed under control. I hurried forward, not wanting to be too far from the bulk of our firepower if any more of the beasts were attracted to the sounds of combat.

'No more than half a dozen,' Logash finished, panting in my wake. No

25 Such beliefs became remarkably widespread as the turn of the millennium approached. Cain wasn't superstitious enough to place any credence in such folk tales, of course, but like many others used the phrase metaphorically to mean the start of M42, which of course at that point was still sixty-eight standard years in the future.

doubt he felt the same urge, only stronger than I did, as he was the only member of our party who was completely unarmed. Whether he still had enough meat on him to actually interest an ambull was a moot point, of course, but I declined to consider it at the time. 'Probably fewer by now,' he added, as the firing stopped.

Well, that was a relief. These creatures weren't all that tough, compared to some of the things I'd faced, and the news that we weren't likely to run into too many more of them was undeniably welcome.

The carcass of our latest victim was lying a few metres further on in a wider tunnel that opened out from the one we followed. It was surrounded by chattering troopers and riddled with the cauterised craters of las-bolt impacts. Vorhees was breathing heavily, trembling from the reaction, and shrugging off the attentions of the squad medic. The front of his flak armour was deeply scored, visible through the rents in his greatcoat. I gathered from the conversations around me that the ambull had just managed to get within arms' reach of him before he finally succeeded in dropping it.

'Well done,' I said, clapping him on the back; it never hurt to show the troopers I cared – even if I didn't. He grinned weakly at me.

'Persistent little frakkers, aren't they sir?' I nodded.

'Take a bit of putting down,' I agreed. Which of course indirectly reminded everyone I'd taken mine down hand-to-hand. I glanced at the carcass, wondering if it was the one I'd shot before, but Vorhees had made such a mess of it blazing away on full auto that there wasn't really enough left intact to tell.

'Fast, too,' Vorhees agreed. It seemed that the thing had come at him along the main tunnel almost as soon as he'd entered it. He'd just been able to bring his weapon up before it was on him.

'Interesting,' Logash said. He was looking at the walls of the tunnel, and messing around with his auspex again. After a moment he turned back to me. 'I think we've found one of the main runs.' Well it certainly seemed a lot wider than the tunnels we'd been following before.

'Which means?' I asked. The tech-priest shrugged, his white robe beginning to look distinctly grubby now, I noticed. Hardly the most practical garment for tunnel fighting, but evidently it hadn't occurred to him to get changed before setting out. Either that or he didn't have anything else to wear in any case.

'The main chamber should be at one end of this passageway.' He glanced uncertainly up and down it. I considered his words carefully.

'Main chamber meaning...?' I asked. Logash responded with the eagerness of the enthusiast.

'The central nesting site, or den. Ambulls are social creatures, with strong familial instincts, and tend to congregate when not out hunting or...'

'Vorhees,' I said. 'Which direction did the creature come from?' Logash looked a little hurt at being abruptly cut off (just as he felt he was getting to the interesting bit no doubt). The trooper jerked a thumb past the rapidly cooling chunk of meat, which was now surrounded by a garnet-coloured nimbus of frozen blood.

'That way,' he indicated. My sense of direction kicked in, and I absently noted that it was almost directly towards the ork siege lines. A sense of grim foreboding settled across my shoulders.

'If it was returning to the lair it would have been carrying prey of some kind to share with the others,' Logash chipped in helpfully.

The pool of light from our luminators revealed nothing apart from the dismembered ambull. There was the answer. We weren't going to be able to complete our reconnaissance mission without passing through a cavern full of these monstrosities. Wonderful. But bowel-clenching as the prospect appeared, I liked the idea of a horde of orks pouring through these tunnels to slaughter the lot of us even less.

'Close up,' I ordered. 'Be ready to concentrate your firepower.' Grifen nodded, and went to shout at Hail and Simla, who were blunting their combat knives by trying to hack the ambull's head off. Up to that point I thought she'd been kidding about taking a trophy back with us, but it seemed at least two of her troopers had taken her literally.

'Move out,' she ordered. 'By teams, covering the commissar and the cogboy.'[26] Logash showed considerably more common sense than hitherto by pretending he hadn't heard her. I must confess to feeling a little better, though, knowing everyone else would be watching my back. (In case you were wondering why Grifen should care about my welfare, and Logash's – I was deemed to be the best judge of the value of any intelligence we might gather, and Logash... well, let's just say Kasteen didn't want to have any more dealings with the Adeptus Mechanicus than she already did.)

So we moved out cautiously, heading towards the centre of the maze, our senses alert for any sign of movement in the darkness. We'd debated dousing a few of our luminators in the hope that we'd make ourselves less obvious, but according to Logash it wouldn't make any difference as the creatures could see in the dark anyway. He started to explain how,[27] but it made no sense to me and I soon stopped listening.

Second team still had the lead position. Grifen was already showing a veteran commander's common sense when it came to hanging back enough to keep an objective eye on the whole squad, although Karta (the ASL[28] and corporal in charge of the fireteam) had rotated Vorhees back to where the medic could keep an eye on him, and had put Drere on point. It made a kind of sense, I suppose, as Vorhees was still pretty twitchy after his close encounter with the ambull, but I'd have been inclined to leave him where he was; if he was going to be trigger happy I'd rather have him where there

---

26 A less than complimentary slang term for tech-priests, apparently derived from their symbol of office. It is common among Guard troopers, along with several others, most of which are considerably more offensive.

27 According to the Magos Biologos they can see heat rather than light. Rather an odd concept, I have to say, but having looked through a tau blacklight system recently I can attest from personal experience that such a phenomenon can be achieved by technosorcery, so I suppose it's not beyond the bounds of possibility that it might also occur in nature.

28 Assistant squad leader, a lower-ranking NCO trained to take command if the sergeant becomes a casualty. Where a squad has been divided into fireteams (which, as has already been noted, was standard practice in the 597th) the ASL will normally take command of the second team when it becomes detached from the first, and the direct control of the sergeant.

was nothing but targets in front. I was behind him in any case though, so it was all one to me.

Jurgen, Logash and I trotted along in the middle, keeping a cautious distance between the leading team and the one covering our backs, because if either made contact I wanted to be well out of harm's way. Of course I was still uneasily aware of the ambulls' ability to carve their way straight through the ice to get at us, but I kept my ears open and my paranoia cranked up to maximum, and so far I hadn't noticed any of the telltale vibrations which might betray the approach of another of the beasts.

'So what do they taste like?' Jurgen asked. I stopped tuning out Logash's prattling to gather that his monologue on the subject of the ambulls' life cycle, social structure, and habitat had finally yielded some useful information. Apparently there had been a number of attempts to domesticate the things as a handy source of meat on desert worlds.[29]

'Rather like grox, I'm told.' Logash looked a little uncomfortable, and I clapped him on the shoulder.

'Excellent,' I said. 'We'll send a scavenging party back to recover the carcasses once we've cleaned out the nest.' All the refinery had to offer in the way of cuisine was a dozen different varieties of soylens viridians, which had already begun to pall, despite being fresh from their own vats. Of course, we'd brought our own supplies along, but a nice fresh steak would lift my spirits nicely, I thought. Besides, the creatures had been eating the miners, so it seemed fair enough to return the compliment.

'Good idea, sir,' Jurgen said with relish. Logash looked a little green for someone so heavily augmented. Maybe he was a vegetarian, if he still bothered eating at all.

'I can hear movement,' Drere said, her voice slightly flattened by the comm-bead in my ear.

'Close up. Prepare for contact.' Grifen issued the order with calm authority, and I found myself at the centre of a small knot of troopers as first team caught up with us. We picked up our pace, fell in with them, and began closing on the lights from the luminators of second team.

'There's a cavern here.' Drere's voice tightened a little, the tension she must have felt transmitting itself through the gently hissing comm-bead in my ear.

'Hold position,' Karta said, his own voice calm, but with audible effort. 'Wait for the rest of us.'

'Confirm that,' Drere said, a faint edge of relief entering her voice. The dancing lights ahead of us were closer together now, I thought, refracting more brightly through the crystal shards which rimed the irregular walls of the tunnel. 'I'm not about to stick my... Emperor's guts!'

A lasgun opened up, bright muzzle flashes strobing down the reflective tunnel, and the luminators ahead of us bobbed more wildly than before as their bearers broke into a run. We followed suit, our boot soles crunching on the ice crystals underfoot. Logash slipped from time to time as he lost

---

29 With a conspicuous lack of success, if truth be told. Their burrowing abilities make them almost impossible to confine, with the inevitable result that the colonies which tried soon found themselves overrun with dangerous predators.

traction. The Valhallans, of course, had no such difficulties, and I'd picked up enough expertise in running on ice from them over the years to avoid my own feet slithering out from under me. I drew my laspistol.

'Janny!' Vorhees shouted, and a second weapon opened up in support. A moment later there was a shriek which echoed through the tunnels, raising the hairs on my arms, and a howl of feedback through the comm-bead which made my teeth ache.

'Medic! Trooper down!' Karta yelled, and by that time the rest of us had reached the scene of the carnage. The tunnel had indeed opened out into a large central chamber, about thirty metres across, and with a handful of other passageways visibly piercing the walls at irregular intervals. Drere was down, steaming blood starting to freeze in a slick hard plate over a gaping wound in her torso. Her face was pinched and white from the shock. Vorhees stood over her, pouring lasfire into the monstrosity which had evidently inflicted the damage, driving it back, screaming in rage and frustration.[30]

The cavern was a positive maelstrom of whirling bodies and wild firing. Luminator beams and las-bolts strobed as the troopers swung the muzzles of their weapons to meet the nearest perceived threat. It was no place for me, I decided, standing aside to let Grifen's team join the mêlée. I held an arm across Logash's chest as though I intended to keep him from harm. (In actual fact, of course, if one of the beasts had come anywhere near us it could have had him and been welcome; and if I'd known just how much trouble he was shortly to cause us I'd probably have thrown him to the closest and bidden it *bon appetit*.)

The reinforcements pitched in with a will, targeting the seething mass of enraged monstrosities which were boiling out of the shadows at us. There were too many to count, or at least that's how it seemed at the time. When the ice chips finally settled it transpired that Logash's estimate hadn't been all that far out, with a mere five of the creatures stretched out on the floor. But if you had asked me to take a stab at the numbers amid all that confusion I'd probably have said dozens.

'Pick your targets! Fire for effect!' Grifen yelled, her actions matching her words. She squeezed the trigger methodically, placing single shots on the head of the nearest ambull with commendable accuracy, aiming for the eyes and maw. A las-bolt burst against the roof of the thing's mouth, blowing a large chunk of brain matter backwards which clung to the frozen wall, solidifying like an obscene outgrowth as the creature toppled backwards. It hit the floor with a concussion which I was certain I could hear even over the cacophony of combat.

'Omnissiah protect us!' Logash was shivering in shock, which surprised me with all that metal in him. Evidently looking at holos of exotic species in the comfort of his chambers was rather more fun than having the blood-soaked reality trying to tear his face off.

---

30 It's not entirely clear from this final subordinate clause whether Cain is referring to the ambull or the trooper; sometimes he lets his immersion in his memories run ahead of comprehensibility. After some reflection I've elected to let his wording stand, as under the circumstances either or both seem equally likely.

'Over there. Eight o'clock.' Jurgen swung his hand in a familiar gesture, lobbing a frag grenade over the heads of the nearest monsters to burst among the ones clustered at the back. (Juveniles just out of the nest, according to Logash when he had a chance to examine them, but they looked dangerous enough to me, pushing forward as maddened by bloodlust as any of the others we'd encountered.)

A scream to my right snapped my head round just in time to see a pair of hideous mandibles close around the arm of the medic with a loud crunching sound which spoke of broken bones or worse. As the creature lifted him off the ground I turned, chainsword shrieking, and leapt forward to lop through the distended jaw. He fell heavily, clutching his wounded arm, and scrabbled for a self-injector from his pouch with his uninjured hand. That should have been enough to establish my participation in the battle and allow me to go back to babysitting Logash, but of course the thing came at me. I swung the weapon again, cursing myself for my stupidity. Jurgen hefted the melta uncertainly, unable to get a shot without killing as many of us as the creatures, and I had a moment to wonder if I'd ever get the chance to suggest he settle for something a little more manageable like a hellgun or a flamer next time. Then a line of bloody craters stitched themselves across the ambull's chest.

'Thanks!' I called to Karta, and administered the *coup de grace* to my staggering foe, lopping the head from its shoulders as it fell to its knees. (Probably unnecessarily, but it was a suitably theatrical gesture for a hero of the Imperium to make, and the surrounding troopers seemed to appreciate it.)

Abruptly I became aware of the sudden silence around us, was broken only by the ticking of the re-freezing ice and the groans of the wounded.

'Casualties?' I asked, playing up to my caring image. Grifen made a rapid assessment.

'Two serious. A few cuts and bruises among the rest, but they'll live.' She turned her attention to the medic, who was treating Drere as best he could with his one good hand. He was assisted by a grim-faced Vorhees.

'How is she?' I asked, walking over to them.

'She'll be fine,' Vorhees said flatly, clearly in no mood to accept any other outcome; the memory of him calling her given name as the fight started came back to me, and I smelled trouble. The nature of their relationship, clearly more than purely professional, was pretty obvious. And if she died he'd no doubt blame himself for not having been on point instead of her. Or Karta for switching their positions. Either way, it was clear his mind was no longer on the mission objectives. 'Won't she, doc?'[31]

'Sure she will,' the medic said, the doubt in his voice obvious to everyone but Vorhees. 'Stick in an augmetic lung and a new liver, she'll be good as new.'

Provided we got her back in time. I hesitated. Our mission was far from

31 A traditional nickname for the squad medic in most Guard units. Most aren't qualified doctors, of course, being trained simply in primary aid techniques designed to stabilise casualties long enough to get them back to a properly equipped aid station or chirurgical facility.

over, but we'd seen no sign of any ork presence in these tunnels, and the greenskins weren't exactly subtle. Come to that, they wouldn't have left any ambulls alive down here either. Chances were the tunnel system was fully secure, and there was nothing more to be gained by completing the sweep.

On the other hand, I haven't made it through to my second century by being complacent. We needed to be certain the orks didn't know the tunnels were here, and even the slightest doubt could fatally undermine our plans for the defence of the refinery. But that certainty could only be bought with time; time Drere clearly didn't have if we were going to get her back in time to save her life.

I hate choices like that. There are no good outcomes, all you can do is pick what seems to be the least bad, and so I dithered. The certainty of safety, or the potential loss of my carefully nurtured image as a leader who cared about the troopers he serves with? The illusion that I was one of them had saved my life many times as they repaid the loyalty they believed I held for them.

It was Jurgen who broke the deadlock in my vacillating mind. As instructed, he'd stuck close to Logash, who, predictably, was ignoring the carnage around him. He was now pottering around the chamber waving his auspex about and digging chunks of ice out of the walls with his augmetic fingers for reasons entirely beyond me.

'Commissar. You'd better take a look at this.' As usual my aide's voice betrayed no excitement, but I knew him well enough to recognise the undercurrent of urgency in his tone. I walked over to the corner where the tech-priest was crouched, grubbing in the ice like a holidaying infant in the coastal sand.

'What have you found?' I asked, then got a good look over Logash's shoulder and wished I hadn't.

'It appears to be a midden,' he said, his voice curiously like a juve comparing scrumball statistics. He picked up a fragment of bone, which looked uncomfortably human in origin.

'A what?' Jurgen asked, his brow furrowing.

'A spoil heap,' Logash explained. 'Ambulls are quite organised, disposing of their waste in a specific part of the den...' I took a step backwards as it occurred to me just what the discolorations in the ice that he was so blithely digging through consisted of. The tech-priest prattled on. 'With proper analysis we should be able to determine what they were eating...'

'We know what they were eating. The miners.' Grifen came over to join us, and lowered her voice. 'Drere's in a bad way, commissar. Do we go on, or go back?' It was clear which alternative she preferred.

'I doubt that would have represented a sufficient food source,' Logash said, still digging, absently responding to the only part of her remark which interested him. He began to work something large out of the ice. 'What have we here?'

'It's a skull,' Jurgen responded helpfully, unable to identify a rhetorical question if one sat up and bit him. I glanced at it, idly wondering which of the luckless miners this was, then froze as something about the shape triggered warning bells in my mind. The cranium was low browed and heavy, the jaw prognathous, and as Logash brushed the obscuring ice away jutting tusks became visible protruding from the lower mandible.

'From an ork,' I added unnecessarily.

So I had my answer. Whether or not the greenskins were aware of it, there was a way down into this labyrinth somewhere beyond their lines, and any other choice I might have made was now moot. I turned back to Grifen.

'We go on,' I said.

SEVEN

The next decision I had to make was the all-important one of how best to maintain morale. I didn't think any of the troopers would actively defy a commissar, even Vorhees, whose concern for Drere looked like outweighing pretty much every other consideration, but simply abandoning our wounded wasn't going to be an option. It would leave everyone demoralised, wondering if they'd be the next to be left to die.

That's not a thought you want your troopers to start brooding on. It makes them jumpy and sloppy, and the next thing you know they're so concerned with preserving their own skins they're losing focus on the important stuff: fulfilling the mission objectives, and preserving mine.

I made a big show of consulting Logash where everyone could hear me.

'Are we likely to run into any more of these creatures?' I asked. He frowned uncertainly.

'Possibly,' he said at last. 'But I doubt it. We seem to have a breeding pair and their offspring here, and given the average size of a family group...'

'I'll take that as a no,' I said firmly, cutting him off before he could bog us all down in extraneous detail. 'Which means we can safely divide our forces.' As I'd expected, a flicker of interest passed around the faces surrounding me, except of course for Drere and the medic, who were too busy bleeding to take much notice. And Jurgen, who rarely showed much sign of interest in anything apart from porno slates.

'Divide how?' Grifen asked. I indicated the wounded, and Vorhees hovering anxiously over his recumbent girlfriend.

'Second team's down to three effectives, and it'll take two of those to carry Drere,' I said. Vorhees's head came up like a hound hearing a ration pack being opened, a spark of hope kindling in his eyes. 'That'll leave one to take point, and pick off any of the creatures we might have missed.' Grifen nodded, understanding and relief mingled in the gesture.

'You're sending them back,' she said, a statement rather than a question. I nodded.

'The sooner the better,' I added, before turning to Karta. 'Better get moving, corporal. We're counting on you.' Not that I gave a frak, you understand, but it sounded good, and it passed the buck nicely; if anyone died before making it to the medicae at least it was out of my hands now. Karta saluted.

'We'll make it,' he asserted, and peeled off to organise his people.

'Am I to understand we're moving on at half strength?' Logash asked, clearly wondering what in the warp I thought I was playing at. I indicated the skull he'd dug up.

'First team, Jurgen and I are,' I said. 'There's obviously a way down here from behind the ork lines, even if the greenskins haven't noticed it yet, and we're not going back until we've found it and plugged the hole in our defences.' Needless to say I wasn't expecting to actually encounter any of the brutes, or run into anything else down here capable of harming us now that we'd slaughtered the ambulls, or I'd never have dreamed of doing such a thing. At the time, though, I was just trying to find a reasonable excuse to linger down here for a while and avoid the gargant.

'I see.' Logash considered it carefully, taking on that half-lost look again. 'Then I assume I should continue to accompany you.'

I hadn't actually considered it, to be honest. I'd have welcomed the chance to get rid of him if the thought had occurred to me, but on reflection he would only slow the wounded down if he tagged along with them, and I supposed his auspex might come in handy. All in all it was marginally preferable to keep him with us, I decided.

'I suppose so,' I said, leaving Jurgen to keep an eye on him, and turning back to watch the wounded depart. I had a final word with Karta, making sure Kasteen would hear about the ork skull we'd found and reinforce the mine entrance until we got back. Then we wished them the Emperor's speed and watched the bobbing lights from their luminators recede up the tunnel.

'Well,' Grifen said after a while, summing up what we all felt. 'Best get to it then. No point waiting around, is there?'

Despite my confidence that we were alone down here, we moved out in full combat order. Hail was on point, her lasgun held with the casual readiness of the veteran, and I found the sight reassuring. Simla followed her. The two of them worked well together, sharing an intuitive understanding which probably meant they had a personal association going as well; only to be expected in a mixed unit, of course. Behind him was Lunt, the squad heavy weapon specialist, who carried a flamer. That was something else I was pleased to find ahead of me rather than behind, although he had shown enough restraint to refrain from using it during the fight in the ambull den, relying instead on the laspistol he wore holstered at his belt.[32] (Just as well, really, as he'd probably have barbecued his squad mates as easily as the animals.) Tall and heavy-set, he carried the weight of his twin promethium tanks with ease, the liquid within them sloshing quietly as he walked.

I came next, along with Logash, Jurgen and Grifen, who kept a little behind us and as far from my aide as possible, while Trooper Magot, a small redheaded woman with disturbingly hard eyes, took up the rear. Out

32 Although not prescribed by regulations, many support weapon troopers and vehicle crews carry a back up sidearm in case they have to abandon their heavy equipment or it malfunctions in the heat of the battle. (Of course if a flamer malfunctions there isn't likely to be all that much left of the trooper carrying it, but Lunt was evidently an optimist.)

of the entire squad she was the only one to address Grifen as 'sarge' instead of 'sergeant,' and moved with the easy grace of an experienced soldier. (I learned later that they'd served together for some time, and she'd requested a transfer to Grifen's squad when her friend was promoted; beyond that I felt it prudent not to enquire.)

Despite everyone's unspoken apprehension we encountered no more of the ambulls, which came as an immense relief believe you me, and the only footfalls we heard were our own. Like everyone else, I kept my ears open for the harsh guttural sounds of ork voices and the crunch of iron-shod boots in the rime ahead of us, but the only noises to be heard were the almost subliminal creaks and pops of the slowly-shifting ice. We must have been moving for some time, I recall, as the vox messages from second team had faded to inaudibility by this point, when Logash stopped to examine the walls of the tunnel.

'How very curious,' he said.

'What is?' I asked, caution taking precedence over the surge of irritation I felt when his metallic elbow jabbed into my ribs as I stumbled into him. By way of reply he scraped a handful of ice from the wall. It crumbled, to reveal the dark grey surface of some kind of rock behind it, still grooved with the marks of the ambull's claws.

'We're below the ice layer. Actually down into the bedrock of the planet. Quite fascinating.'

'I'm glad you're finding the trip so entertaining,' I said, but the tech-priest was almost as impervious to sarcasm as Jurgen, and nodded in response.

'Not quite the word I'd choose, but it certainly beats recalibrating the interociters,' he said cheerfully. I had no idea what he meant, of course, so I smiled and suggested we get moving again. Unfortunately getting his legs going didn't slow down his mouth, and he prattled on about the underlying geology of the mountain range at inordinate length.

'Mountains are just there, aren't they?' Jurgen asked after some time had passed, blinking in befuddlement. Logash shook his head.

'To our limited perception of time, yes. But on a geological timescale, which is to say on the order of millions of years, a planet's crust is as fluid as a pan full of stew on the stove.' Well he understood which metaphors would appeal to Jurgen, I had to give him that. 'The lower strata rise to the surface, and are gradually worn down again by the processes of erosion.'

'So what you're saying,' Jurgen said slowly, 'is that these mountains are like a very large carrot?' I kept my face straight with an effort, although a strangulated snort escaped from Magot who was behind me.

'In a manner of speaking.' Logash was clearly unsure whether Jurgen was taking the frak or not. 'Floating on the surface of the pot. A few million years ago this whole area would have been an open plain, or the bottom of an ocean.'

'How can you have an ocean when everything's frozen?' Jurgen asked, all innocence. But Logash nodded as though pleased with a promising student.

'A good question.' He went on after a moment's thought, ignoring my aide's expression of pleased surprise. 'In its early history this would have been a far more hospitable world. But it's just too far from the sun, and it cooled down gradually. Where we are now is on a continental shelf, which is why we've penetrated as far as the bedrock. The ice goes down for tens of kilometres just out from the mountain range, which would have been an island chain in those days. Or perhaps this was a coastal plain which flooded as the oceans froze and increased in volume.'[33]

'There's something up ahead,' Hail reported a moment later, and I hurried forward to join her, grateful for the excuse to get away from the endless babbling. That may sound harsh, but believe me, after several hours of non-stop logorrhoea you'd have felt the same. As I did so I felt the palms of my hands begin to tingle.

'What is it?' I asked, joining her. She was halted next to the entrance to a side tunnel and peering round it. The luminator taped to the barrel of her lasgun skipped its cone of light around the walls and floor.

That was when it hit me. Unlike the irregular ambull tunnels we'd been following, this corridor was squared off, composed of regular lines and angles beneath its coating of ice. There was no telling who might have built it, of course, or anything else for that matter, as the frozen epidermis effectively obscured every detail.

'Lunt,' I ordered after a moment's thought. 'Get up here.' The hulking trooper ambled across to us, and aimed his flamer down the mysterious passageway, seeking a target. It stretched into the distance, swallowing our luminator beams as though they were the most tenuous of candle flames. After a moment he triggered the weapon, sending a gout of burning promethium down the corridor ahead of us, blasting the shadows from the corners and replacing them with flickering orange spectres. Steam hissed and water dripped from the walls as the pool of burning accelerant roared away on the floor, melting the ice around it.

The hairs on the back of my neck rose. It's an odd sensation, and one I've seldom felt. Grim memories from years before came flooding back as I recognised the obsidian architecture surrounding us, finely polished stone of absolute blackness seeming somehow to suck the light into itself, all the darker and more forbidding for the faint reflective sheen which coated it.

'Omnissiah preserve us,' Logash breathed at my elbow, and for a moment I thought he'd recognised it too. But the words that followed betrayed an ignorance that was almost blissful. 'We must make a full record of this at once. We had no idea that the planet was once inhabited...'

'Everyone out,' I commanded. 'Break out the demo charges and prepare to seal this now.'

'Commissar?' Grifen looked a little confused. I suppose she might have been forgiven for wondering if I'd gone a bit siggy,[34] but by that point the

33 Almost certainly the latter, given Cain's subsequent discovery.

34 A colloquial reference to the Guard medicae sanitorium in the Sigma Pavonis system where troopers suffering from mental illness and combat fatigue are sent for assessment and rehabilitation. The less chronic cases are returned to duty after treatment, while the more severe ones can receive long-term care,

last thing on my mind was how I appeared to the other ranks. 'Those are supposed to be used to seal the tunnels off from the orks.'

'There are worse things than greenskins,' I said. Grifen looked a little sceptical at this, what with the orks being the Valhallans' ancient blood enemy and all that (don't get me wrong, they'd happily pile into any of the Emperor's enemies who happened along, but give them a choice and they'd kill greenies every time), but took my word for it.

'Are you mad?' Logash raised his voice, clearly determined to challenge me. 'The knowledge contained in there could be priceless. We don't know why this structure was built, or by whom...'

'I do,' I said and pointed to one of the walls, where a curious arrangement of lines and circles was partially visible through a curtain of half-melted ice. It was illuminated by the dying flames of the promethium pool. 'The necrons built it.'

The name didn't mean anything to most of them, of course. Only Jurgen had encountered them before aside from myself, and that far less up close and personal than the terrors I'd escaped from on Interitus Prime. But the troopers seemed willing to take my word for it, at least. If only I could say the same for the tech-priest.

'But you can't just blow up a discovery of this magnitude!' Logash was practically beside himself. 'Think of the archeotech that must be down there! Destroying it would be a crime against the Omnissiah!'

'Frak the Omnissiah,' I said, finally shutting him up. 'I swore an oath to serve the Emperor, not a bucket of bolts, and that's exactly what I intend to do. Have you any idea what would happen if there are dormant necrons down there and we did something to disturb them?'

'I'm sure your soldiers could deal with them whatever they are,' Logash replied stiffly.

'Well I'm not,' I said without thinking. Then I remembered who else was there and carried on as though I'd meant to say more all along. 'I'd back this regiment against everything from eldar to daemons, but even the best soldiers in the Guard couldn't stand long against a full-scale necron incursion. These things aren't even alive as we understand the term. They can't be reasoned with, they can't be intimidated, and if they have the numbers on their side they simply can't be stopped. They'll just keep coming until every living thing on this planet is dead!' I was uncomfortably aware as I finished that my voice had risen in pitch. I fought it back to a semblance of calm.

'You're not being rational about this,' Logash said. 'If there were active necrons down here they would have killed the ambulls, surely?'

'Just for starters,' I said. My old nightmare of orks pouring through these narrow passageways bent on plunder and destruction seemed positively comforting now. I fought down memories of those blank metallic faces, fashioned in the semblance of skulls, advancing through a hail of hellgun fire as though it were a refreshing spring rain, and shuddered in horror.

---

sometimes for years. Co-incidentally, the system's other claim to fame is as a manufactoria of combat servitors, many of which find their way into Inquisitorial service.

Logash might have a point, I supposed, the temple or whatever it was might well be abandoned, but then we'd thought that on Interitus Prime as well. And look how that had turned out. Entering so unhallowed a place was simply too dangerous to contemplate, and if Logash and his pals were that keen to take such an insane risk they could damn well do it once the orks were taken care of and we were long gone.

Not that I intended waiting around on this iceball until we'd got rid of the greenskins. Finding a necron artifact changed everything, and our best course of action was simply to evacuate our forces back to the *Pure of Heart*, turn the whole matter over to the Inquisition, and have done with it. I might even get to renew my acquaintance with Amberley, which would at least be one blessing in the affair – assuming she didn't drag me off on another suicidal escapade in the name of the Ordo Xenos of course.

Grifen didn't need telling twice, and was already breaking out the demo charges. Once again my undeserved reputation was working to my advantage, and she no doubt thought that anything bad enough to leave a hero of the Imperium in need of clean undergarments was something she didn't want to meet.

'You can't do this! I simply won't let you!' Logash practically screamed like a petulant child as Simla and Hail placed the charges. He stepped forward as if to interfere. Jurgen barred his way with the melta, and shook his head.

'Best to keep out of the way, sir,' he said. Logash raised a hand to the barrel, as though about to slap it out of the way. I was suddenly uneasily aware of how much strength he might have in his augmetic limbs, and Emperor alone knew what other little alterations the baggy robe might conceal. I stepped forward, ostentatiously loosening the laspistol in the holster at my belt.

'Might I remind you,' I said levelly, 'that this world is currently under martial law. That means you're as subject to my authority as any member of the Guard, and I'm fully within my rights to deal summarily with any attempt to interfere with the protection of this installation.' He took my meaning at once, but with ill grace, and subsided. He glared at me with an expression of malevolent disgust completely at odds with the demeanor of cheerful idiocy I'd come to expect. I suppose I might have found it intimidating if I hadn't been glared at by experts in my time (and trust me, until you've hacked off a daemon you've got no idea of what a real glare is), so I returned his gaze levelly until he broke eye contact.

'Typical meatbag[35] behaviour,' he sneered, failing miserably to regain any dignity. 'Just trample on anything you don't understand. You're no better than the orks.' Considering he was surrounded by heavily armed Valhallans it wasn't exactly the most tactful thing he might have said, but to their credit the troopers continued working with undiminished efficiency, merely breaking off for a second to stare sullenly at him. He must have realised he'd overstepped the mark, though, because he was quiet

---

35 A derisive Adeptus Mechanicus slang term for the unaugmented, who they hold in noticeable contempt. Which, to be fair, is generally reciprocated.

after that, apart from occasional barely audible mutterings about meat-bag barbarians.

'If it's any consolation,' I reassured him, 'we're not destroying anything.' Not from choice, mind, but if the necron architecture I'd come across before was anything to go by the strange black stone would simply be too resilient to be seriously damaged by the meagre quantities of explosive we had at our disposal. 'We're merely sealing it off as a precaution. Once the refinery's safe you can grub around down here to your heart's content.' Just so long as I was at least a sector away by that point. Logash still looked sulky, but slightly mollified.

'Fire in the hole!' Magot bellowed, with rather too much relish for my liking, and we retreated to what I hoped would be a safe distance before she hit the detonator.

The explosion was satisfactorily loud, bringing down a chunk of the corridor ceiling, which proved to be composed of cubical blocks of the strange black stone roughly the length of my forearm. They tumbled down in disarray, followed by chunks of ice and bedrock that formed a solid-looking seal over the mouth of the corridor, reducing the ambull run we'd been following, to half its original width for a dozen paces or so.

'Shady!' Magot said, with evident satisfaction. 'I'd like to see anything get past that.'

'No you wouldn't,' I said. Solid as the blockage seemed, if there really were necrons beyond it they wouldn't take long to dig their way out. Those metal bodies were tireless and implacable, their weapons and equipment so powerful they made the most sophisticated toys of the Adeptus Mechanicus look like sharpened sticks. I forced the image of ancient horrors out of my mind again.

'Well if that was the way the ambulls got an ork down here it's pretty well sealed,' Grifen said. I nodded. It seemed likely, but I supposed we had to be sure. With an effort I dragged my mind back to the mission at hand.

'We'll make a final sweep and head back,' I decided, to everyone's relief. 'We have to report this. It takes priority over everything.'

'Commissar!' Simla called, from the other side of the spoil heap. 'Take a look at this!'

Cursing, I rounded the pile of rubble, homing in on the light from his luminator to find the sharp-featured trooper crouching over something metallic which had evidently been frozen into the floor of the tunnel and dislodged by the explosion. A crudely made bolter of some kind, the barrel sheared off by what looked like claw marks.

'An ork shoota,' I said unnecessarily. 'It must have been dropped by the one the ambulls killed while they were dragging it back to the den.' Simla nodded.

'So it must have come from further up the tunnel.'

Great. The hole in our defenses was still wide open. I dithered for a moment, but in the end there was really no other choice. The necron threat, though terrible, was only a potential one, and had been contained for the time being. But the orks remained a clear and present danger, and would do so until we'd completed our mission. Slowly and reluctantly I stood.

'Sergeant!' I called. 'Move them out. We're going on.'

Editorial Note:

Again I must apologise for inflicting another example of Sulla's overly purple prose on my patient readers (except for those of you who, quite understandably, may choose to skip it.) I do so because events were still moving along on the surface of the planet even as Cain made his disturbing discovery in the depths of the mine. And, as before I feel it important to present a little more background detail than Cain's typically self-centred narrative provides.

We pick up her account of events at a point where her platoon had been rotated back from the front lines for rest and recuperation, after taking a number of casualties while repelling a series of increasingly determined ork assaults.

Extracted from Like a *Phoenix From the Flames: The Founding of the 597th,* by General Jenit Sulla (retired), 097.M42

I'm proud to say that despite the loss of so many gallant comrades in arms, whose sacrifice will ever be remembered,[36] our morale remained high and our determination resolute. Though the greenskins were undeniably a nuisance, we had sent them packing on every occasion they troubled us, and it was almost with a sense of reluctance that we pulled back from our beleaguered redoubt and gave it into the care of Lieutenant Faril and the eager warriors under his command.

Wiser heads than ours had made the decision to relieve us, however, so there was no point in appealing it, and so we picked up our wounded and joined the trickle of tired but still resolute soldiery and headed back to the main refinery complex for a hot meal and a few hours of sleep. We were secure in the knowledge that the fray was far from over and that we would shortly once again have our chance to wreak the Emperor's vengeance on the greenskin barbarians who had had the effrontery to encroach on His sacred dominions.

36 Though not, apparently, their names, as she doesn't bother to record them.

As we trudged through the snow the sky above us was bright with the trails of the shuttles from our sturdy transport ship, and I reflected how beneficent fate, or the guidance of His Glorious Majesty, had so arranged matters that even now, as we faced and bested His bestial foes, His loyal subjects were being taken to the safety which our doughty vessel afforded. Indeed, the truth of the soldier's maxim, 'The Emperor Protects,' had seldom been made manifest to me with such crystal clarity.

It was while I was reflecting thus, and enjoying an unexpectedly lavish meal of the soylens viridians which the tech-priests who ran this palace of wonders had so generously provided from their own resources, that Colonel Kasteen summoned me to the command centre.

Upon my arrival my attention was immediately seized by the hololithic display, which the colonel was consulting along with Major Broklaw, Captain Federer of the engineering contingent, and a civilian I was given to understand had something to do with the mining operation here.[37]

As I listened to the plan which the colonel began to unfold, I was stunned by its boldness and elegance. For it was nothing less than to lure the loathsome greenskins into a trap which would surely annihilate both them and their awesome engine of war which, even as we spoke, was edging ever nearer. How fitting it seemed to use the creatures' impetuosity and overconfidence to lure them to their own destruction!

As I considered the plan in detail the keen intelligence behind the order to pull my platoon back became instantly apparent to me. By replacing the weary units at the front with fewer numbers of fresh soldiers our forces could maintain the illusion of remaining at full strength, at least for the few hours necessary to prepare our trap, while we could continue to gradually reduce the number of defenders. When the time came we could easily pull the remainder back to lure our enemies in, covering our own forces' retreat from our positions on either side, and catching the orks in a withering crossfire which ought to distract them for long enough to detonate the mine.

From the sombreness of Colonel Kasteen's demeanour I had expected to be given the honour of acting as the lure in this most cunning of stratagems, but it seemed even greater glory was to be ours. The colonel explained that within the hour she had received a message from the gallant Commissar Cain, who even as she spoke was continuing his heroic reconnaissance of the lowest levels of the mine, to the disturbing effect that it was possible the greenskins had found a way into the tunnels. Though all were confident that a hero of his stature would easily repel any of the bestial foe incautious enough to venture there, it was felt necessary to provide an armed escort for the sappers and miners who were to prepare our trap; and since Second Squad of my own platoon had ventured into those very tunnels no more than a day before, with the commissar himself, we were the obvious choice for this vital assignment.

37 Undoubtedly Morel.

I must own up to it, my breast swelled with pride as I contemplated the honour of the task with which we had been entrusted, and assured the colonel that we would indeed prove worthy of her confidence.

EIGHT

Needless to say the decision to continue our assignment was far from universally popular, although no one apart from Logash voiced any dissent. Grifen and her team were professional enough to understand the necessity of ensuring the safety of our comrades, not to mention ourselves, and so we pushed on in uneasy silence. The only sounds were the crunching of our boot soles in the thick frost that still coated the tunnel floor and the tech-priest's *sotto voce* imprecations. Besides which, no one in our party could have been more reluctant to proceed than me, you can depend on it. Every instinct of self-preservation I possessed urged me to flee the caverns at once, and find some excuse to board the first shuttle back to the relative safety of the *Pure of Heart*.

'Commissar?' Jurgen asked, and I suddenly became aware that I was murmuring one of the Catechisms of Command under my breath, something I swear I'd never done consciously since leaving the schola. Just goes to show how spooked I was.

'Nothing,' I said hastily, hawking a gob of rapidly cooling phlegm into the encircling darkness. 'Just clearing my throat.'

'Oh. Right.' He nodded, in his usual imperturbable fashion, and walked on, melta held ready across his body. Logash gave me a nasty look.

'"Fear is the mind killer," eh?' he asked, which at least told me his hearing was preternaturally augmented. 'I think you've already proved that today.' I could hardly believe it: here we were, caught between two of the nastiest foes you could ever hope not to meet, and he was still sulking about not being allowed to loot the bloody tomb.

'At least I've still got enough of a mind to know I ought to be scared,' I snapped back. We glared at each other like pre-schola juves whose vocabulary is too limited to prolong an exchange of verbal abuse, and for all I knew we'd have descended to shoving and finger-poking if Hail hadn't cut in on my comm-bead.

'I can see light up ahead.'

A shiver of apprehension shot through me. We were still deeply underground, and although the tunnel floor had been rising gently for the last couple of kilometres my natural affinity for these conditions told me we should be nowhere near the surface.

'Hold position,' I ordered, my irritation with the truculent tech-priest already forgotten, and hurried forward to join her. Jurgen's familiar odour followed, and we overtook Lunt and Simla. The big heavy weapons specialist watched as we passed, and began to ready his flamer, which now we were in front it was rather less comforting than his show of initiative might otherwise have been.

As we approached Hail's position I clicked off my luminator, and a moment later Jurgen did the same. As was my habit I closed my eyes as we did so, knowing my dark vision would adjust a little faster, for such things can mean life or death in these situations and all too often do. To my relief Hail had doused her own light, either from training or common sense, so there was nothing to impede my perceptions as I moved up to join her.

'Over here, sir.' The whisper came from one of the deeper shadows, into which the woman had blended almost invisibly. Her skin was very dark, almost the colour of recaff, and she used this natural advantage to the fullest.[38] As she moved her silhouette came into focus, backlit by a soft, greyish radiance from somewhere further down the tunnel. I sighed with relief. I'd been dreading the sight of the sick, greenish glow which had permeated the necron tomb I'd penetrated before, and the realisation that whatever we were coming to had nothing to do with them hit me with an intensity akin to euphoria.

'Any sign of movement?' I asked, and Hail shook her head, a barely-visible motion in the darkness which I sensed as much as saw.

'Nothing yet,' she said.

'Good.' I stood still for a moment, letting my tunnel rat's senses attune to this change in our environment. As my eyes adjusted fully the pale glow seemed to strengthen, a faint, irregular disc about the size of my thumbnail throwing the darker stone around it into stark relief. And there was a faint current of air on my face too, sharp with the smell of cold and heavy with damp. Impossible as it seemed, it looked very much like a fissure to the surface. 'I think this is it,' I concluded.

'Surely we're far too far underground?' Logash queried at my elbow. Lost in my reverie I hadn't noticed him tagging along, and I started momentarily, to his unconcealed amusement.

'Could be the bottom of a crevasse,' Jurgen volunteered. It sounded plausible to me, and he had grown up on a world like this, so I nodded.

'That would explain our dead ork,' I said. 'It just fell down into the tunnels here.' Maybe the fall had killed it and the ambull who brought it home just got lucky, although in my experience it would take more than dropping a few hundred metres down a hole to finish off a greenskin for sure, especially if it landed on its head.

'So this whole expedition has been a colossal waste of time,' Logash concluded. I shook my head.

'Far from it. If one ork found the hole, others could, and they can climb down a rope just as easily as any other species.' That's not entirely true, of

38 This was extremely unusual for a Valhallan; perhaps as a result of living underground they generally tend to the lightest of complexions. Hail's colouration is the norm on many other worlds in the sector, however, where the white skin typical of her homeworld would seem equally unusual, so it's probable that an ancestor or two of hers settled there after relocating for some reason.

course, they're clumsy brutes at the best of times, but they're determined and resilient, and sometimes that's enough.

'Best go on and check it out then,' Hail said, more for the pleasure of contradicting the tech-priest than supporting me I suspected, but the display of solidarity was welcome nevertheless.

'I think so,' I said, and moved on, the others taking up their positions around me as we continued on towards the gradually intensifying glow. As we got closer the faint current of air grew stronger, and the almost tolerable low temperatures of the tunnels began to drop rapidly, so that I found myself shivering again even through the thick weave of my greatcoat.

'Smells like snow,' Grifen said cautiously. 'We must be getting close.' I was prepared to take her word for it, after all she knew snow and ice the way I did tunnels. I was mildly surprised to see even the stoic Valhallan pulling her greatcoat just a little tighter. If I could trust her instincts as strongly as I believed, that didn't augar well.

In the event we were even closer than we realised. We turned a corner, skirting an outcrop of some deeply-veined rock I didn't bother listening to Logash identify, and the full force of the blood-chilling cold I'd experienced after the shuttle crash hit me in the face along with a weak shaft of sunlight which seemed almost dazzling after the gloom of the tunnels.

'Emperor's bowels!' I said, pulling my scarf up over my mouth and nose, feeling sharp shards of pain skitter through my abused lungs. Somehow, incredibly, the ambull tunnel had broken the surface, hundreds of metres deeper than should have been possible. But we were undeniably outside again.

'Interesting,' Logash said, not even shivering, Emperor rot his augmented hide. Snow whirled in around us, stinging our eyes, and obscuring everything in front of us from sight. He pondered for a moment. 'Perhaps a small valley, cutting into the mountains...'

I considered it, overlaying a rough estimate of our position on the orbital images I'd seen in the *Pure of Heart's* hololithic bridge display. It was perfectly possible that we'd come right through the heart of the ridge forming one of the sides of the valley protecting the refinery complex, and found ourselves at the bottom of a defile of some kind that cut into it from the other side.

If so, that was both good and bad news. Bad in that there was indeed a way through the tunnels which breached our defences, but on the plus side we would be a long way from the main body of the besieging orks. The only ones this far down the other side of the ridge would be stragglers or scouting parties like the one we'd encountered before.

Even shivering as I already was, the thought was enough to send an additional chill through me. There was no telling how many such groups had struck out ahead of the main advance,[39] and if one had already discovered

39 Not that many, in all likelihood. 'Kommandos' as they're known (a loan word from some human culture according to the Ordo Diologus, as orks aren't able to conceptualise anything to do with subtlety for themselves) are quite rare among the greenskin forces. Most lack the patience or, to be blunt, intelligence for anything other than a brute force frontal attack. Which makes these occasional exceptions a danger out of all proportion to their limited numbers, as they generally succeed in taking their targets completely by surprise.

the tunnel entrance and reported back the entire army could be on its way to take advantage of it. Well, perhaps not that many, but a large enough force to cause us some real problems if they got loose behind our defensive line. (Not that it was going to hold for a second once the gargant arrived, of course, so I was just having to thumb my palm[40] that Kasteen had come up with some strategy to deal with it while we were running around in the tunnels.)

'Tracks.' Magot was kneeling on the ice a few metres back from the curtain of whirling snow, staring at it intensely. I couldn't see a thing myself, but once again I found myself putting my full confidence in the Valhallans' natural affinity for these dreadful conditions. Grifen moved to join her, squatting beside her friend.

'Looks like,' she agreed. 'Ork boots, I'd say.'

'How many?' I managed to ask, through the muffling scarf and my rapidly numbing facial muscles. Magot shrugged.

'One pair?' She didn't sound terribly sure. 'The floor's chewed up around here something awful.'

'One ork,' Logash confirmed, scanning the floor with his metal eyes, a hint of impatience entering his voice. 'And ambull tracks. The greenskin must have wandered in, disturbed it, and ended up as lunch.'

'Only one ork?' I asked. 'You're absolutely sure?'

'Of course,' Logash said. 'It's completely clear to anyone with the right eyes to see these things.' Normally I'd have found the hint of the typical tech-priest arrogance returning to his voice irritating, I admit, but at the time it almost came as a relief. I assumed it meant he was getting over his sulkiness. But I had more pressing concerns to consider.

'Then what happened to the others?' I wondered aloud. Orks were obnoxious and quarrelsome, but they were curiously sociable in their own brutal fashion, and our solitary ambull victim wouldn't have been out here alone. True, his friends wouldn't waste all that much time looking for him once they noticed he was missing, but they might still be in the vicinity. And that meant they could stumble in here just as easily as their erstwhile companion.

'A good question,' Logash conceded. 'I suppose you'll want to scout around and make sure there are no more of them outside?'

Well actually that was the last thing I wanted to do, but it was necessary, and I couldn't back down in front of the troopers now that someone had verbalised the thought, so I nodded.

'It's the only way to be sure,' I agreed, managing to conceal my reluctance tolerably well I believed. I was not quite sure whether I detected the ghost of a vindictive smile on the tech-priest's face.

Conditions outside were even worse than I could possibly have imagined. The snow continued to flurry all around us, driven by a wind keener than an eldar wych's flensing knife, and I found my eyes shutting reflexively before I was a handful of paces from the cave mouth. With a thrill of panic I realised I couldn't open them again: the wind-driven tears had frozen on my face and sealed them closed. I was just about to give way to the impulse to

40 A good luck gesture Cain appeared to have retained from his early childhood, wherever that was actually spent.

retrace my steps (a sure way of stumbling to my death down a crevasse or terminal hypothermia away from the vigilance of my companions), when a reassuring arm settled across my shoulders. I inhaled Jurgen's acrid odour gratefully, as though it were the bouquet of a fine vintage, mildly surprised to find that my nose was still working.

'Hold on, commissar.' Something settled across my face, and the stinging in my eyes abated a little. I blinked them clear, forcing them stickily apart, feeling the partially-melted ice crystals slither round the corners of my eye sockets. Jurgen's face came blearily into focus, the portion of it between his scarf and thick fur hat obscured by a pair of snow goggles identical to the ones I now realised were protecting my own sight. 'That should do it.'

'Thank you, Jurgen,' I managed to force out through practically immobilised face muscles. His scarf twitched as though concealing a smile.

'Lucky I usually carry a spare.' That was the closest he would ever come to uttering a reproof, but he had every right to do so of course. The goggles were standard kit in a Valhallan regiment, and I had a pair of my own packed away somewhere in my quarters, but it had never occurred to me I might need them in the depths of the mine where whiteout conditions weren't exactly common. So once again I had cause to thank the Emperor for my aide's streak of thoroughness.

To my complete lack of surprise every trooper in first team had donned a pair as well, but, like Jurgen, these conditions were common to them. Warp it, judging by their body language, most of them were actually enjoying these hellish temperatures.

'Chill enough for you, sir?' Magot asked cheerfully, seemingly genuinely unaware of just how intolerable I was finding it.

'Wouldn't mind a pot of tanna about now,' I conceded, deciding the best approach was game but suffering a little more than I was willing to admit (rather than a hell of a lot more.) That way they'd keep a closer eye on me without resenting it.

'Wouldn't mind a brew myself,' she admitted, before trotting away to take her turn on point.

'This is all a complete waste of time you know,' Logash grumbled. I swear I would have missed him entirely if he hadn't spoken: his white robe was almost invisible in the swirling snow, and only his pale face and metallic eyes appeared wholly in focus. He appeared to hang in the air in front of me like an extreme version of Mazarin's levitation act. 'If there were any more orks around they'll be kilometres away by now. Or frozen to death.'

He was a fine one to talk, I thought, barely even seeming to notice the sub-zero temperatures. Once again I found myself wondering precisely what that robe concealed.

'They're a lot more resilient than you might think,' I pointed out, and Lunt nodded in passing.

'My grandfather found one frozen in a glacier once, back home, left over from the invasions. When they got it back to their camp and thawed it out it came back to life and tried to kill them. It's true, that's what he said.'

Him and every other Valhallan's grandfather, of course, 'The ork in the ice' is one of the most popular folktales on the planet, but I doubted that Logash would know that, so I nodded confirmation.[41]

'So I'd keep looking over my shoulder if I were you,' I added. I can't be sure, but I think Lunt winked at me, enjoying winding up the outsider and treating me as if I was Valhallan myself. Of course I've spent so much of my career serving with them I often find that I've picked up something of their speech patterns, dietary preferences, and so on. I suppose it's not all that surprising that they seem to have adopted me as one of their own in many ways.[42]

'We're in a defile, all right,' Grifen told me, glancing around at the barely visible topography. 'You can tell by the pattern of the snowflakes.' They just looked like a swirling wall of white to me, but I nodded as though I understood. I didn't actually need to know, of course: one of the most important principles of leadership is knowing when to rely on the judgement of your subordinates. But it's always a good idea to look interested.

'Can you tell which way the orks would have gone?' I asked. She nodded.

'They won't have left any tracks we can follow in this blizzard, but that way,' she gestured in what looked to me like a random direction, 'is closed off by the head of the valley. My best guess would be downslope.'

'Fair enough,' I decided. 'We'll check as far as the mouth of the defile. If there are any greenskins out here we'll find them. If not we can pull back and collapse the cave behind us.'

'That might be difficult,' she pointed out. 'We used most of our demo charges to seal the... whatever it was back down the passage.'

'We'll think of something,' I said, with more confidence than I felt. The constant swirling of the snow was making me feel vaguely nauseous, the cold was cramping my stomach muscles painfully, and my head felt as though someone was squeezing it in a vice. The sooner we got this over with the better. 'Jurgen's still got the melta, and I'm sure our cogboy friend will be able to point out a few weak spots in the ceiling.'

'I suppose you're right,' the sergeant said, and I glanced around, expecting some response from Logash, but the surly young tech-priest had vanished into the storm as thoroughly as though he'd never even existed.

---

41 And like many folk tales, there may be an element of truth to it. Although there's no way to be sure, there are still occasional reports of solitary orks being sighted in the Valhallan wilderness, sometimes even backed up by bodies. Chances are these are just corpses left over from the invasion preserved by the cold, but you can never take anything for granted where these creatures are concerned.

42 Actually, given the relationship between most commissars and the troops they serve with, this is pretty remarkable. As so often in his memoirs, Cain gives himself far too little credit for his own achievements.

NINE

'We're going to have to search for him,' I said, resenting every extra second that was going to mean staying out in the bitter cold. For good measure I filled my lungs with the burning air, and called the tech-priest's name as loudly as I could. To no avail, of course, as the screaming wind and the muffling snow combined to stifle all but the loudest noise. Fortunately, I had more than my own lungpower to call on, as the comm-bead in my ear was still tuned to the general squad frequency, and I lost no further time in appraising everyone else of the problem.

'We've lost the tech-priest,' I broadcast, suppressing the impulse to add a number of qualifying adjectives. 'Anyone seen him?'

To my complete lack of surprise a chorus of negatives was the only response.

'At least it'll be quieter on the way back,' Magot added, with rather more candour than tact. That was hardly the point, though, however much I might have agreed with her.

'Complete the sweep,' Grifen ordered, with just enough emphasis to discourage any more flippancy, and the troopers responded, sounding off in turn with a noticeable lack of enthusiasm. She turned back to me. 'If he's ahead of us we'll run into him. And if he's behind we should pick him up on the way back.'

I have to admit to feeling rather less sanguine on that point than she seemed to be. He was, after all, effectively invisible to us in the swirling snow, and I didn't think we stood a chance of finding him under these conditions in any way other than stumbling over him by accident. But if anyone could pick up his trail I supposed it would be the Valhallans, so I nodded in return.

'Better get moving then,' I said, echoing her words of a couple of hours before.

It wasn't that simple, of course. As I've already mentioned, the wind was sweeping up the defile, which was liberally strewn with grey, jagged rocks. These loomed up suddenly out of the swirling blanket of snow, promising a moment of respite from the razor-edged wind which, time and again, proved to be merely a delusion. The irregular topography simply broke the onrush of air into flurries and eddies which dashed handfuls of snow into these pockets of illusory shelter, adding a sudden unexpected lash of stinging ice crystals to an already miserable experience. The only consolation, if that was the right word, was that what little exposed skin I still had was completely numb by this time.

I slipped and slithered down the slope behind Grifen, grateful for the stolid presence of Jurgen behind me; several times he reached out a supporting hand just in time to prevent me from sprawling face down in the knee-deep snow. The Valhallans remained completely sure-footed, but any amusement they may have felt at my floundering progress was well concealed. Glancing back I could see that the furrows we'd left behind us were already beginning to fill with the ever-shifting drifts, and that without my companions' sure instinct for these ghastly conditions we would almost certainly never find the cave mouth again. That, at least, was something of a relief, as the chances of any greenskins stumbling across it were beginning to look reassuringly remote.

On the downside though, any tracks Logash had left would be obscured as completely as our own, so once again it seemed we weren't likely to stumble across him by any means other than sheer blind luck.

At least with all those augmetics I supposed he wasn't likely to freeze to death, in the short term at any rate, but right now I was beginning to think that was a very mixed blessing.

I had, by this time, lost sight of all my companions save for the reassuring presence of Jurgen, their camouflage greatcoats blending so perfectly into the snowstorm that they were effectively invisible. For that matter so was I; my dark commissar's uniform being so coated with the wind-driven flakes that I resembled one of those misshapen effigies children throughout the galaxy sculpt with the onset of winter. (On Valhalla, building snowmen is something of a cross between a serious art form and a competitive sport, with some quite astounding creations to marvel at, but that's beside the point.)

I was just on the verge of deciding that this was futile and ordering everyone to turn back, letting Logash take his chances with the elements as best he could, when Magot's voice crackled over my comm-bead.

'Contact, ninety metres down slope.' I could hardly see an arm's length in front of my own eyes, but she sounded confident enough. I was still trying to force my numb lips to form a reply when Grifen's voice cut into the net.

'Is it the cogboy?'

'Negative.' Magot's voice was tense. 'I can see a lot of movement down there.'

That could mean only one thing, of course, and I was already scrabbling for my laspistol with numb and nerveless fingers when she spoke again, confirming it.

'Greenies. Lots of them.'

'How many?' I asked, keeping hold of my weapon Emperor knows how, my fingers feeling thick and swollen in the cold. Luckily the augmetic ones were working as well as ever, at least enabling me to maintain my grip on the stock, but whether I'd be able to squeeze the trigger with my very real and probably frostbitten index finger would be problematic at best.[43]

'Hard to tell,' Magot replied. 'They're well spread out.' That was hardly surprising under the circumstances, the terrain being less than conducive to their normal habit of charging forward in a disorganized mob. 'But a dozen at least.'

43 Since Cain makes no subsequent mention of any medical treatment, we can infer that this is either exaggeration for effect or hypochondria rather than an accurate diagnosis.

'Contact.' Simla cut in too, and with a sudden thrill of horror I realised he was over to the left side of the defile, three hundred metres at least from Magot's position. No way he was seeing the same group. 'I've got seven. No, eight. Maybe more.'

'Me too,' Hail added, from our right flank. 'Looks like a full squad from here.'[44]

'Pull back,' I ordered. That made at least thirty, probably more, too many for us to take out here even with the Valhallans' ability to make use of the terrain and weather conditions to mount an effective ambush. It also confirmed my worst fear (apart from the thought that the necrons were stirring down in the darkness beneath our feet.) The comrades of the dead ork we'd found had indeed made contact with the bulk of their army, and were on their way back with a full-scale raiding force intent on exploiting the gap they'd discovered in our defences. 'We have to secure the cave whatever happens.'

'Confirm that,' Grifen said, overriding whatever objections her subordinates might be on the verge of expressing. Not that I really expected any, but Valhallan antipathy to the greenskins ran deep, and the temptation to take a pot-shot at them before withdrawing must have been acute. To their credit no one gave way to it though, so I began to breathe a little more easily as we made our way back up the slope towards the welcome refuge of the cave. With any luck we'd be able to slip away before they even knew we were here.

I must confess that the thought of getting out of the bone-numbing wind was so strong, and so all-pervading, that I quite lost track of my surroundings. I stumbled through the snow like an automaton, following in the tracks ploughed by Jurgen, intent only on putting one leg in front of the other. The image of the tunnel mouth and the respite from the cold it represented loomed ever larger in my thoughts, driving out everything but the determination to keep my numbed and frozen limbs moving. So it was with a shock of genuine surprise that I heard the unmistakable report of a bolter round detonating against an outcrop of rock a few metres away.

Spurred by a sense of imminent danger I dropped out of my fugue state at once, bringing the laspistol in my hand around, seeking a target. A hulking shape loomed out of the snow, bounding forward with incredible speed, swinging a crudely-fashioned axe. So eager was it to spill my blood it seemed to have forgotten the primitive bolt pistol clutched in its other hand. I fired by reflex, finding that my panic-spurred finger was able to tighten on the trigger just fine now that the question was a practical one, blowing a hole through its torso. The creature staggered and came on, then dropped to the ground, already cooling, as a second las-bolt took it from the side.

'Sergeant.' I acknowledged Grifen's assistance with a nod, and she gestured with her left hand, the right still holding her lasgun ready to fire.

'This way,' she said. I stumbled in her direction, sure that Jurgen would be with me as always, and in this I was soon proved correct. The unmistakable hiss of the melta opening up behind me made me turn, just in time to see my aide cut down a small group of the creatures that had evidently been following the first with a single ravening blast of thermal energy.

44 Presumably meaning a group the size of an Imperial Guard squad, as ork mobs can vary greatly in size, and wouldn't recognise the concept of any formation as organised as this in any case.

After a moment spent scanning our surroundings he lowered the weapon and began slogging through the knee-high drifts towards us as implacably unconcerned as though he were out for an afternoon stroll. Maybe by the standards of his homeworld he was.

'Up here, commissar.' Lunt reached down from atop a tangle of rocks, grasping my outstretched hand, and lifting me bodily to the top without any apparent effort. Grifen scrambled up after us, barely slowing down, and a moment later Jurgen heaved himself over the rim, the bulky weapon now slung to facilitate climbing, and preceded as always by his unmistakable odour.

'I thought this would be a good spot to regroup,' Grifen said. I glanced around, feeling almost warm now that we were partially sheltered from the relentless wind, and nodded approvingly. She'd chosen an elevated position surrounded by tumbled boulders, from which we could look down on the tunnel entrance from an elevation of a couple of metres or so. That was good thinking: if the orks had made it there ahead of us after all there was no sense in walking up to the cave mouth wearing a big sign saying 'shoot me I'm here.' As I strained my eyes through the whirling snow I wasn't able to discern much, but as I've said before I'd trust her instincts where the greenskins were concerned.

Hail and Simla had made it to our refuge too, I was pleased to see, each raising a hand in greeting as Jurgen and I appeared before going back to scanning the horizon over the sights of their lasguns. I was just about to try contacting Magot and asking her position when a flurry of las-bolt detonations and a bellow of orkish pain somewhere off to our left answered that question quite satisfactorily. The diminutive redhead appeared in person a few moments later, grinning with malevolent amusement.

'There was this greenie over that way making a latrine stop,' she reported gleefully, 'so I shot him right up the...'

'Is it dead?' I interrupted. She nodded, still enjoying the approbation of her comrades, who seemed to think this was as hilarious as she did.

'Deader than Horus,' she confirmed. Good. Her tracks would have been all but obliterated by now, and with any luck the orks wouldn't have a clue where we were or how many of us they faced. Unless they found and interrogated Logash, of course, in which case it was credits to carrots they'd learn everything they needed to know in pretty short order. That left me with only one choice.

'We're pulling back to the cave as soon as we know it's clear,' I said. 'And prepare to collapse it behind us.'

'What about the tech-priest?' Grifen asked, clearly not terribly concerned, but sticking to the letter of her mission brief with admirable tenacity.

'He'll just have to fend for himself,' I said. Catching her look, I added 'I'll take the responsibility.' It went without saying, of course, that went with the scarlet sash.

'It's your call, commissar.' Well, she was right about that, but I could see abandoning a human to the mercy of the orks wasn't going to go down too well with the rank and file, even if he was an annoying little grox-fondler who'd brought it on himself, so I went all solemn.

'It goes against the grain I know,' I said. 'But our first duty is to the Emperor, the regiment, and our mission. The colonel has to know about the necron presence here. It changes everything, and until then the lives of all our comrades are at risk.'

Everyone nodded solemnly at that, apparently perfectly happy to hang the little tech-priest out to dry now I'd been able to make it seem like a noble sacrifice, and we prepared to move out.

As I glanced back down slope, straining my eyes through the swirling blanket of snow for some sign of another party of orks, I thought I caught a glimpse of something moving smoothly and silently through the frozen landscape. I inhaled, intending to call out, then dismissed the impulse as the blur of apparent motion vanished in the kaleidoscope of white. Chances were it was only wishful thinking on my part, I thought, and even if it was Logash he'd never hear me over the howling of the wind. Later, when I had the leisure to reflect on that moment, I was to shudder at how close I had probably come to dooming us all.

'It seems clear enough,' Grifen said, after a few more moments spent observing the cave entrance. So we moved cautiously towards it, putting our trust in the obscuring snow and what little concealment the rocks afforded. The troopers were well disciplined, I found, moving by stages as though we were already in combat, waiting until one of their comrades was in position to provide covering fire before moving to the next place of refuge. I did the same, falling into the rhythm with the instinct born of long practice.

At length we were ranged around the mouth of the cave. I stepped into it gratefully, feeling the barbed wind let go of my flesh, and gasping with the agony of returning circulation. For a moment or two my entire body felt as though I'd been hit by a flamer, then the pain subsided from unbearable to merely excruciating. Even so my survival instinct remained strong, and I was able to override the discomfort for long enough to sweep the tunnel before me with the beam of my luminator, keeping the barrel of my laspistol in line with it. (Under most circumstances, of course, there's no better way to make a target of yourself than that, but I was backlit by the tunnel mouth in any case so it wouldn't make any difference to an assailant lurking in the dark. If anything I might dazzle them for long enough to get a shot off.) As it happened there was nothing waiting to shoot me, and after a second or two I relaxed.

'All clear,' I called, and Jurgen joined me at once, his melta pointing away down the tunnel before us. Bearing in mind what we'd have to pass to get back to our comrades that eased my mind as much as was possible under the circumstances. I turned back to check on the rest of the troopers, who had all taken up positions behind what cover they could find in the immediate vicinity of the cave mouth. Grifen turned to wave at me, from behind a small boulder, and then froze at the unmistakable sound of bolter fire crackling towards us on the wind.

'What the hell?' she asked, seemingly forgetting for a moment that she was still broadcasting on the whole squad net rather than the command channel. Lunt grinned, readying his flamer.

'Sounds like a difference of opinion to me.' He could have been right, of course, greenskins have a definite propensity to settle disputes in the most basic of ways, but the sheer volume of fire I could hear argued against it. It sounded like a full-scale firefight to me. Well, good if it was, the more of each other they slaughtered the better. On the other hand... I strained my ears for the sound I most dreaded, the unmistakable ripping noise of a necron gauss weapon, but if it was there to be heard it was swallowed by the wind.

'Maybe they've found the cogboy,' Hail said slowly, clearly not relishing the idea. I nodded, sharing the same mental picture of the tech-priest fleeing blindly through the snow, howling greenskins in pursuit, firing their ramshackle weapons excitedly as they ran. That seemed unpleasantly plausible.

'Shouldn't we try to help him?' Simla asked. I shook my head, with as much reluctance as I could feign.

'I wish we could,' I lied. 'But we'll never get to him before they do. And unless we want his sacrifice to be in vain we have to report back what we've found.'

'The commissar's right,' Grifen said. 'Pull back, and prepare to blow the entrance.'

Before anyone could move, though, hulking silhouettes could be discerned through the swirling snow, charging towards us with the berserk fury of their kind. By some freak of the weather conditions the eddies of snow were lighter here, affording us an uncomfortably clear view of them as the visibility increased. Crude bolters barked, and chips of stone flew from the outcrops of stone surrounding the cave mouth. Grifen levelled her lasgun.

'Fire at will,' she said.

'Wait!' I ordered, an instant later, and thank the Emperor everyone had the presence of mind to obey. 'Just stay down and don't move!' It had suddenly struck me they weren't firing at us; the bulk of the bolter impacts were off to our left, and it seemed to me that they weren't charging the cave so much as fleeing towards it. And that, my tingling palms and a sudden spasm of the bowels told me, probably meant only one thing. The Valhallans froze, melting into the icy landscape in the way only they could, and even knowing where they were I found them hard to pick out.

A second later my worst suspicions were confirmed, as a vivid green beam, the colour of a festering wound, ripped through the air with the all too vividly remembered sound of tearing cloth, striking one of the orks full on. In less than a second he seemed to dissolve; skin, muscle, and skeleton whipping away to vapour, leaving only the echo of a howl of inhuman agony to mark his passing.

'Emperor on Earth!' Grifen breathed, horror suffusing her voice, and I have to admit to trembling with terror myself. The beam swept on, transfixing another victim, and was joined by another, then another.

The orks scattered, and began to fire back, a little more accurately now that their assailants had so considerately revealed their positions. The swirling snow parted, revealing the sight I had so dreaded, and yet had dared to hope I might be spared after collapsing the entrance to the tomb: eerie metallic warriors, striding silently forward, their carapace sculpted to resemble skeletons. These were surely death incarnate come to claim us all.

'So that's what they look like up close.' Jurgen, imperturbable as ever, his faith in the Emperor's protection still absolute despite taking a bolt to the head on Gravalax, raised the melta, sounding no more than mildly curious. Then again, given some of the horrors we'd faced together over the years, I suppose he just thought it was business as usual. One thing I can say for Jurgen, despite his unprepossessing appearance, he had reserves of courage greater than any man I've ever met. Either that, or he was just too stupid to understand the magnitude of the dangers threatening us.[45] I raised a hand to forestall him.

'Wait,' I breathed. 'Our only chance is to avoid being seen.' That I could attest to from personal experience, my natural propensity for running and hiding being the only thing that had saved me on Interitus Prime when everyone else had been slaughtered. To my relief Jurgen nodded, but kept the heavy weapon aimed, ready for use if it should prove necessary.

The orks had gone to ground by now, taking cover behind the nearest rocks, shooting back at the necron warriors with their usual lack of accuracy. Inevitably the sheer weight of firepower began to tell, however, a number of shells finding their targets regardless. As I'd seen before, the implacable metal warriors simply shrugged off the impacts, the detonations against their metal hides seeming to do no more than discolour whatever unholy alloy they were made of.

A few of the shots were more effective than the rest, though, more by luck than judgement. As we watched, one of the ork bolts detonated against the power pack attached to the weapon of the leading automaton, and an instant later an explosion ripped apart both the weapon and the necron carrying it.

At this the orks set up a great roar of triumph, and a few of the more incautious broke from cover to race forwards, apparently intent on tackling their gleaming metal assailants in hand to hand combat. Inevitably most died, ripped apart by the gauss flayers, but incredibly a couple closed the distance, swinging their crude, heavy axes as they did so.

One was unlucky, or too slow, his target turning with eerie precision to spit him on the combat blade mounted on the end of its weapon. Thick brackish blood poured from a gash which opened the creature from groin to shoulder blade, and the necron shook the eviscerated body from the end of its weapon with an air of weary disdain. The gutted ork fell heavily to the snow, where a slowly-spreading pool of blood began freezing into a thick, icy scab.

The other greenskin parried the blow aimed at it, and whirled around to strike at the necron's neck. Crudely-forged metal met aeon-old sorcery in a blinding flash of discharged energy, and the unliving warrior's head fell heavily to the snow. The ork's triumph was short-lived, however, as the concerted beams of the two surviving necrons ripped it to vapour in a heartbeat.

'Never thought I'd be rooting for the greenies,' Magot said quietly, sentiments I imagined we all shared. The surviving orks stood their ground with the brutish defiance of their kind, pouring inaccurate small arms fire into the area

45 I must confess to remaining undecided about that myself, despite having fought alongside him on a number of occasions.

around the skeletal metallic figures, blowing gouts of snow and ice up around them for the most part, but still inflicting a number of hits which, for the first time, appeared to give the walking nightmares some pause for thought. More distant weapons fire could be heard over the wind now, speaking of other, equally desperate battles, and I allowed myself to feel a surge of hope.

'Everyone pull back,' I ordered quietly. 'Stay under cover. With any luck we can disengage while they're too busy to notice us.'

'Confirm that,' Grifen said, with heartfelt relief evident in her voice. The other troopers began to retreat deeper into the safety of the cave, crawling backwards for the most part, keeping their weapons trained on the unequal battle in front of us.

While the two necrons had concentrated their fire on the orks behind the boulders they'd maintained their position, a big mistake, as I would have been happy to point out if anyone had asked me. Orks are remarkably resilient creatures, driven purely by rage and aggression, so I was scarcely surprised when the one left sprawling in a sorbet of its own blood suddenly grabbed the ankle of its erstwhile assailant and yanked hard on it with all its feral strength. Mortally wounded as it was it clearly had no intention of dying with unfinished business left behind, and the necron fell heavily, its right shin now detached from its knee joint.

Bellowing in triumph the ork began belabouring the fallen warrior with the stump of its own leg, raising a clangour like a peal of cathedral bells (if they were horribly out of tune) and inflicting a remarkable array of dents on its torso and skull. I was under no illusion that this would be enough to incapacitate the hideous thing, though, so I was unsurprised when it swung its combat blade around with the same unhurried precision I'd seen before and sheared through the greenskin's neck. A brief flicker of bewilderment seemed to enter the creature's eyes as its head detached from its shoulders, with the concomitant geyser of gore, and it slumped across the battered metal torso of its murderer.

Abruptly the distant firing we'd heard since just before we first saw the orks ceased, to be followed at once by a howl of barbaric euphoria. It seemed that the main body of the greenskin force had won their battle, though no doubt at a terrible cost. (Not that it would bother them in the slightest, of course, they're not a particularly sentimental species by any stretch of the imagination.) The two necrons before us stopped moving abruptly, as though listening to something, and then simply vanished, along with the remains of their fallen comrades. No doubt their departure was marked by the same crack of air rushing in to fill the sudden vacuum I'd noticed when Amberley was teleported to safety by her displacer field, but if so I was unable to hear it over the howling of the wind.

'Emperor's bowels!' Grifen shook her head, clearly trying to comprehend what we'd just seen. 'Where did they go?'

'Straight back to hell, I hope,' Magot said.

'Close enough,' I confirmed. Even now they'd be reporting what they'd seen, and drawing up their plans for a major incursion, I knew that for a stone cold certainty.

The remaining orks were emerging from cover now, stamping about where the necrons had vanished, and looting the bodies of their fallen companions. Guttural expressions of surprise and confusion drifted towards us on the wind.

'What about the greenies?' Simla asked. I hesitated. They weren't our most urgent priority now, and with any luck would divert any necron attention from us as we scuttled back through the tunnels to warn Kasteen and the others. But then again they'd already found the mouth of the cave, and would be too close behind us for comfort if they felt the urge to do any exploring.

Abruptly the decision was taken out of my hands. The biggest ork in the group, who I took to be the leader,[46] pointed straight at the mouth of the tunnel and bellowed an order of some kind. With a last look back at the bodies of the fallen, half a dozen greenskins started moving towards us. I had no choice; the security of the mission, and more importantly myself, demanded it.

'Kill them all,' I ordered.

46 Generally a safe assumption.

TEN

That was an order the Valhallans were eager to respond to, and they did so with alacrity, opening fire on the greenskins while they were still caught in the open. We took them by complete surprise, the first couple falling under a hail of lasfire before they even had a chance to react.

The others were quick, though, assessing the situation with remarkable acuity for such imbecilic creatures,[47] and scattering again to make themselves more difficult targets. A couple of them went to ground behind a tangle of rocks, and began to shoot back at us. Fortunately their marksmanship was no better than usual so they inflicted no casualties, but they managed to come close enough to make us take full advantage of our own cover, their bolts bursting uncomfortably close to our position. Something stung my cheek, and I wiped away a smear of blood where a chip of stone had caught me. That was too near for comfort and I retreated further into the darkness of the cave, bracing my laspistol against a convenient outcrop of rock to improve the accuracy of my retaliation.

Seeing that we were effectively suppressed the four remaining in the open ran forwards brandishing their blades and screaming at the top of their voices in the way that they do. As they closed with us they fired their hand weapons sporadically, without even bothering to aim, which made a lot of noise but had little practical effect other than making even more sure that we kept our heads down.

'Lunt!' I yelled. 'Take the ones in the rocks!'

'Commissar.' His acknowledgement was crisp as he raised the barrel of his flamer cautiously over the outcrop he was sheltering behind. I directed a flurry of lasbolts at the snipers, if the perpetrators of such inaccurate shooting could be dignified with such a term, and to my relief Hail and Simla followed my lead. Grifen and Magot concentrated their fire on the charging orks in front of us, slowing them momentarily as the big ork in front with the horns on his helmet[48] took a las-bolt to the knee. He stumbled, falling face down in the snow, and a couple of his subordinates tripped over him. For a moment the hail of incoming fire dwindled as the fallen greenskins

47 Though brutal and primitive by the standards of other races, orks have an instinctive understanding of combat second to none.

48 A common symbol of authority among the greenskins, apparently meant to prove that they've overcome something even bigger and nastier than they are.

flailed at one another, exchanging guttural profanities and blows which would have stunned a grox, before floundering to their feet again.

The delay was enough for Lunt, however; he rose to his full height, and directed a searing jet of burning promethium at the tangle of rocks which concealed the shooters. With a roar which sounded more like rage than pain the two orks burst out into the open, like living torches, charging towards our position. Four lasguns spat as one, targeting them as they moved and the trailing one fell, but the one in front just kept coming, wreathed in steam from the snow which evaporated about him, charred bone becoming visible through the sizzling flesh.

'Emperor's guts!' Lunt swung the barrel, trying to line up another shot, then fell back, an expression of pained surprise on his face as a bloody crater exploded in his chest. I swung my gaze back to the main group of orks, who were now on their feet again, their crude weapons kicking up a flurry of snow and debris around the fallen heavy weapons trooper. Typically for their kind they concentrated only on the most visible threat, ignoring the rest of us for the moment; a fatal mistake.

'Jurgen!' I ordered, gesturing to the group which was now close enough to be a target for the melta. Smiling grimly, my aide took careful aim, sighting directly at the limping leader, who was still snarling in triumph at the death of our fellow trooper. (I'd seen enough bolter wounds in my time to know that such a hit would have been instantly fatal, smashing through the flak armour beneath his greatcoat to detonate inside his ribcage. There was nothing to be done for Lunt now other than avenge his demise.) The heavy weapon hissed once more, flashing the intervening curtain of snow into vapour, and reducing the ork leader and the two standing next to him to a rank pile of gently steaming offal. The sole survivor turned, blinking in what looked like stunned stupefaction, its left arm hanging limp and charred from flash burns, then turned and bolted (which just goes to show that at least a few of them aren't as stupid as they look).

I rose fully to my feet and took careful aim, bracing the laspistol in my hand across my left forearm as though I were on the firing range, and trying to still the trembling which seemed to have taken control of my body. Whether it was a delayed reaction to the terror the sight of the necrons had inspired in me, anger at Lunt's sudden and brutal death, or simply my abused body starting to respond to the relative rise in temperature I couldn't say, but I was grimly determined to slay the foul creature myself in spite of it. I squeezed the trigger, thankful for the steadiness my augmetic fingers imparted to my aim, and was rewarded with a gout of ichor from between the greenskin's shoulder blades. Grifen and Magot joined in as it stumbled, bellowing in pain, and between us we dispatched it like the beast it was.

It was only as I stood there, exhaling slowly as the tension eased from my aching body and the trembling gradually came under control, that I noticed the burning ork was still stumbling towards us, its steps faltering now as it staggered drunkenly to the left and the right, but still forging forward, fixated on reaching its tormentors. It was a ghastly sight to behold, I must admit, and I was on the verge of ordering the troopers to finish it off when it dropped abruptly to the ground in a gout of steam from the melting snow around it and at last lay still.

Silence descended, save for the relentless keening of the wind, and the rasping of my breath in my throat.

'Lunt?' Grifen asked, the flatness of her tone already answering her own question.

'Dead,' Hail confirmed, standing over his broken body, the spilled blood and viscera already glazed with ice. I forced myself to join her, looking down at the dead trooper, feeling I knew not what. (Other than my usual sense of profound relief that it wasn't me lying there, as it so easily could have been, of course.)

'He did his duty,' I said, the highest praise I could think of, and everyone nodded soberly. Grifen gestured to Hail and Simla.

'Bring him,' she said. 'We'll take turns.' I shook my head, conscious of how she must feel losing a trooper under her command for the first time. It never gets easy, I can tell you that, but after a while you learn to accept it. Despite what they say, the Emperor can't protect everyone, which is why I take such good care to do the job myself.

'I wish we could,' I said, as gently as I could manage. 'But we don't have the time. We have to get back as fast as possible.' I half expected her to argue, but she nodded, reluctantly.

'We'll come back for him later then,' she said. I shook my head again.

'I'm afraid we can't,' I said, explaining as tactfully as I could. I was suddenly aware of four pairs of eyes boring into me. (Jurgen, of course, would simply go along with whatever I said without argument, his dogged and unimaginative deference to authority being foremost among his well-hidden virtues.)

'Why not?' She wasn't challenging my decision, I was pleased to note, just asking for an explanation, which I supposed they were all entitled to.

'We can't leave any trace of our presence here,' I pointed out. 'Right now, the necrons are only aware of the greenskins.' At least I hoped they were. 'Our best hope of making it back to warn the others is by sneaking past while they concentrate on the threat they know about.'

'The orks.' Grifen nodded in reluctant understanding. 'But if they find Lunt's body they'll come after us too. I see.'

'I'm sorry,' I said again. 'But it's the only way.' I motioned Jurgen forwards, and he readied the melta. I briefly considered trying to salvage the flamer, but it would be more trouble than it was worth; the tanks were too bulky for anyone to add to their kit, and the firing mechanism looked damaged by bolter fire anyway. I checked Lunt's pockets for any personal effects which his family back on Valhalla might want (if he actually had any, I had no idea really, just taking comfort in the familiar routine), and collected his laspistol as an afterthought, giving it to Jurgen to carry. He might as well get the benefit of something less dangerous to the rest of us in case we found ourselves in close quarter combat again. Then I nodded to my aide, stepped back, and he pulled the trigger. Lunt's body boiled into vapour in a matter of seconds, helped by the volatile promethium left in the flamer tanks, and I led the others in a few ritual words commending his soul to the Emperor.

We were a sombre group as we turned away, you can be sure of that, the drifting snow already beginning to obscure the scar in the rock where the heat of the melta had sent our comrade to join His Majesty. Sometimes, when I sit in my study here at the schola and watch the flames in the grate through a glass of amasec, I can't help thinking of all the brave men and women I've seen fall on a battlefield somewhere without even a grave marker left behind to show they were ever there, and reflect that I'm probably the last man alive who even remembers they existed, and that when I'm gone the last trace of them will fade with me. Then I thank the Emperor that I've lasted as long as I have, and that I've seen my last war, and I might just defy the odds long enough to die in bed after all (someone else's, with any luck).[49]

We paused in the mouth of the cave, and Grifen started to take a quick inventory of our remaining stock of explosives.

'There's no time for that now,' I said, urging our party on without, I hoped, too obvious a show of impatience. 'Every minute counts.'

'Right.' She fell into step beside me. 'And there's no point in tipping off the tinheads, is there?'

'Exactly,' I said. Not only would collapsing the passage alert the next necron patrol to our presence, it would close them off from the orks, and the last thing I wanted to do was redirect their attention to the rest of the tunnel complex. Of course they could have found their way into the mines by now in any case, but I was betting that once they'd discovered an exit, and an enemy waiting beyond it, they'd ignore everything else until they'd exterminated the greenies; or at least as many of them as they could find in the vicinity. I explained this to Grifen, and she nodded.

'Makes sense to me,' she said.

'What I don't understand,' Jurgen said slowly, 'is how they got out of the tomb in the first place.' That had been worrying me too. I thought we'd brought down enough of the roof to keep them penned in for a great deal longer than this, but they had access to technosorceries which made the tau look like stone-age barbarians, so it never paid to underestimate them.

'We'll find out soon enough,' I said, apprehension settling across me like a shroud.

Normally I would have been profoundly relieved to have returned to the tunnels where I felt reasonably at home, but the knowledge that there were necrons abroad, possibly even sweeping the same narrow passageways we were so cautiously navigating, knotted my stomach with fear. I would have preferred to move on in the dark, relying on the eerie green glow given off by their gauss weapons to warn us of their presence, but none of the others had the advantage of my hiver's tunnel sense; they'd have been stumbling blindly in the darkness, and making more noise than a grox in a ceramics emporium to boot. So we moved at the double, the easy loping stride of the veteran trooper which eats up the kilometres without dragging

49 Ironically this part of the archive appears to have been composed only a matter of months before the thirteenth Black Crusade engulfed most of the segmentum, and Cain found himself dragged out of retirement despite his advancing years.

you down with exhaustion, our luminator beams reflecting just as brightly from the frozen walls as before.

'There's something up ahead,' Simla said, a couple of kilometres later, taking his turn on point. My palms tingled with dread anticipation as the formation slowed, weapons coming to bear down the tunnel.

'What is it?' I asked.

'I don't know.' His voice on the comm-bead sounded puzzled rather than alarmed. 'There's a lot of blood.'

Well that was something at least: if it bled it wasn't a necron. We closed up into a tighter formation, moving ahead a couple of hundred metres to join him as he walked cautiously forward, his luminator playing on what looked like a large pile of butchered meat. The ice around it was crimson, slick with frozen blood as he'd said. Absently, I realised there was too much there for the body to be human, then as we got closer the full size of it became apparent.

'It's an ambull,' Hail said, surprise suffusing her voice.

'Not any more,' Magot added helpfully.

'Where did it come from?' Jurgen asked, as ever displaying his talent for the obvious question. Grifen shrugged.

'Cogboy must have got his head count wrong.' That much was clear, of course. I was more concerned with how it had died. I moved closer to examine the cadaver, and almost immediately wished I hadn't. Beneath its glaze of ice, raw, bloody wounds slashed across its body. Whatever killed it had done so in close combat, wielding razor-sharp blades with surgical precision.

'Where's its hide?' Simla wondered aloud. Grifen shrugged.

'Do necrons use hearth rugs?'

'Not that I ever noticed,' I said, getting everyone moving again. Something about the dead animal spooked me, I don't mind admitting it. The necrons I'd seen before had killed efficiently and dispassionately, but this mutilated carcase spoke of a refined and gleeful sadism of the kind I associated with the eldar renegades who prey on their own kind with as much abandon as they do upon humanity.[50]

As we left the grisly trophy behind us, all trace of it soon swallowed by the suffocating darkness which closed in around the tiny refuge of light cast by our luminators, my apprehension grew even greater. Every step we took was taking us closer to that hidden tomb, and whatever horrors it might conceal. (I had a better idea than most, after my experiences in the depths of their catacombs, so you'll have to forgive me if I confess that taking those steps became progressively harder as I had to exert every iota of willpower I possessed not to turn and flee, screaming, towards the daylight.)

At length a fatalistic numbness settled over me. Retreat was clearly impossible in any case, as the orkish armies would kill us just as surely as the necrons if we tried to go back the way we'd come, and our only hope of

---

50 If not more so. The eldar corsairs appear to be touched by the Dark Powers in some way, and the enmity between them and their untainted kin seems to run as deep as that between the loyal subjects of His Divine Majesty and the traitors who seek to subjugate humanity in the name of their blasphemous gods.

safety lay in returning to the refinery complex and the protection it afforded. (Meagre as that looked right now, caught between a gargant and who knew what terrors from the dawn of time.)

My sense of direction, reliable as always, was telling me we should be almost on top of the entrance we'd found by now, and I urged my companions to even greater caution. To my relief they needed little urging, the oppressiveness of the tunnels and the knowledge of what awaited us no doubt weighing on their minds as heavily as it did upon my own. I'd kept my laspistol in my right hand ever since the firefight with the orks, and I reached across with my left to loosen my trusty chainsword in its scabbard. Like the pistol I'd carried it for more years than I cared to remember, so long that it had ceased to exist in my mind as a weapon, or even an object in its own right; now when I drew it the humming blade was simply an extension of my own body.[51] Knowing it was there was curiously reassuring, and I breathed a little easier as we rounded the last bend in the tunnel before the roof fall we'd caused.

We'd doused all the lights except Simla's, allowing our eyes to get a little more used to the gloom and covering him from the concealing darkness as he advanced, and at first all seemed well: the tumbled heap of rock, stone and ice lay across the tunnel, narrowing it to half its width as I remembered. The palms of my hands were tingling though, usually a reliable indicator that something my conscious mind hasn't picked up on yet isn't quite right, so I slowed my pace, scanning the pile of debris in the light from Simla's luminator, and waited for my tunnel rat's instincts to provide the missing clue.

The rubble seemed undisturbed, however hard I stared at it, so it couldn't be that. My gaze flickered across a deep patch of shadow a few metres from it, and then on to the dimly-seen texture of the tunnel wall, where the light of our luminators bounced back in the sparkling reflections we'd grown so used to by now they scarcely registered...

'Simla. Tunnel wall, about five metres from the cave-in,' I directed, and waited for our point man to swing his luminator round.

'Emperor's bowels!' Grifen brought up her lasgun, her shocked exclamation putting all our reactions into words. The shadow was no such thing, of course, the texture of the tunnel wall should have been visible there too, as my subconscious had been trying to tell me. A fresh passageway was now gouged out of the rock, leading off Emperor knew where. The work, presumably, of our butchered ambull.

'Claw marks,' Simla confirmed, shining the beam of his luminator around the mouth, and then into the depths of the new tunnel. His posture altered suddenly, the lasgun the luminator was taped to coming up into the firing position. 'Golden Throne!'

---

51 I can attest from my personal association with him that Cain was one of the most accomplished swordsmen in the sector. Even well into his retirement, and his second century, none of the combat instructors at the schola were able to match his skill, honed as it was by innumerable victories in the field. (Much to their chagrin, I might add.) Oddly, his memoirs give little detail about the actual techniques he employed in the mêlées he describes; probably because his fighting style was so instinctive he never bothered to analyse it.

We ran forward to join him, anticipating Emperor knew what, and clustered at the tunnel mouth. At first it seemed no different from the other ambull runs we'd been travelling through. Then I followed the beam of light, saw what was illuminated by it, and swallowed hard.

'Orks,' Jurgen said, as phlegmatically as if he were handing me a fresh bowl of tanna leaf tea.

'You think?' Magot chipped in, with grisly relish. 'Kind of hard to tell without their skins.'

There were six of them in total, all dead, all flayed the way the ambull had been. Beneath their thin glazing of ice they looked for all the world like anatomical models, laid out for the instruction of apprentice medicae (if the greenskins ever bothered with such niceties as chirurgery, of course).[52]

'What killed them?' Hail asked, paling as much as she was able to. At that point I was past caring, to be honest. Their presence here was a strong indication that at least one group had made it into the tunnels ahead of us, and that an indeterminate number of the brutes might even now be wreaking havoc behind our defensive lines. Not to mention standing between us and safety. All I knew was that the necrons must somehow be responsible, and that whatever tomb-spawned horror had killed them like this was something I didn't want to meet. With a premonitory tingle I realised that the new tunnel was running almost parallel to the necron one we'd blocked, and suddenly felt a violent urge to be somewhere else as quickly as possible.

'Look at this, sir.' Jurgen held up one of the crude bolters the orks had carried, an expression of mild curiosity on his face. It had been sheared clean through, the metal bright where a blade of unimaginable sharpness had sliced it in two, along with the hand that had held it if the amount of blood frozen to the stock was anything to go by. Automatically I scanned the scattered equipment around the bodies, looking for some kind of clue as to what their purpose had been. It was hard to be sure, but something about the weapons they carried and the few pieces of rag which hadn't been stained with blood reminded me of the scouts who'd shot down our shuttle.

That was a logical inference, of course, but quite disturbing in its way. It meant we could be up against orks who, untypically for their kind, were skilled at moving quietly and waiting in ambush rather than announcing their presence with loud voices and indiscriminate weapons fire.

'Shouldn't we see what's at the end of the tunnel?' Grifen asked, reluctance audible in her voice. I shook my head.

'No.' It took all the self-control I could muster to sound calm and collected, instead of screaming the word. 'Nothing's more important than reporting back what we've found.'

'Besides,' Magot chipped in, indicating the mutilated orks with a casual wave, 'that looks like a pretty definite Keep Out sign to me.'

'Then let's take the hint,' I said. Grifen nodded.

'You'll get no argument from me.'

'Hold it.' Hail had moved back to the main tunnel, and was now guarding

---

52 Actually they do, although not in any fashion we would recognise as good medical practice.

our rear, standing next to the rockfall which had buried the entrance to the tomb. (And which, thanks to our stray ambull, had turned out to be a complete waste of time.) 'I think I can hear something.'

'Can you be a little more specific?' I asked, lowering my voice instinctively, even though no one else would hear it through the comm-bead in her ear.

'Movement. Beyond the rockslide.' Her voice was equally hushed. Simla scuttled forward to support her, dousing our last remaining luminator, and plunging us into darkness. I've never been prone to claustrophobia, a consequence of my upbringing I suppose, but at that moment the weight of the gloom around us seemed crushing. I found myself obscurely grateful for Jurgen's familiar odour, which reassured me that I had at least one ally down here I could trust, and drew my chainsword from its scabbard.

I strained my ears, listening for any change in the ambient noise around me, tuning out the sounds of my own breathing and my hammering heart. At first I heard nothing except the susurration of the lungs of my companions, and the faint rustling of their clothes as they moved into positions of readiness. Then it came to me, rising up out of the echoes: the sound of boots crunching on hoarfrost, and guttural voices whispering in orkish.

'Let them get close,' I sub-vocalised, hearing the reassuring murmur of response from the rest of the team, and hunkering down to present the smallest possible target. 'Take them when they come round the rockslide.'

It was a good strategy, and probably would have worked, except for my companions' inexperience of tunnel fighting and moving stealthily in the dark. I never knew if Hail or Simla was to blame, but as they settled into the shelter of the tumbled heap of rubble one of them dislodged a small piece of debris.

I held my breath as it skittered away across the ice, and the advancing footsteps halted. A loud sniffing sound echoed through the dark, followed by a muttered conversation in what, for greenskins, were hushed tones. I picked out the word, '*humiez*,'[53] which I'd heard often enough before to be sure of, and knew that our ambush had been discovered.

A glimmer of orange light was now visible behind the rockslide, flickering like fire, and a sick presentiment gripped me. One of the approaching greenskins apparently had a flamer, the pilot light providing illumination for the group as well as heavy support, and a vivid mental image of the immolated orks Lunt had killed rose up unbidden in my mind. I determined to make the bearer my highest priority target; of all the ways to die I'd seen on the battlefields of the galaxy, burning to death looked among the least pleasant.

'Stay back,' I sub-vocalised, probably unnecessarily, as I'm sure the others were all thinking the same. Then I levelled my laspistol at the constriction in the passageway where the greenskins must surely appear, and waited.

To my surprise, however, they didn't charge blindly forward into combat as I'd expected. A couple of small objects flew through the gap, bouncing on the frost-covered floor, and skittering wildly in random directions.

'Grenade!' Simla yelled, just before they detonated, and a storm of shrapnel ripped through the air. He fell backwards, ugly wounds peppering his body.

---

53 The closest the orkish larynx can come to the Gothic word 'humans.'

Even the flak armour beneath his greatcoat couldn't stop all of the shards, and crimson stains began seeping across it as he tried to get to his feet. Hail was luckier, her partner taking most of the blast, but I could see her left arm was bleeding heavily and hung limply at her side. She leapt forward into the gap, screaming in anger, and fired her lasgun one-handed on full auto at the no doubt surprised greenskins beyond. She must have hit at least one, too, judging by the howls of rage and pain which echoed round the confined space.

'Hail! Get back!' Grifen shouted, but she was too late; a volley of bolts tore Hail apart in a rain of blood and viscera, and then the orks were among us. Simla tried to raise his lasgun as the first bounded through the narrow opening, but before he could pull the trigger a massive cleaver swung down to bisect his skull. The greenskin bellowed in triumph, but it was short-lived as Magot and I shot it almost simultaneously, and it dropped, most of its head blown away. Grifen kept up a steady suppressive fire against the opening through which they had to come, attempting to dissuade any more from following, but it was a futile hope. When the blood of an ork is up they have almost no sense of self-preservation, seeming happy to die if they can take a few of their enemies with them. Another greenskin dived through the choke point, spitting bolts from the crude pistol in its hand, and to my horror the flickering glow of the incendiary weapon was growing brighter, indicating that its operator would be the next to emerge.

'Jurgen!' I shouted, pointing, 'take out the flamer!' He nodded, and sighted the melta carefully. I had no more time to consider his actions after that, or anyone else's for that matter, because the greenskin was upon me, swinging its heavy blade at my head.

I ducked, bringing up the screaming chainsword to block it instinctively, and felt the sturdy mechanism shudder as adamantium teeth met crudely forged metal. Sparks flew, miniature orange suns melting tiny craters in the ice which coated the floor, before I turned my body, deflecting the brute's headlong charge into the wall. It roared as its head impacted with the unyielding ice-coated stone, and turned back towards me, thick ropes of drool hanging from its tusks. Now it was really hacked off.

Good. I cut at its leg, slashing a wound that would have disabled a human, but which seemed to affect it little more than a scratch. It brought its cumbersome blade down to block the strike, as I'd anticipated, and I slashed upwards, taking the loathsome creature in the neck. It looked startled for a moment, as if wondering where all the blood was suddenly coming from, and dropped heavily to its knees. With any other species this would have been a mortal blow, but I'd faced greenies too often before to underestimate their resilience. I swung the blade again, laterally this time, and took its head from its shoulders.

The whole fight could only have lasted a second or two. As I turned away my eyes were stabbed by the searing flash of the melta.

'Got him,' Jurgen confirmed, as I tried to blink my retina clear of the dancing after-images, and cursed myself for my carelessness. That degree of disorientation could cost me my life down here.

'Look out!' The breath was suddenly driven from my lungs as Magot dived forwards, catching me around the waist, and barging me out of the way of a large and unfriendly rock which had become detached from the ceiling. It crashed to the ground where I'd been standing less than a second before.

'Thanks,' I said, still trying to pick out the image of the redheaded trooper from the bright green haze which seemed to float between me and the rest of the world. I thought I could make out a grin, and realised she'd switched her luminator on again.

'Any time,' she said.

'The whole roof's coming down!' Grifen yelled, and I became aware of the creaks and rumblings which told me she was right. Apparently the explosion we'd touched off here earlier had left things even more unstable than we'd realised, something I suppose an old tunnel rat like me should have spotted if I hadn't been too busy being terrified of the necrons.

'Back!' I shouted, my childhood instincts kicking in at last; the worst of it sounded as if it was ahead of us. So we ran back to the shelter of the fresh ambull tunnel, and waited for the noise to stop.

'Emperor on Earth!' Grifen said, when the dust had finally settled. I can't say I blamed her. Of the nine troopers she'd set out with only Magot was now left, and she must have felt the loss of so many of her subordinates keenly. Scintillating ice motes danced in our luminator beams as we took in the full import of the sight ahead of us. Where half the passageway had once been blocked, an impenetrable wall of debris now barred our way. Of the orks, and our fallen comrades, there was no sign at all.

'We're frakked, aren't we?' Magot asked. I shook my head, afraid to speak. It looked to me as if she was right.

'I can try another shot,' Jurgen suggested. 'See if that might clear it.' More likely it would bring down even more rubble, and finish us off into the bargain. I shook my head again.

'Probably a bad idea,' I said, surprised at my restraint under the circumstances.

'We could go back,' Grifen suggested. 'Try to get to the refinery overland.' Over a mountain range, swarming with orks. In a blizzard. That would be suicide, and the dubious tone of her voice told me she realised that even as she spoke.

'We've got one chance,' I said, my mind skittering reluctantly away from the thought even as I voiced it. I tried to picture the map of the ambull tunnels Logash had been compiling on his auspex, and overlaid the mental image with the fresh one we'd just discovered. With a lot of luck it might intersect one of the others before too long, and allow us to bypass the blockage ahead of us.

On the other hand, it was also running more or less parallel with the passageway we'd been trying to block off in the first place, and it seemed pretty obvious that the necrons were already using it. If we went ahead we'd almost certainly die.

Well, almost certainly offers a bit more hope than definitely, which was what our other options amounted to, so in the end it was the only choice to make. It was a grim and silent group which started out, already half the size we had been when we passed this way before, and with the gravest peril we had to face still in front of us.

I averted my eyes from the mutilated orks as we filed past their silent and frozen bodies, and wondered if I'd doomed us all.

ELEVEN

By that point we'd given up any attempt at maintaining a proper skirmish formation, advancing instead as a single group, huddled together for protection like the natives of some feral world scared of the daemons beyond the circle of firelight. The difference, of course, was that we knew the daemons were real, and that we were walking straight into their infernal realm. (And speaking as someone who's met a daemon or two in his time, I can assure you that the sensation was not at all dissimilar.)

We had by some unspoken agreement left all the luminators apart from Magot's switched off, so that only a single beam of light preceded us down that narrow and forbidding passageway. As a result, the shadows closed in around us even more suffocatingly than before, despite the reflective qualities of the ice which still coated the walls, intensifying the sense of brooding menace surrounding us. Moreover, my tunnel rat's instincts told me we were descending slowly once again, ever deeper into the bowels of the planet, and the deeper we went, the closer the enshrouding gloom seemed to wrap itself around us, until the air against my face seemed thick and warm, almost choking in its closeness.

Abruptly I became aware that the two phenomena were real, not psychological. The ambient temperature was gradually rising, and our single beam was reflecting less and less from the walls around us as dark rock began to emerge from behind its coating of translucent ice. The resultant humidity was making the air seem damp and thick, a faint mist rising from the floor ahead of us. It was still pretty chilly by any normal measure, you understand, but compared to the temperatures we'd been exposed to on the surface it began to feel almost tropical. The Valhallans certainly seemed to notice it, both women loosening their greatcoats and Jurgen removing his thick fur hat, which he stuffed into one of the equipment pouches he was habitually festooned with.

'Wherever we're going, I think we're here,' Magot volunteered, after an indeterminate period of silence during which we heard nothing apart from our cautious footsteps which seemed to ring like thunder with every pace, echoing all the louder in our ears for every pain we took to muffle them. I nodded, my mouth dry. A faint humming was discernable in the air now, hovering just on the edge of audibility, and a faint acrid tang tickled the membranes of my nose. All things I remembered only too well, and had hoped never to experience again.

'Move carefully,' I warned everyone, completely superfluously no doubt. I gestured to Magot. 'Kill the light.'

She complied, and with a sense of mounting horror I realised that the darkness around us was no longer absolute. A faint luminescence was visible from up ahead, percolating into the tunnel; a sick, gangrenous hue which turned my stomach.

'Down that way.' There could be no doubt at all now: whatever secrets the necrons had buried down here were waiting for us, and there seemed no way to avoid confronting them.

'I'll go first,' Jurgen offered, swinging the bulk of the melta up into a firing position. 'This ought to clear a way for us if we need it.' Frankly I doubted it, where we were going no amount of firepower would make a difference, but the thought that he might at least buy us a little time was a comforting one, so I nodded.

'Good man,' I said, somehow finding the time to enjoy the expression of perplexity on Grifen and Magot's faces. Jurgen was an easy man to underestimate until you got to know him, and few people ever bothered. I tried to look calm, but I'd be surprised if I fooled them for a second; both women looked almost sick with apprehension, and knowing what awaited us I have no doubt my appearance was even worse. 'Ready?' I asked.

'Ready.' Grifen gave Magot's upper arm an encouraging squeeze, and the redheaded trooper nodded.

'As I'll ever be,' she confirmed, and snapped a fresh power cell into her lasgun, more for the comfort the familiar action afforded than because she needed to reload, I suspected.

We emerged into a vast shadowy cavern, full of machinery of strange design and incomprehensible function. Vast geometric slabs rose into the gloom about us, leaking that rancid illumination from vents and thick pipes of stuff which looked like glass but undoubtedly wasn't, suffusing the whole space with shadows and flat, directionless light. In the pale green glow we looked like corpses, long dead and rotting, and I found myself wondering how I had ever hoped to come through this unscathed.

We probed forward cautiously, scuttling from one deep shadow to the next like mice on a cathedral floor, our minds assailed almost to the point of physical nausea by the sense of wrongness everything exuded. This was no place for the living, that much was plain.

'Emperor protect us,' Grifen breathed. We had come through a doorway high enough to admit a Titan, hugging the walls of that vast chamber whose roof rose up beyond sight, and stopped short, our breath stilled by the prospect which awaited us. For those walls were composed of niches, each the height and width of a man, and in each stood a necron warrior, the sickly light gleaming from its metal surface. As we moved the shadows seemed to ripple across those blank, inhuman features, imparting expressions of utter malevolence.

For a moment we stood, transfixed by horror, until I realised with a surge of relief that this apparent motion was an illusion, and that each warrior stood utterly immobile.

'They're in stasis,' I breathed, as though saying the words aloud might alone be enough to wake them.

'Then they're harmless?' Magot asked, clearly not expecting the answer she wanted to hear.

'No,' I confirmed. 'Just dormant. If they were to wake...' I swept my eyes up and along that dizzying vista, seeing nothing but metal bodies receding to infinity, and gave up trying to calculate how many there were. Hundreds of thousands, at the very least, in this one chamber alone. I tried to envisage the havoc which such an army would wreak if it were ever unleashed upon the galaxy, and cringed inwardly at the scale of the carnage that would ensue. 'They have to be destroyed.'

'I think we'll need bigger guns,' Grifen said dryly, wrenching her eyes away from that all but infinite legion, and hefting her lasgun as though ready to fire. Nerves taut, we flicked our gazes left and right, alert for any sign of movement which might betray a threat, but the vast tomb seemed utterly empty apart from us.

'Then we'll get bigger guns,' I reassured her. Nothing in our inventory would even come close to doing the job, but an astropathic message to the nearest naval unit would bring a task force here within weeks, and a flotilla of battleships ought to be enough to level the continent. A couple of barrages from their lance batteries would be enough to excise this cancer, however deeply it was buried.

Of course the planet would be rendered uninhabitable for generations, but no one in their right mind would be willing to set foot here once the necron presence was known in any case, so the question was pretty moot. And if anyone were foolish enough to demur, I had no doubt that Amberley would bring the full force of the Inquisition to bear on the objectors the moment I appraised her of the situation.[54]

We pushed on cautiously, trying to keep the outer walls of the cavern in sight as much as we could; if there was indeed a way out of here I intended to find it. I simply refused to consider the alternative, that the ambull tunnel we'd come in by had been the only entrance left, as that way lay nothing but madness and despair.

'Movement!' Jurgen warned, melting into the shadows at the base of some vast mechanism which hummed away to itself oblivious of our presence. The rest of us went to ground too, finding what concealment we could. I crouched behind some metallic outgrowth which looked both regular and organic, and which felt warm to the touch. A moment later I saw it too, harsh angular shadows at first, presaging our initial sight of the necrons themselves as they rounded the corner of the metal canyon in the depths of which we lurked.

As the monsters themselves came into sight I could scarcely suppress a gasp of pure horror. I'd seen terrors enough on Interitus Prime, but these monstrous creations exceeded even those. At first I took them for ordinary necron warriors, fearsome enough in themselves as I knew only too well,

54 He was not wrong in this assumption.

but these were something far worse. Their fingers ended in long, gleaming blades, smeared with a substance which looked black in this pestilential light but which I had no doubt was truly red. Most terrifying of all, their metal torsos were hidden from view. For a second, as my appalled mind refused to acknowledge the sight before it, I found myself wondering why in the name of the Emperor these unfeeling automata would have donned clothing against the cold; then the realisation hit me, along with a spasm of nausea. They were draped in the flayed hides of the dead orks we'd found. (If one of them was wearing the ambull I failed to notice it, which believe me was quite easy to have done under the circumstances. If the Emperor Himself had tapped me on the shoulder at that moment it probably wouldn't have registered.)

'Golden Throne!' Grifen breathed, unable to contain her revulsion, and I froze, terrified that she might have been heard, but to my unutterable relief the hideous apparitions strode on oblivious,[55] with the inhumanly fluid motion I'd come to associate with all their forms, and after a moment they slipped away down a wide boulevard between arcane devices the size of a warehouse.'

'Should we follow them?' Jurgen asked, phlegmatic as always, as though he'd seen nothing more disturbing than my morning's messages, and I was instantly grateful for the sound of his voice in my comm-bead. It was a welcome touch of the ordinary which I seized on gratefully, and I felt my shattered sensibilities begin to stabilise. I glanced across at Grifen, who was breathing shallowly, her face pale in the ghastly light, and Magot, who was muttering prayers to the Emperor under her breath, all trace of her usual cockiness gone. If I didn't do something to snap them out of it fast they were likely to lose it completely, or go catatonic on me, and neither was an appealing prospect at the moment. And Jurgen's suggestion at least had the merit of keeping the monstrosities in front of us, so I nodded.

'Good a plan as any,' I conceded, then turned to Grifen. 'Sergeant. We're moving out.' To her credit she responded almost at once, turning slowly to face me with wide eyes into which I could see a measure of hard-fought self control begin to return.

'Right,' she confirmed, and reached across to take Magot by the arm again. The trooper failed to respond. Grifen increased the pressure a little, forcing her to take a single step to retain her balance, and after a moment she broke off her muttering to look at the sergeant. 'Mari. Mari, we're going now.'

'We shouldn't be here,' Magot said, an undercurrent of hysteria too close to the surface for my liking. 'We have to get out.'

'That's just what we're going to do,' I assured her, with more confidence than I felt. 'But we need your help to do it. We need you alert, all right?'

'Right. Yes.' She swallowed, incipient panic still bubbling under the surface, but fighting it now. She took a couple of deep breaths. 'I'm on it.'

---

55 Despite decades of intensive study by both the Ordo Xenos and the Adeptus Mechanicus the sensory mechanisms of the necrons remain a mystery. Sometimes they seem almost preternaturally able to detect an enemy, while at others, as in this instance, they overlook targets almost literally under their noses. At this time the Inquisition has no explanation to offer for this paradox; and if the Adeptus Mechanicus has one they're not sharing it.

'Good. Because we're relying on you,' I said, in my most sincere voice. 'If we stick together we'll make it, you have my word.'

'I won't let you down,' she said, a hair's breadth from hyperventilation, and Grifen patted her on the shoulder, a brief, supportive show of human contact.

'I know you won't,' she said kindly. 'So get your arse in gear and let's try to make it back before hell thaws out, OK?'

'OK, sarge.' Whatever the bond between them it seemed to outweigh the terror of the necrons, at least for the time being, so I signalled to Jurgen.

'Move out,' I said.

How long we followed those ghastly apparitions for I had no idea, but it seemed like an eternity, time shifting and blurring until it had no meaning, a phenomenon I'd also noticed in the catacombs of Interitus Prime. At times we passed through forests of glowing tubes, uncannily reminiscent of plague-ridden trees, and at others we scuttled along in the shadows of blank-sided metal slabs the size of a starship. At least twice we passed through more stasis chambers, as full of dormant horrors as the one we'd first encountered, but looking back I find my recollections hazy, as though my mind was simply refusing to accept what it was seeing (probably just as well for my sanity). Abruptly I became aware of a fluttering of motion in my peripheral vision, and dived for cover again, with a sibilant warning to my companions.

And just in time, too. A group of ordinary necron warriors appeared from a side passage, which, like the one we travelled, seemed more like a street than a gap between warehouse-sized machines, and, turning as one with a precision which would have left any Imperial Guard drill instructor worthy of the name seething with envy had they been there to witness it, followed their charnel brethren towards whatever destination awaited them.

As I looked closer I could see faint traces of combat damage on their shiny metal torsos, the dents and craters left by the weapons of the orks already fading as the metal seemed to flow together, healing their wounds by some sorcerous process I was at a loss to understand.[56]

From somewhere up ahead, at the end of that cyclopean thoroughfare, we could now discern a glow brighter than the rest but no less repellent in its hue, and something about the shape of the mechanisms surrounding us seemed vaguely familiar. I began to feel a formless sense of recognition, which hardened into certainty as we approached that vivid corpse-light, and the source came into view in the centre of a broad open space the size of a starport landing pad.

'It's an active warp portal,' I breathed, making the sign of the aquila by reflex. Not that I expected to invoke any additional protection by doing that, of course, but believe me, under those circumstances every little helps.

'Are you sure?' Grifen asked, clearly awestruck at the prospect. Feeling this wasn't the time for lengthy explanations I simply nodded.

---

56 An understanding which the Ordo Xenos would give a great deal to achieve, incidentally. It goes without saying that whatever inroads the Adeptus Mechanicus may have made into the problem, they're keeping to themselves.

'Absolutely,' I said.[57] Ahead of us the flayed ones, as I later learned the Inquisition classified the trophy-takers, stepped into that eldritch glow and vanished, no doubt to some hell hole elsewhere in the galaxy. I must admit to wondering, for a panic-stricken instant, if they were merely teleporting to some starship in orbit, but a moment's reflection was enough to reassure me that no vessel could have emerged from the warp early enough to be here already without registering on the *Pure of Heart's* sensor array long before we set out on our ambull hunt, what seemed like a lifetime ago now. (But which my chronometer stubbornly insisted had been less than a day.)[58] A moment later the warriors followed suit, evaporating from our sight like the vestiges of a nightmare on waking, and the warp portal dimmed back to the level of the ambient illumination.

'Emperor on Earth!' Magot said, a faint trace of her old bravado beginning to return. 'How's that for an exit?'

'It'll do me,' Grifen said grimly. 'Especially if it's permanent.'

'Maybe the greenskins were too much for them,' the redhead said hopefully.

'I wouldn't count on it,' I said. 'This was just a scouting party. They'll be back.'

'How soon?' Jurgen asked, his tone, as usual, no more than mildly curious. I shrugged.

'Emperor alone knows,' I said. 'Long enough for us to get the frak out of here I hope.'

Magot muttered in agreement. I stole a glance at the portal, which, though dormant now, seemed to pulsate with malevolence, as though ready to vomit a tidal wave of metal warriors across the planet at any moment. I thought briefly of trying to rig up something to destroy it from our remaining stock of explosives, but dismissed the idea at once. For one thing, if it was as robust as the equipment I'd seen on Interitus Prime we'd barely be able to scratch it with what little we still carried, and for another, the time it would take us to try would be far better spent looking for an exit. (If I'm honest, the thought of lingering for even a moment longer, certainly for the amount of time it would take to set the charges, was almost enough to start me running in panic; only the realisation that such a course would probably doom us prevented it.) And any attempt to interfere with the mechanisms here would most likely draw attention to us, which would be best avoided to say the least. Though many of the machines around us appeared to be powering down with the departure of the scouting party, which suggested we were alone down here now, there could be any number of alarms or sensors an explosion might trigger, and necron guards or their mechanical lackeys lurking in a corner somewhere prepared to deal with us if alerted to our presence.

'Which way, sir?' Jurgen asked, as though we were simply in the middle of a park somewhere looking for the quickest way back to the barracks. I

57 Cain is almost certainly the only human in the galaxy to have survived a transit through a necron warp portal, during the adventures on Interitus Prime to which he has previously referred. His account of the incident is elsewhere in the archive, and need not detain us further at this time.

58 Cain is generally imprecise about the passage of time in his memoirs; it's usually possible to infer roughly how much time has passed between the incidents he describes, but this is about as specific as he ever gets.

hesitated. My instincts hadn't entirely deserted me, however arcane our surroundings, and after a moment's thought I pointed off to our left.

'The mines should be over that way, if I don't miss my guess.' Jurgen had been down enough holes with me to trust my sense of direction underground, and even if he didn't it was close enough to an instruction for him to follow without thinking about it, so he nodded, and began to move off in that direction. Grifen and Magot began to drift after him so I picked up my pace and fell in between my aide and the two women, feeling a little more secure (if that were even remotely possible considering where we were) now that I had armed troopers on either side of me.

Despite my growing conviction that we were unlikely to meet any more of the metallic monstrosities unless we did something to attract their attention I wasn't about to let my guard down, you can depend on that. In fact the closer we came to safety, or at least the promise of it, the more paranoid I became, starting at every minute sound, real or imagined. I scanned every shadow we passed, increasingly certain that every crevice concealed a swarm of scuttling metal insects or that a vast arachnoid construct lurked above our heads, but every time my apprehensions proved to be groundless.

'I can see the cavern wall,' Jurgen voxed, and we picked up the pace a little, an unspoken agreement sparking among us to quit this hellish place as quickly as we could. I began to see patches of smooth finished stonework ahead of us through the tangle of incomprehensible mechanisms and tried to estimate how far away we were, but my sense of perspective was confused by the strange geometries around us and I was still taken by surprise when we slipped through a grove of pipe-work the breadth of trees and found ourselves up against naked bedrock.

'It's completely smooth,' Magot said, running her hand along it, a tint of wonder entering her voice. She was right, the surface was sheer as glass, and I found myself trying to picture how the work had been done with such precision. The only explanation I could come up with was sorcery of some kind, which fitted right in with everything else I'd seen here since we arrived. I glanced to the left and right, hoping to find some sign of a tunnel, but in this I was predictably disappointed.

'Which way now?' Grifen asked. I didn't have a clue, to be honest, but I had a vague memory of the projected run of the ambull tunnels on Logash's auspex being more numerous off towards the right of where I estimated us to be, so I gestured in that direction with all the authority I could muster.

'That way,' I said. 'And pray to the Emperor for a miracle.'

'This whole place is a miracle, is it not?' a new voice asked. I whirled, bringing up my laspistol, and froze an instant away from pulling the trigger. The speaker sounded vaguely familiar, and a moment later I caught sight of a human figure in an emerald robe (which was actually white, of course, out of that ghastly illumination), whose eyes flashed dazzlingly green as they caught the light. 'All praise the Omnissiah, whose bounty has been revealed to the worthy despite the worst efforts of the unbeliever.'

'Logash,' I said, not quite sure if he'd gone barmy or not. 'We thought you were dead.' But he wasn't, worse luck; the treacherous little weasel had given us the slip in the snowstorm and come scuttling back here as fast as he could. Emperor alone knows what he was hoping to achieve with a couple of tonnes of rubble sealing the entrance to the tomb, but fanatics are like that, no common sense at all, and our stray ambull had solved the problem for him anyway. Of course he took that as a sign from His Divine Majesty, or the clockwork parody they worship, that he was intended to get in here all along, and didn't he just crow about that.

'The Omnissiah guided my steps,' he said, 'and the barriers were thrown down ahead of me. All praise the Omnissiah!' His voice rose, and I cringed inwardly, certain that he'd attract unholy attention. I hushed him with a gesture, and turned to find Magot's lasgun pointed straight at him.

'How come the tinheads didn't get you?' she asked, her finger a little too tight on the trigger for my peace of mind. Frankly, the way I felt now she could have shot him and welcome, but the sound of gunfire would echo around here like an Earthshaker barrage and I wasn't prepared to risk it. I deflected her aim gently with a hand on the weapon's barrel. Logash didn't seem to take offence, though, beaming broadly at the question.

'The holy guardians failed to notice me, as I would expect given my unworthiness. There are mysteries here far beyond my abilities to fathom, but no doubt those of greater wisdom can commune with the machine spirits of this wondrous place.'

'Assuming we ever manage to get out of here to tell them,' Grifen chipped in sourly.

'The Omnissiah will provide, you can depend on it,' Logash said, completely siggy beyond a doubt. (Even though with tech-priests it's often hard to tell.) I found it hard to credit that the necrons had simply ignored him, but I suppose it was a vast complex and it wasn't entirely unfeasible that they had simply failed to notice him as they had the rest of us, even though I had no doubt that he'd been wandering around in the open gawping like some hick up from the sump on his first trip to a guilder trade station instead of hiding like anyone with a micron of sense would have done.

'They certainly noticed the orks,' Magot pointed out. Logash nodded eagerly.

'Vile desecrators of these holy precincts. The guardians cut them down as they deserved.' There he went again, I thought, with a tingle of unease. Anyone who could use the word 'holy' to refer to this chamber of horrors had clearly become unhinged. I suppose the sight of all that technology lying around had overloaded his brain or something.

'Well that's good,' I said, a little too heartily, and prodded him experimentally in the back. To my relief he fell into step beside me. 'It'll still be safe when we tell the others all about it.'

'Oh yes, we must do that.' Logash nodded eagerly, and pulled out his auspex. It's probably a measure of how far gone I was that I was actually glad to see it. The rest of us clustered around anxiously as he called up the image of the ambull tunnels we'd mapped before, the ones in red extrapolated from the ones we'd actually walked.

'Is there another tunnel near here?' Magot asked, raising herself onto her toes to peer over the tech-priest's arm. He nodded, pointing off to the left.

'There should be another ambull run about two hundred metres in that direction.' Luckily no one said anything to me, although to be fair there did seem to be some other tunnels a bit further away in the direction I'd originally chosen. This wasn't the time to stand on my pride, however, so I nodded and patted the tech-priest on his shoulders (which were hard under the robe, and thudded dully under the blows).

'Good,' I said. 'Then let's find it.'

Editorial Note:

Despite my understandable reluctance to resort to this secondary source again I'm afraid it's necessary to fill a gap in Cain's narrative, which breaks off at this point only to resume after some time has passed. No doubt he felt nothing of significance had occurred in the interim, despite the passage of several hours.

As ever, my apologies for the style (or lack of it), and my assurance that readers with a refined appreciation for the Gothic language are perfectly at liberty to skip it.

It is, however, mercifully short.

Extracted from *Like a Phoenix From the Flames: The Founding of the 597th*, by General Jenit Sulla (retired), 097.M42

Vital as the task with which we had been entrusted undeniably was, it could hardly be described as challenging. Once the miners had directed Captain Federer's sappers to the part of the workings where the flaws and stresses in the ice ensured our planned booby trap would work to best effect, there was little for us more practical soldiers to do other than fan out through the galleries to secure our perimeter against the remote possibility of infiltration by the orks. This we did, and although I have to admit that the task was a tedious one, to the credit of the women and men under my command they remained as alert after half the day had crawled by as they had at the commencement of our vigil.

This was disturbed at length by a vox message from deep in the lower galleries, so attenuated by the layers of intervening ice that I could scarcely discern it; and a moment's perusal of the tactical slate was enough to confirm what I'd already deduced. The source of the message was far deeper than the most far-flung of our patrols.

There could be only one explanation, and taking my command squad with me I made haste to respond, finding as we descended and the vox signal became clearer that my suspicions were correct; this was indeed a message from none other than Commissar Cain himself, returning with news of dire import, and demanding, as soon as communications became reliable enough, to be put through to Colonel Kasteen at once.

While my vox operator made haste to comply, his powerful backpack transmitter easily able to boost the tenuous signals of the commissar's comm-bead, I directed my troopers to his aid as rapidly as I could. Though the conversation had moved to a command frequency of a far higher level than those to which I, as a lowly lieutenant, had access, it was clear from the urgent tone of his voice that the tidings he brought were of such importance they must be disseminated as rapidly as possible.

The carrier wave was enough to lead us to the commissar's party, however, and I must confess to a moment of shock as I beheld the bedraggled survivors of what must surely have been a journey of epic endurance. Commissar Cain was, of course, the very picture of martial heroism he always presented, his bearing erect and eye steady, undaunted by whatever horrors he had faced, although his companions all too clearly showed the terrible ravages of the perils they'd fought their way through. The commissar's aide, in particular, looked as though he had come through hell, dishevelled in a way I had seldom seen in a trooper still living.[59] The other soldiers with him stumbled with exhaustion, horror written across their faces, and only the tech-priest at the rear of the party appeared to be in good spirits, doubtless because his augmentations had protected him from whatever had so afflicted the others.

'Help them,' I ordered, and my troopers made haste to obey, providing much-needed support for all.

It was only after I'd spoken that the commissar appeared to recognise me, looking in my direction for the first time, and I must confess to an overwhelming sensation of pride as he spoke my name, quite overcome at the confidence he so evidently had in my qualities as an officer.

'Sulla,' he said, in a voice clearly meant for no ears other than his own. 'Of course. Who else would it be?'

---

59 Sulla had clearly had little prior contact with Jurgen.

TWELVE

As you'll readily appreciate, all I wanted to do when we finally made it back to the refinery was eat, sleep, and grab a hot shower (preferably aboard the *Pure of Heart* while it was heading for deep space as fast as its engines would take it), but events were moving too fast to allow any such luxury. I managed to get rid of Sulla, who'd picked up my increasingly frantic attempts to contact the surface and been predictably unable to resist sticking her nose in, by asking her to make sure Grifen and Magot got to the medicae as fast as possible (which didn't hurt my reputation for taking care of the troops either, never a bad thing), and staggered off to meet Kasteen and Broklaw. At least I'd been able to get a tactical update from Sulla before she went, so I could concentrate on the immediate problem secure in the knowledge that the orks were still being held at our outer defensive line and the gargant was still too far away to open fire on us. For the time being at any rate.

'You look like hell,' the major said cheerfully as I entered the command post, but he held out a mug of tanna leaf tea as he said it, so I let him live.[60]

'You should see me from this side,' I told him, and dropped into a seat at the conference table. Now I was back in the warmth and relative safety of the refinery all the fear and accumulated fatigue of the last day or so bludgeoned me between the shoulder blades, and it was all I could do to keep my head from dropping onto the glossy wooden surface. As I tilted my head back to try and ease the tension in my neck something struck me as odd about the ceiling. 'Merciful Emperor! Did the greenskins get in here?' Broklaw followed the line of my gaze to the bolter holes filigreeing the plasterwork above his head.

'Just a small crowd control problem,' he said, smiling at some private joke. Well if he wasn't too bothered about it neither was I, and asking any more questions might complicate my life even further, so I returned my attention to the matter at hand.

'You should get some rest,' Kasteen said, looking at me with evident concern. I nodded.

'I should. Just as soon as we've dealt with the current situation.' I drank deeply, feeling the cobwebs lift a little from my mind as the tanna started to kick in. 'Did you get the old survey reports I asked for?'

60 Cain is, of course, joking here. Probably.

'Right here.' She skimmed a data-slate across the surface of the table. I glanced at it, but the charts and technical data meant nothing to me. 'Scrivener Quintus has been remarkably helpful.' Broklaw grinned and winked at me, but in my dazed state I hadn't a clue what he was getting at.

'What does it all mean in plain Gothic?' I asked. Kasteen shrugged.

'I ran it by a couple of the engineseers in the transport pool.' That had been a calculated risk; they were cogboys, of course, so their first duty would be to the Adeptus Mechanicus, but they were our cogboys, and had fought alongside the rest of us for long enough to feel at least as loyal to the regiment as to their tech-priest colleagues. So long as we didn't force them to pick sides they'd tell us what we needed to know, or so I hoped. 'It's not really their field, but they seem to think you're right. There are other deposits of refinable ice on Simia Orichalcae much richer than this one.'

'Then why build the refinery here?' Broklaw asked. I shrugged.

'The magos would undoubtedly reel off a dozen different reasons why this particular deposit was easiest to process, or the topography of the valley made construction simpler, or why it was the will of this clockwork Emperor of theirs. He might even believe it himself. But if it smells like a sump rat and it squeaks like a sump rat...'

'Someone in the Adeptus Mechanicus knew that tomb was there,' Broklaw said. 'Someone placed highly enough to make sure the mine was put on top of it.'[61]

'But why?' Kasteen was aghast. 'Surely they wouldn't be mad enough to think they could take on a planet full of necrons?'

I thought of Logash, who'd been driven all but insane by the desire to examine such a rich cache of archeotech, and tried to picture a cabal of high-ranking tech-priests pulling strings to set up the mine over so tempting a prize. It wasn't hard to do at all. If they even suspected such a thing existed they'd take any risk, however great, to get their sticky little mechadendrites on it. I'd learned that much at least from the Interitus Prime debacle.

'They probably assumed the tomb was abandoned,' I said. It wouldn't be the first time they'd made that mistake either, as I knew to my cost.

'The real point,' Broklaw said, 'is how many of the tech-priests here we can trust. Whether or not there was a conspiracy to start with, they all know what's down the bloody hole now.'

That much was true. If I'd had my wits about me I'd have got Sulla to detain Logash as soon as she brought us back up to the surface, but of course she ignored him (only a civilian, and a tech-priest to boot), so by the time I realised what was going on he'd already disappeared. No doubt filling Ernulph's head with visions of sorcerous bounty unseen in millennia even as we spoke.

'None of them,' I said. My head was hurting, the grim, relentless migraine that goes with utter fatigue, and I wasn't looking forward to the next few hours at all.

* * *

61 The identification of those responsible for the decision wasn't difficult, but, as Cain surmised, hard evidence of conspiracy rather than an unfortunate coincidence continues to be elusive. Anyone with information which may prove helpful in resolving this matter will find an interested listener in Inquisitor Kuryakin of the Ordo Hereticus.

I got through them, of course, due in no small part to Jurgen's skill at fending off unwanted interruptions. By the time Kasteen called a full meeting to discuss the situation I'd managed to grab a little sleep, a lot of recaff, and a hot meal (just soylens viridians again, but for some reason I'd gone off the idea of retrieving an ambull steak), and was beginning to feel tolerably human once more. A bath would have topped things off nicely but sleep was even more urgent, and I just had to resign myself to the fact that I was probably beginning to smell as bad as my aide. Jurgen, naturally, looked no worse than usual, probably as a result of a catnap somewhere. He accompanied me, partly to underline my status, and partly to take the blame if my suspicions about my personal freshness were correct.

Of course I'd done a lot more than take care of my personal needs. Even before I staggered off to the mess hall and bed, in that order, I'd roused the refinery's resident astropath and sent the most urgently-worded communiqué I could to both the lord general's office and the rather more guarded channels Amberley had suggested I use if I ever came across something which merited Inquisitorial attention. Well, a tomb full of necrons definitely qualified if anything did, but to my vague disappointment (though complete lack of surprise given the time lag inherent in even the most urgent interstellar communications) neither had responded by the time the briefing was scheduled to start.

The conference room was the most crowded I'd ever seen it as I entered the command post, the babble of conflicting voices almost loud enough to drown out the muffled explosions from the battlefield beyond the large picture window. My eye was drawn to it at once, searching for some sign of the gargant, and despite the ever-present snow whirling against the glass like a disconnected pict screen I was sure I could make out a dark, hulking shape against the mountains in the distance which hadn't been there before. Merciful Emperor, it was almost close enough to open fire on us, a handful of kilometres distant now. I thought of the havoc the massive belly gun would surely wreak, blowing apart buildings and storage tanks alike, and shuddered. Of course the greenskins would be trying to take the installation relatively intact, or at least the vast reserves of refined promethium it contained, so it couldn't really do its worst, but no one ever said orks were rational.[62] If the ork princeps, or whatever he called himself,[63] got over-excited this whole affair could end very loudly and suddenly.

'Commissar.' Colonel Kasteen looked up from her place at the head of the table, and indicated a vacant seat next to her. I dropped into it gratefully, while Jurgen went to find me some more tanna tea, and exchanged a nod of greeting with Broklaw who was seated on the other side of her. 'I'm pleased to see you looking so much better.'

'Thank you,' I said, as Jurgen materialised behind me with a large steaming bowl of the fragrant liquid. I glanced up and down the table, seeing all

62 Actually there have been a few xenologists who argued precisely this, claiming their actions make perfect sense in the context of their own barbarous society, but such views are generally considered eccentric at best.

63 Probably some variation of 'Nob' or 'Boss,' which appear to be the only major signifiers of rank and status their language possesses.

the faces I remembered from the previous meeting, and a lot more besides. 'Shall we get started?'

'By all means.' She nodded to Broklaw, who cleared his throat loudly, and to my astonishment everyone shut up and looked at him expectantly.

'Thank you for coming at such short notice,' he began, with barely a trace of sarcasm. 'As most of you are no doubt aware, the commissar's scouting trip has uncovered a much greater problem than the orks.' At this point he glanced meaningfully at the little knot of tech-priests clustered around Ernulph. Logash was sitting next to him, still wearing the imbecilic grin he'd been sporting ever since we found him in the tomb below our feet. I'd invoked my commissarial privileges to unlock some highly classified files, so that everyone who needed to would know precisely what we were up against, but now the seed of suspicion had been planted it was hard not to wonder if the magos had known most of it already.

'How sure are we that it's a problem?' Ernulph asked, an edge of eager acquisitiveness in his voice. 'If the necrons are in stasis we can surely concentrate our efforts on repelling the immediate threat.' Meaning let the poor bloody Guardsmen keep the orks off their backs while he and his cronies pillaged the tomb, of course.

'They are the immediate threat,' I said, as mildly as I could. I sipped my bowl of tea while the sudden flare of apprehension in my gut at the very thought of those mechanical killers subsided. 'If we were up to our armpits in orks, with a side order of kroot and eldar backing them up, I'd turn my back on the lot of them to take out a single necron. I've fought them before, and they're the biggest single menace in the entire galaxy.'

'Surely you exaggerate,' Pryke said, looking at me sternly, as though I was making the whole thing up. 'I've accessed the records of previous encounters with these... whatever they are, and reports of them are practically non-existent.'

'That's because they hardly ever leave any survivors to report anything,' I rejoined, feeling my hand begin to tremble as old memories came rushing back. A small gobbet of tea escaped the bowl to pool on the polished wooden tabletop, and Jurgen leant forward to mop up the spillage with a handkerchief that left the surface even grubbier than before. 'Everything else in the galaxy fights for a reason, whether it's for territory, honour, or souls for the dark gods.' I heard a satisfying intake of breath at that, having deliberately invoked the most shocking image I could think of to wrong-foot any objectors. 'Necrons don't. They exist purely to kill, and they know we're here now.'

'Are you sure about that?' Ernulph persisted. 'They certainly know about the greenskins. But you escaped unscathed, I gather.' He glanced at Logash for confirmation.

'The Omnissiah guided our steps,' the young tech-priest declared, 'so that we might claim the bounty prepared for us.'

'The only preparation you'll get from the necrons is if one of them fancies your skin as a waistcoat,' I said, having the slight satisfaction of seeing him blench for a moment before his fanaticism kicked in again.

'The commissar is convinced that the party he encountered were simply scouts,' Kasteen said, determined to keep the business of the meeting moving. 'And while the warp portal remains active down there we can expect a full-scale incursion at any time.'

'What I don't understand,' Morel declared, cutting through the subsequent babble of consternation, 'is why now? They've been down there for Emperor knows how long. What got them so stirred up all of a sudden?'

'I think I can answer that.' As everyone turned to look at him, Quintus cleared his throat a little nervously.

'If you can make any sense of this mess I'd like to hear it,' Kasteen prompted after a moment. Quintus flushed even more, and stood, grinning nervously at the colonel. He produced a data-slate from the recesses of his robes, and projected a page onto the main hololith, which still jumped annoyingly as I tried to make sense of what I was looking at.

'These are the sensor logs from the traffic control system,' he began, before Ernulph interrupted.

'Those are technical documents which fall under the purview of the Adeptus Mechanicus. You have no business dabbling in theological matters!'

'I think you'll find,' Pryke rejoined, equally forcefully, 'that they are archive material, and therefore clearly the responsibility of the Administratum.'

'Their care and maintenance, possibly,' Ernulph persisted. 'But interpretation and consultation are the business of those appointed to commune with the numinous, not some jumped-up inky-fingered quill-pusher!' Pryke seemed on the verge of responding in equally trenchant tones, when Broklaw cleared his throat again. The room went suddenly quiet.

'Might I remind everyone,' Kasteen said mildly, 'that I'm in charge here and I decide who does what. And I want to hear what the scrivener has to say. Are there any objections?' Surprisingly there weren't, which might have had something to do with the way both officers had a hand resting casually on the butts of their bolt pistols; I began to suspect they'd been hanging around me a bit too much lately. She smiled at Quintus, who looked quite flustered for a moment, and nodded judiciously. 'Please continue.'

'Ah. Right. Yes.' Quintus cleared his throat again, and pointed to something in the middle of the display which looked like a stain of ackenberry juice. 'This is the flare of warp energy released when the greenskins' space hulk emerged into the materium.' Ernulph harrumphed disapprovingly at the young scrivener's use of the technical term, and a faint, fleeting grin appeared on Quintus' face just long enough for me to realise he'd done it on purpose to irritate the magos. 'And there was another one almost as strong when it dropped back into the warp.'

'We already knew this,' Ernulph said dismissively. 'Our instrumentation was practically overloaded. It's how we knew they were coming in the first place.'

'Precisely,' Quintus said. 'And because of the strength of the flare we missed that.' He pointed to something else with an air of triumph, undermined a little by the almost total inability of anyone else at the table to see what was hidden by his finger.

'Could you magnify it a little?' Kasteen asked. Quintus flushed, and complied, revealing another, almost imperceptible ackenberry stain. A murmur of voices rippled around the table, and Ernulph at least had the grace to look surprised.

'We missed that,' he admitted grudgingly.

'Quite understandably,' Kasteen assured him diplomatically. 'But can you tell us what it is?'

'I can guess,' the magos admitted reluctantly. Then he grimaced, as though biting into a bitterroot pasty someone had assured him was filled with sweet-briar,[64] and gestured to Quintus to continue. 'But I'm sure the young man has worked it out already. He seems quite bright for a bureaucrat, and we'd never have noticed this anomaly at all if it wasn't for his diligence.' I suppose for all his bluster he was a fair-minded man, but it must have pained him to swallow his pride like that. His colleagues looked positively dyspeptic, and Pryke was gazing at him in open-mouthed astonishment. Kasteen just nodded coolly.

'Thank you magos. I'm glad to see we all seem to be on the same side at last. Quintus?' For some reason the young scrivener became flustered all over again as she looked in his direction, and stuttered for a moment before resuming.

'Well it's outside my realm of expertise, as the magos pointed out, but it seems logical to assume that the flare of warp energy somehow activated the dormant portal in the tomb.' Ernulph was nodding in agreement.

'That would be my interpretation,' he conceded.

'Of course!' Logash butted in with the single-minded enthusiasm of the obsessive. 'That's how the ambulls got down there! They came through the portal, and dug their way out of the tomb! That explains the anomalous habitat...' He trailed off, suddenly conscious of how very much nobody else in the meeting cared.

'And somehow the necrons noticed that it had reactivated.' Broklaw nodded. 'So they sent a scouting party through. That makes sense.'

'But where from, though?' Pryke asked, anxious to establish that her department was fully involved in things.

'Could be anywhere in the galaxy,' I said. 'Somewhere with ambulls, by the look of it, but that doesn't narrow it down much.'[65]

'That's not really the question at the moment,' Kasteen said, dragging everyone back to the point. 'What we need to decide now is what we do about them.'

'There's only one thing we can do,' I said, as calmly and decisively as I could. 'Evacuate the planet, while we still have enough time to get clear.'

'Evacuate?' Kasteen echoed, clearly stunned. I nodded, conscious that I was risking my whole fraudulent reputation, but that it was precisely that reputation for heroism which might just do the trick now. I adopted an expression of barely-contained frustration.

'I know how you feel. I've never run from a fight yet,' (which was not entirely

64 Cain was evidently still hungry at this point, judging by the sudden flurry of culinary metaphors; hardly surprising given the amount of energy he had expended over the last couple of days.

65 Indeed not. As yet the world or worlds at the other end of the necron portal remain unidentified, despite the best efforts of the Ordo Xenos.

true, of course, but no one needed to know that), 'and it goes against the grain to start now. But there are wider issues at stake here. The necrons in that tomb outnumber us by hundreds to one, and that's assuming we could disengage from the orks cleanly enough to take them on in a stand-up fight.'

'They'd still know they'd been in a scrap,' Kasteen said grimly. I nodded again.

'I don't doubt the fighting spirit of anyone in the regiment. But if we stand and fight now we will all die. That's a plain, simple fact. They'll overrun us in a matter of hours.' More like minutes, if the ones I'd seen before were anything to go by, but if I told her that she'd never believe me. 'And that's just the start.'

'The portal,' Kasteen said, the coin dropping. I nodded again.

'Hundreds of thousands of them would be let loose on the galaxy. We simply can't allow that to happen.' I paused for a moment, letting the implications sink in. 'We have to call in the Navy to sterilise the whole site from orbit. It's the only way to be sure.'

'You can't do that!' Pryke and Ernulph both shouted at the same time, then broke off to boggle at one another, completely taken aback to find themselves in agreement for once.

'I can, and will,' I contradicted them. 'This facility is under martial law, which means the commissariat is the final arbiter of what can or cannot be done.'

'Have you any idea of the economic value of this installation?' Pryke asked, recovering first.

'None at all, and I care even less,' I said. 'So far as I'm concerned it's not worth the life of one soldier.' The soldier I had in mind being me, of course.

'But the archeotech!' Ernulph spluttered. 'Think of the knowledge, the spiritual advancement of mankind that you'd be sacrificing...'

'All we'd be sacrificing if we left that tomb intact is our lives,' I rejoined. 'Not to mention the millions of others who'd be slaughtered if the necrons down there revive and escape through the portal.'

'But they're in stasis,' the magos persisted. 'While they're dormant we can safely examine...'

'We don't know that,' Kasteen cut in. 'For all we know they're up and about by now. And even if they aren't, their friends could be flocking through the portal from somewhere else. We simply can't risk sending anyone back down there, and that's final.'

'On the contrary,' Ernulph replied. 'I don't think you can risk not sending anyone back.'

'Explain,' Kasteen said, although in a sudden agony of panic I realised what the magos was driving at. The worst of it was that he was right, damn it, and the spasming of my bowels told me who was by far the most likely candidate to get stuck with the job.

'You said it yourself,' he said triumphantly. 'The portal's still active. Even if you called in your naval strike it would be left intact and functioning for months before a flotilla could get here, possibly even years. The necrons would be long gone.'

'Emperor's bowels, he's right.' Broklaw looked more shaken than I'd ever seen him. 'We have to blow the portal before we pull out.'

I felt every pair of eyes at the table lock on to me like the targeting auspex of a hydra battery. The air grew tense with expectation, while my mind whirled frantically, trying to find some plausible reason why this was a truly terrible idea. But inspiration had, for once, deserted me. At length I nodded, my mouth dry.

'I can't see any alternative.'

'Neither can I.' Kasteen turned to me, solemnly pronouncing what I truly believed to be my death sentence. 'Can you lead a team back down to the tomb, commissar?'

THIRTEEN

Of course I couldn't refuse, could I? Not in front of all those people. I'd been neatly impaled on my own rhetoric, and pulling out at this stage would have ruined the reputation I didn't deserve. More to the point it would have lost me the respect of the troops, which was probably the only thing I had left capable of preserving my miserable hide. So I made a few appropriately modest comments about appreciating everybody's confidence and hoping I wouldn't let them down before sinking into a torpor of absolute terror which, as luck would have it, was generally mistaken for fatigue.

As a result the rest of the meeting went by in a blur so far as I was concerned, and if anything else of consequence was discussed I must have missed it.[66] I did rouse myself for long enough to listen to a progress report into some suicidal scheme for disabling the gargant, which Broklaw assured everyone would be effective if the orks in command of it were spectacularly stupid enough to blunder into an obvious trap, but given the intelligence of the ones I'd encountered before in my chequered career this seemed like a safe enough bet. Other than that I took no interest in anything apart from my bowl of tea, which Jurgen, attentive as ever, refilled at intervals.

So it came as something of a surprise when all the civilians stood up and filed out, the quill-pushers and cogboys predictably butting heads at the door over which of them had precedence while Morel and the miners guild delegation sailed serenely past them, and finally the room fell quiet.

'That went well,' Broklaw said, clearly not meaning it. Kasteen nodded.

'They've agreed to the evacuation, anyway. Not that they had a choice, but at least we won't have to waste any manpower herding them onto the shuttles at gunpoint.'

'Don't count on it,' I said. 'Once they've had time to think it over the tech-priests probably won't go without a fight.' At least most of the miners and Administratum staff had already gone, which only left a couple of hundred civilians still planetside. A couple of shuttle flights, no more than that, although lifting the regiment would be a lot more time consuming when the time came for us to pull out.

'Then they can stay and fight the necrons,' Kasteen said. 'I'm not putting any of our people at risk if they start playing silly frakkers.'

---

66 Quintus's minutes of the meeting are singularly unhelpful in filling in this gap, concerned as they are chiefly with the way the overhead lighting struck highlights from Kasteen's hair.

'Glad to hear it,' I said. Not that it would make any difference to me, with my molecules scrambled by a necron gauss gun. And that would be if I was lucky; I thought of the other monstrosities in their coats of ork hide, and hoped fervently never to meet them again. I turned my thoughts in more productive directions with an effort. I wasn't dead yet, and by the Emperor I didn't intend to be if I could find the slightest chance of weaselling out of the suicidal assignment I'd backed myself into. 'What's the tactical situation?' We hadn't discussed that in front of the civvies, of course, they were best being jollied along with vague generalities, and a resolute avoidance of phrases like 'we're frakked' which would only upset them.

By way of an answer Kasteen activated the hololith again and Mazarin appeared at her station on the bridge of the *Pure of Heart*, bobbing slightly in the current from a nearby air vent.

'None of this makes a lot of sense to me,' she admitted cheerfully. 'But you're the soldiers. What do you think?' Kasteen, Broklaw and I stared at the latest sensor downloads from the orbiting starship. The ork advance had unmistakably faltered, breaking against our battle line, and pulling back in places to cluster on their left flank. Broklaw frowned.

'The gargant's veered off,' he said. Well, thank the Emperor for that, I thought, at least I wouldn't have to worry about the booby trap they'd laid for it bringing the whole mine in on top of me while I was down there in the dark facing the necrons again... My hands began to tremble slightly as I thought about that, so I stuffed them into the pockets of my greatcoat and studied the hololith grimly. Something about the redistribution of the ork forces was nagging at my subconscious, and I felt my scalp prickling as I finally realised what it was.

'The tunnel entrance we found was about here,' I said, indicating a point on the opposite flank of the mountain from the valley we were so successfully defending. The bulk of the greenskin forces were moving in that direction, the gargant's unexpected diversion merely a part of the general drift. And there was only one obvious reason why the orks' attention would have been distracted from the ongoing battle with us.

'Frakking warp!' Kasteen breathed, coming to the same conclusion. 'The tinheads are attacking the greenies!'

'In some force, too, judging by the number of reinforcements moving up,' Broklaw said, studying the display in more detail. That wasn't necessarily the case, of course, orks will gravitate naturally to wherever they expect the fighting to be fiercest, but it was certainly suggestive.

'Perfect!' Kasteen said, to my absolute astonishment. 'You know what this means?'

'Nope.' Mazarin shrugged in the corner of the hololith, her image shrunk to the size of my hand. 'Not my department.' But of course Kasteen hadn't been talking to her in any case.

'It means the bloody necrons are awake!' I said, a strange mixture of terror and relief dancing down my spine. 'We haven't a hope in hell of getting to the portal now.' I tried to feign disappointment, while wondering how best to ensure I was on the first shuttle up to the freighter.

'Not necessarily,' Mazarin chipped in, and the flare of hope in my chest withered and died. Luckily it was only her image in the room with us, or I'd probably have throttled her with my bare hands. (Not that it would have done me much good, I suppose, given the amount of metal she seemed to have in what was left of her body.) 'If I'm reading these energy spikes right the portal's being activated roughly every seventeen minutes.'

'Which means what, exactly?' Kasteen asked, taking far too much interest in what the bisected woman had to say for my liking. Mazarin shrugged, unless it was the air conditioning behind her kicking up another notch and bouncing her around.

'The necrons here are probably still in stasis. The ones fighting the orks are being shipped in from somewhere else.'

'Securing the tomb before they wake the others,' Broklaw said. Kasteen nodded.

'Sounds plausible.' She looked across at me. 'And they still have no idea we're behind them. You can be in and out before they even know you're there.'

'Lucky me,' I said, clenching my fists in my pockets until the nails drew blood.

'I'm not going to lie to you,' I said. I felt a vague sense of disconnectedness after that, the reason for which continued to elude me for a while, until I realised that contrary to the habit of a lifetime the subsequent statement was actually true. The harsh arc luminators of the main staging area just inside the mouth of the mine flattened the colours of the scattered equipment around us, including the power lifter against which I leaned in what I hoped was a casual manner rather than revealing the weakness of my knees. 'Our chances of coming back from this assignment are practically non-existent. But it's also no exaggeration to say that the lives of everyone else on the planet, not to mention uncountable others, hang on whether we succeed or not.' I flicked my eyes along the impassive faces in front of me. Not one of them blinked. I ploughed on, feeling vaguely wrong-footed. 'I think you're the best team for the job, which is why I asked for you. But I'll only take willing volunteers. If anyone wants to pull out you have my word there won't be any disciplinary action taken or a word about it on any of your records.' Because I'd be too busy being dead to worry about it... I forced the thought away.

'We're up to it,' the storm trooper sergeant said, the unlit cheroot in the corner of his mouth waggling disconcertingly as he spoke. I gathered that it was some kind of tradition in his squad that he wouldn't light it until the mission was completed. The little knot of men behind him nodded in silent agreement. Not one of them broke ranks, which I would have found astonishing had I not spent a couple of hours combing the records for the most aggressive and disciplined squad in the entire regiment.

And Sergeant Welard and his squad were it: old school storm troopers (quite literally, they'd been together since the Schola Progenium assessors back on Valhalla had decided they were natural born cannon fodder). They were, accordingly, one of the few teams to have remained single-sex following the amalgamation of the two former regiments which now made up the 597th, since there was no point rotating in replacements for the casualties they'd taken on Corania[67] and wherever else they'd fought before. Schola-raised storm trooper squads generally fight better than most because they've been together so long and know each other so well that they share an instinctive rapport no outsider can ever fully share, but the downside of that is that once their numbers drop below a handful they become pretty much useless, and I've never understood why the Guard persists with the tradition.[68] Right now though, men who'd follow orders without thinking were precisely what I needed, and Welard and his team fit the bill nicely.

'I'm pleased to see my confidence wasn't misplaced,' I said. Apart from Welard there were five regular troopers left out of the original ten, so they were on the verge of falling below the critical threshold at which they would cease to be an effective fighting unit. Nevertheless, they would do. Numbers wouldn't help us on this mission, our only hope was to move fast and stealthily, and that, I knew, was something they were bound to be good at. (In the constant round of rivalries and practical joke playing between the different factions in my days at the schola the storm trooper cadets were by far the most adept at sneaking into the other dorms and common rooms to make mischief, and always set the most inventive booby traps, although I still maintain we had the edge over them on the scrumball pitch. In fact the only team that ever regularly beat the commissar cadets were the novitiates of the Adepta Sororitas, who seemed to think the point of the game was sending the greatest number of opponents they could to the sanitorium rather than scoring goals.)

'We'll get the job done,' Welard said, moving the cheroot to the opposite corner of his mouth, and the quintet behind him nodded in unison. Their silence was unnerving, but I suppose it was a natural consequence of the rapport they shared. Not a word or a gesture was wasted, to the point where, swathed in their greatcoats and hats, their faces partly obscured, they seemed almost as emotionless as servitors. Or the necrons themselves. An aura of almost palpable lethality played about them, which I began to feel almost comforted by, until I remembered the odds stacked against us.

'Any questions?' I asked. Answer came there none, so I drew myself up, straightened my cap, and tried to sound confident. 'Good. Then let's go.'

The evacuation was well under way as we set out for the lower levels, a steady flow of miners, Administratum drones and tech-priests walking towards the landing pads with the tense not-quite trot of barely-contained panic, lasgun-wielding troopers guarding the tunnels they thronged through. We strode against the tide, which parted almost miraculously in front of us, each step further from safety seeming like walking on knives to me. A babble of voices surrounded us like syrup, battering the eardrums but overlapping so much that individual words and phrases were indistinguishable.

---

67 The system where a tyranid attack had decimated the imperial defenders, necessitating the amalgamation of the 296th and 301st to create the 597th in the first place.

68 Because the real reason for the practice is to provide properly indoctrinated foot soldiers for the Inquisition. Of course fewer than five per cent reach the exacting standards required, leaving the ones who don't make the grade to be palmed off on the Guard.

'Comms check,' I said, more to distract myself than anything, and Welard and the other storm troopers sounded off one by one, although truth to tell, and I ought to be ashamed of it, I was so busy battling my own apprehension that none of their names registered with me. Everyone's comm-bead seemed to be working, though, so I nodded briskly. 'Very good.'

'General order.' Kasteen's voice cut in. 'Anyone in sight of Magos Ernulph report now.' There was an irritable pause, broken only by a faint hiss of static. 'Anyone with an idea of his whereabouts?' Another pause. 'Anyone seeing him, report at once.'

Great. It seemed the tech-priests weren't about to leave their prize behind after all, and were going into hiding until we'd left. Just so long as they stayed out of our way, though, it wasn't my problem.

The passageways we strode through were getting narrower now, the air cooler as we entered the mine workings themselves, and I told myself the shivering which seemed to be gripping my body was simply a result of the falling temperatures. Before long the walls around us were filmed with ice, and shortly after that there was nothing for the ice to coat; we were in the mine itself again.

Ahead of us a cavern opened out, harsh with the glare of luminators mounted on poles around its perimeter, the dark mouths of the main tunnels puncturing the walls at intervals. Equipment and storage crates littered the floor, and I recognised it as one of the main utility areas we'd passed through on our ambull hunt, little guessing the horrors we'd find in the depths below. Beyond this point our journey would truly begin.

'Movement.' One of the troopers raised his hellgun, and the others melted into the industrial detritus around us with breathtaking speed, leaving me feeling uncomfortably exposed. A lone figure was lurking at the mouth of the tunnel ahead of us, half hidden in the gloom beyond. After a moment to recover my composure, as the rational part of my mind kicked in to remind me that orks or necrons wouldn't be bothering with concealment, I strode forward unconcerned expecting to find some stray miner or tech-priest finishing off a last-minute job prior to joining the evacuation. As I got closer to the solitary figure I felt my spirits inexplicably lifting as I caught the faint whiff of a familiar odour.

'Jurgen,' I called out. 'What the frak are you doing here?' My aide stepped fully into view, and the storm troopers emerged from the cover they'd taken, looking mildly sheepish. 'I thought you were stowing our kit on the shuttle.'

'All taken care of, sir.' He produced a thermal flask. 'I thought you might like a bit of tea for later. And a sandwich.' He burrowed in one of his pockets for a moment. 'It's in here somewhere...'

'I see,' I said, silencing the barely audible snickering from a couple of the storm troopers behind me with a quick glance before turning back to Jurgen again. 'And the melta?' He shrugged, the heavy weapon slung across his back shifting as his shoulders moved.

'I couldn't let you carry your own provisions, sir. Wouldn't be fitting.'

'Quite,' I said, astonished yet again at the depth of his loyalty. For the first time I began to feel that I might actually get out of this ludicrous expedition in one piece after all. 'I suppose you'd better come with us, then.'

'Very good, sir.' He saluted as smartly as he ever did, which wasn't very to be honest, but more than made up for that in enthusiasm, and fell into step beside me. I motioned Welard and his men to the front and we set off into the darkness, towards the terrors which lay in wait for us in the frozen depths below.

Editorial Note:

As the attentive reader will readily appreciate, the overall tactical situation was now becoming increasingly complex. The unexpected necron attack on the orkish flank had thrown the greenskins into disarray, but, typically, they responded with the single-minded aggression of their kind, flinging themselves against this new and deadly foe with what can only be described as enthusiasm. The resulting carnage can barely be imagined.

However, the lessening of the pressure on the beleaguered Valhallans was undoubtedly of great benefit, enabling the evacuation of the Imperial forces to take place relatively unhindered, especially as most of the front-line units had already been given their orders to disengage in preparation for luring the gargant into the now abandoned booby trap.

As to the fate of this formidable war machine, the following extract from Sulla's memoirs may prove illuminating despite her best efforts to render it unreadable.

Extracted from *Like a Phoenix From the Flames: The Founding of the 597th*, by General Jenit Sulla (retired), 097.M42

Notwithstanding the flood of rumours which had swept the regiment, most of them contradictory, but which all agreed in the main particular that Commissar Cain had discovered some new and potent threat in the bowels of the mine, I held fast to my duty and resumed my post at the front line. Whatever the truth of the matter I had my orders, and as a loyal officer that was enough for me. No doubt those better placed to evaluate the intelligence the commissar had so heroically gathered would inform us of whatever we needed to know to meet and overcome this latest vile stain on His Glorious Majesty's blessed dominions in the fullness of time, or so I told my subordinates, and until such information was furnished wild speculation about daemons, tyranids, or walking metal statues was merely a waste of time. This last flight of fantasy would, of course, turn out to have more than a grain of truth in it, but in the closing years of the forty-first millennium, with the true horror of the necron menace still unknown to all but a few, such talk seemed naught but the most febrile of fantasies.

My platoon had resumed its position in the forward line, with strict instructions to fall back at the specified time to draw the gargant into our carefully laid trap, and we had been engaging the main bulk of the greenskin army with a gratifying amount of success. So much so, in fact, that I began to fear that we were thinning them out too quickly, and that we would be forced to engage the towering war machine ourselves before the time came to disengage. The shadow of that grim colossus was falling across us as we gazed in awe at it, the shrieks of thousands of tonnes of unlubricated metal sliding across one another as it tottered forward on unfeasibly stubby-looking legs setting the teeth of every woman and man among us on edge, and I found myself comparing it most unfavourably to the swift darting elegance of the eldar walkers and the majestic nobility of our own blessed Titans.[69]

I was on the verge of ordering those fortunate enough to be manning the forward trenches to engage those members of its crew who could quite clearly be discerned scurrying about on the main hull when the vast cannon nestled in the construct's belly spoke, the concussion sufficient to drive the breath from our lungs and cause cracks to appear in our stout fortifications even at this distance. I turned my head, expecting to see the most grievous havoc wreaked among the precious buildings of the refinery, only to see instead the distant gout of a vast explosion somewhere among the slopes of the mountains surrounding this vital outpost of the Imperium.

'It's veering off!' my communications specialist yelled, angling his head so I could read his lips, for the awesome sound of that titanic explosion had left my ears still ringing, and to my astonishment I beheld the truth of his words. It had clearly faltered, almost on the point of engaging our forward line, and was now turning ponderously towards the looming peaks it had so inexplicably attacked.

At that moment we received our orders to withdraw, so I cannot be sure of what I witnessed next, seeing it as I did at an ever-increasing distance in short, snatched glances over my shoulder as we ran, and through a curtain of falling snow. However, it seemed to me that the terrifying construct was surrounded by small structures, no higher than its knee, which had appeared by sorceries so arcane I was at a loss to explain them. Blank metal pyramids they were, dully reflective, and surrounded by a crackle of lightning which blurred their outline still further; sorcerous lightning without a doubt, for it lashed forth to scourge the hull of that mountain of metal, striking sparks so bright they hurt to look upon. Chunks of metal larger than Chimeras fell lazily to the snow, and the burning bodies of its luckless crew pattered down around them, so that I cannot for the life of me conceive how it could ever have prevailed. But whether it did or not I cannot truly answer, for the snow whirled in around that epic confrontation, and I saw no more.

69 Most unlikely, as at this point in her career she had yet to see either. Unless you count holo-picts, of course.

FOURTEEN

One thing I have to say for Welard and his storm troopers, they were as fast and stealthy as I could have wished for. Jurgen and I had to work hard at keeping up with them even though they advanced as cautiously as though the enemy were already in plain sight. Two or three of them covered the tunnel ahead while the others darted forward to conceal themselves in crevices or patches of shadow before taking up the duties of guardians themselves to allow their comrades to move forward in their turn. They did all of this with an eerie precision apparently unhindered by the bulk of the melta bombs they carried, communicating only by hand signals and eschewing the use of the comm-beads, for which I was grateful, starting in dread at every superfluous sound which might call attention to us. But as we hurried on, following the route which had etched itself indelibly on the synapses responsible for my ability to navigate underground, we saw none of the signs I so dreaded. No gleam of metal in the darkness ahead, no green charnel glow forewarning us of the presence of death incarnate.

We advanced in semi-darkness, our luminators shrouded, so that the dazzling highlights which had been struck from the ice surrounding us on my previous trip into the depths were almost entirely absent. Now, instead of the refulgent background glow I'd grown used to, the walls threw back no more than a slick, almost organic-looking sheen, as though we were passing down the gullet of some warp-spawned leviathan. The thought was hardly a comforting one, and I shuddered from more than the cold.

At length we reached the dead-end passage where Penlan had fallen, revealing the existence of the ambull tunnels below the mine, and we paused to regroup.

'This is it,' I warned everyone. 'From now on our chances of meeting a necron are greatly increased.' What I meant was 'practically inevitable,' but I shied away from pronouncing those words. Not out of deference to the feelings of Welard and his men, who I had no doubt would have responded with the same lack of emotion that they had displayed thus far, but because I didn't want to face that thought myself. Welard waggled his cheroot, which had by now acquired a thin scum of frost over the tightly-packed tabac leaves it was composed of, and which crunched irritatingly between his teeth as he spoke.

'We'll be ready for them.' He gestured with his left hand. 'Hastur.' One of the troopers stepped forward to cover the hole with his hellgun while the rest rappelled down into the darkness with display team precision. I heard a couple of clicks in my comm-bead, almost as if it were picking up some stray interference from somewhere but which I knew was the signal from the advance party confirming that it was all clear down there, and the sergeant grinned at me. For the first time it struck me that he was actually enjoying this. 'Coming?' he asked, and disappeared down the hole after his men.

Why I simply didn't shake my head and run for the surface, intent only on making it to the next shuttle out, I'll never know. There was still my fraudulent reputation to consider, of course, double-edged weapon though that had become in the last few years, dragging me into these ghastly situations almost as readily as I was able to turn it to my advantage, but even now I found myself reluctant to surrender it. And it couldn't be denied that my chances of survival would be marginally better with a screen of storm troopers between me and the necrons instead of wandering around these catacombs alone. I glanced round the narrow chamber, steeling myself, and met Jurgen's eyes. The sight of him was instantly reassuring, despite his usual unprepossessing appearance, a visible (and olfactory) reminder of all the perils we'd faced and bested together. He grinned at me, and hefted the bulk of his melta.

'After you, sir,' he said. 'I'll watch your back.' A task, I have to say, which he performed admirably throughout our years of service together. I forced a smile to my face.

'I don't doubt it,' I said, then before I could change my mind I seized the line and slithered down into the bowels of hell.

I landed heavily, but retained my footing, and was able to step aside as Jurgen lurched down the rope behind me. The storm troopers looked mildly disdainful at our performance, the awkwardness of which was underlined a moment later by Hastur's descent, which he managed with the dexterity of an acrobat.

'Where to?' Welard asked.

'This way.' I indicated the right direction and waited while the storm troopers went through the gap first, falling into place behind them. With every step we took the knot in my stomach wound itself tighter, the memory of where we were going insinuating itself into my forebrain, inextricably intertwined with images of the massacre I'd witnessed on Interitus Prime. This would be different, I kept telling myself. I wasn't fleeing in panic through an unknown labyrinth this time, I was heading for a known location, which, by the Emperor's grace, I had already entered before and escaped to tell the tale. Kasteen was right, the necrons would be concerned entirely with the greenskins, they didn't even know we were here...

'Found something,' the pointman said, snapping me out of my reverie and back to the claustrophobic confines of the ambull run. We closed up, the faint light from our shrouded luminators glinting from some detritus on the tunnel floor.

'What do you make of that, sir?' Jurgen asked, his feeble beam picking out something only he had noticed. Apart from myself, he was the only one of our party who had walked these narrow tunnels before, and would be able to notice any changes. The hairs on the back of my neck rose, something that happens in popular fiction far more often than it does in real life, and which I can assure you is a remarkably uncomfortable sensation. My aide was shining his luminator down a narrow cylinder punched into the ice lining the tunnel, about the width of my forearm and deep beyond the strength of the lamp he carried to pick out the end.

'They've been here,' I murmured. The only possible explanation was a stray gauss flayer shot striking the tunnel wall. I looked about us, finding several more of the sinister indentations.

'Then who were they shooting at?' Jurgen asked. That was a good question. If the orks had made it this far into the tunnels our job was about to get a great deal more complicated. I moved up to join Welard and the point man, who were staring in perplexity at a small mound of metal objects embedded in ice, ominously streaked with red.

'What do you think these are, sir?' he asked, the air of unassailable confidence taking a dent for the first time since I'd met him. I looked at the assemblage of tubes and wires for a moment, then the bile rose into my throat as I realised what I was looking at.

'They're augmetics,' I said, swallowing heavily. 'They've been ripped out of someone.' So that was where Ernulph had disappeared to. These might not be his remains, of course, but it was carrots to credits he'd led whatever foolhardy expedition this pathetic revenant had been a part of. I wondered vaguely if we'd find traces of any other victims, or if they'd all simply been vaporised.

One thing was certain, though. Thanks to these idiots the necrons would know there were humans on Simia Orichalcae now, and were most likely waiting in ambush ahead of us. This was just getting better and better.

Well, there was no point in standing around worrying about it, time was most definitely of the essence here, so I got everyone moving again and dropped back to walk beside Jurgen.

'Be ready,' I warned him, 'things could be about to get–'

I was interrupted by the dying shriek of our point man as he flared and dwindled to nothing in the necrotic glow of one of those hellish gauss weapons, and then the metallic warriors whose appearance I'd so dreaded were upon us.

'Place your shots,' Welard said calmly, and the surviving storm troopers unleashed a hail of hellgun fire against our attackers. The glare of the lasbolts impacting on the leading necron dazzled my eyes, then its chest gave way, seared and blasted by the precision volley, and it tumbled to the ice-slick floor revealing a fresh target behind it, already levelling another gauss flayer.

Credit where it's due, Welard and his men certainly knew their stuff. As I've mentioned before, the ambull tunnels were narrow, forcing the hideous automata to come at us almost in single file. But the storm troopers' discipline was excellent, and with the death of our first casualty they'd dropped into a practiced routine, the men at the front falling prone, those behind kneeling, and the ones at the rear standing up so that the whole squad was able to concentrate their fire as one. The second necron lost its head, quite literally, and fell heavily across the first with a sound not unlike someone kicking a bin full of scrap metal. As I watched it fall I realised, with a thrill of horror, that the first metallic warrior we'd all thought destroyed was rising slowly to its feet again.

'Jurgen,' I called, and my aide stepped forward levelling the melta. The storm troopers slipped easily out of his way, keeping up a barrage of hellgun fire to cover him while he aimed, and shielding their eyes as he squeezed the trigger.

The flare of actinic energy stabbed my retina, even through my closed eyelids, and the roar of ice flashing instantly into steam echoed all around us. The air against my face was suddenly warm and wet, as though I'd been teleported into a rain-forest somewhere. As I blinked my vision clear I could see nothing but puddles of molten metal surrounded by grotesque lumps of statuary, some of which still twitched, freezing almost at once into the rapidly-reforming ice. Then, in an instant, they faded away as though they'd never been, leaving behind nothing but drifting vapour and some oddly-shaped indentations in the tunnel floor.

'Clear,' Hastur called, taking the place of the disintegrated point man, and leading us on into the darkness. Welard nodded at Jurgen, an almost imperceptible tilt of the head as he passed my aide, the closest I suppose he could come to expressing thanks to an outsider, and jogged along in the wake of his men. I couldn't help contrasting the reaction of Grifen's team to the loss of Lunt with the storm troopers' matter-of-fact dismissal of the loss of one of their own, and mentioned as much to the sergeant.

'The mission comes first,' he said, his face hard, and that's all he would say on the subject. I wasn't exactly in the mood for idle conversation either, so I let it drop, and resumed straining my ears for the slightest sound which might indicate the approach of more of those monstrous guardians.

Luck or the Emperor must have been with us, though, as all too soon I beheld the baleful glow which forewarned us that we were about to reach our goal. We flattened ourselves against the ice-covered bedrock of the tunnel wall as we approached the entrance to that mighty cavern, through which I'd escaped only a few hours before, and strained our senses for any sign that we had been discovered.

All seemed quiet, except for that damnable humming and the artillery barrage pounding of my heart, so we crept out into the chamber I had so fervently hoped never to see again. My scalp crawled with apprehension, and I had to exert every micron of self-control I possessed to appear calm in front of Welard and his men. They kept their weapons trained on every patch of cover, every green-tinged shadow in the lee of those towering and incomprehensible mechanisms. If they were at all disconcerted by the sheer sense of wrongness surrounding them they gave no sign of it.

'Which way?' the sergeant asked, and I indicated the direction of the portal. He nodded. 'Move out.'

We scurried through that vast space as Jurgen and I had mere hours before, still sticking to the shadows of the towering machines, that ghastly charnel light bathing everything in a sheen of putrescence. Some of them were marked with the peculiar stick and circle hieroglyphics I'd seen on Interitus Prime, and you can be sure the memories the sight of them stirred up did little to calm my fears. By this time my nerves were stretched tighter than harp strings, and it was probably this sense of heightened paranoia which let me hear an almost inaudible sound, a faint scraping which reminded me of scuttling vermin. I signalled the sergeant.

'Five metres, two o'clock. Behind that... Whatever the hell it is.' Welard nodded, and gestured a couple of troopers to flank the gleaming tangle of green-glowing pipes. The rest of us closed up, ready to face whatever the threat was, and I drew my laspistol and chainsword. Not that I expected the latter to be much good against metal rather than flesh, but it had served me well on many occasions before now, and the weight of it felt comforting in my hand.

'Contact. No threat,' said one of the storm troopers, his voice slightly attenuated in my comm-bead, and fell silent again. I hurried forward to join them, cursing their taciturnity.

'Explain,' I said, equally terse, and afraid of transmitting for long enough to be triangulated on. If the trooper was surprised he gave no sign of it.

'It's a cogboy,' he explained flatly.

Not just any cogboy, of course, the Emperor has more of a sense of humour than that. Even before I joined them I had a sense of foreboding, which was amply justified as I looked down at the quivering bundle trying to wedge itself under the largest pipe.

'Logash,' I said. The young tech-priest must have recognised my voice, because he turned and looked up at me. Though his metal eyes made any expression hard to read, a sense of recognition began to surface through the expression of stark terror suffusing his face.

'Commissar Cain?' His voice trembled, wavering in pitch like a boy in early adolescence. If he wasn't bonkers before, I thought, he certainly was now. 'You were right, you were right. We were unworthy to trespass on the sacred mysteries of the Omnissiah–'

'Where are the others?' I interrupted, squatting down to his level, and keeping my voice calm. I haven't had that much experience with madmen, give or take the odd Chaos cultist, but I've seen enough cases of combat fatigue and his symptoms seemed similar; overwhelmed by the horrors he'd witnessed he'd simply retreated inside himself. 'Where's Magos Ernulph?'

'Dead,' he moaned, his blank eyes roving aimlessly, 'struck down by the guardians for our hubris. We should have listened to you, we should have listened...'

Resisting the temptation to say 'told you so,' albeit with some difficulty, I raised him to his feet as gently as I could manage. (Which wasn't very, to be honest, he was all but catatonic, but I succeeded in the end.)

'You're bringing him with us?' Welard asked, in tones which left me in no doubt what he thought of that idea. I nodded.

'We can't just leave him here,' I said. The sergeant looked dubious, and for a moment I wavered, thinking our mission here was hanging by a thread as it was, and adding a babbling lunatic to our number wasn't likely to help any.

Then again, Logash had been down here longer than any of us, and might have information which could save our lives, or at least help us blow up the portal. As so often in my life it was an almost impossible decision to make, and one which no one else could, but that's why I get to wear the fancy cap. I pulled on the tech-priest's arm, reminded of Grifen's attempt to snap Magot out of her stupor not far from this very spot. 'We have to go,' I said. To my relief Logash nodded, and fell into step beside Jurgen and myself.

'I take it Ernulph asked you to guide him down here?' I asked, and the tech-priest nodded.

'I remembered the way. The Omnissiah guided–'

'Yes, quite,' I interrupted. 'Then what happened?' His face twisted.

'We entered the temple, and the guardians fell upon us. Some were cut down where they stood, in the very act of making obeisance to the machine god, while others fled. But the guardians pursued them without mercy.' That explained the remains we'd found in the tunnel anyway, a few of them must have made it that far out of here before they were cornered. Logash turned a pinched, anguished face to me. 'They were swift and terrible,' he whispered, 'and shrouded in horror.'

Well that sounded pretty much like every form of necron I'd ever encountered, and I dismissed his words as a figure of speech at the time, although I was soon to discover how right he was.

'Contact,' Hastur said, and opened fire. The other storm troopers followed suit, and I dived for cover, dragging Logash into the shadows with me. A moment later an acrid odour of unwashed socks indicated that Jurgen had joined us.

I levelled my laspistol, seeking a target, and was gratified to see that the storm troopers were doing sterling work in engaging the advancing party of metallic warriors. They were the skin-hunters we'd seen before, or identical copies of them, advancing with terrifying speed, their long blades whispering through the air as they swept back and forth. Instead of ork hides, though, the leading ranks were swathed in human skins, still wet and leaking, thin runnels of blood turned black by the corpse-light, which illuminated everything here, veining the metal torsos beneath. As I tracked the leading one, placing a las-bolt squarely in the centre of its forehead, I realised with a shudder that the obscene covering it wore still had the vestige of a face; a face, moreover, which I recognised.

'Ernulph!' I whispered, revulsion twisting my stomach, as the creature inside his skin staggered backwards. I made sure of it with a flurry of follow-up shots, then turned my attention to the monstrosity behind it. The magos had been a pompous fool, it was true, but no one deserved a fate like that.

'They're behind us!' Hastur warned, before his voice rose in a throat-rending scream. I turned just in time to see him borne down by one of the razor-wielding automata, eviscerated in seconds, his blood left streaming down the sides of the bulky metal cabinet from behind which, a heartbeat before, he had been pouring hellgun fire into the main body of our vile assailants. A moment later the flayed one rose from a crouch, the still wet skin of the deceased storm trooper clinging to its metal torso by the stickiness of its own blood.

'Frak this!' I shouted. 'Jurgen!' On cue my aide unleashed another blast from his melta into the centre of the group, cutting a swathe through them as efficiently as before. Once again the necrons caught by the full force of the blast were simply annihilated, flashing into vapour as thoroughly as the victims of their own terrible weapons, while the ones at the fringe of that ravening burst of energy staggered, limbs and torsos seared and softened like candle wax. For a moment I expected them to rally, restoring themselves in that unnerving fashion I'd seen before, but the survivors simply vanished into thin air. For some reason Hastur's body went with them, but why they would want it was a mystery I was sure I would never want to know the answer to.[70]

'How far to the objective?' Welard asked, as the surviving storm troopers regrouped. Beyond a single glance at the coating of blood on the metal surfaces marking the spot where Hastur had died he seemed utterly unperturbed by the terrible fate which had befallen his comrade, and the rest seemed equally focussed on the outcome of our mission, scanning the halls around us for any sign of renewed necron activity. I was grateful for their vigilance, but I was beginning to find their complete lack of emotion somewhat unnerving.

'About three hundred metres,' I said, forcing my mind back to the issue at hand. Welard nodded, and waved to his remaining squad mates to move out. Jurgen and I fell in behind them as before, although I was now acutely aware that an attack could come from any direction, and you can be sure that I scanned our surroundings with even more diligence than before. I got Logash moving again with a relatively light tug on the arm, and he trotted along with us, apparently perfectly happy to follow whatever orders I gave now I'd been proven to be right about the inadvisability of being here in the first place.

After a few moments I caught sight of a bright glow from beyond the concealing bulk of one of those vast machines, and indicated it to the sergeant.

'That's it,' I said, watching it pulse like the beating of a diseased heart, and fighting down the surge of dread which suddenly suffused me. 'The portal.' The glow intensified for a moment, with an accompanying thunder crack of displaced air which rumbled and echoed through that city-sized cavern as though presaging a tropical downpour. 'And it's active.' I tried not to think about how many reinforcements had suddenly arrived; rather too many, judging by the amount of air that had been elbowed out of their way as they materialised.

'Not for long,' Welard said, his confidence apparently undiminished by the loss of a third of his squad already.

'Movement,' one of the troopers cut in, as blandly unemotional as before. 'Eleven o'clock, thirty metres.' We turned to face this new threat, the quartet of storm troopers raising their hellguns, while Jurgen lifted the melta into a firing position. Logash was trembling violently.

---

70 Presumably for the same reason their harvester fleets abduct the populations of isolated colony worlds. Whatever that is.

'Omnissiah protect thy circuits,' he mumbled, 'let this unworthy relay speed the electrons of thy great computation, preserving us from burnout...' and other tech-priest gibberish. I glanced back at the storm troopers, and was astonished to see them quivering almost as badly.

'Emperor be with us,' the closest was muttering under his breath, 'protect us with the shield of thy will...'

Something was seriously wrong, I thought. After everything they'd already shrugged off it was hard to credit that they would be spooked so badly by a single group of warriors who barely outnumbered us. But Willard's jaw was clenched, bisecting the cheroot, most of which had fallen unnoticed to the floor. The hellgun jittered in his hands, wavering almost too wildly to aim, and he was muttering too, one of the catechisms of command which had evidently been drummed into him by the schola tutors, and rather more effectively than it had been with me judging by his demeanour up to this point.

He began firing wildly at the approaching warriors, and as if that were a signal the others opened up too, badly-aimed las-bolts detonating all round the necrons with barely a single hit scored, almost as inaccurate as orks. There was something about these warriors which was different from the others we'd seen, a more resolute, self-aware quality, which sent shudders down my spine as I took in more of the details of their appearance. Less skeletal than the others they seemed composed of ceramics as much as metal, and with writhing pipes and cables corded around their metallic bones which flexed like living muscles as they moved. Thin tendrils of despair seemed to wrap themselves around my very soul as they approached us, bringing not mere death but annihilation in their wake. Fear I was used to, could master and control at least to some extent, but this was different, a primal terror which rose up from somewhere deep within me, and threatened to swamp my very sense of self. Levelling the laspistol in my hand, and ironically grateful for the augmetics which steadied my grip in spite of the treachery of my own body, I fired at the leading one, gouging a neat crater in the centre of its forehead.

'The horror! The horror!' Logash was going foetal on me again, clinging to my ankles, and the storm troopers were breaking, fleeing in all directions with cries of terror. 'The horror returns!'

'Jurgen, get him off me!' I yelled, restrained from following only by the dead weight of the gibbering tech-priest. I fought against that rush of primal emotion, feeling my very sense of self under threat in a way I hadn't experienced since the Slaaneshi witch tried to sacrifice my soul to her perverted deity on Slawkenberg over a decade before, and shooting entirely by instinct now. The green lance of a gauss flayer beam missed me by a couple of centimetres, and punched a neat hole through the smooth-sided cabinet beside me. I shot back, taking my assailant in the chest, and making it stagger for a moment before resuming its unhurried advance.

'Come along, sir.' My aide was at my side now, prising Logash's fingers away from my boot, which wasn't easy given that they were closed by a rictus of terror and augmetic into the bargain. The pressure against my soul eased abruptly, as though cut off by the slamming of a door. I hustled Logash to his feet, and moved behind Jurgen as he aimed and fired the melta.

Once again the powerful weapon did its work, taking down our most immediate assailants, but this time there was to be no reprieve from them teleporting out to lick their wounds. The group had scattered to hunt down the fleeing storm troopers, and we only got a couple of them. As I looked around for some sign of our erstwhile companions I saw two of them taken down with gauss flayer shots, screaming into vapour even as I watched. Welard was backed into a corner between two blocky structures the size of Chimeras, eyes unfocussed, his mind clearly gone, hellgun hanging forgotten from his hand, babbling incoherently. He was still crying out to the Emperor for help which never came when the leading automaton swung the heavy blade of its polearm-like weapon and took his head off cleanly with a single sweep, spraying itself with a thick coating of his blood.

'Come on,' I said urgently. 'We have to get out of here!' Logash was beginning to recover whatever was left of his wits, and shook his head slowly.

'What happened?' he asked. I was beginning to understand, but there was no time now for lengthy explanations, and at our last meeting Amberley had impressed on both Jurgen and myself the paramount importance of not revealing his gift to anyone, so I just grabbed him by the arm to get him moving.

'Stay close to Jurgen,' I instructed, and we went to ground between a blank-faced metal cabinet about three storeys high and a loop of conduit which resembled a glowing green intestine. A faint shriek, abruptly cut off, confirmed the loss of the last storm trooper.

With pounding pulses we stayed put for some time, as Logash had undoubtedly done before, while those ghastly apparitions began what had every appearance of a methodical search for us. To my relief, however, they seemed to become mildly disorientated every time they approached our hiding place, veering off before they had come within a handful of metres of us, a deliverance I could only attribute to Jurgen's peculiar qualities.[71]

At length, when everything seemed quiet again, I decided it was time to move. The evacuation must be well under way by now, and I meant to be on a shuttle and safe aboard the *Pure of Heart* before anything else had a chance to go wrong.

'What about the portal, sir?' Jurgen wondered aloud. I shrugged.

'Nothing we can do about it now.' Which was actually true, as the storm troopers had been carrying the melta charges which were the only things which might have stood some chance of destroying it, and they'd been vaporised along with the soldiers. 'We'll just have to call in the Navy after all.' Tough luck on the galaxy, of course, but it's a big place, and even a necron army couldn't put that big a dent in it. I hoped. So we made our cautious way back to the tunnel we'd come in by, scurrying from cover to cover as we had done before, and freezing into immobility at every sign of movement.

---

71 Perhaps correctly. The aura of terror projected by necron pariahs appears to be at least partly a psychic phenomenon, so it's quite reasonable to assume that a blank would repel them and mask the effect. However, since no other record exists of a blank coming into such close proximity to a group of pariahs, and they're far too rare and valuable to risk in deliberately testing this hypothesis, it must remain conjectural.

To my immense relief we encountered no more of those terrible apparitions, catching sight of the more common warriors only at a distance. The aperture left by the ambulls was unguarded, to my delighted surprise, and I regained the sanctuary of the ice tunnels with a lightness of spirit which was almost intoxicating.

It was too good to last, of course, and inevitably it didn't.

Editorial Note:

As Cain began to make his way back to the surface, things were beginning to take an unfortunate turn there too. The tech-priests' incursion into the necron tomb had indeed, as he feared, drawn their attention to the existence of the human colony above their heads, while the orks, outmatched as they were, had begun to break, only to find the Valhallan defences weakened or abandoned altogether as they fell back. Not unnaturally many of the routing greenskins took advantage of the new line of retreat thus opened up, and began to threaten the refinery itself.

Under this renewed pressure the evacuation began to falter. Even though almost two full companies had thus far been ferried up to the orbiting starship the converted civilian shuttles aboard the Pure of Heart *simply weren't up to the challenge of embarking an entire regiment in a matter of hours. As the following extract from Captain Durant's log makes clear, the loss of well over half the men and women deployed just a few days before seemed almost inevitable.*

+++Vox-log record of Captain Durant, Merchant fleet freighter *Pure of Heart,* 651.932 M41+++

Still stuck in orbit around this miserable iceball. At the last count we had most of the civilian staff and their families stowed away somewhere, only a couple of hundred still cluttering up the corridors with their carcasses and personal effects, but Bosun Kleg has promised to sort that out so I'm leaving him to it.

The Guardsmen have started arriving back up here too, although at least they've got somewhere to bunk. The officers are having a hard time keeping order, as most of them seem concerned about the majority still stranded planetside. Can't say I blame them, as Mazarin says there's no way our shuttles can get many more runs in before the refinery's overrun by the greenskins or these metal creatures, or possibly both. She keeps checking the sensor net and calling the surface with updates, but so far she says the gropos[72] keep losing ground, and I can't see any way of stopping that.

72 A contraction of 'ground pounders,' a Navy term for the Imperial Guard units sometimes billeted aboard their warships. Less common among merchant crews, Durant's use of it here implies that this wasn't the first time the *Pure of Heart* had been pressed into service as a fleet auxiliary.

But then I'm only a starship captain, thank the Emperor, so what I know about soldiering you could write on the back of a holocard. I told Mazarin not to worry, that colonel looks as though she knows what she's doing and their commissar's supposed to be some kind of hero, but I can tell she wasn't convinced...

FIFTEEN

After making our way through the ambull tunnels without so much as a sniff of the necrons I began to think we might just be lucky enough to rejoin our comrades without further incident, and I must confess to a sensation akin to euphoria as we scrambled up the rope to emerge into the lower galleries of the mine itself. After the cramped ambull runs the high ceiling and the wide tunnels of the man-made workings seemed as broad and open as a city boulevard. We made good time back towards the surface, proceeding in line abreast at a rapid trot. Logash seemed to be a little more rational now we'd left that hive of the damned behind us at last, although being a tech-priest that was only relatively speaking of course, and he kept up with Jurgen and myself without any obvious difficulty.

Jurgen and I had set our luminators to full refulgence now we were back on what I fondly imagined was safer ground, and the beams were lighting our way some considerable distance in front of us. The surrounding ice was bouncing the light as it had before, throwing back the photons in the shimmering blues and star cluster sparkles I remembered so well, so it was a second or two before I realised that the gleam up ahead had come not from the walls but from a reflective metal surface.

'Kill the lights!' I shouted as the coin finally dropped, and twisted to the side as I did so, a reflex which undoubtedly saved my life. A bilious green beam cut through the space in which I'd been standing an instant before, illuminating for an instant the darkness which now enshrouded us, Jurgen having followed my lead, and throwing the three of us into sharp relief before it vanished again, evanescent as lightning. The situation was as grim as any I'd faced; to remain where we were would make us sitting targets as the necrons advanced, whereas the slightest glimmer of light would betray our position. A couple more dazzling green flares flickered past us to emphasize the point. Fleeing blindly down the tunnel would merely ensure we were shot in the back, if we didn't simply slip and fall on the icy surface. Our only option seemed to be to stand and fight, although judging by the positions of their weapon flashes the metal warriors were too spread out to make an obvious target for Jurgen's melta, negating the only advantage we had.

I had just drawn my laspistol, preparing for a bit of speculative fire myself in the no doubt vain hope that the necrons would think twice about rushing us (from what I'd seen of them before they didn't strike me as being easily intimidated), when I felt a light tap on my arm.

'This way,' Logash whispered, and I heard the faint scurrying sound of rapid crawling movement to my left. A moment later I heard the same murmur from somewhere in Jurgen's immediate vicinity (which wasn't hard to pinpoint, as my sense of smell was still unimpeded), and I realised with a thrill of hope that the young tech-priest's augmetic eyes were somehow able to function in the darkness which enveloped us.

Having nothing to lose I crawled rapidly in the direction of his voice, guided by occasional murmurs of 'straight ahead,' and 'left a bit... No, the other left, I meant mine...' until I found myself against the frozen surface of the wall. I was just about to ask what now when a gloved hand accompanied by Jurgen's unmistakable odour reached out to seize my arm.

'In here, commissar,' he whispered, giving me the full benefit of his halitosis, and I found myself squeezing through a narrow crevice in the ice. After a few metres it angled sharply, concealing us completely from the main shaft, and we held our collective breath as a clatter of metal feet echoed past our hiding place.

'Well spotted,' I said, when I was sure it was quiet out there, and adjusted my luminator to minimum refulgence. My companions' faces emerged out of the gloom, Logash's pale, and Jurgen's as impassive as ever. The tech-priest nodded.

'Praise the Omnissiah for our deliverance...' he began, and I hushed him quickly.

'Yes, good, thanks very much,' I said. 'Any idea where this goes?' It wasn't on the chart I'd seen before, but that was hardly surprising, showing as it did every sign of being a natural fault rather than having been dug.[73] Logash pondered a moment.

'It seems to be bearing towards the main processing area,' he said at last. 'Assuming it doesn't just peter out.' Well that was a risk I was willing to take, since the alternative was be facing Emperor knew how many necron patrols. I hoped they were simply scouting the mine rather than invading it in force, but I wasn't keen to hang around and find out one way or the other. At least this way we stood a better chance of avoiding them.

An hour or so later I was beginning to think we'd have done better taking our chances playing tag with the necrons. The fault was narrow and jagged, so we were climbing up slopes or slithering down them more often than we were walking, and chunks of ice kept catching at our feet or projecting from the walls at heights and angles calculated to bruise or worse. On several occasions we had to crawl, as the ceiling descended too low for us to walk, and once we were forced to worm our way forwards on our stomachs as the passage became too constricted even for that. Jurgen's bulky melta became wedged with monotonous regularity, requiring some laborious chipping away of the ice with our combat blades before we could free it. (My chainsword would have done the job in a tenth of the time, of course,

73 How Cain came to this conclusion he doesn't bother to explain; it was probably something to do with his affinity for underground environments.

but in that confined space one of us could all too readily have lost a limb by accident, so it remained in its scabbard.) Each time it happened I considered simply abandoning the cumbersome weapon, but it had proven its use too often to be lightly discarded, so I simply gritted my teeth at the delay and carried on.

My sense of direction was no less sure down here than in any other underground passageway, so at least I had the consolation of knowing that we'd come almost a kilometre from our encounter in the main gallery and were moving in the general direction of the centre of the complex, when Logash paused. He was continuing to lead us simply because the passageway was too narrow for any of us to change position, which had left me trailing in Jurgen's wake, uncomfortably aware that if the metal warriors found the entrance to the cleft and came after us I'd be the first one to know about it. The thought was an unpleasant one, producing an itching sensation between my shoulder blades, so I tried not to dwell on it.

'What's the matter?' I asked. The tech-priest shrugged.

'Dead end,' he said. I could have throttled him, but fortunately Jurgen was in the way. I shook my head, unwilling to believe it.

'It can't be.' The words were a reflex denial, but as I said them I was sure that I was right, all of my tunnel rat's instincts told me so. I wondered for a moment why I was so sure, then realised I could feel a faint current of air on my face. 'There's a draft in here.'

'The passage seems to continue,' Logash agreed. 'But it won't do us any good unless you can get through a five centimetre gap.' That really was hard to believe. The passage had constricted before, of course, but that it could narrow so much, so fast, went against all my experience in such an environment. I said so, possibly a little more forcefully than necessary, and Logash squeezed against the ice wall to let me see for myself. Our way was indeed blocked, by a regular convex surface which curved down to just above the floor. Something about the shape struck me as familiar, and then I realised that it was the lower part of a vast cylinder some three or four metres in diameter.

'What the hell's that?' I asked. Logash thumped it with his hand, producing the unmistakable dull thud of thick metal.

'One of the main extraction pipes,' he said. 'Runs up to the processing plant on the surface.'

'And what's in it at the moment?' I asked, an idea so audacious I could barely acknowledge it beginning to form even as I spoke. Logash shrugged.

'Nothing now the plant's shutting down...' His voice trailed off as he evidently came to the same conclusion as I had. I reached an arm out towards him, past my aide.

'Can you get behind Jurgen?' I asked.

'I can try.' It wasn't easy, I can tell you that, but after what seemed to be an eternity of wriggling and swearing he and I were crouched behind what little cover we could find, and Jurgen was aiming the heavy weapon at the pipe. As before we were engulfed in a roar of steam as he fired, so it was a moment or two before our vision cleared enough to show us the metre-diameter hole he had successfully blasted in the wall of the conduit.

'That'll have to be logged for the repair crews,' Logash remarked conversationally, as if the place would ever be back in operation now the necrons were here, and after a moment to let the metal cool Jurgen hoisted himself through the hole and into the pipe.

I followed suit, the tech-priest bounding up ahead of me, to find myself in an echoing metal tube at least twice my own height floored with rapidly-refreezing slush where the metal had conducted the heat of the melta blast away. Stalactites of ice descended from the curved ceiling, where the uniform coating of rime had been disturbed by our blazing entry.

'This way,' I said, taking the lead again, and moving as rapidly up the gentle slope as I could manage on the treacherous surface. Jurgen had no trouble matching my pace, of course, having been born to conditions like these, and Logash apparently had some sort of augmetic balance enhancer, as he seemed as sure-footed as the Valhallan. Despite my tendency to slip unnervingly from time to time, and the faint curvature underfoot doing nothing to make the job any easier, I found the wide, unhindered passageway almost exhilarating after the cramped confines of the defile and set a good pace if I do say so myself.

After a while I became aware of a faint susurration in my ear, and realised that my comm-bead had come within range of the regimental vox net. We were closer to the surface than I'd realised, and a flood of relief almost knocked the breath from my lungs. If someone was still here I wasn't too late to get a shuttle out.

Not that they'd wait if they all thought I was dead, of course, so I lost no time in contacting Kasteen and passing on the status of our mission.

'Commissar!' She sounded surprised and pleased in almost equal measure. 'We were beginning to think you hadn't made it.'

'I nearly didn't,' I admitted. 'They were waiting for us. We never got close to the damn portal.'

'I see.' Resignation tinged her voice. 'How many survivors?'

'Just me and Jurgen.' No point in going into lengthy explanations now, so I glossed over Logash's presence. 'The necrons are moving through the mine. Have they broken out onto the surface yet?'

'No.' Her voice faded for a moment, as she presumably turned her head away from the voxcaster to talk to someone else, then returned with an edge of urgency. 'Wait one...' The link went dead.

Absorbed in my conversation with the colonel I'd hardly noticed that the pipe had come to an apparent dead end. As I craned my neck and shone my luminator upwards, I could see that it had made an abrupt turn to the vertical, soaring away out of sight.

'What now?' I asked. Logash grinned, and indicated a set of metal rungs protruding from the frost, slick with a coating of ice. 'You have got to be kidding.'

He wasn't, of course. He just grabbed a bar and started climbing, sure-footed as a Catachan up a tree, and after a moment I shrugged and went after him. Jurgen followed, as always.

'Why are these here?' he asked.

'The maintenance servitors use them when the pipes shut down,' Logash explained. 'There should be an access panel up here somewhere...'

Concentrating only on maintaining my grip on the treacherous, ice-slick rungs I was startled by the sound of Kasteen's voice suddenly in my ear again. I almost slipped, hanging on purely by the Emperor's grace and the strength of my augmetic fingers.

'We've lost contact with two of the pickets in the middle levels,' she said. 'We're reinforcing...'

'No!' I cut in, a little too loudly. 'Pull everyone back out of the tunnels! It's the only chance they have!' Bottled up in a confined space, unable to concentrate their fire, they'd be picked off easily. I'd seen that all too clearly before. 'Cover the entrances with everything you've got, and engage them as they emerge.' It probably wouldn't do us any good in the long run, but at least that way they'd be the ones held up by the bottleneck. I tried not to think about their ability to teleport, or move through walls...

'Acknowledged,' Kasteen said, clearly willing to defer to my greater experience with these hideous foes, and cut the link. I considered what she'd just told me, not liking the conclusions I was drawing. It was obvious the necrons were moving through the mines in considerable force if they'd been able to take out two of our squads before they even managed to get a vox message off. Maybe the ones in stasis were beginning to revive, and join the new arrivals...

'Found it,' Logash said above me, unnaturally cheerful under the circumstances, and began scraping the covering of frost from the wall, sprinkling me with a light dusting of powdered ice as he did so. He evidently knew what he was doing though, extending a thin metal probe from one of his fingers, and prodding hopefully at an indentation in the side of the pipe. 'Ah. That should do it...'

A section of the wall next to his hand withdrew suddenly, with a loud hum that set my teeth on edge, letting a blast of light and warm air into our frigid enclosure. The tech-priest vanished from sight, and after a moment of scrambling upwards I followed gratefully, heaving myself out onto a metal mesh floor illuminated by a dim electrosconce in the nearest wall. Despite its feebleness the yellow glow seemed incredibly welcoming as I turned to reach down and haul Jurgen up after me.

The chamber we stood in was small, barely large enough for the three of us, and glancing around I realised that it was merely a landing on a vast metal staircase which rose dizzyingly above us as well as descending to a vertiginous depth below. Logash glanced at some runes stencilled on the outside of the access panel we'd exited the pipe by, and nodded in satisfaction.

'Good,' he said.

'What is?' I asked suspiciously. Given his level of mental stability that could have meant just about anything by this stage. The young tech-priest indicated our surroundings with a casual wave.

'We're in one of the primary maintenance shafts. We should be able to get into the main control shrine a few levels up.'

'Best news I've had all day,' I said. 'Lead on.'

* * *

It was more than a few levels, of course, we must have been climbing for almost half an hour before Logash stopped at another access panel in the plain metal wall, and I'd lost count of how many flights of stairs we'd climbed. My knees hadn't though, and ached abominably, but it's surprising how motivated you can be with an army of murderous automata at your heels and I kept going. Jurgen, of course, showed no sign of strain or discomfort, even lugging the heavy weapon.

'This should be it.' Logash hesitated, and I noticed the door was larger and more elaborate than any of the ones we'd passed on the way up, decorated with the cogwheel symbol of the priesthood.

'Good,' I said. 'Then let's get out of here.'

'I'm not sure I should open it,' the tech-priest said slowly, eyeing Jurgen and myself with a speculative expression on his face. 'This is a holy place. Only ordained and sanctified personnel are permitted beyond this point...'

'Fine,' I said. 'We're on a mission for the Emperor. Can't get much holier than that, right?' Logash looked confused.

'That would be an ecumenical matter,' he said. 'I'm not sure I'm qualified to judge...'

'Don't worry,' I said. 'I am. Now are you going to open the frakking door or will Brother Jurgen do it?' My aide stepped forward, raising the melta, and Logash hit the activation rune with almost indecent haste.

I'm not sure what I expected to find inside, but my first impression was one of overwhelming technological sophistication. Unlike the necron tomb below us, though, whose incomprehensible sorceries pulsed with palpable malevolence, this was a shrine suffused with the benevolence of the machine spirit, harnessed for the good of humanity and blessed by the tech-priests who normally worked here. I made an automatic gesture of obeisance to the large stained glass window depicting the Emperor (in His aspect of the Omnissiah, of course, but the Emperor still for all that) which spilled patches of colour across the serried ranks of dark wood and polished brass lecterns, each one inlaid with a pict screen displaying some aspect of the plant's function.

'Try not to touch anything,' Logash warned, brushing past Jurgen, who was making the sign of the aquila, his jaw even slacker than usual. No fear of that, I thought, shying away from the nearest lectern, when my eye was caught by the image on the pict screen. It showed a blurry, flickering image of what looked like one of the mine galleries, and to my horror the unmistakable shadow of a necron warrior passing swiftly out of sight. A moment later another of the metal monstrosities appeared, then a third.

'Logash,' I called. The tech-priest left off genuflecting to the alter in the corner with every sign of annoyance and ambled over to join me. I indicated the pict. 'Where's this?'

'Sector five, level fourteen,' he said after a moment spent consulting some runes on the lectern. He adjusted the controls, and the picture changed, showing another gallery. After a moment the leading necron appeared there. 'Moving towards sector three.'

'Can you see the whole mine from here?' I asked. He nodded.

'The rituals of focusing are very similar to those of your hololith. You may use this lectern if it will help.' After a few moments of instruction, the lighting of an incense stick, and muttering a few prayers over me he left me to it with an air of evident relief.

The picture I started to build up was grim, to say the least. It didn't take me long to establish that the lower levels were crawling with necrons, hundreds at least, and that they were systematically combing the tunnels, moving ever higher as they went. I voxed Kasteen.

'By my estimate we've got about half an hour before they reach the surface,' I said. 'If we're lucky.' At least the few troopers I'd found were already in the upper levels and pulling back, so she'd heeded my earlier advice. An external pictcaster had shown me the landing pad, already crowded with hundreds of our men and women, not to mention vehicles, waiting patiently for their turn to board one of the shuttles. With a sudden sinking feeling in my stomach I began to realise that the vast majority of them would still be there when the necrons emerged.

'We'll be ready,' Kasteen promised, but I already knew how hollow that promise was. They'd be massacred, no doubt about it, and more to the point I'd never make it to the safety of the starship either. There had to be something we could do to hold them off, if only I could think of it...

'Logash,' I called, but this time he ignored me, intent on some task at one of the other lecterns. I walked over and seized his arm. 'Logash, this is important.'

'So is this,' he said, a trace of irritation in his voice. 'The stabilisation rituals for the storage tanks have to be performed every six hours, and are already overdue. You must realise how volatile refined promethium is...'

'Oh yes,' I said, an idea so audacious I could hardly credit it myself beginning to form. I glanced past the glowing glass Emperor to the complex outside, where the huge storage tanks squatted, bulky as hab blocks. 'How much is in the tanks at the moment?'

'Roughly eight million litres,' he said. 'Since the tankers can't land with the orks about it's built up rather. But still within acceptable safety parameters, I can assure you.'

'I was rather hoping it was unsafe,' I said, and if he had any eyebrows I'm sure he would have raised them at that point. I pointed to the tangle of pipe work around the storage tanks. 'Do any of those pipes connect directly to the mine?'

'Not directly, no.' He looked at me quizzically. 'Why do you ask?'

'Because if we could dump all that liquid down the shaft it should really give the necrons something to worry about,' I said. A slow smile began to spread across the tech-priest's face.

'It would mean overriding a number of safety rituals,' he said, considering the idea. 'But it can be done.'

'Excellent,' I said, feeling a flare of optimism returning at last. 'Then you'd better get to it.'

'Indeed.' He huddled over the lectern, muttering gibberish, and what sounded suspiciously like an occasional high-pitched giggle, as he manipulated the controls. The chance to strike back at the creatures who had massacred his friends was obviously stirring up a lot of emotion, and I began to wonder if his fragile sanity would hold for long enough to implement our plan. Still, there was nothing to do but watch in silence while the minutes dragged by, and the automata in the pict screen moved ominously closer to the surface.

'Tanna tea, sir?' Jurgen materialised at my shoulder, proffering the flask he'd brought as a transparent excuse to join the expedition, and I took the fragrant liquid gratefully, suddenly aware of how tired and hungry I was. He still couldn't find the sandwich he'd stowed somewhere, to my barely-concealed relief, so we contented ourselves with the standard ration bars which tasted reassuringly of nothing particularly identifiable.

'Ready!' Logash said at last, another giggle rising to the surface. His face was preternaturally flushed, and his fingers trembled over the controls of the lectern, the first time I had ever seen augmetics do so. I nodded.

'In the name of the Emperor,' I said solemnly.

'In nominae Ernulph!' The tech-priest squeaked vindictively, and flicked a switch.

For a moment nothing seemed to happen, then I became aware of a low rumbling sound which seemed to suffuse the complex. Runes on several of the lecterns began to glow red, and a powdering of snow dislodged itself from the rim of the window outside. Then, for interminable moments, nothing seemed to happen at all.

'Look, sir!' Jurgen pointed to the pict screen, which I'd left tuned to one of the upper levels. A torrent of liquid became momentarily visible, filling the width of the gallery, sweeping all before it, tearing chunks of ice the size of Baneblades from the walls as it came and tumbling them casually ahead of itself. Then the pictcaster was ripped from its mounting, and the screen went dark. I switched to another just in time to see a party of necron warriors, far closer to the surface than I would have thought possible, trapped by the onrushing tsunami, picked up and thrown around like so many rag dolls. If I believed them capable of emotion I might have thought they stood dumbstruck before it before turning to flee, but it engulfed them all the same. I wondered if they'd fade away, smashed to pieces by that irresistible tide of pure promethium. Much good would it do them if they did; their tomb was at the lowest point of the tunnel complex and would surely flood in time, even though Logash had calculated that it would take the torrent around twenty minutes to seep down that far. Not that they needed to breathe, of course, but at the very least it should stop them using the portal until they found some way to pump the chamber out, by which time with any luck the Navy would be here to sterilise the planet.

All in all, I felt, a rather satisfying result.

I was still feeling pretty pleased with myself as I joined Kasteen and Broklaw on the landing pad a short while later, so buoyed with euphoria that for once I didn't even mind the bone-biting cold. The plain of ice was swarming with activity, Chimera engines rumbling as the engineseers marshalled them for embarkation and commenced the services of mothballing, and platoons marshalled by squads ready to take their place on the outgoing shuttles. A blur of motion in the corner of my eye resolved itself into a Sentinel, trotting eagerly round our flank, keeping an eye out for hostiles.

'Well done, commissar.' Broklaw shook me firmly by the hand. 'I don't think anyone else could have come close to achieving what you did today.'

'Well the next time we run across a necron tomb you're welcome to try,' I told him. He grinned, taking the remark for a joke, but any reply he made was drowned by the scream of a shuttle engine as one of the utility vessels from the *Pure of Heart* rose into the sullen air. Kasteen gestured at it as it howled over our heads and began to diminish into the leaden sky above.

'That was the fifth one,' she told me, raising her voice slightly over the ringing in our ears. 'Two full companies embarked already.' Which still left well over half our number, around six hundred troopers, stranded on the ground. Another half dozen flights still needed. I estimated the time that would take, and didn't like the answer. Even if the necrons had been dealt with, there were still plenty of orks around...

'What's the situation with the orks?' I asked Broklaw, but before he could respond a titanic explosion detonated among the refinery buildings, reducing the main Administratum block to rubble in an instant. Debris pattered down around us, mixed with chunks of ice and what looked uncomfortably like fragments of human tissue.

For a moment I was at a loss, my ears still ringing, and cast around for some sign of damage to the storage tanks, convinced that something must have touched off the leaking promethium. Then I saw it, tall as the building it had just destroyed, lurching forward through the rubble. Its hull was seared and breached in a dozen places, its main gun gone, but at least one of the secondaries was evidently still capable of wreaking havoc. Despite being delayed by the necrons, the gargant had arrived at last.

SIXTEEN

So horrifying was the sight of that gigantic war machine, battered, scarred, but still lurching forward almost unstoppably, that for a moment none of us noticed the ant-like scurryings around its feet. Only as the ear-splitting cry of 'WAAAAAAGGGHHHH!' forced itself through the echoes of the explosion still fuzzing up the inside of my skull did I become aware of the horde of greenskins racing across the frozen ground ahead of it. They were afoot mostly, with just a handful of bikes and trucks bouncing forwards to pull clear of the main pack, and I was pleased to see our Sentinels peeling off to engage the light vehicles. Their lascannons cracked repeatedly, punching holes in the crudely welded armour, and a gratifying number of the ramshackle vehicles slewed to a halt leaking smoke.

But my attention remained fixed on the gargant, which loomed over everything like a shadow of doom. Despite the great rents in its metre-thick armour plate and the fused wreckage of its primary armament it still looked unstoppable, lurching forward uncertainly with a shriek of tortured metal, the left leg dragging slightly as though limping from its wounds.

'Fire at will!' Kasteen roared, suiting the action to the word, and hundreds of lasguns crackled repeatedly, sending echoes booming like surf from the structures still standing. The orks replied enthusiastically, but, praise the Emperor, no more accurately than usual, so our casualties remained light in comparison to the scores who were falling and being trampled underfoot by their comrades.

'Target the gargant!' Broklaw ordered the Chimera crews, and dozens of heavy bolters began to hose down the looming tower of metal which continued to plod towards us, cracking the ice of the landing field under its weight with every tottering step. They didn't seem to be bothering it much, but at least they were keeping the crew's heads down, and the open galleries on its shoulders clear of the heavy weapon crews who would otherwise have been adding a hail of supporting fire to its own formidable armament.

'They're consistent at least,' Kasteen muttered at my elbow. True to their nature the orks were attacking us directly across the landing field, sweeping down the length of it parallel to the line of storage tanks, now shimmering behind a haze of promethium vapour from their rapidly-draining contents. At the sight of that wavering shroud my blood ran even colder than it already was. It would only take one stray round landing next to them for the entire complex to be engulfed in an explosion almost impossible to imagine. And us along with it, of course.

'Keep our fire directed away from the storage tanks,' I cautioned, and she nodded grimly, perceiving the danger too. Not that it would make a lot of difference in the long run, I thought. The gargant was swinging its remaining gun around to target the centre of our formation, which of course meant me along with the senior officers, and I began to think we only had moments left if that. The ork advance seemed almost unstoppable, for every greenskin that fell another dozen continuing to charge forward slavering with bloodlust.

'Shuttle three requesting landing co-ordinates.' A new voice cut into the comm-net, and I became aware of the roar of a powerful engine becoming audible even over the din of the ongoing battle. A flare of hope rose within me...

'Shuttle three, abort your approach.' Mazarin's voice cut in abruptly, shattering it, her tone calm and authoritative. 'The greenskins are all over the pad.'

'I can still make it,' the unseen pilot argued, and the blocky shape of the shuttle suddenly appeared over the refinery, banking sharply round to run in over the main bulk of the ork army. Something about his voice sounded familiar, and I wondered if it was the same one who'd got us down here in the first place. Sporadic small arms fire bounced off his hull, and I stilled my breath remembering our abrupt arrival here, but the orks didn't get lucky this time and he came in low over our heads, his landing thrusters screaming. A few of the troopers waved and yelled, but most kept firing grimly into the onrushing horde of blade-waving barbarity. Another couple of moments and they'd be on us. I drew my chainsword, preparing for the shock of impact, and continued spitting las-bolts into the wall of screaming ork flesh bearing down on us almost as fast as the tidal wave of promethium still scouring the mine beneath our feet.

The gargant lurched forward again, and impelled by panic or instinct I finally noticed the deep gash in its leg. It was a slim chance, but...

'Target its left leg!' I yelled, and the Chimera crews switched their aim, pouring a concentrated barrage of heavy bolter rounds against that single, vulnerable spot. For a moment I thought the desperate gamble would fail, but as the torrent of explosive fire chewed away at the torn and overstressed metal the towering leviathan began to sway alarmingly. The damaged limb seemed to seize up entirely, then failed altogether with a crack of rending metal which echoed like thunder between the encircling hills, audible even over the din of battle surrounding us.

Abruptly it lost its equilibrium entirely, toppling absurdly slowly at first, then faster and faster as more of that titanic bulk neared the ground. The orks around it scattered in panic, like ants beneath a descending boot, and a gratifying number of them failed to make it.

The impact shook the ground beneath us, cracking the ice for hundreds of metres around the huge wreck, swallowing almost a third of that vast bulk and opening chasms which engulfed the vast majority of the fleeing greenskins. From deep within that mountain of metal the dull thud of secondary explosions going off echoed like bronchitic coughs, and the lurid red glow of spreading flames began to join the smoke I'd seen earlier.

'Finish them off!' Kasteen ordered, and the Valhallans responded with a will, surging forward to engage the stunned survivors. After a short exchange of weapons fire it was all over, the few remaining orks fleeing beyond the effective range of our lasguns and Kasteen reining in the more enthusiastic platoon commanders who seemed on the verge of going after them with a display of profanity verging on the pyrotechnic. I'd expected Sulla to be leading the charge, but it turned out her company was the first to have been shuttled back up to the ship, so for once she didn't have the chance to do something stupid, which made a refreshing change.

'I think we should board as soon as we can,' I said, feeling our luck had already been stretched far thinner than we had any right to expect, and Kasteen nodded.

'I think you're right,' she said. 'Simia Orichalcae's rather lost its charm for me.'

'You and me both,' Broklaw agreed, and hurried off to organise the next stage of the embarkation as the incoming shuttle grounded at last.

I have to admit that the surge of relief I felt as I hurried up the cargo ramp and heard the comforting clang of metal beneath my boot soles once more left me almost giddy. Nevertheless I couldn't shake a strong sense of foreboding which intensified with every extra minute we remained on the pad, and continued to hover by the open hatch as a steady stream of Guardsmen and women made their way on board. Kasteen joined me there after a while, her face pensive.

'Looking for something?' she asked.

'Hoping I don't see it,' I admitted. 'It'll take more than a bath to see off the necrons if I'm any judge.' All the time we spoke I kept an amplivisor trained on the edge of the complex, dreading the sight of a flash of moving metal. Kasteen nodded ruefully.

'Shame you couldn't blow up the portal,' she said. I echoed the gesture.

'Shame you never got the chance to blow up the gargant,' I echoed. We looked at one another, the same thought occurring to us both simultaneously, and went to find Captain Federer.

'We were going to detonate it by vox pulse,' Federer confirmed. He was a thin-faced, dark-haired man, whose enthusiasm for problem-solving was matched only by his lack of social skills. Rumour among the regiment had it that he'd once aspired to become a tech-priest but been expelled from the seminary for his morbid fascination with pyrotechnics, and he certainly seemed to have an almost instinctive understanding of the arcane technologies of the combat engineer. If the rumours were true, the Adeptus's loss was very definitely our gain.

We found him in the shuttle's main cargo bay fussing over the stowage of the small amount of equipment he'd been able to salvage; under the circumstances Kasteen had decided to abandon our vehicles and stores and use the space we saved to bring up another couple of platoons at a time. Riding back here would be hideously uncomfortable, but far better than still being around if the necrons stirred again.

'So you could still set the charges off from here?' I asked, raising my voice slightly to carry over the babble of voices from the troopers beginning to file in to the echoing hold. A few of them had evidently been in a similar situation before, unfurling their bedrolls into improvised acceleration couches as they settled. Federer nodded. 'Oh yes. You'd just need a sufficiently powerful transmitter. You could even do it from orbit if you wished.'

'That might be safer,' Kasteen suggested. 'After all, it's going to be a pretty big bang.'

'Oh yes.' Federer's face lit up with what I can only describe as unhealthy enthusiasm. 'Huge. Massive in fact. On the order of gigatonnes.' His eyes took on something of a dreamy quality.

'We didn't place anything remotely that powerful,' Kasteen said, looking vaguely stunned. 'We'd have blown ourselves to pieces along with the gargant.' Federer nodded, his voice taking on something of the quality of Logash discussing ambulls.[74]

'That was before the commissar flooded the mine with promethium,' he explained. 'The liquid will have settled to the bottom levels by now. That means the upper galleries would be full of vapour. In effect you've created an FAE bomb several kilometres wide.'[75]

'Assuming the explosives you placed weren't washed away by the flood,' I said. Federer shook his head.

'We anchored them pretty firmly. We were expecting a gargant to tread on them, don't forget. We allowed for stresses in the region of...'

'Never mind,' I said, cutting him off before he could get properly started. Once enthused, as I knew from experience, he was hard to bring back to the point. 'If you say it'll work I'm sure it will.'

'Oh yes,' he said, nodding eagerly.

I must confess that, despite the uneventful journey back to the orbiting starship, I didn't feel entirely safe until I heard the docking clamps engage at last and felt the reassuring solidity of the *Pure of Heart's* deck plating beneath my feet.

'You're back, then,' Durant greeted us as we arrived on the bridge. It was much as I remembered it from our last visit, except that the hololith was now showing a panoramic view of the snowscape outside the refinery. From the height and angle I judged that the pictcaster was mounted somewhere above the main hull of the last shuttle to leave that benighted place, the final few pickets withdrawing to the safety of its cargo hold even as I watched.

---

74 This is the last time Cain mentions the tech-priest in his account of these events. His subsequent career in the Adeptus Mechanicus can best be described as unspectacular, rising to the rank of Magos without doing anything further to draw attention to himself. His last known assignment was at the Noctis Labyrinthus mine complex on Mars.

75 Fuel/Air Explosive, a type of bomb which releases a volatile gas before detonation to magnify its power and area of effect.

The refinery complex still seemed as deserted as ever, but I kept an apprehensive eye on the distant line of structures nevertheless.

'You seem pleasantly surprised,' I said. Durant made the almost-shrug I'd noticed before.

'Yes, well. The Munitorum might have argued about our charter fee if we'd left you behind,' he said, a little too gruffly to have meant it.

'Shuttle one preparing to lift, captain,' a junior officer called from a lectern somewhere to our left, and a palpable air of relief swept the whole chamber.

'Good,' the captain said. 'We've been sitting next to this damned planet so long I'm beginning to put down roots.' He gestured to Mazarin, who was huddled over her workstation with Federer, deep in discussion about something. 'Take us out of orbit as soon as they dock.'

'Aye aye, captain,' she responded, and hummed across to another console, where she busied herself with the rituals of engine activation.

'Better make it fast,' I said. As I'd feared, a glint of moving metal had appeared among the refinery buildings, moving rapidly towards the pict-caster. As it got closer I was able to discern a squadron of speeders, each one with what looked like the top half of a necron welded to it. All of them had a heavy weapon apparently incorporated into their right arm, and as I watched, dazzling green beams of malevolent energy lanced out to strike the hull of the slowly-rising shuttle.

'They're scratching the paintwork!' Durant roared, outraged. Truth to tell they were doing rather more than that, scoring visible channels in the metal. They were a long way from actually breaching it, shuttle hulls are sturdy to say the least, but the fact that they were able to inflict any damage at all spoke volumes for the power of the weapons they carried.

'They're going after the shuttle,' Kasteen said, her eyes on the skimmers which began to rise after it, wheeling about the slowly-climbing slab of metal like flies round a grox. They were growing in number too, I noticed with a quiver of unease, more and more of them rising to the join the swarm.

'They're not going to make it,' I said, alarmed. The pilot was making what evasive manoeuvres he could, but the craft was built for durability rather than agility, and several more of the deadly beams struck home. It could only be a matter of moments before something vital was hit...

'Don't be too sure,' Durant said. A moment later the main engines flared into life, vaporising any of the skimmers unfortunate enough to be behind the craft in a burst of superheated plasma, and lifting it cleanly away on an escape trajectory.

'They're falling behind,' Mazarin confirmed, and the projection obligingly rotated to show the remaining skimmers tumbling aimlessly in the wake of the shuttle's passage. A few moments later the image showed the reassuring refuge of our docking bay, and everyone breathed an audible sigh of relief. (Except for Mazarin, possibly, who may have had her lungs augmetically replaced.)

With our shuttle out of danger Durant had retuned the hololith to the aerial view of the refinery complex which he'd treated us to when we first made orbit.

As he magnified the tangle of buildings and storage tanks, now reassuringly far below us, my breath caught in my throat. A glittering tide of moving metal was emerging from the mouth of the mine, more warriors than I could count, blurring into a single amorphous entity which flowed between the buildings like flood water.

'They've woken!' I gasped, a spasm of fear gripping my bowels. They'd prevented the tide of promethium from flooding their temple, Emperor knew how, which meant their portal was probably still active...

'Broklaw!' I yelled, blessing the hurry that had left the comm-bead still in my ear. 'Stand to! Prepare to receive boarders!' Everyone looked at me as though I'd gone mad. 'They can teleport, remember?' I snapped, and Kasteen nodded grimly.

'They can swim, too, by the look of it.'[76]

'Federer!' I called. 'Now would be a good time!' The sapper grinned happily, exchanged a few more words with the hovering tech-priest, and prodded a rune with his finger. All eyes remained fixed on the cluster of buildings in the hololith. Nothing seemed to be happening.

'It didn't go off...' I began to say, then a gout of ice erupted from the plain at the mouth of the valley. Mazarin did something to enhance the clarity of the image, and in front of our eyes a vast, growing crater spread to engulf the nearby metal warriors. They tumbled into it like broken toys, more and more of them as the ground crumbled away faster than they could flee, and Federer punched the air as though he'd just scored the winning goal of a scrumball match.

'That would have seen off the gargant,' he said cheerfully.

'That it would,' I agreed, awestruck at the amount of devastation he'd wrought. But that had only been the prelude. Deep in the bowels of the pit a sudden flare of light erupted as the promethium vapour trapped in the caverns below ignited. A gout of flame fully a kilometre in height burst from the rupturing ground and raced across the snowscape at the speed of thought, melting the fleeing warriors in an instant, throwing blazing fissures ahead of itself as it went.

There were other explosions now too, the entire surface of the valley erupting like pyroclasts, vaporised rock, ice, and necrons forming a low, looming cloud riven with thunderbolts as electrostatic discharges of incredible power jumped between the particles. The refinery disappeared, sliding into the hellish inferno below, and vanishing as though it had never been...

'Brace for impact!' Durant called out, as though this were just a minor inconvenience, and the *Pure of Heart* was suddenly picked up and shaken like a child's toy by the titanic shockwave as the very atmosphere of the planet bulged under the force of the energies released. Even the crew grabbed for handholds, and I found myself bracing Kasteen, who had fallen back against me (something I had no complaints about at all).

'Just a minute,' Mazarin called, playing the controls in front of her like the keyboard of a forte, and the shuddering gradually ceased. She grinned

76 More likely they simply waded through the flooded levels until they broke the surface.

again, and I began to suspect she enjoyed the chance to push the limits of her engines. 'Lucky we were so high. If we'd been down where the atmosphere's thicker it would have been a bit trickier.'

'Is that it, then?' Kasteen asked, her eyes riveted on the scene of destruction below. Even from orbit the dust cloud could still be seen staining half the planet, and in spite of all the horrors I'd endured down there I couldn't help feeling a spark of regret at the scar across the face of the pristine world I'd first looked upon from this very spot a few short days before.

'I hope so,' I said, although the twist of apprehension in my gut didn't fade entirely until we'd dropped back into the warp and were well on our way back to the safety of the Imperium.

Although, of course, where the necrons are concerned nowhere is ever remotely safe, as we now know to our cost. At least that particular nest appears to have been dealt with, even if no one can ever go back to check; the first thing Amberley did when my message finally caught up with her was to place the whole system under Inquisitorial quarantine.[77]

If there was one bright spot in the whole affair it was that I got to spend a little free time with her, after the interminable debriefing sessions were finally over and she'd finished going round every trooper in the regiment who'd seen or heard anything of what we'd found on that miserable iceball and threatened them with the wrath of the Emperor if they ever breathed a word of it again. Or the wrath of the Inquisition, which, trust me, is even scarier.

Amberley was in an uncharacteristically sombre mood on the last night we spent together, the occasional table in her hotel suite covered in data-slates as she collated all the witness reports, and looked up with a wan smile as I entered.

'You were damn lucky,' she said, the blue of her eyes clouded with fatigue. I nodded, and stood aside to let the room servitor trundle in with a tray of food. She saw it and raised an eyebrow.

'I took the liberty of ordering,' I said. 'You seemed busy.'

'Thank you,' she said, stretching, so I wandered across and massaged some of the tension from her shoulders as the servitor set out dishes and cutlery on the dining table. She smiled as the covers came off.

'Ackenberry sorbet. One of my favourites.' That hadn't been hard to remember, so I smiled in return.

'You did say you'd live on the stuff if you could the last time you ordered it.'

'So I did.' The smile widened as the main course came into view. 'What's that?'

'Ambull steak,' I said. 'I think they owe me that much.'

[Cain's narrative continues for several more paragraphs, but since it only covers personal matters of no interest to anyone else I've chosen to end this extract from the archive right here.]

---

77 Subsequent examination of the site showed no signs of an active necron presence, although if anything was left of their installation it would have been burried far too deeply to have left much trace of anything. I for one would not be at all keen to start digging holes to find out for sure.

HELSREACH

AARON DEMBSKI-BOWDEN

PART ONE

THE EXILED KNIGHT

PROLOGUE

KNIGHT OF THE INNER CIRCLE

I will die on this world.

I cannot tell where this conviction comes from. Whatever birthed it is a mystery to me, and yet the thought clings like a virus, blooming behind my eyes and taking deep root within my mind. It almost feels real enough to spread corruption to the rest of my body, like a true sickness.

It will happen soon, within the coming nights of blood and fire. I will draw my last breath, and when my brothers return to the stars, my ashes will be scattered over the priceless earth of this accursed world.

Armageddon.

Even the name twists my blood until burning oil beats through my veins. I feel anger now, hot and heavy, flowing through my heart and filtering into my limbs like boiling poison.

When the sensation – and it is a physical sensation – reaches my fingertips, my hands curl into fists. I do not make them adopt this shape, it simply happens. Fury is as natural to me as breathing. I neither fear nor resent its influence on my actions.

I am strong, born only to slay for the Emperor and the Imperium. I am pure, wearing the blackest of the black, trained to serve as a spiritual guide as well as a warleader. I am wrath incarnate, living only to kill until finally killed.

I am a weapon in the Eternal Crusade to forge humanity's mastership of the stars.

Yet strength, purity and wrath will not be enough. I will die on this world. I will die on Armageddon.

Soon, my brothers will ask me to consecrate the war that will be my death.

The thought plagues me not because I fear death, but because a futile death is anathema to me.

But this is no night to think such things. My lords, masters and brothers have gathered to honour me.

I am not sure I deserve this, but as with my sick sense of foreboding, this is a thought I keep to myself. I wear the black, and glare from behind the skulled visage of the immortal Emperor. It is not for one such as I to show doubt, to show weakness, to show even the whispering edges of blasphemy.

In the holiest chamber of our ancient flagship, I lower myself to one knee and bow my head, because this is what is asked of me. The time has come after a century and a half, and I wish it had not.

My mentor – the warrior who was my brother, father, teacher and master – is dead. After one hundred and sixty-six years of his guidance, I am on the edge of inheriting his mantle.

These are my thoughts as I kneel before my commanders, this bleak mesh of my master's death and my own yet to come. This is the blackness that festers unspoken.

At last, unaware of my secret torments, the High Marshal speaks my name.

'Grimaldus,' High Marshal Helbrecht intoned. His voice was a guttural rumble, rendered harsh from yelling orders and battle cries in a hundred wars on a hundred worlds.

Grimaldus did not raise his head. The knight closed his disquietingly gentle eyes, as if this gesture could seal the doubts within his skull.

'Yes, my liege.'

'We have brought you here to honour you, just as you have honoured us for so many years.'

Grimaldus said nothing, sensing it was not his time to speak. He knew why they were honouring him now, of course, and the knowledge was bitter. Mordred – Grimaldus's mentor, a Reclusiarch of the Eternal Crusade – was dead.

After the ritual, Grimaldus would take his place.

It was an honour he had waited one hundred and sixty-six years to receive.

A century and a half of wrath, courage and pain since the Battle of Fire and Blood, when he drew the eye of the revered Mordred – who was already ancient but unbowed, and who saw within the young Grimaldus a burning core of potential.

A century and a half since he was inducted into the lowest ranks of the Chaplain brotherhood, rising through the tiers in his master's shadow, knowing that he was being forged in war to replace his ageing guardian.

Over a century and a half of believing he would not deserve the title when it finally rested upon his shoulders.

Now the time had come, and his conviction had not changed.

'We have summoned you,' Helbrecht said, 'to be judged.'

'I have answered the summons,' Grimaldus said in the silence of the Reclusiam. 'I submit myself before your judgement, my liege.'

Helbrecht wore no armour, but his bulk was barely diminished. Clad in layered robes of bone-white and bearing his personal black heraldry, the High Marshal stood in the Temple of Dorn, his hands clutching an ornate helm with all due respect.

'Mordred is dead,' Helbrecht's voice was a deep murmur. 'Slain by the Archenemy. You, Grimaldus, have lost a master. We have all of us lost a brother.'

The Temple of Dorn, a museum, a Reclusiam, a sanctuary of hanging banners from ten thousand years of crusading, briefly came alive as the knights in the shadows intoned their agreement with their liege lord's words.

Silence returned, and Grimaldus kept his gaze on the floor.

'We mourn his loss,' the High Marshal said, 'but honour his wisdom in this, his final order.'

It comes to this. Grimaldus tensed. *Show no weakness. Show no doubt.*

'Grimaldus, warrior-priest of the Eternal Crusade. It was the belief of Reclusiarch Mordred that upon his death, you would be worthiest of our Brother-Chaplains to stand in his stead. His final decree before the returning of his gene-seed to the Chapter was that you, of all your brethren, would be the one to rise to the rank of Reclusiarch.'

Grimaldus opened his eyes and licked lips that had suddenly turned dry. Slowly he raised his head, facing the High Marshal, seeing Mordred's helm – a grinning steel skull – in the commander's scarred hands.

'Grimaldus,' Helbrecht spoke again, no hint of emotion colouring his voice. 'You are a veteran in your own right, and once stood as the youngest Sword Brother in the history of the Black Templars. As a Chaplain, your life has been without cowardice or shame, your ferocity and faith without equal. It is my belief, not merely the wish of your fallen master, that you should take the honour we offer you now.'

Grimaldus nodded, but uttered no words. His eyes, so deceptively soft in their gaze, did not waver from their stare. The helm's slanted eye lenses were the rich, deep red of arterial blood. The death mask was utterly familiar to him – the face of his master when the knights went to war, making it the face of his master for most of his life.

Its skullish visage smiled.

'Rise, if you would refuse this honour,' Helbrecht finished. 'Rise and walk from this sacred chamber, if you wish no place in the hierarchy of our most noble Chapter.'

He tells me to rise if I want to turn my back on the great honour being offered to me. Leave if I wish no place among the commanders of the Eternal Crusade.

I don't move. Despite my doubts, my muscles remain locked. The steel mask sneers, a dark leer that is soothing for its brutal familiarity. From beyond the grave, Mordred grins at me.

He believed I was worthy of this. That is all that matters. I had never known him to be wrong.

I feel the edge of a smile creeping across my own lips. It will not fade, no matter how I try to quell it. As I kneel in this hallowed hall, I know I'm smiling, but it's a private moment despite the dozens of fellow warriors watching from the banner-lined walls.

Perhaps they mistake my smile for confidence?

I will never ask, because I do not care.

Helbrecht approaches at last, and with the silken rasp of steel stroking steel, he draws the holiest blade in the Imperium of Man.

The sword was as ancient as human relics could be, given form and purpose in the forges of Terra after the great Heresy. In those nights of saga and legend, it was carried into battle by Sigismund, the first Emperor's Champion, favoured son of the Primarch Rogal Dorn.

The blade itself, as long as a mortal man is tall, was wrought from the broken remains of Lord Dorn's own sword. In this temple, where the Chapter's greatest artefacts are kept in reverently maintained stasis fields to ward off the corrosive touch of time, the High Marshal held the most sacred treasure in the Black Templar armoury.

'You will have your own rituals within the Chaplain brotherhood,' Helbrecht said, his voice solemn with respect. 'For now, I recognise you as the inheritor to your master's mantle.'

The blade's silver tip lowered, pointing directly at Grimaldus's throat. 'You have waged war at my side for two hundred years, Grimaldus. Will you stand at my side as Reclusiarch of the Eternal Crusade?'

'Yes, my liege.'

Helbrecht nodded, sheathing the blade. Grimaldus tensed again, turning his head and baring his cheek.

With the force of a hammer, the back of Helbrecht's fist crashed into the Chaplain's jaw. Grimaldus grunted, tasting the coppery vitality of his own blood – his primarch's blood – and he grinned up at his commander through blood-pinked teeth. Helbrecht spoke again.

'I dub thee Reclusiarch of the Eternal Crusade. You are now a leader of our blessed Chapter.' The High Marshal raised his hand, showing the flecks of Grimaldus's blood marking his curled fingers. 'As a knight of the inner circle, let that be the last blow you receive unanswered.'

Grimaldus nodded, unclenching his jaw, calming his heart and fighting the sudden flood of his killing urge. Even expecting the ritual strike, his instincts cried at him to respond in kind.

'It... will be so, my liege.'

'As it should be,' said Helbrecht. 'Rise, Grimaldus, Reclusiarch of the Eternal Crusade.'

ONE

ARRIVAL

For some hours after his ritual entrance into the highest echelons of the Chapter, Grimaldus stood alone in the Temple of Dorn.

Without a breeze to breathe life into the austere chamber, the great banners hung unmoving, some faded with the years, others brightly woven, still others even bearing dried bloodstains. Grimaldus looked upon the heraldry of his brothers' crusades.

Lastrati, piles of skulls and burning braziers depicting the war of attrition on the surface of that accursed heretic world...

Apostasy, showing the aquila chained to the globe, when the Templars were recalled to Holy Terra for the first time in thousands of years, to shed the blood of the false High Lord Vandire...

And on into the more recent wars in which Grimaldus himself had played a part – *Vinculus*, with the sword impaling a daemon, where the knights had crashed against the tainted followers of the Archenemy in the great Battle of Fire and Blood – when Grimaldus himself had been taken from the ranks of the Sword Brethren and begun his gruelling rise through the tiers of the Chaplain brotherhood.

Dozens of banners hung in the still air, descending from the ornately carved ceiling, telling the tales of the glories won and the lives lost in each single facet of the Eternal Crusade.

The only noise except for Grimaldus's own breathing was the crackling hum of stasis fields enclosing Templar relics. Grimaldus passed one, a blurry field of smoky blue force revealing through its milky surface a bolter that had once belonged to Castellan Duron two thousand years before. The kill-markings scratched into the firearm's surface, etched in the tiniest Gothic lettering, covered the entire weapon like holy scripture.

Grimaldus stood by the plinth displaying the bolter for some time, his fingers itching to enter the release code on the keypad built into the shield's column. Such secrets were the purview of the Chaplain brotherhood that maintained this shrine, and even before he had risen to his current rank, Grimaldus had honoured the machine-spirits of the chamber's relics through ritual blessings and reconsecrations.

There was great succour in bearing the weapons of champions, even if only to cleanse and purify them after a warp jump.

Only one of the plinths – and in the Temple of Dorn, there were over a hundred occupied displays – bore what Grimaldus had come for. He stood before the short column, reading the silver plaque beneath the pulsing stasis shield.

Mordred
Reclusiarch
'We are judged in life for the evil we destroy.'

Beneath the words was a keypad, each key bearing a Gothic sigil in gold leaf. Grimaldus entered the nineteen-digit code for this specific column, and the stasis field powered down with a grinding of ancient engines inside the stone plinth.

Upon the flat surface of the white stone column, a weapon rested, deactivated and silent, freed of the blue illumination that had protected it.

Without any ceremony at all, Grimaldus clutched the maul's haft and raised it in his sure grip. The head was a hammer of holy gold and blessed adamantium fashioned into the shape of eagle wings over a stylised Templar cross. The haft was darkened metal as long as the knight's own arm.

The weapon's ornate head caught the dim glow from the lume-globes ensconced in the walls, and was painted briefly in flashes of reflected light as he turned it in his hands.

The warrior-priest stood like this for some time.

'Brother,' came a voice from behind. Grimaldus turned, instinct bringing the weapon to bear.

Despite never holding the relic before, his scarred fingertips found the activation rune along its handle before his heart could even beat once. The eagle-winged hammerhead flared with threatening brightness, serpents of hissing electricity flickering over the gold and silver metal.

The figure smiled to be revealed in such stark illumination. In a face pockmarked and crevassed by decades of battle, Grimaldus saw the amusement in the younger knight's pale eyes.

'Reclusiarch,' the figure inclined his head in greeting.

'Artarion.'

'We draw near to our destination. Estimates put translation back into realspace within the hour. I took the liberty of readying the squad for planetfall.'

Artarion's grin, much like Artarion himself, was ugly to look upon. In contrast, Grimaldus finally returned the smile, but as with his eyes there was an unsuspected gentleness in the expression.

'This world will burn,' the warrior-priest said, not even a shadow of doubt creeping into his voice.

'It will not be the first.' Artarion's scratched lips parted to reveal steel teeth – implanted replacements due to a sniper shot fifteen years before. The rifle round had taken him in the side of the face, shattering his jaw. The mess of scar tissue webbing the flesh around the left side of his lips added to the thin, sneering image he projected when his helm was removed. 'It will not be the first,' he said again, 'nor the last.'

'Have you seen the projections? The fleet auguries, the number of vessels in the local systems already, the reports of those yet to arrive?'

'I lost interest when the numbers became too high for me to count on my fingers.' Artarion snorted at his own weak jest. 'We will fight and win, or fight and die. All that ever changes is the colour of the sky we fight under, and the shade of the blood on our blades.'

Grimaldus lowered the crozius hammer, as if only then realising he still held it at the ready. A rich darkness settled over their sight as the relic's crackling illumination faded. In the wake of the brightness, the sharp scent of ozone – that strange freshness after a storm – filled the air. The power cells within the maul's haft whined as they reluctantly cooled down. The weapon's spirit hungered for war.

'You speak with a soldier's heart, but you are wrong to be so dismissive. This campaign... This has the weight of history about it. It would be the gravest of errors to consider this merely another conflict to add to the honour rolls.'

The softness had left Grimaldus's voice now. When he spoke, it was with the bitter passion Artarion was all too familiar with, fierce and thick with anticipation – the growled challenge of a caged animal. 'The surface of this world will burn until all of mankind's great achievements upon it are naught but ash and memory.'

'I have never heard you claim we would lose before, brother.'

Grimaldus shook his head, his voice still low and fevered. 'The planet will burn regardless of our triumph or defeat. I speak of the coming crusade's underpinning truth.'

'You are so certain?'

'I feel it in my blood. Win or lose,' the Chaplain said, 'come the final day on Armageddon, those of us that still stand will realise no war has ever cost us so dearly.'

'Have you shared these concerns with the High Marshal?' Artarion scratched the back of his neck, his fingertips soothing the itching skin around a spinal socket.

Grimaldus chuckled, momentarily blindsided by his brother's naivety. 'You think he needs me to tell him?'

Few ships in the Imperium of Man matched the lethal grandeur of *The Eternal Crusader.*

Some ships sailed the heavens like the seaborne vessels of ancient Terra, journeying between the stars with solemnity and a measured grace. *The Eternal Crusader* was not one of these. Like a spear hurled into the void by the hand of Rogal Dorn himself, the flagship of the Templars had been slicing through space for ten thousand years of war. Its engines raged, streaming plasma contrails in their wake as they powered the vessel from world to world in echo of the Emperor's Great Crusade.

And the *Crusader* was not alone.

At her back, the capital vessels *Night's Vigil* and *Majesty* burned their engines hard, striving to keep pace and fall into a lance formation with their flagship. In the wake of these heavy cruisers – a battle-barge and smaller strike cruiser respectively – a wing of support frigates formed the rest of the lance. Seven in total, each of these faster interceptor vessels powered forward with less of a struggle to maintain formation with the *Crusader.*

The ship burst back into reality, trailing discoloured warp-smog from its protesting Geller field, the brilliance of its plasma drives flaring with gaseous leakage that misted around the void shields of the vessels which slammed back into realspace just behind.

Ahead of them lay an ashen globe, darkened by unclean cloud cover, strangely at peace despite the turmoil surrounding it.

If one were to look into the void around the bitter, punished world of Armageddon, one would see a thriving subsector of Imperial space where even the most prosperous hive planets bore more than their fair share of slowly-healing wounds.

It was a region of space where the worlds themselves were scarred. War, and the fear of another colossal sector-wide conflict, hung over the trillions of loyal Imperial souls like the threat of a storm forever on the edge of breaking.

It was always said by some that the Imperium of Man was dying. These heretical voices spoke of mankind's endless wars against its manifold foes, and decreed that humanity's ultimate fate was being decided in the fires of a million, million battlefields across the countless stars within the God-Emperor's grip.

Nowhere were the words of these seers and prophets more evident than the ravaged – yet rebuilt – Armageddon subsector, named for its greatest world, a world responsible for production and consumption on an immense and unmatched level.

Armageddon itself stood as a bastion of Imperial strength, churning out regiments of tanks from manufactories that never ceased activity by day or night. Millions of men and women wore the ochre armour of Armageddon's Steel Legions, their features hidden behind the traditional respirator masks of this honoured and renowned division of the Imperial Guard.

The hives of this defiant planet reached into the pollution-rich cloud cover that wreathed the world in perpetual twilight. No wildlife howled on Armageddon. No beasts stalked their prey outside the ever-growing hive-cities. The call of the wild was the rattle and clank of ten thousand ammunition manufactories that never halted production. The stalking of animals was the grinding of tank treads across the world's rockcrete surfaces, awaiting transport into the sky to serve in a hundred and more distant conflicts.

It was a world devoted to war in every way imaginable, made bitter by the scars of the past, soured by the wounds gouged into its face by humanity's enemies. Armageddon always rebuilt after each devastation, but it was never permitted to forget.

The first and foremost reminder of the last war, the almighty Second War that saw billions dead, was a deep space installation named for one of the Emperor's Angels of Death.

Dante, they called it.

It was from there that the mortals of Armageddon stared into the blackness of space, watching, waiting, praying that nothing stared back.

For fifty-seven years, those prayers had been answered.

But no longer. Imperial tacticians already had reliable figures from early engagements that confirmed the greenskin fleet bearing down on Armageddon as the largest xenos invasion force in the history of the segmentum. As the alien fleets closed around the system, Imperial reinforcements raced to break the blockaded sectors and land their troops on Armageddon before the invasion fleet arrived in the heavens above the doomed world.

A battle-barge of no standard design, the *Crusader* was a princely fortress-monastery, charcoal-black and bristling with gothic cathedral spires like a beast's spines along its back. Weapons capable of pounding cities into dust – the claws of this night-stalking predator – aimed into the void. Along the ship's length and clustered across its prow, hundreds of weapons batteries and lance cannons stood with mouths open to the silent darkness of space.

Aboard the ships, a thousand warriors cast off the shackles of training, preparation and meditation. At last, after weeks of passage through the Sea of Souls, Armageddon, beating heart-world of the subsector, was finally in sight.

My brothers' names are Artarion, Priamus, Cador, Nerovar and Bastilan.

These are the knights that have waged war beside me for decades.

I watch them, each in turn, as we make ready for planetfall. Our arming chamber is a cell devoid of decoration, bare of sentiment, alive now with the methodical movements of dead-minded servitors machining our armour into place. The chamber is thick with the scholarly scent of fresh vellum from our armour scrolls, coppery oils from our ritually-cleansed weapons, and the ever-present cloying salty reek of sweating servitors.

I flex my arm, feeling my war plate's false muscles of cable and fibre buzz with smooth vibration at the cycle of motion. Papyrus scrolls are draped over the angles of my armour, their delicate runic lettering listing the details of battles I could never forget. This paper, of good quality by Imperial standards, is manufactured on board the *Crusader* by serfs who pass the technique down generation to generation. Every role on the ship is vital. Every duty has its own honour.

My tabard, the white of sun-bleached bone, offers a stark contrast to the blacker than black plate beneath. The heraldic cross stands proud on my chest, where Astartes of lesser Chapters wear the Emperor's aquila. We do not wear His symbol. We *are* His symbol.

My fingers twitch as my gauntlet locks into place. That was not intentional – a nerve-spasm, a pain response. An invasive but familiar coldness settles over my forearm as my gauntlet's neural linkage spike sinks into my wrist to bond with the bones and true muscles there.

I make a fist with my hand armoured in black ceramite, then release it. Each finger flexes in turn, as if pulling a trigger. Satisfied, its dead eyes flashing with an acknowledgement of a job complete, an arming servitor moves away to bring my second gauntlet.

My brothers go through the same rituals of checking and rechecking. A curious sense of unease descends upon me, but I refuse to give it voice. I watch them now because I believe this is the last time we will go through this ritual together.

I will not be the only one to die upon Armageddon.

Artarion, Priamus, Cador, Nerovar and Bastilan. We are the knights of Squad Grimaldus.

Within his veins, Cador carries the blessed blood of Rogal Dorn with what seems like weary honour. His face is shattered and his body tormented – now half-bionic due to untreatable wounds – but he remains defiant, even indefatigable. He is older than I, older by far. His decades within the Sword Brethren are behind him now; he was released with all honour when his advancing age and increasing bionics left him less than the exemplar he had been before.

Priamus is the rising sun to Cador's dusk. He is aware of his skills in the unsubtle and undignified way of many young warriors. Without even the ghost of humility, his roars of triumph on the battlefield sound like cries for attention, a braggart's declarations. A blademaster, he calls himself. Yet he is not mistaken.

Artarion is... Artarion. My shadow, just as I am his. It is rare among our number for any knight to lay aside personal glory, yet Artarion is the one who carries my banner into battle. He has joked more times than I care to remember that he does so only to provide the enemy with a target lock on my location. For all his great courage, he is not a man blessed with a skilful sense of humour. The mangling wound that fouled his face was a sniper shot meant for me. I carry that knowledge with me each time we go to war.

Nerovar is the newest among us. He holds the dubious honour of being the only knight I chose to stand with me, while all others were appointed to fight by my side. The squad required the presence of an Apothecary. In the trials, only Nerovar impressed the rest of us with his quiet endurance. He labours now over his arm-mounted narthecium, blue eyes narrowed as he tests the flickering snap of surgical blades and cutting lasers. A sickening *clack!* sounds as he fires his reductor. The giver of merciful death, the extractor of gene-seed – its impaling component snaps from its housing, then retracts with sinister slowness.

Bastilan is last. Bastilan, always the best and least of us all. A leader but not a commander – an inspiring presence, but not a strategist – forever a sergeant, never fated to rise as a castellan or marshal. He has always said his role as such is all he desires. I pray he speaks the truth, for if he is deceiving us, he hides the lie well behind his dark eyes.

He is the one who speaks to me now. What he says chills my blood.

'I have heard from Geraint and Lograine of the Sword Brethren,' he chooses his words carefully, 'that there is talk of the High Marshal nominating you to lead a crusade.'

And for a moment, everyone stops moving.

The skies over Armageddon were rich and thick with a sick, greyish-yellow cast. Sulphurous cloud cover was nothing new to the population, with their hive walls treated and shielded against the storm season's downpours of acid rain.

Around each hive-city across the planet's surface, vast landing fields were cleared, either hurriedly paved with rockcrete or simply ground flat under the treads of hundreds of landscaper trucks. Around Hades Hive, rain scythed down onto the cleared areas and sparked off the dense heat-shimmer of the city's protective void shields. Across the world, the heavens were in turmoil, weather patterns ravaged by the atmospheric disturbance caused by countless ships breaking cloud cover every day.

Yet at Hades Hive, the storms were especially fierce. Hundreds of troop carriers, their paint already melted to reveal bare, dull metal in places, endured the rainfall as they rested on the landing fields. Some were disgorging columns of men into the hastily-erected campsites that were spreading across the wastelands between the hives, while others sat in silence, awaiting clearance to return to orbit.

Hades itself was little more than industrial scar tissue blighting Armageddon's face. Despite efforts to repair the city after the last war over half a century before, it still bore a ragged share of memories. Toppled spires, broken domes, shattered cathedrals – this was the skyline after the death of a hive.

A squadron of Thunderhawk gunships pierced the caul of cloud cover. To those manning the battlements of Hades, they were a flock of crows winging down from the darkening sky.

Mordechai Ryken scanned the gunships through his magnoculars. After several seconds of zoom-blur, green reticules locked onto the streaking avian hulls and transcribed an analysis in dim white text alongside the image.

Ryken lowered the viewfinder scope. It hung on a leather cord around his neck, resting on the ochre jacket he wore as part of his uniform. His breath was hot on his face, recycled and filtered through the cheap rebreather mask he wore over his mouth and nose.

The air still tasted like a latrine, though. And it didn't exactly smell any better. The joys of high sulphur content in the atmosphere. Ryken was still waiting for the day he would be used to it, and he'd been stuck on this rock so far for every day of his thirty-seven years of life.

A way down the battlements, working on getting an anti-air turret operational, a team of his men clustered with a robed tech-priest. The multi-barrelled monstrosity dwarfed the half a dozen soldiers standing in its shadow.

'Sir?' one of them voxed. Ryken knew who it was despite the shapeless overcoats they all wore. Only one of them was female.

'What is it, Vantine?'

'Those are Astartes gunships, aren't they?'

'Good eyes.' And they were, at that. Vantine would've made sniper a long time ago if she could aim worth a damn. Alas, there was more to sniping than just seeing.

'Which ones?' she pressed.

'Does it matter? Astartes are Astartes. Reinforcements are reinforcements.'

'Yes, but which ones?'

'Black Templars.' Ryken took a breath, tonguing a sore cut on his lip as he watched the fleet of Thunderhawks touching down in the distance. 'Hundreds of them.'

An Imperial Guard column rolled out from Hades to meet the newest arrivals. A command Chimera, flying no shortage of impressive flags, led six Leman Russ battle tanks, their collective passage chewing into the newly laid rockcrete.

Bulky troop landers were still setting down elsewhere on the landing field, the wash from their engines blasting wind and gritty dust in all directions, but General Kurov of the Armageddon Steel Legion did not make personal appearances to greet just anyone.

Despite his advancing age, Kurov cut a straight-backed figure in his grimy uniform of ochre fatigues and black webbing, with flak padding on the torso. No sign of his many medals, not a hint of gold, silver, ribbon, or the other trappings of pomp. Here was the man that had led the Council of Armageddon for decades, and earned the respect of his people by wading knee-deep in the sulphur marshes and bracken forests after the last war, hunting xenos survivors in the infamous Ork Hunter platoons.

He stomped down the ramp, setting his cap to guard his eyes against the heatless, yet annoyingly bright, afternoon sunlight. A team of Guardsmen, each as raggedly attired as their commanding officer, clanged down the ramp after the general. As they moved, misshapen skulls clacked and rattled together from where they hung on belts and bandoliers. Across their chests, they gripped lasguns that hadn't resembled standard-issue for some time – each bore its own display of modifications and accoutrements.

Kurov marched his ramshackle gang of bodyguards in decent parade order, yet without any conscious effort. He led them to the waiting Thunderhawks, each of which was still emitting a dull machine-whine as their boosters cycled into inactivity.

Eighteen gunships. Kurov knew that from the initial auspex report as the Templars had landed. They sat now in disorganised unmoving ranks, ramps withdrawn and bulkheads sealed. Their undersides, blunt noses and wing edges still showed a glimmer of cooling heat shields with the after-effects of planetfall.

Three Astartes stood before the gunship fleet, still as statues, with no evidence of which vessels they'd disembarked from.

Only one wore a helm. It stared through ruby eye lenses, its faceplate a skull of steel.

'Are you Kurov?' one of the Astartes demanded.

'I am,' the general replied. 'It is my h–'

In unison, the three inhuman warriors drew their weapons. Kurov took an involuntary step back, not out of fear but surprise. The knights' weapons went live in a humming chorus of wakening power cells. Lightning, controlled and rippling, coated the killing edges of the three artefacts.

The first was a giant clad in armour of bronze and gold against black, the surface of his war plate inscribed with retellings of his deeds in miniscule

Gothic runes, as well as trinkets, trophies and honour badges of red wax seals and papyrus strips. He clutched a two-handed sword, its blade longer than Kurov was tall, and drove its point into the ground. The knight's face was shaped by the wars he had fought – square-jawed, scarred, blunt-featured and expressionless.

The second Astartes, clad in plainer black war plate, wore a cloak of dark weave and scarlet lining. His sword in no way matched the grandeur of the first knight's relic, but the long blade of darkened iron was no less lethal for its simplicity. This knight's face lacked the expressionless ease of the first. He fought not to sneer as he drove his own sword tip into the ground.

And the last, the knight who still wore his helm, carried no blade. The rockcrete beneath their feet shivered slightly under the pounding of his war-mace thudding onto the ground. The mace's head, a stylised knightly cross atop Imperial eagle wings, flared in protest, lightning crackling as the metal kissed the ground.

The three knights knelt, heads lowered. All of this happened at once, in the space of no more than three seconds since Kurov last spoke.

'We are the Emperor's knights,' the giant in bronze and gold intoned. 'We are the warriors of the Eternal Crusade, and the sons of Rogal Dorn. I am Helbrecht, High Marshal of the Black Templars. With me is Bayard, Emperor's Champion, and Grimaldus, Reclusiarch.'

At their names, both knights nodded in turn.

Helbrecht continued, his voice a growled drawl. 'Aboard our vessels in orbit are Marshals Ricard and Amalrich. We come to offer you our blades, our service, and the lives of over nine hundred warriors in the defence of your world.'

Kurov stood in silence. Nine hundred Astartes... Entire star systems were conquered with a fraction of that. He had greeted a dozen Astartes commanders in recent weeks, but few had brought such significant strength with them.

'High Marshal,' the general said at last. 'There is a war council forming tonight. You and your warriors are welcome there.'

'It will be done,' the High Marshal said.

'I'm glad to hear it,' Kurov replied. 'Welcome to Armageddon.'

TWO

THE ABANDONED CRUSADE

Ryken was not smiling.

He'd been a lifelong believer in not shooting the messenger, but today that tradition was in danger of expiring. Behind him loomed an anti-air turret, blanketing them all in its shadow and shielding them from the dim glare of the morning sun. A squad of his men worked on this turret, as they had worked on countless others along the walls in the space of the last two months. It was almost operational. They weren't techs, by any means, but they knew the basic maintenance rites and calibration rituals.

'One minute to test fire,' Vantine said, her voice muffled by her rebreather mask.

And that was when the messenger showed up. It was also when Ryken stopped smiling, despite the fact the messenger was easy on the eyes, as over-starched, narrowed-eyed tactica types went.

'I want these orders rechecked,' he demanded – calmly, but a demand nevertheless.

'With all due respect, sir,' the messenger straightened her own ochre uniform, 'these orders come from the Old Man himself. He's reorganising the disposition of all our forces, and the Steel Legion are honoured to be first in that reappraisal.'

The words stole Ryken's desire to argue. So it was true, then. The Old Man was back.

'But Helsreach is half a continent away,' he tried. 'We've been working on the Hades wall-guns for months.'

'Thirty seconds to test fire,' Vantine called.

The messenger, whose name was Cyria Tyro, wasn't smiling either. In her position as adjutant quintus to General Kurov, grunts and plebeians were forever questioning the orders she relayed, as if she would ever dare alter a single word of the general's instructions. The other adjutants had no difficulties in this area, she was sure of it. For some unknown reason, these lowborn dregs just simply didn't take well to her. Perhaps they were jealous of her position? If so, then they were more foolish than she'd have given them credence for.

'I have long been entrusted with certain aspects of the general's plans,' Tyro lied, 'that frontliners such as yourself are only now being made aware of. I apologise if this is a surprise to you, major, but orders are orders. And these orders come with the highest mandate imaginable.'

'Are we not even going to defend the damn hive?'

At that moment, Vantine test-fired the turret. The floor beneath their feet shook as four cannon barrels blared their anger up at the empty sky. Ryken swore, though it was drowned out in the ear-ringing thunder of the gun's echo. Tyro also swore, though unlike Ryken's general lament, hers was aimed at Vantine and the gun crew.

The major was close to yelling over the ache in his ears. It was fading, but not fast.

'I said, *are we not even going to defend the damn hive?*'

'*You* are not,' Tyro almost pouted, her mouth compressed in restrained irritation. '*You* are going to Helsreach with your regiment. Your transports leave tonight. All of the 101st Steel Legion is to be aboard and ready for transport by sunset in six point five hours.'

Ryken paused. Six and a half hours to get three thousand men and women into heavy lifter transports, gunships and land trains. It was the kind of bad news that made the major feel the need to be overwhelmingly honest.

'Colonel Sarren is going to be furious.'

'Colonel Sarren has dealt with this assignment with grace and solemn devotion to his duty, major. Your commanding officer still has much to teach you in that regard, I see.'

'Cute. Now tell me *why* it's us being sent all the way to Helsreach. I thought Insan and the 121st were kings of that shitpile.'

'Colonel Insan had a terminal failure of his augmetic heart infusers this morning. His second officer requested Sarren by name, and General Kurov agreed.'

'That old bastard's finally dead? That'll teach him to lay off the garage-brewed sauce. Ha! All those expensive augmetics he had done, and he keels over six months later. I like that. That's delicious.'

'Major! Some respect, if you please.'

Ryken frowned. 'I don't like you,' he told Tyro.

'How grievous,' the general's assistant replied, and there was no mistaking the dark, unamused scowl on her face. 'For you have been appointed a liaison to aid in dealings with the Astartes and the conscripted militia.' She looked as if she'd eaten something sour and it was still wriggling on her tongue. 'So... I will be coming with you.'

A moment of curious kinship passed between them, almost going unspoken. They were being exiled to the same place, after all. Their eyes met in that moment, and the foundations of something like a reluctant friendship almost bloomed between them.

It was broken when Ryken walked away.

'I still don't like you.'

'Hades Hive will not survive the first week.'

The man speaking is ancient, and he looks every hour of his age. What keeps him on his feet is a mixture of minimal rejuvenat chem-surgeries, crude bionics, and a faith in the Emperor founded in hatred for the enemies of Man.

I liked him the moment my visor's targeting reticules locked onto him. Both piety and hate echo in his every word.

He should not hold rank here - not to the degree he does. He is merely a commissar in the Imperial Guard, and such a title does not tend to make generals, colonels, Astartes captains and Chapter Masters remain in polite silence when it comes to tactical planning. Yet to the humans at this war council, and the citizens of Armageddon, he is the Old Man, a beloved hero of the Second War fifty-seven years ago.

Not just a hero. *The* hero.

His name is Sebastian Yarrick. Even we Astartes must respect that name.

And when he tells us all that Hades Hive will be destroyed within a matter of days, a hundred Imperial commanders, human and Astartes alike, hang on his every word.

I am one of them. This will be my first true command.

Commissar Sebastian Yarrick leans over the edge of a hololithic display table. With his remaining hand - the other arm is nothing but a stump - he keys in coordinates on the numeric datapad, and the hololith projection of Hades Hive widens with flickering impatience to display both of the planet's hemispheres in insignificant detail.

The Old Man, a gaunt and wizened human of sharp features and skeletally-obvious facial bones, gestures to the blip on the map that represents Hades Hive and its surrounding territories. Wastelands, in the main.

'Six decades ago,' he says, 'the Great Enemy met his defeat at Hades. Our defence here was what won us that war.'

There are general murmurs of assent. The commissar's voice carries around the expansive chamber through floating skull drones equipped with vox-speakers where their jaws had once been.

I am surrounded by the familiar hum of active power armour, though the scents and faces that meet my eyes are new to me. Standing to my left at a respectful distance, his face raggedly proud around extensive bionics, is Chapter Master Seth of the Flesh Tearers - known to his men as the Guardian of the Rage. He smells of sacred weapon oils, his primarch's potent blood running beneath his weathered skin, and the spicy, unwholesome reptilian scent of the lizard predator-kings that stalk the jungles of his home world. Seth is flanked by his own officers, each one bareheaded and with faces as pitted and cracked as their master's. Whatever wars have occupied the Flesh Tearers in recent decades, the conflicts have not been kind to them.

To my left, my liege Helbrecht stands resplendent in his battle armour of black and bronze. Bayard, the Emperor's Champion, is by his side. Both rest their helmets on the table's surface, the stern helms distorting the edge of the hololithic display, and give their full attention to the ancient commissar.

I cross my arms over my chest and do the same.

'Why?' someone asks. Their voice is low, too low to be human, and carries over the chamber without the need of vox-amplification. A hundred heads turn to regard an Astartes in the bright red-orange of a lesser Chapter, one unknown to me. He steps forward, leaning his knuckles on the table, facing Yarrick from almost twenty metres distance.

'We recognise Brother-Captain Amaras,' an Imperial herald announces from his position at Yarrick's side, smoothing the formal blue robes of his office. He bangs the butt of his staff on the ground three times. 'Commander of the Angels of Fire.'

Amaras nods in thanks, and fixes Yarrick with his unblinking gaze.

'Why would the greenskin warlord simply annihilate the greatest battlefield of the last war? Surely our forces should muster at Hades and stand ready to defend against the largest assault.'

Murmurs of agreement ripple throughout the gathered commanders. Emboldened, Amaras smiles at Yarrick.

'We are the Emperor's Chosen, mortal. We are His Angels of Death. We have centuries of battle experience compared to these human commanders at your side.'

'No,' another voice replies. This one is distorted into a vox-born snarl, filtered through a helm's speakers. I swallow as the herald bangs the staff another three times.

I had not realised I'd spoken out loud.

'We recognise Brother-Chaplain Grimaldus,' he calls out. 'Reclusiarch of the Black Templars.'

Grimaldus shook his head at the gathered commanders. Over a hundred, human and Astartes, all standing around the huge table in this converted auditorium once used for whatever dreary theatre performances occurred on a manufactory world. A riot of colours, heraldry, symbols of unity, varied uniforms, regimental designations and iconography. General Kurov stood at the commissar's shoulder, deferring to the Old Man in all things.

'The xenos do not think as we do,' Grimaldus said. 'The greenskins do not come to Armageddon for vengeance, or to seek to bleed us for the defeats they have suffered at Imperial hands in the past. They come for the pleasure of violence.'

Yarrick, a skeleton wreathed in pale flesh and a dark uniform, watched the knight in silence. Amaras pounded his fist onto the table and pointed at the Templar. For a moment of deathly calm, Grimaldus considered drawing his pistol and slaying him where he stood.

'That lends credence to *my* belief,' Amaras almost snarled.

'Not at all. Have you inspected what remains of Hades Hive? It is a ruin. There is nothing to fight over, nothing to defend. The Great Enemy knows this. He will be aware that Imperial forces will put up no more than a token resistance here, and fall back to defend hives that are still worth defending. It is likely the warlord will obliterate Hades from orbit, rather than seek to take it.'

'We cannot let this hive fall! It is a symbol of mankind's defiance! With respect, Chaplain–'

'Enough,' Yarrick said. 'Peace, Brother-Captain Amaras. Grimaldus speaks with wisdom.'

Grimaldus inclined his head in thanks.

'I will not be silenced by a mortal,' Amaras growled, but the fight was gone from him. Yarrick – the thin, ancient commissar – just stared at the Astartes captain. After several moments, Amaras looked back to the hololithic topography around the hive. Yarrick turned back to the gathered officers, his one human eye stern and his augmetic one whirring in its socket as it refocussed on the faces before him.

'Hades will not survive the first week,' he said again, this time shaking his head. 'We must abandon the hive and spread the forces here to other bastions of strength. This is not the Second War. What is coming in-system now far exceeds what has laid waste to the planet before. The other hives must be reinforced a thousand times over.' He took a moment to clear his throat, and a cough stole over him, dry and hoarse. When it subsided, the Old Man smiled without even the ghost of humour.

'Hades will burn. We must make our stand elsewhere.'

At this cue, General Kurov stepped forward with a data-slate.

'We come to the divisions of command.' He took a breath, and pressed on. 'The fleet that will besiege Armageddon is too vast to repel.'

A chorus of jeers rose. Kurov rode them out. Grimaldus, Helbrecht and Bayard were among those that remained absolutely silent.

'Hear me, friends and brothers,' Kurov sighed. 'And hear me well. Those of you who insist this war will be anything more than a conflict of bitter attrition are deceiving yourselves. At current estimates, we have over fifty thousand Astartes in the Armageddon subsector, and thirty times the number of Imperial Guardsmen. And it will still not be enough to secure a clean victory. At our best estimations, Battlefleet Armageddon, the orbital defences, and the Astartes fleets remaining in the void will be able to deny the enemy landing for nine days. These are our *best* estimates.'

'And the worst?' asked an Astartes officer bedecked in white wolf furs, wearing the grey war plate of the Space Wolves. His body language betrayed his impatience. He almost paced, like a canine in a cage.

'Four days,' the Old Man said through his grim smile.

Silence descended again. Kurov didn't waste it.

'Admiral Parol of Battlefleet Armageddon has outlined his plan and uploaded it to the tactical network for all commanders to review. Once the orbital war is lost, be it four days or nine, our fleets will break from the planet in a fighting withdrawal. From then on, Armageddon will be defenceless beyond what is already entrenched upon the surface. The orks will be free to land whatever and wherever they wish.

'Admiral Parol will lead the remaining Naval ships of the fleet in repeated guerrilla strikes against the invaders' vessels still in orbit.'

'Who will lead the Astartes vessels?' Captain Amaras spoke up again.

There was another pause, before Commissar Yarrick nodded to a dark-armoured cluster of warriors across the table.

'Given his seniority and the expertise of his Chapter, High Marshal Helbrecht of the Black Templars will take overall command of the Astartes fleets.'

And once more, there was uproar, several Astartes commanders demanding that the glory be theirs. The knights ignored it.

'We are to remain in orbit?' Grimaldus leaned closer to his commander and voiced the question.

The High Marshal didn't take his eyes from Yarrick. 'We are the obvious choice to command the Astartes elements in the orbital battles.'

The Chaplain looked across the chamber, at the various leaders and officers of a hundred different forces.

I was wrong, he thought. I will not die in futility on this world. Eagerness, hot and urgent, flushed through his system, as real and vital as a flood of adrenaline gushing through his two hearts.

'The *Crusader* will plunge like a lance into the core of their fleet. High Marshal, we can slaughter the greenskin tyrant before he even sets foot on the world below us.'

Helbrecht lifted his gaze from the ancient commissar as his Chaplain spoke. He turned to Grimaldus, his dark eyes piercing the other knight's skull mask with their intensity.

'I have already spoken with the other marshals, my brother. We must leave a contingent on the surface. I will lead the orbital crusade. Amalrich and Ricard will lead the forces in the Ash Wastes. All that remains is a single crusade, to defend one of the hive cities that yet remains ungarrisoned by Astartes.'

Grimaldus shook his head. 'That is not our duty, my liege. Both Amalrich and Ricard have a host of honours inscribed upon their armour. Each has led greater crusades alone. Neither will relish an exile to a filthy manufactorum hive while a thousand of their brothers wage a glorious war in the heavens. You would shame them.'

'And yet,' Helbrecht was implacable, his features set in stone, 'a commander must remain.'

'Don't.' The knight's blood ran cold. 'Don't do this.'

'It is already done.'

'No,' he said, and meant it with every fibre of his being. *'No.'*

'This is not the time. The decision is made, Grimaldus. I know you, as I knew Mordred. You will not refuse this honour.'

'No,' Grimaldus said again, loud enough that other commanders began to stare.

Helbrecht said nothing. Grimaldus stepped closer to him.

'I would burst the Great Enemy's black heart in my hand, and cast his blasphemous flagship to the surface of Armageddon wreathed in holy fire. Do not leave me here, Helbrecht. Do not deny me this glory.'

'You will not refuse this honour,' the High Marshal said, his voice as stony as his face.

Grimaldus wanted no further part in the proceedings. Worse, he knew he was irrelevant here. As deliberations and tactics were discussed for the coming orbital defence, he turned from the hololithic display.

'Wait, brother.' Helbrecht's voice made it a request, not an order, and that made it easy to refuse.

Grimaldus stalked from the chamber without another word.

* * *

Their destination was called, with bleakness so typical of this world, Helsreach.

'Blood of Dorn,' Artarion swore with feeling. 'Now that's a sight.'

'This is… huge,' Nerovar whispered.

The four Thunderhawks tore across the sulphurous sky, parting sick yellow clouds that drifted apart in their wake. From the cockpit of the lead aircraft, six knights watched the expansive city below.

And *expansive* barely covered it.

The four gunships, boosters howling, veered in graceful unison around one of the tallest industrial spires. It was slate-grey, belching thick smoke into the dirty sky, merely one of hundreds.

A wing of escorts, small and manoeuvrable Lightning-pattern air superiority fighters, coasted alongside the Astartes Thunderhawks. They were neither welcome nor unwelcome, merely ignored.

'We cannot be the only Astartes strength sent to this city,' Nerovar removed his white helmet with a hiss of venting air pressure and stared with naked eyes at the metropolis flashing beneath. 'How can we hold this alone?'

'We will not be alone,' Sergeant Bastilan said. 'The Guard is with us. And militia forces.'

'Humans,' Priamus sneered.

'The Legio Invigilata has landed to the east of the city,' Bastilan said to the swordsman. 'Titans, my brother. I don't see you sneering at that.'

Priamus didn't answer. But nor did he agree.

'What is that?'

The knights leaned forward at their leader's words. Grimaldus gestured down at a vast stretch of rockcreted roadway, wide enough to accommodate the landing of a bulk cruiser or a wallowing Imperial Guard troop carrier.

'A highway, sir,' the pilot said. He checked his instruments. 'Hel's Highway.'

Grimaldus was silent for several moments, just watching the colossal road and the thousands upon thousands of conveyances making their way along it in both directions.

'This roadway splits the city like a spine. I see hundreds of capillary roads and byways leading from it.'

'So?' Priamus asked, his tone indicating just how little he cared about the answer.

'So,' Grimaldus turned back to the squad, 'whoever holds Hel's Highway holds the beating heart of the city in their hands. They will have unprecedented, unstoppable ability to manoeuvre troops and armour. Even Titans will move faster, at perhaps twice the speed than if they had to stalk through hive towers and city blocks. '

Nerovar shook his head. He was the only one without his helm covering his features. Insofar as it was possible for an Astartes to look uncertain, he was doing so now.

'Reclusiarch.' He spoke Grimaldus's new title with hesitancy. 'How can we defend… all *this*? An endless road that leads into to a thousand others.'

'With blade and bolter,' said Bastilan. 'With faith and fire.'

Grimaldus recognised his own words spoken from the sergeant's mouth.

He looked down in silence at the city below, at the insane stretch of road that left the entire hive open, accessible.

Vulnerable.

THREE

HIVE HELSREACH

The Thunderhawks touched down on a landing pad that was clearly designed for freight use. Cranes moved and servitors droned out of their way as the gunships came down in a hovering shower of engine wash and heat shimmer.

Ramps clanged onto the landing pad's surface and the four gunships disgorged their living cargo – one hundred knights in orderly ranks, marching into formation before their Thunder-hawks.

Watching this display, and desperately trying not to show how impressed he felt, was Colonel Sarren of the Armageddon 101st Steel Legion. He stood with his hands clasped together, fingers interlaced, over his not inconsiderable stomach. Flanking him were a dozen men, some soldiers, some civilians, and all nervous – to varying degrees – about the hundred giants in black armour forming up before them.

He cleared his throat, checked the buttons on his ochre greatcoat were fastened in correct order, and marched to the giants.

One of the giants, wearing a helm shaped into a grinning skull mask of shining silver and steel, stepped forward to meet the colonel. With him came five other knights, each carrying swords and massive bolters, but for one who bore a towering standard. Upon the banner, which waved lazily in the dull breeze, a scene of red and black depicted the skull-helmed knight bathed in the golden purity of a flaming aquila overhead.

'I am Grimaldus,' the first knight said, his gem-like eye lenses staring down at the portly colonel. 'Reclusiarch of the Helsreach Crusade.'

The colonel drew breath to make his own greeting, when the hundred knights in formation cried out a chant in skin-crawling unity.

'Imperator Vult!'

Sarren glanced at the ranks of knights, formed up in five ranks of twenty warriors. None of them seemed to have moved, despite their cry in High Gothic: *The Emperor wills it.*

'I am Colonel Sarren of the 101st Steel Legion, and overall commander of the Imperial Guard forces defending the hive.' He offered a hand to the towering knight, and turned the gesture quite smartly into a salute when it became clear the knight was not going to shake hands.

Muted clicks could be heard every few seconds from the helms of the knights standing closest to him. Sarren knew full well they were speaking with each other over a shared vox-channel. He didn't like it, not at all.

'Who are these others?' the first knight asked. With a war maul of brutal size and weight, he gestured to Sarren's staff arrayed in a loose crescent behind the colonel. 'I would meet every commander of this hive, if they are present.'

'They are present, sir,' Sarren said. 'Allow me to make introductions.'

'Reclusiarch,' Grimaldus growled. 'Not "sir".'

'As you wish, Reclusiarch. 'This is Cyria Tyro, adjutant quintus to General Kurov.' Grimaldus looked down at the slender, dark-haired female. She made no effort to salute. Instead, she spoke.

'I am to act as liaison between off-planet forces – such as yours, Reclusiarch, and the Titan Legion – and the soldiers of Hive Helsreach. Simply summon me if you require my aid,' she finished.

'I will,' Grimaldus said, knowing he would not.

'This is Commissar Falkov, of my command staff,' Colonel Sarren resumed.

The officer named clicked his heels together and made an immaculate sign of the aquila over his chest. The commissar's dark uniform singled him out with absolute clarity among the ochre-wearing Steel Legion officers.

'This is Major Mordechai Ryken, second officer of the 101st and XO of the city defence.'

Ryken made the aquila himself, and offered a cautious nod of greeting.

'Commander Korten Barasath,' Sarren introduced the next man, 'of the Imperial 5082nd Naval Wing.'

Korten, a lean figure still dressed in his grey flightsuit, saluted smartly.

'My men were in the Lightnings that guided you down, Reclusiarch. A pleasure to serve with the Black Templars again.'

Grimaldus narrowed his eyes behind his helm's false grin. 'You have served with the Knights of Dorn before?'

'I have personally – nine years ago on Dathax – and the Fifty-Eighty-Twos have on no fewer than four separate occasions. Sixteen of our fighters are marked with the heraldic cross, with permission given by Marshal Tarrison of the Dathax Crusade.'

Grimaldus inclined his head, his respect solemn and obvious, despite the helm.

'I am honoured, Barasath,' he said.

The squadron leader suppressed a pleased smile and saluted again.

And on it went, through the ranks of senior Steel Legion officers. At the end of the line stood two men, one in a clean and decorated uniform of azure blue, the shade of skies on worlds much cleaner than this one, and the other in oil-stained overalls.

Colonel Sarren gestured to the thin man in the immaculate uniform.

'The most honourable Moderati Primus Valian Carsomir of the Legio Invigilata, crewman of the blessed engine *Stormherald*.'

Grimaldus nodded, but made no other outward show of respect. The Titan pilot inclined his gaunt face in turn, utterly emotionless.

'Moderati,' the knight said. 'You speak with the voice of your Legion?'

'A full battle group,' the man replied. 'I am the voice of Princeps Majoris Zarha Mancion. The rest of Invigilata is committed to other engagements.'

'Fortune favours us that you still remain,' the knight said. The Titan pilot made the cog sign of the Mechanicus, his knuckles interlinked over his chest, and Sarren finished the final introduction.

'And here is Dockmaster Tomaz Maghernus, lead foreman of the Helsreach Dockers' Union.'

The knight hesitated, and nodded again, just as he had for the soldiers. 'We have much to discuss,' Grimaldus said to the colonel, who was sweating faintly in the stifling afternoon air.

'Indeed we do. This way, if you please.'

Tomaz Maghernus wasn't sure what to think.

Back at the docks, as soon as he walked into the warehouse, his crew flocked around him, barraging him with questions. *How many Astartes were there? How tall were they? What was it like to see one? Were all the stories true?*

Tomaz wasn't sure what to say. There had been little grandeur in the meeting. The towering warrior with his skull face had seemed more dismissive than anything else. The ranks of knights in their black armour were silent and inhuman, utterly separate from the hive's delegation and not interacting at all.

He answered the questions with a level of vagueness lessened by a convincing false smile.

An hour later, he was back in his crane's command cabin, strapped to the creaking leather seat and turning the axis wheel to bring the loading claw around again. Levers controlled the claw's vertical position and the grip of its magnetic talons. Tomaz slammed the claw onto the deck of the tanker ship closest to his station, and hauled a cargo crate into the air. The markings alongside the sturdy metal crate marked it as volatile. More promethium, he knew. The final imports of fuel for the Imperial Guard's tanks were arriving this week. Dried food rations and shipments of fuel were all they'd been unloading on the docks for months now.

He tried not to dwell on his meeting with the Astartes. He'd been expecting a rousing speech from a warrior armoured in gold. He'd expected plans and promises, oaths and oratory.

All in all, he decided, it had been a disappointing day.

A city.

I am in command of a *city*.

Preparations have been underway for months, but estimates pit the Great Enemy arriving in-system within a handful of days. My men, the precious few knights that remain with me on the surface of Armageddon, are spread across the sprawling hive. They are to serve as inspiration to the human soldiers when the fighting becomes thickest.

I recognise the tactical validity of this, yet lament their absence. This is not how a holy crusade should be fought.

The hours pass in a blur of statistical outlays, charts, hololithic projections and graphs.

The food supplies for the entire city. How long they will last once nothing can be brought in from outside the hive. Where the food is stored. The durability of these silos, buildings and granaries. What weapons they can withstand. How they appear from the air. Ration projections. Sustainable food ration planning. Unsustainable food ration planning, with appended lists of estimated sacrificial casualties. Where food riots are likely to break out once starvation is a reality.

Water filtration centres. How many are required to be fully operational in order to supply the entire population. Which ones are likely to be destroyed first, once the city walls fall. Underground bunkers where water is currently stored. Ancient wellsprings that might be tapped in times of great need.

Estimates of disease once the city is shelled and civilian casualties are too heavy to be dealt with efficiently. Types of disease. Symptoms. Severity. Risk of contagion. Compatibility with the ork genus.

Lists of medical facilities. Endless, endless screeds of how each one is supplied as of the most recent stock reports, to the most minute detail. New stock-checks are constantly performed. Updated information cycles in all the while, even as we review the previous batch.

Militia numbers, conscripted and volunteer. Training regimes and training schedules. Weapon supplies. Ammunition supplies for the civilian population currently under arms. Projections for how long those supplies will last.

Hive Defence Forces, straddling the line between militia and Guard. Who leads the individual sector forces. Their weapons. Their ammunition. Their proximity to significant industrial targets.

Imperial Guard numbers. Throne, what numbers. Regiments, their officers, their live fire training accuracy records, their citations, their shames, their moments of greatest glory and ignominy on a host of distant worlds. Their insignia. Their weapon and ammunition supplies. Their access to armour units, ranging from light scout vehicles such as Sentinels and Chimeras, through to super-heavy Baneblades and Stormswords.

The Guard figures alone take two days to file through. And this, they say, is merely the overview.

Landing platforms come next. Hive Defence landing platforms, civilian sites already in use by the Guard, and civilian sites currently in use for the importation of essential supplies, either from Navy vessels, traders in orbit, or elsewhere on the planet. The access to and from these sites is critical, regarding reinforcements making it into the hive, refugees making their way out, and the enemy capturing them as bases when the siege begins.

Air superiority. The numbers of light fighters, heavy fighters, and bombers at our disposal. The records of every pilot and officer among the Imperial 5082nd Skyborne. These, I skip past. If they wear the Templar cross with permission of a marshal, then there is little need to review their acts of valour. It is already clear. The projections move on to simulated displays of how long our air forces can prevent enemy landings, and what situations would merit the use of bombers beyond the city walls. On and on, the simulations roll in flickering hololithic imagery. Barasath is relieved to go when it is complete, complaining of a dozen headaches at once. I smile, though I let none of the humans witness it.

Helsreach heavy defence emplacements. What anti-air turrets are stationed on the walls, and where they are. Their optimal firing arcs. The make and calibre of each barrel and shell. The number of crew appointed to man these positions. Estimated projections on damage they can inflict upon the enemy, run through countless scenarios of varying greenskin offensive strength. The teams resupplying their ammunition, and from where that ammunition comes. Freight routes from manufactories.

And the manufactories themselves. Industrial plants churning out legions of tanks, all of various classes. Other manufactories where shells are made and dispatched for use. Which industrial sites are the most valuable, the most profitable, the most reliable and the most likely to suffer assault in a protracted siege.

The Titan Legion, most noble and glorious Invigilata. What engines they have on the Ash Wastes outside the city. Which ones will walk in the defence of Helsreach, and which ones are promised to reinforce the hordes of Cadian Shock and our brother Astartes, the Salamanders, out in the wilds of Armageddon.

Invigilata keeps its internal records from our sight, but we are fed enough information to thread into yet more hololithic charts and simulations, adding the might of Titans - of various grades and sizes - to the potential carnage.

The docks. The Helsreach Docks, greatest port on the planet. Coastal defences - walls and turrets and anti-air towers - and trade requirements and union complaints and petitions arguing over docking rights and warehouses appropriated as barracks for soldiers and complaints from merchants and dock-officers and...

And I endure this for nine days.

Nine. Days.

On the tenth day, I rise from my chair in Sarren's command centre. Around me in the colonel's armoured fortress at the heart of the city, three hundred servitors and junior officers work at stations: calculating, collating, transmitting, receiving, talking, shouting, and sometimes quietly panicking, begging for aid from those around them.

Sarren and several of his officers and aides watch me. Their necks crane up as they follow my movement. It is the first time I have moved in seven hours. Indeed, the first time I have moved since I sat down this morning at dawn.

'Is something wrong?' Sarren asks me.

I look at the sweating, porcine commander; this man unable to shape his body into a warrior's fitness, confined as he is - and totally at home - with this relentless trial of a million, million numbers.

What kind of question is that? Are they blind? I am one of the Emperor's Chosen. I am a knight of Dorn's blood, and a warrior-priest of the Black Templars. *Is something wrong?*

'Yes,' I say to him, to them all. 'Something is wrong.'

'But... what?'

I do not answer that question. Instead, I move to walk from the room, not caring that uniformed humans scatter before me like frightened vermin.

With a volume that would put a peal of overhead thunder to shame, a siren starts to wail.

I turn back to the table.

'What is that?'

They flinch at the rough bark from my helm's vocaliser. The siren keeps whining.

'Throne of the God-Emperor,' Sarren whispers.

Hive Helsreach did not have city walls. It had battlements.

When the citywide siren began to ring, Artarion was standing in the shadow of a towering cannon, its linked barrels aiming into the sick sky. Several metres away, the human crew worked at its base, performing the daily rituals of maintenance. They hesitated at the sound of the siren, and talked among themselves.

Artarion briefly looked back in the direction of the tower fortress in the city's centre, blocked as it was from view by distance and the forest-like mess of hive spires between here and there.

He felt the humans casting occasional glances his way. Knowing he was distracting them from their necessary mechanical rites, he moved away, walking further down the wall. His gaze fell, as it did almost every hour since coming to the hive a week before, on the endless expanse of wasteland that reached to the horizon and beyond.

Blink-clicking a communication rune on his visor display, he opened a vox-channel. The siren rang on. Artarion knew what it signalled.

'About time.'

From vox-towers across the city, an announcement was spoken in deceptively colourless tones. Colonel Sarren, not wishing to incite the populace to unrest, had tasked a lobotomised servitor to speak the words to the people.

'**People of Hive Helsreach. Across the planet, the first sirens are sounding. Do not be alarmed. Do not be alarmed. The enemy fleet has translated in-system. The might of Battlefleet Armageddon and the greatest Astartes fleet in Imperial history stands between our world and the foe's forces. Do not be alarmed. Maintain your daily rites of faith. Trust in the God-Emperor of Mankind. That is all.**'

In the control centre, Grimaldus turned to the closest human officer sat at a vox-station.

'You. Hail the Black Templar flagship *Eternal Crusader,* immediately.'

The man swallowed, his skin paling at being spoken to so directly and with such force by an Astartes.

'I... my lord, I am coordinating the–'

The knight's black fist pounded into the table. *'Do it now.'*

'Y-yes, my lord. A moment, please.'

The human officers of Sarren's staff shared a worried look. Grimaldus paid no attention at all. The seconds passed with sickening slowness.

'The *Eternal Crusader* is making ready to engage the enemy fleet,' the officer replied. 'I can send a message, but their two-way communications are in lockdown without the proper command codes. D-do you have the codes, my lord?'

Grimaldus did indeed have the codes. He looked at the frightened human, then back at the worried faces of the command staff as they sat at the table.

I am being a fool. My fury is blinding me to my sworn duty. What did he expect, truly? That Helbrecht would send down a Thunderhawk and allow him to take part in the glorious orbital war above? No. He was consigned here, to Helsreach, and there would be no other fate beyond this.

I will die on this world, he thought once more.

'I have the codes,' the knight replied, 'but this is not an emergency. Simply send the following message to their incoming logs, with no need for a reply: "Fight well, brothers."'

'Sent, lord.'

Grimaldus nodded. 'My thanks.' He turned to the gathered officers, and leaned over the hololithic display, his gauntleted knuckles on the table's surface.

'Forgive me a moment's choler. We have a war to plan,' the knight said, and breathed out the most difficult words he had ever spoken. 'And a city to defend.'

Until their dying nights, the warriors of the Helsreach Crusade bore their lamentations and rage with all the dignity that could be expected of them. But it was no easy feat. No easy feat to be consigned to a city of several million frightened souls while above the stained clouds, hundreds upon hundreds of their battle-brothers were carving their glory from the steel and flesh of an ancient and hated foe. The Black Templars across the city looked skyward, as if their helms' red eye lenses could pierce the wretched clouds and see the holy war above.

Grimaldus's own anger was a physical ache. It burned behind his eyes, and beat acid through his veins. But he mastered it, as was his duty. He sat at the table with the human planners, and agreed with them, disagreed, nodded and argued.

At one point, a whisper made its way through the room. It was serpentine thing, as if it threaded its way from human mouths to human ears seeking to avoid enraging the black-clad Astartes knight. When Colonel Sarren cleared his throat and announced that the two fleets had engaged, Grimaldus simply nodded. He'd heard the very first whispers thirty seconds before, of crackled voices coming over the vox-headsets of those at the communication stations.

It was beginning.

'We should give the order,' Sarren said quietly, to murmured agreement among the officer cadre.

Grimaldus turned to the vox-officer he had spoken to before. This time, he glanced at the man's rank badge. The officer saw the silver skull helm nod once in his direction.

'Lieutenant,' the knight said.

'Yes, Reclusiarch?'

'Give the order to Imperial forces throughout Helsreach. Martial law is in immediate effect.' He felt his throat dry at the gravity of what he was saying.

'Seal the city.'

* * *

Four thousand anti-air turrets along the hive's towering walls primed and aimed their multiple barrels into the sky.

Atop countless spires and manufactory rooftops, secondary defence lasers did the same. Hangars and warehouses converted for use by the Naval air squadrons readied the short rockcrete runways necessary for STOL fighters. Grey-uniformed Naval armsmen patrolled their bases' perimeters, keeping their sites enclosed and operating almost independently of the rest of the hive.

Across the city, recently-established makeshift roadway checkpoints became barricades and outposts of defence in readiness for the walls falling to the enemy. Thousands of buildings that had been serving as barracks for the Imperial Guard and militia forces sealed themselves with flakboard-reinforced doors and windows.

Announcements from vox-towers ordered the citizens of the hive who weren't engaged in vital industrial duty to remain in their homes until summoned by Guard squads and escorted to the underground shelters.

Hel's Highway, lifeline of the hive, was strangled by Guard checkpoints clearing the way of civilian traffic, making room for processions of tanks and Sentinel walkers, a rattling, grinding parade stretching over a kilometre. Clusters of the war machines veered off as they dispersed across the hive.

Helsreach was locked down, and its defenders clutched their weapons as they stared into the bleak sky.

Unseen by any of the humans within the city, one hundred knights – separated by distance but united by the blood of a demigod in their veins – knelt in silent prayer.

Eighteen minutes after the sirens started to wail, the first serious problem with force deployment began. Representatives of Legio Invigilata demanded to speak with the hive's commanders.

Forty-two minutes later, born entirely of panic, the first civilian riot broke out.

I ask Sarren a reasonable question, and he responds with the very answer I have no wish to hear.

'Three days,' he says.

Invigilata needs three days. Three days to finish the fitting and arming of their Titans out in the wastelands before they can be deployed within the city. Three days before they can walk through the immense gates in the hive's impenetrable walls, and station themselves within the city limits according to the agreed upon plan.

And then Sarren makes it worse.

'In three days, they will decide if they are to come to our aid, or deploy along the Hemlock River with the rest of their Legio.'

I quench the rush of fury through a moment's significant effort. 'There is a chance they will not even walk in our defence?'

'So it seems,' Sarren nods.

'Projections have the enemy breaching the orbital defences in four to nine days,' one of the other Steel Legion colonels – his name is Hargus – speaks from across the table. 'So we have time to allow them the largesse they require.'

None of us are seated now. The siren's drone has been lowered to less inconvenient levels, and speech is a realistic possibility for the unenhanced human officers once again.

'I am going to the view-tower,' I inform them. 'I wish to look upon this problem with my own eyes. Is the moderati primus still within the hive?'

'Yes, Reclusiarch.'

'Tell him meet to me there.' I pause as I stride from the room, and look back over my shoulder. 'Be polite, but do not ask. Tell him.'

INVIGILATA

Moderati Primus Valian Carsomir scratched at the greying stubble that darkened his jawline. His time was limited, and he had made that clear.

'You are not alone in that position,' Grimaldus pointed out.

Carsomir smiled darkly, though not without empathy. 'The difference, Reclusiarch, is that I do not intend to die here. My princeps majoris is still in doubt if Invigilata will walk for Helsreach.'

The knight moved to the railing, his armour joints humming with the gentle motions. The viewing platform was a modest space atop the central spire of the command fortress, but Grimaldus had spent much of his time up here each night, staring over the hive as it made ready for war.

In the faded distance, over the city walls, his gene-enhanced sight could make out the skeletal details of Titans on the horizon. There, in the wastelands, Invigilata's engines also made ready. Fat-hulled landers made the wallowing journey back into orbit as part of the final phase of Imperial deployment. Soon, within a matter of days, there would be no hope of landing anything more on the planet's surface.

'This is the greatest of Armageddon's port cities. We are about to be assaulted by the largest greenskin-breed xenos invasion ever endured by the Imperium of Man.' The Astartes did not turn to the Titan pilot. He watched the gigantic war machines, blurred by the sandy mist of distant dust storms. 'We must have Titans, Carsomir.'

The officer stepped alongside the Astartes, his bionic eyes – both with lenses of multifaceted jade set in bronze mountings – clicking and whirring as he followed the knight's gaze over the city and beyond.

'I am aware of your need.'

'*My* need? It is the hive's need. Armageddon's need.'

'As you say, the hive's need. But I am not the princeps majoris. I report on the hive's defences to her, and the decision is hers to make. Invigilata has received strong petitions from other cities, and other forces.'

Grimaldus closed his eyes in thought. Unblinking, his skulled helm continued to stare at the distant Titans.

'I must speak with her.'

'I am her eyes, ears and voice, Reclusiarch. What I know, she knows; what I say, she has bid me speak. If you wish, I could – perhaps – arrange a conversation over the vox. But I am here – a man of not inconsiderable station myself – to show that Invigilata is earnest in its dealings with you.'

Grimaldus said nothing for several seconds.

'I appreciate that. I am not blind to your rank. Tell me, moderati, is it permissible to speak with your princeps majoris in person?'

'No, Reclusiarch. That would be a violation of Invigilata tradition.'

Grimaldus's brown eyes opened once more, drinking in the scarce detail of the war machines on the horizon.

'Your objection is noted,' the knight said, 'and duly ignored.'

'What?' the Titan pilot said, not sure he heard correctly.

Grimaldus didn't answer. He was already speaking into the vox.

'Artarion, ready the Land Raider. We're going out into the wastelands.'

Four hours later, Grimaldus and his brothers stood in the shadows cast by giants.

A light dust storm sent grit rattling against their war plate, which they ignored as easily as Grimaldus had ignored Carsomir's offended protests about the nature of this mission.

Crews of servitors laboured at the ground level, and while they were mind-wiped never to process or acknowledge physical discomfort, the abrasive wasteland grit was rubbing their exposed skin raw, and crudely sandblasting mechanical parts.

The Titans themselves stood watch over the wastelands in austere vigil – nineteen of them in total, ranging from the smaller twelve-crew Warhound-classes, to the larger Reaver- and Warlord-classes. Godlike, immune to the elements, the Titans were bedecked in the crawling forms of tech-adepts and maintenance drones performing the rites of awakening.

Despite their slumber, it was anything but silent. The grinding, deafening machine-whine of internal plasma reactors trying to start was a sound from primordial nightmare, ripped right from worlds where humans feared gigantic reptilian predators and their ground-shaking roars.

It was all too easy to imagine hundreds of robed tech-priests within the fleet of Titans, chanting and praying to their Machine-God and the spirits of these slumbering war-giants. As Grimaldus and his brothers walked in the shade cast by one Warlord, the relentless grind of metal on metal became a full-throated thunderclap that broke the air like a sonic boom. Heated air blasted outwards from the Titan's hull, and around the site, thousands of men instantly fell to their knees in the sand, facing the Titan and murmuring their reverence in the aftershock of its rebirth.

The Titan's birth cry rang out through its warning sirens. The sound was somewhere between pure mechanical sound and organic exultation; as loud as a hundred manufactories with a full workforce, and as terrible as the wrath of a newborn god.

It moved. Not with speed, but with the halting, unsure strides of a man that has not used his muscles in many months. One splayed claw of a foot, easily huge enough to crush a Land Raider, rose several metres off the ground. It crashed back to earth a moment later, blasting dust in all directions.

'Sacrosanct awakens!' came the cry from hundreds of vox-altered voices. *'Sacrosanct walks!'*

The Titan answered the worshipful cries of its cult below. It roared again, the cry blaring from its speaker horns and echoing across the wastelands.

As impressive as the sight was, it was not why Grimaldus had led his men out here. Their goal was larger still, dwarfing even these mighty Warlords, paying them no heed as they stood or walked around at the height of its weapon-arms.

It was called *Stormherald.*

The battle-class Titans were walking weapons platforms, capable of levelling hive blocks. *Stormherald* was a walking fortress. Its weapons could level cities. Its legs, capable of supporting the weight of this colossal sixty-metre war machine, were bastions – barracks – with turrets and arched windows for the troops transported within to fire at the foe even as their Titan crushed them underfoot. Upon its hunched back, *Stormherald* carried crenellated battlements and the seven spires of a sacred, armoured cathedral devoted to the Emperor in His aspect as the Machine-God. Gargoyles clung to the edges of the architecture, carved around defence turrets and stained glass windows, their hideous mouths open as they wailed silently at the enemy from their holy castle above the ground.

Banners hung from its cannon arms and the battlements themselves, listing the names of enemy war machines it had slain in the millennia since its birth. As the birth cry of *Sacrosanct* faded, the knights could hear the sound of religious communion in the fortress-cathedral on *Stormherald's* giant shoulders, as pious souls no doubt beseeched their ethereal master for the blessing of the greatest god-machine waking once more.

The Titan's clawed feet were tiered stairs leading into the armoured chambers of its lower legs. With the immense structure still unmoving, Grimaldus made his way through scores of scurrying menial tech-priests and servitors. As his booted foot thudded down on the first stair layer, the resistant welcome he was expecting finally made itself known.

'Hold,' he said to his brothers. Troops, their features covered, filed from the archways into the Titan's limb-innards. The knights' attempted entrance was blocked by Mechanicus minions.

The soldiers facing them were called skitarii. These were the elite of the Adeptus Mechanicus infantry forces – a fusion of integrated weapon augmetics and the human form. Grimaldus, like many Astartes, regarded their unsubtle flesh-manipulation and the crude surgeries bestowing weapons upon their limbs as making them little more than glorified servitors, and equally wretched in their own way.

Twelve of these bionic creatures, their skin robed against the wind, levelled thrumming plasma weapons at the five knights.

'I am Grimaldus, Reclusiarch of the Black Tem–'

—Your identity is known to us— they all spoke at once. There was little unity in the chorus of voices, with some sounding unnaturally deep, others inhuman and mechanical, still others perfectly human.

'The next time I am interrupted,' the knight warned, 'I will kill one of you.'

—We are not to be threatened— all twelve said, still in unison, still in a chorus of unmatching voices.

'Neither are you to be addressed. You are nothing; slaves, all of you, barely above servitors. Now move aside. I have business with your mistress.'

—We are not to be ordered into submission. We are to remain as duty demands—

A human would have missed the division within their unified speech, but Grimaldus's senses could trace the minute deviations in the way they spoke. Four of them started and finished words a fraction of a second later than the others. Whatever mind-link bound the twelve warriors, it was more efficient in some than others. While his experience with the servants of the Machine-God was limited, he found this a curious flaw.

'I will speak with the princeps majoris of Invigilata, even if I have to shout up to the cathedral itself.'

They had no orders pertaining to such an action, and lacked the cognition to make an assessment of how it would matter to their superiors, so they remained silent.

'Reclusiarch...' Priamus voxed. 'Must we bear this foolish indignity?'

'No.' The skull helm scanned the skitarii each in turn, its red eyes unblinking. 'Kill them.'

She floated, as she had floated for seventy-nine years, in a coffin-like tank of milky amniotic fluid. The metallic, chemical tang of the watery, oxygen-rich ooze had been the only constant in almost a century of life, and its taste, its feel, its intrusion into her lungs and its replacement of air in her respiration had never ceased to feel somewhat alien.

That was not to say she found it uncomfortable. Quite the opposite. It was forever unsettling, but not unnatural.

In moments of battle, which always seemed too few and far between, Princeps Majoris Zarha believed with cold certainty that this was what gestation within the womb must have felt like. The cooling fluid supporting her would become warm in sympathy with the plasma reactor at *Stormherald's* core. The pounding, world-shaking tread echoed around her, magnified like the beat of a mighty heart.

A feeling of absolute power coupled with being utterly protected. It was all she needed to focus on to remain herself in those frantic, bladed moments when *Stormherald's* broken, violent mind knifed into her consciousness with sudden strength, seeking to overpower her.

She knew that there would come a day when her assistants unplugged her for the last time – when she would be denied a return to the machine's soul, for fear its ingrained temperament and personality would swallow her weaker, too-human sense of identity.

But that was not now. Not today.

No, Zarha focussed on her simulated regression to the womb, and it was all she ever needed to push aside the clinging insistency of *Stormherald's* blunt and primal advances.

Voices from the outside always reached her with a muffled dullness, despite the vox-receivers implanted where the cartilage of her inner ears once were, and the receptors built into the sides of her confinement tank.

They spoke, those voices, of intrusion.

Princeps Majoris Zarha did not share their appraisal of the situation. She turned in her milky fluid, as graceful as a sea-nymph from the tales of the impious Ancient Terra, though the augmented, wrinkled, hairless creature within the spacious coffin was anything but lovely. Her feet had been removed, for she would never need them again. Her bones were weak and soft, and her body curled and hunched.

She replied to them, to her minions and brothers and sisters, with a stab of thought.

I wish to speak with the intruders.

'I wish to speak with the intruders,' the vox-emitters on her coffin droned in a toneless echo of her silent words.

One of them came closer to the clear walls of her amniotic chamber, looking in at the floating husk with great respect.

'My princeps,' it was Lonn speaking, and though she liked Lonn, he was not her favourite.

Hello, Lonn. Where is Valian?

'Hello, Lonn. Where is Valian?'

'Moderati Carsomir is returning from the hive, my princeps. We thought you would still sleep for some time.'

With all this noise? What was left of her face turned into a smile.

'With all this noise?'

'My princeps, Astartes are seeking to gain entrance.'

I heard.

'I heard.'

I know.

'I know.'

'Your orders, my princeps?'

She twisted in the water again, in her own way as graceful as a seaborne mammal, despite the cables, wires and cords running from the coffin's mechanical generators into her spine, skull and limbs. She was an ancient, withered marionette in the water, serene and smiling.

Access granted.

'Access granted.'

—Access granted— said twelve voices at once.

The crackling edge of the maul remained motionless, no more than a finger's thickness above the lead skitarii's skull. A small spark of electrical force snapped at the soldier's face from the armed power weapon, forcing him to recoil.

—Access granted— they all intoned a second time.

Grimaldus deactivated his crozius hammer and shoved the augmented human soldiers aside.

'That is what I thought you would say.'

* * *

The journey was short and uneventful, through narrow corridors and ascending in elevator shafts, until they stood outside the sealed bulkhead doors of the bridge. The process of reaching the control deck involved a great deal of silently staring tech-adepts, their green-lens replacement eyes rotating and refocusing, either scanning or in some eerie mimicry of human facial expressions.

The interior of the Titan was dark, too dark for unaugmented humans to work by, lit by the kind of emergency-red lighting the knights had only seen before in bunkers and ships at war. Their gene-enhanced eyes would have pierced the gloom with ease, even without the vision filters of their helm's visors.

No guards stood outside the large double bulkhead leading onto the command deck, and the doors themselves slid open on clunking rails as the knights waited.

Artarion gripped Grimaldus's scroll-draped pauldron.

'Make this count, brother.'

The Chaplain looked at the bearer of his war banner through the silver face of his slain master.

'Trust me.'

The command deck was a circular bay, with a raised dais in the centre surrounded by five ornate and heavily-cabled thrones. At the edges of the chamber, robed tech-adepts worked at consoles filled with a dizzying array of levers, dials and buttons.

Two vast windows offered a grand view across the harsh landscape. With a shiver of realisation, Grimaldus knew he was looking out from the god-machine's eyes.

Upon the dais itself, a huge, clear-glass tank stood supported by humming machinery. Within its milky depths floated a naked crone, ravaged by her years and the bionics necessary to sustain her life under such conditions. She stared through bug-eyed augmetic replacements where her human eyes once were.

'Greetings, Astartes,' the vox-speakers built into her coffin spoke.

'Princeps Majoris,' Grimaldus nodded to the swimming husk. 'An honour to stand in your presence.'

There was a distinct pause before she replied, though her gaze never left him. **'You are keen to speak with me. Waste no time on pleasantries. *Stormherald* wakes, and soon I must walk. Speak.'**

'I am told by one of this Titan's pilots, as an ambassador to Helsreach, that Invigilata may not walk in our defence.'

Again, the pause.

'This is so. I command one-third of this Legio. The rest already walks in defence of the Hemlock region, many with your brothers, the Salamanders. Do you come to petition me for my portion of mighty Invigilata?'

'I do not beg, princeps. I came to see you with my own eyes and ask you, face to face, to fight and die with us.'

The withered woman smiled, the expression both maternal and amused. **'But you have not yet completed your intended duty, Astartes.'**

'Is that so?'

This time, the pause was longer. The old woman laughed within her bubbling tank. **'We are not face to face.'**

The knight reached up to his armoured collar, disengaging the seals there.

Without my helm, the scent of sacred oils and the chemical-rich tang of her amniotic tank are much stronger. The first thing she says to me is something I am not sure how to respond to.

'You have very kind eyes.'

Her own eyes are long-removed from her skull, the sockets covered by these bulbous lenses that twist as she watches me. I cannot return the comment she made, and I do not know what else I could say.

So I say nothing.

'What is your name?'

'Grimaldus of the Black Templars.'

'Now we are face to face, Grimaldus of the Black Templars. You have been bold enough to come here, and honour me with your face. I am no fool. I know how rare it is for a Chaplain to reveal his human features to one not of his brotherhood. Ask what you came to ask, and I will answer.'

I step closer and press my palm against the casket's surface. The vibration is twinned with that of my armour. I can feel the eyes of the Mechanicus minions upon me, upon my dark ceramite, their reverent gazes showing their longing to touch the perfection of the machinesmith's craft represented by Astartes war plate.

And I look into the mechanical eyes of the princeps as she floats in the milky waters.

'Princeps Zarha. Helsreach calls for you. Will you walk?'

She smiles again, a blind grandmother with rotten teeth, as she presses her own palm against mine. Only the reinforced glass separates us.

'Invigilata will walk.'

Seven hours later, the people of the city heard a distant mechanical howl from the wastelands, eclipsing the cries of the lesser Titans. It echoed through the streets and around the spiretops, chilling the blood of every soul in the hive. Street dogs barked in response, as if sensing a larger predator nearby.

Colonel Sarren shivered, though he smiled at the others in his command meeting. Through bloodshot eyes, heavy with sleeplessness, he regarded them all.

'*Stormherald* has awoken,' he said.

Three days, just as promised, and the city shook with the tread of the god-machines.

Invigilata's engines walked, and the great gates in the northern wall rumbled open to welcome them. Grimaldus and the hive's command staff watched from atop the viewing platform. The knight blink-clicked a rune on his retinal display, accessing a coded channel.

'Good morning, princeps,' he said softly. 'Welcome to Helsreach.'

In the distance, a walking cathedral-fortress pounded its slow, stately way through the first city blocks.

'Hail, Chaplain.' The crone's voice was laden with barely-contained energy. **'I was born in a hive like this, you know.'**

'It is fitting then, that you'll be dying here, Zarha.'

'Do you say so, sir knight? Have you seen me today?'

Grimaldus watched the distant form of *Stormherald,* as tall as the towers surrounding it.

'It is impossible not to see you, princeps.'

'It's impossible to kill me, as well. Remember that, Grimaldus.'

No human had ever dared use his name so informally before. The knight smiled for the first time in days.

The city was finally sealed. Helsreach was ready.

And as night fell, the sky caught fire.

FIVE

FIRE IN THE SKY

Its name had been, in nobler years, *The Purest Intent.*

A strike cruiser, constructed on the minor forge world Shevilar and granted to the Shadow Wolves Chapter of the Adeptus Astartes. It had been lost with all hands, captured by xenos raiders, thirty-two years before the Third War for Armageddon.

When a huge and shapeless amalgamation of scrap and flame came burning through the cloud cover above the fortified city, warning sirens sounded once more across the hive. The squadron of fighters in the air – commanded by Korten Barasath – voxed their inability to engage. The hulk was burning up already, and far out of their capability to damage with their Lightnings' lascannons and long-barrelled auto-cannons.

The wing of fighters broke away as the hulk burned through the sky.

Thousands of soldiers manning the immense walls watched as the wreckage blazed its way overhead. The air itself shook with its passage, a palpable tremor from the thrum of overworked, dying engines.

Exactly eighteen seconds after it cleared the city walls, *The Purest Intent* ended its spaceborne life as it ploughed a new scar into Armageddon's war-torn face. All of Helsreach shook to its foundations as the massive cruiser hammered into the ground and carved a blackened canyon in its wake.

It took a further two minutes for the crippling damage inflicted by the impact to kill the immense, howling engines. Several booster rings still roared gaseous plasma and fire as they tried to propel the vessel through the stars, unaware it was half-buried in the stinging sulphuric sands that would be its grave.

But the engines failed.

The flames cooled.

At last, there was silence.

The Purest Intent was dead, its bones strewn across the wastelands of Armageddon.

'The ship registers as *The Purest Intent,*' Colonel Sarren read out from the data-slate to the crowded war room. 'An Astartes vessel, strike cruiser-class, belonging to the–'

'Shadow Wolves,' Grimaldus cut him off. The knight's vox-voice was harsh and mechanical, betraying no emotion. 'The Black Templars were with them at the end.'

'The end?' asked Cyria Tyro.

'They fell at the Battle of Varadon eleven years ago. Their last companies were annihilated by the tyranid-breed xenos.'

Grimaldus closed his eyes and relished the momentary drift of focus into memory. *Varadon*. Blood of Dorn, it had been beautiful. No purer war had ever been fought. The enemy was endless, soulless, merciless... utterly alien, utterly hated, utterly without right to exist.

The knights had tried to fight their way to join up with the last of their brother Chapter, but the enemy tide was unrelenting in its ferocity. The aliens were viciously cunning, their swarming tides of claws and flesh-hooked appendages smashing into the two Astartes forces and keeping them isolated from each other. The Wolves were there in full force. Varadon was their home world. Distress calls had been screamed into the warp by astropaths weeks before, when their fortress-monastery fell to the enemy.

Grimaldus had been there at the very end. The last handful of Wolves, their blades broken and their bolters empty, had intoned the Litanies of Hate into the vox-channel they shared with the Black Templars. Such a death! They chanted their bitter fury at the foes even as they were slain. Grimaldus would never, *could* never, forget the Chapter's final moment. A lone warrior, a mere battle-brother, horrendously wounded and on his knees beneath the Chapter's standard, keeping the banner proud and upright even as the xenos creatures tore into him.

The war banner would never be allowed to fall while one of the Wolves yet lived.

Such a moment. Such honour. Such *glory,* to inspire warriors to remember your deeds for the rest of their own lives, and to fight harder in the hopes of matching such a beautiful death.

Grimaldus breathed out, restoring his senses to the present with irritated reluctance. How filthy this war would be by comparison.

Sarren continued. 'The latest report from the fleet lists thirty-seven enemy ships have breached the blockade. Thirty-one were annihilated by the orbital defence array. Six have crashed onto the surface.'

'What is the status of Battlefleet Armageddon?' the knight asked.

'Holding. But we have a greater comprehension of enemy numbers now. The four to nine day estimate has been abandoned, as of thirty minutes ago. This is the greatest greenskin fleet ever to face the Imperium. The fleet's casualties are approaching a million souls. One or two more days, at best.'

'Throne of the Emperor,' one of the militia colonels swore in a whisper.

'Focus,' Grimaldus warned. 'The crashed ship.'

Here, the colonel paused and gestured to Grimaldus. 'I suggest we hold, Reclusiarch. A handful of greenskin survivors cannot hope to survive an assault against the walls. They would be insane – even for orks – to try.'

'We are comfortable letting these survivors add their numbers to their brethren when the enemy's main forces make planetfall?' This, from Cyria Tyro.

'A handful of additional foes will make no difference,' Sarren pointed out. 'We all saw the *Intent* hit. Not many of its crew are walking away from that.'

'I have fought the greenskins before, sir,' Major Ryken put in. 'They're tougher than a marsh lizard's hide. Almost unbreakable. There'll be plenty who survived that crash, I promise you.

'Send a Titan,' Commissar Falkov smiled without any humour whatsoever, and the room fell quiet. 'I am not making a jest. Send a Titan to obliterate the wreckage. Inspire the men. Give them an overwhelming victory before the true battle is even joined. Morale among the Steel Legion is mediocre at best. It is lower still among the volunteer militia, and barely existent among the conscripts. So send a Titan. We need first blood in this war.'

'At least get Barasath's fighters to scan for life readings,' Tyro added, 'before we commit to sending any troops outside the city.'

Throughout all of this, Grimaldus had remained silent. It was his silence that eventually killed all talk, and had faces turning towards him.

The knight rose to his feet. Despite the slowness of his movement, his armour's joints emitted a low snarl.

'The commissar is correct,' he said. 'Helsreach needs an overwhelming victory. The benefit to morale among the human forces would be considerable.'

Sarren swallowed. No one around the table enjoyed Grimaldus pointing out the difference in species between the humans and the genetically-forged Astartes.

'It is time my knights took to the field,' the Reclusiarch said, his deep, soft voice coming out from his skull helm as a machine-growl. 'The humans may need first blood, but my knights hunger for it. We will give you your victory.'

'How many of your Astartes will you take?' Sarren asked after a moment's thought.

'All of them.'

The colonel paled. 'But surely you don't need–'

'Of course not. But this is for appearances. You wanted an overwhelming display of Imperial force. I am giving you that.'

'We can make this even better,' Cyria said. 'If you can have your men stand in formation before they move out of the city, long enough for us to arrange live pict-feeds to all visual terminals across Helsreach...' she trailed off, a pleased smile brightening her features.

Falkov slammed a fist on the table. 'Let's get started. The first charge of the black knights!' He smiled a thin, nasty grin. 'If that doesn't light a fire in the heart of every man breathing, nothing will.'

Priamus twisted the blade, widening the wound before wrenching the sword clear. Stinking blood gushed from the creature's chest, and the alien died with its filthy claws scratching at the knight's armour.

Within the crashed ship, stalking from room to room, corridor by corridor, the Templars hunted mongrels in the name of purification.

'This is bad comedy,' he breathed into the vox.

The reply he received was punctuated by the dull clang of weapons clashing together. Artarion, some way behind.

'Fall back, damn it.'

Priamus sensed another lecture about vainglory in his future. He walked on, his precious blade held at the ready, moving deeper into the darkness that his red visor pierced with consummate ease.

Like vermin, the orks scrambled through the tunnels of the wrecked ship, springing ambushes with their crude weapons and snorting their piggish war cries. Priamus's contempt burned hot on his tongue. They were above this. They were Black Templars, and the morale of the puling humans was none of their concern.

Grimaldus was spending too much time among the mortals. The Reclusiarch was beginning to think like them. It had galled Priamus to stand in ranked formation for the pict-drones to hover around and capture the knights' images, just as it galled him now to hunt the scarce survivors of this wreck. It was beneath him, beneath them all. This was work for the Imperial Guard. Perhaps even the militia.

'We will draw first blood,' Grimaldus had said to them all, as if it was something to care about – as if it would affect the final battle in any way at all. 'Join me, brothers. Join me as I shake off this disgust at the stasis gripping my bones, and slake my bloodthirst in holy slaughter.'

The others, as they stood in their foolish ranks for the benefit of the mortals, had cheered. They had *cheered.*

Priamus remained silent, swallowing the rise of bile in his throat. He had known in that moment, with clarity sharper than ever before, that he was unlike his brothers. They *cared* about shedding blood now, as if this pathetic gesture mattered.

These warriors who called him vainglorious were blind to the truth: there was nothing vain in glory. He was not rash, he merely trusted in his skills to carry him through any challenge, just as the great Sigismund, First High Marshal of the Black Templars, had trusted his skills to do the same. Was that a weakness? Was it a flaw to exemplify the fury of the Chapter's founder and the favoured son of Rogal Dorn? How could it be considered so, when Priamus's deeds and glories were already rising to eclipse those of his brothers?

Movement ahead.

Priamus narrowed his eyes, his pupils flicking across his field of vision to lock targeting reticules on the brutish shapes swarming in the darkness of the wide, lightless corridor.

Three greenskins, their xenos flesh exuding a greasy, fungal scent that reached the knight from a dozen metres away. They lay waiting in a puerile ambush, believing themselves hidden by fallen gantries and a half-destroyed bulkhead door.

Priamus heard them grunting to one another in what passed for whispers in their foul tongue.

This was the best they could do. *This* was their cunning ambush against warriors made in the Emperor's image. The knight swore under his breath, the curse never leaving his helm, and charged.

Artarion licked his steel teeth. I heard him doing it, even though he wears his helm.

'Priamus?' he asks. The vox answers with silence.

Unlike the swordsman, I am not alone. I walked with Artarion, the two of us slaying our way through the enginarium decks. Resistance is light. Most of our venture so far has consisted of kicking xenos corpses out of our path, or butchering lone stragglers.

Most of the Templars were sent across the wastelands in their Rhinos and Land Raiders, chasing down the crash survivors who sought to hide in the wilderness. I have given them their head, and let them hunt. Better the greenskins die now, rather than allow them to lie in wait and rejoin their bestial kin in the true invasion. I took only a handful of warriors into the downed cruiser to purge whatever remains.

'Leave him be,' I say to Artarion. 'Let him hunt. He needs to stand alone for now.'

Artarion pauses before answering. I know him well enough to know he is scowling. 'He needs discipline.'

'He needs our trust.' My tone brooks no further argument.

The ship is in pieces. The floor is uneven, torn and wrenched from the crash. We turn a corner, our boots clinging to the sloping decking as we head into a plasma generator's coolant chamber. As huge as a cathedral's prayer chamber, the expansive room is largely taken up by the cylindrical metal housing that encases the temperamental and arcane technology used for cooling the ship's engines.

I see nothing alive. I hear nothing alive. And yet...

'I smell fresh blood,' I vox to Artarion. 'A survivor, still bleeding.' I gesture to the vast coolant tower with my crozius. The mace flashes with lightning as I squeeze the trigger rune. 'The alien lurks beneath there.'

The survivor is barely deserving of the description. It lies pinned under metal debris, impaled through the stomach and pinned to the floor. As we approach, it barks in its rudimentary command of the Gothic tongue. Judging from the pool of cooling blood spreading from its sundered form, the alien's life will end in mere minutes. Feral red eyes glare at us. Its porcine face is curled in a rictus of anger.

Artarion raises his chainsword, gunning the motor. The saw-teeth whine as they cut through the air.

'No.'

Artarion freezes. At first, my brother knight isn't sure what he'd heard. His glance flicks to me.

'What did you say?'

'I said,' I'm stepping closer to the dying alien even as I speak, looking down through my skulled mask, '...no.'

Artarion lowers his sword. Its teeth stutter to a halt.

'They always seem so immune to pain,' I tell him, and I feel my voice fall to a whisper. I place a boot upon the creature's bleeding chest. The ork snaps its jaws at me, choking on the blood that runs into its burst lungs.

Artarion must surely hear the smile in my voice. 'But no. Look into its eyes, brother.'

Artarion complies. I can tell from his hesitation that he does not see what I see. He looks down and sees nothing but impotent rage.

'I see fury,' he tells me. 'Frustration. Not even hatred. Just wrath.'

'Then look harder.' I press down with my boot. Ribs crunch with the sound of dry twigs snapping, one after the other, as the weight descends harder. The ork bellows, drooling and snarling.

'Do you see?' I ask, knowing the smile is still evident in my voice.

'No, brother,' Artarion grunts. 'If there is a lesson in this, I am blind to it.'

I lift the boot, letting the ork cough its lifeblood through its blood-streaked maw.

'I see it in the creature's eyes. Defeat is pain. Its nerves may be dead to torment, but whatever passes for its soul knows how to suffer. To be at an enemy's mercy... Look at its face, brother. See how it dies in agony because we are here to watch such a shameful end.'

Artarion watches, and I think perhaps he sees it, as well. However, it does not fascinate him the way it does me. 'Let me end it,' he says. 'Its existence offends me.'

I shake my head. That would not do at all.

'No. Its life's span is measured in moments.' I feel the dying alien's gaze lock with my red eye lenses. 'Let it die in this pain.'

Nerovar hesitated.

'Nero?' Cador called over his shoulder. 'Do you see something?'

The Apothecary blink-clicked several visualiser runes on his retinal display.

'Yes. Something.'

The two of them were searching the ruined enginarium chambers on the level beneath Grimaldus and Artarion. Nerovar frowned at what the digital readouts across his eye lenses were telling him. He looked to the bulky narthecium unit built into his left bracer.

'So enlighten me,' Cador said, his voice as gruff as always.

Nerovar tapped a code into the multicoloured buttons next to the display screen on his armoured forearm. Runic text scrolled in a blur.

'It's Priamus.'

Cador grunted in agreement. Nothing but trouble, that one. 'Isn't it always?'

'I've lost his life signs.'

'That cannot be,' Cador laughed. 'Here? Among this rabble?'

'I do not make mistakes,' Nerovar replied. He activated the squad's shared channel. 'Reclusiarch?'

'Speak.' The Chaplain sounded distracted, and faintly amused. 'What is it?'

'I've lost Priamus's life signs, sir. No heightened returns, just an immediate severance.'

'Confirm at once.'

'Confirmed, Reclusiarch. I verified it before contacting you.'

'Brothers,' the Chaplain said, his voice suddenly ice. 'Maintain search and destroy orders.'

'What?' Artarion drew breath to object. 'We need–'

'Be silent. *I* will find Priamus.'

* * *

He wasn't sure what they hit him with.

The greenskins had melted from their hiding places in the darkness, one of them carrying a weighty amalgamation of scrap that only loosely resembled a weapon. Priamus had slain one, laughing at its porcine snorting as it fell to the deck, and launched at the next.

The scrap-weapon bucked in the greenskin's hands. A claw of charged, crackling metal fired from the alien device and crunched into the knight's chest. There was a moment of stinging pain as his suit's interface tendrils, the connection spikes lodged in his muscles and bones, crackled with an overload of power.

Then his vision went black. His armour fell silent, and became heavier on his shoulders and limbs. Out of power. They'd deactivated his armour.

'Dorn's blood...'

Priamus tore his helm clear just in time to see the alien racking his scrap-weapon like a primitive solid-slug launcher. The claw embedded in his chest armour, defiling the Templar cross there, was still connected to the device by a cable of chains and wires. Priamus raised his blade to sever the bond even as the alien laughed and pulled a second trigger.

This time, the channelled force didn't just overload his armour's electrical systems. It burned through the neural connections and muscle interfaces, blasting agony through the swordsman's body.

Priamus, gene-forged like all Astartes to tolerate any pain the enemies of mankind could inflict upon him, would have screamed if he could. His muscles locked, his teeth clamped together, and his attempt to cry out left his clenched jaw as an ululating, shuddering *'Hnn-hnn-hnn'*.

Priamus crashed to the ground fourteen seconds later, when the agony finally ceased.

The greenskins hunch over his prone form.

Now they have managed to bring him down, they seem to have no idea what to do with their prize. One of them turns my brother's black helm over in its fat-knuckled hands. If it means to turn Priamus's armour into a trophy, it is about to pay for such blasphemy.

As I walk down the darkened corridor, I drag my mace along the wall – the ornate head clangs against the steel arches. I have no wish to be subtle.

'Greetings.' I breathe the word from my skulled face.

They raise their hideous alien faces, their jaws slack and filled with rows of grinding teeth. One of them hefts a heavy composite of detritus and debris that apparently serves as a weapon.

It fires... something... at me. I do not care what. It's smashed from the air with a single swing of my inactive maul. The clang of metal on metal echoes throughout the corridor, and I thumb the trigger rune on the haft of my crozius. The mace flares into crackling life as I aim it at the aliens.

'You dare exist in humanity's domain? You dare spread your cancerous touch to our worlds?'

They do not answer this challenge with words. Instead, they come at me in a lumbering run, raising cleaver swords; primitive weapons to suit primitive beings.

I am laughing when they reach me.

Grimaldus swung his mace two-handed, pounding the first alien back. The sparking force field around the weapon's head flashed as it reacted with opposing kinetic force, and amplified the already inhuman strike to insane levels of strength. The greenskin was already dead, its skull obliterated, as it flew twenty metres back down the corridor to smash into a damaged bulkhead.

The second tried to run. It turned its back and ran, hunched and ape-like, back in the direction it had come.

Grimaldus was faster. He caught the creature in a handful of heartbeats, hooked his gauntleted fingers in the ork's armoured collar to halt its flight, and smashed it against the corridor wall.

The alien grunted a stream of curses in Gothic as it struggled in the knight's grip.

Grimaldus clutched at the creature's throat, black gauntlets squeezing, choking, crunching bone beneath his grip.

'You *dare* defile the language of the pure race...' He slammed the alien back, breaking its head open on the steel wall behind. Foetid breath steamed across Grimaldus's faceplate as the ork's attempt to roar came out as a panicked whine. The Astartes would not be appeased. His grip tightened.

'You dare desecrate our tongue?'

Again, he bashed the greenskin back, the alien's head splitting wide as it struck a girder.

The ork's struggles died immediately. Grimaldus let the creature fall to the metal decking, where it hit and folded with a muffled thud.

Priamus.

The fury was fading now. Reality asserted itself with cold, unwanted clarity. Priamus lay on the deck, head to the side, bleeding from his ears and open mouth. Grimaldus came to his side, kneeling there in the darkness.

'Nero,' he said quietly.

'Reclusiarch,' the younger knight returned.

'I have found Priamus. Aft, deck four, tertiary spine corridor.'

'On my way. Assessment?'

Grimaldus's targeting reticule flicked over his brother's prone body, then locked onto the scrap-weapon carried by the orks he'd killed.

'Some kind of force-discharging weapon. His armour is powered down, but he's still breathing. Both his hearts are beating.' This last part was the most serious aspect of the downed knight's condition. If his reserve heart had begun to beat, there must have been significant trauma done to Priamus's body.

'Three minutes, Reclusiarch.' There was the dampened suggestion of bolter fire.

'Resistance, Cador?' Grimaldus asked.

'Nothing of consequence.'

'Stragglers,' Nerovar clarified. 'Three minutes, Reclusiarch. No more than that.'

It was closer to two minutes. When Nerovar and Cador arrived at a run, they smelled of the chemical combat stimulants in their blood and the acrid tang of discharged bolters.

The Apothecary knelt by Priamus, scanning his fallen brother with the medical auspex bio-scanner built into his arm-mounted narthecium.

Grimaldus looked at Cador. The oldest member of the squad was reloading his bolt pistol, and muttering into the vox.

'Speak,' the Chaplain said. 'I would hear your thoughts.'

'Nothing, sir.'

Grimaldus felt his eyes narrow and teeth grind together. He almost repeated his words at an order. What held him back was not tact, but discipline. His rage still boiled beneath the surface. He was no mere knight, to give in to his emotion and remain flooded by it. As a Chaplain, he held himself to a higher standard. Putting the chill of normality into his voice, he said simply:

'We will speak of this later. I am not blind to your tensions of late.'

'As you wish, Reclusiarch,' Cador replied.

Priamus opened his eyes, and did two things at once. He reached for his sword – still chained to his wrist – and he said through tight lips, 'Those whoresons. They shot me.'

'Some kind of nerve weapon.' Nerovar was still scanning him. 'It attacked your nervous system through the interface feeds from your armour.'

'Get away from me,' the swordsman said, rising to his feet. Nerovar offered a hand, which Priamus knocked aside. 'I said *get away*.'

Grimaldus handed the knight his helm.

'If you are finished with your lone reconnaissance, perhaps you can stay with Nero and Cador this time.'

The pause that followed the Chaplain's words was pregnant with Priamus's bitterness.

'As you wish. My lord.'

When we emerge from the wrecked ship, the weak sun is rising, spreading its worthlessly dim light across the clouded heavens.

The rest of my force, the hundred knights of the Helsreach Crusade, is assembling in the wastelands around the broken ship's metal bones.

Three Land Raiders, six Rhinos, the air around them all thrumming with the chuckle of idling engines. I think, for a strange moment, that even our tanks are amused at the pathetic hunting on offer last night.

Kill-totals scroll across my visor display as squad leaders report the success of their hunts. A paltry night's work, all in all, but the mortals behind the city walls have the first blood they so ardently desired.

'You're not cheering,' Artarion voxes to me, and only me.

'Little was cleansed. Little was purified.'

'Duty is not always glorious,' he says, and I wonder if he refers to our exile on the planet's surface with those words.

'I presume that is a barbed reference for my benefit?'

'Perhaps.' He clambers aboard our Land Raider, still speaking from within. 'Brother, you have changed since inheriting Mordred's mantle.'

'You are speaking foolishness.'

'No. Hear me. We have spoken: Cador, Nero, Bastilan, Priamus and myself. And we have listened to the talk among the others. We must all deal with these changes, and we must all face this duty. Your darkness is spreading to the entire Crusade. One hundred warriors all fearing that the fire in your heart is naught but embers now.'

And for a moment, his words ring true. My blood runs cold. My heart chills in my chest.

'Reclusiarch,' a voice crackles over the vox. I do not immediately recognise it – Artarion's words have stolen my thoughts.

'Grimaldus. Speak.'

'Reclusiarch. Throne of the God-Emperor... It's truly beginning.' Colonel Sarren sounds awed, almost eager.

'Elaborate,' I tell him.

'Battlefleet Armageddon is in full retreat. The Astartes fleet is withdrawing alongside them.' The colonel's voice broke up in a storm of vox-feedback, only to return a moment later. '...breaking against the orbital defence array. Breaking *through,* already. It's beginning.'

'We are returning to the city at once. Has there been any communication from *The Eternal Crusader*?'

'Yes. The planetary vox-network is struggling to cope with the influx. Shall I have the message relayed to you?'

'At once, colonel.'

I embark and slam the Land Raider's side hatch closed. Within the tank, all is suffused in the muted darkness of emergency lighting. I stand with my squad, gripping the overhead rail as the tank starts with a lurch.

At last, after the vox-clicking of several channels being linked together, I hear the words of High Marshal Helbrecht, the brother I have fought beside for so many decades. His voice, even on a low-quality recording, is filled with his presence.

'Helsreach, this is the *Crusader.* We are breaking from the planet. The orbital war is lost. Repeat: the orbital war is lost. Grimaldus... once you hear these words, stand ready. You are Mordred's heir, and my trust rides with you. Hell is coming, brother. The Great Enemy's fleet is without number, but faith and fury will see your duty done.'

I curse him, without giving voice to my spite. A silent oath that I will never forgive him for this exile... For damning me to die in futility.

Behind his words, I hear the cacophony of a ship enduring colossal assault. Dull explosions, horrendous and thunderous shaking – *The Eternal Crusader's* shields were down when he sent me this message. I cannot conceive of any enemy in history that has managed to inflict such damage to our flagship.

'Grimaldus,' he says my name with cold, raw solemnity, and his final words knife into me like a bitter blade.

'Die well.'

SIX

PLANETFALL

Grimaldus watched Helsreach erupting in fury.

They came through the morning clouds, fat-bellied troop landers that streaked with fire from atmospheric entry and the damage they had sustained breaking through the orbital defences.

Burning hulks juddered as their boosters fired, slowing them before they ploughed into the ground. They came from the horizon, or descended from stretches of cloud cover far from the city. Those few that sailed overhead, close enough for the city's defence platforms to reach, were subjected to horrendous battery fire, destroyed with such swift force that flaming wreckage rained upon the city below.

He stood with his command squad, fists resting on the edge of the battlements, watching the bulk landers coming down in the northern wastelands. Imperial fighters of all classes and designs flitted between the sedate troop ships, unleashing their payloads to minimal effect. The ships were too big for fighter-scale weapons to make any significant difference. As more alien scrapships broke the poison-yellow cloud cover, xenos fighter craft descended with their motherships. Barasath and his Lightning squadrons engaged these, punching them out of the air like buzzing insects.

Across the city, almost drowned out by the booming rage of the battlement guns, a siren wailed between automated announcements that demanded every soul take up arms and man their appointed positions.

The walls.

During the opening phase, Helsreach's defenders would stand upon the city's walls and be ready to repel an archaic siege. Hundreds of thousands of soldiers and militia, standing vigil on walls that were as tall as a Titan.

Several bold ork drop-ships sought to land within the city. Spiretop platforms, wall guns and cannon batteries mounted upon the tops of towers annihilated those that made the attempt. The luckier failures managed to climb with enough altitude to escape the city's reach and crash on the wastelands. Most were torn apart by unrelenting weapons fire, pulled apart and cast to the ground in flames.

Guard units stationed throughout the hive and pre-selected for the duty moved in on the downed hulks, slaughtering any alien survivors. Across the city, fire containment teams worked to put out blazes that spread from the crashing junkers.

Grimaldus looked along the walls to either side, where thousands of uniformed men stood in loose groups, every one clad in the ochre of the Armageddon Steel Legion. These were not Sarren's own 101st. The colonel's regiment remained at the command centre, as well as being spread across the city in platoons to defend key areas.

Artarion's words still burned behind the Chaplain's eyes.

'Brothers,' he spoke into the vox. 'To me.'

The knights drew closer – Nerovar watching the distant landings without a word; Priamus, his blade already in his hands, resting on one pauldron; Cador, projecting a sense of implacable patience; Bastilan, grim and silent; and Artarion, holding Grimaldus's banner, the only one of them without his helmet. He seemed to enjoy the uncomfortable glances he received from the human soldiers as they saw his shattered face. Occasionally, he'd grin at them, baring his metal teeth.

'Helm on,' Grimaldus said, the words emerging from his vocaliser as a low growl. Artarion complied with a chuckle.

'We must speak,' Grimaldus said.

'You have chosen a curious moment to realise that,' Artarion said. The wall shivered beneath their feet again as the turrets unleashed another volley at an alien scrap-cruiser shaking the sky overhead.

'The city has awoken to its duty,' Grimaldus intoned. 'It is time I did the same.'

The knights stood and watched as xenos landers touched down on the plains several kilometres from the city. Even from this distance, the Templars could make out hordes of greenskins spilling from the grounded ships, mustering on the wastelands.

Reports clashed with each other over the vox, telling of similar landings being made to the east and west of the city.

'Speak,' Grimaldus demanded in the face of his brothers' silence.

'What would have us say, Reclusiarch?' asked Bastilan.

'The truth. Your perceptions of this doomed crusade, and the way it is being led.'

The ork ship that had passed overhead minutes before now came down in the wasteland with slow, grinding, earthshaking force. It ploughed into the dusty ground, throwing up a trail of dust in its wake, and Helsreach shook to its foundations.

A cheer went up along the wall – thousands of soldiers crying out at the sight.

'We hold the largest city on the planet, with hundreds of thousands of soldiers,' Cador said, 'as well as countless experienced Guard and militia officers. And we have Invigilata.'

'Your point?' Grimaldus asked, watching the crashed ship burn. 'Do you think that will be even half of what we would need to repel the siege that we'll soon suffer?'

'No,' Cador replied. 'We are going to die here, but that is not my point. My point, brother, is that the city has a command structure already in place.'

Bastilan pitched in. 'You are not a general, Grimaldus. And you were not sent here to be one.'

Grimaldus nodded, his mind flashing back from the fire on the wastelands, snapping into recollections of the endless command staff meetings when the mortals had requested his presence.

He had thought it was his duty to be present, to grasp the full situation facing the hive. When he said these words to his brothers, he was answered with curses and smiles.

The Chaplain watched the greenskin swarm growing in size as more landers came down. The alien vessels darkened the sky, such was their number. Like steel beetles, they infested the wastelands in every direction, disgorging hosts of xenos warriors.

'It *was* my duty to study every soul, every weapon, every metre of this hive. But I have erred, brothers. The High Marshal did not send me here to command.'

'We know,' Artarion said softly, his skin tingling at the change in Grimaldus's tone. He sounded almost himself again.

'Until this moment, until I looked upon the enemy myself, I had not resigned myself to dying here. I was... enraged... with Helbrecht for damning me to this exile.'

'As were we all,' Priamus said, his voice rich with the sneer he wore on his face. 'But we will carve a legend here, Reclusiarch. We will make the High Marshal remember the day he sent us here to die.'

Good words, Grimaldus thought. Fine words.

'He will always recall that day. It is not he who must be forced to remember the Helsreach Crusade.' The Chaplain nodded out to the massing army. 'It is them.'

Grimaldus looked to his left, then his right. The Steel Legion stood in organised ranks, watching the mass of enemies coming together on the plains. When his own gaze returned to the foe, he couldn't help a smile creeping its way across his features.

'This is Grimaldus of the Black Templars,' he voxed. 'Colonel Sarren, answer me.'

'I am here, Reclusiarch. Commander Barasath reports–'

'Later, colonel. Later. I am looking at the enemy, tens of thousands, with more landing each moment. They will not wait for their wreck-Titans to be landed. These beasts are hungry for bloodshed. The first strike will come at the north wall, within the next two hours.'

'With respect, Reclusiarch, how will they reach the wall without Titans to breach it?'

'Propulsion packs to gain the battlements. Ladders to climb. Artillery to pound holes in the walls. They will do whatever they can, and as soon as they are able. These creatures have been imprisoned on bulk ships for weeks, and in some cases, months. Do not expect sense. Expect madness and rage.'

'Understood. I will have Barasath's squadrons ready for bombing runs on enemy artillery.'

'I would have suggested the same, colonel. The gates, Sarren. We must watch the gates. A wall is only as strong as its weakest point, and they will come at the north gate with everything they have.'

'Reinforcements are already being rerouted to–'

'No.'

'Pardon me?'

'You heard me. I will not require reinforcement. I have fifteen of my knights with me, and an entire Steel Legion regiment. I will provide updates as the situation evolves.' Grimaldus killed the vox-link before Sarren could argue more.

The Templar watched the enemy massing in the distance for several more minutes, listening to the chatter of the Guard soldiers nearby. The men around him wore the insignia of the 273rd Steel Legion. Their shoulder badges showed a black carrion bird, clutching the Imperial aquila in its claws.

The Reclusiarch closed his eyes, recalling the personnel data meetings he'd endured. The 273rd. The Desert Vultures. Their commanding officer was Colonel F. Nathett. His second officers were Major K. Johan, and Major V. Oros.

In the distance, a great cry was raised. It barely reached the defenders' ears over the powerful refrain of wall-guns firing, but it was there nevertheless. Thousands upon thousands of orks bellowing their racial war cry.

They were charging.

Charging alongside grumbling, rickety vehicles; troop-carriers stolen from the Imperium and subsequently junked in the spirit of alien 'improvement'; growling tanks that already lobbed shells that fell far short of the city walls; even great beasts of burden, the size of scout-class Titans, with scrap-metal howdahs on their rocking backs, filled with howling orks.

'We have sixteen minutes before they reach the range of the wall-guns,' Nerovar said. 'Twenty-two before they reach the gates, if their rate of advance remains unaltered.'

Grimaldus opened his eyes, and took a breath. The humans were muttering amongst themselves, and even though they were trained veterans, Grimaldus's gene-enhanced senses could scent the reek of sudden sweat and fear-soured breath through their respirators. No mortal could fail to be moved by the horde of devastation rumbling their way. Even without their greater war machines, the first ork assault was vast.

The city was ready. The enemy was coming. It was time to face up to why he was exiled here.

Grimaldus took a step up onto the battlements.

The wind was strong – an atmospheric disturbance from so many heavy craft making planetfall – but despite the powerful gale that whipped the greatcoats of the human soldiers, Grimaldus remained steady.

He walked along the edge of the wall, his weapons drawn and activated. The generator coils on the back of his plasma pistol burned with fierce light, and his crozius maul sparked with lethal force. As he moved, the eyes of the soldiers followed him. The wind tore at his tabard and the parchment scrolls fastened to his armour. He paid no heed to the anger of the elements.

'Do you see that?' he asked quietly.

At first, only silence followed. Hesitantly, the Guard soldiers began to cast glances to each other, uncomfortable with the Chaplain's presence and confused by his behaviour.

All eyes were on him now. Grimaldus aimed his mace out at the advancing hordes. Thousands. Tens of thousands. And only the very beginning.

'Do you see that?' he roared at the humans. The closest ranks flinched back from the mechanical bark that issued almost deafeningly loud from his skull helm.

'Answer me!'

He received several trembling nods. 'Yes, sir...' uttered a handful of them, the speakers faceless within the masses behind their rebreather masks.

Grimaldus turned back to the wasteland, already dark with the teeming, chaotic ranks of the enemy. At first, his helm emitted a low, vox-distorted chuckle. Within a few seconds, he was laughing, laughing up at the burning sky while aiming his crozius hammer at the enemy.

'Are you all as insulted as I am? *This* is what they send against us?'

He turned back to the men, the laughter fading, but amused contempt filling his voice even through the inhumanising vocalisers of his helm.

'This is what they send? This *rabble?* We hold one of the mightiest cities on the face of the planet. The fury of its guns sends all skyborne enemies to the ground in flames. We stand united in our thousands – our weapons without number, our purity without question, and our hearts beating courage through our blood. And *this* is how they attack us?

'Brothers and sisters... A legion of beggars and alien dregs wheezes its way across the plains. Forgive me when the moment comes that they whine and weep against our walls. Forgive me that I must order you to waste ammunition upon their worthless bodies.'

Grimaldus paused, lowering his weapon at last, turning his back on the invaders as if bored by their very existence. His entire attention was focussed upon the soldiers below him.

'I have heard many souls speak my name in whispers since I came to Helsreach. I ask you now: Do you know me?'

'Yes,' several voices replied, several among the hundreds.

'Do you know me?' he bellowed at them over the firing of the wall-guns.

'Yes!' a chorus answered now.

'I am Grimaldus of the Black Templars! A brother to the Steel Legions of this defiant world!'

A muted cheer greeted his words. It wasn't enough, not even close.

'Never again in life will your actions carry such consequence. Never again will you serve as you serve now. No duty will matter as much, and no glory will taste as true. We are the defenders of Helsreach. On this day, we carve our legend in the flesh of every alien we slay. Will you stand with me?'

Now the cheers came in truth. They thundered in the air around him.

'Will you stand with me?'

Again, a roar.

'Sons and daughters of the Imperium! Our blood is the blood of heroes and martyrs! The xenos dare defile our city? They dare tread the sacred soil of our world? We will throw their bodies from these walls when the final day dawns!'

A wave of noise crashed against his armour as they cheered. Grimaldus raised his war maul, aiming it to the embattled heavens.

'This is *our* city! This is *our* world! Say it! *Say it! Cry it out so the bastards in orbit will hear our fury! Our city! Our world!*'

'OUR CITY! OUR WORLD!'

Laughing again, Grimaldus turned to face the oncoming horde. *'Run, alien dogs! Come to me! Come to us all! Come and die in blood and fire!'*

'BLOOD AND FIRE!'

The Reclusiarch cut the air with his crozius, as if ordering his men forward. *'For the Templars! For the Steel Legion! For Helsreach!'*

'FOR HELSREACH!'

'Louder!'

'FOR HELSREACH!'

'They cannot hear you, brothers!'

'FOR HELSREACH!'

'Hurl yourselves at these walls, inhuman filth! Die on our blades! I am Grimaldus of the Black Templars, and I will cast your carcasses from these holy walls!'

'GRIMALDUS! GRIMALDUS! GRIMALDUS!'

Grimaldus nodded, still staring out over the wastelands, letting the cheering chant mix with the howling wind, knowing it would carry to the advancing enemy.

A vox-voice pulled him from his reverie. 'That is the first time since we landed,' said Artarion, 'that you have sounded like yourself.'

'We have a war to fight,' the Chaplain replied. 'The past is done with. Nero, how long?'

The Apothecary tilted his head, watching the horde for several moments. 'Six minutes until they are within range of the wall-guns.'

Grimaldus stepped down from the edge of the wall, standing among the Guard. They backed away from him, even as they all still cheered his name.

'Vultures!' he called, 'I must speak with Colonel Nathett, and Majors Oros and Johan. Where are your officers?'

A great deal can happen in six minutes, especially when one has the resources of a fortress-city to call upon.

Dozens of fighters in the gunmetal grey of the 5082nd Naval Skyborne streaked over the advancing horde, punishing them from above with strafing runs. Autocannons chattered, spitting into the tide of enemy flesh. Lascannons beamed with eye-aching brilliance, destroying dozens of the few heavy tanks present in this initial ork host.

Grimaldus stood upon the battlements, weapons in hands, watching Commander Barasath's Lightnings and Thunderbolts unleashing devastation from the sky. He was a veteran of two hundred years. He knew, with cold clarity, when something was wasted effort.

Every death counts, he thought, seeking to force himself to believe it as the immense sea of foes came crashing closer.

Priamus was similarly unmoved. 'Barasath's best attempt is no more than spitting into a tidal wave.'

'Every death counts,' Grimaldus growled. 'Every life lost out there is one less enemy assailing our walls.'

A great beast, some kind of stomping mammoth covered in scales, cried out as it went down, lanced through its legs and belly by a volley of lascannon fire. The orks fell from the howdah on its back, vanishing into the swarm of warriors. Grimaldus prayed they were crushed underfoot by their allies.

On his retinal display, a runic countdown began to flicker red.

He raised his crozius.

Along the north wall, hundreds of multi-barrelled turrets begin their realignment. On grinding joints, they cycled down to aim at the wastelands, leaving the city vulnerable from above.

Around each turret, a cluster of soldiers stood ready – loaders, sighters, vox-officers, adjutants, all ready for the order.

'Wall-guns,' Nero voxed to Grimaldus. 'Wall-guns, now.'

Grimaldus sliced the air with his blazing maul, screaming a single word.

'Fire!'

Craters appeared in the enemy horde. Huge explosions of dirt, scrap metal, bodies and gore erupted from the army. With the numbers facing them, the gunners on Helsreach's walls couldn't miss.

Thousands died in the first barrage. Thousands more came on.

'Reload!' a lone figure, armoured in black, shouted into the vox.

The walls themselves shook again, tremors pulsing through the rockcrete as the second volley fired. And the third. And the fourth. In a sane army, the annihilation inflicted upon them would be catastrophic. Entire legions would be breaking and running in fear.

The aliens, blood-maddened and howling their throaty war cries, didn't even slow down. They ignored their dead, trampled their wounded, and crashed against the towering walls like a peal of thunder.

With nothing capable of breaching the metres-thick sealed gates in the northern wall, the berserk aliens began to climb.

I have always believed there is something beautiful in the very first moments of a battle. Here are the moments of highest emotion; the fear of mortal men, the frustrated bloodlust and screaming overconfidence of mankind's enemies. In the moments when a battle is joined, the purity of the human species is first revealed to the foe.

In organised union, the hundreds of Steel Legion soldiers step forward. They move like different limbs of the same being. Like a reflection stretching into infinity, every man and woman down the line aims their lasguns over the wall, down at the greenskins howling and clambering. The aliens drag themselves up by their own claws; they climb on ladders and poles; they boost up on the whining thrusters of jump-packs.

And all of it so delightfully futile.

The *crack!* of thousands of lasguns discharging in a chorus is a strangely evocative song. It sings of discipline, defiance, strength and courage. More than that, it's a furious response – the first time the defenders can vent their rage at the invaders. Every soldier in the line squeezes their triggers, letting their lasrifles shout for them, spitting death down at the foe. Las-bolts tear into green flesh, ripping orks open, throwing them to the ground far below to be pulped under the boots of their kin.

Barasath's fighters streak overhead, their weapons still stuttering into the massed horde. Their targets have changed – more often than not, they rain their viciousness upon the artillery tanks that were unloaded last from the landers, and are only now catching up to the back to the besieging army.

I watch as the first of our fighters is brought down. Anti-air fire rattles up from a junked Hydra, its two remaining turrets tracking a group of Lightnings. The explosion is almost ignorable – a crumpled pop of fuel tanks detonating, and the protests of engines as the fighter spirals down.

It impacts in a burning wreck, wings shorn off, spinning and crashing through the ranks of the enemy. Some might consider it tragic that the pilot likely killed more of the enemy with his death than he did in life. I care only that more of the invaders are dead.

The first of the enemy to gain the ramparts does so alone. A hundred metres and more down the wall, a lone ork crashes down with his back-mounted propulsion pack streaming smoky fire. The others that were with him are either dead or dying, falling from their ascent as their bodies and thruster fuel tanks are riddled with las-fire. The one alien that touches down on the wall lasts less than a heartbeat. The creature is bayoneted in the throat, the eye, the chest and both legs by half a dozen soldiers, and their rifles blast the beast back over the edge.

First blood to Helsreach.

The minutes became hours.

The orks hurled themselves against the walls, still lacking any ability to secure a hold there, clambering up the hulls of wrecked tanks, mounds of their own dead, and ladders of twisted metal in a vain effort to reach the battlements.

Word was filtering through the wall commanders now; the east and west walls were enduring similar sieges. In the wasteland around the city, more landers were making planetfall, unloading fresh warriors and legions of tanks. While plenty of these new forces committed themselves immediately to the first attack already in progress, many more remained far from the city, making camps, clearing more landing zones and organising for a far more coordinated assault in the future.

The hive's defenders could make out individual banners among the ork swarm – clans and tribes united under the Great Enemy – many of which were now holding back rather than hurl themselves into this first, doomed attack.

Grimaldus remained with the Steel Legion troops on the northern wall, his knights spread out among the Guard's ranks, the Astartes' own squad unity suspended. Occasionally, greenskins would manage to reach the battlements rather than being slaughtered as they climbed. In those rare moments, Templar chainblades would shear through stinking alien flesh, before Guard-issue lasrifles would finish the job with precision beams of laser light.

At some point during the endless firing downward, Major Oros had voxed Grimaldus in bemusement.

'They're just lining up to die,' he'd laughed.

'These are the most foolish, and the least in control of themselves. They hunger to fight, no matter the odds or the war being waged. Look out onto the plains, major. Witness the gathering of our real enemies.'

'Understood, Reclusiarch.'

Grimaldus heard the Legion officers shouting to their men then, ordering another change of rank. The soldiers at the battlements fell back to reload, to clean their weapons and cool down overheating power-packs. The next line advanced to take their comrades' vacated positions, stepping up to the ramparts and immediately opening fire on the climbing orks.

The smell of the siege was drifting into the city now. Mountains of alien dead lay at the foot of the walls, their bodies ruptured and their tainted fluids leaking into the ashy soil. While the Templars and the Legionnaires were spared the worst of the stench by their helms and rebreathers, within the city itself, the civilians and militia forces were getting their first, foul taste of war against the ork-breed xenos. It was an unpleasant revelation.

Night was threatening to fall before the aliens finally fled.

Whether the mountain of their own dead had turned their fury to futility, or whether some cognition finally dawned over them all that the true battles were yet to come, the green tide retreated en masse. Horns sounded across the wasteland, hundreds of them, signalling a retreat that otherwise lacked even a hint of cohesion. Las-bolts flashed down from the walls as the Legion kept up a savage rate of fire, punishing the orks for their cowardice now just as they had punished them for their eager madness before. Hundreds more of the xenos collapsed to the ground, slain by the day's last, bitterest volley.

Soon, even the stragglers were out of range, limping their way behind the horde back to their landing sites.

Ork ships covered the wasteland now from horizon to horizon. The largest ships, almost as tall as hive spires themselves, were opening to release colossal, stomping scrap-Titans. Like hunched, fat-bellied aliens in shape, the junk-giants crashed across the plains, their pounding tread raising dust clouds in their wake.

These were the weapons that would bring the wall down. These were the foes that Invigilata had to destroy.

'That,' Artarion nodded at the sight as the knights remained on the wall, 'is a bleak picture.'

'The real battle begins tomorrow,' Cador grunted. 'At least we will not be bored.'

'I believe they will wait.' It was Grimaldus who spoke, his voice less bitter now the war cries and speeches were over. 'They will wait until they have overwhelming force with which to crush us, and they will strike like a hammer.'

The Chaplain paused, leaning on the battlements and staring at the army as sunset claimed the surrounded city.

'I requested we withdraw all Guard forces from the wasteland installations across all of southern Armageddon Secundus. The colonel agreed in principle.'

Bastilan joined the Reclusiarch at the wall. The sergeant disengaged his helm's seals and stood barefaced, ignoring the cool wind that prickled at his unshaven scalp.

'What's worth guarding out there?'

The Reclusiarch smiled, his expression hidden.

'The days and days of briefings were a necessary evil to answer questions like that. Munitions,' Grimaldus said. 'A great deal of munitions, to be used when the hive cities fall and need to be reclaimed. But that is not all. The Desert Vultures spoke of a curious legend. Something buried beneath the sands. A weapon.'

'We are involving ourselves in this world's mythology now?'

'Do not dismiss this. I heard something today that gave me hope.' He took a breath, narrowing his eyes as he watched the sea of enemy banners. 'And I have an idea. Where is Forgemaster Jurisian?'

SEVEN

ANCIENT SECRETS

Cyria Tyro leaned back in her chair, closing her eyes to rid her vision of the numbers she'd been staring at.

Casualties from the first day's engagement were light, and damage to the wall was minimal. Flamer teams had been lowered to drag the alien dead away from the city walls and burn them in massive pyres. It was a volunteer-only duty, and one that came with an element of risk – if the orks decided to attack in the night, there was no guarantee the hundreds of pyre-lighters outside could be brought back in time.

The funeral fires burned now, an hour before dawn, and though there were far too many bodies to complete the duty in a single night, the mounds of xenos dead were at least reduced.

For now, she sighed.

The ammunition expended on the first day alone had been... Well, she'd seen the numbers and could scarcely believe her eyes. The city was a fortress and its weapon reserves had seemed inexhaustible, but on a day of relatively sporadic fighting with only three regiments engaged, the logistical nightmare soon to be facing them was all too apparent. Their ammunition stocks would last months, but supplying it to regiments scattered throughout the city, ensuring they were aware of boltholes, weapons caches and...

I'm tired, she thought with a dry smile. She'd not even fought today.

Tyro signed a few data-slates with her thumbprint, authorising the transferral of reports to Lord General Kurov and Commissar Yarrick, far off in distant hives, already engaged in their own sieges.

The door's proximity chime pulsed once.

'Enter,' she called out.

Major Ryken walked in. His greatcoat was unbuttoned, his rebreather mask was hanging from its cord around his neck, and his black hair was scruffy from the rain.

'It's hurling it down out there,' he grumbled. He'd come all the way from the east wall. 'You wouldn't believe what the orbital disturbance has done to the atmosphere. What did you want that couldn't be done over the vox?'

'I couldn't reach Colonel Sarren.'

'He'd not slept in over sixty hours. I think Falkov threatened to shoot him unless he got some rest.' Ryken narrowed his eyes. 'There are other colonels. Dozens of them.'

'True, but none of those are the city commander's executive officer.'

The major scratched the back of his neck. His skin was cold, itching and grimy with the faintly acidic rainwater.

'Miss Tyro,' he began.

'Actually, given my rank as adjutant quintus to the planetary leader, I'll settle for "ma'am" or "advisor". Not "Miss Tyro". This is not a society function, and if it were, I would not be spending it talking to a drowned rat like you, major.'

Ryken grinned. Tyro didn't.

'Very well, *ma'am,* how may this lowly rodent be of service? I have a storm to get back out into before dawn.'

She looked around her own cramped but warm office in the central command tower, hiding her guilty flush by faking a cough.

'We received these from Acheron Hive an hour ago.' She gestured at several printed sheets of paper featuring topographic images. Ryken picked them up from her messy desk, flipping through them.

'These are orbital picts,' he said.

'I know what they are.'

'I thought the enemy fleet had destroyed all our satellites.'

'They have. These were among the last images our orbital defence array was able to send. Acheron received them, and sent them on to the other cities.'

Ryken turned one of the images to face her. 'This one has a caffeine stain on it. Did Acheron send that?'

Tyro scowled at him. 'Grow up, major.'

He spent a few more moments regarding the printed picts. 'What am I looking for here?'

'These are picts of the Dead Lands to the south. *Far* to the south, across the ocean.'

'I paid attention in basic geography, thank you, ma'am.' Ryken went through the picts a second time, lingering over the images of massive ork planetfall discolouring the landscape. 'This makes no sense,' he said at last.

'I know.'

'There's nothing in the Dead Lands. Not a thing.'

'I know, major.'

'So do we have any idea why they landed a force there that looks large enough to take a city?'

'Tacticians suggest the enemy is establishing a spaceport there. Or a colony.'

Ryken snorted, letting the picts drop back onto her desk.

'The tacticians are drunk,' he said. 'Every man, woman and child knows why the xenos come here: to fight. To fight until either they're all dead, or we are. They don't raise the greatest armada in history just to pitch tents at the south pole and raise ugly alien babies.'

'The fact remains,' Tyro gestured to the prints, 'that the enemy is there. Their distance across the ocean puts them out of reach for air strikes. No flyers would reach us without needing to refuel several times. They could just as easily set up airstrips in the wastelands much nearer the hive cities. In fact, we can already see they're doing just that.'

'What about the oil platforms?' he asked.

'The platforms?' she shook her head, not sure where he was leading with this.

'You're kidding me,' Ryken said. 'The Valdez oil platforms. Didn't you study Helsreach before you were posted here? Where do you think half of the hive cities in Armageddon Secundus get their fuel from? They take it in here from the offshore platforms and cook it into promethium for the rest of the continent.'

Tyro already knew this. She let him have his moment of feigned indignity.

'I paid attention,' she smiled, 'in basic economics. The platforms are protected from these southernmost raiders by the same virtue we are. It's just too far to strike at them.'

'Then with all due respect, ma'am, why did you pull me off the wall? I have duties to perform.'

And here it was. She had to deal with this matter delicately.

'I... would appreciate your assistance. First, I must disseminate this information among the other officers.'

'You don't need my help for that. You need access to a vox-caster, and you're sitting in a building full of them. Why should they care, anyway? What does a potential colony of the enemy on the polar cap have to do with the defence of the hive?'

'High Command has informed me that the matter is to be considered Helsreach's problem. We are – relatively speaking – the closest city.'

Ryken laughed. 'Would they like us to invade? I'll get the men ready and tell them to wrap up warm and lay siege to the south pole. I hope the orks outside the city respect the fact we'll be absent for the rest of the siege. They look like sporting gentlemen. I'm sure they'll wait for us to return to the hive before attacking again.'

'Major.'

'Yes, ma'am.'

'High Command has informed me to spread the information and let all officers be aware of the concern. That is all. No invasions. And it is not what I require your aid with.'

'Then what is it?'

'Grimaldus,' she said.

'Is that a fact? Problems with the Emperor's finest?'

'This is a serious matter,' Tyro frowned.

'Fair enough. But talk from the Vultures said that he was finally getting involved. They apparently got one hell of a speech.'

'He performed his duties on the wall with great skill and devotion.' She still wasn't smiling. 'That is not the problem at hand.'

Ryken let his raised eyebrow do the talking.

Tyro sighed. 'The problem is one of contact and mediation. He refuses to talk to me.' She paused, as if considering something for the first time. 'Perhaps because I'm female.'

'You're serious,' Ryken said. 'You truly believe that.'

'Well... He has bonded with the male officers, hasn't he?'

Ryken thought that was debatable. He'd heard that the only commander in the city Grimaldus had treated with anything more than disdainful impatience was the ancient woman that led the Legio Invigilata. And even that was just rumour.

'It's not because you're female,' the major said. 'It's because you're useless.'

The pause lasted several seconds, during which Cyria Tyro's face hardened with each passing moment.

'Excuse me?' she asked.

'Useless to them, shall we say. It's simple. You're the liaison between a High Command that is too busy to care what happens here, too distant to make much difference even if it did care, and offworld forces that have no need or interest in playing nice with the grunts of the Guard. Does the Crone of Invigilata need to pass orders through you? Does Grimaldus? No. Neither group cares.'

'The chain of command...' she started, but trailed off.

'The chain of command is a system both the Legio and the Templars are outside. And above, if they choose to be.'

'I feel useless,' she finally said. 'And not just to them.'

He could see how much that admission cost her. He could also see that she didn't seem such a haughty bitch when her defences were down. Just as Ryken drew breath to speak – and tell her a more polite version of his current thoughts – her desk vox-speaker buzzed.

'Adjutant Quintus Cyria Tyro?' asked a deep, resonant male voice.

'Yes. Who is this?'

'Reclusiarch Grimaldus of the Black Templars. I must speak with you.'

The Crone of Invigilata floated in her fluid-filled coffin, appearing to listen to the muffled sounds outside.

In truth, she was paying little attention. The muted sounds of speech and movement belonged to a world of physicality that she barely remembered. Linked with *Stormherald,* the god-machine's ever-present rumbling anger infected her like a chemical injected into her mind. Even in moments of peace, it was difficult to focus on anything but wrath.

To share a mind with *Stormherald* was to dwell within a maze of memories that were not her own. *Stormherald* had looked upon countless battlefields for hundreds of years before Princeps Zarha was even born. She had only to shut down the imagefinders that now served as her eyes, and as the hazy image of her milky surroundings faded to nothing, she could remember deserts she had never seen, wars she had never fought, glories she had never won.

Stormherald's voice in her mind was an unrelenting murmur, a hum of quiet tension, like a low-burning fire. It challenged her, with wordless growls, to taste of the victories it had tasted for so long – to swim beneath the surface memories and surrender to them. Its spirit was a proud and indefatigable machine-soul, and it hungered not only for the fiery maelstrom of war, but also the cold exaltation of triumph. It felt the banners of past wars that hung from its metal skin, and it knew fierce, unbreakable pride.

'My princeps,' came a muffled voice.

Zarha activated her photoreceptors. Borrowed memories faded and vision returned. Strange, how the former were so much clearer than the latter, these days.

Hello, Valian.

'Hello, Valian.'

'My princeps, the adepts of the soul are reporting discontent within *Stormherald's* heart. We are getting anomalous readings of ill-temper from the reactor core.'

We are angry, moderati. We yearn to bring the thunder down upon our foes.

'We are angry, moderati. We yearn to bring the thunder down upon our foes.'

'That is understandable, my princeps. You are... operating at peak capacity? You are sanguine?'

Are you querying if I am at risk of being consumed by Stormherald's heart?

'Are you querying if I am at risk of be*kkrrssshhhhh* heart?'

'Maintenance adept,' Valian Carsomir called to a robed tech-priest. 'Attend to the princeps's vocaliser unit.' He turned back to his commander. 'I trust you, my princeps. Forgive me for troubling you.'

There is nothing to forgive, Valian.

'There is noth*kkkrrrrrsssssssssh*.'

That would become annoying after a while, she thought, but did not pulse the sentiment to her vocaliser. *Your concern touches me, Valian.*

'Your concern touches me, Valian.'

But I am well.

'B*krsh* I am well.'

The tech-adept stood by the side of Zarha's amniotic tank. Mechanical arms slid from his robe and began to do their work.

Moderati Primus Valian Carsomir hesitated, before making the sign of the cog and returning to his station.

We will see battle soon, Valian. Grimaldus has promised it to us.

'We will see battle soon, Valian. Grimaldus has promised it to us.'

Valian didn't reply at first. If the enemy was going to amass its numbers first, shelling the foe from the safety of the city walls was hardly seeing battle, in his eyes.

'We are all ready, my princeps.'

Tomaz couldn't sleep.

He sat up in bed, swallowing another stinging mouthful of amasec, the cheap, thin stuff that Heddon brewed in one of the back warehouses down at the docks. The stuff tasted more than a little of engine oil. It wouldn't have surprised Tomaz to learn that was one of the ingredients.

He swallowed another burning gulp that itched its way down his throat. There was, he realised, a more than good chance he was going to throw this stuff back up soon. It had a habit of not sitting too well on an empty stomach once it went down, but he didn't think he could manage another dry meal of preserved rations. Tomaz glanced at several packets of unopened, densely packed grain tablets on the table.

Maybe later.

He'd not been anywhere near the north and eastern walls. At the south docks, there was little difference between today and any other day. The grinding joints of his crane drowned out any of the distant sounds of the war, and he'd spent his twelve-hour shift unloading tankers and organising distribution from the warehouses in his district – just as he spent every shift.

The backlog of docked tankers, and those awaiting docking clearance, was beyond a joke. Half of Tomaz's crew was gone, conscripted into the militia reserves and sent across the city to play at being Guardsmen, kilometres away from where they were really needed. He was the elected representative of the Dockers' Union, and he knew every other foreman was suffering the same lack of manpower. It made a difficult job completely laughable, except none of them were smiling.

There had been talk of limiting the flow of crude coming in from the Valdez platforms once the orbital defences fell, under fears the orks would bombard the shipping lanes.

Necessity outweighed the risk of tanker crews dying, of course. Helsreach needed fuel. The flow continued. Even with the city sealed, the docks remained open.

And they were somehow busier than before, despite the fact there was only half the manpower on the crews. Teams of Steel Legionnaires and menial servitors manned the many anti-air turrets along the dockside and the warehouse rooftops. Hundreds upon hundreds of warehouses were now used to house tanks, converted into maintenance terminals and garages for war machine repair. Convoys of Leman Russ battle tanks shuddered through the docks, strangling thoroughfares with their slow processions.

Half-crewed and slowed by constant interference, the Helsreach docks were almost at a standstill.

And still the tankers arrived.

Tomaz checked his wrist chronometer. Just over two hours until dawn.

He resigned himself to not getting any sleep before his shift began, and took another drink from the bottle of disgusting amasec.

Heddon really should be shot for brewing this rat piss.

She stood in the storm, her Steel Legion greatcoat heavy around her shoulders.

The lashing rainfall did little to clean the streets. The reek of sulphur rose from the wet buildings around her as the acidic rain mixed with the pollution coating the stonework and rockcrete across the city.

Not a good time to forget your rebreather, Cyria...

Major Ryken escorted her along the north wall. In the dim distance to the east, the sun was already bringing dawn's first glimmer to the sky. Cyria didn't want to look over the wall's edge, but couldn't help herself. The dim illumination revealed the enemy's army, a tide of darkness that reached from horizon to horizon.

'Throne of the God-Emperor,' she whispered.

'It could be worse,' Ryken said, guiding her onward after she'd frozen at the sight.

'There must be millions of them out there.'

'Without a doubt.'

'Hundreds of tribes... You can make out their banners...'

'I try not to. Eyes ahead, ma'am.'

Cyria turned with reluctance. Ahead of her, fifty metres down the wall, a group of giant black statues stood in the rainfall, the deluge making the edges of their armour shine.

One of the giants moved, his boots thudding on the wall as he walked towards her. The harsh wind whipped the soaked scrolls tied to his armour, and drenched his tabard with its black cross upon the chest.

His face was a grinning silver skull, the eyes staring a soulless red, right through her.

'Cyria Tyro,' he said in a deep, vox-crackling voice, 'greetings.' The Astartes made the sign of the aquila, his dark gauntlets banging against his chestplate as they formed the symbol. 'And Major Ryken of the 101st. Welcome to the north wall.'

Ryken returned the salute. 'I heard you gave the Vultures a speech earlier, Reclusiarch,' he said.

'They are fine warriors, all,' Grimaldus said. 'They needed none of my words, but it was a pleasure to share them, nevertheless.'

Ryken was caught momentarily off-guard. He'd not expected an answer, let alone this unnerving humility. Before he could reply, Cyria spoke up. She looked up at Grimaldus, shielding her eyes from the downpour. The hum of his armour made her gums itch. The sound seemed to be louder than before, as if reacting to the bad weather.

'How may I be of service, Reclusiarch?'

'That is the wrong question,' the knight said, his vox-voice a low growl. The rain scythed onto his armour, hissing as it hit the dark ceramite. 'The question is one you must answer, not one you must ask.'

'As you wish,' she said. His formality was making her uncomfortable. In fact, everything about him was making her uncomfortable.

'We have defensive positions in the wastelands, manned by the Steel Legion. Platoons of the Desert Vultures, among other regiments, have dug in to hold these against the enemy. Small towns, coastal depots, weapons caches, fuel dumps, listening stations.'

Tyro nodded. Most of these outposts, and their relative strategic value, had been covered in the command meetings.

'Yes,' she said, for want of anything else to say.

'Yes,' he repeated her reply, sounding amused. 'I was informed today exactly what is stored in the underground hangar of the D16-West outpost, ninety-eight kilometres to the north-west of the city. None of our briefings mentioned it was a sealed Mechanicus facility.'

Tyro and Ryken exchanged a glance. The major shrugged a shoulder. Although most of his face was masked by his rebreather, his eyes showed he had no idea what the Chaplain was inferring. Cyria's glance fell back to the towering knight's crimson gaze.

'I've seen little data on D-16 West's storage consignments, Reclusiarch.

All I know is that a deactivated relic from the era of the First War is stored in the sub-level compound. No Guard personnel are permitted access to the innards of the facility. It is considered sovereign Mechanicus territory.'

'I learned the same today. That does not intrigue you?' the Astartes asked.

It was a fair question. In truth, no, it didn't interest her at all. The First War had been won almost six hundred years ago, and the planet's face was one of different cities and different armies now.

'Whether I find it fascinating or not is hardly of consequence,' she said. 'Whatever is stored there is impounded under orders of the Adeptus Mechanicus – I suspect for a damn good reason – and is a secret even from Planetary High Command. Even our Guard force there is a token battle group. They are not expected to survive the first month.'

'Do you know your history, Adjutant Tyro?' Grimaldus's voice was calm, low and composed. 'Before we made planetfall here, a great deal was committed to our memories. All lore is useful in the right hands. All information can be a weapon against the enemy.'

'I have studied several of the decisive battles of the First War,' she said. All Steel Legion officers had.

'Then you will know what Mechanicus weapon was designed and first deployed here.'

'Throne,' Ryken whispered. 'Holy Throne of Terra.'

'I... don't think you can be right...' Tyro told the Astartes.

'Perhaps not,' Grimaldus conceded, 'but I intend to learn the truth for myself. One of our gunships will carry a small group to D-16 West in one hour.'

'But it's sealed!'

'It will not be sealed for long.'

'It's Mechanicus territory!'

'I do not care. If I am right in my suspicions, there is a weapon there. I want that weapon, Cyria Tyro. And I will have it.'

She pulled her greatcoat tighter around her body as the storm intensified.

'If it was something that would help with the war,' she said, 'the Mechanicus would have deployed it by now.'

'I do not believe that, and I am surprised that you do. The Mechanicus has committed a great deal in the defence of Armageddon. That does not mean they have the same stake in the war that we do. I have battled alongside the Cult of Mars many times. They breathe secrecy instead of air.'

'You can't leave the city before dawn. The enemy–'

'The enemy will not break the city walls in the first day. And Bayard, Emperor's Champion of the Helsreach Crusade, will command the Templars in my absence.'

'I can't allow you to do this. It will enrage the Mechanicus.'

'I am not asking for your permission, adjutant.' Grimaldus paused, and she swore she could hear a smile in his next words. 'I am asking if you wish to come with us.'

'I... I...'

'You informed me upon my arrival that you were here to facilitate interaction between the offworld forces and those of Armageddon.'

'I know, but–'

'Mark my words, Cyria Tyro. If the Mechanicus has reasons for not deploying that weapon, they may not be reasons that other Imperial commanders will find acceptable. I do not care about those reasons. I care about winning this war.'

'I'll accompany you,' she almost choked on the words. Throne, what was she doing…

'I thought you would,' said Grimaldus. 'The sun is rising. Come, to the Thunderhawk. My brothers already wait.'

The gunship shuddered as its boosters lifted it from the landing platform.

The pilot, an Initiate knight with few honour markings on his armour, guided the ship skyward.

'Try not to get us shot down,' Artarion said to him, standing behind the pilot's throne in the cockpit. They were set to fly above the clouds anyway, and take a course over the ocean and the coast before veering inland once they were clear of the besieging army and its fighter support.

'Brother,' the Initiate said, watching the city falling below as he applied vertical thrust, 'does anyone ever laugh at your jokes?'

'Humans sometimes do.'

The pilot didn't reply to that. Artarion's answer said it all. The gunship gave a kick as its velocity boosters fired, and through the cockpit window, the toxic cloud cover began to slide past.

EIGHT

OBERON

Domoska muttered the Litany of Focus as she looked through the sight of her lasrifle. She blinked behind her sunglare goggles, then raised them to look through the gunsight again without the tinted lenses darkening her vision.

'Uh, Andrej?' she called over her shoulder.

The two soldiers were at their modest camp on the perimeter of D-16's boundaries. Sat on the desert sands, cleaning their rifles, the fact they were away from the main base also set them apart from the other forty-eight Steel Legionnaires assigned to this pointless, suicidal duty.

Andrej didn't look up from his lap, where he was wiping laspistol power cell packs with an oily rag.

'What is it now, eh? I'm busy, okay?'

'Is that a gunship?'

'What are you talking about, eh?' Andrej was from Armageddon Prime, on the far side of the world. His accent always made Domoska grin. Almost everything he said sounded like a question.

'That,' she pointed into the sky, close to the horizon. Nothing was visible to the naked eye, and Andrej groped on the coat laid out on the ground, reaching for his detached gunsight.

'Listen, okay, I am trying to respect the spirit of my weapon, yes? What is this you want? I see no gunship.' He stared through his sight, squinting.

'A few degrees above the horizon.'

'Oh, hey, yes that is a gunship, okay? You must report it at once.'

'This is Domoska, at Boundary Three. Contact, contact, contact. Imperial gunship inbound.'

'That is the Black Templars, yes? They are from Helsreach. I know this. I listen to my briefings. I do not sleep, like you.'

'Be quiet,' she murmured, waiting for confirmation over the vox.

'I will be the one with so many medals, I think. You have nothing, eh?'

'Be quiet!'

'Acknowledged,' the reply finally came. Andrej took that as his cue to speak again.

'I hope they are saying we may return to the city, okay? That would be good news. High walls! Titans! We might even survive this war, eh?'

Neither of them had ever seen a Thunderhawk gunship before. As it came in on howling thrusters, slowing down and hovering over the almost abandoned facility of empty warehouses and storage bunkers, Domoska had a sinking sensation in her stomach.

'This can't be good.' She bit her lower lip.

'I do not agree, you know? This is Astartes business. It will be good. Good for us, bad for the enemy.'

She just looked at him.

'What? It will be good. You will see, eh? I am always right.'

Storm Trooper Captain Insa Rashevska glanced at the soldiers on either side of her as the gunship's front ramp lowered on hissing hydraulics.

One thought had been rattling around her mind in the five minutes since Domoska had voxed in the sighting, and that was a very simple, clear: *Why in the hells are the Astartes here?*

She was about to get her answer.

'Should we... salute?' one of her men asked from his position at Rashevska's side. 'Is that what you're supposed to do?'

'I don't know,' she replied. 'Just stand at attention.'

The gang ramp clanged as boots descended. A human – from the Legion, no less – and two Templars.

Both Astartes wore the black of their Chapter. One was draped in a tabard showing personal heraldry, and his helm showed an ornate death mask as the faceplate. The other wore much bulkier armour, with additional layers of ablative plating, and the war plate whirred and clanked as its false-muscles moved.

'Captain,' the Legion officer said. 'I'm Adjutant Quintus Tyro, seconded to Hive Helsreach from the Lord General's command staff. With me are Reclusiarch Grimaldus and Master of the Forge Jurisian, of the Black Templars Chapter.'

Rashevska made the sign of the aquila, trying not to show her unease in the presence of the towering warriors. Four machine-arms, their servo-joints grinding, unlocked from Jurisian's thrumming back-mounted power pack. Their metal claws clicked open and snapped closed while the arms themselves extended as if stretching.

'Greetings,' Jurisian rumbled.

'Captain,' Grimaldus said.

'We have come to enter the installation,' Cyria Tyro smiled.

Rashevska said nothing for almost ten seconds. When she did speak, it was with a stunned and disbelieving laugh.

'Forgive me, is this a joke?'

'Far from it,' Grimaldus said, striding past her.

On the surface, D-16 West wasn't a particularly grand site. Rising from the wasteland's sandy soil were a cluster of buildings, all of which were solidly built and armoured – almost bunker-like in their squat construction. All were empty, save for those now occupied by the small Steel Legion force stationed here. In those buildings, bedrolls and equipment were arranged in an order that spoke of discipline. Two expansive landing platforms, easily big enough for the bulky Mechanicus cruisers that could even carry Titans, were half-buried in sand, as the desert slowly reclaimed the facility.

The only architecture of significant interest was a roadway over a hundred metres in width that led into the ground beneath the surface complex. Whatever colossal doors had once opened into the underground complex were long buried beneath the wasteland's shifting tides. It would only be a handful of decades before the last evidence of the roadway itself was covered over.

One of the bunker buildings contained nothing but a series of elevators. The bulkhead doors to each lift were sealed, and the machinery lining the walls and connected to the shafts was all powered down. Keypads with runic buttons of various colours were installed on the wall next to each closed door.

'There is no power here,' the Reclusiarch said as he looked around. 'They left this place entirely devoid of energy?' That would make reactivation – if this installation was even ever meant to be reactivated – an incredibly difficult operation.

Jurisian walked around the interior of the bunker, his thudding tread making the floor tremble.

'No,' he said, his vox-voice a slow, considering drawl. 'There is power. The installation sleeps, but does not lie dead. It is locked in hibernation. Power still beats through its veins. The resonance is low, the pulse is slow. I hear it, nevertheless.'

Grimaldus stroked his fingertips along the closest keypad, staring at the unknown sigils that marked each button. The language of the runes was not High Gothic.

'Can you open these doors?' he asked. 'Can you get us down into the complex?'

Jurisian's four machine-arms extended again, their claws articulating. Two of the servo-arms came over the Techmarine's shoulders. The other two remained closely aligned with his true arms. The Master of the Forge approached one of the other elevator bulkheads, already reaching for his enhanced auspex scanner mag-locked to his belt. The arms reaching over his shoulders took Jurisian's bolter and blade, gripping them in claw clamps and leaving the knight's hands free.

'Jurisian? Can you do this?'

'It will necessitate a great deal of rerouting power from auxiliary sources, and those will be difficult to reach from a remote connection point here. A parasitic feed is required from–'

'Jurisian. Answer the question.'

'Forgive me, Reclusiarch. Yes. I will need one hour.'

Grimaldus waited, statue-still, watching Jurisian work. Cyria quickly grew bored, and wandered through the complex, speaking with the stormtroopers on duty. Two were returning from their shift at a boundary post, and the adjutant waved them over as she stood in the avian shadow cast by the gunship.

'Ma'am,' the female trooper saluted. 'Welcome to D-16 West.'

'Now we have Helsreach brass coming to visit, okay?' said the other. He made the sign of the aquila a moment later. 'I told you it would be good.'

Cyria returned their salutes, not even a little off-guard at their nonchalance. Storm troopers were the best of the best, and their distance from regular troops often bred a little... uniqueness... into their attitudes.

'I'm Adjutant Quintus Tyro.'

'We know. We were told this on the vox. Digging for secrets in the sand, yes? That is not going to make the Mechanicus smile, I think.'

Whether the Mechanicus would be pleased or not evidently didn't matter to this man. He was smiling, either way.

'A big risk,' he added, nodding sagely as if this was some hidden truth he had worked out alone. 'It may bring much trouble, eh?' He still seemed entertained by the concept.

'With respect,' the female trooper – her stormcoat badge read DOMOSKA in flat black letters – said, looking uncomfortable, 'Will this not anger the Legio Invigilata?'

Tyro stroked a stray lock of her dark hair from her face, tucking it behind her ear. She repeated exactly what Grimaldus had said to her when she'd asked the same question during the Thunderhawk flight here.

'Perhaps,' she said, 'but it's not like they can leave the city in protest, is it?'

The doors opened.

The motion was smooth, but the noise of resistant machine-innards was immense: a squealing, unlubricated whine that split the air. Inside the elevator, the spacious car had enough room for twenty humans. Its walls were a matte, gunmetal grey.

Jurisian stepped back from the control console.

'It was necessary to power down all other ascent/descent systems. This one shaft will function. The others are now soulless.'

Grimaldus nodded. 'Will we be able to return to the surface once we go down?'

'There is a thirty-three point eight per cent chance, given current system destabilisation, that a return ascent will require additional maintenance and reconfiguring. There is a further twenty-nine per cent chance that no reconfiguring will restore function without access to the primary installation power network.'

'The word you're looking for, brother,' Grimaldus stepped towards the open doors, 'is "maybe".'

They wandered down there for hours.

The underground complex was a silent – and initially lightless – series of labyrinthine corridors and deserted chambers. Jurisian brought the installation's overhead lighting back online after several minutes at a wall console.

Cyria clicked her torch off. Grimaldus cancelled his helm's vision intensifier settings. With flickering reluctance, dull yellow lighting illuminated their surroundings.

'I have resuscitated the spirits of the illuminatory array,' Jurisian said. 'They are weak from slumber, but should hold.'

The bland greyness all around them soon grew uninspiring as they ventured deeper into the complex. Around corners, through silent chambers with inactive engines, motionless machinery and generators of unknowable purpose.

Jurisian would occasionally pause and examine some of the Mechanicus's abandoned technology.

'This is a magnetic field stabiliser housing,' he said at one point, walking around what looked to Cyria like an oversized tank engine as big as a Chimera APC.

'What does it do?' she made the mistake of asking.

'It houses the stabilisers for a magnetic field generator.'

Her fear of the Astartes had dimmed some way by this point. She fought the urge to sigh, but failed.

'Do you mean,' Jurisian enquired, 'what application does this have in Imperial technology?'

'That's close to what I meant, yes. What is its purpose?'

'Magnetic fields of significant size and intensity are difficult to create and a struggle to maintain. Many of these units would be required to work in synchronicity, stabilising a powerful field of magnetic force. Such standard constructs as this housing are used in anti-gravitational technology, much of which is kept sealed by Mechanicus secrecy. More commonly, the Imperial Navy would use these units in the construction and maintenance of starship-sized magnetic accelerator rings. Plasma weapon technology, on a grand scale.'

'No,' Cyria shook her head. 'It can't be.'

'We shall see,' Jurisian rumbled. 'This is only the installation's first level. From the angle of the buried roadway, I would conjecture that the complex proceeds beneath the earth for at least a kilometre. From my knowledge of template patterns used in Mechanicus facility construction, it is more likely to be two or three kilometres deep.'

Nine hours after Grimaldus, Jurisian and Cyria had entered the installation, they reached the fourth sublevel. The third level had taken almost six hours to traverse, with sealed doors requiring more and more intensive manipulation to coax open. At one point, Grimaldus had been certain they were thwarted. He hefted his crozius in both hands, triggering it live, ready to vent his anger on the unopening door.

'Don't,' Jurisian said, without looking up from the controls.

'Why not? You said this might be impossible, and time is not our ally down here.'

'Do not apply force to the doors. These are, as you have seen, each no less than four metres thick. While you will eventually hammer through to the other side, it will not be a rapid endeavour, and such violence is likely to activate the installation's significant defences.'

Grimaldus lowered his mace. 'I see no defences.'

'No. That is their strength, and the primary reason no living and augmetic guards are required.'

He still did not look away from his work as he spoke. Four of Jurisian's six arms all worked at the console: hitting buttons, pulling clusters of wires and cables, tying them, fusing them together, replacing them, tuning dead screens. His lower servo-arms were now coiled close to his back-mounted power pack, carrying his bolter and power sword.

'There are,' Jurisian continued, 'twelve hundred needle-thin holes in the walls, spaced ten centimetres apart, in this corridor alone.'

Grimaldus examined the walls. His visor locked onto one immediately, now he knew they were there.

'And these are...?'

'A defence. Part of one. The application of force, no matter how righteous, brother, will trigger the machinery behind these holes – and the same holes in many other corridors and chambers throughout the complex – to release a toxic gas. It is my estimation that the gas would attack the nervous system and respiration above all, making it especially lethal to fully biological intruders.'

The Master of the Forge nodded pointedly to Cyria.

Grimaldus's crozius went dead as he released the trigger. 'Have there been other defences that escaped our attention?'

'Yes,' Jurisian said. 'Many. From automated las-turrets to void-shield screens. Forgive me, Reclusiarch, this code manipulation requires my full attention.'

That had been three hours ago.

Finally, the doors opened to the fourth sublevel. To Cyria, the air was painfully cold, and she pulled her stormcoat tightly closed.

Grimaldus failed to notice her discomfort. Jurisian merely commented, 'The temperature is at a survivable level. You will not suffer lasting harm. This is common in Mechanicus facilities that are left on minimal power.'

She nodded, her teeth chattering.

Ahead of them, the corridor widened to end in a huge double doorway, sealed as every other door had been so far. On this one, etched into the dull, grey metal, was a single word in bold Gothic.

- OBERON -

This was why Grimaldus hadn't noticed Cyria's shivering. He could not take his eyes off the inscription, with each letter standing as tall as a Templar.

'I was right,' he breathed. 'This is it.'

Jurisian was already at the door. One of his human hands stroked the surface of the sealed portal, while the others accessed the wall terminal nearby. Its complexity was horrific compared to those stationed at the previous doors.

'It is so beautiful...' Jurisian sounded both hesitant and awed. 'It is magnificent. This would survive orbital bombardment. Even the use of cyclonic torpedoes against nearby hives would barely harm the protection around this chamber. It is void-shielded, armoured like no bunker I have ever seen... and sealed with... with a billion or more individual codes.'

'Can you do it?' Grimaldus asked, his gauntleted fingertips brushing the 'O' in the inscribed name.

'I have never witnessed anything so complex and incredible. It would be like mapping every particle within a star.'

Grimaldus withdrew his hand. He seemed not to have heard.

'Can you do it?'

'Yes, Reclusiarch. But it will take between nine and eleven days. And I would like my servitors sent to me as soon as you return. '

'It will be done.'

Cyria Tyro felt tears standing in her eyes as she stared at the name. 'I don't believe it. It can't be here.'

'It is,' Grimaldus said, taking a last look at the doors. 'This is where the Mechanicus hid the Ordinatus Armageddon after the First War. This is the tomb of *Oberon.*'

As they returned to the surface, Cyria's hand-vox crackled for her attention, and a signal rune pulsed on Grimaldus's retinal display.

'Tyro, here,' she said into her communicator.

'Grimaldus. Speak,' he said within his helm.

It was the same message, delivered by two different sources. Tyro had Colonel Sarren, his voice more of an exhausted sigh than anything else. Grimaldus heard the clipped, imperious tones of Champion Bayard.

'Reclusiarch,' the champion said. 'The Old Man's predictions were correct, as you suspected. The enemy is annihilating Hades Hive from orbit. It is crudely done. Standard bombardment, with mass drivers to hurl asteroids at a defenceless city. A dark day's work, brother. Will you return soon?'

'We are on our way back now,' he said, and killed the link.

Tyro lowered her communicator, her face pale.

'Yarrick was right,' she said. 'Hades is burning.'

NiNE

GAMBITS

The enemy did not come on the second day.

The defenders watched from the walls of Helsreach as the wastelands turned black with enemy vessels and clans of orks establishing their territory, making primitive camps and raising banners to the sky. More landers brought new floods of troops. Bulk cruisers disgorged fat-hulled wreck-Titans.

Upon the enemy banners, thousands of crudely painted symbols faced the city, each one depicting a bloodline, a tribe, a xenos war-clan that would soon be hurling itself into battle.

From the battlements, the Imperial soldiers marked these symbols, and responded in kind. Standards flew above the walls – one for every regiment serving inside the city. The Steel Legion banners flew in greatest number, ochre and orange and yellow and black.

After he returned from D-16 West, Grimaldus himself planted the banner of the Black Templars among those already standing on the north wall. The Desert Vultures gathered to watch the knight ram the banner pole into the rockcrete, and swear an oath that Helsreach would never fall while one defender still lived.

'Hades may burn,' he called to the gathered soldiers, 'but it burns because the enemy fears us. It burns to hide the enemy's shame, so they need never look upon the place where they lost the last war. While the walls of Helsreach stand, so stands this banner. While one defender draws breath, the city will never be lost.'

In echo of his gesture, Cyria Tyro persuaded a moderati to plant the banner of the Legio Invigilata nearby. Lacking a banner suitable for handling by humans rather than the huge standards that were borne by the god-machines, one of the weapon-arm pennants from the Warhound Titan *Executor* was used in absentia – mounted on a pole and driven into the wall between two Steel Legion banners.

The soldiers on the wall cheered. Unused to such attention outside the cockpit of his beloved Warhound, the moderati seemed awkwardly pleased by the reaction. He made the sign of the cog to the officers present, and made the sign of the aquila a moment later, as if anxiously covering a mistake.

At night, the winds blew harder and colder. It almost cleared the air of the sulphuric stench that was forever present and, at its strongest, it dragged the standard of the 91st Steel Legion from the battlements of the west wall.

Preachers attached to the regiment warned that it was an omen – that the 91st would be the first to fall if they did not stand defiant when the true storm struck.

As the sun was setting, Helsreach shook with thunder to match the maelstrom taking place on the wastelands. *Stormherald* was leading several of its metal kin to the walls, where the largest – the battle-class Titans – could fire over the battlements once the enemy came in range.

The Guard were ordered to abandon the walls for hundreds of metres around the god-machines. The sound of their weapons discharging would be deafening to anyone too close, and even being near the gigantic guns could be lethal, with the amount of energy they unleashed as they fired.

No one in Helsreach would be sleeping tonight.

He opened his eyes.

'Brother,' a voice called to him. 'The Crone of Invigilata requests your presence.'

Grimaldus had returned to the city hours ago. He had been expecting this summons.

'I am in prayer,' he said into the vox.

'I know, Reclusiarch.' It was not like Artarion to be so formal.

'Did she *request* my presence, Artarion?'

'No, Reclusiarch. She, ah, "demanded" it.'

'Inform Invigilata I will attend Princeps Zarha within the hour, once my ritual observations are complete.'

'I do not believe she is in the mood to be kept waiting, Grimaldus.'

'Nevertheless, waiting is what she will do.'

The Chaplain closed his eyes again as he kneeled on the floor of the small, empty chamber in the command spire, and once more let his mouth form the whispered words of reverence.

I approach the amniotic tank.

My weapons are not in my hands, and this time, in the close confines of the Titan's busy cockpit chamber, the tension from before is distilled into something altogether more fierce. The crewmen, the pilots, the tech-priests... they stare with unconcealed hostility. Several hands rest on belts close to sheathed blades or holstered firearms.

I refrain from laughing at this display, though it is no easy feat. They command the greatest war machine in the entire city, yet they concern themselves with ceremonial daggers and autopistols.

Zarha, the Crone of Invigilata, floats before me. Her lined, matronly face is twisted by emotion. Her limbs twitch in gentle spasm every few moments – feedback from the link with *Stormherald's* soul.

'You requested my presence?' I say to her.

The old woman suspended in the fluid licks her metallic teeth. **'No. I summoned you.'**

'And that was your first mistake, princeps,' I tell her. 'You are granted permission to make only two more before this conversation is over.'

She snarls, her face hideous in the milky fluids. **'Enough of your posturing, Astartes. You should be slain where you stand.'**

I look around the cockpit, at the nine souls in here with me. My targeting reticule locks onto all visible weapons, before returning to focus on the Crone's withered features.

'That would be an unwise solution,' I tell her. 'No one in this room is capable of wounding me. Should you call the eight skitarii waiting outside the doors, I would still leave this chamber a charnel house. And you, princeps, would be the last to die. Could you run from me? I think not. I would tear you from your artificial womb, and as you choked in the air, I would hurl you from the eye-windows of your precious Titan, to die naked and alone on the cold ground of the city you were too proud to defend. Now, if you are quite finished with the exchange of threats, I would ask you to move on to more important matters.'

She smiles, but the hatred curling her lips is all I see. It is, in its own way, beautiful. Nothing is purer than hatred. With hatred, humanity was forged. Through hatred, we have brought the galaxy to its knees.

'I see you do not show your face this time, knight. You see me revealed, yet you hide behind the death mask of your Emperor.'

'*Our* Emperor,' I remind her. 'You have just made your second mistake, Zarha.'

I disengage my helm's collar seals and lift the mask clear. The air smells of sweat, oil, fear and chemical-rich fluids. I ignore the others, ignore all but her. Despite the bitterness around me that deepens with each moment, it is comfortable to stand without my senses enclosed by my helm. Since planetfall, the only time I have removed my helm in the company of others has been on the two occasions I have spoken with the Crone.

'I said when last we met,' she watches me carefully, **'that you had kind eyes.'**

'I remember.'

'It is true. But I regret it. I regret ever speaking a fair word to you, blasphemer.'

For a moment, I am not sure how to respond to that.

'You stand on difficult ground, Zarha. I am a Chaplain of the Adeptus Astartes, sworn into my position with the grace of the Ecclesiarchy of Terra. In my presence, you have just expressed the notion that the Emperor of Mankind is not your god, as He is for the entire glorious Imperium. While I am not blind to the... separatist... elements within the Mechanicus, the fact remains that you are speaking heresy before a Reclusiarch of the Emperor's Chosen.

'You are speaking heresy, and I am charged with the responsibility of ending any heresy I encounter in the Eternal Crusade. So let us tread carefully, you and I. You will not insult me with false accusations of blasphemy, and I will answer the questions you have regarding D-16 West. This is not a request. Agree, or I will execute you for heresy before your crew can even soil themselves in fear.'

I see her swallow, and despite herself, her smile shows her amusement.

'It is entertaining to be spoken to in this manner,' she says, almost thoughtful.

'I can imagine that your perceptions offer a much grander view than mine,' I meet her optic augments with my own gaze. 'But the time for misunderstandings is over. Speak, Zarha. I will answer what you ask. This must be resolved, for the good of Helsreach.'

She turns in her tank, swimming slowly in the fluid-filled coffin before eventually coming back to face me.

'Tell me why,' she says. **'Tell me why you have done this.'**

I had not expected such a base question. 'It is the Ordinatus Armageddon. It is one of the greatest weapons ever wielded by Man. This is a war, Zarha. I need weapons to win it.'

She shakes her head. **'Necessity is not enough. You may not harness *Oberon* on a whim, Grimaldus.'** She floats closer, pressing her forehead to the glass. Throne, she looks tired. Withered, tired and without hope. **'It is sealed now because it must be sealed. It is not used now because it cannot be used.'**

'The Master of the Forge will determine that for himself,' I tell her.

'No. Grimaldus, please stop this. You will tear the Mechanicus forces on the world apart. It is a matter of the greatest import to the servants of the Machine-God. *Oberon* cannot be reactivated. It would be blasphemy to use it in battle.'

'I will not lose this war because of Martian tradition. When Jurisian accesses the final chamber, he will examine the Ordinatus Armageddon and evaluate the trials ahead in awakening the spirit within the machine. *Help us,* Zarha. We do not have to die here in futility. Throne of the Emperor, *Oberon* would win us this war. Are you too blind to see that?'

She twists in the fluid again, seeming lost in thought.

'No,' she says at last. **'It cannot, and will not, be reawakened.'**

'It grieves me to ignore your wishes, princeps. But I will not have Jurisian cease his ministrations. Perhaps *Oberon's* reactivation is far beyond his skills. I am prepared to die with that as an acceptable truth. But I will not die here until I have done all in my power to save this city.'

'Grimaldus.' She smiles again, looking much as she did at our first meeting. **'I am ordered by my superiors to see you dead before you continue this course of action. This can only end one way. I ask you now, before the final threats must be spoken. Please do not do this. The insult to the Mechanicus would be infinite.'**

I reach to my armoured collar and trigger the vox-link there. A single pulse answers – an acknowledgement signal.

'You have made your third mistake by threatening me, Zarha. I am leaving.'

From the pilots' thrones, voices begin to chatter. 'My princeps?' one calls.

'Yes, Valian.'

'We're getting auspex returns. Four heat signatures inbound. From directly above. The city's wall-guns are not tracking them.'

'No,' I say, without taking my eyes from Zarha. 'The city defences wouldn't shoot down four of my Thunderhawks.'

'Grimaldus... No...'

'My princeps!' Valian Carsomir screams. '*Forget him!* We demand orders at once!'

It is too late. Already, the chamber starts to shake. The noise from outside is muted by the Titan's immense armour plating, but remains nevertheless: four gunships on hover, their boosters roaring, black hulls eclipsing the moonlight that had beamed in through the eye-windows.

I look over my shoulder, seeing the four gunships align their heavy bolter turrets and wing-mounted missiles.

'Raise shields!'

'Don't,' I say softly. 'If you try to raise the shields and prevent my attempt to leave, I will order my gunships to open fire on this bridge. Your void shields will never rise in time.'

'You would kill yourself.'

'I would. And you. And your Titan.'

'Keep the shields down,' she says, the bitterness returning to her visage. Her bridge crew comply, reluctance evident in their every movement and whispered word. **'You do not understand. It would be blasphemy for *Oberon* to enter battle. The sacred war platforms must be blessed by the Lord of the Centurio Ordinatus. Their machine-spirits would be enraged without this appeasement. *Oberon* will never function. Do you not see?'**

I see.

But what I see is a compromise.

'The only reason the Mechanicus is not committing one of its greatest weapons to the war to save this world is because it remains unblessed?'

'Yes. The soul of the machine will rebel. If it even awakens, it will be wrathful.'

Within these words, I see the way through our stalemate. If their rites require a blessing that is impossible to give, then we must alter our demands to the most basic, viable needs.

'I understand, Zarha. Jurisian will not reactivate the Ordinatus Armageddon and bring it to Helsreach,' I tell her. She watches me closely, her visual receptors clicking and whirring in poor mimicry of human expression.

'He will not?'

'No.' The pause lasts several heartbeats, until I say, 'We will remove the nova cannon and bring it to Helsreach. It is all we needed, anyway.'

'You are not permitted to defile *Oberon's* body. To remove the cannon would be to sever its head or remove its heart.'

'Consider this, Zarha, for I am finished with standing here and posturing over Mechanicus banalities. The Master of the Forge was trained on Mars, under the guidance of the Machine Cult and in accordance with the most ancient oath between the Astartes and the Mechanicus. He reveres this weapon, and counts his role in its reawakening as the greatest honour of his life.'

'If he was true to our principles, he would not do this.'

'And if you were true to the Imperium, you would. Think on that, Zarha. We need this weapon.'

'The Lord of the Centurio Ordinatus is en route from Terra. If he arrives in time, and if his vessel can break the blockade, then there is a chance Helsreach will see *Oberon* deployed. I can give you no more support than that.'

'For now, that is all I need.'

I thought that would end it. Not end it *well,* by any means. But end it nevertheless.

Yet as I walk away, she calls me back.

'Stop for a moment. Answer me this one question: Why are you here, Grimaldus?'

I face her once more, this twisted, ancient creature in her coffin of fluids, watching me with machine-eyes.

'Clarify the question, Zarha. I do not believe you speak of this moment.'

She smiles. **'No. I do not. Why are you here, at Helsreach?'**

Strange to be asked such a thing, and I see no reason to lie. Not to her.

'I am here because one who was brother to my dead master has sent me to die on this world. High Marshal Helbrecht demanded that one Templar commander stay to inspire the defence. He chose me.'

'Why you? Have you not asked yourself that question? Why did he choose you?'

'I do not know. All I know for certain, princeps, is that I am taking that cannon.'

'I find it difficult to countenance,' Artarion said, 'that your plan actually worked.' The knights stood together on the wall, watching the enemy. The aliens were massing, forming into clusters and chaotic regiments. It still resembled a swarm of vermin more than anything else, Grimaldus thought, but he could make out distinct clan markings and the unity of tribal groups standing apart from others.

It would be dawn soon. Whether or not that was the signal the xenos were waiting for didn't matter. The flow of landers had fallen to a trickle, no more than one every hour now. The wastelands were already home to millions of orks. The attack would come today. The overwhelming force they needed to take the city was here.

'It has not worked yet,' Grimaldus replied. 'Ultimately, it comes down to what they will allow. We need their cooperation.' The Chaplain nodded to the gathering horde. 'If we do not have Mechanicus aid in reactivating the cannon, these alien dogs will already be gnawing on our bones within a handful of months.'

A cry went up from further down the wall. Few Guardsmen remained posted on the battlements, and those that were served mainly as sentries. Two more of them shouted, and the call was taken up along the entire northern wall. The general vox-channel came alive with eager voices. The city's siren once more began to wail.

Grimaldus said nothing at first. He watched the horde sweeping closer like a slow tide. What little order had been evident within the enemy's ranks was broken now, and in the sea of jagged metal and green flesh, scrap-tanks and wreck-Titans powered forward – the former dense with aliens clinging to their sides and howling, the latter shaking the wastelands with their waddling tread.

'I have heard it said,' Artarion noted, 'that the greenskins raise their Titans as idols to their strange, piggish gods.'

Priamus grunted. 'That would explain why they are so hideous. Look at that one. How can that be a god?'

He had a point. The wreck-Titan was an iron effigy of a corpulent alien, its distended belly used to house the arming chambers for the proliferation of cannons thrusting from its gut.

'I would laugh,' Nero said, 'if there weren't so many of them. They outnumber Invigilata's engines at a ratio of six-to-one. '

'I see bombers,' Cador noted, neither interested nor disinterested, merely stating a fact. A wing of ugly aircraft, over forty of them, rose from landing platforms hidden behind the landers of the main force. Grimaldus could hear their engines from here, labouring like a sick elder ascending the stairs.

'We should abandon the walls, brothers.' Nero turned to watch the last Guardsmen making their way down the ramps and ladders leading from the battlements. 'The Titans will be firing soon.'

'So will theirs,' Priamus smiled within his helm. 'And these mighty walls will be reduced to so much powder.'

At that moment, a squadron of fighters soared overheard – the sleek metal hulls of Barasath's Lightnings turned silver by the reflections of the rising sun.

'Now that is courage,' said Cador.

Commander Barasath had argued long and hard for permission to make his first attack run. This was principally because anyone with even a vague grasp of tactics could see full well it would almost definitely be not only his first attack run, but also his last.

Colonel Sarren had been against it. Adjutant Tyro had been against it. Even the Emperor-damned dockmaster had been against it. Barasath was a patient man; he prided himself on tact and the willingness to deliberate being among his chief virtues, but to have to sit there and listen to a *civilian* complaining and questioning his tactical expertise was beyond galling.

'Won't we need your planes to protect the tankers still coming from the Valdez platforms?' the dockmaster, Maghernus, had asked. Barasath gave the man a feigned smile and a nod of acknowledgement.

'It is unlikely the orks have the presence of mind to seek to cut our supplies of fuel, and even if they have, they would need to take the long route around the city, and risk running out of fuel themselves long before they reached our shipping lanes over the ocean.'

'It is still not worth the risk,' Sarren said, shaking his head and seeking to conclude the matter.

'With all due respect,' he said, none of his inner turmoil showing through to his demeanour, 'This attack run offers us too much to merely dismiss out of hand.'

'The risks are too great,' Tyro said, and Barasath was fast coming to hate her. A petulant little princess from the Lord General's staff – she should go back to her clerical duties and leave war to the men and women who were trained to deal with it.

'War,' Barasath mastered his temper, 'is nothing but risk. If I take three-quarters of my squadron, we can destroy the enemy's first waves of bombers and fighter support. They will never even reach the city.'

'That is exactly why this is a fool's errand,' Tyro argued. She was less skilled at controlling her agitation. 'The city's defences will annihilate any aerial attack. We don't even need to risk a single one of our fighters.'

My fighters, Barasath said silently.

'Adjutant, I would ask you to consider the practicalities.'

'I am,' she scoffed.

Uppity bitch, he added to the previous thought.

'This is a two-bladed attack that I suggest.' Barasath looked at his fellow commanders gathered here in the briefing room. While the chamber itself was a bustling hive of activity, with staff and servitors manning vox-consoles, scanner decks and tactical displays, the main table that had once seated the entire city's command section was almost deserted. Almost every regimental leader was with his or her soldiers now, standing ready.

'I'm listening,' Colonel Sarren said.

'If we engage the enemy above the city, a great deal of burning wreckage will fall to the streets and spires below. Add to that the fact we will be under fire from our own defensive guns. Anti-air turrets on spires will be firing up at the sky battle, and have a significant chance of hitting my pilots with their flak-bursts. But if we take the fight to them, their precious junk-fighters will rain down upon their own troops in flames. Once my first wave has pierced their formation, send a second and a third. We can cut overhead to perform strafing runs on their airstrips.'

Silence met this statement. Barasath capitalised on it. 'Their aerial capabilities will be butchered *in a single hour.* You cannot tell me, colonel, that such a victory isn't worth the risk. This is how we must strike.'

He could tell the colonel wasn't convinced. Tempted, yes, but not convinced. Tyro shook her head slightly, half in thought, half already preparing her advised refusal.

'I have spoken with the Reclusiarch,' Barasath said suddenly.

'What?' from both Sarren and Tyro.

'This plan. I have discussed it with the Reclusiarch. He commended me on it, and assured me that city command would allow it.'

Of course, Barasath had done no such thing. The last he'd heard of the knight leader was that Grimaldus was evidently involved in some sort of difficult negotiation with the Crone of Invigilata. But it turned Tyro's head, and that was all he needed. A wedge of doubt. A sliver of her interest.

'If Grimaldus advises this...' she said.

'Grimaldus?' Sarren arched an eyebrow. His jowly face was caught between amusement and alarm. 'A trifle familiar of you to use his name like that.'

'The Reclusiarch,' she swallowed. 'If he believes this is a sound plan, perhaps we should take that into consideration.'

Barasath was adept at hiding all emotion, not just the negative ones. He battled down the urge to grin now.

'Colonel,' he said, 'and Adjutant Tyro. I can see why you wish to hold as much of our forces in reserve as is tactically viable. This is a defensive war, and aggressive attacks will play little part in it. But my pilots and I are useless once the walls are breached and the enemy floods the city. Even the hololithic simulations made that clear, did they not?'

Sarren sighed as he linked his fingers over his belly.

'Do it,' he'd said. And Barasath had. His squadron was airborne an hour later, tearing over the city streets below before powering low over the wastelands.

In the tight confines of his Lightning's cockpit, he was more than just comfortable. He was home. Both control sticks in his hands were extensions of his own body. They said infantry felt the same about their rifles, but by the Holy Throne, there was no comparison. A rifle to a Lightning was like a spear to an angel of iron and steel.

The mass of the alien invasion darkened the ground beneath them.

'Need I remind anyone,' he said over the squadron's vox, 'that bailing out over this mess is extremely ill-advised?'

A volley of 'No sirs' was his answer.

'If you're hit – and by the Throne, some of us will be – then bring your bird down into one of their fat-arsed god-walkers. Take as many of the bastards with you as you can.'

'Gargants, sir.' That was Helika's voice. 'The orks call their Titans "gargants".'

'Duly noted, Helika. Fifty-Eighty-Twos, on my mark, you will break formation and open fire. The Emperor is with us, boys and girls. And the Templars are watching. Let's show them how we earned the knights' crosses painted on our hulls.

'For Armageddon,' he narrowed his eyes, breathing in a lungful of the recycled oxygen offered by his facemask, 'and Helsreach.'

TEN

SIEGE

When the wall is first breached, it dies in an avalanche of pulverised rockcrete.

Dark powdery dust blasts into the air, thicker than smoke and expanding like a stormcloud, blinding in its density.

I watch this from hundreds of metres away, standing with my brothers and the soldiers of the Desert Vultures. At the end of the street, the wall is no more. Our defences are broken, and behind the dust cloud, the breach gapes wide.

The true siege has begun. On every rooftop, in every alley, on every street and from every window – for kilometres around – Imperial guns stand ready, clutched in loyal hands, ready to slay the invaders.

Road by road, home by home. This was always how the Battle of Helsreach would be fought, and it is what every soul in the city stands ready for.

The great figures of the Titans begin to withdraw. Their first duty is done; they stood at the walls and pounded the enemy forces with their immense artillery. Invigilata's engines fall back now, not in defeat, nor even willingly – but because they must reload for the true battle. The Crone updated the commanders' shared tactical grid with the locations of the Mechanicus landers within the city limits that serve as Invigilata's rearming stations. Her Titans trudge back to the closest ones now, their tread shaking the city around them. They are tall enough to darken the rising sun as they pass, even though they walk through distant streets.

Reports filter in from across the vox-network. The wall is falling to pieces, crumbling under the insane firepower of so many tanks and wreck-Titans. Around me, the smell of fear rises from the human soldiers. It is a foul musk; the sourness of breath, the tangy reek of liquid waste, and the rich, stinging scent of cold sweat. This fear-smell emanates from several of them, and while I do not hold them to the standards of Astartes, while I acknowledge the fact the human body will always react in this way even with the bravest of souls inhabiting it, it is still hard to stand in their presence. Their fear disgusts me.

Above the dust cloud, the head and shoulders of a wreck-Titan emerge, its bulbous head of scrap metal shaped into a roaring alien maw. Throne of the Emperor, it would have towered above the wall even if our insignificant barricade was still there. Glass shatters in every window along the street as its slow march brings it closer.

A moment later, the street thunders beneath our feet. Every one of the human soldiers with us falls to the ground, their curses lost amid the noise. I maintain my balance only because of my armour's joint stabilisers compensating for the tremors. With the brightness of a flaring sun, the wreck-Titan's head detonates, showering debris into the dust cloud below.

The cheer that rises around me is the loudest sound yet.

'Engine kill,' comes Zarha's voice over the vox, sounding amused despite the interference. **'You owe me for that, Grimaldus.'**

I do not answer. The shot must have been a truly difficult challenge, but I do not care where *Stormherald* is, nor that it is retreating. My focus is here and now. Tension burns through my body like superheated blood. I feel it in my brothers, as well. Twenty of us, our breathing fast, our hands clutching weapons that are ritually chained to our armour. Chainswords complain as they rev, cutting only air. Last-minute oaths are whispered, or sworn to the sky.

Emerging from the dust cloud, snorting their porcine war cries, come the hunched silhouettes of the enemy.

Hundreds of them, flooding into the street.

'Fire at will!' calls one of the Steel Legion officers.

'Hold your fire!' I scream, my helm's vocalisers piercing the surrounding noise.

'They're in range!' the officer, Major Oros, yells back.

'Hold your fire!'

I am already running, sprinting, my armour joints snarling as I leave the humans behind. Proximity runes, my brothers' life-markers, flicker on my retinal display, but I have no need for them. I know who follows me.

'Sons of Dorn! Knights of the Emperor! Charge!'

The first of the aliens runs from the dust, its green skin plastered grey from the cloud. It raises a junk weapon in its brutish fists, and dies with my crozius annihilating its malformed face a moment later.

The two battle lines meet with a discordant crunch of weapon against weapon and flesh against armour. The sick, fungal stench of ork blood fills the air. Chainswords chew through xenos flesh. Bolters discharge their lethal loads – the crashing bangs of release followed by the muffled thumps of shells detonating within bodies.

The creatures howl and laugh as they die.

My knights remain silent as they slaughter.

Perception fades, as it always does in war, to flickering images that come moment to moment. Concentration is impossible, anathema to the holy rage that fills my senses. I grip my master's relic weapon in both hands, and swing at three aliens before me. They are hurled back from the mace's crackling power field, all three slain by the impact with their chests shattered, each of them tumbling across the road to end in limp, lifeless heaps.

I kill, and kill, and kill. It does not concern me that there is no end to this horde. The enemy fall before us, thrown to the floor by the righteous arcs of sacred weapons, and all that matters is how much blood flows before we are forced to retreat.

Over the vox, I hear Oros and the men cheering. It is an easy sound to ignore.

Artarion suffers more than the rest of us. He sacrifices one hand to hold my banner aloft, his chainblade held in his other. The standard draws the enemy to him. *They want our banner. They always do.* Without even a grunt of effort, he hacks left and right, parries clumsy strikes and lashes back with vicious ripostes.

Priamus saw the danger first. I see one of the aliens behind Artarion fall in two pieces, the young knight's sword splitting the creature in twain through the torso. He kicks the biological wreckage from his blade and cleaves his way to fight side by side with Artarion.

'Reclusiarch,' Nerovar is still with me, tearing his sword free from the belly of a disembowelled greenskin. His boots crush the viscous, stinking ropes of intestine that spill to the road. 'We are being overwhelmed.'

A spear crashes against my helm, reducing my visor display to static for a moment. I swing back at the creature that hurled it, and my sight flickers back online to see the beast's skull demolished beneath my crozius. More discoloured blood spatters over my armour in a light rainfall.

Two more orks fall, one to Nero's chainsword ripping across its throat, the other to my maul, hammered into its chest and sending it flying against the wall of a nearby building. Blood of Dorn, Mordred's weapon is an incredible gift. It slays with effortless ease.

I can feel its charge and release with each alien that dies. There is a split second before every impact as the energy field around the head pulses in a low growl, conflicted by the closeness of other material, before it unleashes its force in a snapping burst of kinetic power.

The enemy have encircled us, but that is little worry. Fighting our way free will be no effort.

'Oros,' I breathe into the vox. 'We are preparing to fall back to you.'

'Give me the mark,' he says. 'We're itching for a turn ourselves.'

With the true siege underway, the Imperial forces fell into their prepared defensive strategies.

Every road had a barricade, where Steel Legion soldiers arrayed in ranks would unleash las-fire at the swarming foe. Snipers worked their deadly duties from rooftops. Battle tanks of every pattern and class ground their way down streets, shelling the first waves of enemy infantry pouring into the outlying sectors of the city.

Every road and building had its assigned piece to play in the battle. Every section had its orders to hold and inflict as much punishment upon the advancing foe as possible, before falling back to the next barricade.

Rearmed Titans stood as vigilant sentinels over entire city blocks, their weapons reaping life from the creatures that swarmed around their feet. The enemy gargants were still engaged in pulling down and breaking through the wall. In these first hours, Invigilata was unrivalled in its destruction.

The invaders spilled into Helsreach, and died in their thousands. Every metre they took was bought with foul alien blood.

Colonel Sarren watched the battle unfolding on the hololithic table. Stuttering images relayed the position of Imperial forces at the very edges of the city, inexorably withdrawing from the walls. Larger locator runes showed the position of Invigilata's engines, or battalions of Steel Legion tanks. He had formulated this endless, relentless fighting withdrawal over the course of the past weeks, and by the Emperor, it was a fine thing to see it in action.

In this first phase, it was imperative that casualties be kept to a minimum. The grind of army against army would come in time. For now, losses must be kept light and the death toll suffered by the enemy must be kept high. Let the invaders claim the outlying city sectors. Let them purchase these abandoned, worthless zones with their lives. It was all part of the plan.

The wave would break soon.

Sarren watched the flickering icons depicting his forces across the immense map. It would come soon, that perfect moment in the shifting winds of battle when the enemy's first push would falter and slow as the advance elements outpaced their slower support units. The initial hordes of infantry would crash against Steel Legion resistance in the outer city streets that they could never break without support from their tanks and wreck-Titans.

And at that moment, the wave would break like the tide against the shore. With the ferocious momentum of the first attack lost, the defence would begin in earnest.

Counterattacks would be mounted in some streets, especially those close to Invigilata's engines or Legion armour units. In other zones, the Guard would stand fast, unable to take ground back but entrenched well enough to hold it.

All that mattered was keeping the enemy from reaching Hel's Highway.

At the last meeting, when the commanders had gathered in their battle armour, Sarren had outlined once more the necessity to holding the highway.

'It is the key to the siege,' he'd said. 'Once they reach Hel's Highway, the city becomes twice as difficult to defend. They will have access to the entire hive. Think of it as an artery, ladies and gentlemen. *The* artery. Once it is severed, the body will bleed out. Once the enemy takes the highway, the city is lost.'

Grave expressions had answered this statement.

The colonel hunched over the table now, his squinting eyes taking the scene in, road by road, building by building, unit by unit.

He watched the war in silence, waiting for the wave to break.

Barasath had hit the ground hard.

He'd seen Helika fall from the sky – and heard her, too. That'd been difficult to deal with. The night they'd spent together sharing a bunk had been almost three years ago now, when they'd both pretended to be drunker than they were, but Korten had never forgotten it, nor had he wished it to be the only one. Hearing her die had chilled his blood, and he had to fight not to deactivate his vox as she screamed on the way down, her engine trailing fire.

Her Lightning, with its white-painted wings, had ploughed into the chest of an alien god-walker. The Titan had shuddered for a moment, then vented flames and wreckage from its spine as Helika's bird – now nothing more than spinning debris – burst through its back.

The gargant kept walking as if unharmed, even with a hole blown clear through it.

That had been in the first run. Helika didn't even get time to fire.

A wicked, weaving scrap of a battle through the alien fighters saw most of them spiralling groundward on dying engines. He'd taken cannon-fire along his hull, but a lucky shot saw him bleeding fuel instead of turned into a fireball in the sky. With the way clear and only a handful of his flyers down, Barasath's second and third waves were inbound.

That's when things had gotten really nasty.

The enemy god-walkers weren't marching idly. Turrets on their shoulders and heads aimed up into the sky spat both laser fire and solid shells at the Imperial fighters. Dodging these alone would have been a chore. Dodging these when they were joined by more ork scrap-flyers and anti-air fire from the tanks below turned the situation into the nightmare that Colonel Sarren had promised.

Barasath's first wave scattered, boosting toward the primitive landing strips the enemy had formed in the desert.

Hundreds of ork fighters still waited on the ground, unable to take off yet, consigned to waiting their turn on the scraped-flat runways. A more pessimistic man might have noted there was little he could do to such a massive, grounded force when he led the remaining birds of an air superiority squadron. A more pessimistic man might also have circled the enemy airbase and waited for his Thunderbolt bombers in the second wave.

Korten Barasath was not a pessimistic man, and his patience took a backseat when it came to necessity. In graceful arcing dives and strafing runs, he unloaded his autocannons and drained his lascannon power packs, hurling everything he could down at the grounded fighters below. Dozens sought to take to the skies in panicked defence – most of these crashed during their ill-attempted takeoffs as their landing gear became fouled in the sandy wasteland soil. Those few that managed to get airborne were easy prey for Imperial cannons.

His second wave arrived, unleashing their payloads. Thunderbolts, much larger and heavier armed than the Lightnings, sent great plumes of smoke and dust rising from the wasteland's surface as their incendiaries impacted.

'Bomb this place to ashes,' Barasath voxed, and watched his pilots do exactly that.

Fire ripped across the wastelands in hungry trails, consuming the ragged airstrips that would never be allowed to take shape after this. Grounded junk-fighters exploded in succession.

Of course, the site wasn't completely defenceless, even with most of it in flames. A few tanks fired gamely up at the strafing Imperial flyers, with all the grace and accuracy of old men trying to swat flies.

He'd taken fire on his last banking swoop over the airbase. A lucky – or unlucky, as Barasath saw it – shot sheared off the best part of his left wing. There would be no climbing from this death-dive. No aiming for a wreck-Titan as Helika and a handful of others had done.

He pulled the cockpit release as the fighter started to spin, ditching above the burning site. There was a moment of disorientation, the push of the wind, the world coming into focus after the twisting plunge of the falling fighter... and then he was falling into black smoke and dust clouds.

Darkness embraced him. His respirator saved him having to breathe the choking smog, but his flight goggles were unenhanced and couldn't pierce the smoke. Barasath pulled his cord, feeling himself jerked upward as his grav-chute opened.

With no idea where the ground was, he was lucky to hit the earth without breaking both of his legs. His ankle flared up in protest, but he considered that to be getting off lightly.

Cautiously, aware of the fact that the smoke hid him as much as it hid the enemy, he pulled his laspistol and moved through the blinding darkness. It was hot, a savage heat all around him that spoke of burning planes and landers nearby, yet not enough light to offer direction.

When he finally broke through the black cloud, pistol in his sure grip, he blinked once at what stood before him, and started to fire.

'Oh Throne,' he said with surprising politeness, right before the orks lumbering ahead shot him through the chest.

Stormherald hungered.

It ached with each pounding step, its roiling plasma core burning in its chest as it reluctantly turned its back on the enemy and marched through the streets.

Its way was clear, its path already set. Buildings had been demolished earlier in the week – their foundations blown up and the hab-blocks themselves fallen to rubble – to make way for its passage.

The need to turn around and pour its hatred into the enemy was fierce, a hunter's urge, almost strong enough to overwhelm the Crone's whispers in its mind.

The Crone. Her presence was a savage irritant. Again, *Stormherald* leaned as it walked, seeking to turn with its ponderous, striding slowness. And again, the Crone's claws in its mind forced its body to comply with her intent.

We move, she whispered, *to fight a greater battle soon.*

Stormherald's rage faded at her voice. There was something new in her words, something its predator's mind clutched and recognised immediately. A fear. A doubt. A plea.

The Crone was weaker now than she ever had been before.

Stormherald knew nothing of pleasure or amusement. Its soul was forged in ancient rites of fire, molten metal, and plasmic energy that churned with the ferocity of a caged sun. The closest it came to an emotion approximating pleasure was the rush of awareness and the dimming of its painful anger as enemies died under its guns.

It felt a ghost of that sensation now. It complied with her urgings now, still bound to her control.

But the Crone was weaker.

Soon, she would be his.

Nightfall found Domoska with her storm trooper platoon holed up in the ruins of what had once been a hab-block.

Greenskin heavy armour had rolled through and changed all that. Now it was a tumbledown ruin of rockcrete and flakboard, and Domoska crouched behind a low wall, clutching her hellgun to her chest. Strapped to her back, her power pack hummed. The cable-feeds between her hellgun's intake port and the backpack were vibrating and hot.

She was glad the skull-faced Astartes and that prissy adjutant quintus had ordered them back to the city. She didn't want to admit it, but travelling in an Astartes gunship – even just in the bay with the racked jump-packs and attack bikes – had been a thrill.

She was less delighted with her platoon's assigned position in the urban war, but she was a storm trooper, the Legion's finest, and she prided herself on her devotion to duty without raising a complaint.

With the bulk of Imperial forces in slow, fighting withdrawals and protracted holding actions, units across the city were tasked with lying in wait as the orks advanced, or stalking past undetected to take positions behind the enemy.

Across Helsreach, it was almost uniformly veteran outfits and storm-trooper squads tasked with these movements. Colonel Sarren was using his best soldiers to achieve the most difficult operations.

And it was working.

Domoska would have preferred to be safely crouched behind a barricade, with Leman Russ tanks in support, but such was life.

'Hey,' Andrej whispered as he ducked next to her. 'This is better than sitting on our arses in the desert, yes? Yes, it is, that's what I think.'

'Be quiet,' she whispered back. Her auspex returns were coming back clear. No enemy heat signatures or movement nearby. Still, Andrej was being annoying.

'The last one I gutted with my bayonet, eh? I am tempted to go back for his skull. Sand it down, wear it on my belt like a trophy. That would get me much attention, I think.'

'It would get you shot first, most likely.'

'Hm. Not the right kind of attention. You are too negative, okay? Yes, I said it. It is true.'

'And I said to be quiet.'

Miraculously, he was. The two of them moved on, keeping crouched and low, moving from cover to cover. Sounds of battle were coming from the adjacent street – Domoska could hear the guttural roars and piggish snorts of embattled orks.

'This is Domoska,' she whispered into her hand-vox. 'Contact ahead. Most likely the second group that passed us an hour ago.'

'Acknowledged, Scout Team Three. Proceed as instructed, with all due caution.'

'Yes, captain.' Domoska clicked her vox off. 'Ready, Andrej?'

Andrej nodded, crouched next to her once again. 'I have three det-packs left, okay? Three more tanks must die. Then I get that caffeine the captain promised.'

The holographic table told its tale with reassuring accuracy. Sarren could not look away, despite how staring at the flickering light-images stung the eyes after a while.

The wave was breaking.

His bulwark units were digging in and holding their ground. Already, the pincer platoons were moving into position behind the first horde of invaders, ready to drive them forward and crush them between the hammer and anvil.

Sarren smiled. It had been a fine day.

Jurisian had not moved from his position in almost twenty-four hours.

He had said he would need over a week, and closer to two. He no longer believed this. This would take weeks, months... perhaps even years.

The codes that kept the impenetrable bunker doors sealed were beautiful in their artistry – clearly the work of many masters of the Mechanicus. Jurisian feared no living being, and had slain in the name of the Emperor for twenty-three decades. This was the first time he had loathed his duty.

'I need more time, Grimaldus,' he had spoken into the vox several hours before.

'You ask for the one thing I cannot give,' the Reclusiarch had answered.

'This might take me months. Perhaps years. As the code evolves, it breeds sub-ciphers that – in turn – require dedicated cracking. It breeds like an ecology, always changing, reacting to my intrusions by evolving into more complex systems.'

The pause had been laden with bitten-back anger. 'I want that cannon, Jurisian. *Bring it to me.*'

'As you will, Reclusiarch.'

Gone was the thrill of hoping to look upon *Oberon*, and being the soul to reawaken the great Ordinatus Armageddon. In its place was cold efficiency and undeniable disgust. This sealing code was one of the most complex creations humanity had pieced together from its various spheres of knowledge. Destroying it afflicted him with a pain akin to that which an artist would feel in destroying a priceless painting.

Runes spilled across his retinal display in green lettering. He solved six of the scrolling codes in the space of a single breath. The final five involved additional calculations based on the parameters established by the previous ones.

The code evolved. It reacted to his interference like a living thing, its ancient spirit fighting against his manipulations. So, so beautiful, Jurisian thought as he worked. Damn Grimaldus for asking this of him.

His servitors stood behind him, slack-jawed, dull-eyed and slowly starving to death.

Jurisian paid no heed.

He had a masterpiece to slay.

ELEVEN

THE FIRST DAY

The shaking no longer bothered Asavan Tortellius.

His presence was an honour, and one he thanked the Mechanicus for in his daily prayers. In his eleven years of service, he'd quickly grown used to the shaking, the lurching tread, and even the rattling of weapons fire against the walls of his monastery. What Tortellius had never grown used to was the Shield.

In many ways, the Shield replaced the sky. He had been born on Jirrian – an unremarkable world in an unremarkable subsector a middling distance from Holy Terra. If Jirrian could be said to possess any attribute of note, it was its weather in the equatorial regions. The sky over the city of Handra-Lai was the deep, rich blue that poets spent so much time trying to capture in words, and imagists spent so much time trying to capture in picts. In a world of tedious tradition and the greyness of infinite societal equality – where everyone was just as poverty-stricken as everyone else – the skies above the slum hive Handra-Lai were the one aspect of his early life worth remembering.

The Shield had stolen that from him. He still had the memories, of course. But every year, they became duller, as if the Shield's overreaching presence caused all else to fade.

It wasn't that the Shield had any particular colour, because it didn't. And it wasn't that the Shield was brazenly oppressive, because it wasn't.

Most of the time it wasn't even visible, and at the best of times, it wasn't even *there*.

And yet, in a way, it always was. It was oppressive. It was always there. It did discolour the sky. Its existence was betrayed by the abrasive electrical fizz in the air. Static would crackle between fingertips and metal surfaces. After a while, one's teeth began to ache. It was most irritating.

And to think that it could be raised any moment. Looking up at alien skies held no pleasure at all, and it was all because of the Shield. It severed any real enjoyment of the heavens. Even when deactivated, there was forever the risk of it slamming up into life without notice, cutting Tortellius off from the outside world once more.

In moments of battle, the Shield was more beautiful than threatening. It would ripple like breaking waves, the colours of oil on water cascading across the sky. The smell of the Shield as it suffered attack was a heady clash of ozone and copper that, if one stood outside on the monastery's battlements, would actually begin to make you feel light-headed after a time. Tortellius made a point of standing outside when the Shield was under siege, not for the stimulant effects of the Shield's electrical charge, but because it was a dark pleasure to see his prison's limits, rather than fear the invisible oppression.

Sometimes he would wonder if he was watching it in the secret hope it would fail. If the Shield came down... then what? Did he truly desire such a thing? No. No, of course not.

Still. He did wonder.

As he leaned on the battlements of the monastery, watching the city below, Tortellius reflected on the loathsomeness of this particular breed of xenos. The greenskins were filthy and bestial, their intelligence generously described as rudimentary, and more accurately as feral.

The mighty *Stormherald,* instrument of the God-Emperor's divine will, had come to a halt. Tortellius noticed only because of the relative silence in the wake of its crashing tread.

His monastery, only part of the cathedral of spires and battlements adorning the Titan's hunched shoulders, remained silent. Fifty metres below, he could hear the rattling of the leg turrets killing the aliens in the street. But the domed weapon mounts – each one bristling with granite gargoyles and stone representations of the angelic primarchs, those blessed slain sons of the God-Emperor – merely moved in their set alignments, their cannons ready.

Tortellius scratched his thinning hair (a curse he blamed entirely on the harsh electro-static charge of the Shield), and summoned his servo-skull. It hovered along the battlements towards him, its miniature suspension technology purring as it stayed aloft. The skull itself was human, sanded smooth and modified after it was removed from a corpse, now showing augmetic pict-takers and a voice-activated data-slate for recording sermons.

'Hello, Tharvon,' said Tortellius. The skull had once belonged to Tharvon Ushan, his favoured servant. How noble a fate, to serve the Ecclesiarchy even in death. How blessed Tharvon's spirit must be, in the eternal light of the Golden Throne.

The skull probe said nothing. Its gravity suspensors hummed as it bobbed in the air.

'Dictation,' said Tortellius. The skull emitted an acknowledgement chime as its data-slate – no larger than a human palm and built into its augmented forehead – blinked active.

What little breeze penetrated the Shield wasn't enough to cool his sweating face. The Armageddon sun might have been weak compared to the star that burned down on equatorial Jirrian, but it was stifling enough. Tortellius mopped his dark-skinned brow with a scented kerchief.

'On this, the first day of the Siege of Hive Helsreach, the invaders have spilled into the city in unprecedented numbers. No, hold. Command word: Pause. Delete "unprecedented". Replace with "overwhelming". Command word: Unpause. The skies are clogged with pollution from the world's industry, flak hanging in the clouds from the hive's defences, and smoke from the outlying fires that ravage the outermost districts where the invaders have already conquered ground.

'It is my belief that few chronicles of this immense war will survive to be interred in Imperial archives. I make this record now not out of a desire to spread my name in pomposity, but to accurately detail the holy bloodshed of this vast crusade.'

Here he hesitated. Tortellius struggled for the words, and as he chewed his lower lip, musing over dramatic description, the monastery shook beneath his feet again.

The Titan was moving.

Stormherald strode through the city, its passage unopposed.

Three enemy engines – the scrap-walkers that the aliens called gargants – had already died to its guns. In her prison of fluid, Zarha felt the stump at the end of her arm aching with a dull heat.

Once, she thought with an ugly smile, I had hands.

She aimed her next thought with care. *The annihilator is overheating.*

'The annihilator is overheating.'

'Understood, my princeps,' replied Carsomir. He twitched in his restraint throne, accessing the status of the weapon through his hardwired link to the Titan's heart-systems. 'Confirmed. Chambers three through sixteen show rising temperature pressure.'

Zarha turned in her milky coffin, feeling instinctively what every other soul on board needed to perceive through calculations on monitors or slower hardwire links. She watched Carsomir twitch again, feeling the orders pulsing from his mind through willpower alone, reaching into the cognitive receptors at the Titan's core. 'Coolant flush, moderate intensity,' he said. 'Commencing in eight seconds.'

Zarha moved her right arm in the ooze, feeling pain in fingers that no longer existed.

'Flushing coolant,' said a nearby adept, hunched over his wall-mounted control panel.

The relief was immediate and blissful, like a sunburned hand plunged into a bucket of ice. She cancelled the vision feed from her photoreceptors, immersing herself in blackness as relief washed through her arm.

Thank you, Valian.

'Thank you, Valian.'

Her vision flickered back into existence as she reactivated her optical implants. It was the work of a moment to readjust her perceptions, filtering out the immediacy of her surroundings. She took a breath, and stared out across the city with a god's eyes.

The enemy, ant-like and amusing, swarmed in the street around her ankles. Zarha lifted her foot, feeling both the rush of air on her metallic skin and the swirling of fluid around her footless limb. The aliens fled from her crushing tread. A tank died, pounded into scrap.

Incidental fire from *Stormherald's* leg battlements spilled into the road, cutting the orks down in droves.

'My princeps,' Moderati Secundus Lonn was twitching in his throne as he spoke, his muscles spasming in response to the flood of pulses from his connection to the Titan.

Speak, Lonn.

'Speak, Lonn.'

'We are venturing ahead of our skitarii support.'

Zarha was not blind to this. She hunched her shoulders, wasted muscles tensed and trembling, striding forward through the street.

I know. I sense... something.

'I know. I sense something.'

The hab-towers on either side of the marching Titan were abandoned – this sector was one of the few lucky enough to be within easy range of the city's scarce subterranean communal bunker complexes.

Inform Colonel Sarren I am pressing ahead with phase two.

'Inform Colonel Sarren I am pressing ahead with phase two.'

'Yes, my princeps.'

This sector, Omega-south-nineteen, had been one of the first to fall when the walls came down the day before. The aliens had been crawling through the area for many hours, but significant scrap-Titan strength was – as yet – unseen. It represented the perfect opportunity to slaughter legions of the enemy while their gargant groups were engaged elsewhere.

A feeling grew in the back of her head – something invasive and sharp, blooming through the webbing of veins in her brain. It was something she had not heard in many, many decades.

Someone was weeping.

Zarha felt her face locked in a rictus as the feeling blossomed and grew fangs. The sharpness was jagged now, an acidic pulse through her skull.

'My princeps?'

She didn't hear at first.

'My princeps?'

Yes, Valian.

'Yes, Valian.'

'We're receiving word from *Draconian.* He's dying, my princeps.'

I know... I feel him...

A moment later, Zarha felt the full shock grasp at her senses. The mortis-cry slashed through her cognitive link like a hurricane, shrieking at a soundless pitch of pain. *Draconian* was down. The princeps aboard her, Jacen Veragon, was screaming as the aliens scuttled over his corpse, pulling at his armoured metal skin as he lay prone.

How had he fallen?

And there it was. In the screaming cry was the memory she sought. The lurching of vision as the Reaver-class engine was dragged to its knees. The sense of infuriating immobility. He was a god... How could this happen... Why would his limbs no longer function...

Everywhere around was rubble and smoke. It was impossible to see clearly.

The scream was fading now. *Draconian's* reactor-heart, a boiling cauldron of plasmic fusion, was growing cold and still.

'We've lost contact,' said Valian, a second after Zarha sensed it herself. She was weeping, though the saltwater secreted from her tear ducts was immediately dissolved in the fluid entombing her.

Lonn had his eyes closed, accessing an internal hololithic display within the cognitive link. '*Draconian* was in Omega-west-five.' His dark eyes flicked open. 'Reports show the site is the same as here: evacuated habitation towers, minimal engine resistance.'

The adept manning the scanning console, his mouth replaced by a scarab-like vocaliser, blurted a screed of machine code across the cockpit.

'Confirmed,' Carsomir said. 'We're getting an auspex return to the south. Significant heat signature. Almost definitely an enemy engine.'

Zarha heard almost none of this. Images of *Draconian's* death played out behind her false eyes like scenes from a play, coloured by the stinking taint of black emotion beneath. She sobbed once, her heart aching like it would burst. Hearing only that an enemy was nearby, she walked in the fluid, her limbs moving.

The Titan shook as it took another step.

'My princeps?' both moderati said at once.

I will have vengeance. Even in her own mind, she could barely hear herself in the words. A mechanical overtone twinned with her thoughts – and it was protective in its overwhelming rage. *I will have vengeance.*

'We will have vengeance.'

Tower blocks passed by its shoulders as the Titan strode on.

'My princeps,' began Carsomir, 'I recommend we hold here and wait for the skitarii to scout ahead.'

No. I will avenge Jacen.

'No,' the vox-voice was harsh. **'We will avenge *Draconian*.'**

Blind to the disparity between her thoughts and the emerging voice, Zarha pushed onward. Voices assailed her, but these she cast aside with a brush of willpower. Never before had she felt it so easy to disregard the chattering, needy voices of her lesser kin. Valian's voice, coming from the cockpit chamber rather than the cognitive link, was another matter.

'My princeps, we are receiving requests for Communion.'

There will be no Communion. I hunt. Communion with the Legio can come tonight.

'There will be no Communion. We hunt. Communion with the Legio can come tonight.'

With effort, Valian turned around in his restraint throne. The cables snaking from his skull's implant sockets turned with him, like a beast's many tails.

'My princeps, Princeps Veragon is dead and the Legio demands Communion.' In his voice was the edge of concern, but never panic, nor fear. The rest of the battle group desired the momentary sharing of focus and purpose – the unity of princeps and the souls of their engines – that was tradition in the aftermath of loss.

The Legio will wait. I hunger.

'The Legio will wait. We hunger.'

Forwards. Ready main weapons. I smell the xenos from here.

Her voice emerged as a crackle of static, but *Stormherald* marched on.

While Carsomir was not a man prone to extremes of emotion, something cold and uncomfortable crawled through his thoughts as he turned back to watch the cityscape through the Titan's huge eye lenses.

He may not have been as connected to *Stormherald's* burning heart as the princeps was, but his own bonds with the god-walker were not devoid of intimate familiarity. Through his weaker tie to the engine's semi-sentient core, he felt a depth of fury that was almost addictive in its all-encompassing purity. The passion transferred through his empathic link into grim irritability, and he had to resist the urge to curse the inefficiency of those around him as he guided the Titan onwards. Knowing the cause of his distracted irritation was no balm for it.

The Titan's right foot came down on a street corner, pulverising a cargo conveyer truck into flat scrap. *Stormherald* turned with a majestic lack of speed, and hull-mounted pict-takers panned to show a wider avenue, and the afternoon sunlight glinting from *Stormherald's* burnished iron skin. Valian was immersed, just for a moment, in the wash of exterior imagery fed through the mind-link. Hundreds of pict-takers, each one showing pristine silvery skin, or dense armour – cracked and pitted with its legacy of small arms fire.

Ahead, down the wide avenue, was the enemy engine that blinked like a red-smeared migraine on the cockpit's auspex scanners. Valian shuddered at the sight of it, breathing deeply of the scent-thick cockpit air. As always, living within *Stormherald's* head smelled of oiled gears, ritual incense and the burning reek of crew members sweating and bleeding, their bodies exerted despite remaining motionless in their thrones.

The enemy scrap-Titan was grotesque – unappealing on a level that went far beyond mere design distaste to Valian. Its junk metal appearance showed no reverence, no respect, no care in its construction. *Stormherald's* iron bones were thrice-blessed by tech-ministers even before they were brought together as the skeleton of a god-machine. Each of the million cogs, gears, rivets and plates of armour used in the Imperator's birth was honed to perfection and blessed before becoming part of the Titan's body.

This avatar of perfection incarnate faced its hideous opposite, and every crewmember piloting the Titan felt disgust flow through them. The enemy engine was fat, big-belled to hold troops and ammunition loaders for its random array of torso cannons. Its head, in opposition to the Gothic-style machine skull worn by *Stormherald,* was stunted and flat, with cracked eye lenses and a heavy-jawed underbite. It stared pugnaciously down the street at the larger Imperial walker, its cannons covering its body like spines, and roared a challenge of its own.

It sounded exactly like what it was: an alien warleader within the cockpit head blaring into a vox-caster. *Stormherald* laughed in response, its warning sirens slamming back with a wall of sound.

In her tank of fluids, Zarha raised her arms, her handless stumps facing forward.

In the street, with an immense grinding of gear joints, *Stormherald* mirrored the motion.

It never fired. The trap, as crude and simple as it was, exploded around the great Titan.

'Your request for reinforcement is acknowledged,' the voice crackled.

Ryken lowered the vox-mic, readying his lasrifle again.

'They're coming,' he hissed to Vantine. The other trooper was with him, crouched with her back to the wall, sharing his slice of cover. Her expression was unreadable, masked by her goggles and rebreather, but she gave the major a nod.

'You said that half an hour ago.'

'I know.' Ryken slammed a fresh cell into his lasgun. 'But they're coming.'

The wall behind them buckled as it took the brunt of another shell. Debris from the ceiling clattered down onto their helmets.

Ryken's platoon was up to their necks in trouble, and no amount of hard fighting alone was going to get them out of it. Most of his men, the ones that weren't bleeding to death on the ground, were at the windows on the various floors of this hab-block, pouring their fire into the street outside. The rooms were still full of furniture, left by the families who were taking shelter in local underground bunkers. It was, as last stands went, a pretty terrible place to be holed up in, but their barricade had fallen half an hour before, and it was every squad for themselves until they could regroup at the next junction.

The problem was that Ryken's platoon was cut off much too fast when the last bastion fell. As rearguard covering the other squads' escapes, they'd been encircled and forced to find whatever cover they could.

'They're climbing the damn walls!' someone cried out. Ryken scrambled to the nearest window, keeping low and bracing to fire into the street again. As he rose to fire, he found himself face to face with a green-skinned creature hauling its way through the second-storey window. It reeked of mould and gunsmoke, and its piggish eyes were glazed by whatever alien emotions it felt in the heat of battle.

Ryken bayoneted the beast in the throat, firing three shots even as he stabbed. The alien was hurled back from the window to fall on its companions below.

They were indeed climbing the damn walls.

Ryken ordered three of his men to cover the window, and raced for the stairs leading down to the ground floor. The snapping *crack* of lasrifles firing was even louder from downstairs, where the bulk of the platoon was entrenched.

'Reinforcements are en route!' he called down the stairs.

'You said that half an hour ago!' Sergeant Kalas called back up.

Ryken caught a glimpse of the sergeant, his bolt pistol clutched in a two-handed grip, kneeling at a window and firing booming shots out into the road. He retreated back to a nearby window himself, adding his fire to the onslaught.

In the street, a riot of alien flesh was taking place. Only the most foolish or bloodthirsty orks were seeking to race across the road and scale the building's walls. Most of the xenos – and Ryken thanked the Emperor for small mercies – possessed enough intelligence to remain in cover themselves, behind their own junk-transports or shooting from windows of adjacent habitation blocks. They laughed and jeered as the barrage continued, and great howls of porcine laughter would rise up when another pack of baying aliens would charge across the street only to be cut down by the Steel Legion's defences. Raucous enjoyment of their own kin's death was a barbarous madness Ryken had long come to associate with this accursed xenos breed.

There was no understanding such creatures.

'We can't hold here,' Vantine crouched under cover again, whispering a rapid litany of devotion as she reloaded her rifle. 'You hear those engines? More are coming, major.'

'We're not breaking out anytime soon,' he spoke the words as a bitter curse, setting his rebreather straight. 'So we *will* hold.'

'Or we die.'

'That's not an option, and I'll shoot you the next time you give voice to it.'

She smiled behind her own gas mask, but Ryken saw none of it. He had risen to his feet and was leaning against the wall, his lasgun braced against his chest. He kept close to the wall, risking a look out of the window. What he saw made him curse more colourfully than Vantine had ever heard before.

'So,' she rose close to him, taking position on the other side of the window, 'not good news, then?'

'Tanks. The bastards are rolling armour up the road.'

Vantine chanced a look herself. Three tanks, Imperial Leman Russ chassis looted and 'improved' with crooked armour panels bolted on and painted in mismatched hues. The jagged fronts of the three tanks showed alien glyphs of allegiance that meant nothing to human eyes.

'We're dead,' she shook her head. 'And there's no need to shoot me. They'll shell this block to rubble and do it for you.'

Ryken ignored her. 'Nikov,' he keyed his vox-bead live. 'Nikov, how's the launcher coming?'

Nikov was on the hab-block's top floor, where he'd retreated with his missile launcher ten minutes before. The weapon had taken a beating when the barricade had fallen earlier.

'It's still jammed,' Nikov's reply came over the vox in a crackling hiss. After a pause of several moments, he added, 'Did I hear you shouting about reinforcements again?'

'They're coming! Throne, why is everyone whining about that?'

'I think it's because we'd rather not die, sir.'

The west wall chose that moment to explode. Debris burst into the room, filling it with stone dust. Through his goggles, Ryken stared at a hole the size of three grown men in hab-block's wall. Most of the soldiers nearby picked themselves up off the floor. Two stayed where they were, mangled and unmoving.

'Get that launcher working,' Ryken said in the moment of eerie calm. Vantine scrambled to her feet and ran from the gaping hole in the wall.

Outside offered alien laughter, the grinding of tank treads and a distant thrum of racing engines.

'More?' Vantine called out.

'That's not the enemy,' Ryken said. 'Those aren't tank engines.'

And they weren't. His vox-bead screeched a distorted chatter of mixed channels, but one voice broke through. 'Your request for reinforcement,' it said, much too deep to be human, 'is acknowledged.'

The room darkened as the gunship rattled past on whining turbines. It swooped low, strafing the street, opening up with its weapons. From its cruising angle, it clearly didn't intend to stay long, but the pilot was inflicting all the punishment he could while the Thunderhawk remained.

Heavy bolters mounted on its wings and cheeks spat a torrent of lethal shells into the visible groups of enemy warriors. Inhuman blood misted the air as packs of the creatures burst under the explosive ammunition. Snarling, the diminishing groups of survivors returned fire – their stubbers chattering, the solid shells raining off the black gunship's hull like harmless hail.

The tanks were another matter. The first shell crashed into the gunship's side with a storm's force, and Ryken flinched back from the detonation. It spun the gunship on its axis, sending burning wind breathing from its boosters as it turned. In reaction to the attack, the avian shape gained altitude in a sudden thrust, banked over the first of the tanks, and at last dropped its cargo.

Dark figures clanged onto the surface of the tanks, as black as beetles crawling on the metal skin.

The first to fall – a figure on the roof of the lead tank – wore a silver-faced helm and wielded a mace with a sparking power field around its eagle-winged head. The weapon descended in a slice to shatter the vehicle's turret. It broke clean off and fell into the horde of aliens that mobbed the tanks from below.

'Good morning, Reclusiarch,' Ryken's voice was breathless with relief.

The knight didn't answer at first. He and his standard bearer were already engaged by the greenskins swarming up over the useless tank's hull, clambering higher in a desperate need to shed the blood of the black knights.

Artarion's bolter emitted its stuttering crash, blowing the aliens back down to the street. With the brilliance of a sun-flare, Grimaldus's plasma pistol disintegrated two of the climbing beasts, letting their burning skeletal remains tumble in pieces back into the horde.

The second tank was dead in its tracks, smoke pouring from vents and cracks in its armour. The Templars had dropped grenades into the interior, and Ryken saw two knights leaping clear, ignoring the slain vehicle as they waded into the aliens massing on the street.

'Forgive the delay, major.' The Reclusiarch wasn't even out of breath. 'We were required at the barricade breaches in south section ninety-two.'

'Better late than never,' Ryken replied. 'The last word from central command suggested that Sarren's plan in this sector was working better than almost all hololithic estimations. Are we getting redeployed for a counterattack?'

On top of the tank, Grimaldus swung his mace in a vicious arc, pummelling an ork into ruined biological matter.

'You are still breathing, major. Let that be enough for now.'

Dawn brought nothing more than a continuation of the night's bloodshed.

The Helsreach Crusade begins its first bloody day. Across the city, millions of us now fight for our lives.

The noise is like no other sound I have ever heard. In two centuries of life, I have waged war at the heels of god-machines whose weapons were louder than the death-cries of stars. I have stood against armies of thousands, while every soul that stood against us screamed their hatred. I have seen a ship the size of a hive tower crash into the open ocean on a far distant world. The plume of water it threw into the sky and the tidal wave that followed were like some divine judgement come to flood the land and erase all humanity beneath its salt-rich depths.

Yet nothing has matched the sound of Helsreach's defiance.

In every street, humans and aliens clash, with their weapons and voices merging into a gestalt wave of senseless noise. On every rooftop, turrets and multi-barrelled defence cannons bark into the sky, their loaders never ceasing, their rate of fire never slowing. The machine-roars of Titans duelling can be heard from entire districts away.

Never before have I heard an entire city fighting a war.

As we fight to clear the streets of Major Ryken's besiegers – and as the Legionnaires themselves leave their havens and join us in the slaughter – I keep an edge of focus for the general vox-channels.

Ryken was not wrong. While we are locked in our planned fighting withdrawal across the entire hive, precious few sectors are in unplanned retreat.

The wreck-Titans are in the city now. Coldly delivered kill ratios from Invigilata commanders are a recent addition to the chaos of communication traffic, but they are a welcome one. Helsreach stands defiant as the sun rides the sky into noon.

My brothers remain scattered across the city, reinforcing the weakest parts of the Imperial chain, supporting the defences where the orkish tide breaks into the city with overwhelming force. I regret that we did not have the chance to gather together one last time. Such a lost opportunity is another of the failings I must atone for.

The reports of their engagements reach me hourly. As yet, no casualties blacken our record. I cannot help but wonder who the first to fall will be, and how long the hundred of us will last as the hours become days, and the days become weeks.

This city will die. All that remains to be learned is just how long we can defy fate. And above all, I want the weapon buried beneath the wasteland's sands.

I am drawing breath to recall our gunship when the vox explodes with panic. It is difficult to make any sense from the maelstrom of noise. Key words manage to break through the mess: Titan. Invigilata. *Stormherald.*

And then, a voice so much stronger than all others, speaking a single word. She sounds in pain as she says it.

'Grimaldus.'

TWELVE

IN A PRIMARCH'S SHADOW

The gunship bursts across the sky, rattling around us in its ferocious race southward. It is all too easy to imagine the thick Armageddon clouds left in turmoil in our wake.

Wind roars into the crew compartment through the open bulkhead door. As is my right, I am first at the portal, gripping the edge of the airlock with one hand as the wind claws at my tabard and parchment scrolls. Beneath us, the city slides by – towers aiming up, streets laid flat. The former are aflame. The latter are flooded by ash and the enemy.

Already, many of the city's outermost sectors are burning. Helsreach is what it is: an industrial city devoted to the production of fuel. There is much that will burn, here.

The flames choke the sky as the ring of fire swallowing the hive's edges creeps ever inward. Reports of refugees spilling into the city's core have increased tenfold. Housing them is no longer even the greatest problem; the trouble in the avenues where the civilians flock is that Sarren's redeployment of his armour divisions suffers crippling congestion.

I do not judge him for this. His mastery of the city after arriving in the final weeks – only barely before we did – has been as efficient as could be expected from a human mind under such duress. I recall the initial briefings, when he was stifled by large sections of the civilian populace refusing to abandon their homes even in the face of invasion. In truth, it is not as if the city was built with an abundance of bunkers to house refugees anyway. With reluctance, he had allowed them to remain where they were, knowing the problem was – in part – a self-correcting one. As districts fell to the invaders, the civilian death toll would be catastrophic.

'Well,' he had said one night to the gathered commanders, 'it will mean fewer refugees in the siege itself.'

I had admired him greatly in that moment. His merciless clarity was most commendable.

With a lurch, the Thunderhawk begins its descent. I brace myself, whispering words of reverence to the machine-spirit within the propulsion engines now attached to my armour. The jump pack is bulky and ancient, the metal pitted and scarred and in dire need of repainting, but its link to my armour is without flaw. I blink-clink the activation rune, and the hum of the backpack's internal systems joins the growl of my active armour.

I see *Stormherald.*

Over my shoulder, Artarion sees the same. 'Blood of Dorn,' he says, his voice uncharacteristically soft.

The entire scene is tainted by the grey dust clouds in the air from fallen buildings. In this cloud of grey, half-buried in the debris of the exploded buildings, the Titan kneels in the street.

Sixty metres of walking lethality – an unstoppable weapons platform with the ornate cathedral adorning its shoulders – *kneels in the street,* defeated. Around it is the devastation of several fallen habitation towers. The invaders, curse their soulless lives, had set the surrounding hab-blocks to detonate and collapse on the Titan.

'They have brought an Emperor-class Titan to its knees,' Artarion says. 'I never thought I would live to see such a thing.'

Hundreds of them swarm the streets now, climbing onto the defeated god-machine's back with grappling hooks and boosting up there on burning thruster packs. They crawl across its dust-coated armour like insectile vermin.

'Grimaldus,' the Titan hails me, and suddenly it is so obvious why the voice is pained. Not from agony. From shame. She has advanced ahead of her skitarii phalanxes, and is undefended against this massed infantry assault.

'I am here, Zarha.'

'I feel them, like a million spiders across my skin. I... cannot stand. I cannot rise.'

'Make ready,' I vox to my brothers. Then, to the humbled princeps, 'We are about to engage the enemy.'

'I feel them,' she says again, and I cannot tell from her machine-voice if she is bitter, delirious, or both. **'They are killing my people. My prayer-speakers... my faithful adepts...'**

I am not blind to the meaning in her words. To the Machine Cult, each death was more than a mortal tragedy – it was the loss of knowledge and perspective that might never be recovered.

'They are inside me, Grimaldus. Like parasites. Violating the Cathedral of Sanctuary. Climbing inside my bones. Drilling toward my heart.'

I do not reply to her as I watch the crumbled cityscape below. Instead, I tense myself for a moment's sensory dislocation, and hurl myself out into the sky.

Grimaldus was first to leap from the circling Thunderhawk.

Artarion, ever his shadow and still bearing his banner, was only seconds behind. Priamus, his blade in hand, came next. Nerovar and Cador followed, the first of them leaping into a dive, the latter merely stepping out in an uncomplicated plummet. Last of all was Bastilan, the sergeant's insignia on his helm catching the dull evening light. He voxed to the pilot, wishing him well, and drew his weapons before falling into air.

Altitude gauges on retinal displays showed fast-falling numbers, the digital readouts a blur as the knights dropped from the sky. Beneath them, the kneeling god-machine presented a huge target. The multi-levelled cathedral on its shoulders was like a city in miniature – a city of spires – bristling with weapons batteries and crawling with alien vermin.

The knights saw the aliens as they descended: the beasts clambering up on tethered lanyards, or flying up on primitive rocket packs, laying siege to the stricken Titan. *Stormherald* itself was a pathetic statue depicting its own failure. It was driven to one knee, buried to the waist in the debris of six or seven fallen hab-block towers. The avenue was in ruin around it, where the detonated buildings had collapsed and levelled the city flat. The Titan's arm-guns, as large as some habitation towers themselves, were grey-white with dust and resting on the mounds of broken brick, twisted steel supports, and rockcrete stone.

Grimaldus held off firing his boosters to slow his freefall.

'Come down in the courtyard in the centre of the cathedral,' he voxed to the others. Their acknowledgements came immediately. In turn, each of them engaged their jump packs, arresting their dives into more controlled descents.

Grimaldus was the last to fire his boosters, and the first to hit the ground.

His boots thudded onto the paved courtyard, smashing the precious mosaics into gravel beneath his feet. Immediately, he leaned to the side, compensating for the angle of the ground. *Stormherald's* defeated posture was tilting the entire cathedral forward almost thirty degrees.

The courtyard was modest, ringed by nine plain marble statues that each stood four metres tall. In each of the cardinal directions, a set of open doors led into the cathedral itself. The mosaic tiles on the floor depicted the black and white bisected, cyborged skull of the Machine Cult of Mars. Grimaldus had come down onto the dark eye socket of the skull's human side, crushing the black tiles to powder underfoot.

Nothing moved nearby. The sounds of battle, of looting, of desecration – these all came from within the surrounding building.

Priamus landed with a skid, his armoured boots tearing at the mosaics and shearing them off in a wave of broken pebbles. His blade, chained to his wrist, crackled into life.

Nerovar, Cador and Bastilan were altogether more graceful in their landings. The sergeant came down in the shadow of one of the tilted statues. Its stern face eclipsed the setting sun.

'These are the primarchs,' he said to the others as they readied their weapons.

All heads turned towards Bastilan. He was right.

As representations of the primarchs went, they were plain to the point of almost being crude. The sons of the Emperor were usually depicted in grandeur and glory, rather than by sculptures so subtle and austere.

There was Sanguinius, Lord of the Blood Angels, prominently unwinged, with a childlike face lowered in repose. And there, Guilliman of the Ultramarines, his robed form so much slenderer than any other depiction of him that the knights had seen before. In one hand, he clutched an open tome. The other was raised to the sky, as if he was caught and forever frozen in a moment of great oratory.

Jaghatai Khan was bare-chested, bearing a curved blade in his hands and looking to the left, as if staring at the distant horizon. His hair was shaggy and long, whereas in so many masterpieces it was shaven but for a topknot. Next to him, Corax, the Prince of Ravens, wore a plain mask that was utterly featureless but for the eyes. It was as if he was unwilling to show his face in the company of his brothers, hiding his visage behind an actor's mask.

Ferrus Manus and Vulkan shared a plinth. The brothers were bareheaded, and the only two primarchs sculpted here in armour. Both wore vests of mail, the fine links of chain on Manus's breast a counterpoint to the larger scales adorning Vulkan's. They stood back to back, facing in opposite directions, both carved to bear hammers in each hand.

Leman Russ of the Wolves stood with legs apart, head cast back, facing the sky. Whereas the other sons of the Emperor wore robes or armour, Russ was clad in rags sculpted over his chiselled musculature. He was also the only primarch with tensed fists, as if he stared into the heavens, awaiting some grim arrival.

A robed figure, hooded yet visibly slender to the point of emaciation, clutched the hilt of a winged blade, its tip between the statue's bare feet. Here was the Lion, depicted as a warrior-monk, eyes closed in silent contemplation.

And, last of all, rising above Bastilan, was Rogal Dorn.

Dorn stood apart from his brothers, neither facing his kin, nor looking into the skies above. His regal visage was aimed at the ground to his left, as if the primarch stared at something vital only he could see. The robe he wore was plainer that those adorning his brothers' icons, though it showed a cross on its breast, sculpted with care. Although he had been the Golden Lord, the commander of the Imperial Fists, his personal heraldry had inspired that of his Templar sons who followed.

His hands were what drew the knights' eyes more than any other aspect in this gathering of demigods. One was held to his chest, the fingertips joined to the cross there, frozen in mid-stroke. The other was held out in the direction Dorn stared, palm up and kindly, as if offering aid to one who would rise from the floor.

It was quite the most humble and exquisite rendition of their gene-father Grimaldus had ever laid eyes on. He fought the sudden burning urge to fall to his knees in reverent prayer.

'This is an omen,' Bastilan continued. Grimaldus could barely believe only a handful of seconds had passed since the sergeant last spoke.

'It is,' the Reclusiarch replied. 'We will purify this temple under the gaze of our forefather. Dorn watches us, brothers. Let us make him proud of the day he sired the first Templar.'

We move without hesitation, and without caution, through the cathedral.

The angled floor is an irritation that I've managed to blank from my mind by the time the third alien is dead. Room by room, we move in unison. The cathedral is a divided into a series of chambers ringing the courtyard, each one with its own stained glass windows now shattered and gaping like missing teeth, each room reaching high up with a pointed ceiling ending in the spire above.

The slaughter is easy, almost mindless. Priamus is like a wolf on the leash, eager to run ahead on his own.

My patience is wearing thin with him.

Each chamber also shows its own unique desecration. Tech-adepts and Ecclesiarchy priests lie dead and butchered, their bodies in pieces across the mosaic floors. Unarmed as they were, they offered little resistance to the rampaging invaders. Bookshelves are overturned, ceramic ornaments shattered... I would never put feral destruction past this xenos-breed, but it almost seems as if the greenskins sought something specific in their rabid assault.

'The articulation structures are sealed. My bones are defended by internal forces. My heart-core is cut off from the parasites.'

Ambush or not, it is disgusting that it took them even this long to achieve such basic necessities.

'We are retaking the Cathedral of Sanctuary,' I tell her. 'Resistance is minimal, Zarha. But you must stand. They are still coming. Bring the cathedral out of range of boarders, or we will be overwhelmed.'

'I cannot stand,' she says.

What a sin it is, for such a majestic warrior to speak with such shameful defeat tainting her words. Were she one of my men, I would kill her for such dishonour. Slowly. By strangulation. Cowardice does not deserve the rush of a blade.

'I have tried,' she intones.

The emotion colouring her machine-voice brings my bile rising. For all I know, she could be weeping. My disgust is so powerful I must fight the need to vomit.

'Try harder,' I breathe into the vox, and sever the link.

We fight our way to the outer battlements at *Stormherald's* front, where the incline allows for easy boarding. An ork's fat hand slaps on the red metal of the battlement's edge, and the brute hauls itself up. My pistol meets its face, the heat exchanger vanes hissing against its skin. It has a moment to bawl its hatred at me before I pull the trigger. What remains of the alien falls from its handholds, tumbling to the ground, burning briefly on its way down as a living torch of white-hot fire.

The battlements resemble a true siege in all respects. The last remaining tech-adepts and priests defend the cathedral against boarding aliens, though no more than a small cluster remain. Few humans, augmented or otherwise, are a match for one of these beasts.

Priamus slips the leash of discipline. His charge carries him ahead, his sword flaring with light each time its power field saws into alien flesh. My brothers lay into the enemy along the besieged wall with bolter and blade. The few servitor-manned spire turrets that had been spitting solid shots into the mass of orks fall silent, not willing to risk striking any of us.

'You will do penance for this, Priamus.'

He doesn't answer. 'For the Emperor!' he cries into the vox. 'For Dorn!'

In the pockets of battle where none of us stand, the turrets open fire once again. At least their servitors are worth something, then. The orks turn from butchering the few priests still standing. Their bestial faces are afire with brutish, eager emotion as they come for us.

One of them... Throne of the Emperor... One of them dwarfs his piggish brethren. His armour makes him twice the size of us, looking like scrap metal and primitive, chugging power generators bolted onto an exoskeletal frame. His hands are industrial claws that look as if they could peel a tank apart without effort. He even kills his own kin as he strides towards us on the inclined floor. His claws swing, battering his lesser allies aside, hurling them against the cathedral wall or over the battlement's edge.

I raise my crozius in a two-handed grip.

'That one is mine,' I tell my brothers.

Dorn is watching this.

'You asked to see me, sir?'

Tomaz didn't bother to straighten his crumpled work overalls as he stood at what could loosely be called attention. Around him, the command chamber was its usual bustling hive of activity. A junior staff officer bumped him as she passed.

Tomaz said nothing. He'd worked fifteen hours straight today, on a dock backed up with dozens and dozens of ships, with almost no room to unload. Fifteen hours of shouting, of broken vox-casters and no techs spare to fix them, of cargo being dumped wherever it could be dumped – which was inevitably the wrong place (and the most inconvenient one for someone else) – necessitating its removal minutes later when another worker's already fouled-up work was fouled-up even further.

Frankly, he didn't much care if he got shoved over onto the ground. Maybe he could curl up and get some damn sleep.

'Sir,' he prompted.

Sarren finally looked up from the hololithic table. The colonel had aged in the last week, Maghernus could see it clearly. He looked as tired and bone-achingly sick of it all as Tomaz felt.

'What?' Sarren asked, narrowing his bloodshot eyes. 'Oh. Yes. Dockmaster.' Sarren looked back down at the hololithic display. 'I need your crews to speed up. Is that understood?'

Maghernus blinked. 'I'm sorry, sir. I didn't quite hear you.'

'I need,' Sarren didn't look up, 'your crews to speed up their work. The reports I'm getting from the docks show they are at a standstill. We are talking about significant portions of the north and east perimeters of the city, dockmaster. I need to move troops. I need to store materiel. I need you to do your job.'

Maghernus looked around the room in disbelief, unsure how to respond.

'What would you have me do, colonel? What is there that I can possibly do?'

'Your *job*, Maghernus.'

'Have you even seen the docks recently, colonel?'

Sarren looked up again, laughing without even a shred of humour. 'Do I look like I have seen anything except casualty reports recently?'

'I can't do anything about the docks,' Maghernus shook his head, a sense of unreality settling over him. 'I'm not a miracle worker.'

'I appreciate you have an... intense... workload.'

'That's not the half of it. We're dealing with a backlog of weeks, months even, and no room to handle anything.'

'Nevertheless, I need more from you and your crews.'

'Of course, sir. I'll be back in a moment, I feel the sudden need to piss expensive white wine and turn everything I touch into gold.'

'This is no laughing matter.'

'And I'm not laughing, you pompous son of a bitch. "Work harder"? "Do more"? Are you insane? There's nothing I can do!'

Nearby officers glanced his way. Sarren sighed and rubbed his closed eyes with the tips of his fingers.

'I respect the difficulties of your position, dockmaster, but this is the first week of the siege. This is only going to get worse. We are all going to sleep much less, and we are all going to work much harder.

'Furthermore, I understand that you are sweating blood in an under-appreciated duty, but you are not the only one suffering. You, at least, are guaranteed to live longer than many of us. I have men and women in the streets, fighting and dying for your home, so that you may continue to complain at how I crack the whip over you. I have hundreds of thousands of citizens under arms, facing the greatest alien invasion force the world has ever seen.

'Sir,' Maghernus took a breath. 'I will–'

'You will shut up and let me finish, dockmaster. I have platoons of men and women lost behind the advancing enemy line, no doubt hacked to pieces by the axes of barbarous xenos monsters. I have armour divisions running out of fuel because of resupply difficulties in the embattled sectors. I have an Emperor-class Titan on its knees, because its commander was too angry to think clearly. I have a city with its edges on fire, and its population in rout with nowhere to run to. I have tens of thousands of soldiers dying to prevent the enemy from reaching the Hel's Highway – people dying for a *road,* dockmaster – because once the beasts reach the city's spine, we are all going to die a great deal faster.

'Now, am I making myself perfectly clear when I tell you that while I have sympathy for your difficulties, I also expect you to work through them? We are, just to be sure, no longer speaking past one another? We are, for the record, now on the same page?'

Maghernus swallowed and nodded.

'Good,' Sarren smiled. 'That's good. What can you do for me, dockmaster?'

'I'll... speak to my crews, colonel.'

'My thanks for understanding the situation we are in, Tomaz. You are dismissed. Now, someone raise a reliable vox-signal to the Reclusiarch. I need to know how close he is to getting that Titan walking.'

In the cognition chamber, Grimaldus stood before the crippled Zarha.

His armour's calm, measured hum was marred by a mechanical ticking sound at random intervals. Something, some internal system linking the power pack to the suit of armour was malfunctioning. His skull helm with its silver faceplate was painted with alien blood. His armour's left knee joint clicked as he moved, the servos inside damaged and in need of reverent maintenance by Chapter artificers. Where scrolls of written oaths had hung from his pauldrons, the armour was burned, the ceramite cracked.

But he was alive.

At his side, Artarion looked similarly battered. The others remained in the cathedral above, maintaining a vigil now the orks were punished and slain for their blasphemy.

'Your Titan,' Grimaldus uttered the words, 'is purged. Now *stand*, princeps.'

Zarha floated in the milky waters, not hearing him, not even moving. She looked as if she had drowned.

'*Stormherald* has taken her,' Moderati Carsomir said, his voice low. 'She was ancient, and had oppressed her will over the Titan's core for many years.'

'She still lives,' the knight noted.

'Only in the flesh, and not for much longer.' Carsomir looked pained even explaining this. His eyes were bloodshot and rimmed by dark circles. 'The machine-spirit of an Imperator is so much stronger than any soul you can imagine, Reclusiarch. These precious engines are born as lesser reflections of the Machine-God Himself. They carry His will and His strength.'

'No machine-spirit is the equal of a living soul,' said Grimaldus. 'She was strong. I sensed it in her.'

'You understand nothing of the metaphysics at work here! Who are you to lecture us in this way? We were linked to the Titan's core at the end. You are nothing, an... an *outsider*.'

Grimaldus turned to the crewmembers in their control seats, his broken armour joints snarling.

'I shed blood in the defence of your engine, as did my brothers. You would be torn from your thrones and buried in the rubble of your own failure, had I not saved your lives. The next time you call a Templar *nothing* is the moment I kill you where you sit, little man. You are nothing without your Titan, and your Titan lives because of me. Remember to whom you speak.'

The crew shared uncomfortable glances.

'He meant no offence,' one of the tech-priests mumbled through a facially-implanted vox-caster.

'I do not care what he intended. I deal in realities. Now. Make this Titan walk.'

'We... can't.'

'Do it anyway. *Stormherald* was supposed to move in synergy with the 199th Steel Legion Armoured Division over an hour ago, and they are in full retreat due to being unsupported. The delay is finished with. Get back in the fight.'

'Without a princeps? How are we to do that?' Carsomir shook his head. 'She is gone from us, Reclusiarch. The shame of it all, the rage of defeat. We all felt the Titan rush into her. Her mind has joined the union of all previous princeps, amalgamated in the Titan's core. Her soul is buried as surely as her body would be in a grave.'

'She lives,' the knight narrowed his eyes.

'For now. But this is how princeps die.'

Grimaldus turned back to the amniotic coffin, and the unmoving woman within. 'That is unacceptable.'

'It is the truth.'

'Then the truth,' the Reclusiarch growled, 'is unacceptable.'

She wept in the silence – the way one weeps when truly alone, when there is no shame to be found in being seen by others.

Around her was nothingness absolute. No sound. No movement. No colour. She floated in this nothingness, neither cold nor hot, with no reference of direction or sensation.

And she wept.

Upon opening her eyes moments before, a thrill of fear had sliced up her spine. She did not know who she was, where she was, or why she was here.

Her memories – the fractured, flashing images that were all that kept her mind from being completely hollow – were of a hundred worlds she could not recall seeing, and a hundred wars she could not remember fighting.

Worse, they were each tainted by an emotion she had never felt – something inhuman, abrasive, sinister... and partway between exaltation and terror. She saw these moments of memory, and felt the unnerving presence of another being's emotions instead of her own.

It was like drowning. Drowning in someone else's dreams.

Who had she been before? Did it even matter? She slipped deeper. What remaining sense of self existed began to break away and diminish, sacrificed to buy a peaceful, silent death.

Then the voice came, and it ruined everything.

'Zarha,' it said.

With the word came a weak understanding, an awareness. She had memories of her own – at least, she had once possessed such things. It suddenly seemed wrong to no longer have access to her own recollections.

As she resurfaced slowly, the infiltrating memories returned. The wars. The emotions. The fire and the fury. Instinctively, she pulled away again, preparing to return deeper within the nothingness. Anything to escape the memories belonging to another soul.

'Zarha,' the voice clawed after her. 'You swore to me.'

Another layer of comprehension returned. Within the revelation were her own emotions, waiting for her to reclaim them. The overwhelming sensory storm of the other mind's memories no longer frightened her. They angered her.

She would not be so easily shackled. No false-soul's thoughts would conquer her like this.

'You swore to me,' the voice said, 'that you would walk.'

She smiled in the nothingness, rising through it now like an ascending angel. *Stormherald's* memories assailed her with renewed vigour, but she cast them aside like leaves in the wind.

You are right, Grimaldus, she told the voice. *I did swear I would walk.*

'Stand,' he demanded, stern and cold and glowering. 'Zarha. Stand.'

I will.

* * *

The voice came without warning, emerging from the vox-speakers on the coffin.

'I will.'

Crew members flinched back from the sound, their hands white-knuckled as they clutched the backrests of their thrones. Only Grimaldus remained where he was, face to face with the glass sarcophagus, his blood-smeared skull mask glaring into the milky depths.

The old woman's body twitched once, and her head rose. She looked around slowly, her augmetic gaze at last coming to rest on the knight before her.

Rubble scattered in an avalanche, and a dust cloud rose again as the wreckage of fallen buildings went tumbling aside. With a thunderous grinding of gears and the clanging-hammering of a multitude of tank-sized pistons in its iron bones, *Stormherald* raised its immense bulk, metre by painful machine-squealing metre.

The avenue shuddered as its bastion of a right foot pounded onto the road. The sound was loud enough that the nearby buildings still untouched by orkish demolition charges lost their windows in a blizzard of breaking glass.

As the crystal rain fell to the scarred streets below, the Imperator raised its weapons, standing – once more – defiant.

'Shields up,' the Crone of Invigilata demanded.

'Void shields active, my princeps,' responded Valian Carsomir.

'Make ready the heart.'

'Plasma reactor reports all systems at viable integrity, my princeps.'

'Then we move.'

The chamber shuddered with a familiar rhythm as the god-machine took its first step. Then a second. Then a third. Throughout the metal giant's bones, hundreds of crew members cheered.

'We walk.' The ancient woman turned in her tank, looking at the tall knight once more. **'I heard you,'** she told him. **'As I was dying, I heard you calling me.'**

Grimaldus removed his filthy helm. Although he didn't look a day over thirty, his eyes told his true age. Like windows into his thoughts, they showed the weight of his wars.

'There is a story of my father,' he said to Zarha.

'Your father?'

'Rogal Dorn, the Emperor's son.'

'The primarch. I see.'

'It is a tale of a once-strong brotherhood, broken by Horus the Betrayer. Rogal Dorn and Horus were close before the Great Heresy. None of the Emperor's sons were bonded as truly in the years before the malignant darkness took hold of Horus and his kin.'

'I am listening,' she smiled, knowing how rare this moment was. To hear a warrior of the Adeptus Astartes speak of their gene-sire's life outside of their Chapter's secret rituals.

'It has always been told among the Black Templars that when the two brothers crusaded together, they would compete for the greater glory. Horus was legendarily hungry for triumph, while my father was – it is told – a more reserved and quiet soul. Each time they made war together, they were said to have made an oath in blood. Clasping hands, they would each swear that they would stand until the final day dawned. "Until the end", they would say.'

'That is a touching legend.'

'More than that, princeps. Tradition. It is our most binding oath, spoken only between brothers who know they will never see another war. When a Templar knows he will die, it is the promise he gives to his brothers that he will stand with honour until he can no longer stand at all.'

She said nothing, but she smiled.

'Yes, I called you back to this war.' He nodded, his gentle eyes fixed upon her bionic replacements. 'Because you made a similar oath to me. Promises like that – they matter more than anything else in life. I could not let you die in shame.'

'Until the end, then.'

'Until the end, Zarha.'

PART TWO

KNIGHTFALL

THIRTEEN

THE THIRTY-SIXTH DAY

DARGRAVIAN.
The 5th day. Meritorious defence of the Torshav refuelling complex.
Gene-seed: **Recovered.**

FARUS.
The 7th day. Discovered in the Kurule Junction surrounded by no fewer than twelve of the slain enemy.
Gene-seed: **Recovered.**

THALIAR.
The 10th day. Lost in the petrochemical explosions at White Star Point.
Gene-seed: **Unfound / Unrecovered.**

KORITH.
The 10th day. Lost in the petrochemical explosions at White Star Point.
Gene-seed: **Unfound / Unrecovered.**

TORAVAN.
The 10th day. Lost in the petrochemical explosions at White Star Point.
Gene-seed: **Unfound / Unrecovered.**

AMARDES.
The 11th day. Unable to survive 83% body tissue immolation suffered at White Star Point. Granted the Emperor's Peace.
Gene-seed: **Ruined / Unrecovered.**

HALRIK.
The 13th day. Eyewitness reports from Armageddon 101st Steel Legion relate intense personal courage and heroism in the face of overwhelming odds. Awarded posthumous Crusade Mark of Valiant Conduct for rallying Guard forces at the fall of Cargo Bridge Thirty.
Gene-seed: **Recovered.**

ANGRAD.
The 18th day. Single-handedly destroyed five enemy tanks at the Breach of the Amalas Concourse. Brought down by alien treachery and lost beneath enemy tank treads.
Gene-seed: **Ruined / Unrecovered.**

VORENTHAR.
The 18th day. Fought at the Breach of the Amalas Concourse.
Gene-seed: **Recovered.**

ERIAS.
The 18th day. Fought at the Breach of the Amalas Concourse.
Gene-seed: **Recovered.**

MARKOSIAN.
The 18th day. Fought at the Breach of the Amalas Concourse. Notably slew an enemy warlord in single combat, atop the alien's command tank. Awarded posthumous Crusade Mark of Unbroken Courage. Body was incinerated by the enemy in wrathful response.
Gene-seed: **Ruined / Unrecovered.**

It was always going to happen.

That did not make the reality any easier to bear, or the defeat any less bitter. But preparations were in place. When it happened, the Imperials were ready.

It happened first on the eighteenth day, at the Amalas Concourse, Junction Omega-9b-34. That was its assigned identifier according to the Imperial hololithic displays.

Colonel Sarren was watching through heavy, fatigue-dulled eyes as the flickering holo-images moved silently back from the location of their barricade. It was such a small thing – no more than a few marking runes blinking back a few centimetres, moving away from the point of the map marked *Amalas Concourse, Junction Omega-9b-34.*

Behind the flickering holo-runes was an illusory ramp, which in turn threaded into a much, much, much wider road. Sarren watched the runes falling back along this ramp, and tried to breathe in. In took four attempts, his breath catching in his throat on the first three.

'This is Colonel Sarren,' he spoke into his hand-vox. 'All units in Omega Sector, Subsector Nine. All units, prepare to retreat. Cancel assigned fallback locations, repeat: cancel withdrawal to assigned fallback locations. When the order comes, you will retreat, retreat, retreat to contingency positions.'

He ignored the storm of demands for confirmation, letting his vox-officers respond on his behalf.

'We did well,' he said to himself. 'We did damn well to keep the bastards away for this long.' Eighteen days – over half a month of siege warfare. He had every reason to colour his bitterness with that fierce core of pride.

The minutes passed in unblinking slowness. An aide came to his side, and quietly asked for his attention.

'Sir, your Baneblade stands ready.'

'Thank you, sergeant.'

She saluted and moved away. Finally, Sarren reached for his vox-mic again.

'All units in Omega Sector, Subsector Nine. Retreat, retreat, retreat. The enemy has reached Hel's Highway.'

MALATHIR.
The 19th day. Missing in action since the successful enemy siege of the Yangara Installation.
Gene-seed: **Unfound / Unrecovered.**

SITHREN.
The 20th day. Fell in personal combat with an enemy Dreadnought at the Danab Junction, Titan rearming site.
Gene-seed: **Recovered.**

THALHAIDEN.
The 21st day. Fell in personal combat with an enemy Dreadnought at the Danab Junction, Titan rearming site. Survival depended on extensive and immediate surgical augmentation. Granted the Emperor's Peace.
Gene-seed: **Recovered.**

DARMERE.
The 22nd day. Body discovered with massacred elements of the 68th Steel Legion at the Mu-15 barricades.
Gene-seed: **Recovered.**

IKARION.
The 22nd day. Body discovered with massacred elements of the 68th Steel Legion at the Mu-19 barricades.
Gene-seed: **Recovered.**

DEMES.
The 30th day. Missing in action since the fall of the Prospering Haven habitation sector. Significant civilian casualties recorded.
Gene-seed: **Unfound / Unrecovered.**

GORTHIS.
The 33rd day. Led a counterattack after the defences at Bastion IV were overrun. Also lost in the engagement were two Warlord-class Titans of the Legio Invigilata.
Gene-seed: **Recovered.**

SULAGON.
The 33rd day. Missing in action since the failed defence of Bastion IV. Last

sighting reported his honourable conduct in the face of overwhelming enemy numbers.
Gene-seed: **Unfound / Unrecovered.**

NACLIDES.
The 33rd day. Orchestrated and inspired the last stand defence at Bastion IV, seeking to hold the militia fortress until reinforcements could arrive.
Gene-seed: **Recovered.**

KALEB.
The 33rd day. Part of the counterattack at Bastion IV. Body suffered extreme mutilation and dismemberment at the hands of the enemy.
Gene-seed: **Ruined / Unrecovered.**

THORIAS.
The 33rd day. Pilot of the Thunderhawk *Avenged* – vehicle destroyed by gargant anti-air fire on routine patrol.
Gene-seed: **Unfound / Unrecovered.**

AVANDAR.
The 33rd day. Co-pilot of the Thunderhawk *Avenged* – vehicle destroyed by gargant anti-air fire on routine patrol.
Gene-seed: **Unfound / Unrecovered.**

VANRICH.
The 35th day. Lost in an action to mine the road before an enemy armour division.
Gene-seed: **Recovered.**

Nerovar lowers his arm, his attention drifting from his narthecium bracer-gauntlet.

Cador lies on the cracked road, the old warrior's armour broken and split.

'Brother,' I tell Nero, 'now is not the time to grieve.'

'Yes, Reclusiarch,' he says, though I know he does not hear me. Not really. With mechanical dullness, his movements are leaden as he lowers his hand to Cador's chest.

Around us, the shattered highway is deserted but for the bodies of our latest hunt. The war here is a distant thing, and though the sound of battle in other sectors reaches our ears, this far behind enemy lines, all is quiet and still. The skies are calm and untroubled – unbroken by wrathful turrets.

The sharp *crack!* of the reductor doing its work splits the silence. First once, then again. The meaty, wet sound of flesh being pulled open follows.

Nero lifts his arm, the surgical gauntlet's armour-piercing flesh drills buzzing, spraying dark, rich Astartes blood against his armour. In his hand, with great care, he holds the glistening purplish organs that had rested within Cador's chest and throat. They drip and quiver, as if still trying to feed their host with strength. Nero slides them into a cylinder of preserving fluids, which is in turn retracted into his gauntlet's protective housing.

I have seen him perform this ritual too many times in the past month.

'It is done,' he says, dead-voiced, rising to his feet.

He ignores me as I approach the corpse, occupying himself with entering information on his narthecium's screen.

CADOR.
The 36th day. Ambush along enemy-controlled portions of Hel's Highway.
Gene-seed: **Recovered.**

The thirty-sixth day.

Thirty-six days of gruelling siege. Thirty-six days of retreat, of falling back, of holding positions for as long as we are able until inevitably overwhelmed by the insane, impossible numbers arrayed against us.

The entire city smells of blood. The coppery, stinging scent of human life, and the sickening fungal reek of the foulness purged from orkish veins. Beneath the blood-scent is the stench of burning wood, melted metal, and blasted stone – a city's death in smells. At the last gathering of commanders in the shadow of Colonel Sarren's Baneblade, the *Grey Warrior,* it was estimated that the foe controlled forty-six per cent of the city. That was four nights ago.

Almost half of Helsreach, gone. Lost to smoke and flame in bitter, galling defeat.

I am told we lack the force to take anything back. Reinforcements are not coming from the other hives, and the majority of the Guard and militia that still fight are exhausted remnants of the regiments, forever falling back, time and again, road by road. Hold a junction for a few nights, then withdraw to the next position when it finally falls.

Truly, we are fated to die in the most uninspired crusade ever to blight the name of the Black Templars.

'Reclusiarch,' the vox calls me.

'Not now.' I kneel by Cador's defiled body, seeing the holes in his armour and flesh – some from alien gunfire, two from the ritual surgery of Nerovar's flesh-boring tools.

'Reclusiarch,' the voice comes again. The rune blinking at the edge of my retinal display signifies it as from the *Grey Warrior.* I suspect I am to be begged, again, to fall back to Imperial lines and help in the defence of some meaningless roadway junction.

'I am administering the rites of the fallen to a slain knight. Now is not the time, colonel.'

At first, the colonel had replied to such words with the worthless, polite insistence that he was sorry for my loss. Sarren no longer says such things. The tens of thousands of lives lost in the last four weeks have utterly numbed him to such personal sentiment. That, too, is almost admirable. I see the strength in the way he has changed.

'Reclusiarch,' Sarren's voice betrays how ruined by exhaustion he is. Were

I in the room with him, I know I would feel the weariness in his bones like an aura around where he stands. 'When you return from your scouting run, your presence is required in the Forthright Five district.'

Forthright sector. The southernmost docks.

'Why?'

'We are receiving anomalous reports from the Valdez Oil Platforms. The coastal auspex readers are suffering from offshore storms, but there *are* no storms off the coast. We suspect something is happening at sea.'

'We will be there in an hour,' I tell him. 'What anomalies are we speaking of?'

'If I could give you specifics, Reclusiarch, I would. The auspex readers look to be suffering some kind of directed interference. We believe they're being jammed.'

'One hour, colonel.' Then, 'mount up,' I say to my brothers. It is not a short ride down the Hel's Highway, especially when it crawls with the enemy. Scouting teams are more often mounted on motorcycles now – the risk of Thunderhawks being shot down in enemy territory is too great.

'It is strange,' Nero says, cradling Cador's helm in his hands, as if the old warrior merely slept. 'I do not wish to leave him.'

'That is not Cador.' I rise from where I have been kneeling next to the body, anointing the tabard with sacred oils, before tearing it from the war plate. In better times, the tabard would be enshrined on the *Eternal Crusader*. In this time, here and now, I rip it from my brother's body and tie it around my bracer, carrying it with me as a token to honour him. 'Cador is gone. You are leaving nothing behind.'

'You are heartless, brother,' Nero tells me. Standing here, in this annihilated city, with the bodies of so many dead aliens around us, I almost burst out laughing. 'But even for you,' Nero continues, 'even for one who wears the Black, that is a cold thing to say.'

'I loved him as one can love any warrior that fights by your side for two hundred years, boy. The bonds that form from decade upon decade of shared allegiance and united war are not to be ignored. I will miss Cador for the few days that remain to me, before this war kills me, as well. But no, I do not grieve. There is nothing to grieve over when a life has been led in service to the Throne.'

The Apothecary hangs his head. In shame? In thought?

'I see,' he says, apropos of nothing.

'We will speak of this again, Nero. Now mount up, brothers. We ride south.'

Half of the city was a wasteland, one way or the other. Some of it burned, some of it was silent in death now that the xenos had moved onto other sectors, and some of it was simply abandoned. Habitation towers stood under Armageddon's yellow sky, lifeless and deserted. Manufactories no longer churned out weapons of war, or breathed smoke into the heavens.

Packs of orks – the jackal-like stragglers who had fallen behind the main advance – looted through the empty sectors of the city. While there was little of calculated malice in the beasts' minds, what few human civilian survivors remained were slain without mercy when they were found.

Five armoured bikes growled their way down Hel's Highway. Their sloped armour plating was as black as the war plate worn by each rider. Their engines emitted healthy, throaty roars that told of a thirst for promethium fuel. The boltguns mounted on the motorcycles were linked to belt-feeding ammunition boxes contained within the vehicles' main bulks.

Priamus throttled back, falling into formation alongside Nerovar. Neither warrior looked at the other as they rode, weaving through a shattered convoy of motionless, burned-out tank hulls spread across the dark rockcrete of the highway.

'His death,' the swordsman began, his vox-voice crackling from the distortion of the engines. 'Does it trouble you?'

'I do not wish to speak of this, Priamus.'

Priamus banked around the charred skeleton of what had once been a Chimera trooper carrier. His sword, chained to his back, rattled against his armour with the bike's vibrations.

'He did not die well.'

'I said I have no desire to speak of this, brother. Leave me be.'

'I only say this because if I were as close to him as you were, it would have grieved me, also. He died badly. An ugly, ugly death.'

'He killed several before he fell.'

'He did,' the swordsman allowed, 'but his death-wound was in the back. That would shame me beyond measure.'

'Priamus,' Nerovar's voice was ice cold and heavy with both emotion and threat. 'Leave me alone.'

'You are impossible, Nero.' Priamus revved his engine and accelerated away. 'I try to sympathise with you. I try to connect, and you rebuke me. I will remember this, brother.'

Nerovar said nothing. He just watched the road.

The Jahannam Platform.

Six hundred and nineteen workers stationed on an offshore industrial base. Its skyline was a mess of cranes and storage silos. Beneath it, only the deep of the ocean and the richness of the crude oil that could be refined into promethium.

A new shadow entered the depths.

Like a black wave under the water's surface, it drifted closer to the support struts that held the gigantic platform above the water. Lesser shadows, fish-like and sharp, spilled ahead of the main darkness like rainfall falling from a storm cloud.

The platform shuddered at first, as if shivering in the chill winds that always howled this far from shore.

And then, with majestic slowness, it began to fall. A town-sized, multilayered platform fell into the ocean, crashing down into the water. The ships around it began, one by one, to explode. Each one, once breached, sank alongside the Jahannam Platform.

Six hundred and nineteen workers, and one thousand and twenty-one crewmembers from the ships died in the freezing waters over the course of the following three hours. The few men and women that managed to reach vox-casters shouted into their machines, little realising their voices were carrying no further.

The platform was eventually submerged except for a fleet of floating detritus. The ocean no longer teemed with potential profit, but the scrap metal of destroyed enterprise.

Helsreach heard nothing of this.

The Sheol Platform.

In a central spire, nestled between tall, stacked container silos, Technical Officer Nayra Racinov cast an annoyed look at her green screen, and the sudden fuzzy wash of distortion it was displaying for her.

'You're joking,' she said to the screen. It replied with white noise.

She thumped the thick glass with the bottom of her fist. It replied with slightly angrier white noise. Technical Officer Nayra Racinov decided not to try that again.

'My screen's just died,' she called out to the rest of the office. Looking over her shoulder, she saw that the 'rest of the office,' which usually consisted of an overweight ex-crane driver called Gruli who monitored the communications system, had gone for a mug of caffeine.

She looked back at her console. Warning lights were flickering cheerily around the confused screen. One moment, the green wash showed a chaotic burst of incoming presences on the sonar. Hundreds of them. The next, it showed a clear ocean. And the next, nothing but distortion again.

The room shuddered. The entire platform shuddered, as if in the grip of an earthquake.

Nayra swallowed, watching the screen again. The presences under the water, hundreds of them, were back once again.

She dived across the shaking room, hammering the vox-station's transmit button with the heel of her hand.

She managed to say 'Helsreach, Helsreach, come in…' before the world dropped out from under her and the second of the Valdez Oil Platforms was brought down, with its steel bones burning, bending and screaming, into the icy sea.

The Lucifus Platform.

The largest of the three offshore installations was manned by a permanent work crew population twice the size of those at Jahannam and Sheol. While they were powerless to prevent their own destruction, they at least saw it coming.

Across the platform, sonar auspex readers were suddenly captured by the storm of distortion that had preceded the deaths of Sheol and Jahannam. Here, a fully-staffed control office reacted quicker, with a low-ranking tech-acolyte managing to restore a semblance of clarity to the screens.

Technical Officer Marvek Kolovas was on the vox-network immediately, his gravelly voice carrying directly to the mainland.

'Helsreach, this is Lucifus.' Massive, repeat, massive incoming enemy fleet.

At least three hundred submersibles. We can't raise Sheol or Jahannam. Neither platform is responding. Helsreach? Helsreach, come in.'

'Uh...'

Kolovas blinked at the receiver in his hand. 'Helsreach?' he said again.

'Uh, this is Dock Officer Nylien. You're under attack?'

'Throne, are you deaf, you stupid bastard? There's a fleet of enemy submersibles launching all kinds of hell at our support gantries. We need rescue craft immediately. *Airborne* rescue craft. Lucifus Platform is going down.'

'I... I...'

'Helsreach? Helsreach? Do you hear me?'

A new voice broke over the vox-channel. 'This is Dockmaster Tomaz Maghernus. Helsreach hears and acknowledges.'

Kolovas finally let out the breath he'd been holding. Around him, the world shook as it began to end.

'Good luck, Lucifus,' the dockmaster's voiced finished, a moment before the link went dead.

'This is the situation,' Colonel Sarren began.

The Forthright Sector dockmaster's office was, putting it politely, a pit. Maghernus was not a tidy man at the best of times, and a recent divorce wasn't helping his state of cleanliness. The sizeable room was a hovel of old caffeine mugs that were growing furry mould-masses in their depths, and unfiled stacks of papers were scattered everywhere. Here and there were some of Maghernus's cast-off clothing from the nights he'd slept in his office rather than go back to his depressing bachelor hab – and before that, back to the woman he'd taken to calling The Cheating Bitch.

The Cheating Bitch was a memory now, and not a pleasant one. He found himself worrying against his will. Had she already died in the war? He wasn't sure his bitterness stretched quite far enough to wish something like that.

His dawdling thoughts were dragged back in line by the arrival of the Reclusiarch. In battered black war plate, the knight stalked into the room, sending menials and Guard officers scurrying aside.

'I was summoned.' The words blasted rough from his helm's vox-speakers.

'Reclusiarch,' Sarren nodded. The colonel's bone-tiredness bled from him in a slow drip. In his weary majesty, he moved like he was underwater. The officers gathered around the room's messy table, poring over a crinkled paper map of the city and the surrounding coast.

Room was made at the table as Grimaldus approached.

'Speak to me,' he said.

'This is the situation,' Colonel Sarren began again. 'Exactly fifty-four minutes ago, we received a distress call from the Lucifus Platform. They reported they were under attack by an overwhelming submersible fleet numbering at least three hundred enemy vessels.'

The gathered officers and dock leaders variously swore, made notes on the map, or looked to Sarren to provide an answer to this latest development.

'How long until they reach–'

'...must move the reserve garrisons–'

'...storm trooper battalions to assemble–'

Cyria Tyro stood alongside the colonel. 'This is what the bastards were doing in the southern Dead Lands. It's why they touched down there. They were taking their landing ships to pieces and building this fleet.'

'It's worse than that,' Sarren gestured to the portable hololithic table with a control wand, zooming out from the city and showing a much wider spread of the southern coast of the Armageddon Secundus landmass.

'Tempestus Hive,' several officers muttered.

Enemy runes flickered as they drew nearer to the other coastal hive. Almost as many as those bearing down on Helsreach.

'They're dead,' Tyro said. 'Tempestus will fall, no matter what we do. A hive half our size, and with half our defences.'

'We're all dead,' a voice spoke out.

'What did you say?' Commissar Falkov sneered.

'We have done all that can be done.' The protests came from an overweight lieutenant in the uniform of the conscripted militia forces. He was calm, sanguine even, speaking with what he hoped was measured wisdom. 'Throne, three hundred enemy vessels? My men are stationed at the docks, and we know what we can do there. But the defences are as thin as... as... damn it, there *are* no defences there. We must evacuate the city, surely. We've done all we can.'

Commissar Falkov's dark stormcoat swished as he reached for his sidearm. He never got the chance to execute the lieutenant for cowardice. A snarling, immense blur of blackness sliced across the room. With a crash, the lieutenant was slammed back against the wall, held a metre off the ground, short legs kicking, as the Reclusiarch gripped his throat in one hand.

'Thirty-six days, you wretched worm. Thirty-six days of defiance, and *thousands upon thousands of heroes lie dead.* You dare speak of retreat when the day finally comes for you to spill the enemy's blood?'

The lieutenant gagged as he was strangled. Colonel Sarren, Cyria Tyro and the other officers watched in silence. No one turned away.

'Hnk. Agh. Ss.' He fought for breath that wouldn't come as he stared into the silver replica of the God-Emperor's death mask. Grimaldus leaned closer, his skulled face leering, blocking out all other sight.

'Where would you run, coward? *Where would you hide that the Emperor would not see your shame and spit on your soul when your worthless life is finally at an end?*'

'Pl– Please.'

'Do not shame yourself further by begging for a life you do not deserve.' Grimaldus tensed his hand, his fingers snapping closed with wet snaps. In his grip, the lieutenant went into spasms, then thumped to the floor as the knight released his grip. The Reclusiarch strode back to the table, ignoring the fallen body.

It took several seconds for conversation to resume. When it did, Falkov saluted the Reclusiarch. Grimaldus ignored it.

Maghernus tried to make sense of the lines being drawn across the map showing troop disposition, but it might as well have been in another language to him. He cleared his throat and said, above the din, 'Colonel.'

'Dockmaster.'

'What does this mean? In the simplest terms, please. All of these lines and numbers mean nothing to me.'

It was Grimaldus who answered. The knight spoke low, staring down at the map with his helm's unblinking scarlet eyes.

'Today is the thirty-sixth day of the siege,' the Templar said, 'and unless we defend the docks against the tens of thousands of enemy that will arrive in under two hours, we will lose the city by nightfall.'

Cyria Tyro nodded as she stared at the map. 'We need to evacuate the dockworkers in the most efficient manner possible, allowing for the arrival of troops.'

'No,' Maghernus said, though no one was listening.

'These avenues,' Colonel Sarren pointed out, 'are already clogged by inbound/outbound supply traffic. We will struggle to get all of the dock menials – no offence, Dockmaster – out in time. Let alone get troops in.'

'No,' Maghernus said again, louder this time. Still, no one paid him any attention.

One of the Steel Legion majors present, a storm trooper set apart by his dark uniform and shoulder insignia, traced a finger along a central spine road leading from Hel's Highway.'

'Evacuate the drones down the other paths and leave the highway route clear. That'll be enough to fill the central docks with trained bodies.'

'That still leaves almost two-thirds of the dock districts,' Sarren frowned, 'with no defence except the garrisoned militia. And the militia will suffer from the fleeing dock menials being in their way.'

'Hello?' said Maghernus.

'We can reroute the traffic through to these secondary veins,' Tyro pointed out.

'Troops would trickle in,' Sarren nodded. 'That might not be enough, but it may be the best we can ask for in the situation.'

A sound emerged, machine-like and harsh, like the engine of a Chimera troop transport choking on the wrong fuel. One by one, heads turned to Grimaldus. The sound was emitted from his helm's vocalisers. He was chuckling.

'I believe,' said the knight, 'the dockmaster has something to say.'

All heads turned to Maghernus.

'Arm us,' he said.

Colonel Sarren closed his eyes. The others watched the dockmaster, unsure if they had heard correctly. Maghernus continued, as the silence spread out, 'There are over thirty-nine thousand of us on those docks – and that's just the workers, not including the militia. If you need time, arm us. We'll give you the time.'

The storm trooper major snorted. 'You'll be dead in an hour. All of you.'

'Maybe,' said Maghernus. 'But we were never going to win this war, were we?'

The major wasn't done, and his voice had less of a sneer now. 'Brave, but insane. If we allow the enemy to butcher the dockworker forces, the city won't be able to function for decades after this war. We're fighting to preserve our way of life, not just survive.'

'Let us focus,' Sarren opened his eyes, 'on surviving first. The fact remains that the majority of the Steel Legion cannot be moved. They are holding the city, and pulling them back from their positions will see the city fall as surely as if we leave the docks undefended. Invigilata and the militia can't hold everything.'

'There's little choice,' said Tyro. 'The dockworkers will die unsupported.'

'Arm them first,' Grimaldus said, his vox-voice heavy with finality. 'Then argue how long they have left to live.'

'Very well. Our course is clear.' Colonel Sarren cleared his throat. 'Dock-master. I thank you.'

'We'll fight like... like... We'll fight damn hard, colonel. Just don't take too long getting the troops to back us up.'

'We have immense stockpiles of materiel in the dock districts.' The colonel nodded to Cyria Tyro. 'You heard the Reclusiarch. Arm them.'

She saluted with a grim smile, and left the table.

'We can hold,' Sarren told everyone that remained. 'After all we have done, I refuse to believe this will be the treacherous blow that breaks our back. We can hold. Major Krivus, the movement of storm trooper squads to the docks is already under way, but I need you to take personal command of that process immediately. Grav-chute them in if you have to. Drop them from the Valkyries that remain. Every rifle counts.'

The major saluted, and moved out of the office with all the grace and speed his bulky carapace armour allowed.

'The civilians,' Tyro murmured, staring at the hololithic. Almost all of the city's reinforced shelters were situated – and sealed – within and beneath the docks district. Sixty per cent of the hive's population, crowded in civilian shelter bunkers, now no longer away from the front lines. 'We can't have that many people left in the direct line of fire.'

'No? We can't release them onto the streets.' Sarren shook his head. 'There is nowhere for them to run, and the panic would choke the byways, preventing the Steel Legion ever reaching the docks. They are as safe as they can be in their shelters.'

'The beasts will tear down those shelters,' Tyro argued.

'Yes, they will. Nothing can be done now.' Sarren would not be deterred. 'There will be no evacuation. We can't arm them in time, and we can't protect them if they leave the shelters. They will do nothing but die in the streets and clog the veins of reinforcements.'

Tyro didn't raise another objection. She knew he was right.

Sarren continued, 'I need insurgency walkers and light armour battalions riding in from the tertiary arterial roads here, here, here and here. Sentinels, my friends. Hellhounds and Sentinels. Everything we can muster.' More officers left the table.

'Reclusiarch.'

'Colonel.'

'You know what I am going to ask of you. There is only one way we will survive this assault long enough to flood the docks with tried and tested troops. I cannot order you, but I would ask it nevertheless.'

'There is no need to ask. My knights will deploy from our remaining gunships. We will stand with the civilians. We will hold the docks.'

'My thanks, Reclusiarch. Now, we are as ready as it is possible to be, given the nature of this unwelcome surprise. We are, however, placing a great deal of pressure on Invigilata and the bulk of the Imperial Guard. The city will bleed while we divert our elite infantry to the docks, and this fight... it'll take days. At best.'

'Let Invigilata hold the city,' Grimaldus said, gesturing to the map with a black gauntlet. 'Let the Steel Legion stand with them. Focus on what matters in the here and now.'

'No grand speech? I'm almost disappointed.'

'No speech.' The Templar was already stalking from the room. 'Not for you. You won't be dying this day. I save my words for those who will.'

FOURTEEN

THE DOCKS

They came as the sun began its downward arc in the sky.

The Helsreach docks took up almost a third of the hive's perimeter. Thousands of uninspiring warehouses and harbour office towers stood watch over an expansive bay which featured an endless number of quays and piers that stabbed out into the sloshing, filthy greyish water.

The air across the entire world might have always reeked of something faintly sulphuric, but here – at the heart of Helsreach's industry – the reek bordered on petrochemically unhealthy. It only took an hour for a person's clothes and hair to become saturated with the greasy, heavy stink of spilled oil and ammoniac seawater. Lifers, the dockworkers who spent their entire careers here, hacked up a fair share of blackness when they hawked and spat. Respiratory tumours were the second-largest cause of death among the populace, only behind industrial accidents by a small margin.

The chaos of the docks was a natural deterrent to the enemy assault, but not a true defence. The first sign of the enemy came as crews leaped from their vessels, risking a kilometre-long swim through pollution-foul waters to reach the docks. On dry land, the defenders of Helsreach watched as the hundreds of undocked tankers, lurking offshore with their volatile manifests, began to explode.

The men and women of Helsreach stood together on cargo crates, on the paved groundways, on steel piers, all eyes turned to the seas and the fleet of enemy vessels breaching the surface of the water, powering closer to the city. A horde of humanity, looking out to sea.

Maghernus was close to the front of one crowd, leading his worker gang in their filthy overalls, clutching a newly-forged lasgun to his chest. They were being handed out by Guard officers from weapon crates stored in warehouses across the dock districts. Every dock gang was treated to a short, simple talk on how a lasrifle was loaded, unloaded, set to safety and fired after aiming. Maghernus had felt his palms sweating as he collected the rifle and extra power cells, which now sat in a small sack hanging from the side of his belt. The hurried Guard sergeant had shouted his way through a quick demonstration, and now here Maghernus was, gun in hand, dry-mouthed.

'Follow your assigned leaders,' the sergeant had yelled above the noise of so many men and women gathered in one place. 'Every dock gang, and every group of fifty people, will have a storm trooper with them. Follow that storm trooper the way you'd follow the Emperor Himself if He descended from the sky and told you what to do with your sorry arses. He will tell you when to fight, when to run, when to hide and when to move. If you do what this trooper tells you to do, you've got a much greater chance of getting through this in one piece, and not messing up another unit's movements. If you don't listen, there's a greater chance you'll be fouling it up for everyone else, and getting your friends killed. Understood?'

General assent answered this.

'For the next few days, you're in the Imperial Guard. First rule of the Guard: Go forward. If you get lost, *you go forward.* You lose your way? *You go forward.* You fall away from your group? *You go towards the enemy.* That's where you'll do the most good, and that's where you'll find your friends. Understood?'

General assent answered this, too. It came with a little more reluctance.

'Right. Next groups!'

With that, Maghernus's gang and several others filed from the warehouse, making room for others to get exactly the same lecture.

Outside, dozens of Steel Legion storm troopers in their ochre jackets and heavy, thrumming power generator backpacks were directing the flow of human traffic. Maghernus led his gang to one that waved him over. The man was slender, unshaven, scratching his forehead under the domed helmet he wore. His goggles were raised up, fastened around the helmet, and his rebreather mask was hanging slack around his neck. He had the look of someone who, if not lost, was at least not entirely sure where he was.

'Hello,' Maghernus swallowed. 'We need an assigned soldier.'

'Ah, I know this already. That is me. I am Andrej.'

'Thank you, sir.'

The storm trooper laughed, slapping the dockmaster on the shoulder. 'That is funny. "Sir". I may keep you after the war is done, to make me feel good, eh? I am not Sir. I am Andrej. Perhaps I will be Sir after I make sure none of you are dead. I would like that. It would be nice.'

'I...'

'Yes, it is a big pressure. I understand this. I would like a promotion, so you must all stay alive. We play for big stakes now, no? I thank you for this idea you have given me. You have made the day more fun.'

'I...'

'Come, come. No time for making friends now. We will talk much soon. Hey! All of you dock-working people, come with me, yes?'

Without waiting for an answer, Andrej began to walk through the crowds, followed by Maghernus's gang. The storm trooper would occasionally wave at other soldiers, most of whom offered silent nods or gruff greetings. One of them, a pale beauty with black hair so thick and rich it had no business being leashed in a plain ponytail, smiled and waved back.

'Throne, who was that?' Maghernus asked as he trailed just behind Andrej. 'Your wife?'

'Ha! I wish. That is Domoska. We are squadmates. She is nice to look at, no?'

She was. Maghernus watched her leading another group through the masses. As Domoska was lost in the teeming crowds, his gaze fell on the men she was leading. Maghernus prayed he didn't look as nervous as they all did.

'It is very funny, I think. Her brother is the ugliest man I have ever seen, yet the sister is touched by fortune with great beauty. He must be very bitter, no?'

Maghernus just nodded.

'Come, come. Time is running away from us.'

That had been an hour ago. Now, they stood with Andrej, unfamiliar weapons held to their chests, pressed against quickened heartbeats. Andrej was occupying himself by picking his nose. This was something he struggled to do in gloves of thick, brown leather, but he went about the task with a curiously stately tenacity.

'Sir,' Maghernus started.

'A moment, please. Victory is almost mine.' Andrej flicked something grotesque from his fingertip. 'I can breathe again. Emperor be praised.'

'Sir, shouldn't you say something to us?' He lowered his voice, stepping closer. 'Something to inspire the men?'

Andrej frowned, absently biting his cut lip as he looked around at the other groups spread down the dock lines. 'I do not think so. No other Legionnaire is talking. I was going to wait for the Reclusiarch's speech, you know? Would you prefer me to speak now?'

'The Reclusiarch will speak?'

'Oh, yes. He is good at this. You will like it. It will happen soon, I am thinking.'

A blast of screeching feedback slashed through the air as across the docks – kilometre upon kilometre of them – every vox-tower came alive in a distorted whine.

'See?' Andrej grinned. 'I am always right. It is what I do best.'

For several seconds, the people of Helsreach heard nothing but breathing – low, heavy, threatening – over the vox-speakers.

'Sons and daughters of Hive Helsreach,' the voice boomed across the shore districts, too low and resonant to be human, flavoured by the slight crackle of vox-corruption. *'Look to the water. The water from which you draw the wealth of your city. The water that now promises nothing but death.*

'For thirty-six days, the people of your world, the people of your own city, have been selling their lives to defend you. For thirty-six nights, your own mothers and fathers, your own brothers and sisters, your own sons and daughters have been fighting the enemy to ensure that half of the hive remains in human hands. They have battled, road by road, sweating and fighting and dying so you can enjoy a handful of days of freedom.

'You owe them. You owe them for the sacrifices they have made so far. You owe them for the sacrifices they will make in the days and nights yet to come.

'Here and now, you will have the chance you deserve, the chance to repay them all. More than that, you will have the chance to punish the enemy for daring to lay siege to your city, for breaking your families apart and destroying your homes.

'Watch the tides. See the scrap fleet that sails into your port, bearing a horde of howling beasts. When the sun sets at the end of this week, every single invader in those surfacing ships will no longer draw breath from the sacred air of this world. They will fall because of you. You are going to save this city.

'Fear is natural. It is human. Feel no shame for a heart that beats too fast in this moment, or fingers that tremble as you hold a weapon you have never wielded before. The only shame is in cowardice – in running and leaving others to die when everything comes down to your actions.

'You are led by Guard veterans – the best of your Steel Legions – Imperial storm troopers. But they are not alone. The forces of Helsreach are coming. Stand and defy the enemy for long enough, and you will soon see thousands of tanks constructed in this very city grinding the invaders into dust. Help. Is. Coming. Until then, stand proud. Stand resolute.

'Remember these words, brothers and sisters. "When death comes, the good we have done will mean nothing. We are judged in life for the evil we destroy".

'That time of judgement is upon you. I know every man and women here feels it in their blood, in their bones.

'I am Grimaldus of the Black Templars, and this is my vow to you all. While one of us stands, these docks will never fall. If I have to kill a thousand of the enemy myself, the sun will rise once more over an unconquered city.

'Look for the black knights among you. We will be where the fighting is fiercest, at the heart of the storm.

'Stand with us, and we will be your salvation.'

Silence descended once more.

Maghernus sighed, tension ebbing from him as his breath misted in the cool air. Andrej was adjusting the slide rack settings on his modified lasrifle. The weapon emitted a pulsing, charged hum that set the dockmaster's teeth on edge.

'That was a stern talking-to, no? Not many will run now, I am thinking.'

Maghernus nodded. It took him several moments to speak. 'What's that rifle?'

'This?' Andrej finished his ministrations, gesturing to the thick power cables feeding from the rifle's bulky stock to the humming metal power pack he wore between his shoulders. 'We call them hellguns. Like yours, only brighter and louder and hotter and meaner. And no, you cannot have one. This is mine. They are rare, and only given to people who are right all the time.'

'And what's that?'

'This is a det-pack.' He tapped the hand-sized detonator disc hanging from his belt. 'Used for sticking to tanks and making them explode into many pretty pieces. I once had many, now I have only one. When I use it, I will have none, and that will be a sad day.'

Maghernus wanted to ask if Andrej was really a storm trooper. He settled for saying 'You are not exactly what I expected.'

'Life,' the soldier said, looking off to the side in what appeared to be distracted consideration, 'is a series of very wonderful surprises, until a final bad one.' Turning to the entire group, Andrej buckled his helmet's chin strap with a grin.

'My handsome new friends, it is soon to be time for war. So, my beautiful ladies and fine gentlemen, if you want to remain beautiful and fine, keep your heads down and your rifles up. Always aim from the cheek, with your eyes down the barrel. Do not be firing from the hip – that is the best way to feel excellent about yourself and yet hit nothing. Oh, and it will be loud and scary, no? Much panic, I think. Always wait one second before pulling your trigger, to make sure you are aiming at something you should be aiming at. Otherwise you may be shooting other people, and that is bad news for you, and worse news for them.'

The gangs of workers began to disperse across the docks, taking up positions in alleys between warehouses, behind crate stacks, around the edges of buildings and on the various floors of multi-storey hangars and work blocks facing the sea.

'Come, come.' Andrej led his group into the shadows of a loader crane, ordering them to spread out and take cover around the huge metal strut columns and cargo containers close by.

'Sir?' called one of the men.

'My name is Andrej, and I have said this many times. But yes, what is the problem?'

'My gun's jammed. I can't get the power cell back in.'

From where he crouched at the head of the group, Andrej shook his head with a melodramatic sigh. With his goggles over his eyes and the infantile grin plastered across his features, he looked like some breed of gigantic, amused fly.

'One has to wonder why you would be taking it out in the first place.'

'I was just–'

'Yes, yes. Be nice to the weapon's machine-spirit. Ask it nicely.'

The dockworker looked awkward as he turned his gaze down at the rifle. 'Please?' he said, lamely.

'Ha! Such reverence. Now click that lock switch on the other side. That is the release catch, and you need to slide it back to get the cell back in.'

The man dropped the power cell from his shaking hands, but slapped it home on the second try. 'Thank you, sir.'

'Yes, yes, I am a hero. Now, my brave friends, a siren will soon begin to sing. When it does, it means the enemy is within range of our artillery defences, which are sadly too few in number to make me smile. When I say it is time to be ready, you are all to sit up and start looking for huge and ugly beasts to shoot.'

'Yes, sir,' they chorused.

'I could become used to that, oh yes. Now, listen with both ears my wonderful fellows. Aim for the bodies. It is the biggest target, and that is what counts if you are new to this.'

'Yes, sir,' they said again.

'There is a very beautiful woman I would like to marry after this war. She will almost certainly be saying no to my proposal, but hey, we will see. If she says yes, you are all invited to my wedding, which will be in the eastern territories where the weather is much less like being pissed on by the sky every day. Also, the drinks will be free. You have my word on this. I am always truthful, this being one of my many glorious virtues.'

A few of the men smiled, despite themselves.

The siren began to wail. A banshee's keen across kilometres of docks, howling over tens of thousands of frightened Imperial souls. Muffled thumps started up in response as the Sabre-class defence platforms opened fire on the incoming fleet.

'It is time,' Andrej grinned again, 'to earn some very shiny medals.'

'For the Emperor,' one man breathed the words like a mantra, his eyes closed. 'For the Emperor.'

'Oh, no. Not for Him.' Andrej fastened his rebreather mask, but they could still hear the smile in his voice. 'He is happy on His Golden Throne, a long way from here. This is for me, and it is for you, and that is more than enough.'

The sirens began to fade, one by one, until a last lone wail sputtered out.

'Any moment now,' Andrej said, leaning up to aim over the top of the container he'd been kneeling behind. 'We will have company.'

The first vessels crashed into the docks with the noise of a storm wave breaking against the shore. With no finesse, without even slowing down, they crunched into the gangways and loading platforms, ferociously beaching themselves. Doors and portals immediately blasted open, disgorging a tide of foul alien flesh onto the docks.

The very first of the alien beasts to spill from its underwater scrap-pod was a brute, easily half again the size of its lesser brethren, bearing a trophy rack on its hunched shoulders with human skulls and Astartes helms from other wars on other worlds. It had been leading its tribe across the edges of the Imperium for decades, and in a fight with all else even, would have been more than a match for a lone Astartes.

Its face, shoulder and torso disintegrated in a ruthless volley of las-fire that sent the burning remains spinning off the edge of the docks and into the polluted water below. Less than a hundred metres away, Domoska shouted encouragement to the dockworkers she led, and ordered them to fire again. Many had missed, but more than enough had struck home. It was a pattern being repeated along the Helsreach docks now, as the first wave of xenos creatures howled and laughed their way into the city.

From his makeshift cover within the den of loosely-stacked cargo containers, Maghernus fired shot after shot, feeling the rifle in his hands growing warmer with each *crack* of release. He lowered himself below the lip of the crate he knelt behind, and reloaded his lasgun with inexpert fingers. The bastard thing was stuck.

'Use force,' Andrej said from his place next to the dockmaster. The stormtrooper didn't look at him, didn't even glance away from where he was aiming and firing. Another migraine-bright beam of overcharged energy spat from the soldier's hellgun. 'The slides often jam on new rifles. This is a sad truth with the rifles of our home world. Their spirits take time to wake up.'

Maghernus was amazed he could even hear the other man over the din of beaching vessels, alien roars and discharging lasguns filling the air with a scattered chorus of mechanical cracks.

'I fired a Kantrael rifle once,' Andrej was continuing, his words punctuated by slight shifts in his posture and aim as he tracked target after target, releasing round after round. 'It was a very keen weapon, oh yes. That world forges eager guns.'

Maghernus slotted the fresh power cell home and raised himself back into position. His back already ached from his first two minutes as a soldier. How the Steel Legion crouched like this for days on end and got used to battle was a mystery to him. He fired at distant figures, lumbering alien hulks that ran with almost no sense of direction or purpose, as if hunting for a scent – lost until they found it. Others in the emerging packs would race to the source of the las-fire being thrown at them, and were cut down in their headlong run. A few, clearly cunning by the standards of these creatures, remained back and loaded heavy weapons. These last beasts sent shrieking missiles into the entrenched Imperial lines, exploding stacks of cargo crates or pulverising the sides of warehouses.

Slowly but surely, with an insidious creep, the docks were being enveloped by thick smoke from the destroyed submersibles and burning buildings.

'We will have to move soon,' Andrej called over his shoulder to the others.

The words proved prophetic. With a crash of metal on stone and a wave of flooding water, a submersible beached itself on the docks not thirty metres from their position. Saltwater splashed down on the crouching dockworkers. Alien growls came from the wrecked sub as its doors blasted open.

'That is far from good,' the storm trooper scowled behind his rebreather as he slammed back into his firing position, drawing a bead on the first creature to emerge. It dropped like a puppet with its strings cut as the harsh beam lanced through its face and blew out the back of its head.

Maghernus and the others joined their fire to his. Still more beasts came spilling from the submersible. The greenskins were charging now, having sniffed out the nearby cluster of humans behind the barricade, and following the streams of laser fire.

'Sir...' one of the men stammered, his eyes wide and bloodshot. 'Sir, they're coming...'

'That is a fact I am aware of,' Andrej replied, not stopping his stream of fire for a moment.

'Sir–'

'Please *shut up* and *keep firing*, yes?'

The beasts reached the cargo containers. They reeked of blood, smoke, bitter sweat and the alien stench of fungal corruption. Bunched muscles hauled the beasts over the barricades, and the brutes roared down at the humans – no longer in cover, but hemmed in by the cargo pods.

Las-rounds sliced up, punching dozens of the scrambling beasts back. The remnants of the first wave were joined by the second, and the creatures dropped in amongst the dockworkers, scrap-pistols barking and heavy axes swinging.

'Fall back!' Andrej shouted, firing his hellgun at point-blank range, using it to slash a way through the erupting melee. 'Run!'

The dockworkers were already in a panicked flight. 'With me, you idiots!'

the storm trooper yelled, and for a wonder, it actually worked. The dockers with enough presence of mind to clutch their lasguns in the chaos moved with Andrej, adding their fire to his again.

He left a third of his team in the shelter of the containers and crane struts. Screaming dockworkers, unable to escape the invaders. Andrej sensed a momentary hesitation in those that remained with him; a handful of seconds where they ceased against all logic, some freezing rather than open fire on their dying friends, and others mesmerised in astonished fear by the sight of such slaughter.

'They're already dead!' Andrej slammed his gloved palm into the side of Maghernus's head, jolting him back into the moment. 'Fire!'

It was enough to break the spell. Las-fire opened up again, streaming into the embattled aliens.

'Fall back only when you must reload! Stand and fire until then!'

Andrej swore under his breath after he gave the order. The orks were already scrambling closer in an avalanche of green flesh, axe blades and ragged armour. Around the retreating team, the docks burned and thundered with the sounds of more submersibles beaching themselves. Andrej caught a momentary glimpse of another team of dockworkers through the smoke some distance away, breaking into flight as they were chopped to pieces by the orks in their midst.

The same was about to happen to his ragtag gang, and he swore again. He hoped Domoska was faring better.

What a stupid place to die.

Kilometres away from Helsreach, beneath the sands of the wastelands to the north-west, there was a loud and unprecedented *clunk* of heavy machinery.

Jurisian, Forgemaster of the *Eternal Crusader,* rose to his feet with a slowness born of exhaustion. Tears stood in his eyes – a rarity indeed for a being that had not wept in over twenty decades. His mind pulsed with a thundering ache, a dull and thudding heat that had nothing to do with physical weakness.

He could smell his servitors now that his senses were returning from their focusless lock on his primary task. Turning to regard them where they lay, Jurisian could smell the decay setting into their organic parts. They had been dead for weeks, starved of sustenance. He hadn't noticed. They had proven useless after the first few hours, over a month ago, their internal cognitive processors unable to keep up with the ever-evolving code. Jurisian had needed to work alone, cursing Grimaldus all the while.

Another deep clunk of grinding machinery restored his attention to the present. His joints ached – both the mechanical ones and his still-human ones – from such a period of inactivity. He had been a statue in place for four weeks, his mind alive and his body in hunched, tense stasis by the console.

He had not slept. He knew that on several occasions, as his closing, exhausted mind had drifted close to shutting down, he had almost lost grip on the code. With his thoughts moving sluggishly, the code had outpaced him just as it had done to his servitors. In these moments of panicked intensity, he had resisted by silencing sections of his mind with clinical meditation, operating at a lessened capacity, but at least he was still awake.

Jurisian stared ahead at the vast doors.

- OBERON -

That word burned itself into his core, written in towering letters, more a warning than a tomb marker.

A last resonant machine-sound signalled the grinding rollback of the final interior lock. Pressurised coolant vapour flushed into the corridor as the door's seal systems vented it. It reeked of chlorine – not poisonous, but stale from being cold-cooked for so many years while the door remained silent and still. In a ballet of rumbling, shuddering technology, the portal began to open.

'Reclusiarch,' Jurisian voxed, horrified at the dull scratchiness of his voice. 'The defences are broken. I am in.'

FIFTEEN

BALANCE

The chamber offered nothing at first. Nothing except a powerless darkness that was blacker than black, even to Jurisian's visor lenses. A whispered keyword cycled his vision filters through a thermal-seeking infrared, through to a crude echolocation that falsified an auspex scanner's silent chimes to detect movement. He had made these modifications himself, with the proper respect to the machine-spirit of his wargear.

It was this last sense that produced a response. A vague grey blur passed his vision, and with it, the whirring of internal mechanisms. Hinges. Cogs. Fibre muscles. The sound was as familiar to Jurisian as his own breathing, but brought with it an edge of disconcerting curiosity.

Joints. He was hearing joints.

Something was wrong. The suggestion of static interference at the edges of his vision display told a tale of interference, obfuscation, more than a darkness born from a lack of light. He was being jammed, and the manipulation was insidiously subtle.

Jurisian's bolter came up in steady hands, panning left and right in the darkness as his eye lenses continued to cycle through filters. At last, a targeting monocle slid over his right eye lens – the mechanical echo of a lizard's nictitating membrane.

Better. Not perfect, but better.

'I am Jurisian,' he said to the creature before him, as it resolved into focus. 'Master of the Forge for the *Eternal Crusader,* flagship of the Black Templars.'

The creature didn't answer immediately. The size of a man, it smelled of ancient machinery and sour breath.

It was likely the thing had once been human – or some part of it was organic, even if only the smallest aspect. Hunched, robed in a ruined cloak of woven fabric, misshapen lumps in its surface area suggested additional limbs or advanced modification. It remained faceless, either refusing to look up or unable to do so.

Jurisian lowered his bolter. The servo-arms extending from his back-mounted power generator still clutched a host of weaponry, aiming it at the robed being before him. He voiced his next words through his helm's vox-speakers, letting his armour's spirit twist the human language into a universal, bluntly simple machine code – a basic program for communication which he had acquired during his long years of tuition and training on Mars, home world of the Mechanicus.

'My identity is Jurisian,' the code pulsed, 'of the Astartes.'

The reply came in a burst of snarled code, the words and meanings bleeding into each other. It was akin to machine-slang, evolved from the viral program that sealed the doors. This creature, whatever it was, had an accent born of hundreds of years of isolation here.

'Affirmative,' Jurisian responded in the foundation code. 'I can see you. Your interference should be aborted. It is no longer relevant.'

The creature raised itself higher, no longer lurking on all fours. It now reached Jurisian's chestplate, though it came no closer, remaining a dozen metres away. The weapons in the Forgemaster's servo-arms tracked the being's movements.

It pulsed another tangled mess of accented code.

'Affirmative,' Jurisian replied again. 'I destroyed the sealant program.'

This time, the creature's response was rendered through a more simple code. Jurisian narrowed his eyes at this development. Like the chamber's virus lock, the creature was adapting and working with new information at a faster rate than standard Mechanicus constructs.

'This is the sanctuary of *Oberon*.'

'I know.' The Forgemaster risked a panning glance left and right, seeking any resolution in the artificial darkness. His targeting monocle couldn't pierce the gloom more than a few metres ahead. Flickering static was beginning to crawl across his eye lenses. 'Deactivate the interference,' Jurisian raised his bolter again, 'or I will destroy you.'

Against his will, emotion coloured the code-spoken declaration. To be limited like this was an affront to his sense of honourable conduct – there was no glory or prudence in allowing oneself to be kept at an enemy's mercy.

'I am the guardian of *Oberon*. Your presence generates negligible threat to me.'

Jurisian tasted anger on his tongue, bitter and metallic. His finger tensed on the thick trigger of his bolter.

'Deactivate the interference. This is your final warning.' Static mottled his vision now, like a thousand insects clustering on his eye lenses. He could make out no more than the barest silhouette as the Mechanicus warden moved closer.

'Negative,' it said.

Jurisian's servo-arms, answering his mind's impulses a fraction of a second after his true limbs, had raised his axe and other weapons in a threatening display, almost akin to some feral world arachnid predator increasing its size to warn off prey.

The knight's final threat was spoken with conviction, the machine-cant laced with numerical equations indicating emphasis.

'Then die.'

Their saviour was one of the black knights.

He charged the enemy from the sky with a whining howl of protesting thrusters. Fire streaked from his flight pack as he landed in the aliens' midst, a dark blur of movement outlined in flame.

Andrej immediately scrambled back, ordering his gang into the relative cover provided by an overturned cargo loader truck.

'Do not dare cease fire,' he shouted over the sound of alien bellowing and thousands of guns crying out. He doubted any of them heard him, but they went back to firing as soon as they slid into cover.

The Templar cut left and right with his chainsword, ripping stinking green flesh from malformed orkish bones. His bolt pistol sang out in a thudding refrain, embedding fist-sized bolts in alien bodies which detonated a moment later. Andrej, who had seen Astartes fight before, did all he could to keep up his rate of fire in support of the suicidal bravery taking place. Several of his dockworker crew lowered their guns in slack-jawed, frightened awe.

Perhaps, Andrej cursed, they believed the Astartes would actually survive unaided.

'Keep firing, damn you!' the storm trooper yelled. 'He's dying for us!'

The ferocious advantage of surprise did not last long. The greenskins turned to the deadly threat among them, laying about with their crude axes and firing their clattering pistols at close range. Several of them hit each other in their fury, while stragglers and those on the edges of the melee were punched down by las-fire from Andrej's gang.

The Templar screamed – a vox-distorted cry of wrath that went crawling across the skin of every human in earshot. His chainblade fell from his black hand, hanging loose on the thick chain that bound the blade to his forearm.

Behind the staggering warrior, one of the few remaining greenskins tore a crude spear back out from the knight's lower spine. The beast had no more than a moment to enjoy its victory: a searing lance of headache-bright energy dissolved its face and blew the contents of its skull over the dying knight's armour. Andrej recharged his weapon without even needing to look away from the melee.

The Templar regained his balance, then recovered his grip on the revving chainsword a heartbeat after. He lasted for three more savage cuts, tearing gobbets of flesh and shattered armour from the orks closest to him, before the remnants of the alien pack impaled him on their spears and bore him to the ground. His flight pack crashed to the floor, rent from his body. They aimed with brutal efficiency, ramming blades into his armour joints and using their immense strength to force him to his knees. The Templar's pistol came up one final time to hammer a bolt into the chest of the nearest beast, spraying those nearby with inhuman gore as it primed and exploded.

The last three orks were scythed down by Andrej's dock team, collapsing next to the Astartes they had slain. The scene before them was a slice of eerie calm, the heart of a storm, while the rest of the docks burned.

'Throne,' the storm trooper hissed. 'Stay here, yes?'

Maghernus didn't even have time to agree before the soldier was making a break across the rockcrete platform, crouched low, moving to the downed knight's body.

'What's he doing?' asked one of the dockworkers.

Maghernus wanted to know that himself. He moved after the storm trooper, doing his best to mimic the crouching run Andrej had just performed. Something hot and angry buzzed past his ear, like the passage of a poisonous insect. It took several seconds to realise he'd almost had his head taken off by a stray shot.

'What are you doing?' He knelt by the storm trooper.

What he was doing seemed obvious to Andrej. His gloved fingers quested under the chin of the knight's helm, seeking some kind of catch, or lock, or release. Throne, there must be something...

'Seeing if he lives,' the soldier muttered, clearly distracted. 'Ayah! Got you.'

With a muted hiss almost drowned out by nearby gunfire, the helm's seals parted and the expressionless helmet came loose. Andrej pulled it off, handing it to Maghernus. It was about three times as heavy as the dockmaster had been expecting, and he'd been expecting it to weigh a hell of a lot.

The knight wasn't dead. His face was awash in blood, the dark fluid filming over his eyes and darkening his features as it ran from his nose and clenched teeth. Astartes blood was supposed to clot within instants, so the tales told. It wasn't happening here, and Andrej doubted that was a positive sign.

'Can't move,' the Templar growled. His voice was wet from a burbling throat. 'Spine. Hearts. Dying.'

'There is something inside you, I know,' Andrej spared a glance around, making sure they weren't in immediate danger. 'Something important inside you, that your brothers must reclaim, yes?'

'Progenoid,' the knight's breathing was as raw as a chainsword's snarl. The warrior's oversized armoured hand gripped the front of Andrej's armour. It was strengthless.

'I do not know what that is, sir knight.'

'Gene-seed,' the Templar spat blood as he forced the words through numbing lips. His eyes were lolling now, half-closed and rolling back. It was clear he was blind. *'Legacy.'*

Andrej nodded to Maghernus. 'Help me move him. Do not argue. It is important that his brothers find his body. Important for their rituals.'

'Emperor...' the knight grunted, *'Emperor protects.'*

With those words, the hand gripping Andrej's chestguard went slack, thumping to rest on the heraldic cross on the warrior's own breastplate.

Their eyes met once, and the dockworker and the career soldier started dragging the dead knight.

We are dying.

We are dying, scattered across kilometres of docks, mixed in with the humans, torn from the unity of brotherhood.

'Wear your helm,' I say to Nero without looking over my shoulder at him. 'Do not let the humans see you like this.'

With tears in his eyes, our healer does as I order. The list of failing life signs is transferred from his wrist display to his retinal readouts. I hear him draw a shaking breath over the vox.

'Anastus is dead,' he says, adding another name to those that came before.

I lean forward, the racing wind clawing over the surface of my armour, sending my parchment scrolls and tabard streaming in its grip. We are several hundred metres up, making ready to drop on the beasts below. The Thunderhawk's turbines lower their growl as they throttle down.

The docks below us are already in ruin. They burn – black and grey, amber and orange – making the view from the polluted skies like staring down into the mouth of some mythical dragon. Percussive thumps signal the crash landings of more submersibles, or our own munitions stores going up in flames.

'Helsreach will fall tonight,' Bastilan says, giving voice to something we must all be thinking. I have never, in over a century of waging war at his side, heard him speak such a thing.

'And do not lie to me, Grimaldus,' he says, sharing the bulkhead's space with me. 'Save your words for the others, brother.'

I tolerate such familiarity from him.

But he is wrong.

'Not tonight,' I tell him, and he doesn't look away from the skull I wear as my face. 'I swore to the humans that the sun would rise over an unconquered city. I do not mean to break that vow. And you, brother, will help me keep it.'

Bastilan turns away at last. What closeness had been near to the surface cools fast, leaving us distant again. 'As you command,' he says.

'Make ready to jump,' I vox to the others. 'Nero. Do you stand ready?'

'What?' He lowers his narthecium, retracting surgical saws and cutting blades. I see the empty sockets for gene-seed storage withdraw and lock under smooth armour plating.

'I need you, Nero. Our brothers need you.'

'Do not lecture me, Reclusiarch. I stand ready.'

The others, Priamus especially, are taking note now. 'Cador is dead. Two-thirds of the Helsreach Crusade will not live to see the coming dawn. You will carry their legacy, my brother. Grief has its place – none of us have suffered such losses before – but if you are lost in sorrow then you will be the death of us all.'

'I said I stand ready! Why do you single me out like this? Priamus is likely to see us all dead because he cannot follow orders! Bastilan and Artarion are not half the fighters Cador was. Yet you lecture *me* about being the weak one, the crack in the blade?'

My pistol is aimed at his head, at the faceplate marked white as a symbol of his expertise and valuable skills.

'Bitterness is taking root within you, brother. Much longer, and it will bore through you, hollowing out your heart and soul, leaving naught but empty bones. When I tell you to focus and stand with your brothers, you respond with black words and treacherous thoughts. So I tell you again, one last time, that we need you. And you need us.'

He doesn't stare me down. When he looks away, it's not in defeat or cowardice, but in shame.

'Yes, Reclusiarch. My brothers, forgive me. My humours are unbalanced, and my mind has been adrift.'

'"A mind without purpose will walk in dark places,"' Artarion quotes. A human philosopher; one I don't recognise.

'It is fine, Nero,' Bastilan grunts. 'Cador was one of the Chapter's finest. I miss him, just as you do.'

'I forgive you, Nerovar,' Priamus says, and I thank him on a private vox-channel for not sounding like he is sneering for once.

The Thunderhawk slows, thrusters keeping it aloft as we make ready to jump. In the air around us, snapping explosions decorate the sky.

'Anti-air fire? Already?' Artarion asks.

Whether they've beached several submersibles with surface-to-air weapons or taken control of wall defence cannons is irrelevant. The gunship swings violently, shaking as the armour plating takes its first hit. They're firing up through the smoke, tracking the gunship through primitive methods that are apparently effective enough to work.

'Incoming missiles,' the pilot voxes to us. The Thunderhawk re-engages its forward thrust, boosting forward. 'Dozens, too close to evade. Jump now or die with me.'

Priamus goes. Artarion follows. Nero and Bastilan next, launching out of the airlock.

The pilot, Troven, is not a warrior I know well. I cannot judge his temperament the way I can with my closest brothers, except to say that he is a Templar, with all the courage, pride and resolution that honour entails.

In a human, I'd call such behaviour stubbornness.

'There is no need to die here,' I say as I enter the cockpit. I have no idea if I'm right to say such a thing, but if this hope can be forged into the truth, I will make it happen now.

'Reclusiarch?'

Troven has chosen to wrench the Thunderhawk through evasive manoeuvres, rather than disengage himself from the pilot's throne and try to leap from the gunship. Both choices, such as they are, are likely to fail. I still believe he chose wrong.

'Disengage *now*.' I haul him from the throne, power feeds snapping from connection ports in his armour. He spasms with the electrical feedback of an unsafe and flawed disconnect, half of his perception and consciousness still melded with the gunship's machine-spirit. His protests are reduced to garbled, wordless grunts of pain as his armour's power supply kicks back in and the union with the gunship's systems dims.

The Thunderhawk tilts, diving from the sky on dead engines. Nausea fades as soon as it threatens, balanced by the gene-forged organs replacing my standard human eyes and ears. Troven's genetic compensators take a moment longer to adjust, ruined by the disorientation of the severed connection. I hear him grunting through his helm's vox-speakers, swallowing his bile.

This freefall will delay the missiles' impact. I hope.

In this weakened state, he's easy to drag from the cockpit to the open bulkhead. The visible sky is twisting as the gunship plummets. Mag-locked step by mag-locked step, my boots adhere to the iron floor, preventing the spiralling death-dive from hurling us around the cabin.

As I face the air-rushing portal, my targeting display overlays the spinning sky. I blink at a flashing rune of crossed blades pulsing in the centre. A propulsion gauge spills across my retinas, and the jump pack weighing my shoulders down whines into life.

'You'll kill us both,' Troven almost laughs. I spare no more than a second's thought for the two servitors operating the other flight stations.

'Brace,' is all I have time to say. The world around us dissolves into jagged metal and screaming fire.

Once the noises had faded and the air reeked of the powdery, familiar scent of bolter fire, Jurisian hauled himself back to his feet.

The immediate area around him was illuminated by flashing sparks and energy flares vented by his broken servo arm and savaged armour. The expulsions of electrical force from wounded metal were bright enough to leave violent smears across his sensitive eye lenses. Jurisian blanked the filters with a command word, restoring standard vision mode.

A moan of pain emerged from his vox-speakers as a harsh crackle. Even with no one nearby, it shamed him to voice his weakness in such a way. He would seek out the Reclusiarch and perform penance when... Well, there would be no *when.* This war would never be won.

Retinal displays showed in grim detail the damage to his internal biological and mechanical components. The Forgemaster spared several seconds to examine the flashing warning runes, indicating leaking vital oxygenated haemo-plasma from areas near several organs. Jurisian felt a grin steal over his face as his pain-drunk mind latched onto an altogether more human explanation.

I'm bleeding.

He barely cared. It wasn't terminal damage, neither to his living components nor his augmetic modifications. He stepped forward, crushing underfoot one of the many segmented blade-arms the warden had deployed as it launched at him only minutes before.

It lay in motionless repose, its internal power generators cycling down, descending into silence. In death, the truth was revealed with an almost melancholic clarity. The warden was no more than a shadow of what it had claimed to be.

Certainly, the creature would have been a match for most intruders – be they alien or human. But with its robe parted to show the decrepit truth it had concealed, what was once a stalwart Mechanicus tech-guardian was revealed as little more than an ancient, degrading magos, long-starved of the supplies it needed to maintain itself. Once, it had been human. And in an era after that, it had been a powerful sentinel for the Mechanicus, watching over this most precious of secrets.

Time had robbed it of a great deal.

The ancient warden had leapt at Jurisian, its limb-blades snapping into life, stabbing and cutting as they descended on flailing mechadendrites.

The knight's own servo-arms had hit back, slower, weightier, inflicting pounding and lasting damage in opposition to the scrapes and gouges inflicted by the warden. By the time the sentinel creature had severed one of the knight's machine-limbs, Jurisian's bolter was hammering shot after shot into the guardian's torso, detonating vital systems and rupturing the human organs that yet remained. Suspension fluid and chemical lubricants ran in place of blood that would no longer flow.

Piercing pain signalled the moments that the warden punctured Jurisian's ceramite armour. It still possessed enough of its attack routines to stab for his joints and armour's weak points, but just as often as it struck a gouging hit, its efforts were deflected by the customised, revered war plate that Jurisian had modified himself so long ago on the surface of Mars.

He rose after it had finally fallen. Damaged, but unashamed. Regretful, but with his conviction burning.

Already, the creature – the sentinel that had come so close to ending his life – was forgotten. The interference had cleared with its destruction.

Jurisian stared into the resolving darkness of the colossal chamber, and became the first living being in over five hundred years to see *Oberon,* the Ordinatus Armageddon.

'Grimaldus,' he whispered into the vox. 'It's true. It's the holy lance of the Machine-God.'

The thrusters kicked in with desperate force, arresting their insane descent. The jolt was savage – without his armour's fibre bundle musculature, Grimaldus's neck would have snapped as soon as the boosters fired to bring them both stable.

They were still falling too fast, even with the jump-pack's engines howling hot.

'Acknowledged, Jurisian,' the Reclusiarch breathed. *Of all the accursed times...*

Grimaldus grunted at the weight of Troven's armour. His pistol dangled on its wrist-bound chain, while he gripped the other knight's vambrace. Troven, in turn, hung in the air, holding to Grimaldus's own wrist. Their burning tabards slapped against their armour, caught in the wind.

With retinal gauges flashing scarlet, the Reclusiarch and the prone knight descended into the atmosphere of black smoke rising from the docks. Before their vision was blocked entirely, Grimaldus saw Troven reaching with his free hand, drawing the gladius sheathed to his thigh.

Interference crackled thick from the surrounding chaos, but Bastilan's vox-voice made it through the distortion, coloured by brutal eagerness.

'We saw that, Reclusiarch. Dorn's blood, we all saw it.'

'Then you are unfocussed on the battle, and will do penance for it.'

He bunched his muscles, negating thrust in the moment before thudding into the ground with bone-shaking force. The two knights skidded across the rockcrete surface of the docks, sparks spraying from their armour.

As they both regained their footing, the hulking silhouettes of alien beasts ambled through the surrounding smoke.

'For Dorn and the Emperor!' Troven cried, and brought his bolter to bear from where it hung at his side, forever bound to his armour by the ritual chains. Grimaldus twinned his cries with Troven's, laying into the enemy.

If these docks could be saved, then by the Throne, they would be.

SIXTEEN

A TURNING TIDE

A wing of fighters bolted overhead, their engines leaving smoke-smears across the darkening sky. In pursuit, alien craft rattled after them, tracer rounds spitting across the clouds in futility as they tried to hunt the Imperial fighters back to one of the city's few remaining airstrips.

Beneath the aerial chase, Helsreach burned. Avenue by avenue, alley by alley, the invaders flooded through the docks district, gaining ground with the death of every defender.

Where the fighting was fiercest, vox-contact was a broken, unreliable mess of lucky signals breaking through the interference. The Imperials fell back through the night, sector by sector, leaving thoroughfares packed with their dead. The city added new scents to its reek of sulphur and saltwater. Now, Helsreach had come to smell of blood and flame, of a hundred thousand lives ending in fire between a single sunrise and sunset. Poets from the impious ages of Old Terra had written of a punitive afterlife, a hell beneath the world's surface. Had that realm ever existed, it would have smelled like this industrial city, dying in fire on the shores of Armageddon Secundus.

In unconnected catacombs below the ground, the citizens of Helsreach remained shielded from the slaughter above. They clustered together in the darkness, listening to the erratic drumbeat of factories, workshops, tanks and munitions stores exploding. Although the walls of the subterranean shelters shook with tremors that bled down through the ground, the booms and thumps on the surface echoed down like peals of thunder. Many parents told their young children that it was just a violent storm above.

Across the embattled world, the besieged cities were visible from orbit as blackened patches scarring the planet's surface. As the planetary assault entered its second month, Armageddon's atmosphere was turning thick and sour with smoke from the burning hives.

Helsreach itself no longer resembled a city. With the docks under siege, the last pristine sectors of the hive were aflame, wreathing the city in a black pall born of burning oil refineries.

The hive's spine, Hel's Highway, was a wounded serpent winding through the city. Its skin was mottled with patches of light and dark: pale and grey where the fighting had ceased, leaving graveyards of silent tanks, and blackened where conflict still raged, pitting the armoured fist of the Steel Legion against the junk-tanks of the invading beasts.

The city walls were half-fallen, resembling some archaeological ruin. Half of the hive was surrendered, abandoned to defeat's lifeless silence. The other half, held by Imperial forces that diminished by the hour, burned in battle.

And so dawned the thirty-seventh day.

'Hey, no sleep for you.'

Andrej kicked at Maghernus's shin, jolting the dockmaster back to the waking world. 'We must move soon, I am thinking. No time for sleeping.'

Tomaz blinked the stickiness of exhaustion from his eyes. He'd not even realised he'd fallen asleep. The two of them were crouched behind a stack of crates in a warehouse with the remaining nine men of Maghernus's dock gang. He met their faces now, each in turn, barely recognising any of them. A day of war had aged them all, gifting them with sunken eyes and soot-blackened skin that brought out the lines in their middle-aged faces.

'Where are we going?' Maghernus whispered back. The storm trooper had removed his goggles to wipe his own aching eyes. They'd not slept – they'd barely even stopped fighting – in over twenty hours.

'My captain wishes us to move west. There are civilian shelters above ground there.'

One of the men hawked and spat on the ground. His eyes were red-rimmed and bloodshot. Andrej didn't think any less of him for the fact he'd been weeping.

'West?' the man asked.

'West,' Andrej said again. 'That is my captain's order, and that is what we will do.'

'But the beasts are already there. We saw them.'

'I did not say the order was what I wished to do with my retirement years. I said it was an order, and obeying orders is what we are going to do.'

'But if the aliens are already there...' another worker piped up, snapping Andrej's patience.

'Then we will be behind enemy lines and see many dead civilians we were too late to save. Throne, you think I have good answers for you all? I do not. I have no good answers, not for you, not for anyone else. But my captain has ordered us to go there, and go there we most certainly shall. Yes? Yes.'

It did the trick. A ghost of focus returned to their slack, weary gazes.

'Let's do it, then,' Maghernus said, his knees clicking as he rose up. He was amazed he could still stand. 'Blood of the Emperor, I've never ached like this.'

'Why are you complaining, I wonder,' the storm trooper refastened his goggles with a grin. 'You worked insane shifts on these docks. This is surely no more tiring, I think.'

'Yeah,' one of the others grunted, 'but we were getting paid then.'

With muted laughter, the team moved back out onto the docks.

Colonel Sarren's injured arm was securely fastened in a makeshift sling. What annoyed him most was the loss of his right arm to gesture with to the hololithic display, but then, that was the price to pay for foolishly leaving the *Grey Warrior* in hostile territory. Shrapnel in the arm was a lucky break, all things considered. The enemy sniper team had killed four of his Baneblade's command crew as they surfaced from the bowels of their tank for much-needed fresh air after countless hours breathing the rank, recycled fumes of the internal filtration scrubbers.

Another sector cleared, only to be wormed through again by bestial scavengers mere hours later.

In the low-ceilinged confines of the tank's principal command chamber, Sarren sat on his well-worn throne, letting the tension ebb from him and trying to forget the column of pain that had been a perfectly normal arm only an hour before. The sawbones, Jerth, had already recommended amputation, citing the risk of infection from dirty shrapnel and the likelihood the limb would never return to – as he put it – 'full functionality.'

Bloody surgeons. Always so keen to graft on some cheap, jury-rigged bionic that would click every time he moved a muscle and seize up because of low-grade components. Sarren was no stranger to augmetics in the Guard, and they were a far cry from the modifications afforded to the rich and decadent.

He stared at the hololithic table now, watching the docks recede from Imperial control with agonising, desperate slowness. Seeing the flickering regiment runes and location sigils, it was hard to translate the skeletal vision to the fierce fighting that was truly taking place.

More and more Steel Legion infantry units were reaching the docks, but it was like holding the sea back with a bucket. The Guardsmen being sent in did little but bolster the general retreat. Reclaiming ground was a distant fiction.

'Sir?' the vox-officer called out. Sarren looked over to him, drawn from his reverie, not realising the man had been trying to get his attention for almost a minute.

'Yes?'

'Word from orbit. The Imperial fleet is reengaging again.'

Sarren made the sign of the aquila – at least, he tried to, and ended with a grunt of pain as his bound arm flared up in pained protest. One-handed, he made a single wing of the Imperial eagle instead.

'Acknowledged. May the Emperor be with them all.'

This scarce acknowledgement made, he lapsed back into watching the deployment of his forces throughout the city. Around him, the tank's crew worked at their stations.

So the Imperial fleet was reengaging.

Again.

Every few days, the same story played out. The joint Astartes and Naval fleet would break from the warp close to the planet, and hurl themselves at the ork vessels ringing the embattled world. The engagement would hold for several hours as both sides inflicted horrendous losses on the other, but the Imperials would inevitably be hurled back into a fighting retreat by the immense opposition.

Once they'd fallen back to the safety of a nearby system, they'd regroup over time, under the command of Admiral Parol and High Marshal Helbrecht, and make ready for another assault. It was blunt, and crudely effective. In a void war of such magnitude, there was little place for finesse. Sarren wasn't blind to the tactics at play – lance strikes into the heart of the enemy fleet, bleed them for all that was possible before a retreat back to safety. It was a necessary grind, a war of attrition.

It was also hardly inspiring. The hive cities were on the edge now. Without reinforcements in the coming weeks, many would fall outright. The infrequent transmissions from Tartarus, Infernus and Acheron were all increasingly grim, as were Sarren's reports of Helsreach to them.

If there was no–

'Sir?'

Sarren glanced to his left, to where the vox-officer sat at his station. The man held his headphone receivers to his ear with one hand. He looked pale.

'Emergency signal from the *Serpentine* in orbit. She requests immediate cessation of all anti-air weaponry in the docks district.'

Sarren sat forward in his chair. There was barely any anti-air firepower left in the docks district, but that wasn't the point.

'What did you say?'

'The *Serpentine,* Astartes strike cruiser, sir. She requests–'

'Throne, send the order. Send the order! Deactivate all remaining anti-air turrets in the docks district!'

Around him, the tank's crew was silent. Waiting, watching.

Sarren breathed a single word, almost fearful giving voice to it would shatter the possibility it was true.

'Reinforcements...'

One ship.

The *Serpentine.*

Sea green and charcoal black, it dived like a dragon of myth through the enemy fleet while the rest of the Imperial warships hammered into the orkish invaders, breaking against the ring of alien cruisers surrounding the planet.

One ship broke through, running a gauntlet of enemy fire, its shields crackling into lifelessness and its hull aflame. The *Serpentine* hadn't come to fight. As the Astartes vessel tore through the upper atmosphere, drop-pods and Thunderhawks rained from its ironclad belly, streaming down to the world below.

Its duty complete, the *Serpentine* powered its way back into the fight. Its captain gritted his teeth against a screed of damage reports signalling the death of his beloved ship, but there was no shame in dying with such a vital duty done. He had acted under the orders of the highest authority – a warrior on the surface below whose deeds were already inscribed in a hundred annals of Imperial glory. That warrior had demanded this risk be taken, and that reinforcements be hurled down to the Armageddon no matter the odds facing them.

His name was Tu'Shan, Lord of the Fire-born, and the *Serpentine* did his will.

The *Serpentine's* end never came. A black shape eclipsed the fat-hulled orkish destroyers cutting the Astartes vessel to pieces. Another ship, a far greater ship, pounded the alien attackers into wreckage with overwhelming broadside fire, buying the *Serpentine* the precious moments it needed to escape the gauntlet it had run a second time.

As they broke clear, the *Serpentine's* captain breathed out a prayer, and signalled across the bridge to the master of communications.

'Send word to the *Eternal Crusader,*' he said. 'Give them the sincerest thanks of our Chapter.'

The response from the *Eternal Crusader* came back almost immediately. The grim voice of High Marshal Helbrecht echoed across the *Serpentine's* bridge.

'It is the Black Templars that thank you, Salamander.'

The beasts have cracked open another of the above-ground civilian shelters.

Like blood spilling from a wound, humans flood into the streets through the destroyed wall. When the choices are to die cowering, or die fleeing to a safety that may not even exist, any human can be forgiven for giving in to panic. I tell myself this as I watch them dying, and do all I can not to judge them, to hold them to the exalted standards of honour I would demand of my brothers. They're just human. My disgust is unfair, unwarranted. And yet it remains.

As they die, families and souls of all ages, they squeal like butchered swine.

This war is poisonous. Trapped here, locked away from my Chapter, my mind echoes with bleak prejudices. It is becoming hard to accept that I must die for these people to live.

'Attack,' I tell my brothers, my voice barely carrying over the ranting of the engine. Together, we run from the moving Rhino transport, smashing into the enemy's rearguard.

My crozius rises and falls, as it has risen and fallen ten thousand times in the last month. The adamantium eagle chimes as it cuts through the air. It flares with unleashed energy as its power field connects with flesh and armour. The brazier orb built into the weapon's pommel breathes sacred incense in a grey mist, like coils of smoke weaving between us all – friend and foe.

The weariness ebbs. The grudges fade. Hatred is the greatest purifier, the truest emotion overriding all others. Blood, stinking and inhuman, rains across my armour in discoloured spurts. As it marks the black cross I wear on my chest, my revulsion flares anew.

Crunch. The crozius maul ends another alien's life. *Crunch.* Another. My mentor, the great Mordred the Black, wielded this weapon in battle against mankind's foes for almost four centuries. It sickens me to know it may never be recovered from Helsreach. Nor our armour. Nor our gene-seed. What legacy will we leave once the last of us falls to the filthy blades of these beasts?

One of them roars into my face, spattering my visor with his unclean saliva. Less than a second later, my crozius annihilates his features, silencing whatever pathetic alien challenge I was supposed to be answering.

My secondary heart has joined the primary. I feel them thudding in concert, but not in unison. My human heart pounds like a tribal drum, fast and hot. Twinned to it in my chest, my gene-grown heart supports it in a slow, heavy thud.

They swarm over each other in their mindless fervour to claw at us. Fistfuls of scrap metal that have no right to function as weapons cough solid rounds that clang off our armour. Each shot tears more of the black paint from our war plate but sheds none of Dorn's holy blood.

At last, they recognise the threat we represent. The aliens abandon their wanton slaughter of the fleeing civilians that still spill from the shell-broken wall. The mob of beasts, flooding the street, has turned to more tempting prey. Us.

Our banner falls.

Artarion's cry of pain carries across the close-range vox as a roar of distortion, but I hear his voice beneath the interference.

Priamus is with him before the rest of us can react. Throne, he can fight. His blade lunges and cuts, every gesture a killing blow.

'Get up,' he snarls at Artarion without even looking.

I crash the faceplate of my helm into the barking maw of the alien before me, shattering his jaw and the rows of shark-like teeth. As he falls back, my crozius crunches into his throat, hammering his wrecked corpse to the ground.

The banner rises again, though Artarion favours his left leg. The right is mauled, his thigh punctured by an alien spear. Curse the fact these beasts have the strength to violate Astartes war plate.

Another vox-distorted growl signifies Artarion has pulled the lance free from his leg. I have no time to witness his recovery. More beasts shriek before me – a thrashing wall of sick, jade flesh.

'We're losing this road,' Bastilan grunts, his signal marred by the sound of weapons crashing against his armour. 'We are but six, against a legion.'

'Five.' Nerovar's voice is strained as he fights with his chainblade two-handed, hewing down the beasts with none of Priamus's artistry but no less fury. 'Cador is dead.'

'Forgive me, brother,' Bastilan's voice breaks off as he fires a stream of bolter shells at point-blank range. 'A moment's lack of focus.'

Ahead, our targets – three junkyard tanks that have long since ceased to resemble their original Imperial Guard hulls – continue shelling the shelter block. These have none of the security offered by the subterranean shelters, for they are not civilian evacuation shelters at all. Each of these squat domes houses a thousand at capacity, designed to resist violent sandstorms and the tropical cyclones all too common on the equatorial coast – not sustained shelling from enemy armour. They are used now because there is nothing else to use, with the city grown far beyond its capacity to shelter all its citizens beneath the ground.

The beasts know us well. They seek to draw the city's forces into the most fevered fighting, so they hurl themselves at our defenceless civilians with sick cunning, knowing we will do all we can to defend these sites above any others.

How easy it is, to despise them.

'Gnnh,' Nerovar voxes, his voice wet and ruined by pain. I vault the falling corpse of the alien closest to me, and stand by his side – maul swinging with relentless motion – as our Apothecary struggles to rise again.

He fails. The beasts have brought him to his knees.

'Gnnnnnh. Not coming out,' he coughs. His hands clutch weakly at the axe hammered into his stomach. His gauntlets stroke without strength along the haft, gaining no grip. Blood from the sunder in his armour is painting his tabard scarlet. 'Can't do it.'

'In the name of the Emperor,' my chastisement comes forth as no more than a low growl, 'stand and fight, or we all die.'

With Nerovar wounded and prone, he becomes a lodestone for the creatures desperate to deliver the death blow to one of the Emperor's knights. They bellow and charge.

My crozius kills one. A kick to the sternum sends another staggering back long enough for me to bring the maul down on his head. A third is claimed by plasma fire, tumbling back as a blur of white-hot flame. Stinging ash, all that remains of the wretched alien, blasts back into the eyes of its bestial comrades.

Too many.

Even for us, this is too many.

I have a momentary glimpse of human families fleeing in all directions down the burning streets, able to escape while the horde focuses its fury on us. Several of the civilians are cut down by sponson fire from the junk-tanks, but many more survive – even if only to run blind into the unsafe labyrinth of their dying city. Before this war, I would never have counted such a thing to be a victory.

With a cry that mixes anger and pain, Nero tears the axe blade from his abdomen. Any relief I feel is swallowed, for he has no time to rise before the beasts are on us.

'I see some knights,' Andrej said. This announcement was followed by a whispered *'Damn it,'* and the humming of his hellgun powering up again.

The work gang kept their backs to the rooftop's low wall, with only Andrej peering over the edge to look down into the street. 'Everybody, load rifles and be very ready.'

'How many?' Maghernus asked. 'How many knights?'

'Four. No, five. One is injured. I also see thirty of the enemy, and three tanks that were once our Leman Russes. Now, no more talking. Everybody take aim.'

The dockworkers did as ordered, drawing beads on the melee unfolding below.

'Aim low,' Maghernus told his men, drawing a silent smile from Andrej. 'Aim for legs and torsos.' No one needed to be told to be careful with their fire and not hit the Templars.

The storm trooper fired first, his bright lance of laser the signal for the others to join in. Lasguns bucked in increasingly sure hands, focusing lenses burning as they spat their lethal energy into the street below. The tearing laser fire punched into shoulders, legs, backs and arms, and the Imperials had managed three volleys before the beasts ripped their hungry attention from the knights and returned fire up at the men crouching on the warehouse rooftop.

'Down!' Andrej ordered the others. They obeyed, sinking back into cover. The storm trooper hunched lower, but remained where he was. He risked another shot, and another, splitting two aliens through the skull with pinpoint fire.

Around him, around them all, the low wall edging the roof was shredding under the surviving aliens' fire, but it didn't matter. The knights were free. Andrej crouched at last, after seeing the figure of one Templar, the knight's armour more gunmetal grey than black now from battle damage, hurl aside three attackers and lay waste to them with his monstrous, crackling relic hammer.

His last act before falling back was to untrap his last det-pack, and set the timer for six seconds. With a roar of effort, Andrej hurled it down at street towards the tanks. It exploded a half-second after clanging against the lead tank's turret, decapitating the war machine in a burst of noise and fire.

The Templars could deal with the other two.

'Back!' the storm trooper was laughing. 'Back across the roof!'

'What the hell is so funny?' one of the dockworkers, Jassel, was complaining as they ran in crouches away from the disintegrating roof edge.

'They weren't just knights,' Andrej's voice was coloured by a sincere grin. 'That was the Reclusiarch we just saved. Now, quick quick, down to the street again.'

In the calm that followed, the streets gave birth to an atmosphere that was somewhere between serene and funereal. A very different warrior greeted Maghernus this time. The towering figure was far from the regal, impassive statue that merely acknowledged his existence with a nod.

The Reclusiarch's armour still set his teeth on edge, its active hum making his eyes water if he stood too close. But Maghernus knew machines, even if he didn't know ancient artefacts of war, and he could hear the faults in the war plate now. Its once-smooth, angry purr had a waspish edge to its tone now, and intermittent clicks told of something internal no longer running at full function. The joints of the battered armour no longer snarled with tensing fibre-cable muscles – they growled, as if reluctant to move.

Five weeks. Five weeks of fighting, night and day, in the same suit of armour, with the dock assault rising as the most punishing week yet. It was a miracle the armour still functioned at all.

The tabard was ripped and stained grey-green with alien blood. The scrolls that had adorned the warrior's shoulders were gone, with only snapped chains showing they were ever held there at all. The armour itself was still impressive in its violent potential and faceless inhumanity, but where it had been blacker than black before the war, most of the blackness remaining was from scorch marks and laser burns marking the armour like bruises and claw wounds. Much of the war plate was revealed in a dull, unpolished grey now that the paint was lost to a thousand weapon chops and glancing gunshots.

Somehow, it had the inelegant presence of a rifle or tank churned out of an Armageddon factory: plain, simple, but utterly brutal.

The other Templars looked no better. The one who bore the Reclusiarch's standard now bore battle damage akin to his leader. The banner itself was a ragged ruin, little more than scraps hanging from the pole. The one with the white helm was barely able to stand, supported by two of the others. The voice that rasped from his mouth grille was a wordless, hacking cough.

And rather than humanise them, rather than reveal the warriors beneath the trappings and the knightly war gear, this damage instead stole what little personality had ever been in evidence to human eyes. How could any men, even ones shaped by genetic forges on a distant world, withstand so much punishment and survive? How could they stand before others of their own species and seem so utterly unlike them?

'Hello, Reclusiarch,' said Andrej. He carried his hellgun, uncharged now, resting on his shoulder. He thought this made him look rakish and casual, and he was right. He looked that way to the dockworkers, at least.

Grimaldus's voice didn't growl or boom – it intoned, a low and bleak and grim drawl. It was all too easy to imagine this man back aboard a great, gothic warship, speaking a sermon to his brothers in the endless cold of void travel.

'You have the thanks of the Black Templars, storm trooper. And you, dockworkers of Helsreach.'

'It was good timing, I think,' Andrej continued, a vague nod and the same smile showing he thought nothing of conversations with badly-wounded towering inhuman warriors surrounded by slaughtered aliens. 'But the docks, they are not looking good. I am hearing no orders anymore. So I see you, noble sirs, and I am wondering: perhaps they can give me orders.'

There was a pause, but not a silent one. The city was never silent, offering up a background chorus of gunfire rattles and the *crump* of distant explosions.

'All units are called to the shelter blocks. Guard, militia, Astartes. All.'

'Even without my captain's voice, we have followed that path. But there is more, sir.'

'Speak.' Grimaldus looked away now, the silver skull that served as his face glaring in the direction of a burning commerce district several streets away.

'One of your knights fell at the docks. We have hidden his body from the enemy jackals. The etchings on his armour named him as Anastus.'

The white-helmed Astartes spoke, his voice emerging like a man speaking through a mouthful of gruel.

'Anastus died... as we deployed... last night. Life signs faded fast. Warrior's death.'

Grimaldus nodded, his attention restored to the humans.

'What is your name?' the Reclusiarch asked the storm trooper.

'Trooper Andrej, 703rd Steel Legion Storm Trooper Division, sir.'

'And yours?' he asked the next man in line, taking every name until the last, whom he recognised without needing to ask. 'Dockmaster Tomaz Maghernus,' the knight grunted, finally. 'It is good to see you on the field. Courage such as yours belongs at the vanguard.'

Maghernus's skin crawled, not with distaste but raw awkwardness. How does one reply to such a thing? To say he was honoured? To admit that every muscle in his body ached and he regretted ever volunteering for this madness?

'Thank you, Reclusiarch,' he managed.

'I will remember your names and deeds this day. All of you. Helsreach may burn, but this war is not lost. Every one of your names will be etched into the black stone pillars of the Valiant Hall aboard the *Eternal Crusader*.'

Andrej nodded. 'I am very honoured, Reclusiarch, as are these handsome and fine gentlemen with me. But if you could tell my captain about this, I would be even happier.'

The harsh sound emitted from the Reclusiarch's vox-speakers was somewhere between a bark and a snarl. It took Maghernus several moments to realise it had been a laugh.

'It will be done, Trooper Andrej. You have my word.'

'I am hopeful this will also impress the lady I intend to marry.'

Grimaldus wasn't sure how to reply to that. He settled for 'Yes. Good.'

'Such optimism! But yes, I must find her first. Where do we move now, sir?'

'West. The shelters in Sulfa Commercia. The alien dogs are taunting us.' The Reclusiarch gestured with his massive hammer, the weapon's power field deactivated for now. Between warehouses and manufactories, distant domes were aflame.

'See them. Already, they burn.'

Priamus didn't look where the others did. His attention was lifted higher, to the smog-thick skies.

'What's that?' He gestured skyward, to a ball of flame trailing down. 'It can't be what it looks like.'

'It is,' Grimaldus replied, unable to look away from the sight.

'Ayah!' Andrej cheered as several similar objects appeared, blazing earthward, leading fiery contrails like comets.

'What are they?' asked Maghernus, caught off-guard by the storm trooper's capering and the knights' reverence.

'Drop-pods,' said the Reclusiarch. His silver skull turned amber with the reflection of the burning tank hulls nearby. 'Astartes drop-pods.'

SEVENTEEN

INTO THE FIRES OF BATTLE, UNTO THE ANVIL OF WAR

The Sulfa Commercia district had been a bastion of militia reserves and a strongpoint for the docks' anti-air defences.

The few turrets that remained atop buildings, both automated and manned, fell silent. Around them, the district burned. Above them, ork fighters and bombers dropped their payloads with abandon, barely held in check even when the defence turrets were operational.

Sulfa Commercia, as a trading hub for the western docks that was always densely populated in times of peace, was home to a particularly large concentration of above-ground storm shelters, most of which were already broken by the besieging orks. The enemy advance was at a standstill in this section of the dockyards, not because of Imperial resistance, but because there was so much blood to shed, and so much to destroy. To leave the area devoid of life and in utter ruin meant the aliens had to linger here, slaying with wild joy in their feral eyes.

When writing of the siege in a personal journal some years after the war, Major Lacus of the 61st Steel Legion lamented the 'unbelievable loss of life' that occurred with the dock breaches, citing the destruction of the Sulfa Commercia as 'among the bloodiest events in the Helsreach siege, which no man, no tank battalion, no legion of Titans could have dreamed of preventing.'

The trading concourse resembled little of its former grandeur. While warehouses were less in evidence here, the houses of the wealthy mercantile families of Helsreach burned just as well, and those citizens that had elected to remain in their homes rather than seek out the subterranean municipal shelters now fell to the same fate as the civilians trapped in the cracked-open storm shelters. The aliens descended without mercy, and no contingent of house guards, no matter how well-trained they were, were capable of defending their lords' estates against the xenos tide that swarmed the docks districts.

The most notable defence – one that captured the spirit of defiance surging throughout the hive's stunted propaganda machine – was not, as might be suspected, the one that inflicted greatest harm upon the enemy. The estate defence that did the most damage numerically-speaking was performed by the House Farwellian Constabulary, employed for seven generations by the noble Farwell bloodline. Their extended survival wasn't quite the soul-lifting story that Commissar Falkov and Colonel Sarren were seeking, as the esteemed House Farwell were, in truth, considered decadent pigs in the public eye, and its various scions were no strangers to political scandal, financial investigation, and rumours of trade double-dealing. In short, they performed so well in this district war because they had shrewdly cheated their way to immense wealth, and had a standing army of six hundred soldiers at their beck and call.

A standing army that, it was noted in Imperial records, the Farwells refused to lend to the defence of the docks or the city's militia.

This sizable force was also their bane. As words flashed through the orkish ranks that there was a nexus of defence formed at the House Farwell compound, the aliens stormed it en masse, ending the tenacious resistance – and the bloodline itself.

The most notable defence, as stated, was a far cry from this exercise in doomed selfishness. House Tarracine, with only five off-world mercenaries hired as protection, defended their modest estate through a series of guerrilla strikes and automated security traps for nineteen hours. Although their home was destroyed by the invaders, seven family members emerged unscathed in the days after the dock battle, leaving them in a relatively strong position for the rebuilding of the city, with Lord Helius Tarracine's four daughters suddenly pursued with great vigour by weakened and heirless noble bloodlines.

At shelter CC/46, one of the few shelters still intact as the second day of the dock war stretched on, annihilation was averted at the very last moment.

The first drop-pod came down with a thunderbolt's force, striking into the roadway leading to the front doors of the sanctuary dome. The ork rabble that had been clamouring in the street was thrown into disarray, and several of the beasts were incinerated in the pod's retro burst or crushed beneath its hammering weight.

The pod's sides blasted open, slamming down into descent ramps which pulverised the beasts that had recovered enough to start beating their axe blades against the green hull.

Across the docks, several more pods rained down, their arrival mirroring the destruction unleashed by the first.

With bolters raised, crashing out round after round, and flamers breathing dragon's breath in hissing gouts of chemical fire, the Salamanders joined their Templar brothers in defence of Hive Helsreach.

'We are seventy in number,' he says to me. Seven squads.

His name is V'reth, a sergeant of the Salamanders' 6th Company. Before I speak, he says something both humbling and unexpectedly respectful. 'I am honoured to fight at your side, Reclusiarch Grimaldus.'

This confession throws me, and I am not certain I keep my surprise from my voice when I reply.

'The Templars are in your debt. But tell me, brother, why you have come?'

Around us, my knights and V'reth's warriors stalk among the dead and the dying, slaying wounded orks with sword thrusts to exposed throats. The storm trooper and his dockworkers follow suit, using the bayonets of their rifles.

V'reth disengages his helm's seals and lifts it clear. Even having served with the Salamanders before, it is difficult to look upon one of the sons of Nocturne and feel nothing at all. The gene-seed of their primarch reacts to their home world's viciously radioactive surface. The pigmentation of V'reth's skin is the same charcoal-black as every unhelmeted warrior of the Chapter I've ever seen. His eyes lack pupils and irises. Instead, V'reth stares out at the world around us through orbs of ember red, as if blood has filled his eye sockets and discoloured his eyes in the process.

His true voice is a low, aural embodiment of the igneous rock that leaves the surface of his home world dark, barren and grey. It is all too easy to see how these warriors come from a world of lava rivers and volcanic mountain ranges that turn the sky black.

'We were the last of the Salamanders in orbit. The Lord of the Fire-born called us to him, and we obeyed.'

I am familiar with the title. I have heard their Chapter Master referred to by this name many times before.

'Master Tu'Shan, may the Emperor continue to favour him, fights far from here, brother. The Salamanders bleed the enemy many leagues to the east, and the Hemlock river runs black with alien blood.'

V'reth inclines his head in a solemn nod, and his red-eyed gaze rises to take in the shelter dome at the end of this very street.

'This is so, and it gladdens me to know my brothers fight well enough to earn such words from you, Reclusiarch. The Lord of the Fire-born makes his stand with the war engines of Legios Ignatum and Invigilata.'

'So answer my question, for time is not our ally. Helsreach burns. Will you stay? Will you fight with us?'

'We will not stay. We cannot stay.'

I bite back the wrath that rises from disappointment, and the Salamander continues, 'We are the seventy warriors chosen to make planetfall here and stand with you until the docks are held. My lord and master heard of the assured civilian devastation in the fall of this city's coastal districts.'

'Few messages reach the ears of our allies elsewhere in the world. Few messages from them reach us.'

'The Salamanders were not blind to your plight, honoured Reclusiarch. Master Tu'Shan heard. We are his blade, his will, to ensure the survival of the city's most innocent souls.'

'And then you will leave.'

'And then we will leave. Our fight is along the banks of the Hemlock. Our glory is there.'

This gesture alone is enough to earn my eternal gratitude. For the first time in decades, emotion steals the words I wish to voice. This is all we needed. This is salvation.

We can hurt them now.

I remove my own helm, breathing in the first taste of Helsreach's sulphuric air in... weeks. Months.

V'reth inhales deeply, doing the same.

'This city,' he smiles, teeth white against his onyx features, 'it smells like home.'

The heated wind feels good on my skin. I offer my hand to V'reth, and he grips my wrist – an alliance between warriors.

'Thank you,' I tell him, meeting his inhuman eyes.

'If you are needed elsewhere,' V'reth matches my gaze with his own, 'then go to your duty, honoured Reclusiarch. We stand with you, for now. And together, we will not let these docks fall.'

'First, tell me of the orbital war. What news of the *Crusader*?'

'The deadlock remains. It grieves me to say this, but it is so. We are shattering the enemy, battle by battle, but it is like hurling fire at stone. Little is achieved against such an overwhelming foe. It will take weeks before your High Marshal dares a full assault to reclaim the heavens. He is a shrewd warrior. My brothers and I were honoured to serve with him in the fleet.'

To hear his words is like a lifeline. A connection to existence beyond the broken walls of this accursed city. I press him for more.

'What of Tempestus Hive? They suffered as we did.'

'Fallen. Lost to the enemy, its forces in retreat. The last word from any remnant of command structure was that the city was being abandoned, and its retreating survivors were making their way overland to connect with the Guard regiments serving alongside my lord and master.'

Scattered defence forces and Guard units, crossing hundreds of kilometres of wasteland. Such tenacity was to be admired.

This world will never recover, that much is clear. Fatalism may not be bred into my bones, but there is no valour in living a lie. What we do here is defiance – the selling of life as dearly as possible. We are not fighting to win, but waging war out of spite.

This Salamander, brother though he may be, has a destiny beyond this city. I relent to it.

'Coordinate the dispersal of squads with Sergeant Bastilan. Focus your efforts on the westernmost districts, where the bulk of storm shelters are to be found. Bastilan will provide you with the required vox frequencies to connect with the storm troopers leading the civilian defences. Do not expect clarity in communications. Many of the city's vox-relay towers have fallen.'

'It will be done, Reclusiarch.'

'For the Emperor.' I release V'reth's wrist. His reply is a curious one, betraying his Chapter's unique focus.

'For the Emperor,' he says, 'and His people.'

Jurisian, Master of the Forge and knight of the Emperor, threw his head back and laughed. He had not laughed in many years, for he was not a soul given to humour. What he was seeing now however struck him as immensely funny. So he laughed, without meaning to.

The sound echoed throughout the immense chamber, resounding off metal-reinforced walls of stone and the hulking adamantium shape that stretched for fifty metres into the darkness.

The Ordinatus Armageddon. *Oberon.*

Jurisian's armour had been the only sound in the chamber for hours, the overlaid ceramite plating clacking and whirring as he moved around the great weapon. He'd circled it several dozen times, staring, scanning, taking in every detail with his own eyes and his war plate's auspex sensors.

It was, without question, the most beautiful creation he had ever laid his augmetic eyes upon.

In aesthetics, perhaps it would not appeal to a poet or a painter. But that was hardly the point. In power, it would appeal to any general in the Imperium. It was a triumph of design and intent, a glorious success in mankind's quest to master a greater ability to destroy its enemies.

The great construct consisted of a strong, three-sectioned base that held up a weapons platform on gantries and struts. Atop the platform was the weapon itself. Jurisian considered each aspect of the war machine in turn, silent in its deactivation.

From the front, *Oberon* was as wide as two bulky Land Raider battle tanks side by side. Its length was fifty metres in total, giving it the appearance of a land train, long and segmented. Immense to say the least, it was of approximate size to a towering battle Titan lying on its back.

The war machine's base was divided into three sections – a helm segment, the drive module, with a reinforced cockpit chamber; a thorax section next, pinned under the weight of massive metal stanchions; lastly, an abdomen segment, bearing the same weight as the section before. Each of these base sections was bulked up further by side-mounted power generators, shielded behind yet more armour plating. These, Jurisian knew, were the gravitational suspensor generators. Anti-gravitational technology on such a scale was no longer heard of in the Imperium, except for the deployment of war machines of this calibre.

These generators' rarity made them the most precious thing on the entire planet, bar nothing.

The stanchions and gantries supported the colossal weapons platform, which in turn housed dozens of square metres of energy pods, fusion chambers and magnetic field generators. It was as if an industrial manufactorum had been installed on the back of a column of tanks.

These generators would, if active, supply power to the land train's weapon mount: a tower of a cannon forged of heat-shielded ceramite and joined to the forward power generators. Coolant vents ran the length of the cannon like reptilian scales. Like parasitic worms, nests of secondary power feed cables hung from the barrel, while industrial support claws held the weapon in place.

A nova cannon. A weapon used by starships to end one another across the immensity of the void. Here it was, mounted on priceless and infinitely-armoured anti-gravitational technology from a forgotten age.

'Titan-killer,' the Master of the Forge whispered.

Jurisian reverently stroked his gloved fingertips down the drive section's metallic skin, feeling the thick armour plating, the chunky rivets... down to the miniscule differences in the layers of adamantium: the tiniest variations and imperfections from its forging process hundreds of years before.

He'd withdrawn his hand, and that was when he'd laughed.

Oberon, the Death of Titans. It was real. It was here.

And it was his.

He gained access to the forward command module through a ladder leading to a bulkhead that required opening manually. Once inside the powerless cockpit chamber, Jurisian spared a glance for the winches, levers and black, blank screens along the drive console. It was all new, all alien to him, but nothing he considered beyond his intuition and Mechanicus training. Another bulkhead barred his way to the second module. With the Ordinatus powered down, this one also required him to manually turn the iron wheel on its surface.

The door squealed open with the reluctance of an unused airlock. Jurisian's gaze pierced the blackness beyond with aid from his helm's vision filters. It was confined and claustrophobic, despite there being little in the module beyond armoured pods fixed to the walls that housed the power generators for the anti-grav lifters, and crew ladders leading up into the main generatorium on the platform above. Jurisian ascended, opening another two bulkheads as he rose through the support gantries.

The innards of the platform-top generatorium were familiar enough in their cluttered, industrial layout. He stood within the heart of a spaceship's weapon system, condensed to offer less range and power, but on a more manoeuvrable and manageable scale. The projectiles from this sacred cannon didn't, after all, have to travel across thousands of kilometres of open space to strike a target.

It was, bluntly speaking, the sawn-off shotgun of nova cannon technology. The notion brought a smile to Jurisian's mirthless lips.

It took a further three hours of investigation, feed-checks and generator testing to ascertain whether the Ordinatus Armageddon could be reactivated, and how such a feat could be achieved.

The result at the close of the investigations was a bittersweet one.

This weapon of war should have been crewed by dozens of specialist skitarii, magi and tech-adepts, born and raised for this purpose above all others. It should have been ritually blessed by the Lord of the Centurio Ordinatus and its newest duty inscribed upon its hull alongside the ninety-three prayers of reawakening.

Instead of the chanting and worship due to the spirit of such a war engine, the soul of *Oberon* awoke in silence and darkness. Its vague, reforming consciousness did not detect a gestalt host of abased Centurio Ordinatus minds supplicating themselves for its attention, but a single other soul in union with its own.

This soul was strong: ironclad and dominant.

It identified itself as Jurisian.

In the drive module, his brain, spine and body armour linked via telemetry cables to the interface feeds in the princeps throne, the Master of the Forge closed his eyes. Around him, the systems flared into life. Scanners chimed as they began to see again. Overhead lights flickered and held at low illumination settings.

With a great shudder and the accompanying thrumming of power generators coming back to life, all three modules shook once, twice, and jolted hard.

In the drive section, Jurisian lurched in his seat. He hadn't jolted forward, but *up*.

Five metres up.

There the modules remained, cradled on a pulsing anti-grav field that distorted the ground below with something that was, and was not, a heat-shimmer.

'Activation Phase One,' the war machine's voice issued from vox-speakers around the command module.

Beneath the mechanical tone seethed a roiling, uncoiling hatred. Jurisian bowed his head in respect, but did not cease his work.

'My brothers call me to Helsreach,' he spoke into the cold control pod, expecting no answer and receiving none. 'And though that may mean nothing, I know that war calls to you.'

Through the interface connection, the spirit of *Oberon* growled, the sound inhuman and untranslatable.

Jurisian nodded. 'I thought so.'

Asavan Tortellius lingered over a single phrase.

He had no idea how to describe just how cold he was.

Around him, the deserted cathedral still bore more than its share of wall scars and battle damage. On a fallen block of masonry, the acolyte composed his memoirs of the Helsreach war, while the great Titan pitched slowly forward and back in the rough rhythm of walking. Occasionally, air pressure and gravity would exert themselves on his left or right side, as *Stormherald* rounded a corner. As he had done for years, Asavan ignored these things.

The ruined cathedral around him was altogether harder to ignore. It still appeared much as it had over thirty days ago, when the alien brutes had brought the god-machine to its knees. The statues still lay as alabaster corpses in broken, facedown repose, limbs cracked off to lie several metres distant. The walls were still decorated by gunfire holes and ugly cracks that cobwebbed outwards from impact points. The stained glass windows – his only succour from the irritation of the Shield above – were still gaping holes in the war-blackened architecture, as unpleasant to look upon as missing teeth in the smile of a saint.

Day in, day out, Asavan sat in the lonely, contemplative quiet of the cathedral, and composed what he knew full well were poorly-worded poems commemorating the coming victory in Hive Helsreach. He would destroy well over half of what he wrote, sometimes wincing as he reread the words he'd brought into being.

But of course, there was no one else to witness them. Not here.

The cathedral had stood almost empty since it had been besieged. The Templars had come, 'in purity, protecting us; in wrath, indefatigable,' Asavan had written (before deleting the cringe-worthy words forever), but they had come too late to do much more than preserve the wounded, hollow bones of *Stormherald's* monastery. Weeks had passed since. Weeks during which nothing had changed, nothing had been repaired.

Asavan was one of the few people still living in the cathedral. His fellows consisted mainly of servitors hardwired into the battlement turrets, slaved to the targeting and reloading systems along the walls. He saw these wretches often, because it had become his duty to keep them alive. The lobotomised, augmented once-humans were little more than limbless and slack-jawed automatons installed in life support cradles next to their turret cannons, and had no means to sustain their own existences. Several had lost their feed/waste bio connection cables with the damage taken in the siege, and even all these weeks later, the remaining magi in *Stormherald's* main body had not reached repairs so minor on the long list of abuses in need of correcting. Key systems took priority, and few enough Mechanicus adepts remained alive as it was. The fighting had been fierce below, as well.

So it fell to Asavan, as one of the few cathedral survivors, to spoonfeed these mindless creatures with soft protein-rich paste in order to keep them from dying, and flush their waste filters once a week.

He did this not because he was ordered to, or because he particularly cared about the continuing functionality of the handful of battlement cannons that were still unscathed. He did it because he was bored, and because he was lonely. It was the second week when he started talking to the unresponsive servitors. By the fourth, they all had names and backstories.

At first, Asavan had sought to order one of the seven medial servitors still patrolling the cathedral to perform these actions, but their programming was cripplingly limited. One was mono-tasked with walking from room to room, broom in hand, sweeping up any dust from the boots of the faithful.

Well, there were no faithful anymore. And the servitor had no broom. Asavan had known the servitor before his augmentation, as a particularly dull-witted acolyte that earned his fate for stealing coins from his lay-brothers. His punishment was to be rendered into a bionic slave, and Asavan had shed no tears at the time. Still, it was no joy to see the simple creature stagger from chamber to chamber, clacking the broken end of a brushless broomstick against the rubble-strewn ground, never getting closer to cleaning up the mess, and unable to rest until its duty was done. It refused orders to cease work, and Asavan suspected what was left of its mind had been broken at some point during the battle. An unnoticed head wound, perhaps.

Six weeks in, the servitor had collapsed in the middle of a row of broken pews, its human parts no longer able to function without rest. Asavan had done with it as he'd done with all of the slain. He and the handful of survivors threw the body overboard. A morbid curiosity (and one that he always regretted afterwards) compelled him to watch as the bodies fell fifty metres to rupture on the ground below. Asavan took no thrill or amusement from such sights, but found he could never look away. In work he quickly erased, he confessed to himself that seeing the bodies fall was a means of reminding himself he was still alive. Whatever the truth of the situation, the sights gave him nightmares. He wondered how soldiers could get used to such things, and why they would ever want to.

His main concern this past week was the cold.

With the Titan committed to battle for this prolonged engagement, the damage it had sustained in the ambush weeks ago was forever being repaired, compensated for, and re-aggravated by new war wounds sustained in the conflict. The command crew (*'blessings be upon them as they lead us to triumph,'* Asavan still whispered) were drawing ever-increasing maintenance attention and power from secondary systems throughout the Titan.

Minor systems went unrepaired by the adept tech-teams that were already spread thin throughout the gigantic construct and dealing with the vital systems. Some systems even went powerless as energy feeds were drained and disconnected, their thrumming fuel flooded to the plasma cells used to power the Shield and the main weapons.

A week ago, the heating systems to the cathedral had been drained to the point of no longer functioning. With typical Mechanicus efficiency, there were secondary and tertiary fallback options in the case of such a development. Unfortunately for Asavan and the few acolytes left alive up there, both the secondary and tertiary contingencies were lost. The secondary fallback had been a smaller, self-sustaining generator that fed itself from a power source reserve that was linked to nothing else, and could therefore never be drained for other purposes. The generator was now no more than scrap metal in the ruined mess that had once been the cathedral's maintenance deck.

The generator's destruction also annihilated the tertiary contingency plan, which was for four mono-tasked servitors – good for nothing else – to be activated and set to turn the generator's manual pumps by hand. Even if the generator had been fully functional, all four of the servitors were killed in the battle five weeks ago.

Asavan had gamely tried to turn the first of the hand-cranks himself, but lacking a servitor's strength meant all he achieved was a sore back. The crank never moved a centimetre.

So now, here he sat on a fallen pillar, trying to compose something to describe how bone-achingly cold he was, and how bone-achingly cold he had been for the last six days.

In place of organs, *Stormherald* possessed a generator core of intensely radioactive and fusion-hot plasma. Asavan found it a curious paradox that the heart of a sun was hermetically sealed and insulated many decks below him, yet here he was, on the edge of freezing to death.

These were the kinds of observations that he would write down, and then destroy in shame at daring to complain while so many innocent Imperial souls were out there in the burning city, dying moment by moment.

It was in that moment Asavan Tortellius decided he would change fate himself. He would not freeze to death on the Titan's back, in this hollow monastery. Nor would he gripe about the cold while thousands of deserving and loyal people died in their droves.

His fellow acolytes had never been kind to him regarding his intelligence, but people could say what they wished about his wits, slow or otherwise – Asavan liked to believe he always arrived at the right answer eventually. And now he had.

Yes. It was time to make a difference to the people of Helsreach.

It was time to leave the Titan.

EIGHTEEN

CONSOLIDATION

Three more nights passed as every day had passed before them. The docks were lost at dawn on the sixth day after the submersible assault.

The defeat was unusual enough to bring the Imperial commanders together again. Around the battle-damaged hull of the *Grey Warrior,* Sarren gathered the leaders. In the dawn gloom, most of the Guard colonels were dead on their feet with fatigue, several showing telltale signs of combat narcotics to keep them going – a twitch here, a shiver there. Overtaxed minds and muscles could only be kept active for so long, even with stimulants.

Sarren wouldn't reprimand them for this. In times of need, men did as they must in order to hold the line.

'We've lost the docks,' he said, and his voice was as tired and scratchy as he felt. This was not news to any of the gathered officers. As the colonel outlined the details of what little remained of the dock districts, a Chimera rumbled up to park in the *Grey Warrior's* shadow. The crew ramp slammed down, and two people disembarked. The first was Cyria Tyro, her uniform still clean but clearly ruffled from constant wear. The second was dressed in a pilot's grey flightsuit.

'I've found him,' Tyro said, leading the pilot to the gathered commanders.

'Captain Helius reporting,' the pilot saluted Sarren. 'Commander Jenzen died two nights ago, sir.'

Third in line, after Jenzen and Barasath? They were lucky to have any flyers left.

'A pleasure, captain.'

'As you say, sir.'

Sarren nodded, returning the aquila salute with his wounded arm still aching like a jungle wildfire. A morning breeze, chilling and unwelcome, gusted across the stretch of the Hel's Highway. The Baneblade's hull blocked most of the wind, but not enough as far as Sarren was concerned. Throne, he was tired of aching all over.

'Remaining forces?'

'Three airstrips, though it looks like the Gamma Road will fall today; it's been besieged for days now. At last count, we had twenty-six Lightnings remaining. Only seven Thunderbolts. Gamma Road is already being evacuated and the fighters are landing on the Vancia Chi Avenue.'

Sarren made a grumbling noise. He still lamented the loss of Barasath and the majority of his air power, even after all this time.

'Intentions?'

'Currently, no change from Jenzen's orders. Provide air support for embattled Titan forces and armour battalions. The enemy are still showing next to no offensive capacity in the air. It's reasonable to suggest that, this far in, they've simply got nothing left.'

'Was that a barb, captain?'

Helius saluted again. 'By no means, sir.'

Sarren smiled, the indulgent grin ruined by weariness. 'If it was, it's forgiven. Barasath was right, and he sold his life at great cost to give us an edge in the air. The beasts have thrown up nothing but a handful of scrap-fighters since the siege began, and I've already noted on the campaign record – as well as Barasath's personal file – that he made the right call.'

'Yes, sir.'

'I'm sorry to hear about Jenzen. She was an asset we'll greatly miss: solid, reliable, steady.'

And she had been. Commander Carylin Jenzen, for better or worse, had been a by-the-book flyer, dependable and constant, if rather uninspired. Under her, the city's air forces had maintained a campaign of reliable defensive support for over a month. The Crone of Invigilata herself had commended Jenzen's endeavours in recent weeks.

'Sir–' Helius began.

Here it comes... Sarren thought.

'I had hoped to discuss the possibility of a more aggressive tactical pattern.'

Yes. Yes, of course you had hoped to discuss that.

'In good time. For now, the docks.'

Sarren nodded back to the gathered officers. Cyria Tyro and Captain Helius joined them, standing next to one another. Major Ryken scowled at the pilot, and Sarren resisted the urge to roll his eyes. *Bloody Throne, Ryken. Now is hardly the time for schoolyard jealousy.*

'We did not lose the docks,' one of the Astartes argued, his vox-voice laden with resonant calm. Colonel Sarren had not met Sergeant V'reth of the Salamanders before this morning. He knew from vox-traffic that the green-armoured warriors had deployed close to the remaining civilian shelters and their valour was directly responsible for a great many lives spared. But it seemed his tactical outlook varied wildly from the colonel's.

'I'm not sure I understand, sir,' Sarren offered.

V'reth's armour was dented and scratched, but remained pristine in comparison to the wreckage worn by the Reclusiarch at his side. A golden-eyed helm glared down at the human officers.

'I am merely stating, Colonel Sarren, that we did not lose the docks. The enemy is beaten. The seaborne invasion was denied, for the city still stands. The invaders lie dead at the docks.'

This was and wasn't true, from the way Sarren looked at it. The disparity was the reason the colonel had called this gathering.

'Allow me to amend my appraisal. The docks are gone. As an industrial factor in Armageddon's collective output, Helsreach no longer exists. We're receiving reports now of ninety-one per cent harm to the city's refinery infrastructure, taking into account the loss of the offshore oil platforms.'

The soldiers shared uncomfortable glances. The Imperium demanded heavy tithes of materiel from Armageddon. If the other hive cities suffered as Helsreach had, the grade of Exactis Extremis would be lowered significantly. Certainly to Solutio Tertius, and perhaps to Aptus Non. If Armageddon provided nothing, it would be offered little in return. The Imperium would turn away. Without the support and finances to recover after the war, the world might never recover.

'However, all is not dark. As the noble Sergeant V'reth makes clear, thanks to the tenacity of the dockworker population, our own storm troopers, and our Astartes allies, the xenos were repelled.'

At insane cost, he decided not to add. *Tens of thousands dead in four days. The city's industry reduced to a worthless husk.*

'We have received further word from the Crone of Invigilata,' the colonel continued. What he had to say next almost caught in his throat. 'The most honourable Legio Invigilata has been petitioned by outside forces to leave the city.'

'She will stay.' The Reclusiarch's tone was cold even through his helm's vox-speakers. 'She swore to fight.'

'As I understand it, the Imperial advances along the length of the Hemlock River are grinding to a halt. The settlements there, protected by the Salamanders and regiments of the Cadian Shock, are now considered a higher priority than the city.' Sarren let the words resonate for a few moments. 'This is from the Old Man himself. It came over the vox an hour ago.'

Grimaldus snarled as he spoke, 'I do not care. Our mandate is to defend Helsreach.'

'*Our* mandate, yes. But Princeps Zarha's mandate was to deploy where she desired. Most of the Legio Invigilata is already stationed along the Hemlock and across the wastelands, alongside elements from Ignatum and Metalica.'

'She will not leave,' Grimaldus snorted. 'She is here until the end.'

Sarren felt his ire rising at the way the Reclusiarch dismissed his concerns with such blasé finality. On another day, another morning, after any other week of fighting, he would have reined in his emotions better. As it was, he sighed and closed his gritty eyes.

'Enough, *please,* Reclusiarch. *Stormherald* is embattled seven kilometres down the Hel's Highway, with an enemy scrap-Titan battalion in the Rostorik Ironworks. She has given no further word of her decision.'

Grimaldus crossed his arms over his ruined heraldry. 'Tartarus Hive and the battles along the shores of the Hemlock will be won and lost without us. This war has taken everything from the city, and we are reduced to fighting like desert jackals over Helsreach's bones. The only question that matters to us is: What can we still save?'

Ryken removed his rebreather and took a deep breath. 'It may be time to consider the last fallback point.'

Sarren nodded. 'That's why we're here. We stand in the heart of a dying city, and the time has come to decide where we will make our final stand. What of the... weapon, Reclusiarch?'

'A fool's hope. The Master of the Forge is a single soul. Without Mechanicus support, Jurisian has been able to do nothing more than activate *Oberon's* core systems. He can certainly not crew it alone. As of four nights ago, the Ordinatus has locomotion, and on his own the Forgemaster is able to fire the Oberon Cannon once every twenty-two minutes. But that is all. It cannot be defended by a lone pilot. It is worthless in battle.'

The colonel's ire rose again. 'You waited four days to tell me of this? That the Ordinatus has power once more?'

'I have not waited. I filed coded confirmation across the command network the same night I learned *Oberon* was operational. Yet as I said, it is almost worthless to us.'

'Is your Forgemaster bringing the weapon to the city?'

'Of course.'

'Has the Mechanicus been informed we are defiling their weapon and dragging it into a warzone, almost certain to lose it in its first engagement against the enemy?'

'Of course not. Are you insane, human? The best weapons are those that remain secret until wielded. This truth would force Invigilata to act against us, or to leave the city.'

'You are not the commander of this city. You surrendered that honour to me. This is information I have been eagerly awaiting, only to find it denied to me because of broken vox-traffic?'

The silver skull breathed out a mechanical growl.

'I was knee-deep in alien dead at the docks, Sarren, selling the lives of my brothers to ensure the people of your home world lived to see another sunrise. You are tired. I understand the limitations of the human form, and you have my sympathies for them. But remember to whom you are speaking.'

Sarren bit back his disappointment. It wasn't supposed to be like this, yet with the Astartes, it always was. Compliant and valuable one moment, superior and distant the next, shaped as much by their fierce independence as they were by their loyalty to the Imperium.

It felt... petty. That was the only word that encapsulated it in the colonel's mind. An awkward divide between humans fighting for their home, and once-humans fighting for intangible ideals and heroic codes of conduct.

'Well...' Sarren began, but knew he had nowhere to go with the words.

'I am not to blame for your malfunctioning vox. It is a plague upon the city's defence, and a burden we must bear. I was not about to abandon the docks to deliver the news into your ears like some enslaved courier, nor would I entrust such a development to any other soul. If the Mechanicus learns of this, we lose Invigilata.'

'None of us had much hope pinned on the Ordinatus,' Ryken said, seeking to defuse the tension. 'It was the longest of long shots, any way you slice it.'

'Have you tried the Mechanicus forces again?' Cyria Tyro asked. Her tone didn't hide the fact she still pinned a great deal of hope on the weapon, despite what Ryken had just said.

'Of course.' The Reclusiarch gestured west along the Hel's Highway, in the direction of *Stormherald* fighting out of sight in the Ironworks. 'Zarha refused as she refused before. It is blasphemy to do what we have done.'

'Still no word from Mechanicus royalty,' Sarren put in. 'Wherever this arch-priest of theirs is, he's not responding to any of our astropathic pleas.'

He spat onto the broken roadway beneath his feet. Indeed, whoever this Lord of the Centurio Ordinatus was, his arrival in the Armageddon system would be far too late to make a difference to Helsreach.

'At least the weapon may yet be put to use in the defence of other cities,' the colonel forced a chuckle. 'We stand on the very edge now. The fallback plan is, however, not something I wish to consider anymore. There are few enough surviving Imperial forces left in the city. Let us not gather together for the last days of our lives and offer an easy target.'

'So it's over,' one of the captains said.

'No,' Grimaldus answered. 'But we must keep the enemy locked in the city as long as we can. Each day we survive increases the chances of reinforcement from the Ash Wastes. Each day we hold out costs the enemy more blood, and keeps them here in Helsreach, where they cannot add their axes to the beasts besieging the other cities.'

Ryken scratched at his collar, soothing an itching scar he'd earned the week before.

'Uh. Sir?' he said to Sarren.

'Major?'

Ryken let his expression of disbelief do the talking. Sarren rubbed grit from his eyes with dirty fingertips as he answered. 'I have studied the hololithic projections in the wake of the dock siege. I have managed, blessings upon the Emperor, to actually maintain a conversation over the vox with Commissar Yarrick that lasted for more than ten seconds, and offered more productivity than merely listening to the crackle of static for once. We are following a pattern being used in several of the other hive cities. The Steel Legion will disperse throughout the city, centring at population centres that remain untouched.'

'What about the highway?'

'The enemy already claims most of it, Captain Helius. Let them have the rest. As of this morning, we are no longer fighting to preserve the city. We are fighting to save every life that can be saved. The city is dead, but over half of its people are not.'

The captain scowled, rendering his handsome face immediately unattractive. Unreliable friends borrowed a great deal of money with expressions like that.

'None of our remaining airstrips are anywhere near civilian population centres. Forgive me for pointing it out, colonel, but that was the very point of setting them up where we did. To hide them.'

'You did well. And I'm certain you will hold off the enemy for an admirable space of time before you are overrun. Just like the rest of us.'

'We need to be defended!'

'No. You would *like* to be defended. You do not wish to die. None of us do, captain. But I command the Steel Legion, and the Steel Legion marches in defence of the hive's people now. I cannot spare regiments of men just to continue covering the air squadron's inexorable dance across the city. The plain truth is that there are no longer enough of you to be worth defending. Hide when you must, and fight when you can. If Invigilata stands with us, fly in support of them. If Invigilata leaves, then fly in support of the 121st Armoured Division, who will be based at the Kolav Residentia District, defending the entrances to the subterranean bunkers. Those are your orders.'

The captain's salute was reluctant. 'Understood, sir.'

'The coming weeks will go into Imperial records as the 'hundred bastions of light'. We no longer have the forces required to defend large swathes of territory. So we will fall back to the cores – the most vital points – and die before we ever give another metre of ground. The Jaega District, with its storm shelters. The Temple of the Emperor Ascendant, at the heart of the Ecclesiarchal sector. The Azal Spaceport in the Dis industrial sector. The Purgatori Refinery, that blessedly still stands on the docks. A list of primary and secondary defence points is being circulated over the vox-network and via hundreds of courier teams throughout the city.'

The colonel turned to the hulking figures of the Astartes. 'Sergeant V'reth, the people of Helsreach and Armageddon offer their thanks to you and your brothers for the assistance. You'll quit the city today?'

'The Lord of the Fire-born calls.'

'Quite so, quite so. I offer my personal thanks. Without your arrival, many more would have lost their lives.'

V'reth made the sign of the aquila, his green gauntlets forming the familiar shape to mirror the bronze eagle on his chest.

'You are fighting with ferocity unmatched, Steel Legionnaire. The Emperor sees all and knows all. He sees your sacrifices and your courage in this war, and you are earning your place in the Imperium's legends. It was an honour to fight at your side, on the streets of your city.'

Sarren glanced between the two Astartes – the warrior and the knight. He could not doubt the valour of the Templars in past weeks, but Throne, if only he'd had the Salamanders here. They were everything the Templars were not: communicative, supportive, *reliable*...

He found himself offering his hand. A moment's tension followed the gesture, as the towering warrior remained unmoving. Then, with care, the Salamander held the colonel's small, human hand in a shake. The joints of the sergeant's power armour hummed with the minor movement.

'The honour was ours, V'reth. Hunt well in the wastelands, and give my thanks to your lord.'

The Reclusiarch watched this in silence. No one knew what expression was masked by his relic helm.

Once the discussion is done, I walk from the gathered humans. V'reth remains with me, shadowing my movements. Away from the pitted and cracked hull of Sarren's Baneblade, I slow in my stride to allow him to catch up. Does V'reth not have his own orders to obey? Does the Hemlock not call? Curious that he chooses to remain.

'What do you want, Salamander?'

As we walk along the Hel's Highway, I cannot help but stare at the city below. The platformed road rises above the habitation blocks here, once allowing traffic to rattle through the heart of the city between the spires of its tall residential towers. Now it remains aloft – a rockcrete wave riding above urban devastation. The buildings here are flattened, reduced to rubble by the enemy's scrap-Titans and shelling from our own forces.

Across the city, the Highway has come down in several places. Fortunate that it has not done so here, as well.

'To speak, if you are willing, Reclusiarch.'

'I would be honoured,' I tell him, but this is a lie. We have spent a week fighting together, side by side, and although his presence was invaluable, his warriors are not knights. Too often, they fell back to guard civilian shelters rather than press the attack and prevent the enemy from escaping. Too often they withstood repeated assaults rather than strike first and eliminate any need of further retaliation.

Priamus loathes them, but I do not. Their ways are not our ways. It is not cowardice that drives them to these tactics, but rather tradition. Yet still, their valour is as alien to me as the disgusting savagery of the orks.

It is difficult to hold my tongue. I wish him to leave before honesty stains the deeds we have achieved together, and before truth spoken too brutally threatens the alliance between our respective Chapters.

'My brothers and I came to this city without the illuminating guidance of our Chaplain. We would offer reverent thanks if you would lead us in prayer before we quit the city and rejoin our Chapter by the shores of the Hemlock.'

'I know little of your Chapter's cult and creed, Salamander.'

'We know this, Reclusiarch. Still, we would offer sincere thanks.'

It is a magnificent and bold gesture, and I know it honours me far more than it would honour them if I agreed. To lead brothers from another Chapter in prayer is beyond merely rare. It is almost unheard of. In my life, I can recall only one such instance, and that was with our gene-brothers and fellow sons of Dorn, the Crimson Fists, when the Declates system burned.

'Think of the battle last night,' I tell him. 'Think of the rooftop battle in the Nergal district. There was one moment in the chaos that still preys upon my mind. It casts a shadow over us now, like an enemy's spear threatening to fall.'

He hesitates. This is clearly not the way he thought his request would be answered. 'What aspect of the battle troubles you, Reclusiarch?'

A fine question.

The beast falls from my hands, its skull broken, to die at my feet.

I hear the burning hiss of Priamus's blade tearing through alien flesh. I hear the strained snarls of meat-clogged chainblades. I hear the yelling of panicked humans as they cower in the storm shelter, their fear reaching my senses through the armour plated walls.

Another creature snarls in my face, spitting thick saliva over my faceplate. It dies as Artarion's bolter kicks once from a few metres away, shearing its malformed head off in a burst of gore.

'Focus,' he grunts over the vox.

I return the favour a moment later, my maul pounding into a beast that sought to leap at him from behind.

The battle is close, down to pistols, blades and the crashing beat of fists into faces. In the centre of the expansive plaza, the thickly-armoured storm shelter endures siege from close to two hundred of the enemy.

Footing is treacherous. Our boots are stamping down on pools of cooling blood and the bodies of dead dockworkers. The Salamanders are...

Curse them all...

Priamus blocked a cut from the closest ork, the beast's chopping sword deflected with a shower of sparks from the brief blade contact.

He killed it with the riposte – an ugly strike he felt no pride for, slipping past the creature's non-existent guard and ramming the blade's point into the beast's exposed neck.

The brute's axe slammed with clanging force against the side of his helm. His vision receptors showed angry static for two seconds.

Not deep enough. The swordsman yanked back with the blade, and on the second plunge he hilted it in the ork's collarbone. The beast collapsed in a heap of dead limbs.

Priamus resisted the urge to laugh.

The next ork to leap at him came with two of its brothers. The first fell to Priamus's blade lashing out to carve through its torso, the energised blade going through meat and bone like soft clay. The second and third would have had a fair chance at overpowering him, had they not been battered to the ground by a sweep of the Reclusiarch's maul.

'Where are the Salamanders?' he voxed, his breath coming in ragged gasps.

'They're holding.'

'They're what?'

Bastilan's fist vibrated with the crashing judder of his bolter. Streaks of alien blood painted his battered armour yet again.

Recriminations spilled out over the vox. The Salamanders weren't advancing with the Templars. The Templars were pushing ahead too far, too fast.

'Follow us, in the name of the Throne!' Bastilan added his voice to the vox-chatter.

'Fall back,' came the staid voice of Sergeant V'reth. 'Fall back to the eastern platform and be ready to engage the second wave.'

'Advance! If we strike now, there will be no second wave. We're at the warlord's throat!'

'Salamanders,' V'reth spoke calmly, 'Hold and be ready. Cut down any stragglers that seek to breach the shelter.'

Bastilan kicked a hunched alien in the chest, breaking whatever passed for its rib structure. In the moment's respite, he ejected his spent bolt magazine and slammed a fresh one home.

They were advancing unsupported, away from the shelter, in pursuit of the fleeing orks. Ahead, through the crowd of panicking beasts, Bastilan could see the armoured warlord of this wretched tribe, its staggering gait made all the more pronounced by the ablative armour plating that seemed surgically bolted to its nerveless flesh.

Bolts slashed after the retreating warleader, roaring from the muzzles of Templars fighting their way through a bestial and ferocious rearguard. Several shells detonated against the creature's armour, while others smacked into the backs and shoulders of fleeing orks around their commander.

'He's getting away,' Bastilan grunted. The words shamed him even to speak them.

'Fall back,' came the Reclusiarch's growl.

'Sir,' Bastilan began, coupled with Priamus's decidedly more annoyed 'No!'

'Fall back. This is not worth dying over. We do not have the numbers to spill the warlord's blood now.'

V'reth, to his credit, nods.

'I see. You consider this a stain on your personal honour.'

He does not see. 'No, brother. I consider it a waste of time, ammunition, and life. Two of your own squad were killed in the successive waves that followed. Brother Kaedus and Brother Madoc from my own force were slain. If we had pursued in unity, we could have broken through to the enemy leader and taken his head. The rest of the beasts would have scattered, and the bulk could easily have been purged by kill-teams in the aftermath.'

'It is tactically unsound, Reclusiarch. Pursuit would have left the shelter undefended and vulnerable to regrouping waves attacking from other sectors. Three thousand lives were saved by our defiance last night.'

'There were no attacks from other sectors.'

'There may have been, had we pursued. And there was still no guarantee we would have overpowered the rearguard quickly enough to reach the warlord.'

'We weathered six further assaults, wasted seven hours, lost four warriors, and expended a hoard of ammunition that my knights can ill-afford to throw away.'

'That is one way of seeing the final cost. I see it more simply: we won.'

'I am finished with this... debate, Salamander.' Again, I recall the grinding cut of Nero's medicae-saw, and the puncturing retrieval of cutting tools extracting glistening gene-seed organs from the chests of the slain.

'It grieves me to hear you speak this way, Reclusiarch.'

Listen to him. So patient. So calm.

So blind.

'Get out of my city.'

NINETEEN

FATE

The giant stood above its worshippers in silence.

Its skin and bones were harvested from crashed and salvaged ships, each column, gear, pylon, girder and plate of armour that went into its birth stolen from something else. Although the giant was not alive, living creatures served it in place of blood and organs. They clambered through the god's form, insulated by the armour, hanging from the metal bones, moving like the blood cells in sluggish arteries.

The giant had taken over two thousand labourers over a month to build. It had finally awoken outside the walls of Hive Stygia three days before, to great roars of praise from its devoted faithful.

And then, in its first hours of life, it had wiped the hive city from the face of the planet. Stygia was a modest industrial city, defended by the Steel Legion and its own militia with little in the way of Astartes or Mechanicus support. From the moment the giant awoke to the moment the last vestiges of organised Imperial resistance was crushed, the city lasted a total of five hours and thirty-two minutes.

And now, the giant stood silent, idle, making ready for its journey south.

Its face was piggish and round-eyed, all jagged jaw and red-iron tusks. Behind the broken windows that served as its eyes, hunched crewmembers moved in loping gaits, attending to their bestial imitations of Imperial Titan command.

The giant's name, splattered across its ugly, fat-bellied hull in crude alien hieroglyphs, was *Godbreaker*.

With a slow tread that shook the earth around it, *Godbreaker* began to move south, toward the coast.

Toward Helsreach.

If it could remain mobile without breaking down – a difficult feat given the skills of its creators – it would arrive by dawn the following day.

In a fateful sense of opposed unity with the *Godbreaker*, another powerful war machine drew nearer to Helsreach. Its journey was a far longer one, and its progress was a melancholy fraction of what it might have been in a better age.

Waves of ashy soil blew aside in the land train's wake, as its gravity suppression field exerted its influence on the ground below the rattling, serpentine vehicle. Jurisian felt its resistance in every touch upon its controls. The soul of the machine was rising from its slumber now, finding itself disrespected and on the edge of lashing out at the living being responsible.

'Reclusiarch,' he spoke into the vox again, once more receiving no answer.

Oberon's existence in his mind was akin to a beast alone in the woods. Jurisian could keep it at bay as long as he focussed on its presence, just as a traveller could face down a wolf in the wild if he kept watch for the beast and carried a torch of flame to ward it away. It was a game of focus, and despite his weariness, the Master of the Forge possessed focus in abundance. He was a conscientious and patient soul, devoted to each of his tasks like a predator hunting prey. This demeanour and dedication, coupled with his ability and deeds of honour, had seen him promoted to his rank aboard the *Eternal Crusader* nineteen years before.

Jurisian had been present at Grimaldus's induction into the inner circle, and though it shamed him to admit it now – even silently, even only to himself and the lurking soul of the war machine – he had cast his vote against the Chaplain ascending to Mordred's role as Reclusiarch.

'He is not ready,' Jurisian had said, adding his voice to Champion Bayard's. 'He is a master of small engagements, and a warrior beyond peer. But he is a not a leader of the Chapter.'

'The Forgemaster speaks the truth, High Marshal,' Bayard had added. 'Grimaldus is flawed by hesitation. A second's delay in all he does, and it is no secret why. He holds himself to his master's standards. Doubt clings to him, darkening his place in the Chapter.'

'He is shaken by Mordred's death,' Jurisian had pressed. 'He seeks his place in the Eternal Crusade.'

Helbrecht had sat musing on his throne, his cold eyes lowering the temperature of the room.

'In the coming war, I will give him the chance to find that place.'

Jurisian had spoken no more, and inclined his head in a bow. The Emperor's Champion was not so subdued, and had put forward his recommendations for warriors other than Grimaldus to succeed Mordred.

The High Marshal had kept his own counsel, but the voices of the Sword Brethren around Helbrecht's dais sounded out in jeers as fists crashed against shields. Grimaldus was the chosen of Mordred the Avenger, and skilled in personal combat beyond question. Two centuries of valour and glory; two hundred years of unrelenting courage and a host of enemy dead across a horde of worlds; his short years as the youngest Sword Brother in the history of the Chapter – there was no arguing with such truths.

Jurisian and Bayard had relented. The following night, they watched Grimaldus accept Mordred's mantle.

Oberon tilted as it rose over an ash dune, the anti-grav field changing its tone to a more strained whine.

On the horizon, a blanket of blackness rose from a burning city.

'Reclusiarch,' he voxed, trying once more to speak with the warrior that did not deserve the title he now carried.

* * *

Leaving the Titan had proved less of a trial than Asavan had feared.

He'd managed it two days ago, and had been on the streets of the city ever since. All it had taken was a slow descent through the decks, and what felt like about eight million spiral staircases, each one shaped from dense bronze and riveted heavily to the walls.

Well. Perhaps closer to four staircases. But by the time Asavan was approaching ground level, he was blinking sweat from his eyes and cursing his lack of fitness. On the Titan's lower levels, all was emergency red lighting, narrow corridors, and stuffy air filled with the smell of sacred incense holy to the Machine-God, as well as His disciples chanting blessings in His name. Through their devotion was *Stormherald* empowered. Praise be.

'Halt,' a machine-voice barked, and Asavan did exactly as he was told. He even raised his hands in the air, mimicking some unnecessary surrender. 'What are you doing here?' the voice demanded.

Here was at the base of the Titan's pelvis, in one of the lowest accessible chambers, lit by a flickering yellow siren light. Six augmented skitarii stood stationed around a bulkhead in the floor. The room itself rocked back and forth, tilting with the Titan's tread.

'I'm leaving the Titan,' the priest said.

The skitarii glanced at each other with focus lenses instead of eyes. The air buzzed with inter-vox communication. They were confused. This... this made no sense.

'You are leaving the Titan,' one of them, apparently their leader, said. His eye lenses revolved, scanning the unaugmented human.

'Yes.'

More vox-chatter. The leader, his face noticeably more bionic than the others,' emitted a blurt of machine code. Asavan knew an error/abort complaint when he heard one.

'*Stormherald* is engaged in locomotive activity.'

Asavan was aware of this. The entire room was, after all, moving. 'The Titan is walking. I know. I still wish to leave. This service maintenance ladder will take me down the left leg struts to the shin-fortress, will it not?'

'It would,' the skitarii leader allowed.

'Then please excuse me. I must be going.'

'Halt.' Asavan did, again, but he was growing tired of this. 'You wish to leave the Titan,' the skitarii repeated. 'But... why?'

This was hardly the ideal setting for a debate on crises of faith and the sudden revelatory desire to walk among the city's people and help them with one's own hands.

Asavan reached for the medallion around his neck, marking him as an honoured member of the Ecclesiarchy of Terra and a minister ordained to preach the word of the Emperor in His aspect as the Machine-God of Mars.

The skitarii stared at the icon for several moments – the double-headed eagle and the divided skull backing it – and lowered their weapons.

'My thanks,' the sweating priest said. 'Now if it's not too much trouble, could you open that bulkhead for me?'

His stomach lurched at the sight beyond the opened trapdoor. Beneath, the broken rockcrete of Hel's Highway passed by, a good twenty-five metres down. Pudgy hands gripped the black iron service ladder as he descended, rung by rung, through the wind, hanging on to the Titan's thigh. Above him, the bulkhead slammed with a chime of finality.

So be it. Down, he went.

Behind the god-machine's knee, another bulkhead blocked his descent into the bulky lower leg section. Below, Asavan heard the servos of turrets mounted on the shin-walls panning back and forth, seeking targets.

It took almost a full minute to work the bulkhead's wheel lock, but he was energised now, drawing close to his objective. Once more, he descended into red-lit, downward spiralling corridors, avoiding the troop chambers where ranks of skitarii stood in tomb-like silence.

The Titan's movement now was almost unbearable, slamming him to the wall and rocking him from his feet on several occasions. This low, the gravitic stabilisers were little use against the sheer degree of movement necessary for each leg to make. His surroundings rumbled with sickening violence every eleven seconds, as the foot came down on the road below. Asavan vomited against a wall, and tried not to laugh. He was trying to keep his balance while walking through the steel bones in the ankle of a striding machine giant. Perhaps this wasn't such a wonderful idea, after all.

And now came the hardest part.

This last bulkhead opened onto the Titan's tiered claw-toes, which formed steps by which the skitarii battalions in the leg-fortresses could ascend and descend, when *Stormherald* was at rest.

Disembarking with the Titan in motion was going to be... exciting.

Asavan pulled the door open on squealing hinges, gripping a nearby handrail and watching the ground in bug-eyed horror, waiting for it to level out with the foot touching down. It did, with a bone-jarring rumble of thunder, and the fat priest ran, huffing and puffing, down the tiered stairs.

The other foot came down, shaking the ground and sending Asavan tumbling down the last steps to land in a heap of overweight flesh and filthy robes on the dirty surface of the highway.

A metre away, the stairs rose again as the great war machine lifted its foot to take another step. Squealing without even realising he was doing so, Asavan Tortellius sprinted, with his additional chins shaking, away from the leg's ascent and inevitable descent. He hurled himself the last few metres, landing hard.

As the Titan walked on, monstrous feet still pounding into the ground, the priest lay on his back, breathing in ragged gasps.

And thus was completed the least dignified disembarkation from an Imperator Titan in the history of the Imperium.

That had been two days ago.

Since then, Asavan had not improved his situation by a great deal, but by the Throne, he was doing the Emperor's work. And that was a start.

His journey along the Hel's Highway (which he was resolutely calling his 'pilgrimage') had begun on an uninspiring note. Hauling himself to his unsteady feet and recovering the shoe he had lost in his fall, he began to make his way down the wide road, clutching his bag of dehydrated foodstuffs and electrolyte fluid packs.

Away from the Titan, with *Stormherald* thumping away in the far distance now, he realised how utterly silent a dead city could be. The crashing of weapons and war machines was a muted murmur, seeming a world away. His immediate surroundings were quiet almost to the point of eeriness.

He left the highway to trudge through an abandoned commercia district that had been punished heavily weeks before. Slain tanks littered the central market zone, both Imperial and alien, and each one commanding its own mound of nearby bodies. Red flies – the bloated and oversized tropical vermin that bred like a plague in the jungles to the west – were here in swarms, blanketing the dead and feeding from them.

He'd not been prepared for the smell of a city at war. On the back of a Titan, one strode the battlefield like a colossus, far from what the princeps, blessings upon her, referred to as the 'distasteful biological carnage.'

The smell was somewhere between untreated sewage and spoiled food. He vomited again halfway across the plaza, releasing a stringy ooze that stuck to his teeth. Fluid packs and dehydrated foodstuffs were not wonderful for the digestion.

That night, he'd camped in the broken shell of a Leman Russ. The tank was half-buried in a fallen wall, which evidently it had rammed. Whatever had become of its crew was a mystery Asavan didn't feel like looking into. He was glad enough that they weren't there, slouched and rotting in their seats like so many others had been.

When he finally slept, he dreamed of everything he'd seen that day. After three hours of dreaming that every corpse he'd passed was staring at him, he gave up the attempt to find rest and instead pushed on deeper into the city.

On the second day, he had found his first survivors. In the ground floor of a collapsed habitation block, movement drew his eye.

He'd voiced a tremulous 'Hello?' before he'd even realised he might be calling out to one of the invaders. The sound of scampering footsteps emboldened him. Alien beasts would not run from a lone human's cry. 'I've come to help,' he called.

Silence was the only answer.

'I have food,' he tried.

A filthy face rose from behind a pile of rubble. Narrowed eyes never left him – bright and quick like a scavenger's gaze.

'I have food,' Asavan said again, lowering his voice this time. With no sudden movement, he unslung the satchel from his back and held up a dehydrated food pouch in its silver packaging. 'It's dehydrated. Rations. But it's food.'

The face became a person, a middle-aged woman, as she left her hiding place and drew closer. Gaunt and wild-eyed, she moved with the caution of the forever fearful. It took three attempts for her to speak. Before the words left her mouth in a scratchy whisper, she had to clear her throat repeatedly.

'You're a priest?' she asked, still not coming within arm's reach. She pointed at his white and violet robes, her gesture weak and dismissive.

'I am. The God-Emperor sent me to you.'

She had wept in that moment, and soon after, they shared a small meal in the ruins of her hab-chamber. He asked questions of her life, and the losses she'd suffered. Before he left an hour later, he made sure she had several days' worth of food and fluid, and blessed her in the name of the God-Emperor. It was strange to be ministering to the genuinely needy, and the fully-fleshed. So many of his sermons had been to fellow clerics and machine-altered skitarii that a weeping woman praising the Emperor was quite beyond his experience.

It was strange, but it was good. It was worthy.

Asavan Tortellius's first meeting with a survivor had gone well. He walked on, similar encounters repeating themselves over the next day and night. It was only on the third day that he ran into trouble.

A small group of ragged survivors huddled around a trash-fire, warming their hands as night fell over another tank graveyard along the Hel's Highway. Asavan cleared his throat as he approached, raising a hand in greeting.

The survivors whirled, bringing lasguns to bear. Several of the group were in workers' overalls, blood-spattered and dark with grime. One of them was clad in a Guard uniform, a bulky power pack on his back and a cabled lasrifle aimed at Asavan's face.

'No more surprises, please, yes?' The soldier spat onto the ground, his thin face marked with suspicion. 'I am tired and I am cold and I am sick to my core of shooting looters in the skull.'

'I'm not a looter.'

'That is not a surprise to me, given what I have just said I do to looters.'

'I'm a priest.'

'Explains the robes,' one of the workers chuckled. 'I think he's telling the truth, Andrej.'

'A priest,' the storm trooper repeated.

'A priest,' Asavan nodded.

The storm trooper lowered his rifle. 'That is most definitely a surprise. I am Andrej of the Legion. These are my friends, who were unlucky enough to be born in Helsreach instead of a city worth defending.'

The workers snickered.

'I am Asavan Tortellius, of *Stormherald*.'

'The god-machine?' Andrej barked a laugh. 'You are far from your walking throne, fat priest. Did you fall off and fail to catch up?'

Asavan drew nearer to the fire, and the workers made room for him.

'Tomaz Maghernus.' One of them offered his hand for the priest to shake. 'Don't mind Andrej, sir. He's not all there.'

'All of me is exactly where it needs to be.' The storm trooper shook his head, his dark, weasel eyes glinting with the fire's reflection. 'Throne, I have never been so cold. We are all lucky that our balls have not frozen and cracked by now.'

'Good to see you,' one of the other men muttered to the priest.

'Yeah,' another nodded, his voice sincere despite not meeting the newcomer's eyes. Asavan was touched by their almost-shy gratitude to see a priest amongst all this.

'Looters?' Asavan asked. 'Did I hear that correctly?'

'You did,' Maghernus breathed into his hands, before holding them out to the flames. 'Dockworkers. Militia and Guard deserters. It's ugly out here. They're going through the habs, stealing credits and whatever else they can find.'

'May I ask, why are you out here?'

Andrej shook his head as he joined the group. 'Do not sound so suspicious, holy man. We are not hiding from duty. We are merely the Forgotten, lost in the dead city, making our way back to... wherever the closest front line might be.'

'You have no contact with the rest of the Guard?'

'Ha! I like this. I like the way you think. You fell off your Titan, fat man. Do you have a vox-link back to ask your Mechanicus masters for advice? No. Exactly. You were not at the docks, priest. Half the city died last week. The Guard is broken, and the vox is no more than a hundred frequencies of hissing noise. If I am right, and I hope to be wrong, then no Imperial force is able to contact any other in perhaps half of the city.'

'What do you intend to do?'

'We are moving west. The Templars went to the west, and so shall we. Why are *you* here?'

Asavan shrugged. It wasn't something he could explain with any conviction. 'I wanted to walk the streets and help where I could. I was serving no one on the back of a Titan.'

A few of the group made the sign of the aquila and murmured their admiration.

'You wish to come with us, fat priest? You will like what is in the west, I am thinking.'

'What's in the west?' Asavan asked.

'A great number of burning industrial sectors, too many looters for my innocent heart to consider at this moment in time, and of course, the Temple of the Emperor Ascendant.'

'What is this temple you speak of? A monastery? A cathedral?'

Maghernus shook his head. 'Both. Neither. It's a shrine – built by the original colonists who came to Armageddon.'

In his surprise, Asavan almost ordered a servo-skull to take a dictation. 'You are telling me that the first church ever built in Helsreach still stands? It endured the First War against the daemon armies? It remained unbroken through the Second War, when the Great Enemy first came to this world?'

'Well... yeah,' Maghernus replied.

This was providence. This was why he had left the Titan, and this was why the God-Emperor had guided him through the city to these men.

Andrej snorted at his questions. 'It is not simply the first church built in Helsreach, my fat friend. It is the first church ever raised in the whole world. When the first settlers prayed to the Emperor, they prayed in the Temple of the Emperor Ascendant.'

Asavan felt his hands trembling. 'How do we reach it?'

Andrej gestured to the expansive, raised road in the distance. 'We walk the Hel's Highway. How else?'

* * *

Artarion stood away from the others.

The building they occupied had once been a small temple, serving as the spiritual heart of this industrial sector. Now it was a tumbledown ruin, no longer fit to house dawn and dusk prayers for the local workers. In the altar room, Artarion had paused his bored exploration, finding bloodstains on some of the fallen rubble that had buried the floor in broken architecture.

The blood-scent was old, the stains themselves flaking. Whoever was entombed beneath had been dead for days. Artarion breathed in through his helm's filters. Female. Had not bled much after being crushed. Dead for perhaps three days; the delicate scent of decomposition was little more than spice on the air.

He'd removed himself to perform the rites of maintenance on his weapons, as well as to get away from Priamus muttering about the Salamanders.

As he lowered himself to sit on the dead woman's cairn, the knee joint of his armour locked for several seconds. Runic warnings flickered across his visor display. Instead of blanking them, he disengaged his helm's seals, removed it, and breathed in the smell of the fire, ash and brick dust that was all Helsreach had become. The faulty joint crunched back into motion, eliciting a grunt from the knight as he sat.

His bolter, chained to his thigh and mag-locked in place, was starved of ammunition. He had not spoken of this to the others yet, but knew they must surely be approaching similar difficulties. Before the week of bloodshed at the docks, the supplies brought down by the Helsreach Crusade from the *Eternal Crusader* so long ago had been reduced to a Thunderhawk cargo bay half-full of bolts and an almost-empty crate of replacement tooth-tracks for chainswords.

The gunship itself sat cold and silent in the courtyard of a factory complex, almost two kilometres to the west, in a sector of the city still securely in Imperial control.

Artarion examined the bolter's fire-blackened muzzle, turning the weapon over in his hands as he followed the path of winding, once-gold inlaid scriptures etched along the gun's sides. A list of enemies slain, battles won, worlds defended...

In wordless silence, he lowered the bolter again.

'There is nothing to like in them,' Priamus spat as he paced the prayer room. 'They wage war to defend, to preserve. Everything in their way is devoted to maintaining what humanity already has.'

Bastilan was sharpening his combat blade, running a whetstone along the gladius's killing edges. The small chamber was filled with Priamus's crunching bootsteps and the *resssh, resssh* of the whetstone scraping.

'It is flawed,' the swordsman added. 'I mean no offence to them as warriors. But drop-podding into the city purely to defend civilians? Madness.'

Resssh, resssh.

'Why do you not answer, brother?'

'I have little to say.' *Resssh, resssh.*

'Do you think ill of me for my beliefs? Bastilan, please, you know I am right.'

'I know you are treading on unstable ground. Do not besmirch the honour of our brother Chapter. The Salamanders shed as much blood as we did this week.'

'That is not the point.'

Resssh, resssh. 'That is where you and I disagree, brother. But you are young. You will learn.'

Priamus didn't bother to hide his disgusted sneer from infecting his voice. 'Do not patronise me, old man. You know of what I speak. You are just quietened by the mounting years and too reserved to say it aloud.'

'I am not that old,' Bastilan laughed. The boy was annoying, but he certainly knew how to drag out a smile or two with his misguided fervour.

'Do not laugh at me.'

'Then stop making me laugh. What two Chapters fight the same? What two Chapters wage war according to the same principles? We are all born of different worlds and trained by different masters. Accept the differences and stand with them as allies.'

'But they are *wrong*.' Priamus stared at the older warrior in disbelief. How could he be so obtuse? 'They could have landed anywhere in the city. They could have struck at one of the alien commanders. Instead, they crash down amongst us at the docks to defend the humans.'

'That is why they came. Do not mistake their compassion for tactical idiocy.'

'That is my point.' Priamus resisted the rising urge to draw his blade. There was nothing to cut beyond the air before him, yet he felt a keen need to draw steel. 'They preserve. They defend. We are Astartes, not Imperial Guard. We are the spear thrust to the throat, not the blunt anvil. We are all that remains of the Great Crusade, Bastilan. For ten thousand years, we and we alone have crusaded to bring the Emperor's worlds into compliance. We do not fight for the people of the Imperium, we fight for the Imperium itself. We attack. We *attack*.'

Resssh, ressh. 'Not here. Not at Helsreach.'

Priamus lowered his head, unwilling to concede the point, despite the fact he knew he was defeated. That bastard Bastilan always did this to him. A few quiet words and he'd puncture all of what Priamus was trying to say. It was far, far beyond annoying.

'Helsreach is...' the swordsman's voice was lower now – less bitter, and somehow less confident. 'Nothing about this war has felt right.'

Nerovar had also retreated from the others.

But apparently not far enough.

'Brother,' came a voice. Grimaldus had returned. Nero acknowledged him with a nod, and returned to his feigned examination of the blistered and burned mural on the temple wall. Scenes of the Emperor watching over Helsreach: a golden god with His radiant visage regarding scenes of great industry below. With the wall ruined by flame and the artwork charred, it now resembled the city outside more than it ever had.

'How was the command meeting?'

'A tedious discussion of last stands. In that respect, it was no different from any other time. The Salamanders have withdrawn.'

'Then perhaps Priamus will cease his complaints.'

'I doubt that.'

Grimaldus removed his helm. Nerovar watched him as he examined the paintings, seeing the Reclusiarch's scarred features set in a thoughtful frown.

'How is the wound?' Grimaldus asked, his voice both deeper and softer now, unfiltered by helm vox.

'I will live.'

'Pain?'

'Does it matter? I will live.'

The chains binding his weapons to his armour rattled as the Reclusiarch moved across the chamber. Ceramite armour boots thudded on the dusty mosaics, breaking them underfoot. In the centre of the room, Grimaldus looked up at the holed ceiling, where a stained glass dome had once mercifully blocked the view of the polluted sky.

'I was with Cador,' he said, staring up into the heavens. 'I was with him at the end.'

'I know.'

'So you will believe me when I say that you could have done nothing for him had you been at our side? He was dead the moment the beast struck him.'

'I saw the death wound, did I not? You are telling me nothing I do not already know.'

'Then why do you still mourn his fall? It was a magnificent death, worthy of a vault on board the *Crusader.* He killed nine of the enemy with a broken blade and his bare hands, Nero. Dorn's blood, if only we could all inscribe such deeds on our armour. Humanity would have cleansed the stars by now.'

'He will never rest in that vault, and you know it.'

'That is not worth mourning over. It is just a regrettable truth. Hundreds of our own heroes have fallen and remained unrecovered. You carry Cador's true legacy. Why is that not enough? I wish to help you, brother, but you are not making it easy.'

'He trained me. He taught me the blade and bolter. He was a father in place of the parents I was stolen from.'

Grimaldus had still not looked at the other knight. He watched as an Imperial fighter streaked overhead, and wondered if it was Helius, the heir to Barasath and Jenzen.

'It is the way of the warrior,' he said, 'to outlive the ones that train us. We take their lessons and wield them as weapons against the enemies of Man.'

Nero snorted.

'Did I say something amusing, Apothecary?'

'In a way. Hypocrisy is always amusing.' The Apothecary removed his own helm. As he did so, he could suddenly feel the unwelcome weight of the cryo-sealed gene-seed in his forearm storage pod.

'Hypocrisy?' Grimaldus asked, more curious than annoyed.

'It is not like you to comfort and console, Reclusiarch. Forgive me for saying so.'

'Why would I need to forgive you for speaking the truth?'

'You make it sound so clear and easy. None of us have been truthful with you since… we came here.'

Grimaldus lowered his gaze from the dark skies. He fixed his eyes – eyes that the commander of a god-machine had called kind, of all things – on Nerovar's own.

'You say "Since we came here". I sense another lie.'

'Very well. Since before we came here. Since Mordred died. It is difficult to be near you, Reclusiarch. You are withdrawn when you should be inspiring. You are distant when you would once have been wrathful. I believe you are wrong to lecture me on Cador's death when you have been lost to us since Mordred fell. There are flashes of fire beneath the cold surface, and we have warned you of these changes before. But to no avail.'

Grimaldus chuckled, the sound leaving his lips as a soft exhalation through a reluctant smile.

'I am seeing the world through his eyes,' he said, looking down at the silver skull mask in his hands. 'And I am seeing, night after night, that I am not him. I did not deserve this honour. I am no leader of men, nor am I skilled at dealing with the humans. I should not be wearing the mantle of a Reclusiarch, yet I was certain once the war began, my doubts and discomforts would fade away.'

'But they have not.'

'No. They have not. I will die on this world.' Grimaldus looked at the Apothecary again. 'My master died, and mere days later, I was consigned to die on a world that has no hope of surviving an ugly war, far from my brothers and the Chapter I have served for two centuries. Even if we win, what does victory buy? We will be kings astride a ruined world of dead industry.' He shook his head. 'And this is where we will die. A worthless death.'

'It is glorious, in its own way. The Helsreach Crusade. Our brothers and the people of this world will remember our sacrifice forever. You know this as well as I.'

'Oh, I know it. I cannot escape it. But I do not care for *glory*. Glory is earned through a life lived in service to the Throne. It should not be a consolation gift, or something sought to sate a hunger. I want my life to matter to my brothers, and I want my death to further the cause of the Imperium. Do you not recall Mordred's last words to me? They are written in gold upon the plinth of the statue that honours him.'

'I remember them, Reclusiarch. *"We are judged in life for the evil we destroy"*. And we will be judged well, for a great many have fallen before us already.'

'Our deaths inspire no one. They benefit no one. Do you recall the Shadow Wolves? When we saw the last of that Chapter die, I felt my heart sing. Never before had I craved the taste of alien blood as I did in that moment. Their deaths mattered. Every warrior clad in silver armour died in true glory that day. What of Helsreach? Who will draw courage from a footnote in the archives of a fallen city?'

Grimaldus closed his eyes. He did not open them again, even as he heard Nerovar approaching. The fist crashing against his jaw knocked him to the ground, where he at last looked back at the Apothecary. Grimaldus was smiling, though in truth he had not expected the blow.

'How dare you?' Nero asked, his teeth clenched and his fist still tight. '*How dare you?* You throw filth on our glory here, yet you dare tell me Cador's death means something? It means *nothing*. He died as we will all die: unremembered and unburied. You are my Reclusiarch, Grimaldus. Do not lie to me. If our glory matters to no one, then Cador's death is meaningless and I have every right to mourn him as you mourn for all of us.'

The Chaplain licked his lips, tasting the chemical-rich blood that marked them. In silence, he rose to his feet. Nerovar did not back away. Far from it, he stood his ground, and activated his bracer-mounted storage pod. A plastek vial slid from its secure housing, and Nerovar threw it to Grimaldus.

The Reclusiarch caught it in hands that threatened to shake. NACLIDES, the script on the vial denoted. The gene-seed of a brother fallen days before.

'Nero...'

Nerovar ejected another tube and tossed it to the Reclusiarch. DARGRAVIAN, it read. He had been the first to fall.

'Nerovar...'

The Apothecary ejected a third vial. This one he held in his fist, his gauntlet clutching it just shy of crushing it into shards. CADOR showed between Nero's fingers.

'Answer me,' the Apothecary demanded. 'Is what we do here worthless? Is there nothing to be proud of in our sacrifice?'

Grimaldus didn't answer for several moments. He looked around the modest, broken temple, the light of thought bright in his eyes.

'The city is falling, brother. Sarren and the other humans faced that fact today. The time has come for us to choose where we will die.'

'Then let it be where we will be remembered.' Nerovar reverently handed the vial bearing Cador's cryogenically frozen gene-seed organs to the Chaplain. 'Let it be where our deaths will matter, and give birth to tales worthy of being recorded in humanity's history.'

Grimaldus looked at the three vials resting in his gauntleted palm.

'I know of a place,' he said softly, a dangerous flicker appearing in his eyes as he looked back up at his battle-brother. 'It is far from here, but there is no holier place on this entire world. There, we shall dig our graves, and there, we will ensure the Great Enemy forever remembers the name of the Black Templars.'

'Tell me why you have chosen this place. I must know.'

The truth is... surprising, but as I speak the words, there is no doubt within them. This is what we must do, and it is how we must die. Our lives are sacrifice, from implantation of the gene-seed to its extraction from our bodies.

'We will die where our deaths matter. Where we can spite the enemy with our last breaths, and inspire the warriors of this city.'

'Now those,' Nero says, 'are at last the words of a Reclusiarch.'

'I am a slow learner,' I confess. This brings a smile to my brother's lips.

'Mordred is dead,' Nero said, keeping his voice low. 'But he trusted you as his heir above any other for one reason. He believed you were worthy.'

I say nothing.

'Do not die without ever living up to him, Grimaldus.'

TWENTY

GODBREAKER

Maralin moved across the botanical garden, her fingertips trailing along the dewy leaves and petals of the rosebushes.

They were not hers, but that didn't stop her admiring them. Only one of her sisters had the patience and skill to grow roses in the choking air and sickened soil of the city, and that was Alana. All other blooms in the botanical garden were raised by cultivation servitors, and in Maralin's opinion, it showed. Her fingers danced along the wet petals of the soot-darkened roses, amazed as always at how lovelier and fuller Alana's flowers were in comparison to the modest blooms grown by the augmented slave workers.

They lacked inspiration, clearly, and no doubt the severance of their souls had much to do with it.

Passing through the spacious garden, she entered the rectory. The building's air filters were straining, keeping the main chamber cooled. Prioress Sindal was sat, as she almost always was, at her oversized desk of rare stonewood, scribing away in meticulous handwriting.

She looked up as Maralin entered, peering through the corrective eyelenses that had slipped to the end of her nose.

'Prioress, we've received word from Tempestora.'

Sindal's cataracted eyes narrowed, and she gently sprinkled sand across her parchment, drying the fresh ink. She was seventy-one years old, and she didn't just look it – she also sounded it when she spoke.

'What of the Sanctorum?'

'Gone,' Maralin swallowed.

'Survivors?'

'Few, and most are wounded. The hive has fallen, and the Sanctorum of the Order of Our Martyred Lady is overrun by the enemy. We received word now that there aren't enough survivors to retake their Sanctorum as of yet. Our own sisters in the Ash and Fire Wastes are moving to support.'

'So Tempestora is gone. What of Hive Stygia to the north?'

'Still no word, prioress. They are surely enduring the siege as we are.'

The old woman's hands were palsied, though she found that writing always steadied them for reasons beyond her understanding. They shook now as she set the completed parchment aside, on a loose pile of several others.

'Helsreach has weeks left, but little beyond that. The siege is almost at our own gates.'

'That... brings me to the second of the morning's messages, prioress.' Maralin swallowed again. She was clearly uncomfortable, and resented being the one sent to deliver these messages, but she was the youngest, and often relegated to these tasks.

'Speak, sister.'

'We received a message from the Astartes commander in the city. The Reclusiarch. He sends word that his knights are en route to stand with us in the defence.'

The prioress removed her eyeglasses and cleaned them with a soft cloth. Then, carefully, she placed them back onto her face and looked directly at the young girl.

'The Reclusiarch is bringing the Black Templars here?'

'Yes, prioress.'

'Hmph. Did he happen to say why he felt the sudden wish to fight alongside the Order of the Argent Shroud?'

He had not, but Maralin had been paying close attention to the scraps of information that made it over the vox with any clarity. This, too, was one of her duties as the youngest, while her sisters were preparing for battle.

'No, prioress. I suspect it ties into Colonel Sarren's decision to break up the remaining defenders into separate bastions. The Reclusiarch has chosen the Temple.'

'I see. I doubt he asked permission.'

Maralin smiled. The prioress had fought with the Emperor's Chosen before, and many of her sermons had included irritated mentions of their brash attitudes. 'No, prioress. He didn't.'

'Typical Astartes. Hmph. When do they arrive?'

'Before sunset, mistress.'

'Very well. Anything more?'

There was little. The compromised vox-network had offered several suggestions of severe enemy Titan movement to the north, but confirmation wasn't forthcoming. Maralin relayed this, but she could tell the prioress's mind was elsewhere. On the Templars, most certainly.

'Damn it all,' the old woman muttered as she rose from her chair, placing the quill in the inkpot. 'Well, don't just stand there gawping, girl. Prepare my battle armour.'

Maralin's eyes widened. 'How long has it been since you wore your armour, prioress?'

'How old are you, girl?'

'Fifteen, mistress.'

'Well, then. Let's just say you couldn't wipe your own backside the last time I went to war.' The old woman's forehead barely reached Maralin's chin as she shuffled past. 'But it'll be good to deliver a sermon with a bolter in hand again.'

Elsewhere in the Temple of the Emperor Ascendant, the sisters were making ready for war. The Order of the Argent Shroud were not in Helsreach in any significant force, their contributions thus far being little more than a series of fighting withdrawals from churches across the city.

Ninety-seven battle-ready sisters manned the Temple's walls and halls, standing guard over several thousand menials, servitors, preachers, lay sisters and acolytes. The Temple itself was formed of a central basilica, surrounded by high rockcrete walls bedecked in leering angels and hideous gargoyles staring out at the city beyond. Between the walls and the central building, acre upon acre of graveyard reached out from the basilica in every direction. Thousands of years before, they had been lush garden grounds, grown and tended by the first of Armageddon's settlers. Those same settlers were buried here, their bones long turned to dust and their gravestones weathered faceless by time. Interred alongside them were generations of their descendants; holy servants of the Imperium; and the respected dead of Armageddon's Steel Legions.

No one was buried here now; the graveyard was considered full. Official records numbered the graves around the basilica as nine million, one hundred and eight thousand, four hundred and sixty. Currently, only two people knew this was incorrect, and only one of them cared about the discrepancy.

The first was a servitor who had been a gardener in life, and had devoted several of his living years, before the augmetics had stolen his reason and independence, to counting the graves as he tended the gardens around them. He'd been curious, and it had satisfied him to learn the truth. He kept it to himself, knowing to report it to his superiors might bring down accusations of laxity in his primary duties. He was, after all, a garden-tender and not a stock-counter or cogitator. Three months after he had satisfied himself with the truth, he was found stealing from the Temple's tithe boxes, and sentenced to augmetic reconfiguration.

The second person who knew the truth was Prioress Sindal. She had also counted them herself, over the course of three years. To her, it was a form of meditation; of bringing herself to a state of oneness with the people of Armageddon. She had not been born here, and in her devoted service to the people of this world, she felt her meditative technique was apt enough.

She had, of course, filed amendments to the records, but they were still locked in the bureaucratic cycle. The Temple's cardinal council were notoriously foul at having their staff deal with paperwork.

Most gravestones were stacked close together in clusters of bloodline or fealty, and there was no conformity in the markers – each was a slightly different size, shape, material or angle to those nearby, even in sections where the rows were ordered in neat lines. In other parts of the graveyard district, finding one's way along a pathway was akin to navigating a labyrinth, with weaving a way between the graves taking a great deal of time.

The Temple of the Emperor Ascendant itself was, by Imperial standards, a thing of haunting and gothic beauty. The spires were ringed by stone angels and depictions of the Emperor's primarchs as saints. Stained glass windows displayed a riot of colours, showing scenes of the God-Emperor's Great Crusade to bring the stars into union beneath humanity's vigilant guidance. Lesser depictions were of the first settlers themselves, their deeds of survival and construction exaggerated to deific proportion, showing them as the builders of a glorious, perfect world of golden light and marble cathedrals, rather than the industrial planet they had founded in truth.

The Sisters of the Order of the Argent Shroud had not been idle during the months of warfare that ravaged the rest of the city. Lesser shrines in the graveyard were both heavy weapon outposts and chapels to their founder, Saint Silvana. Angular statues of solid silver – each one of the weeping saint in various poses of grief, triumph and contemplation – stood silent watch over turret pods and barricaded gun-nests.

The walls themselves were reinforced in the same way as the city walls, and bore the same ratio of defence turrets per metre. These remained manned by Helsreach militia.

The Temple courtyard's great gates were not closed. Despite the protestations of the cardinal council, Prioress Sindal had demanded the doors be kept open until the last possible moment, allowing more and more refugees to enter over the weeks of siege. The basilica's undercroft housed hundreds of families who hadn't been able to enter the subterranean shelters, for reasons of criminal activity, administrative error, or outright bad luck. Bunched together in the gloom, they came up for morning and evening prayer, adding their voices to the singing pleas that reached up the immaculately-painted ceiling, where the God-Emperor was depicted staring off into the heavens.

The Temple of the Emperor Ascendant was, in short, a fortress.

A fortress filled with refugees, and surrounded by the largest graveyard in the world.

We are the last to arrive.

Twenty-nine of my brothers already await my arrival, with our cargo gunship grounded nearby. It brings our total force to thirty-five, if one was to count Jurisian labouring on the forlorn hope, bring the weapon across the Ash Wastes.

Thirty-five of the hundred that landed in Helsreach five weeks before.

One of those awaiting our arrival is the one warrior I have done all I can to avoid for the last five weeks.

He kneels before the open gates of the Temple's compound, his black sword plunged into the marble before him, helmed head lowered in reverence. As with the Templars around him, almost all evidence of scripture parchment, wax crusader seals and cloth tabard is gone from his armour. I recognise him because of his ancient armour and the dark blade he prays to.

Jurisian himself has worked on that armour, repairing it with reverence each time he has been honoured with the chance to touch it. Before Jurisian, a host of other Masters of the Forge maintained the relic war plate through the centuries, back to its original forging as a suit of armour for the Imperial Fists Legion.

While our armour shows dull grey wounds under the stripped paint, this knight's war plate, forged in a time when primarchs walked the galaxy, shows gold beneath the battle damage. The legacy of Dorn's Legion is still there if one knows where to look; between the cracks, revealed by war.

The knight rises, pulling the sword from the marble with no effort at all. His helm turns to face me, and a faceplate that once stared out onto the battlefields of the Horus Heresy regards me with eye lenses the colour of human blood.

He salutes me, sword sheathed on his back and his gauntlets making the sign of the aquila over his battered breastplate. I return the salute, and rarely in my life has the gesture been so heartfelt. I am finally ready to stand before him, and endure the judging stare of those crimson eyes.

'Hail, Reclusiarch,' he says to me.

'Hail, Bayard,' I say to the Emperor's Champion of the Helsreach Crusade.

He watches me, but I know he is not seeing me. He sees Mordred, the knight whose weapon I bear, and whose face I wear.

'My liege.' Priamus comes forward, kneeling before Bayard.

'Priamus,' Bayard vox-laughs. 'Still breathing, I see.'

'Nothing on this world will change that, my liege.'

'Rise, brother. The day will never come that you must kneel before me.' Priamus rises, inclining his head in respect once more before returning to my side. 'Artarion, Bastilan, it is good to see you both. And you, Nero.'

Nerovar makes the sign of the aquila, but says nothing.

'Cador's fall tore at my heart, brother. He and I served in the Sword Brethren together, did you know that?'

'I knew it, my liege. Cador spoke of it often. He was honoured to serve at your side.'

'The honour was mine. Know that fifty of the enemy died by my blade the day I heard of his passing. Throne, but he was a warrior to quench the fires of the stars themselves. I miss him fiercely, and the Eternal Crusade is poorer without his sword.'

'You... do great honour to his memory,' Nero's voice is choked with emotion.

'Tell me, brother,' Bayard's tone lowers, as if the refugees standing and staring at us outside the great gates have no right to hear of what we speak. 'I heard his death-wound was in the back. Is this so?'

Nero's nod comes with reluctance. 'It is.'

'I also heard he killed nine of the beasts alone, before succumbing to his wounds.'

'He did.'

'Nine. *Nine.* Then he died facing his enemy, as a knight must. Thank you, Nero. You have brought me comfort this day.'

'I... I...'

'Welcome, brothers. It has been too long since we stood united.' There are general murmurs of assent, and Bayard looks to me.

I smile behind my mask.

They rode in the back compartment of a trundling Chimera armoured personnel transport, their backs thumping against the metal walls with each sharp turn. It had been parked on the highway itself, riddled with bullet holes and las-burns, but still very much fuelled and ready to roll. Andrej and the others had dragged the bodies of dead Legionnaires out onto the road, and the storm trooper had forced the dockers to say a short prayer over the corpses before he would, as he put it, 'steal their ride.'

'Manners cost nothing,' he told them. 'And these men died for your city.'

The troop section in the back of the Chimera was a typical slice of Guard life, smelling of blood, oil and rancid sweat. On creaking benches, Maghernus and his dockers, along with Asavan Tortellius recruited to their cause, sat and waited for Andrej to get them all the way down the Hel's Highway.

He was not a good driver. They had mentioned this to him, and he professed not to know what they were talking about. Besides, he'd added, the left tank tread was damaged. That was why he kept skidding.

Also, he'd amended last of all, they should shut up. So there.

Andrej cycled through vox-channels, still getting no luck on any frequency. Whether every vox-tower in the city was gone or the orks had some intense jamming campaign going on was beside the point at this stage. He couldn't get in touch with his commanders, and that left him to his own devices. As always, he would *go forward.* It was the way of the Legion, and the creed of the Guard.

The way he saw it, the Reclusiarch owed him a favour. In this case, *going forward* meant making a stand with the black knights until he could find someone, anyone, from his command structure.

There'd been a particularly galling moment when he'd managed to contact elements of the 233rd Steel Legion Armoured Division, but they were in the middle of being annihilated by an enemy scrap-Titan formation and had no time for pleasantries. Fate was laughing at him, Andrej was sure of it – the one Imperial force he'd been able to reach were minutes from being wiped out anyway.

This was no way to fight a war. No communication between any forces? Madness!

Smoke and flames were on the horizon ahead, but that indicated next to nothing of any use in determining direction or destination. Smoke and flames were on every horizon. Smoke and flame was all each of the horizons had become.

Andrej was not laughing. This did not amuse him, no sir.

He changed gear with a nauseating grind of metal hating metal. A chorus of complaints jeered from the back as the Chimera juddered in protest and shook his passengers around some more. He heard someone's head clang off the interior wall. He hoped it was the fat priest's.

Andrej sniggered. At least that was funny.

'...ckr... sn... tl...' declared the vox.

Aha! Now this was progress.

'This is Trooper Andrej, of the–'

He closed his mouth as the transmission crackled into a semblance of clarity. The burning district ahead, through which he'd need to pass to reach the distant Temple... it was the Rostorik Ironworks. The vox told of a Titan's death-wails.

'Hold on,' he called back, and accelerated the battered transport along the Hel's Highway, towards the emerging shape of *Stormherald* above the surrounding industrial towers.

The link was savaged by *Bound in Blood's* mortis-cry. Zarha twisted in her coffin, trying to filter the empathic pain from the influx of sensory information she needed to focus on.

Her fistless arm pushed forward in the milky fluid, and the Titan obeyed her furious need.

'Firing,' Valian Carsomir confirmed.

In the centre of the industrial sector, ringed by burning towers and crushed manufactories, the Imperator Titan weathered a hail of enemy fire from scrap-walkers that barely reached its waist. Its shields rippled with searing intensity, corona-bright and almost blinding.

The plasma annihilator amassed power, sucking in a storm of air through its coolant vanes and juddering as it made ready to release. Around the god-machine's legs, the waddling ork walkers blared sirens and howling warnings to one another. Burning vapour clouded around the shaking plasma weapon as it vented pressure, and with a roar that shattered every remaining window in a kilometre-wide radius, *Stormherald* fired.

Three of the lesser scrap-Titans were engulfed in the flood of boiling plasma that surged from the weapon, melting to sludge in the white-hot sunfire.

Zarha's arm was aflame with sympathetic agony. She did her best to blank it from her mind, focusing instead on the rattling crawl of insects over her body. Her shields were taking grave damage now. *Stormherald* could not linger here for much longer.

'*Bound in Blood* isn't rising, my princeps.'

Zarha knew this. She'd heard its soul scream across the Legio's princeps-level link.

He is dying.

'He is dying.'

'Orders, my princeps?'

Stand. Fight.

'Stand. Fight.'

The Titan shuddered as another wreck-walker staggered closer, its shoulder cannons booming. Standing above the downed Reaver-class Titan *Bound in Blood, Stormherald* returned fire with its incidental weapon batteries, flash-frying the lesser machine's void shields in a hail of incendiary fire.

Zarha pushed her other arm forward through the ooze, laughing as she moved. *Stormherald's* other arm, the colossal hellstorm cannon, thrummed as its internal mechanics chambers and drive engines cycled up to firing speed.

'My princeps...' Lonn and Carsomir warned in the same breath. Zarha cackled in her tomb of fluid.

Die!

'Die!'

The enemy scrap-Titan was shredded by five energy lances blasting from *Stormherald's* hellstorm cannon. In less than three seconds, its plasma core was breached and critically venting, and in less than five it had exploded, taking the bulk of the fat-bodied gargant with it. Shrapnel shards the size of tanks hammered off the Imperator's void shields, leaving distortions of bruising while the generators struggled to compensate.

'Secondary impact from the turbolaser batteries... Cog's teeth, we struck the G-71 orbital landing platform. My princeps, I implore you to use caution...'

Engine kill. She licked her cold, wrinkled lips. *Engine kill.*

'Engine kill.'

Half a kilometre behind the dead enemy walker – its foundation struts destroyed by the laser salvo from *Stormherald's* hellstorm cannon – a sizeable landing platform crashed down to the ground, sliding on fouled gantries to smash through the roof of a burning tank manufactorum. An avalanche of rockcrete, broken iron and steel was all that remained of both installations, at the heart of a cloud of grey-black smoke and rock dust.

The ironyard had played host to the pitched battle between Titans and infantry for several days. Little was left, yet neither side was giving ground.

'My princeps...'

No more lectures. I do not care.

'No more lectures. I do not care.'

'My princeps,' Valian repeated, 'new contact. Behind us.'

She spun in the fluid, fish-like and alert. *Stormherald* followed with ponderous slowness, its fortress-legs thudding down onto the ground. The cityscape view through the Titan's eyes panned, showing nothing but devastation.

'The scanner blur is either several walkers together, or a single engine of our size.'

The adept hunched by the auspex console turned to regard the pilot crew with three bionic eyes, each with a lens of dark green glass. A blurt of machine-code disagreed with Lonn's appraisal.

[]Negative. Thermal signature registers distinct single pulse.[]

One enemy engine.

That isn't possible, she thought, but never let it reach her vocalisers. An uneasy tremor was running through the Titan's bones, and she felt it as keenly as she'd once felt the wind on her skin in another lifetime.

'My princeps, we must disengage,' Lonn said, staring out into the burning ironyard. 'We need to rearm and cool the plasma core in standard sustained venting procedure.'

I know that better than you, Lonn.

'I know that better than you, Lonn.'

But I am not abandoning a district I have spent four nights fighting to hold.

'But I am not abandoning a district I have spent four nights fighting to hold.'

'My princeps, there's precious little left standing to defend,' Lonn pressed. 'I repeat my recommendation to withdraw and rearm.'

No. I am sending Regal *and* Ivory Fang *north to hunt the inbound enemy engine and confirm with visual scanning.*

'No. I am sending *Regal* and *Ivory Fang* north to hunt the inbound enemy engine and confirm with visual scanning.'

Lonn and Carsomir shared a glance from across the command deck. Both men were restrained in their control thrones, and both men wore the same expression of frustrated doubt.

'My princeps,' Carsomir tried, but he was cut off.

'See? They move.' On the hololithic display screen, the runes denoting the scout Titans *Regal* and *Ivory Fang* broke away from their perimeter-stalking patrol to the west, and strode northward in search of the incoming thermal pulse.

'My princeps, we do not have the ammunition reserves required to inflict destruction-level damage on an enemy engine of comparable size to us.'

'I am venting the heart-core's excess fusion matter and flushing the heat exchangers.' Even as she vocalised the orders, she was sending empathic pulses through her links to make it so.

'My princeps, that is not enough.'

'He is right, my princeps,' Carsomir had turned in his throne, and was looking back at her fluid tank now. 'You are too close to *Stormherald's* wrath. Return to us and focus.'

'We are defended by three Reavers and our own scout screen. Be silent.'

'Two Reavers, my princeps.'

Yes. Two. She pulled back from the immersion of rage. Yes... two. *Bound in Blood* was silent and dead, its power core cooling and its princeps voiceless. In her confused thinking, she did not mean to vocalise her next words.

'We have lost seven engines in one week of battle.'

'Yes, my princeps. Prudence would serve us best now. If the auspex is true, we must withdraw.'

She floated in her coffin, hearing the curious humanity in their voices. Such emotion. Such curious intensity, affecting their speech tones. She recognised it as fear, without truly recalling what the sensation felt like.

'We have killed almost twenty of the foe's engines... but I concede. Sound the withdrawal as soon as the Warhounds have confirmation.'

The first Imperial engine to bear witness to the *Godbreaker* was *Ivory Fang*. It stalked fast and low on its backwards-jointed legs, the side-to-side pitch of its stomping gait adding a feral, if mechanical, grace to its dawn hunt.

Warhound-class. And it suited the name, lone wolfing its way through the wrecked industrial sector, striding around the shells of tanks destroyed in the week-long struggle for the Rostorik Ironyard. Sometimes, its hooved feet would crunch down on the soft meat of burned bodies and render them into pulped smears along the ground. Dead skitarii, Guardsmen, factorum workers and greenskins littered the district.

Ivory Fang was commanded most ably by a princeps by name of Haven Havelock. Princeps Havelock dreamed, as did most of his ilk, of one day mastering a great battle-Titan, and perhaps even one of Invigilata's precious few Imperators. His fellow princeps – equals and superiors alike – spoke well of him, and he knew his place in the Legio as a solid, reliable scout-Titan commander was assured, valued, and deserved.

Patience was foremost among his virtues – patience and cunning. That reasoned, meticulous hunting instinct bled through the mind-bond into *Ivory Fang*. Twinned, man and machine were past masters at the kind of deep-urban stalks where Warhound Titans most excelled.

The rough link between Titan commanders maintained throughout the city had suffered just as Imperial vox had suffered, but Havelock was reassured by the fragments of meaning that pulsed through the chaos. If there truly was an enemy scrap-Titan out there, it was nothing the battle group could not deal with. *Stormherald* was no more than two kilometres to the south, and with it were *Danol's Retribution* and *The Ghoul,* both Reavers with victory banners descending from their armour plating that would put mid-range Titan princeps from any other Legio to shame.

Nothing the beasts could hurl at them would break such a formation. Even the largest gargant would fall to *Stormherald.*

I see nothing, came the aggravated spurt of machine code from his fellow princeps, Feerna of *Regal.*

Havelock spent a quarter of a second consulting his internal tracking runes. The link to his Titan's auspex sensors formed a rough, instinctive knowledge of his kin's locations in his mind.

Regal was a half-kilometre to the north-east, moving at speed through a small cluster of iron smelteries. It would have been in visual range, had the space between the two Titans not been obstructed by ruined manufactories.

I see nothing, either.

It's the heat, she complained. *Hunting for thermal signatures in this inferno is like seeking black in the night sky. My auspex readers show nothing but thermal disruption. Horus himself could be hiding in here, and I would not kn–*

Feerna? Feerna?

'Registering energy discharge of significant size to the north-east,' Havelock's moderati called out.

'Confirmed,' murmured the tech-adept that hunched in a station behind the princeps throne.

Feerna? Havelock tried once more. 'Bring us about and move north-east at aggressive intent speed. Everyone be ready.' He twitched in his restraint throne as the Titan obeyed his pilot's urgings. The connection feeds were alive with subtle static, itching at his nerves. *Ivory Fang* was keen. It had sensed something.

And then it hit Havelock, too.

'Hnnngh,' he drooled through clenched teeth, shuddering against the leather bindings that restrained him in place. 'Hnn... Hvv...'

The pain of *Regal's* mortis-cry faded, and Havelock breathed again. Feerna was gone, as was her Titan. She'd been a Warhound, and her link to the others was tenuous and weak in comparison to the strength of a bond to the greater god-machines. The pain bled away fast, bringing relief in its wake.

The Titan clanked its way down a subsidiary alley, its weapon-arms rising in readiness. Havelock sent several mental urgings in quick succession, triggering autoloaders, coolant valves and bracing pistons into activity. *Ivory Fang* rounded the corner at the alley's end, stalking out into the main street. As it had been since this morning, this sector was still aflame because of the destroyed refineries and petrochemical stores, with about half the buildings finally quieting into smouldering ruins.

But the fighting was done here.

'Where is the bastard?' Havelock whispered.

The auspex chimed - once, weak.

'We have movement,' the tech-adept grumbled, not looking up from his scanner console. 'There is–'

'I see, it, I see it. Back away *now!*'

It came from the black clouds, rumbling forward on a clumsy mess of tank treads and crushing feet. Its body was slanted, tapering to a head that was all brutal jaw and piggish, alien eye-windows. Every metre of its scrap metal torso bristled with tiered weapons platforms.

It was quite the ugliest and most offensive thing Havelock had ever seen, and that was more than simply because it was an affront to the purity of Mechanicus god-machine creation. No, more than that, it offended him because its manifestation before him made no sense. It... dwarfed *Stormherald.*

It seemed impossibility given form, striding, limping from the oily smoke that blanketed the district.

Havelock pulsed a digitally-translated pict of the enemy gargant across the mind-bond to Princeps Zarha and any other Titan commander in range. It was all the warning he would be allowed to send, for *Godbreaker* opened fire the very moment its main armaments cleared the smoke.

Ivory Fang was pulverised beneath enough solid, laser and plasma weapon fire to level a city block. Its demise, and the end of Havelock's mediocre career, was marked by a vast crater that would remain for decades after the war had bled the whole world almost dry.

Godbreaker moved onward.

TWENTY-ONE

STORMHERALD DOWN

The two engines faced one another across the burning ironyard, as alike in power as they were unlike in dignity. Both were ablaze, both bleeding fire and smoke into the clouded air.

The air between them was a blizzard of weapon fire as secondary turrets and battlement guns spat anti-infantry firepower at each other in the hopes of inflicting as much damage as possible. Inside both Titans, it sounded like a flood of pebbles clattering against the armour-plated hulls.

Inside *Stormherald,* the sirens were wailing long and loud.

Zarha writhed in her fluid-filled tomb, her limbs pushing through the blood-pinked water. Psychostigmata was ravaging her, as *Stormherald's* wounds played out in a map across her naked body. Where the Titan was battered, she was discoloured by bruising or bent by broken bones. Where the god-machine was rent and torn, her flesh smiled and bled in open wounds. Where *Stormherald* burned, she was haemorrhaging internally.

The Titan's command deck smelled of burning oil and rancid sweat.

'Primary shield layer restored,' Carsomir announced, his hands working at his console with a near-furious focus. 'Core containment holding.'

Raise... raise shields...

'Krrrsssshhhhh.'

RAISE THE SHIELDS.

'Raise the shields.'

'Already done, my princeps.'

She was slowing down. The pain stole so much of her attention now. With a moan that was swallowed into silence by the water, she pulsed orders to the various decks and pushed both of her arms forward through the pinkish ooze.

Nothing happened.

She tried again, screaming into the oxygen-rich fluid, the stumps of her hands thumping against the front of her coffin.

Nothing.

'Plasma annihilator venting for sixteen more seconds, my princeps. Fourteen. Thirteen. Twelve.'

Fire the... the... other arm. Fire it.

'Krrrsssssshh.'

FIRE THE HELLSTORM CANNON. Her stunted right limb thudded over and over against the glass side of her amniotic tank.

'Fire the hellstorm cannon.'

'As soon as it has recharged, my princeps,' Lonn replied, half-ignoring her now. She'd given the order to fire at will several minutes before. Drifting in her pain as the Titan fell to pieces, she was barely trustworthy now. Carsomir and Lonn worked almost independently of their princeps's wishes. They only had one more shot at walking away from this – the enemy Titan was already advancing over the mangled body of *The Ghoul,* which had lasted less than a minute beneath the *Godbreaker's* initial volleys.

The scrap-Titan was capable of a merciless amount of firepower. None of *Stormherald's* command crew had seen anything like it before, let alone suffered on the receiving end. Only a few minutes into the god-machines' duel, and the Imperator was wreathed in flame, temperature gauges whining and warning lights flashing throughout the confined corridors threading through the giant's steel bones.

The multitude of layered energy screens that served the Titan as void shields had been torn apart with insane, laughable speed by the ork walker.

'I'm ready,' Carsomir announced. 'Firing.'

'Wait for the stabilisers to come back online!' Lonn yelled. 'They only need another minute.'

Carsomir thought his fellow pilot's faith in the tech-crews working in the shoulder joints was admirable, but unbelievably misguided given the circumstances. He blinked once, wasting precious seconds to even think about listening to Lonn's plea.

'The arm isn't badly damaged. I'm taking the shot. I can make it.'

'You'll miss, Val! Give them thirty seconds, just thirty more seconds.'

'Firing.'

'You son of a bitch!'

Stormherald's knees locked in preparation and the plasma annihilator tower that served as its left arm began its air-sucking inhalation of coolant.

'You've killed us,' Lonn breathed, watching the enemy Titan through the steamed-up view windows. An unremitting torrent of incidental fire rained against *Stormherald's* shields, turning them violet with strain.

'Void shields buckling,' one of the tech-adepts called from a side terminal.

'Enemy engine making ready to fire primary weapons,' another said.

'They'll never get the chance...' Valian Carsomir smiled with a wicked light in his eyes.

Lonn's shouted protest was drowned out in the roar of discharging sunfire. A beam of plasma – roiling, boiling and white-hot – vomited from the cannon's focusing ring, blasting across the four hundred metres separating the two Titans. *Stormherald* stood rigid, defensive, no longer advancing after the first two minutes of punishing exchange. *Godbreaker* had not stopped its thunderous, slow charge.

'You bastard!' Lonn yelled. Carsomir had missed. The jet of plasma blanketed the ground to the left of the closing ork gargant, where it began to dissolve everything it touched in a vast pool of acidic corruption.

Lonn had been right. The arm-weapon had strayed despite targeting locks, as the supreme force of its own firepower sent it veering off-centre.

'I had the shot,' Carsomir shook his head.

'Void shields failing,' the tech-adept announced without any emotion whatsoever.

'I had the shot,' Carsomir repeated, unable to look away from the wreck-Titan bearing down upon them. Behind the moderati thrones, Zarha floated in her suspension tank, slack and unconscious.

'No, no, no...' Lonn worked at his console, his brow furrowed. 'This can't be.'

The Titan began to shudder around them as the void shields died again, the Imperator's dense armour taking the brunt of the alien attack.

Lonn had never worked like this before in his life. It was a flurry of effort, performed half in the flesh and half with the mind. He could feel the Titan falling into slumber, and its dimming consciousness dragged at his thoughts, slowing them to a crawl. Where he met resistance like this in the mind-link, he compensated by overrides on his command console.

The command deck grew dark as he worked. The enemy gargant eclipsed all outside light, looming before the idle *Stormherald.*

'Why hasn't it fired?' Carsomir worked as Lonn did, cooling essential systems, ordering repair teams to afflicted joints, feeding power from the coughing shield generators to the thirsty weapon energy cells.

To Lonn, the reason was obvious. Like the savages that acted as the gargant's puppeteers, the scrap-Titan was built to kill with its hands. Several of the thing's weapon mounts were taken up by crude arms that ended in spears and claws of salvaged metal. It wanted to savour *Stormherald's* death, like some many-armed daemon from the impure millennia of pre-Imperial Terra.

Zarha's augmetic eyes flicked back to active as the chamber grew dark. She awoke, seeing the doom bearing down on her, feeling secondary fire devastating her armour plating like she was being skinned alive.

Through the bloody fluid and maddening pain, she raised her shivering arms. *Stormherald* mirrored the gesture as it was pummelled under *Godbreaker's* guns. Jagged metal fell from the Mechanicus giant like rainfall, ripped from its body and crashing to the ground below. Many of the Imperator's crew that had the sense of self-preservation to flee were killed by the falling chunks of armour plating.

Zarha put the last of her strength, and the last of her life, into throwing both her arms forward. The plasma annihilator did not fire. Neither did the hellstorm cannon. Both were locked in the time-consuming process of recharging from depleted power generators.

Both towering weapon-arms speared forward, hammering through the fat hull of *Godbreaker* and impaling it in place. The cry of tearing scrap metal was cacophonous as *Stormherald's* cannons pushed deeper, stabbing like daggers through meat, seeking to grind and crush the enemy's heart-reactor.

Grimaldus. I stood until the end, as promised. Awaken Oberon. *Awaken it, or die as we have.*

Perhaps her thoughts echoed across the empathic link to her moderati, for one of them voiced something of her sentiments.

'We're dead,' Carsomir murmured. He wanted to rise from his throne, but the restraints and connection cables bound him too completely. He settled for closing his eyes.

Lonn had sensed the Crone's intent. He leaned all his weight on the control levers, adding his demands to Zarha's, plunging the arms deeper into the enemy Titan's chest with scraping, grinding slowness. He felt sick to stare up through the darkened viewports to see the bestial, tusked aliens clambering along the impaling arm-cannons, using them as bridges to board *Stormherald* as they bled from the wounds in their own Titan's body.

With no peaceful fade or foreshadowing, the power died, leaving him in darkness. He eased up on the levers, knowing without needing to look that the Crone was gone.

Stormherald was a statue, joined to the war machine that was slowly carving it to pieces with great chops of its bladed limbs. As endings went, Lonn mused, this was neither grand nor glorious.

As the command deck shook with rhythmic violence from the *pound, pound, pounding* of *Godbreaker's* many weapon-arms, Lonn drew his laspistol, and watched the sealed doors, ready for the aliens to eventually breach them. His skin crawled at the gentle sound of Zarha's corpse bumping against the glass front of her coffin, in time to the Titan's shaking.

'I... I had the shot,' Carsomir stammered from the adjacent throne as he waited to die in the dark. 'I had the shot...'

The side of his head burst open as a las-beam slashed through his skull.

'You bastard,' Lonn said to the twitching body. Then he lowered his pistol, took a deep breath, and began the laborious process of disengaging himself from the control throne.

There was something human in the way *Stormherald* died. The way it went slack, the way it staggered, the way it crashed to the ground, its heart-core cold, swarming with enemy bodies like insects feeding upon a corpse.

The god-machine shook the earth when it finally toppled. The spined, spiked cathedral tumbled from its back in a spillage of priceless architecture, left as no more than rubble and scraps of armour plating in a mountain of wreckage by the Titan's head. *Stormherald's* arms were wrenched from the torso, squealing free of the ruptured shoulder joints when the ancient engine hammered into the ground with enough force to send tremors through the entire city.

The head itself was torn free before the main body fell, leaving a socket of trailing power cables and interface feeds, like a nest of a million snakes. Gripped in the lifter-claw at the end of one of *Godbreaker's* many arms, the Titan's head was clamped and crushed, then hurled aside as a twisted ball of scrap metal. Its landing flattened a small manufactorum, as the armoured command chamber weighing several dozen tonnes blasted through the building's side wall and pulverised several support pillars.

On board *Godbreaker*, the bestial creature in charge ranted at its subordinates for destroying and discarding the Titan's head in such a way. To the beast's mind, it would have made a very impressive trophy to mount on their own god-machine.

The few Legio crew members, skitarii defenders and tech-adepts that survived *Stormherald's* fall scrabbled from exits and breaks in the behemoth's skin. In the midday light of Armageddon's weak sun, they were cut down by the ork reavers around the dead Titan.

Miraculously, Moderati Secundus Lonn was one of these. He had managed to break free of the bindings and interface cables linking him to the dying god-machine, and make it out of the bridge by the time *Godbreaker* decapitated *Stormherald.* In the following fall, he broke his leg in two places, earned a concussion as the tilting corridor sent him falling down a flight of spiral stairs, and busted several of his teeth clear out of his gums when his head smacked off a handrail.

On hands and knees, dragging his dead leg and half-drunk with concussion, Lonn hauled himself out of an emergency bulkhead to lie on the warm armour plating of *Stormherald's* torso. There he remained, panting and bleeding in the thin sunlight for several seconds, before starting to crawl his slow way down the ground. He was killed less than a minute later by the marauding greenskins swarming over the downed Titan.

Through the pain, he was laughing as he died.

Grimaldus came at last to the inner sanctum.

He was no longer a warrior here, but a pilgrim. Of this he was certain, though in the wake of his words with Nero, he felt certain of little else.

It had taken very little time within the Temple of the Emperor Ascendant to bring about this certainty within him, but the feeling was undeniable. He felt home, on familiar and sacred ground, for the first time since he had left the *Eternal Crusader.*

It was purifying.

The cool air didn't taste of fire and blood on a world he had no wish to walk upon. The silence wasn't broken by the drumbeat of a war he had no stake in.

Augmented infants – the lobotomised bodies of children kept eternally young through gene manipulation and hormone control – were enhanced by simple Mechanicus organs and pressed into service as winged cherub-servitors, hovering on anti-grav fields as they trailed prayer banners through the halls and arched chambers.

In the myriad rooms of the basilica, the devoted and the faithful of Helsreach went about their daily reverence despite the war blackening their city. Grimaldus walked through a chamber of monks offering prayer through inscribing hundreds of saints' names on thin parchments that would hang from the weapons of Temple guards. One of the holy men kneeled as the Astartes passed, imploring the 'Angel of Death' to wear the parchment on his armour. Touched by the man's devotion, the knight had accepted, and voxed an order to the rest of his men scattered throughout the temple grounds to acquiesce to any similar charity.

Grimaldus let the lay brother tie the scroll to his pauldron with twine. The offered parchment was a modest but appreciated replacement for the iconography, oathpapers and heraldry that had been scoured from his armour in the last five weeks of battle.

The Reclusiarch had ventured alone into the undercroft, wishing to bear witness to the civilians there in his patrol to examine all defences and locations within the basilica. The subterranean expanse might once have been austere and solemn, featuring little more than infrequently-spaced sarcophagi of black stone. To the knight's eyes, it was a refugee bunker, packed tight with humans that smelled both unwashed and afraid as they sat around in family clusters – some asleep; some speaking quietly; some comforting crying babies; some spreading out meagre possessions on dirty blankets, taking stock of everything they now owned in the world, which was all they had managed to carry with them as they'd fled their homes.

Wordlessly, he'd walked among them. Every one of them had moved from his path; every one of them so openly awed by their first sighting of an Astartes warrior. Parents whispered to children, and children whispered more questions back.

'Hello,' a voice called from behind him as he was moving back up the wide marble stairs. The Reclusiarch turned. A girl-child stood at the bottom of the staircase, clad in an oversized shirt that clearly belonged to a parent or older sibling. Her ratty blonde hair was so dirty that it snarled quite naturally into accidental dreadlocks.

Grimaldus descended again, ignoring the girl's parents hissing at her, calling her back. She was no older than seven or eight. She stood up straight, and reached his knee.

'Hail,' he said to her. The crowd flinched back from the vox-voice, and several of those closest gasped in a breath.

The girl blinked. 'Father says you are a hero. Are you a hero?'

Grimaldus's gaze flicked across the crowd. His targeting cursor danced from face to face, seeking her parents.

Nothing in two centuries of war had prepared him to answer this question. The gathered refugees looked on in silence.

'There are many heroes here,' the Chaplain replied.

'You are very loud,' the girl complained.

'I am more used to shouting,' the knight lowered his voice. 'Do you require something from me?'

'Will you save us?'

He looked at the crowd again, and chose his words with great care.

That had been an hour ago. The Reclusiarch stood with his closest brothers and the Emperor's Champion in the basilica's inner sanctum.

The chamber was expansive, easily able to accommodate a thousand worshippers at once. For now, it stood bare, the hundreds of Steel Legionnaires that were bunking here in recent weeks currently out on their patrols through the graveyard and surrounding temple district.

The few dozen that had been off-duty were ushered out by monks when the Astartes had entered. Almost immediately, the knights were joined by a new presence. An irritated presence, at that.

'Well, well, well,' the irritated presence said in her old woman's voice. 'The Emperor's Chosen, come to stand with us at last.'

The knights turned in the sunlit chamber, back to the entrance where a diminutive figure stood in contoured power armour. A bolter, cased in bronze with gold-leaf etchings, was mag-locked between her shoulders. The gun was a smaller calibre than Astartes weaponry, but still a rare firearm to see in the possession of a human.

Her white power armour was bedecked in trappings that marked her rank in the Holy Order of the Argent Shroud. The old woman's white hair was cut severely at her chin, framing a wrinkled face with icy eyes.

'Hail, prioress,' Bayard acknowledged her with a bow, as did the others. Grimaldus and Priamus made no obeisance, with the swordsman remaining unmoving and Grimaldus instead making the sign of the aquila.

'I am Prioress Sindal, and in the name of Saint Silvana, I bid you welcome to the Temple of the Emperor Ascendant.'

Grimaldus stepped forward. 'Reclusiarch Grimaldus of the Black Templars. I cannot help but notice that you do not sound welcoming.'

'Should I be? Half of the Temple District has already fallen in the last week. Where were you then, hmm?'

Priamus laughed. 'We were at the docks, you ungrateful little harpy.'

'Be at ease,' Grimaldus warned. Priamus replied with a vox-click of acknowledgement.

'We were, as my brother Priamus explained, engaged in the east of the hive. But we are here now, when the war is at its darkest, as the enemy approach the temple doors.'

'I have fought with Astartes before,' the prioress said, her armoured arms crossed over the fleur-de-lys symbol that marked her sculpted breastplate. 'I have fought alongside warriors who would have given their lives for the Imperium's ideals, and warriors that cared only for accruing glory, as if they could wear their honour like armour. Both breeds were Astartes.'

'We are not here to be lectured on the state of our souls,' Grimaldus tried to keep the irritation from his voice.

'Whether you are or not doesn't matter, Reclusiarch. Will you dismiss your fellow warriors from the chamber, please? There is much to speak of.'

'We can speak of the temple's defence in front of my brothers.'

'Indeed we can, and when the time comes to speak of such things, they will be present. For now, please dismiss them.'

'Did you cleanse yourself, by the Stoup of Elucidation?'

This is the question she asks in the silence that descends once my brothers are gone, and the doors are closed.

The stoup she speaks of is a huge bowl of black iron, mounted upon a low pedestal of what looks like wrought gold. It stands by the double doors, which are themselves bedecked in imagery of warlike angels with toothed swords, and saints bearing bolters.

I confess to her that I did not.

'Come then.' She beckons me to the bowl. The water within reflects the painted ceiling and the stained glass windows above – a riot of colour in a liquid mirror.

She dips a bare finger into the water after taking the time to detach and remove her gauntlets. 'This water is thrice-blessed,' she says, tracing her dripping fingertip across her forehead in a crescent moon. 'It brings clarity of purpose, when anointed onto the doubting and the lost.'

'I am not lost,' I lie, and she smiles at the words.

'I did not mean to imply that you were, Reclusiarch. But many who come here are.'

'Why did you wish to speak with me alone? Time is short. The war will reach these walls in a matter of days. Preparations must be made.'

She speaks, staring down into the perfect reflection offered by the bowl. 'This basilica is a bastion. A castle. We can defend it for weeks, when the enemy finally gathers courage enough to besiege it.'

'Answer the question.' This time, I could not keep the irritation from my voice even if I had wished to.

'Because you are not like your brothers.'

I know that when she looks at my face, she does not see me. She sees the death mask of the Emperor, the skull helm of an Astartes Reclusiarch, the crimson eye lenses of humanity's chosen. And yet our gazes meet in the water's reflection, and I cannot completely fight the feeling she is seeing *me*, beneath the mask and the masquerade.

What does she mean by those words? That she senses my doubts? That they drip from me like nervous sweat, visible and stinking to all who stand near me?

'I am no different from them.'

'Of course you are. You are a Chaplain, are you not? A Reclusiarch. A keeper of your Chapter's lore, soul, traditions and purity.'

My heart rate slows again. My rank. That is all she meant.

'I see.'

'I am given to understand Astartes Chaplains are invested with their authority by the Ecclesiarchy?'

Ah. She seeks common ground. Good luck to her in this doomed endeavour. She is a warrior of the Imperial Creed, and an officer in the Church of the God-Emperor.

I am not.

'The Ecclesiarchy of Terra supports our ancient rites, and the authority of every Chapter's Reclusiam to train warrior-priests to guide the souls of its battle-brothers. They do not invest us with power. They recognise we already hold it.'

'And you are given a gift by the Ecclesiarchy? A rosarius?'

'Yes.'

'May I see yours?'

The few Astartes singled out for ascension into the Reclusiam are gifted with a rosarius medallion upon succeeding in the first trials of Chaplainhood. My talisman was beaten bronze and red iron, shaped into a heraldic cross.

'I no longer carry one.'

She looks up at me, as if the reflection of my skull visage was no longer clear enough for her purposes.

'Why is that?'

'It was lost. Destroyed in battle.'

'Is that not a dark omen?'

'I am still alive three years after its destruction. I still do the Emperor's work, and still follow the word of Dorn even after its loss. The omen cannot be that dark.'

She looks at me for some time. I am used to humans staring at me in awkward silence; used to their attempts to watch without betraying that they are watching. But this direct stare is something else, and it takes a moment to realise why.

'You are judging me.'

'Yes, I am. Remove your helm, please.'

'Tell me why I should.' My voice is not pitched to petulance, merely curiosity. I had not expected her to ask such a thing.

'Because I would like to look upon the face of the man I am speaking with, and because I wish to anoint you with the Waters of Elucidation.'

I could refuse. Of course I could refuse.

But I do not.

'A moment, please.' I disengage my helm's seals, and breathe in my first taste of the crisp, cool air within the temple. The fresh water before me. The sweat of the refugees. The scorched ceramite of my armour.

'You have beautiful eyes,' she tells me. 'Innocent, but cautious. The eyes of a child, or a new father. Seeing the world around you as if for the first time. Kneel, if you would? I cannot reach all the way up there.'

I do not kneel. She is not my liege lord, and to abase myself in such a way would violate all decorum. Instead, I lower my head, bringing my face closer to her. The joints of her pristine armour give the smooth purr of clean mechanics as she reaches up. I feel her fingertip draw a cross upon my forehead in cold water.

'There,' she says, refastening her gauntlets. 'May you find the answers you seek in this house of the God-Emperor. You are blessed, and may tread the sacred floor of the inner sanctum without guilt.'

She is already moving away, her milky eyes squinting. 'Come. I have something to show you.'

The prioress leads me to the centre of the chamber, where a stone table holds an open book. Four columns of polished marble rise at the table's cardinal points, all the way to the ceiling. Upon one of the columns hangs a tattered banner unlike any I have ever seen before.

'Hold.'

'What is it? Ah, the first archive.' She gestures to the sheets of ragged cloth hanging from the war banner poles. Each once-white, now-grey sheet shows a list of names in faded ink.

Names, professions, husbands and wives and children...

'These are the first colonists.'

'Yes, Reclusiarch.'

'The settlers of Helsreach. The founders. This is their charter?'

'It is. From when the great hive was no more than a village by the shore of the Tempest Ocean. These are the men and women that laid the temple's first foundations.'

I let my gloved hand come close to the humming stasis field shielding the ancient cloth document. Parchment would have been a rare luxury to the first colonists, with the jungle and its trees so far from here. It stands to reason they would have recorded their achievements on cloth paper.

Thousands of years ago, Imperial peasants walked the ashen soil here and laid the first stone bones of what would become a great basilica to house the devotions of an entire city. Deeds remembered throughout the millennia, with their evidence for all to see.

'You seem pensive,' she tells me.

'What is the book?'

'The log from a vessel called the *Truth's Tenacity*. It was the colonisation seeding ship that brought the settlers to Helsreach. The four pillars house a void shield generator system, protecting the tome. This is the Major Altar. Sermons are given here, among the city's most precious relics.'

I look at the tome's curled, age-browned pages. Then at the archive banner once more.

Last of all, I replace my helm, coating my senses in the selective vision of targeting sights and filtered sounds.

'You have my thanks, prioress. I appreciate what you have shown me here.'

'Am I to expect any more of your kind arriving to bolster us, Astartes?'

I think, for a moment, of Jurisian, bringing the Ordinatus Armageddon overland, uncrewed, at minimal power and of little to no use once it arrives.

'One more. He returns to join us and fight by our sides.'

'Then I bid you welcome to the Temple of the Emperor Ascendant, Reclusiarch. How do you plan to defend this holy place?'

'We are past the point of retreat now, Sindal. No finesse, no tactics, no long speeches to rally the faint of heart and those that fear the end. I plan to kill until I am killed, because that is all that remains for us here.'

Both the Reclusiarch and the prioress turned at the pounding upon the door.

Grimaldus blink-clicked the rune to bring his vox channels live again, but it wasn't any of his brothers seeking his attention.

Prioress Sindal waved her hand in a magnanimous gesture, as if there were a crowd to impress. 'Do come in.'

The great metal-wrought doors rumbled open on clean but heavy hinges. Eight men stood framed by the doors and the austere corridor beyond. Each of them bore a filthy share of blood, mud, soot and oil stains. They carried lasguns with the practiced ease of men who had become utterly familiar with the weapons, and all but two of them wore dirty blue dock-workers' overalls. One of those that did not was dressed in the robes of a priest, but not the cream and blue weave of the temple's own residents. He was from off-world.

The leader of the group raised his goggles, letting them clack back on the top of his helmet. He regarded the knight with wide eyes.

'They said you would be here,' the storm trooper said. 'I beg the many forgivings of this holy place for my intrusion, but I bring news, yes? Do not be angry. The vox is still playing many unamusing games and I could not speak with anyone in any other way.'

'Speak, Legionnaire,' said Grimaldus.

'The beasts, they are coming in great force. Many are not far behind us, and I have heard vox-chatter that Invigilata is leaving the city.'

'Why would they leave us?' the prioress asked, horrified.

'They would quit the city at once,' Grimaldus admitted, 'if Princeps Zarha was gone. Mechanicus politics.'

'She is gone, Reclusiarch,' Andrej finished. 'An hour ago, we saw *Stormherald* die.'

Behind the Guardsman, a warrior-maiden in the white power armour of the Order of the Argent Shroud caught her breath, staring at the prioress with her features flushed.

'Prioress!'

'Take a breath, Sister Maralin.'

'We've received word from the 101st Steel Legion! Invigilata's Titans are abandoning Helsreach!'

Andrej looked at the newcomer as if she had announced that gravity was a myth. He shook his head slowly, a deep and solemn pity written across his face.

'You are late, little girl.'

The first wave to break against the walls was not a horde of the enemy.

Close-range vox detected them first, with reports of elements from three Steel Legion regiments engaged in panicked retreat. Grimaldus responded with the temple's vox-systems, boosted far beyond what the squad-to-squad comms systems were currently capable of.

He gave the order to any Helsreach forces receiving the message to fall back to the Temple of the Emperor Ascendant, abandoning any further struggle to hold the few remaining sectors in the Ecclesiarchy District. Several lieutenants and captains sent affirmative responses in reply, including a captain of the hive militia still leading over a hundred men.

The fleeing Imperials began to arrive less than an hour later.

Grimaldus stood with Bayard at the gates, looking out into the city. A dark-hulled Baneblade command tank rolled past, guided into the graveyard sector by a platoon of Guardsmen waving directions to the driver. Behind it, a cadre of Leman Russ battle tanks with various turret weapons trundled in loose formation. Mingling between the rolling armour and trailing behind were several hundred Legionnaires, ochre-clad and visibly weary. Wounded were being stretchered by their fellows in serious numbers, and there were plenty of wails and moans calling out over the grind of tank engines.

Two soldiers passed by the watching knights, bearing the writhing body of a junior officer on a cloth stretcher. The man had lost an arm and a leg, at the elbow and knee respectively. His face was a contorted mess of whatever he really looked like, his visage ruined by the pain flowing through him.

One of the stretcher-bearers nodded to Grimaldus as he passed, and muttered a respectful 'Reclusiarch.'

The Templar nodded back.

'Fought with them?' Bayard asked over the vox.

'Desert Vultures. I was with them when the first walls fell. Good men, all.'

'Very few left,' Bayard said, a strange edge to his voice.

Grimaldus turned his skulled face to the Champion. 'There will be enough. Have faith in your brothers' blades, Bayard.'

'I have faith. I am sanguine with my fate, Chaplain.'

'My rank is Reclusiarch. Use it.'

'By your will, brother, of course. But we stand vigil over the city's death with a handful of bleeding humans, Reclusiarch. I am sanguine, but I am also a realist.'

Grimaldus's vox-snarl drew stares from the soldiers passing nearby. 'Have faith in the people of this city, Champion. Such condescension is beneath you. We are the last guardians of the relics prized by the first of Armageddon's colonists. These people are fighting for more than their homes and lives. They are fighting for their ancestors' honour, on the holiest ground in the entire world. The survivors of this war across the globe will take heart from sacrifices made by the thousands destined to die here. Blood of Dorn, Bayard... the Imperium was *born* in moments such as this.'

The Emperor's Champion watched him for a long moment, during which Grimaldus found his heart thumping faster. He was angry, and feeling the anger rise was as purgative as his time within the temple's serene halls. Bayard spoke, his voice sincere despite the crackle of vox-breakage.

'My voice was one of the few that spoke against your ascension to Mordred's rank.'

Grimaldus snorted, returning to watching the arriving forces. 'I would have said the same in your place.'

Seventy soldiers of the Steel Legion 101st came together in a battered convoy of Chimera transports. The ramp slammed down as the lead vehicle pulled up to a halt. A squad of Legionnaires disembarked, not a one of them free of bloodstains or bandaging.

'Leave the Chimeras outside,' Major Ryken ordered the others. Half of his face was wrapped in grubby cloth bandages, and he leaned heavily on an aide's shoulder, limping as he walked.

'Shouldn't we take them inside?' Cyria Tyro asked. She looked back over her shoulder at the tanks being abandoned.

'To hell with them,' Ryken spat blood as she led him to the two knights. 'Not enough ammunition in the turrets to make it worthwhile.'

'Grimaldus,' she said, looking up at the towering warrior.

'Hail, Adjutant Quintus Tyro. Major Ryken.'

'We got cut off from Sarren and the others. The 34th, the 101st, the 51st... They're all in the central manufactory sectors...'

'It does not matter.'

'What?'

'It does not matter,' Grimaldus repeated. 'We are defending the last points of light in Helsreach. Fate brought you to the Temple. Fate sent Sarren elsewhere.'

'Throne, there are still thousands of the bastards out there.' He spat pinkish spit again, and Tyro grunted as she took more of his weight. 'And that's not the worst of it.'

'Explain.'

'Invigilata has gone,' Tyro said. 'They left us to die. The enemy still has Titans – and there's one that you'll never believe until you look upon it with your own eyes. We saw it march from the Rostorik Ironworks, collapsing habitation towers in its wake.'

'The 34th Armoured rolled out to stop it,' Ryken winced as he spoke. His bandages were growing more stained, around what was likely an empty eye socket. 'It flattened most of them in the time it takes a desert jackal to howl at the full moon.'

A curious local expression. Grimaldus nodded, catching the meaning, but Ryken had more to add.

'*Stormherald* is down.' he said.

'I know.'

'This *Godbreaker*... it killed the Crone, and slew *Stormherald*.'

'I know.'

'You know? So where's the damn Ordinatus? We need it! Nothing else will kill that gigantic clanking... thing.'

'It is coming. Move inside and see to your wounds. If the end is coming to these walls, you will need to stand ready.'

'Oh, we'll all be ready. The bastards took my face, and that made it personal.'

As they moved away, Grimaldus heard Tyro gently teasing the major for his bravado. When they were beyond the gates but still in sight, the Reclusiarch saw the general's adjutant kiss the major on his unbandaged cheek.

'Madness,' the knight whispered.

'Reclusiarch?' Bayard asked.

'Humans,' Grimaldus replied, his voice soft. 'They are a mystery to me.'

TWENTY-TWO

EMPEROR ASCENDANT

At last, vox reports began to trickle through to the defenders gathered in the temple's graveyard district. Across Helsreach, Sarren's plan, the 'one hundred bastions of light', was in effect, with Imperial forces massing in defensive formations around the most vital parts of the city.

Contact was erratic at best, but the fact it even existed was a boost to morale. Every point of focussed defence was holding well, with all divisions breaking down between storm troopers, Guard infantry, Steel Legion armour units, militia and armed civilians who chose to take to the streets rather than cower in their shelters.

The city was fighting to keep its heart beating, and the orks no longer found themselves advancing against a mobile wave of human resistance. Now the aliens were breaking against a multitude of last stands, hurling themselves against defenders that had nowhere left to run.

Fortunately for the Imperials, enemy scrap-Titans were few in number. With recent engagements such as the Battle of the Rostorik Ironworks, the greenskins' complement of god-machines had suffered furious losses in the face of Legio Invigilata's wrath.

Even as Invigilata recalled its last remaining Titans from the city in the wake of *Stormherald's* death, the Titans were forced to fight their way free of the orks flooding through Helsreach's unprotected streets. Although several Titans escaped through the broken walls and into the Ash Wastes beyond, the Warlord-class engine *Ironsworn* was brought down by a massed infantry assault in an ambush similar to the one that had laid *Stormherald* low all those weeks before.

The last of the Imperial Navy forces in the city had based themselves at the Azal spaceport, where they continued to mount bombing runs and offer limited air support to the tank battalions ringing the Jaega District's surface shelters. The fighting here was among the thickest and fiercest seen in the entire siege to date, and the archives which would catalogue the Third War for Armageddon came to consider many of the glorious propaganda falsehoods born here as cold fact. Many of these heroic twists of the truth were due to the writings of one Commissar Falkov, whose memoir, entitled simply '*I Was There...*', would become standard reading for all officers of the Steel Legions in the years after the war.

Although there was absolutely no truth in the tale, Imperial records would state that acting-Commander Helius sacrificed his own life by ramming his Lightning into the heart-reactor of the enemy gargant classified as *Blood Defyla.* The truth was rather more mundane – like Barasath before him, Helius was shot down and torn to pieces shortly after disentangling from his grav-chute on the ground.

The presence of *Godbreaker* was a bane to any Imperial resolve nearby. Although the god-machine appeared a shadow of its former self, bearing a legion of wounds and missing limbs from its death-duel with *Stormherald,* with Invigilata marching away across the badlands the defenders of Helsreach had little in the way of firepower capable of retaliating against the gargant.

After laying waste to the Abraxas Foundry Complex, the mighty enemy engine adopted a random patrol of the city, engaging Imperial forces wherever it chanced upon them.

Imperial records would state that while the Siege of the Temple of the Emperor Ascendant was entering its second day, the alien war machine *Godbreaker* was destroyed on its way to finish the temple defenders once and for all.

This, at least, was perfectly true.

Jurisian watched the mechanical giants stride from the city, stepping through its sundered walls. There were three – the first escapees of Legio Invigilata – and the Master of the Forge stared from the quiet confines of *Oberon's* command module as the Titans left the burning city behind.

The first was a Reaver-class, a mid-range battle Titan that appeared to have sustained significant damage if the columns of smoke rising from its back were any indication. Its flanking allies were both Warhounds, their ungainly gait rocking their torsos and arm-cannons side to side, step by step across the sands.

The wastelands outside Helsreach's walls resembled nothing more than a graveyard. Thousands of dead orks lay rotting in the weak sun; killed in Barasath's initial attack runs or slaughtered in the inevitable inter-tribal battles that arose when these bestial aliens gathered.

Ruined tanks were scattered in abundance, as was the wreckage from countless propeller-driven planes, each one made out of scrap and reduced back to it. The orks' landing vessels stood abandoned, with every xenos capable of lifting an axe now waging war inside the city. The primitive creatures were here to fight and destroy, or fight and die. They cared nothing for what fate befell their vessels left in the desert. Such forethought and consideration was beyond the mental capacity of most greenskins.

Jurisian made no attempt to hide his presence. There would be little point in making the attempt, for he knew the approaching Titans would be able to read *Oberon's* energy shadow on their powerful auspex scanners. So he waited, all systems active, as the Invigilata Titans drew near. The ground began to shiver with their closing tread, which Jurisian noted by the twisted metal and bodies across the desert floor shaking in rhythm with the god-machines.

The wounded Reaver came to a halt, its immense joints protesting that it was still forced to remain standing. It was damaged enough that a second's focus-drift might see the princeps losing control over the engine's stabilisers. It slowly aimed its remaining weapon arm at the command module, and Jurisian looked up into the yawning maw of a gatling blaster cannon.

With *Oberon's* shields up, the Master of the Forge would have estimated the Ordinatus could tolerate several minutes of sustained assault even from a weapon as destructive as this Reaver's main armament. But *Oberon* had no shields. They were one of many secondary systems that Jurisian had lacked the time, expertise and manpower necessary to reengage.

He knew what a gatling blaster was capable of. He'd seen them devastate regiments of tanks, and rip the faces and limbs from enemy Titans. *Oberon's* armour plating would last no more than a handful of seconds.

The Titan stared down at him in silence, no doubt while the princeps decided how to deal with this unbelievable blasphemy. Hunchbacked and striding with arm-cannons raised in threatening salute, the two Warhounds circled the immobile Ordinatus. Their posturing amused the Forgemaster. How they played at being wolves.

'Hail,' he said into a broad range of vox-channels. In truth, he was growing bored of the silence. He was far, far from intimidated.

'What blasphemy is this?' crackled the reply through the command module's internal speakers. *'What heretic dares defile* Oberon's *deserved slumber?'*

Jurisian leaned back in the control throne, elbows on the armrests and his gloved fingers steepled before his helmed face.

'I am Jurisian of the Black Templars, Master of the Forge aboard the *Eternal Crusader,* and trained by the Cult Mechanicus for years on the surface of Mars itself. I am also in possession of the Ordinatus Armageddon, after subduing its defences and reawakening its soul, force-binding it to my will. And, lastly, I am summoned to Helsreach to aid wherever I am able. Aid me, or stand aside.'

The delay was significant in duration, and in other circumstances, that would have made it insulting. Jurisian suspected his words were being transmitted to all nearby princeps, almost definitely summoning them to this position.

Half a kilometre away, another Reaver Titan was breaching the city walls, emerging into the Ash Wastes. The knight watched it begin its halting stride in this direction, noting that it was relatively undamaged.

'You are blaspheming against the Machine-God and its servants.'

'I am wielding a weapon of war in defence of an Imperial city. Now aid me, or stand aside.'

'Leave the Ordinatus platform, or be destroyed.'

'You are not about to open fire on this holiest of artefacts, and I am not empowered by my liege lord to comply with your demands. That brings us to a stalemate. Discuss useful terms, or I will take *Oberon* into the city unprotected, surely to be destroyed without significant Mechanicus support.'

'Your corpse will be removed from the sacred innards of the Ordinatus Armageddon, and all remnants of your presence will be eradicated from memory.'

As Jurisian drew breath to offer terms, his vox-link flickered into life. Grimaldus, at last.

'Reclusiarch. I trust the time has finally come?'

'We are embattled at the Temple of the Emperor Ascendant. How soon can you bring the weapon to us?'

The Master of the Forge looked out of the reinforced windows at the patrolling Titans, then at the city beyond, beneath a smoke-blackened sky. He knew the hive's layout from studying the hololithics before his exile into the desert.

'Two hours.'

'Status of the weapon?'

'As before. *Oberon* has no void shields, no secondary weapon systems, and suspensor lift capability is limited, hindering speed to a crawl. Alone, I can fire it no more than once every twenty minutes. I need to recharge the fuel cells manually, and regenerate flow from the plasma containment ch–'

'I will see you in two hours, Jurisian. For Dorn and the Emperor.'

'By your will, Reclusiarch.'

'Heed these last words, Forgemaster. Do not bring the weapon too close. The Temple District is naught but fire and ash, and we are surrounded on all sides. Take the shot and flee the city. Pursue Invigilata's retreating forces, and link up with the Imperial assault along the Hemlock.'

'You wish me to run?'

'I wish you to live rather than die in vain, and save a weapon precious to the Imperium.' Grimaldus broke off for a moment, and the pause was filled with the anger of distant guns. 'We will be buried here, Jurisian. There is no dishonour that your fate is elsewhere.'

'Call the primary target, Reclusiarch.'

'You will see it as you manoeuvre through the Temple District, brother. It is called the *Godbreaker*.'

Four Titans soon barred his path.

Mightiest among them – and the last to arrive – was a Warlord, its armour plating black from paint, not battle-scarring. Its weapons trained down – immense barrels aimed at the Ordinatus platform. The numerological markings along the engine's carapace marked it out as the *Bane-Sidhe*.

'I am Princeps Amasat of Invigilata, sub-commander of the Crone's forces and heir to her title in the wake of her demise. Explain this madness immediately.'

Jurisian looked at the city, and thought about his offer carefully before making it. He spoke with confidence, because he knew full well the Mechanicus had little other choice. He was going back into the city, and by the Machine-God, they were going to come with him.

The graveyard – that immense garden of raised stone and buried bone – played home to the storm of disorder that had until recently been raging its way through the Temple District.

The enemy had breached the temple walls at dawn on the second day, only to find that the graveyard was where the real defences stood in readiness. As tanks pounded the walls down and beasts scrabbled over the rubble, thousands of Helsreach's last defenders waited behind mausoleums, gravestones, ornate tombs of city founders and shrines to treasured saints.

Burning beams of las-fire cobwebbed across the battlefield, slicing the alien beasts down in droves.

At the vanguard, a warrior clad in black and wielding a relic warhammer battled alongside a dwindling handful of his brothers. Every fall of his maul ended with the crunch of another alien life ended. His pistol, long since powered down and empty, dangled from the thick chain binding it to his wrist. Where the fighting was thickest, he wielded it like a flail, lashing it with whip-like force into bestial alien faces to shatter bone.

At his side, two swordsmen moved and spun in lethal unison. Priamus and Bayard, their bladework complementing one another's perfectly, cutting and impaling with the same techniques, the same footwork, and at times, even in the very same moments.

With no banner to raise, not even the barest scraps left, Artarion laid about left and right with two chugging chainblades, their teeth-tracks already blunted and choked with gore. Bastilan supported him, precision bolter rounds punching home in alien flesh.

Nero was always moving, never allowed to rest for even a moment's respite. He vaulted the enemy dead, bolter crashing out round after round as he blasted the beasts away from the body of another fallen brother, buying enough time to extract the gene-seed of the honoured dead.

This he did, time after time, with tears running down his pale face. The deaths did not move him; merely the feeling of dread futility that all his efforts would be in vain. Their genetic legacy might never escape this hive to be used in the creation of more Astartes, and no Chapter could afford to bear the loss of a hundred slain warriors with easy dignity.

Around the time Jurisian was entering the city, escorted by five Titans from Legio Invigilata, the Imperial defences were straining to hold the outer limits of the graveyard. Cries of 'Fall back! Fall back to the Temple!' started to spread through the scattered lines.

Assigned squads, appointed teams, random groups of men and women – all began to back away from the unending grind of the alien advance.

The Baneblade exploded, sending flaming shrapnel spinning in a hundred directions. The Imperials nearest to the tank – those that weren't thrown from their feet – started to flee in earnest.

But there is nowhere to fall back to. Nowhere to run.

Like a lance pushed close to breaking point, our resistance is bending, the flanks being forced back behind the centre.

No. I will not die here, in this graveyard, beaten into darkness because these savages have greater numbers than we do. The enemy does not deserve such a victory.

My boots clang on the sloped armour plating as I leap and sprint up the roof of the crippled, burning Baneblade. In the maelstrom around the rocket-struck tank, I see the 101st Steel Legion and a gathering of dockworkers trying to fall back in a panicked hurry, their forward ranks being scythed down by bloodstained axes in green-knuckled fists.

Enough of this.

The beast I am seeking seeks me out in turn. Huge, towering above its lesser kin, packed with unnatural muscle around its malformed bones and reeking of the fungal blood that fuels its foul heart. It launches itself onto the tank's hull, perhaps expecting some titanic duel to impress its tribe. A champion, perhaps. A chieftain. It matters not. The brutes' leaders rarely resist the chance to engage Imperial commanders in full view – they are loathsomely predictable.

There is no time for sport. My first strike is my last, hammering through its guard, shattering its crossed axes and pounding the aquila head of my crozius into its roaring face.

It topples from the Baneblade, all loose limbs and worthless armour, as pathetic in death as it had been in life.

I hear Priamus laughing from the tank's side, voxing it through his helm's speakers, mocking the beasts even as he slays them. On the other side, Artarion and Bastilan do the same. The orks redouble their assault with twice the fury and half the skill, and though I could reprimand my brothers for this indignity, I do not.

My laughter joins theirs.

Asavan Tortellius was serene, and that surprised him given the shaking of the walls and the sounds of war's thunder. This was no Titan's fortress-cathedral back, where he had learned to worship in safety. This was a temple besieged.

It had not taken long to find work to do within the basilica. He quickly came to realise that he was the only priest with experience of preaching on the battlefield. Most of the lay brothers and low-ranking Ecclesiarchy servants spent their time attending to their daily tasks in hurried nervousness, praying the war would remain outside the walls. Several others cowered in the undercroft with the refugees, doing more harm than good and failing to ease a single soul with their stuttering, sweating sermons.

Asavan descended into the sublevel, immediately marked out from the other preachers by his grimy robes and dishevelled hair. He walked among the people, offering gentle words to families as he passed. He was especially patient with the children, giving them the blessing of the God-Emperor in His aspect as the Machine-God, and saying personal prayers over individual boys and girls that seemed the most weary or withdrawn.

There was a lone guard stationed at the bottom of the stairs. She was slight of frame, both short and slender, wearing a suit of power armour that seemed too bulky to be comfortable. In her hands was a boltgun, the weapon held across her chest as she stood to attention.

Asavan moved over to her, his worn boots whispering across the dusty stone.

'Hello, sister,' he said, keeping his voice low.

She remained unmoving, at perfect attention, though he could see the tremor in her eyes that betrayed how difficult she found it to bear this rigid nothingness.

'My name is Asavan Tortellius,' he told her. 'Will you please lower the weapon?'

She looked at him, her eyes meeting his. She didn't lower the bolter.

'What is your name?' he asked her.

'Sister Maralin of the Holy Order of the Ar–'

'Hello, Maralin. Be at ease, for the enemy is still outside the walls. Might I ask you, please, to lower the weapon?'

'Why?' she leaned closer to whisper.

'Because you are making the people here even more nervous than they already are. By all means, be visible. You are their defender, and they will take comfort in your presence. But walk among them, and offer a few kind words. Do not stand there in grim silence, weapon held tight. You are giving them greater reason to fear, and that is not why you were sent down here, Maralin.'

She nodded. 'Thank you, Father.' The bolter came down. She mag-locked it to her thigh plate.

'Come,' he smiled, 'let me introduce you to some of them.'

The *Bane-Sidhe*'s void shields rippled and rained sparks, brought into visibility as another layer was stripped by the explosive shells raining against them. A short growl of accumulating power ended in a blasting discharge of energy as the Warlord annihilated the tanks laying claim to the Hel's Highway ahead.

A black, smoking scorch smear was all the evidence that the tanks had ever existed. Behind the striding *Bane-Sidhe, Oberon* drifted forward on its gravity suspensors, gently cruising over any obstructions in its path. Bringing up the column's rear were the clanking, ungainly Warhounds that *Bane-Sidhe* had ordered back into the city.

The agreement made was monumentally simple, and that was why Jurisian was certain it would work.

'Defend *Oberon,*' he'd said. 'Defend it for long enough to take a single shot, to down the enemy command gargant. Then the Ordinatus will be surrendered into your control during the retreat towards the Hemlock River.'

What choice did they have? Amasat's voice over the vox was harsh with the promise of recrimination should the plan fail to run smooth. Jurisian, for his part, could not have cared less. He had the support he needed, and he had a primary target to destroy.

Infantry resistance was met with punishing and instant devastation. Armour formations endured no longer. Through the Temple District, they encountered precious little in the way of enemy engines.

'That is because, blasphemer, Invigilata left the enemy Titan contingent in ruins.'

'Except for the *Godbreaker,*' the Forgemaster replied. 'Except for the slayer of *Stormherald.*'

Amasat chose not to retort.

'I have nothing on my auspex,' he said instead.

'Nor I,' reported one of the Warhound princeps.

'I see nothing,' confirmed the other.

'Keep hunting. Draw closer to the Temple of the Emperor Ascendant.'

The Mechanicus convoy traversed the urban ruination in bitter dignity for another eight minutes and twenty-three seconds before Amasat voxed again.

'Almost one quarter of the enemy inside this hive is embattled at the Temple of the Emperor Ascendant. You are threatening Oberon *with destruction as well as desecration? Does your heresy know no end?'*

It was Jurisian's turn to abstain from the argument.

'I have a thermal signature,' he said, studying the dim auspex console to the left of his control throne. 'It has a plasma shadow, much too hot to be natural flame.'

'I see nothing. Coordinates?'

Jurisian transmitted the location codes. It was on the very edge of scanning range, and still several minutes away.

'It is moving to the Temple.'

'Locomotion qualifiers?'

'Faster than us.'

The pause was almost painful, broken by Amasat's sneering tone. *'Then I will give you the victory you require. Talisman and Hallowed Verity – remain with the blessed weapon.'*

'Yes, princeps,' both Warhounds responded.

Bane-Sidhe leaned forward, its armoured shoulders hunching as it moved into a straining stride. Jurisian listened to the protesting gears, the overworked joints, hearing the engine's machine-spirit cry out in the stress of metal under tension. He said a quiet word of thanks for the sacrifice about to be made.

TWENTY-THREE

KNIGHTFALL

Andrej and Maghernus skidded into the basilica's first chamber, their bloody boots finding loose purchase on the mosaic-inlaid floor. Dozens of Guardsmen and militia dispersed through the vast hall, catching their breath and taking up defensive points around pillars and behind pews.

The final fallback was beginning in earnest. The graveyard outside was blanketed in enemy dead, but the last few hundred Imperials could no longer hold any ground with their own numbers depleted.

'This room...' the former dockmaster was breathing heavily, '...doesn't have much cover.'

Andrej was unslinging his back-mounted power pack. 'It is a nave.'

'What?'

'This room. It is called a nave. And you are speaking the truth – there is no defence here.' The storm trooper drew his pistol and started running deeper into the temple.

'Where are you going? What about your rifle?

'It is out of power! Now follow, we must find the priest!'

Ryken fired with his autopistol, taking a moment between shots to regain his aim. It was a custom, heavy-duty model that wouldn't have been out of place in an underhive gangfight, and as he crouched by a black stone shrine to a saint he didn't recognise, the gun barked hot and hard in his fist, ejecting spent cartridges that clattered off nearby gravestones.

'Fall back, sir!' one of his men was yelling. The alien beasts crashed through the graveyard like an apocalyptic flood, a unbreakable tide of noise.

'Not yet...'

'*Now*, you ass, come on!' Tyro dragged at his shoulder. It threw off his aim, but to hell with it – it was like spitting into the ocean anyway. He scrambled away from the relative cover of the weeping statue just in time to miss it being shattered into chips and shards by raking fire from a fully-automatic enemy stubber.

'Are they coming?' he shouted to his second officer, limping badly now.

'Who?'

'The bloody Templars!'

* * *

They were not coming.

To the retreating human survivors, it seemed as if the black knights had lost all sense, all reason, cutting their way forward while the humans that had supported them broke ranks and fled back.

No one could see why.

No one was getting a clear answer from the vox.

Bayard was dead.

Priamus saw the great champion fall, and all flair in his killing strokes was abandoned in a heartbeat. He slew with all the grace of a peasant chopping lumber upon the face of some backwater rural world, his masterwork sword reduced to a club with a vicious edge and draped in lethal energy.

'Nerovar!' he screamed his brother's name into the vox. *'Nerovar!'*

Other Templars took up the cry, summoning the Apothecary to extract the gene-seed of a Chapter hero.

Bayard stood almost slouched against the wall of an ornate mausoleum shaped from pink-veined white stone. The body had not fallen only because of the crude spear pinning it through the throat. A killing blow, without a shadow of doubt. Priamus spared a moment of desperate blocks and thrusts, taking an axe blow against his pauldron, risking a second's distraction to pull the spear free. The ork's axe threw off sparks as it crashed aside from the ceramite shoulder guard. The corpse of the Emperor's Champion slumped to the ground, freed of its undignified need to stand.

'Nerovar!' Priamus cried again.

It was Bastilan that reached him first. The sergeant's helm was gone, revealing a face so bloody only the whites of his eyeballs revealed him as human anymore. Torn flaps of skin hung in wet patches, leaving his head open to the bone beneath.

'The Black Sword!'

Priamus deflected another dozen cuts in four beats of his pounding twin hearts. He had no time to reach for the blessed weapon Bayard had dropped in death.

Bastilan's ruined face vanished in a burst of red mist. Priamus had already rammed his power sword through the chest of the bolter-wielding ork behind the sergeant by the time Bastilan's headless body crashed to the ground with the dull clang of ceramite on stone.

'Nerovar!'

With Bastilan's last words, something changed within the Templars.

Twelve remained. Of these, only seven would escape what followed.

The knights pulled together, their blades slashing and carving not only to kill their foes, but to defend their brothers alongside them. It was an instinctive savagery born of so many decades fighting at each others' sides, and it spread through their failing ranks now as they stood on the precipice of destruction.

'Take the sword!' Grimaldus roared. His charge carried him ahead of the

others, hammering his crozius in arhythmic fury, smashing a bloody path through to Priamus. *'Recover the Black Sword!'*

We cannot leave it here. It cannot lie abandoned on a battlefield while one of us yet lives.

Over the vox, the humans are calling us insane and begging us to fall back with them. To them, this bloodshed must seem like madness, but there is no choice. We will not be the only Crusade to violate our most sacred tradition. The Black Sword will remain in black hands until there are none left to bear it.

I have a moment – just a single moment – of reflexive pain when I see Bayard's body next to Bastilan's. Two of the finest Sword Brethren ever to serve the Chapter, now slain in glory. More alien bodies block my view. More xenos bleed as I force my way closer to Priamus.

A sense of bloodthirsty, eerie calm descends between us. The battle rages, weapons clashing against our armour, but I speak in a fierce whisper that I know carries over the vox to him and him alone.

'Priamus.'

'Reclusiarch.'

My maul sends two of the beasts flying back, and for a heartbeat's span, there are no alien barbarians separating us. Our eye lenses meet for that precious second, before we are both forced to turn and engage other foes.

'You are the last Emperor's Champion of the Helsreach Crusade,' I tell him. '*Now recover your blade.*'

Major Ryken spoke into his hand-vox, repeating the same words he'd been saying for almost a minute. His voice echoed around the nave in curiously calm counterpoint to the ragged breathing and moans of pain from the wounded.

'Any armour units still outside the basilica, respond. The *Godbreaker* has been sighted due south of the temple walls. Any armour units still outside, engage, engage.'

From his viewpoint by one of the broken stained glass windows, he watched the gargant's torso rising above the broken graveyard walls in the distance.

He didn't recognise the voice that eventually answered. It sounded both bitter and disgusted, but it still made Ryken grin.

'Engaging.'

'Hello? Identify yourself!'

'I am Princeps Amasat of the Warlord Titan Bane-Sidhe.'

The *Bane-Sidhe*, named for a shrieking monster from ancient Terran mythology, did everything in its power to gain the *Godbreaker's* attention. Opening salvos from its arm-cannons and shoulder-mounted weapon batteries lashed against the larger Titan's force fields. Siren horns, used to warn loyal infantry of the Titan's passing close – or even through – their regiments, blared now at the enemy engine. Whatever primitive communications array passed for a vox system on board the *Godbreaker* was scrambled into white noise by a focussed spike of machine-code from *Bane-Sidhe's* tech-adepts.

All of this was enough to drag the towering beast-machine away from its intent to flatten the Temple of the Emperor Ascendant.

The Warlord, thirty-three metres of armour plating and city-killing weaponry forged into an iconic image of the Machine-God Himself, began its shameful retreat. All guns fired at will as it clanked backwards, drawing the *Godbreaker* away from the last Imperials alive in the hive's most sacred sector.

'May I have a weapon, please?'

Andrej shrugged as he cleaned his goggles with a dirty cloth. 'I have no other pistol, fat priest. For this, I apologise.'

Tomaz Maghernus shook his head when Asavan looked his way. 'I don't, either.'

Several maidens of the Order of the Argent Shroud came down the wide stairs into the undercroft. Prioress Sindal led them, carrying her bolter with ease due to the machine-muscles of her power armour.

'It is time to seal the undercroft,' the old woman said, her voice low. She, at least, knew the merits of not panicking the refugees gathered in the sublevel. 'The beasts have reached the inner grounds.'

'May I have a weapon, please?' Asavan asked her.

'Have you ever fired a bolter?'

'Until this month, I had never even seen a bolter. Nevertheless, I would like a weapon with which to defend these people.'

'Father, with the greatest respect, it would do you no good. My thanks for comforting the flock, but it is time to prepare for the end. Everyone who is staying behind, be ready to be sealed down here within the next three minutes. The oxygen should last a month, as long as the xenos do not destroy the air filtration systems above ground.'

Andrej raised a singed eyebrow. 'And if they do?'

'Use your imagination, Guardsman. And return to the surface, quickly. Every able body is needed in defence of the temple.'

'A moment, please.' Andrej turned back to Asavan. 'Fat priest. You are destined to either survive this, or die at least some time later than I.' He handed the holy man a small leather pouch. Asavan took it, clutching it tight in fingers that would have trembled in this moment only weeks before.

'What is this?'

'My mother's wedding ring, and a letter of explanation. Once this is over, if you are still drawing breath, please find Trooper Natalina Domoska of the 91st Steel Elite. You will recognise her – this, I promise to you. She is the most beautiful woman in the world. Every man says so.'

'*Move*, young man,' the prioress insisted.

Andrej snapped a crisp salute to the overweight priest, and made his way back up the stairs, his laspistol held in both hands. Maghernus followed him, casting a lingering look back at Asavan and the refugees. He waved as the underground bulkheads slammed closed. Asavan didn't seem to see, preoccupied with the refugees who were rising to their feet in panic and protest.

Several of the battle-sisters remained at the base of the stairs, entering codes to seal the doors and imprison the civilians away from harm. The prioress managed to keep up with Andrej and Maghernus. The dockmaster smiled at her, knowing the gesture was meaningless and filled with melancholy. She returned the smile, her expression carrying the same emotions as his. The Temple was shaking as the orks battered at its walls.

The next time Maghernus would see Prioress Sindal of the Order of the Argent Shroud, she would be a mangled corpse in three pieces, spread across the floor of the inner sanctum.

That would be in less than one hour's time, and her body would be one of the last things he saw before he was killed by a bolt round in the back.

Bane-Sidhe tore clean through the Hel's Highway when it fell.

The Warlord had made it half a kilometre before its void shields burst out of existence and its front-facing armour began to suffer the assault from the *Godbreaker's* guns. No matter how thick the ceramite and adamantium plating covering the Warlord's vital systems, the sheer level of firepower hurled at *Bane-Sidhe* meant that once its shields died, its existence was measured in minutes.

It was perhaps unfair that such a noble example of the Invigilata's god-machines met its end as a sacrificial lure, but within the Legio's archives, both *Bane-Sidhe* and her command crew were given the highest honours. The wreckage of the Titan would come to be salvaged by the Mechanicus in the following weeks, and restored to working order fourteen months later. Its destruction at Helsreach was marked upon its carapace with a six-metre square engraved image upon its right shin, depicting a weeping angel over a burning, metallic skeleton.

Unable to withstand any more punishment, with flames pouring from its bridge, the great Warlord fell backwards on howling joints. Its immense weight was enough to break the rockcrete columns holding up the Hel's Highway, sending the *Bane-Sidhe* and a significant section of the main road crashing down to land in a mountain of rubble.

The *Godbreaker* stood over the crater of broken road, as if staring down at the body of its latest kill.

Fourteen seconds after the Warlord's shattered remains came to a rest, a flare of sun-bright and fusion-hot energy screamed across the Hel's Highway. It was the shape of a newborn star, flaring with arcing coils of plasma light and surrounded by a blinding corona.

The *Godbreaker's* shields disintegrated at the sunfire's touch. Its armour disintegrated mere seconds later, as did its crew, skeletal structure, and all evidence that it had ever existed.

Jurisian drooled through clenched teeth, feeling the untamed machine-spirit's quivering rage at being used without being ritually blessed and activated via the correct rituals. As the knifing pain in his skull faded to tolerable levels, he opened a vox-link to Grimaldus, and breathed two words.

They were laden with both agony and meaning – symbolising the completion of his duty, and a final farewell.

'Engine kill,' he said.

* * *

'The *Godbreaker* is dead,' Grimaldus voxed to anyone still listening to the comms channels. The news brought no relief to him, and no joy, even for thought of Jurisian's glory. There was nothing now beyond the next second of battle. Step by step, the Reclusiarch and his last brothers were pushed backwards through the basilica, room by room, hall by hall.

The air reeked of alien breath, spilled innards and the sharp overcooked ozone sent of las-fire.

The walls still shook as xenos tanks shelled the holy temple even while their own forces stormed through it.

A young girl in Argent Shroud battle armour was cut down, wailing as she was disembowelled by the horde. Artarion's two blades, both inactive from meat-clogging and no more use than jagged clubs, ripped across the face and throat of the girl's killer. Then he too was beaten back by the four beasts that took the dead brute's place.

A voice rose above the carnage – harsh and enraged.

'Kill them all! Let none survive! Never has an alien defiled this holiest of places!'

Grimaldus dragged the closest ork against him, gripping its throat and thudding his skulled helm against its face to shatter its hideous bone structure. The voice was the prioress's, and he realised now where he was.

No.

No, how could it all be over already?

We have been beaten back to the inner sanctum in mere hours. Sindal's cries of defiance have the worst effect: they awaken everyone from the mindless heat of battle and bloodshed, dragging us back to face the truth.

The inner sanctum is a gore-slick mess of heaving, slashing, shooting humans and orks. We are beaten. No one in this room is going to survive more than a few more minutes. Already, others have sensed this and I see them through the crowd, trying to run from the room, seeking a way past the orks rather than lay down their lives at the last stand.

Militia. Civilians. Guard. Even several storm troopers. Half of our pathetic remaining force is breaking from the battle and trying to run.

With my hand still at the ork's throat, I drag the kicking beast up with me, standing atop the Major Altar. The beast struggles, but its clawing is weak with its skull broken and its senses disoriented by pain.

My plasma pistol is long gone, torn from me at some point in the last two days of battle. The chain remains. I wrap it around the beast's throat, and roar my words to the painted ceiling as I strangle the creature in full view of everyone in the room.

'Take heart, brothers! Fight in the Emperor's name!' The beast thrashes as it dies, claws scraping in futility at my ruined armour. I tense my grip, feeling the creature's thick spinal bones begin to click and break. Its piggish eyes are wide with terror, and this... this makes me laugh.

'I have dug my grave in this place...' An explosive round detonates on my shoulder, blasting shards of armour free. I see Priamus kill the shooter with the Black Sword in a one-handed grip.

'I have dug my grave in this place, and I will either triumph or I will die!'

Five knights still live, and they roar as I roar.

'No pity! No remorse! No fear!'

The walls shudder as if kicked by a Titan. For a moment, still laughing, I wonder if the *Godbreaker* has returned.

'Until the end, brothers!'

The cry is taken up by those of us that yet draw breath, and we fight on.

'They're bringing the temple down!' Priamus calls, and there is something wrong with his voice. I realise what it is when I see my brother is missing an arm and his leg armour is pierced in three places.

I have never heard him in pain before.

'Nero!' he screams. 'Nerovar!'

The beasts are primitive, but they are not devoid of intelligence and cunning. Nero's white markings signal him as an Apothecary, and they know of his value to humanity. Priamus sees him first, two dozen metres away through the melee. An alien spear has punched its way through his stomach, and several of the beasts are lifting him from the ground, raising him like a war banner above the carnage.

Nerovar dies like no warrior I have ever seen before. Even as I try to kill my way closer to him, I see him gripping the spear in his fists, hauling himself down the weapon, impaling himself deeper on it in an attempt to reach the aliens below.

He has no bolter, no chainblade. His last act in life is to draw his gladius from its sheath at his thigh and hurl it down with a Templar's vengeance at the ork with the best grip on the spear. He'd dragged himself down to get close enough to ensure he wouldn't miss. The short sword bit true, sinking into the beast's gaping maw and rewarding the xenos with an agonising death, choking on a sword blade that had ravaged its throat, tongue and lungs. With the beast unable to keep hold, the spear falls and Nero plunges into a seething mass of greenskins.

I never see him again.

Priamus, one-armed and faltering now, staggers ahead of me. A detonating round crashes against his helm, spinning him back to face me.

'Grimaldus,' he says, before falling to his knees. 'Brother...'

Flames engulf him from the side – clinging chemical fire that washes over his armour, eating into the soft joints and dissolving the flesh beneath. The ork with the flamer pans the weapon left and right, dousing Priamus in corrosive fire.

I am hammering my way with painful slowness to avenge him when Artarion's blade bursts from the ork's chest. He kicks the dying ork from his broken chainsword. With vengeance taken, my standard bearer turns with as much grace as can be salvaged in this butchery, and his back slams against mine.

'Goodbye, brother.' He's laughing as he says the words, and I do not know why, but it brings out my own laughter.

Blocks of the ceiling are falling now, crushing those beneath. The orks in here with us, paying for every human life with five of their own, pay no heed to their kin outside damning them by destroying the temple with them still inside.

Not far from the altar, I catch a final glimpse of the storm trooper and the dockmaster. The former stands above the dying latter, Andrej defending the gut-shot Maghernus while he tries to comprehend what to do with his bowels looping across his lap and the floor nearby.

'Artarion,' I call to him, to return the farewell, but there is no answer. The presence against my back is not my brother.

I turn, laughing at the madness before me. Artarion is dead at my feet, headless, defiled. The enemy drive me to my knees, but even this is no more than a bad joke. They are doomed as surely as I am.

I am still laughing when the temple finally falls.

EPILOGUE

ASHES

They call it the Season of Fire.

The Ash Wastes are choking with dust from roaring volcanoes. Planet-wide, the picts show the same images, over and over. Our vessels in orbit watch Armageddon breathe fire, and send the images back to the surface, so that those there might witness the world's anger in its entirety.

Fighting across most of the world is ceasing, not because of victory or defeat, but because there can be no arguing with Armageddon itself. The ash deserts are already turning dark. In a handful of days, no man or xenos beast will be able to breathe in the wastelands. Their lungs would fill with ashes and embers; their war machines would grind to a halt, fouled beyond use.

So the war ceases for now. It does not end. There is no tale of triumph and victory to tell.

The beasts stagger and crawl back to cities they have managed to hold, there to hide away from the Season of Fire. Imperial forces consolidate the territories to which they still lay claim, and drive the invaders out from those where the orks have managed to grasp no more than a weak hold.

Helsreach is one of these places. That necropolis, in which one hundred of my brothers lie dead alongside hundreds of thousands of loyal souls...

That tomb-city, so much of which is flattened by the devastation of two months' road-by-road warfare, with no industrial output left at all...

Imperial tacticians are hailing it as a *victory.*

I will never again understand the humanity I left behind when I ascended to the ranks of the Templars. The perceptions of humans remain alien to me since the moment I swore my first oaths to Dorn.

But I will let the people of this blighted world claim their triumph. I will let the survivors of Helsreach cheer and celebrate a drawn-out defeat that masquerades as victory.

And, as they have requested, I will return to the surface once more.

I have something of theirs in my possession.

They cheer in the streets, and line Hel's Highway as if in anticipation of a parade. Several hundred civilians, and an equal number of off-duty Guard. They stand in crowds, clustered either side of the *Grey Warrior.*

My helm's aural receptors filter the noise of their cheering to less irritating levels, the way it would do if an artillery battery was shelling the ground around me.

I try not to stare at them, at their flushed faces, at their bright and joyous eyes. The war is over to them. They care nothing for the orbital images that show entire ork armies taking root in other hives. For the people of Helsreach, the war is over. They are alive, so they have won.

It is hard not to admire such simple purity. Blessed is the mind too small for doubt. And in truth, I have never seen a city resist invasion so fiercely. The people here have earned the lives they still have.

This part of the city, not far from the accursed docks, is relatively unscathed. It remained a stronghold firmly in Imperial control. I am given to understand that Sarren and his 101st fought here to the last day.

A gathering of figures clusters by the *Grey Warrior.* Most wear the ochre uniforms of the Steel Legion. One of them, a man known to me, beckons me over.

I walk to him, and the crowd erupts into more cheers. It is the first time I have moved in almost an hour.

An hour of listening to tedious speeches transmitted from the gathered group, over to a vox-tower nearby that blares the words across the sector.

'Grimaldus, Reclusiarch of the Black Templars,' the vox-voice booms. More cheers as I draw close. The soldier that beckoned to me offers quiet greetings.

Major, or rather, *Colonel* Ryken has regained much of his face since I last saw him. Burn scars spread across much of the remaining skin, but over half of his features are dull-metalled augmetics, including significant reconstruction to his skull. He makes the sign of the aquila, and only one of his hands is his own. The other is a skeletal bionic, not yet sheathed in synthetic skin.

I return the salute. The vox-speech – the speaker is a member of General Kurov's staff I have never met before – drones on about my own heroism alongside the Steel Legion. As my name is shouted by thousands of humans, I raise my fist in salute to them all.

And all the while, I am thinking how my brothers died here.

Died for them.

'Did Adjutant Quintus Tyro survive?' I ask.

He nods, his ruined face trying to make a smile. 'Cyria made it.'

Good. I am pleased for him, and for her.

'Hello, sir,' another of the Legionnaires says. I glance behind Ryken, to a man several places down the line. My targeting reticule locks on him – onto his grinning face. He is unscarred, and despite his youth, has laugh lines at the corner of his eyes.

So. He's not dead, either.

This does not surprise me. Some men are born with luck in their blood.

I nod to him, and he walks over, seemingly as bored with proceedings as I am. The orator is declaring how I 'smote the blaspheming aliens as they dared defile the Temple's inner sanctum.' His words border on a sermon. He would have made a fine ecclesiarch, or a preacher in the Imperial Guard.

The ochre-clad soldier offers his hand for me to shake. I humour him by doing the same.

'Hello, hero,' he grins up at me.

'Greetings, Andrej.'

'I like your armour. It is much nicer now. Did you repaint it yourself, or is that the duty of slaves?'

I cannot tell if this is a joke or not.

'Myself.'

'Good! Good. Perhaps you should salute me now, though, yes?' He taps his epaulettes, where a captain's badges now show, freshly issued and polished silver.

'I am not beholden to a Guard captain,' I tell him. 'But con-gratulations.'

'Yes, I know, I know. But I must be offering many thanks for you keeping your word and telling my captain of my deeds.'

'An oath is an oath.' I have no idea what to say to the little man. 'Your friend. Your love. Did you find her?'

I am no judge of human emotion, but I see his smile turn fragile and false. 'Yes,' he says. 'I did find her.'

I think of the last time I saw the little storm trooper, standing over the dock-master's bloody corpse, bayoneting an alien in the throat, only moments before the basilica fell.

I find myself curiously glad that he is alive, but expressing that notion is not something I can easily forge into words. He has no such difficulty.

'I am glad you made it,' he uses my own unspoken words. 'I heard you were very injured, yes?'

'Not enough to kill me.'

But so close. I quickly grew bored of the Apothecaries on board the *Crusader* telling me that it was a miracle I clawed my way from the rubble.

He laughs, but there is little joy in it. His eyes are like glass since he mentioned finding his friend.

'You are a very literal man, Reclusiarch. Some of us were in lazy moods that day. I waited for the digging crews, yes, I admit it. I did not have Astartes armour to push the rocks off myself and get back to fighting the very next day.'

'The reports I have heard indicated no one else survived the fall of the basilica,' I tell him.

He laughs. 'Yes, that would make for a wonderful story, no? The last black knight, the only survivor of the greatest battle in Helsreach. I apologise for surviving and breaking the flow of your legend, Reclusiarch. I promise most faithfully that I and the six or seven others will be very quiet and let you have all the thunder.'

He has made a joke. I recognise it, and try to think of something humorous with which to reply. Nothing surfaces in my mind.

'Were you not injured at all?'

He shrugs. 'I had a headache. But then it went away.'

This makes me smile.

'Did you meet the fat priest?' he asks. 'Did you know him?'

'I confess, I do not recall anyone by that name or description.'

'He was a good man. You would have liked him. Very brave. He did not die in the battle. He was with the civilians. But he died two weeks after, from a problem with his heart. Ayah, that is unfair, I think. To live through the end and die at the new beginning? Not so fair, I am thinking.'

There is a twisted poetry to that.

I would like to speak words that comfort him. I would like to tell him I admire his courage, and that his world will survive this war. I want to speak with the ease Artarion would have done, and thank this soldier for standing with us when so many others ran. He honoured us all in that moment, as did the dying dockmaster, the prioress, and every other soul that faded from life on the night only I survived.

But I say nothing. Further conversation is broken by people chanting my name. How alien it sounds, voiced by human throats.

The orator whips the crowd up, speaking – of course – of the relics. They want to see them, and that is why I am here. To display them.

I signal the cenobyte servitors forward. Augmetic servants, vat-grown by the Chapter's Apothecaries and augmented by Jurisian to haul the Temple's artefacts. None of the mindless wretches bear a name; just a relic that represents all I could do to ease my guilt at such a shameful defeat.

The crowd cheers again as the servitors move from the vulture shadow of my Thunderhawk, each of the three carrying one of the artefacts. The ragged scraps of the banner. The cracked stone pillar, topped by the shattered aquila. The sacred bronze globe, sloshing with its precious holy water.

My voice carries with ease, amplified by my helm. The crowd quietens, and Hel's Highway falls silent. I am reminded, against my will, of the impenetrable silence beneath the mountain of marble and rockcrete when the Temple came down upon us all.

'We are judged in life,' I tell them, 'for the evil we destroy.'

Never my words. Always Mordred's.

For the first time, I have an answer to them. A greater understanding. And my mentor... You were wrong. Forgive me, that it took so long to leave your shadow and realise it. Forgive me, that it took the deaths of my brothers to learn the lesson they each tried to teach me while they yet drew breath.

Artarion. Priamus. Bastilan. Cador. Nero.

Forgive me for living, while you all lie cold and still.

'We are judged in life for the evil we destroy. It is a bleak truth, that there is nothing but blood awaiting us in the spaces between the stars. But the Emperor sees all that transpires in His domain. And we are judged equally for the illumination we bring to the blackest nights. We are judged in life for those moments we spill light into the darkest reaches of His Imperium.

'Your world taught me this. Your world, and the war that brought me here.

'These are your relics. The last treasures of the first men and women ever to set foot upon your world. They are the most precious treasures of your ancestors, and they are yours by right of legacy and blood.

'I return them to you from the edge of destruction. And I thank you not only for the honour of standing by the people of this city, but for the lessons I have learned. My brothers in orbit have asked me why I dragged these relics from beneath the fallen Temple. But you have no need to ask, for you each already know the answer. They are *yours,* and no alien beast will deny the people of this world the inheritance they deserve.

'I dragged these relics back into the sunlight for you – to honour you, and to thank you all. And in humility now, I return them to you.'

This time, when the cheers come, they are shaped by the orator. He uses the title I swore to High Marshal Helbrecht, standing before Mordred's statue, that I would not refuse when it was formally awarded to me.

'I am told,' the High Marshal had said afterwards, 'that Yarrick and Kurov have spoken with the Ecclesiarchy. You are being given the relics, to carry Helsreach's memory and honour with you, in the Eternal Crusade.'

'When I return to the surface, I will offer the icons back to the people.'

'Mordred would not have done so,' Helbrecht said, masking any emotion, any judgement, from me.

'I am not Mordred,' I told my liege. 'And the people deserve the choice. It is for them that we waged that war, for them and their world. Not purely for the holy reaping of inhuman life.'

And I wonder now, as they chant my new title, what they will decide to do with the relics.

Hero of Helsreach, the crowd cheers.

As if there is only one.

THE ONLY GOOD ORK

SANDY MITCHELL

There's never a good time to come face to face with an ork, but doing so while crawling from the wreck of a crashed Salamander is one of the least propitious. What made the surprise even less welcome was that, until that moment, I'd had no idea that any of the creatures were even in the area at all. I suppose I shouldn't have been completely taken aback; Frumenta had been infested with them a few decades prior to the experience, until the Guard had arrived to clear them out – a job they'd performed with commendable efficiency. But, as always, there had been occasional localised outbreaks in the years since, which the Frumentan militia had been more than capable of mopping up. At least until they'd turned out to be infested with genestealers, turned on one another and sparked a full-scale civil war, which the Astra Militarum had been sent back in to deal with.

I'd been dragged into the whole dismal affair, despite being officially retired by now, by virtue of passing through the void station that the task force was assembling around at just the wrong moment. Refusing to tag along at the lord general's personal request would have put more of a dent in my undeserved, but undeniably useful on occasion, reputation than I could afford, not to mention our personal friendship. And then there was Amberley, and my well-concealed avocation as one of her Inquisitorial errand boys – a hitherto unsuspected genestealer infestation on such a scale was sure to be of interest to the Ordo Xenos. Which meant, in turn, that she was liable to be a bit miffed with me if I passed up the chance to acquire some intelligence on the spot, a complication my life could well have done without.

So, with carefully concealed reluctance, I let my waiting sinecure on Perlia slide still further into the indefinite future, and embarked for an unremarkable agri world little different to a score of others. On arrival I attached myself to the general staff, made sure my successor wasn't being too much of a nuisance to Zyvan (which she wasn't, as I'd made sure the Commissariat would appoint someone pragmatic enough to just let him get on with the job before I left) and busied myself making morale-boosting visits to whichever regiments seemed sufficiently far away from the fighting at the moment, picking up whatever scraps of information I could for Amberley along the way.

Which was how I'd eventually found myself in the Cascades, an area of high peaks, deep gorges and spectacular waterfalls, which had been a popular tourist destination away from the intensely cultivated zones in more peaceful times. Many of the genestealer cultists retreating in the face of the Guard advance had sought refuge there, counting on the rugged terrain and sparse population to let them effectively disappear. It might even have worked if the narrow, twisting roads over the mountain passes hadn't funnelled their vehicles into a limited number of transit corridors, making them sitting waterfowl for our air corp's Vendetta gunships. I'd just finished a typical visit to one of the forward airstrips, where I'd dispensed a few platitudes, shaken a few hands and enjoyed an indifferent lunch, when we drove into an ambush, presumably set for the supply trucks which kept the flyboys fed.

My first intimation of trouble was a las-bolt, which impacted on the rim of the Salamander's open passenger compartment, followed by a number of others as I ducked behind the comforting solidity of the armour plate.

'Jurgen,' I voxed, tapping the comm-bead in my ear, 'we're taking fire.' Not that I was particularly concerned. The sturdy little scout vehicle could shrug off a great deal worse than that, and had probably come as a nasty surprise to the insurgents, who'd no doubt been expecting nothing tougher than a lorry or two they could disable and loot.

I scrambled behind the pintle-mounted heavy bolter, which afforded me some protection as I stood, and pulled the trigger, hosing down the cliff face from which, judging by the angle of the incoming fire, the bulk of it had come. I was rewarded with a sudden cessation of the rain of las-bolts, and a few flickers of movement among the scrub clinging hopefully to the near-vertical surface as our assailants scrambled for something more solid to hide behind.

'That seems to have dampened their enthusiasm.'

'Pleased to hear it, sir,' my aide responded from the driver's compartment, opening the throttle as he spoke. If anyone else had been at the controls I'd have found the sudden surge of acceleration distinctly alarming, given that our left-hand tread was mere centimetres from the precipice edging the highway, but I knew Jurgen's exceptional driving skills of old, and merely tightened my grip on the bolter a little to help maintain my balance; a reflex which might well have saved my life. I just had time to register a bright streak in the air ahead of us before a rocket hit the corner of our front armour plate, shredding one of the tracks with the resulting shower of shrapnel.

The Salamander lurched violently. Jurgen swore, or began to, his oath choked off half-finished as the sturdy little vehicle veered over the cliff-edge.

Fortunately, as I've mentioned before, there was a fair amount of scrub, even a tree or two, clinging to the face of the gorge, and, by the grace of the Emperor, the cliff face here wasn't quite vertical. After a heart-stopping moment in which we seemed to be suspended in mid-air, the breath was driven from my lungs by a bone-jarring impact, and our crippled Salamander began slithering down the scree, rocks and shattered vegetation spraying out all around us. I clung to the bolter for dear life, my teeth rattling in my head, while the sky and the rocks around us pinwheeled; then, with a jolt, a bounce and a squeal of abused metal, the entire vehicle tilted over on its side, and at last came to rest, a few metres from the stream running energetically along the floor of the gorge.

After a moment I realised I wasn't dead after all, and crawled out from under the bolter mounting, bumping my head on the way. Still dazed, I rolled off the armoured floor, which until recently had been the Salamander's side plates, feeling gravel and a few larger, harder stones pressing against my back, and looked up into a face that more properly belonged in a nightmare. Indeed, for a moment I thought that was precisely what it was, a hallucination shaken out of my scrambled cortex by the violence of our descent – until I realised that no figment of my imagination could possibly have exuded breath as feculent as that.

'Waaaaaaghhhh!' it bellowed, punching a dent in the armour plate behind me as I rolled out of the way in the nick of time, scrabbling for my laspistol as I moved. My hand closed on nothing at all, the precise distance above an empty holster that the grip should have been, and I rolled again, evading another killing blow, catching sight of the weapon just under the heavy bolter mount, where I couldn't scrabble for it without getting my skull stove in from behind in the process. A loud clanging from the distorted hatch of the driver's compartment, accompanied by a litany of profanity in my earpiece, made it abundantly clear that I wasn't going to get any help from Jurgen in the next few seconds – I was on my own, at least until he managed to force it open.

Fortunately, I still had my chainsword, and I drew it, scrambling to my feet while my orkish assailant remained unbalanced from the failure to connect. Before I could take a swipe at him,[1] however, a fusillade of lasgun fire burst around us, spanging from the mangled metalwork of the Salamander, and gouging a couple of wounds in my attacker which would have put a human down in an instant, probably for good. It simply seemed to enrage him, however, and he whirled around to face this new threat with an even louder bellow of defiance than before.

'What's happening, sir?' Jurgen asked, hardly surprisingly under the circumstances, while I dived for the cover of the overturned passenger compartment, taking the opportunity to grab my laspistol while the ork's attention was diverted.

'Rebels,' I said, taking in the situation with a rapid glance. The squad of troopers advancing up the defile were wearing local militia uniforms, but by now I'd seen enough genestealer hybrids to notice the subtle wrongness about the way a few of their number carried themselves. Emboldened by their presence the survivors of the ambushing party on the road above sent a few las-rounds in our direction too, but what with the extreme range and awkward angle they might just as well not have bothered; all the couple of bolts that actually hit the crippled vehicle did was reinforce my inclination to stay put. Which, with an angry ork practically in punching distance, wasn't really much of an option.

'Be right with you, sir,' my aide assured me, while the banging and swearing

1 Since they appear to reproduce by spore diffusion, orks are technically genderless, but are generally referred to exclusively by the masculine pronoun – which, given the physical strength and spectacular stupidity of most of their kind, is, I suppose, inevitable. *Amberley Vail, Ordo Xenos.*

from the driver's compartment both increased in volume. The ork turned back to me, murder in his eyes, and I brought the laspistol up, hoping I'd be able to find a weak spot in that phenomenally thick skull. Then another possibility occurred to me.

'Oldyt!'[2] I bellowed, as loudly as I could, keeping the pistol on aim in case he didn't. But the results were as successful as I could have hoped for. An expression of almost comic confusion at being addressed in his own barbarous tongue[3] furrowed his bestial visage. I gestured at the advancing hybrids, who were considerate enough to draw his attention to them with another burst of automatic fire, which ricocheted around us, fortunately creating more noise than damage in the process. 'We kill them first. Then each other.'

The ork frowned for a moment, trying to work it out. Then, to my intense relief, he threw back his head to emit a harsh bark of laughter.

'Kill them first,' he agreed. Then his eyes fell on the heavy bolter. 'Shoota!'[4]

'Help yourself,' I said, wondering whether handing an enemy our most powerful weapon was altogether wise. On the other hand, I couldn't use it where it was, firmly attached to the Salamander, and, right this minute, the genestealer brood seemed the greater threat. Marginally. Come to that, I'd never seen an ork without a weapon of some kind before, or on his own, and that worried me. Time enough to think about that later, though, if I got the chance.

A fist large enough to have crushed my head seized the heavy weapon, and wrenched it from its mounting with a groan of protesting metal. Hardened steel twisted and tore, and I found myself once again marvelling at the sheer brute strength of these creatures. The ork hefted the heavy bolter with an unmistakable expression of satisfaction, fumbled for the trigger, and emitted a frustrated grunt as his ploin-thick forefinger proved too bulky to fit through the trigger guard. With an irritated exhalation he pinched the thin strip of metal between finger and thumb, and pulled it away, like Jurgen disposing of a scab. His gaze fell on me, and I have to confess to a shiver of apprehension, which I concealed as best I could, flourishing my own weapons and glancing in the direction of the oncoming enemy.

'Kill them first!' he bellowed, taking the hint. *'Waaaghhhhh!'*

And, to my inexpressible relief, he lumbered off in their general direction, brandishing the bolter. A moment later he'd levelled it, and a withering blast of explosive projectiles made a satisfying mess of the first few hybrid troopers, while the rest scattered, no doubt unpleasantly surprised by this sudden turn of events. Taking advantage of the distraction of both sets of enemies, I turned back to the crippled vehicle behind me.

'Move away from the hatch,' I voxed Jurgen, thumbing the speed selector of my chainsword to maximum, and beginning to hack at the hinges. Thankfully, they gave way almost immediately, in a shower of sparks, and the

---

2 Orkish for 'wait,' or 'I saw it first.' *A.V.*

3 Which, as noted elsewhere in the edited portions of his memoirs, Cain acquired a basic working knowledge of during his successful guerilla war against the orkish occupiers of Perlia's eastern continent early on in his career. *A.V.*

4 A generic Orkish term for any firearm or energy weapon, preferably as noisy and destructive as possible. Since it's unlikely that Cain proposed his truce in plain Gothic, he seems to be translating selectively here in the interests of clarity. *A.V.*

circular slab of metal fell away with a *clang!* that echoed around the narrow valley. My aide emerged, cocooned in the odour of month-old socks, clutching his lasgun and looking around warily.

'Who's firing the bolter?' he asked, flicking the safety off, 'And who at?'

'An ork,' I said, deciding to keep things as simple as possible, 'and some hybrids. This way, while they keep each other busy.' I started to lead the way along the edge of the stream, keeping the bulk of the wrecked Salamander between us and the combatants. The hybrids were returning the greenskin's fire by now, from whatever cover they'd been able to find, and with any luck they'd take care of each other while we made ourselves scarce.

I suppose anyone else would have responded to a statement like that with a stream of questions, but Jurgen, phlegmatic as ever, simply shrugged, and fell in at my shoulder as usual, his lasgun readied for use. 'Knew I should have brought the melta,' he said, spitting ruefully into the stream.

'This sector was supposed to be clear,' I reminded him; this was no time to get distracted with pointless reproaches. 'I can see I'll have to have a little word with our analysts when we get back.' If we got back. But that was a line of thought I had no wish to pursue. And, in all honesty, I could hardly blame anyone else for our predicament – we wouldn't have been out here on our own at all if I'd thought there was the remotest chance of blundering into the enemy. Just our luck to stumble across a handful of stragglers.

'So where did the ork come from?' Jurgen asked, as we rounded a curve in the stream bed, which revealed a wider section of the gorge. There was a small shingle beach here, the walls of the defile covered in vegetation, but the only thing which registered with me was the scattering of dead orks decorating it. All had been killed with Imperial ordnance, and a gratifying degree of thoroughness; judging by the miasma of greasy smoke hanging over everything, and the charred condition of most of the corpses, someone had doused the dead in promethium and set fire to them, a detail which left Jurgen nodding in satisfaction.[5]

'Here would be my guess,' I said, glancing around for any more which might still be twitching. In my experience it was never wise to count any of the creatures out entirely, however chewed up they were, their resilience bordering on the preternatural. But I needn't have worried; these were as dead as they looked, a fact I verified as simply as possible by putting a couple of las-bolts into each of them from a safe distance. 'Looks like they'd set up camp here.' Not that there was much evidence of that left, beyond a crude firepit formed from some of the larger rocks, in which the remains of a fire still smouldered.

Jurgen nodded agreement. 'That looks like a den,' he said, pointing to a tangle of brushwood piled up next to the cliff face. As I took a few more steps towards it, I saw what he meant. The branches had been laced together to form a crude shelter, which, judging by the smell emanating from it, had been in use for some time. A primitive spear, formed from a sapling,

5 Their home world having once been invaded by orks, Valhallans set great store by disposing of their ancestral enemies as comprehensively as possible. *A.V.*

a chipped rock lashed to its tip, lay on the ground nearby, and I prodded it with my foot, feeling somewhat bemused.

'Where's their kit?' I asked.

My aide shrugged. 'We're walking on it.' He stirred the shale underfoot with the tip of his boot, and I belatedly recognised the flakes as the knapped detritus left by the creation of stone tools. 'These must be recently spawned.'[6]

'You'd know,' I said, deferring to his greater knowledge of the creatures, honed over generations of keeping his home world free of any further infestations. The distant sound of bolter fire drifted towards us on the breeze, indicating that my erstwhile companion was still enjoying himself, but he was probably running out of genestealer hybrids to shoot, and would no doubt be turning his attention to us before much longer. By which time I fully intended to be a long way from here, lurking in ambush, or both. I'd seen what a heavy bolter could do far too frequently to have any intention of being on the wrong end of one.

Or lasguns, come to that. The unmistakable crackle of several bursts echoed around the defile, and one of the stones by my boot burst from the sudden thermal shock of a las-bolt hit. More of the genestealer hybrids were charging at us from further up the defile, firing as they came, wild unaimed bursts intended to pin us in position while they closed, or force us to run so they could shoot us in the back. A crude tactic that might possibly have worked against the local loyalists, but Jurgen and I had been on far too many battlefields to make either mistake, throwing ourselves prone behind the nearest smoking greenskin corpse instead; which smelled about as pleasant as you might imagine, but at least it masked my aide's distinctive aroma and soaked up the bulk of the incoming fire perfectly satisfactorily.

'Pick your targets,' I cautioned, quite unnecessarily given the decades Jurgen and I had served together, but my aide nodded, and began placing precise single shots among the onrushing hybrids, dropping the lead one with a neat hit between the fellow's torso armour and helmet. A cauterised crater replaced most of his face, and he fell forwards into the stream, raising a cloud of spray.

'Let 'em waste their ammo,' Jurgen agreed, as several of the troopers switched to full-auto, chewing away determinedly at the ork corpse behind which we were sheltering. 'Frakwits.'

'They're trying to keep our heads down,' I said, apprehending the danger just in time, and turning to shoot at another hybrid rappelling down the cliff face, his lasgun slung over his shoulder, 'while the ones from the road flank us!' I missed him, of course, given the range and the angle, but the las-bolt struck close, and he lost his grip on the rope, falling the last few metres. That wasn't enough to finish him off, but his leg must have been broken, because he flapped about like a recently landed fish until Jurgen administered the *coup de grâce* with another precisely aimed shot.

'Well, they're succeeding,' my aide muttered, abandoning his lasgun for a moment while he fumbled in his collection of webbing pouches, and

---

6 The prevailing theory among the magos biologis studying these creatures is that some innate knowledge, including the construction and use of weapons, is somehow genetically coded within them – if so, this group clearly lacked the resources to build 'shootas' from scratch. *A.V.*

produced a grenade. 'This ought to return the favour.' He lobbed it over our reeking makeshift barricade, following up with a couple of others.

The first detonated in the middle of the squad attempting to pin us down, shredding a couple of the nearest troopers with its spray of shrapnel, and sending the rest scattering left and right in an instinctive scramble to get away from the site of the explosion. Right where Jurgen had placed the other two frag charges, of course, which went off almost simultaneously a second or two later, wreaking similar havoc among the injured and shell-shocked survivors. Not all the tainted squad were down, but the majority were, and I felt a degree of vindictive satisfaction at the realisation that most of the survivors were limping.

'Nicely done,' I said, potting one of the nearer walking wounded for good measure, and turning my attention to the latest threat. Not that the handful of remaining hybrids from the first squad could be counted out, of course – their connection to the brood mind kept them focused on their objective long after most human troopers would have retreated to regroup, or simply fled for their lives – but at least they'd stopped shooting at us for the time being. Which reminded me, the distant sounds of bolter fire had ceased; either the ork had been killed, or he'd run out of ammunition. Either way, that would be a problem for later.

I glanced at the enemy gathering by the cliff face, their boots crunching on the rocky beach as they shrugged free of their rappelling lines: a potential way back up to the road, and help, if we could reach them. The airstrip we'd left so short a time before was only a few kilometres away, and Jurgen and I could walk it in an hour or so; but with any luck someone would have noticed we were missing before then, and sent out a search party we could hitch a ride with. Right now, though, I might as well wish for the Emperor Himself to turn up and offer us a hand – the dangling ropes, and the arduous climb they promised, were well out of reach, cut off from us by a horde of well-armed, human-looking abominations. The battered survivors of the other squad were joining them, and I counted a dozen or so enemy troopers in total.[7]

'Got any more of those grenades?' I asked, and Jurgen nodded soberly.

'Two more frag. And a couple of krak ones.' Which might have been of some use if the enemy had a vehicle, but we both knew the armour-piercing charges would be pretty much useless against dispersed infantry, other than startling them with an unexpectedly loud bang.

'Then frag it is,' I said, eyeing the next dead ork to our left, which seemed to offer a bit more cover against the new direction of the enemy advance than our rapidly decaying current refuge. 'Better make 'em count.'

'I will that.' My aide followed the direction of my gaze, reading the situation just as clearly as I was. 'That one there?'

'That one there,' I confirmed. 'On three.' I took careful aim at the cultist with the sergeant's rank insignia (they were all part of the brood mind, so taking out the nominal leader wouldn't actually make a blind bit of

7 Presumably he'd taken a few of the ambushers on the road out with the heavy bolter before the Salamander crash, or the group had already been severely depleted in earlier clashes with the Imperial Guard. *A.V.*

difference, but I couldn't see any point in overriding my normal targeting priorities) and pulled the trigger. 'Three!'

The shot was a good one, taking him squarely in the chest. I couldn't see if it had penetrated his torso armour from this distance, but I don't suppose it actually mattered. He staggered from the impact, and Jurgen and I moved, running for the next cadaver, crouching low to minimise our profiles, and popping off a few rounds in the general direction of the enemy. A few desultory las-bolts followed us in return, but by the grace of the Throne none came close enough to actually hit.

I threw myself down behind the shielding corpse, driving the breath from my lungs against the hard-edged stones, briefly envying my aide his body armour, an instant before the hybrids found the range again, and the dead ork twitched as though disturbed by dreams as half a dozen las-bolts slammed into it.

'Oh no you don't.' Jurgen snapped off a double tap,[8] and one of the figures by the cliff face folded, the rocket launcher which had presumably done for our Salamander dropping to the ground beside it. He must already have primed the warhead, because it detonated inside the tube, spraying a satisfactory amount of shrapnel in all directions, which more or less halved the number of our opponents in one fell swoop. (Quite literally, in the case of the couple standing nearest to him.) Jurgen nodded, in quiet satisfaction. 'Thought that would be a frag charge.'

'Nicely done,' I told him; it may have been a happy accident, but he might as well get the credit. I began to think we might get out of this after all.

Then a familiar bellow ripped through the air, and the ork reappeared – not dead as I'd hoped after all, but very much the worse for wear. He was limping, his whole torso pockmarked with the stigmata of lasweapons. One ear was missing, along with enough muscle and skin to expose the teeth along that side of his jaw, and an ecstatic grin stretched across what was left of his face. Even by the standards of his own species he seemed remarkably resilient, although I'd seen the like often enough before: I've practically lost count of the number of orks I've encountered too stubborn or stupid to realise they're dead, lumbering on long after they should have dropped, fuelled by nothing but bloodlust and rage.

'Killed them all!' he roared, picking up speed, his eyes fixed on Jurgen and me. 'Now you!' The bolter was still in his hand, but it seemed I'd been right about him running out of ammunition; he was brandishing it like a club, and it seemed to have acquired a patina of congealed blood, to which a few patches of what looked like hair, brain and bone fragments adhered to give it a little variety. He seemed so fixated on ripping Jurgen and me to shreds that he might not even have noticed the remaining hybrids if they hadn't made the obvious mistake of opening fire on him as he closed with us, no doubt in the hope of ridding themselves of all three of us at once.

'Not all!' I yelled back, keeping my aim on the other enemy with an almost preternatural effort of will. If I turned to face him the hybrids would rush

8 Two shots in quick succession. *A.V.*

us, and it would all be over, even if, by some miracle, the ork didn't finish me off first. 'Still them!' I fired in their general direction to reinforce the point. 'Kill them first!'

It was touch and go, I don't mind admitting it; once an ork is carried away by bloodlust, there's practically nothing in the galaxy that'll divert them from their intended target, unless it's some idiot making themselves look like a better one. Or, in this case, half a dozen idiots. Three or four las-bolts impacted on him, the rest hissing by harmlessly, or expending themselves in the corpse I was cowering behind. His head turned.

'Waaaaghhhhh!' he roared again, turning and breaking into a stumbling run. A barrage of las-rounds tore into his chest, exposing his ribcage, but by now he'd picked up so much momentum he could probably have shoulder-charged a Leman Russ and barged it out of the way. The first hybrid to stand his ground fell in an instant, his head reduced to a gore-drenched mist by a single swing of the heavy bolter, the second and third going down an instant later on the backswing. The remaining hybrids broke and ran, affording Jurgen and me an easy target apiece, and then the last went flying against the cliff face, his neck broken by a single blow from a fist the size of my head.[9] He stood there for a moment, trying to force air into his exposed lungs, then turned slowly to face me.

'Killed them all,' he said.

'Killed them all,' I agreed, shifting my stance a little, bracing for what I knew was about to come. The chainsword hummed in my hand, and I slipped the laspistol back into its holster, ready to take a two-handed grip if I needed to. 'Now each other.'

I spoke the fateful phrase at the same moment he did, and then the ork charged.

To this day, I don't know how much difference the damage he'd already taken made; I have, after all, faced so many of his kind in hand-to-hand combat that I honestly have no idea of the number, and at least half of them have been completely uninjured. But in my experience, that doesn't seem to count for much, the brutes' abhuman resilience allowing them to shrug off injuries a man would have found instantly fatal. His charge did seem to me to be a little slower than most, however, and I sidestepped his first blow easily, the teeth of the chainblade whining and raising a shower of sparks as it deflected the mass of metal in his hand.

The makeshift club gouged into the shingle, raising a storm of stinging stones, and I stepped back, anticipating another wild swing, and hoping to open up enough distance between us for Jurgen to get off a shot without running the risk of felling me instead – but the ork followed up almost instantly, bellowing with rage, closing the gap too quickly for my aide to intervene. My boots slithered on the pebbles as I took another step backwards, and the next swipe grazed past my face close enough that I felt the breeze of its passing. If I let the brute continue to press his attack, I'd be dead in a handful of heartbeats.

9 Possibly a slight exaggeration, but maybe not by much. *A.V.*

The only way to regain the initiative was to close the distance, so I stepped in under a vicious downward blow, bringing my blade up to block it, and sliced clean through his forearm. The mangled heavy bolter fell to the shingle, still grasped in the hand that had held it, and I drove in hard, putting all my weight behind a thrust which ripped through his ruined chest cavity, and deep into his heart.

The ork fell to his knees as I tore the blade free through the side of his chest.

For a moment I thought he was about to say something, then his eyes dulled, and he pitched forward, crashing to the stones. I flicked the blade free of the bits of macerated ork still clinging to it, and stepped back, still wary, but the creature remained motionless, and at last I sheathed the weapon, sure that he was dead.

Jurgen slung his lasgun and began rummaging in his collection of pouches again. 'Didn't know there were greenskins around here,' he said.

'No one did.' I shook my head. 'We'll have to send recon teams out. Make sure there aren't any more of them.'

'There are always more of them,' Jurgen said, accurately but unhelpfully. He held out a thermal flask. 'Tanna?'

'Most welcome,' I said. I tapped the comm-bead in my ear hopefully, but, as I'd expected, the vox-gear in the Salamander seemed not to have survived our precipitous descent. It seemed we'd be walking back after all. I sighed and approached the nearest dangling rope. 'It looks like we're in for a strenuous afternoon.'

ORK HUNTER

DAN ABNETT

Keyser, who they call the sergeant but who wears no rank pins I can see, calls a halt. He gets up on the limed trunk of a massive fallen cypress and stands, sniffing the air.

We wait, thigh deep in the stinking soup below.

The wet air seems to fill my lungs with steam, and I want to cough, but the Skinner nearest me, a lean brute with charcoal-blackened eye-sockets and piercings down his ears, fixes me with a savage glare as if he can tell what I'm thinking. Keyser waves three scouts ahead, and that leaves thirty of us, twenty-two Skinners and eight Jopall Indentured. I'm halfway down the file, the swamp water bubbling and oozing around my legs, dust flies swirling round me.

The silent halt seems to last an eternity. There are spiders in my hair. I can feel them.

Captain Lorit, looking as out of place as the rest of us Jopall in his white-flecked, jade green fatigues and white peaked cap, wades forward. 'What are we–' he begins.

The Skinner they call Pig, standing to the captain's left, surges forward and takes my commander in a choke hold, clamping one greasy paw across his mouth. The captain struggles, wild-eyed, and Pig tightens his grip. The reason for Pig's nickname is self-evident – slabby and fat, with vastly developed muscle groups stretching his tattered tunic, he has a face ruined by scars and a ragged snout of flesh where his nose was bitten off.

Pig's muscles tighten further and the captain begins to turn blue. We Jopall look on in silent disbelief.

Keyser drops his hand and the Skinners un-freeze and move again. Pig releases the captain and throws him, gagging, face down into the water.

Keyser's jumped down off the cypress by then, and drags the captain up with one hand.

'He assaulted me! That man assaulted me! Put him on a charge!' The captain spits out weed and slime, indignant. Keyser doesn't put Pig on a charge. He punches the captain in the throat and silences him. The Skinners laugh, an ugly sound. Pig snorts, a far, far uglier noise.

'I thought we covered this in basic back at Cerbera. When I signal silence out here in the Green, I mean silence.' Keyser's voice is as sharp and taut as a wire. He says this to the captain, who is too busy grovelling and vomiting in the liquid mud to listen attentively.

He turns to the rest of us. 'We've got a scent of the 'skins. Close by, no more than a kilometre. Arm, load and follow. No noise. Especially you skinbait.'

That's what we are to them. Not Imperial Guard, not fellow troopers, not noble soldiers from the Jopall Indentured Squadrons. No matter most of us are from good, up-hive stock, no matter our comrades are even now defending the walls of Tartarus Hive against the Invasion.

We are skinbait. Nothing. Lower than scum.

For these Skinners set the value of scum. There are juve-gangs from the Tartarus underhive I'd have more respect for.

It is my considerable misfortune, mine and the other members of my squad, to have been sent to Cerbera Base to undergo jungle warfare training with the ork hunters just as the war for beloved Armageddon began. There is no hope of rejoining our company or hive. We are stuck for the duration, seconded to one of the most notorious units of 'skull-takers', the so-called Keyser's Skinners.

Once in a while, from very far away, we hear the thump of artillery or the scream of ram-jets. Open war is being waged in the lands beyond the jungle, far away. It may as well be on another world. Word is Yarrick himself had returned. Oh to be part of that!

Oh to not be part of this... I believe the Skull-takers have been fighting the feral greenskins for so long, they have begun to mirror what they fight. The least of them are painted and pierced, the worst have implanted tusks jutting from their jawlines. All have ork finger-bones, teeth and ears dangling from them as grisly trophies. They have no official chain of command. They respect no rank or authority other than their own. I have been told they elect their leaders. Think of that!

We edge forward now, slopping through the pools of mire; thick, sticky fluid like mucus. Dragonflies, with stained-glass wings as wide as a man's arm span, cross the glades, beating the air louder than the blade-fans of the air-cars in Tartarus's elite district. Skaters as big as my hand skitter across the sheened water.

Pig tells us we're wading through sap, sap drooled out of the fleshy cycads and root-ferns all around. He snorts again. It's hard to catch my breath, the air is so humid. The Skinners though... they move so silently. They disturb nothing. They make no ripples, leave no trace. Their damn boots never get stuck in the mud-pools. Their sleeves never catch on thorns. Fronds never whip back as they pass. Bark doesn't snap as they climb over it. Even cobwebs remain miraculously intact, as if the Skinners were never there.

For coarse brutes, they move with unimaginable care and enviable skill. We Jopall blunder like fools amongst them. I spent four weeks last summer on a covert training course at the Hades Hive Guard Academy. I did well. I thought I was good. How... how in the name of the Emperor who watches us all do you not make a ripple when you wade through water?

We stop once more, and I lean against the bole of a giant ginkgo. Something has laid a clutch of wet, yellow eggs in the fabric of my jacket cuff. The size of rice grains, they glisten. I shudder and make to wipe them off.

A dirty hand grabs mine and stops me. It is the Skinner with the blackened eye sockets.

'Don't touch them. Rot-wasp eggs. Be thankful they chose your fancy jacket to lay in and not your ear, or your genitals, or your tear-ducts.'

He scrapes the eggs off me with the blade of a rusty shearknife.

I look at him, bewildered.

'You wanna wake up with larvae munching out of your nose? Eating out your brain?'

I shake my head. Who would?

He chuckles.

'What's your name?' I ask.

'Deadhead.'

'No... your real name.'

'Er... Rickles,' he replies, as if he has to think about it. Then he turns away.

'Don't you want to know my name?' I call after him.

He turns back with a shrug. 'No point remembering the name of a skin-bait who'll be dead by tonight. I'll never use your name anyway.'

Anger puffs up inside me, dry and fire-hot despite my sweat. 'I'm Corporal Ondy Scalber of the Jopall Indentured, you scum-sucker! Remember it! Emperor help you that you do ever have to use it!'

He grins, as if my forthright attitude has impressed him.

But he punches me in the mouth anyway.

We press on, the ever-quiet Skinners silently punishing every clumsy stumble of us Jopall. We reach a glade where the vast upper canopy is broken and sunlight streams down bright as lasers. There are flowers here, floating on the frothy, weed-choked water, huge flowers with shocking pink heads. Vast insects too, slow and drowsy, buzzing the air like chainswords and dripping nectar from each hideously limp proboscis. A pallid white serpent with vestigial limbs slides through the murk between my legs. My friend, Trooper Rokar, starts to whimper. He has just discovered that something unseen and submerged has gnawed off the cap of his boot... along with two of his smaller toes.

I was in a scholam with Rokar. I pity him. His injury. His weakness.

The scouts come back, two of them. We never see the third again. They confer with Keyser for a while. Then he tells us, low and mean, there's a nest nearby and we must fan out.

Rokar is whimpering even more now, and begins to climb up into a tree. The captain tries to call him down. Rokar shakes his head, refusing, terrified.

Keyser gets him out of the tree. He throws a stab-knife and impales my old friend through the sternum. Rokar drops and hits the ooze with a wet slap. His body sinks.

'He was no use to us anyway. A liability. Worse than a liability,' Keyser tells the captain.

The captain is speechless with rage and horror. We all are. I don't know what to think or feel any more.

I am sent on the right hand side of the fan advance, with Deadhead and Pig, and another Skinner called Toaster who hefts a heavy flamer unit. Trooper Flinder of the Jopall is with us.

Pig stops us under the shade of a horsetail and smears foul smelling grease over our skin from a dirty pot. Now we smell as bad as the Skinners, and I notice for the first time that they are caked in the stuff. It isn't just dirt. It's deliberate.

'It's skin tallow,' Toaster sneers as he explains while checking the hoses of his sooty flamer. 'Now you won't smell of soap and humans.'

Pig has just daubed us with ork grease, blubber fat from their pestilent bodies. My stomach turns over.

We edge onwards. Flinder and I try to be as silent as the Skinners. Our efforts seem laughable. Then Deadhead stops me again, and points down at the gossamer skein my shin was about to break. He traces it back to a clump of flowering moss and gently exhumes a clutch of stikk-bombs, wired to the cord.

Keyser appears.

'Good work, Deadhead. Good eye.'

'Wasn't me who found it, sir. It was Ondy there.'

I look round, delighted to hear my name used.

'His shin, anyway,' Deadhead adds, and he and the Skinner boss laugh out loud. Curse their filthy hides.

We crouch in sap-water for half an hour, not daring to breathe. Bird calls and insect chirrups wing through the air. Some of them are natural, some are disguised signals. I can't tell them apart.

Deadhead waves us on.

As we cross a deep culvert of mud and slime, I see movement in the far tree-line. I've always had a good eye. It's the one skill I'm still proud of. I make something pustular and green amid the Green.

So I don't hesitate. I raise my lasrifle, and fire a stuttered burst.

Something big and green and tusked and monstrous slumps out of the foliage, its chest cavity exploded, and drops into the mere.

Then hell breaks loose. There are 'skins all around us, throwing themselves up out of the ooze, spitting out the hollow reeds they were breathing through. They are lean, malnourished, pale things, with jutting teeth like anthracite and deep-set eyes like diamonds. They howl and whoop. They stink. They wield heavy cleavers, cudgels and crude sidearms.

We're all firing. Gunfire explodes from the other elements of our formation. The wet air becomes cinder dry with ozone from the laser discharge. Las-rounds pepper through the leaf cover and fill the air with sap-vapour.

Toaster triggers his flamer and wastes the curtain of foliage before us. Swine-shrieks issue from the raging fire, piercingly harsh.

I fire, on full auto now, dropping 'skins around him. A rusty cleaver takes Flinder's head off his shoulders in a welter of blood and frayed tissue. I see Captain Lorit lifted right up out of the water on a primitive spear that transfixes his gut. He screams, piteously, flailing his limbs.

I had fixed my bayonet hours before, as per the Skinners' briefing. Now, with las-rounds expended and no time to change the clip, I stab and gut and slash.

Deadhead is nearby. He has wrested an ork lance from some dead grip, and is splitting skulls and whooping like a 'skin. Toaster fires again, his belch of flamer vaporising a tide of charging 'skins so that nothing but their fused skeletons slump in the steaming water, dribbling molten fat.

I impale a charging 'skin on my rifle-blade. It howls and pulls towards me, dragging the weapon out of my grasp. There is a plate-metal hatchet in its massive paw already wet with human brain tissue.

I pull my autopistol and blow its face apart.

'Throw! Throw!' yells Deadhead, tossing me a clutch of stikk-bombs.

We hurl them together into the densest part of the 'skin press. In the flash-wash, slivers of shrapnel flutter back, stippling the water with a million separate impacts.

The orks turn and melt away, as if they were never there.

We regroup. Five Skinners are dead. I am one of only three Jopall left alive. I slump, hollowed by shock, against a lichen-covered rock with the others of my hive as the Skinners lock down the perimeter and take the spoils.

'What do you want?' Pig asks, and I turn.

He is sawing the head off an ork corpse with a serrated knife.

'What?'

'An ear? A tooth? You earned it.'

My gut tosses in revulsion. 'Skin ichor is leaking from the sawed incision he is working and forms a stinking slick on the water's surface.

'Don't make a mistake now, Ondy Scalber.' It is Deadhead. His voice is low.

'A mistake?'

'Pig's offering you a trophy. Can't remember the last time Pig did that for skinbait. It's an honour. Don't refuse it.'

'A tooth then,' says I, turning back to see the butchery.

'Yeah,' agrees Deadhead. 'He had a good eye back there. Saw them first.'

Pig nods, snorts, and digs his blade in.

'A good eye? Then that's what he'll get. A good eye for Good Eye!' Pig and Deadhead laugh.

Pig hands me the trophy. It dangles like a pendant on its long rope of blood-black optic nerve.

I can't refuse. I take it, tie it to my dog-tags. It thumps against my chest like a rubber ball at every move I make. As soon as Pig is gone, I'll lose it.

The Skinners build what they call warning shrines. Ork skulls and limbs spiked on posts or nailed to trunks. The idea is the 'skins will now shun this area because it stinks of murder and defeat. But the Skinners wire up the remnants to grenades anyway, in case the 'skins decide to recover their dead.

It's what Keyser calls a win-win situation.

Keyser. I see him across the clearing as the Skinners raise the ork heads on display all around us. He is bent over the eviscerated body of Captain Lorit, who is cruelly still alive. Toaster says Keyser is giving the captain last rites. I see the sudden twist of Keyser's hand. That wasn't last rites as we know it.

The nest is close. We move in, forming small groups. I find myself with Pig, Toaster, and two other Skinners called Slipknot and Buck.

In the glade ahead, swathed in vapour, rises a great, ghostly tree. I sense it is not one tree but several that have become wrapped around each other over time. Hundreds of metres tall and thousands of years old, the great, entwined trunks are lifted clear of the water by a vast raft of winding roots. Birds flitter in the upper canopy. Beetles crawl and gnaw on the exposed roots.

We enter the root system, finding a tunnel half-filled with rank water. The roots coil and interlock above our stooped heads, reminding me of the interlocking arch vaults of the glorious Ecclesiarchy chapel back home on Jopall.

Toaster leads the way. We can smell the leaking promethium of his blackened flamer.

Buck shows me how to take a strip of field dressing and soak it in the swamp water to make a breath mask. Already, the pungent smoke of fires deliberately lit by the scouts on the far side of the nest is creeping back to us.

I breathe through wet gauze.

They're on us a moment later. Toaster scours the tunnel with his flamer, but they're pouring out of side turnings we didn't even see. I'm killing them even as I realise these are youngsters, small ork spawn no taller than my waist, weeping and shrieking as they run from the smoke.

Children. That's what we'd call them.

I don't care any more. Slipknot and I push down a side-vent, clawing our way through the tangles of black roots, and engage fierce 'skin youths, who jab at us with short spears and broken blades.

No match for las-fire.

'This way, Good Eye!' I hear Slipknot shout.

Then I'm into a larger root cavity, with Buck and Slipknot on my heels. We can still hear the rasp of Toaster's flamer nearby, and smell the burning promethium.

Feral orks are all around us now, many full-grown and massive. Some have guns. Slipknot is blown apart by a bolt round. His left hand slaps against my shoulder as it is blown clear of his carcass.

I kill the ork with the bolter. Then Buck and I pepper the cavity with random automatic fire. Green blood splats and sprays in the close air.

An ork is right on top of me, howling, raising a blade in a meaty paw bigger then my head. My gun is out. I fumble. It sees the eye bouncing across my chest and it seems to make it pause. I need no further urging. I slam the bayonet up into its jutting chin so the blade-end punches out through the back of its skull. Its huge jaws, spasming shut as it dies, bite the end off my lasgun.

I take up its blade in my right hand, holding my autopistol in my left. With the blade I dash out 'skin brains. With the pistol I wound and cripple and kill. I am plastered with 'skin blood now, as feral as the things I slay, murderous, wanton, out of my mind.

Jopall seems a long, long way away. Further than ever before.

And I know now I can't go back there.

Not now.

Not after this.

Toaster comes in behind us and yells for us to drop. Buck does, and I pull my head down as the flamer wash gusts like a sun's heat over our heads, incinerating the rest of the chamber.

We're all laughing as we clamber out of the nest. Golder and Spaff, the remaining Indentured Squadrons, look as me as if I have run mad. I know how I must look to them, singed and filthy and covered in 'skin blood that is baked like treacle. I don't care. I don't care what they think. I don't care for anything any more.

Keyser is fighting the boss. Driven out by the smoke and carrying a ragged stomach wound, the massive 'skin has found himself cornered in a sap-pool east of the nest. Keyser confronts him. We all group around to watch. No one interferes. We just watch and whoop and chant.

Like orks.

The 'skin boss is one hundred kilos heavier than Keyser, and massively muscled, with molars like daggers and tusks like bayonets. It wears a turtle-shell breast plate, and carries a hooked bill on one paw and a gutting knife in the other. Its torn belly oozes foul-smelling ichor, making the thing crouch.

Keyser, lank and lean in tattered camo-fatigues and webbing, his skin white with paint, has only a shear-knife. They circle and jab. We stand around the clearing, clapping and cheering, chanting 'Key-ser! Key-ser!' like animals. The boss circles in, sidestepping Keyser's blade and taking a decent cut of meat from Keyser's left thigh with its bill. In return, Keyser swings and kicks the monster square in its wounded abdomen, throwing it back into the water in a spray of slime.

The boss rises to its feet awkwardly. Keyser is now limping from the ragged slice in the meat of his thigh, a slice that has flapped the skin open to show pink meat and gleaming white bone.

Another swing with the bill, an evasive deflection from Keyser's knife. How can he go on with a wound that bad, I wonder?

But he does. Keyser splashes through the churning, foamy water and rips his blade along the boss's forearm, causing it to drop its bill.

Then Keyser swings in counter-clockwise and buries his blade up to the hilt in the boss's throat.

Gurgling and aspirating mists of blood, the boss falls on its back, surging water across the clearing under its vast bulk. And dies.

We chant Keyser's name so loud that leaves shake lose and drop from the canopy.

Ondy Scalber is dead. He died somewhere and somewhen in the glades of Armageddon's vicious jungles.

I only barely remember him now. He was a good sort, I suppose.

What I am become now, only time will tell. I hate it, yet I love it too. It is a way of life and of death that appeals to me in its simplicity. To hunt, to kill, to be a better hunter and better killer than the brutes we stalk. To be Good Eye.

One day, perhaps, I'll remember Jopall and the life I had there. Perhaps. I may wake screaming in the night, dreaming of it. I may not.

The Green waits for me. There I will do my work, in the Emperor's name. There I will find my glory.

ONE HATE

AARON DEMBSKI-BOWDEN

I am the future of my Chapter.

My masters and mentors often tell me this. They say I, and those like me, hold the Chapter's soul in our hands. We wear the black, and we are the beating heart of a reborn brotherhood.

It is our duty to remember. We are charged to recall the traditions that came before the moment when our Chapter stood on the edge of extinction.

My name is Argo. In a Chapter with few remaining relics, I am blessed above my brothers in the tools of war in my possession.

My armour was born when the Imperium was born – repaired, amended and maintained in the centuries since by generations of warriors, slaves, servitors and serfs. My bolter roared on the battlefields of the Horus Heresy, and has been carried in the red-marked hands of thirty-seven Astartes since the day of its forging. Each of their names is etched into the dark iron of the weapon, along with the name of the world that claimed their lives. The eyes of my helm have stared out onto ten thousand wars, and seen a million of Mankind's foes die.

Around my neck is a gift from the Ecclesiarchy of Holy Terra: an aquila symbol of priceless worth and imbued with the warding secrets of a technology almost lost to time. My armour is black, for I am death itself. My helm is the skull of every man that died in every battle fought by my Chapter in the ten millennia since our founding.

More than that, my face is the victorious leer of the dying Emperor.

And why am I charged with this responsibility? Why do I wear the black?

Because I hate. I hate more than my brothers, and my hatred runs blacker, deeper, purer than theirs.

One hate stands above all others. One hate that burns in our blood and barks from the mouths of five hundred bolters when we stand together in war. It is a hatred with many names: the greenskin, the ork, the kine.

To us, they are simply the Enemy.

We are the Crimson Fists, the shield-hand of Dorn, and we have survived extinction when all others would have fallen into worthless memory. Our hatred takes us across the stars in service to the Throne.

And now it brings us to Syral.

* * *

Syral. A lone orb around a diminutive sun, on the edge of Segmentum Tempestus.

The single celestial child of a red star that was taking thousands of years to die. The sun's waning would take thousands of years before its eventual expiration, and the planet it warmed was still of great use to the Imperium.

Syral was an agri-world, with the globe's landmasses given over to expansive and fertile continents of foodstuffs and livestock. Syral's great oceans were similarly plundered by Imperial need. Beneath their dark surface, the tides concealed hydroponics facilities the size of cities, harvesting the edible wealth of the depths. As a planet, Syral had but one colossal purpose: to export a system's worth of food ready for purchase by the worlds nearby that lacked such natural bounty. Syral fed three hive-worlds, from the spires of the rich to the slums of the destitute, as well as several Imperial Navy fleets and regiments of the Imperial Guard warring in nearby crusades.

From space, Syral was the blue-green of mankind's ancestral memory, as if drawn from an artist's imaginings of the impious ages of Old Terra. However, the face of a world can change a great deal in a year.

'The Fists are back.'

Lord General Ulviran looked at Major Dace, who had spoken those words. With his thin face, ice-blue eyes and aquiline nose, the lord general was a natural when it came to bestowing withering looks on those among his staff that disappointed him. He gave one of those glances to Dace now. The major looked away, suitably chastised.

The gunship sat idle, as it had for several minutes now, its landing stanchions and velocity thrusters still hissing with occasional jets of steam as they released flight pressure and settled into repose. Across the side of this midnight-blue vulture of a vessel, an engraved symbol stared back at the horde of Guardsmen that waited. A clenched fist, as red and dark as good wine.

The gunship's forward ramp lowered like a mouth opening. Ulviran was put in mind – as he always was when seeing an Astartes Thunderhawk – of a great steel bird of prey. When its forward ramp lowered, just beneath the cockpit window, the bird seemed to roar with the sound of whining hydraulics.

'I count four,' Major Dace said, making this his second most obvious observation that day. Four armoured forms, each more than a head taller than a normal man, tramped down the clanking ramp.

'Just four...' the major added a moment later. Ulviran would gladly have shot him, had he been able to think of a reason to do so. Not even a good reason, just a legal one. Dace was an asset on the battlefield, but at staff meetings his dullard observations were a tedium his fellow officers could easily do without.

The Astartes made no move to approach the crowd of Guardsmen. They stood as still as statues, monstrous bolters held to their eagle-emblazoned chests. Ulviran took stock of the situation. The Astartes were back, and it was not the time to stand around gawping. Control. The scene warranted control. Maybe there could be some dignity salvaged from this whole tawdry development. Having the Astartes arrive would be a cause for celebration right enough, but Ulviran recalled every single word in the missive he'd composed to Chapter Master Kantor of the Crimson Fists. Begging was the only word for it, really. He'd begged for aid, and here it was: deliverance once more. He was not a man who enjoyed resorting to begging. It had galled him even as he'd dictated the distress call.

Ulviran strode forward to meet the giants as they stood stone-still in the shadow of their avian gunship. He noted with unnoticeable displeasure that the heavy bolter turrets on the Thunderhawk's wing tips panned across the camp, as if seeking threats even amongst Imperial forces. Did the Fists not even consider the Guard capable of holding their own base camp secure against the enemy? In that moment, deliverance or not, the lord general hated their damned arrogance.

'Welcome back,' he said to the first of the Astartes, who was undoubtedly the commander of this small team.

The warrior looked at the lord general, his snarling visored helm turning down to regard the human. This close, no more than an arm's length from the towering warriors, Ulviran felt his gums ache from the pressuring hum of the squad's power armour. The whine of energy was more tactile than audible, making his eyes water and prickling the skin on the back of his neck. He swallowed as the Astartes made the sign of the aquila, the warrior's gauntleted hands forming the salute and banging against his armoured chest. Even the smallest of movements made their armour joints purr in a low mechanical snarl.

Ulviran returned the salute. His neck hurt a little, looking up like this, and he unwillingly flinched when the Astartes spoke.

'With all due respect,' the voice was a crackling, vox-distorted growl, far deeper than a normal man's, 'why are you addressing me?'

Ulviran hadn't expected this level of disrespect, nor this degree of informality. He was a lord general, after all. Planets lived and died by his tactical expertise.

The general took in the details of the warrior's armour. The suit was the blue of a starless midnight sky, trimmed in places with a bold red, nowhere more noticeable than the clenched fist on the warrior's shoulder pad. A scroll detailing oaths and matters of unknowable honour was draped from the warrior's other shoulder pad, moving slightly in the gentle wind. Hanging from a thick chain that had been made into a bandolier, oversized, misshapen skulls knocked quietly together as the Astartes moved. From the pronounced lower jaws and brutish bone structure, Ulviran knew they were the skulls of orks. In life, they'd been big orks, most likely leaders among their bestial kind. In death, they were impressive trophies.

This Astartes was clearly the leader of the squad. None of the others wore trophies to match.

'I am addressing you because I assumed you were in command.' He adopted the tone of one speaking to a small child, which his men would have found both laughable and insane had they heard. The thrill of authority over these giants rushed through the lord general's blood. He would, after all, brook no disrespect.

'Do I look like a brother-captain to you?' the Astartes asked, and Ulviran wondered if the warrior's vox-speakers made his voice into a growl, or if it was naturally that low.

Ulviran nodded in response to the question. He was determined not to be intimidated.

'To my eyes, yes, you do.'

'Well, I'm not.' Here the Astartes looked to his fellows. 'Not yet, anyway.' Ulviran heard something at the edge of his hearing – a series of quiet clicks coming from the helms of the armoured men. He assumed, quite correctly, that they were laughing with each other over a private vox-channel.

The Astartes draped in skulls, chains and scrolls detailing his many victories inclined his head at one of the others.

'He's the sergeant.'

Ulviran turned to face this next one, making the sign of the aquila once more.

Before the lord general could speak, this next Astartes – who was clad in a blood-coloured toga draped around his armour – shook his helmed head.

'No, lord general,' the Astartes intoned, his voice as much a mechanical rumble as the first one's had been. 'You do not address me, either.'

Ulviran's patience was reaching its end.

'Then who am I to address?'

The robed warrior nodded in the direction of the Thunderhawk, at the newest arrival striding down the ramp. This Astartes was clad in plate of charcoal-black, and even without much knowledge of Astartes technology it was clear to Ulviran that the dark suit of power armour was an antique, dating back centuries – probably even millennia. The black warrior's helmed face was a grinning skull, the red eye lenses lending it a daemonic cast as he looked left and right, surveying the landing site.

Ulviran swallowed, unaware of how his Adam's apple bobbed and betrayed his nervousness. *Throne,* he thought. *A Chaplain.*

The Astartes in the red toga offered the lord general a slight bow.

'You address him.'

In private, they discussed Syral. The Chaplain stalked around the large table with its map-covered surface. Here in the lord general's command room, aboard his personal Baneblade, *The Indomitable Will,* the human and the Astartes shared words away from the ears of others.

'We handed you this world four months ago.'

Those words chilled the lord general's blood. They were an insult, certainly, but they were also an unarguable truth.

'Circumstances change, Brother-Chaplain.' And they had. Ork reinforcements had come in flooding waves, washing the western hemisphere in a tide of greenskin invaders. The Imperium's easy victory, largely bought by the surgical strikes of the Crimson Fists four months before, was nothing more than a pleasant memory and a tale of what might have been. The Imperial Guard had been falling back ever since.

The Chaplain's vox-voice was edged by growls, as if the man spoke at an octave almost too low for words.

'You are losing Syral,' the Astartes said. His skullish face stared at the human across the room.

'I know better than to argue that assessment,' came the lord general's reply. 'I'd wager that I see it clearer than you, for I've been watching it happen for months.'

Ulviran watched as the Chaplain reached up to his helm and pulled the release catches on his armoured collar. With a serpentine hiss of venting pressure, the locks disengaged and the Astartes removed his skulled helmet, reverently lifting it then laying it on the table before him. Its red eyes were dimmed now the helm was detached from the armour's power supply, but they still glared at the lord general in dull accusation.

'I am not here to chastise you, lord general.'

Ulviran smiled to hear the warrior's true voice. It was deep and resonant, but with a gentility shaping the words. The Chaplain was, by the lord general's best guess, close to thirty years of age, but with the Astartes it was almost impossible to tell. He didn't even know for certain if they *did* age; he'd always taken the trope for granted that one determined a Space Marine's age by the scars on their flesh and the inscriptions etched into their armour.

Had this Astartes been allowed to grow as a normal man, he might have been considered handsome. Even as the product of intensive genetic enhancement since puberty, the Chaplain was a fair example of his kind. The Astartes was almost two heads taller than a normal man, with features and body mass to match, but Ulviran saw something undeniably human within the warrior's dark-blue eyes and the half-smile he wore.

The lord general liked him immediately. For Ulviran, who prided himself on being a fine reader of men, this was a rare development.

'Brother-Chaplain–'

'Argo,' he interrupted. 'My name is Argo.'

'As you wish. I must ask you, Argo, how did you respond so quickly to our...' he didn't want to say *to our plea*, '...to our request for reinforcement?'

Argo met his gaze. The half-smile left his face, and the warrior's eyes narrowed. The silence that followed the general's question bordered on becoming awkward.

'Just good fortune,' the Chaplain said at last, the smile returning. 'We were close to the system.'

'I see. And are you alone?'

The Chaplain spread his hands in beneficence. One gauntlet was the same coal black as the warrior's armour. The other, his left, was painted blood red in keeping with the traditions of his Chapter.

'I bring with me the brothers of Squad Demetrian, of the Fifth Battle Company.'

'Yourself and four others. Nothing more?'

'The Chapter serfs and servitors responsible for the flight and maintenance of our Thunderhawk.'

'No more Astartes.' It was a statement of resignation, not a question.

'As you say,' the Chaplain offered a shallow but sincere bow, 'no more Astartes.'

Ulviran was noticeably ill at ease. 'As much as I thank the Throne and your Chapter Master for any assistance the Fists offer, especially so quickly, I had hoped for a… bolder show of support.'

'Hope is the first step on the road to disappointment. Four months ago, we broke the Enemy's back here. I assume you recall the date.'

'I do. The men still speak of it. They call it Vengeance Night.'

'Very apt. We left the enemy reeling, lord general. We left them bloody, their armies shattered from our assaults across the globe. I was at the Siege of the Cantorial Palace. I was part of the strike force that destroyed the palace itself, and I was there when Brother Imrich of the Fifth took the head of Warlord Golgorrad in the battle amongst the smoking rubble. We are back, lord general, and I humbly suggest you be grateful for even the small blessing one squad of our Chapter represents.'

'I am grateful, to you and your Chapter Master.'

'Good. I apologise for any harshness in my tone. Now, let us talk of strategy.' The Chaplain pointed with his red hand at the largest map spread across the table. 'Southspire, the capital city, unless I am mistaken.'

'You are not.'

'And, according to the sensor sweeps made by my Thunderhawk as we broke orbit, the city – and the site of the Cantorial Palace at the city's heart – is once more in the hands of the enemy.'

'It is.'

Argo's blue eyes met Ulviran's, drilling into the officer with an unblinking lack of mercy.

'So when do we take it back?'

The interior bay of the Thunderhawk echoed with Argo's footfalls, his clanking tread ringing from the iron skin of the inert machinery stored there. Chapter serfs in robes of deep blue stepped aside, making the sign of the aquila as he passed. Argo nodded to each one in kind, whispering benedictions for them all. They thanked him and moved about the business of attending to the gunship's innards and readying the stored machinery. Argo's eyes raked along the heavy digging equipment stored in the hold, and his mood turned black.

Squad Demetrian was training. He heard them long before he saw them. Climbing a ladder to the next deck, Argo thumped the door release to the communal 'quarters', a room where Astartes remained strapped in flight seats when the gunship took to the skies. In the small usable space between the twin rows of seats, two of Squad Demetrian duelled in full armour.

The two warriors could not have been less alike. His armour draped in scrolls of his deeds, bone tokens of fallen foes, and the skulls of seven orks hanging from his chain bandolier, Imrich was a whirlwind of movement. Kicks, punches, elbow thrusts, headbutts – all thrown into a duel with shortswords, added between the moves of the clashing blades.

Opposing him was Toma, embodying pure economy of motion. Where Imrich's fury twinned with his skill, Toma's movements were calculated to the finest degree by a lightning mind that drove his vicious combat reflexes.

His blade snapped into position to block and thrust in a silver blur, stopping precisely at each twist, never overbalancing, never overreaching, with Toma never giving ground.

'I'll wear you down, Deathwatch,' Imrich teased. Their gladius blades locked again, and the two helms glared at each other only half a metre apart.

Toma said nothing. Displayed on the polished iron of his unique shoulder pad was the stylised symbol of the Holy Inquisition. He always fought in silence. His recent return from three years in the specialist Ordo Xenos Deathwatch Chapter hadn't changed that.

The fight came to an end when Argo cleared his throat. Disengaging from one another, Imrich and Toma resheathed their blades.

'I had you, Deathwatch.' Imrich saluted his opponent with his clenched left fist against his heart.

'Sure you did, hero.' Toma's voice was toneless as he returned the gesture.

'I had you.'

'The day you have me is the day the Emperor rises from the Throne and dances all night long.'

Brother-Sergeant Demetrian silenced them both with a fist pounded against the metal wall.

'News, Brother-Chaplain?' the sergeant asked.

Argo removed his helm and gave them his half-smile. 'They think we're here in answer of a distress call.'

The squad looked at the Chaplain, awaiting further explanation. Now this had their interest up.

'You didn't tell them the truth,' said Demetrian. The veteran's scarred face was a map of battles fought across a hundred systems. Both his gauntlets were crimson; he'd served time in the Crusade Company among the best of the best, and on the knee of his armour, a Black Templar cross was proudly displayed. The Declates Crusade, when the Templars and the Fists broke ranks to fight in mixed units, was a point of great honour for both Chapters. Demetrian had been there. A roll of his honours was recorded in acid-etched lettering on a gold tablet in the Chapter's fortress-monastery back home on Rynn's World.

Argo nodded. 'I thought it best to retain the illusion of our compliance. The truth would breed animosity.'

'No surprise,' Demetrian's words were as clipped and to the point as ever. 'The plan remains the same?'

'We fight until the Cantorial Palace. Then we do the duty entrusted to us. I saw the maps of Southspire and the enemy's forces spread across the sector. A new warlord leads the enemy on the far side of the city, and the Guard ready for their last attempt at a big push. The city itself is flooded with roaming bands of foes.'

'Numbers?'

'Thousands within the city. Tens of thousands at the edge, where the warlord waits.'

'I like those odds,' Imrich said. They all heard the smile in his words, even from behind his helm.

Argo shook his head. 'This is not a war we can win without the Guard.'

Now Toma spoke up. He sat in one of the restraining seats, meticulously dismantling and cleaning the sacred bolter given to him by the Ordo Xenos during his tenure in the Inquisitorial kill-teams.

'Will the Guard win this war without us?'

Argo shrugged. 'We have our orders.'

Toma pressed on. 'And once we leave?'

'The Emperor protects,' the Chaplain replied.

Imrich's skulls rattled as he turned. 'So we flee a war that the Imperium is losing? I don't like the thought of running from the kine.'

'Duly noted, but Chapter Master Kantor was clear in his priorities,' Argo said. 'And you will do penance for your disrespect of the Enemy, Brother Imrich.'

It was a matter of small shame among some of the Crimson Fists that they referred to the greenskins as *kine*. On Rynn's World, another agri-world, it was slang for 'cattle'.

'Yes, Brother-Chaplain,' Imrich growled.

'Hate the inhuman, slaughter the impure, and praise the Emperor above all. But always respect the foe.'

'Yes, Brother-Chaplain.' Imrich wanted to insist Argo stopped quoting the litanies at him. Instead he bowed his head. He knew better than to apologise.

'When do we move out?' Demetrian cut in.

'Tomorrow night, the Guard will advance,' Argo said, as he held his golden aquila medallion in his red-fingered gauntlet. 'And we advance with them.'

Dawn found Argo in the cockpit of the Thunderhawk, still in his armour. He sat in one of the command thrones, his elbows on his knees, staring out of the window. He had not slept. He was Astartes. He barely needed sleep.

Toma came to him as he mused on the coming battle. The quiet warrior was a powerful credit to the squad, and Argo – who was over a century younger than the Deathwatch specialist – always welcomed his presence. He suspected it would not be long before the captain of the Fifth selected Toma for promotion into the Crusade Company, or to lead his own squad into the field of war.

'Another dawn, Brother-Chaplain.' Toma took the command throne next to Argo, sitting and holding his helm in his hands. The Deathwatch had aged him, Argo saw. New scars, faded from fast treatment but still noticeable, pitted the warrior's cheek and temple.

'Acid burns,' Argo said, gesturing with a gloved hand, his black one. 'The Deathwatch kept you busy.'

'I can't say,' Toma replied. His face was as expressive as stone.

'Can't or won't?' Argo asked, already knowing the answer.

'Both.'

'The Ordo Xenos keeps its secrets close.'

'It does.' Toma's expression was edged with thought as he replayed hazy recollections, little more than echoes, through his mind. Oaths had been sworn. Promises were made. Memories were torn from the mind by psyk-enhanced meditation and the ungentle scouring of arcane machinery.

It was the first time Argo had seen his fellow Fist's neutral mask slip, and he found it fascinating.

'We go to war today,' the Chaplain said. 'We are a poor portion of the Fifth's strength, but we are the Fifth nevertheless. In the fires of war, we are forged. And yet I sense a burden on your soul, brother.'

Toma nodded. This was why he had come.

'It's Vayne.'

Brother-Apothecary Vayne was in the Thunderhawk's confined apothecarion, little more than an operating table and racks of monitoring equipment fastened to the small room's walls. Already prepared for the battle tonight, he was in full armour with one exception: his head was bare. The white-faced helm that marked him as an Apothecary rested on the surgery table, and this was the first thing Argo saw as he entered. The second thing was Vayne himself, adjusting data readouts on his arm-mounted narthecium. As Argo watched, several surgical spikes and knives snapped back into the bulky medical unit housed on Vayne's forearm.

Vayne eventually turned to the sound of thrumming power armour, though his enhanced senses would have detected the Chaplain's approach long before he came into the room.

'Argo,' he said in subdued greeting.

'Vayne,' the Chaplain nodded back.

The atmosphere between the two men was nothing short of ugly. Seven years before, they'd served together as novices in Nochlitan's Scout squad. Seven years since the final trials to become Astartes, when Argo had been chosen to wear the black, and Vayne the white.

A Chaplain and an Apothecary drawn from the same Scout unit. Sergeant Nochlitan, who like Demetrian had served admirably in the Crusade Company among the Chapter's elite, had been honoured by Chapter Master Kantor himself for honing such excellence in a novice squad.

With the Chapter still in its perilous rebuilding stage, the finest warriors of the Crimson Fists were often charged with the duty of training novice squads. It was no shame to step away from the First Company to the role of Scout-sergeant, and Nochlitan was one of the most respected.

Beyond a few scars, Argo looked no different. The same could not be said for the Apothecary. Half of Vayne's face was gone, replaced by cold, smooth steel shaped to resemble his features. Despite its artistry, the exquisite workmanship was clear evidence of a terrible wound that had almost been Vayne's death. Vayne's left eye, an augmetic lens of synthetic scarlet crystal, whirred in its circular socket as the Apothecary focused his gaze on the Chaplain.

'You're looking well,' he remarked. Argo didn't reply. He watched as Vayne limped around the surgical table, and considered the rest of the Apothecary's newly-restored body.

Daemon-fire had done this to Vayne, during the Cleansing of Chiaro two months before. Fresh from the victory on Syral and the destruction of the Cantorial Palace, the Crimson Fists had entered the warp for several weeks to reach Chiaro, answering a call for aid by the planetary governor. Mutant cults were spreading in the rotting industrial sectors of his world. A true purge was needed to stamp the problem out, after the local defence forces had failed to quell the matter.

The Fists had not failed. It took a month and was not without casualties, but their duty was done. The rest of the strike force returned to Rynn's World at the behest of Chapter Master Kantor. Argo and Squad Demetrian had returned to Syral aboard the support cruiser *Vigil*.

It had been a cold, quiet journey back to Syral. They were the only Astartes on board, except for a single Apothecary from the Fifth Company that remained to preside over Vayne's injuries – and act in his stead if the younger man died.

Vayne had suffered as the servitors and his potential replacement rebuilt his body. He was almost certain to die, given the massive burns sustained and their initial refusal to heal. The Chapter would lose a gifted healer in a time when the Fists most desperately needed to reclaim and preserve their fighting strength. Had Vayne died, it would have been a true loss.

From shoulder to fingertips, his left arm was augmetic. It connected internally to the bionic sections of his spine and collarbone, purring in a smooth hiss of expensive augmentation that Argo's keen hearing could detect even underneath the background hum of their power armour. As with his left arm, so too was his left leg bionic – from hip to toes. The augmentations were still new, still untested in battle, and although Argo doubted a normal human could discern the minute inconsistencies in Vayne's gait and posture, to Astartes senses it registered as a subtle but noticeable hitch in his stride. A limp.

It was temporary, until the augmetics aligned with Vayne's body patterns and wholly fused with his biorhythms. The leg ended in a splayed claw of a foot for enhanced stability: a cross of blackened metal that connected to the well-armoured ankle joint and the heavy musculature of the bionic shin and calf above.

'Your attitude is beginning to create strain within your squad,' Argo began. 'I am told you are melancholic.'

Vayne scowled. His false eye hummed in its socket as it tried to conform to his facial expression.

'Brother-Sergeant Demetrian has said nothing.'

'You were saved because you have value to the Chapter. You stand in high regard for your skills. Why are you unbalanced by wounds which heal even as we speak?'

Vayne watched his own crimson left gauntlet close and open, repeating the motion several times. It was his bionic arm, and feeling was slow in returning.

'I trained a lifetime in my own body. Now I fight in someone else's.'

'It is still your body.'

'Not yet. There is acclimatisation to come.'

'Then you will acclimatise. There is no more to say.'

'You don't see? This is not false pathos, Argo. I was perfect before, made in the Emperor's image in accordance with his ancient and most sacred designs.'

'You still are.'

'No. I am a simulacrum.' He clenched his augmetic hand into a numb fist. 'I am the best imitation we are capable of creating. I am no longer perfect.'

'Our brothers in the Iron Hands would dispute that diagnosis.'

Vayne scoffed. 'Those uninspired slaves of the Mechanicum? They make war at the pace of toothless old men.'

'If you resort to insults against our brother Chapters, I will lose my temper as well as my patience.'

'My point is that I am no Iron Hand. And I have no wish to be some half-flesh imitation Astartes.'

'You will acclimatise,' Argo stepped forward, taking Vayne's helm from the table and looking down at the white faceplate.

'Even so, until then I am a liability to my brothers.'

Argo handed his friend the helmet and shook his head. 'You are petulant beyond my comprehension. Only in death does duty end. We are the Fists. We are the shield-hand of Dorn. We do not weep and cower from battle because of pain or fear or worries of what might yet be. We fight and die because we were made to fight and die.'

Vayne took the helm and smiled without humour. Half of his face didn't follow the expression.

'What amuses you?'

'You are blind, Argo. You may preserve the soul of our Chapter, but I preserve its body. I harvest the gene-seed of the fallen, and I ensure the wounded will fight again. So listen to me, *brother*. I fear nothing but allowing my failures to harm my brethren. I am not at peak performance, and I am unused to the wounds I still wear under this armour. That is the source of my unbalance.'

'You lose your own argument. You fear to let down your brothers because your battle skills are hindered for a short while. Vayne, you are harming your brothers far more with your withdrawn attitude and the bitterness leaking from your every word. You are eroding their trust in you, and destroying their confidence.'

Argo's battle-collar pulsed a single blip. He tensed his neck, activating the pearl-like vox-bead attached to his throat, which picked up the vibrations of his vocal chords.

'Brother-Chaplain Argo. Speak.'

'Brother-Chaplain,' it was Lord General Ulviran. 'I have a request to ask you and your warriors.'

'I will be with you shortly,' Argo said, and killed the link. The silence between Argo and Vayne returned.

'Your point is taken,' Vayne conceded. 'I will not allow my melancholy to taint my squad any longer.'

'That is all I demand.' Argo was already turning to leave.

'I remember a time when you could not make such demands of me, Argo.'

'I remember a time when I did not need to make them.'

* * *

The Fists shed blood before the Guard's night-time advance. Under Ulviran's request, Argo and Demetrian led the squad into the shattered remains of the city's western sector.

In the minutes leading up to deployment, Argo had gathered the warriors together in the shadow of their Thunderhawk. Dozens of Guardsmen around the camp looked on, dallying about their business while they watched the Astartes soldiers perform their rite. The Fists ignored them all.

With his gladius, Argo sliced the palms of each warrior's left hand. They, in turn, pressed their bleeding hands against the chest piece of the Fist next to them.

Imrich rested his hand on the embossed silver eagle decorating Toma's breastplate. The Larraman cells in his blood scabbed and sealed the gash quickly, but not before his palm left a dark smear on Toma's Imperial symbol.

'My life for you,' Imrich said, then removed his hand and fastened his helm. Toma was next, pressing his bleeding hand against Vayne's breastplate.

'My life for you,' the Deathwatch veteran said, before donning his own helm. Vayne forced a smile. He had to perform the rite with his remaining flesh hand, his right instead of his left, and did so without complaint.

When it came to the Chaplain's turn, Argo rested his hand on Demetrian's armour, as tradition necessitated the officiating Chaplain to honour the ranking officer.

'My life for you,' Argo said. A moment later, his senses were submerged in the audiovisual chaos of his battle helm. On the eye lens displays, he saw the flickering readouts of the squad's vital signs, communication runes, lists of vox-channels, sight-altering lens options, thermo-conditional and local atmospheric readouts, and a cluster of information pertaining to the myriad functions of his armour.

All of the information added up to one thing.

'Ready,' he voxed to the others, blink-clicking most of the lens displays into transparency.

'Ready,' they voxed back. They'd started walking then, loping strides that emitted a chorus of mechanical growls from their armour joints. The Guardsmen parted like a split sea as the Astartes neared them.

With blood on their Imperial eagles, the Crimson Fists went to war.

That had been three hours ago. The Fists took a Guard Chimera troop transport to the city limits, and were advancing through the western edge of Southspire. It was a scouting run, and progress was predicted – by Lord General Ulviran – to be fast. Intelligence had pinned enemy resistance in this section of the city to be minimal. Only at the city's centre was resistance expected to pick up.

Intelligence had been wrong about that.

Argo crouched in the ruins of what had once been an Administratum building, where hundreds of barely-educated wage slaves typed their lives away into cogitators that amassed Syral's exportation data. Pressed against a wall half tumbled down months ago from Imperial Basilisk shelling, the Chaplain waited unmoving, listening to the thrum of his power armour and the sounds of several foes breathing nearby.

Roaming bands of greenskins claimed this part of the city. Squad Demetrian had abandoned the Chimera long before, in favour of stalking through the ruins and clearing a path for the Guard's advance tonight.

Argo heard the xenos trampling closer, around the corner. They muttered to each other in their guttural, swinish tongue. The Chaplain tasted bile in his mouth. Their inhumanity repelled him.

He heard the bestial things pause in their lazy search, heard them snuffing at the air and grunting. They had his scent, he was sure of it, and his blood ran hot as he clenched his short combat sword in one hand, his bolter in the other.

At his hip hung his deactivated crozius arcanum, the symbolic weapon of his role in the Chapter. Capped by an eagle-shaped maul fashioned from blackened adamantium, it was a fearsome bludgeon when sheathed in its crackling power field. Argo's crozius had belonged to Ancient Amentus, one of the first Crimson Fist Chaplains; a founder of the Chapter from when the primarch divided the Imperial Fists Legion ten millennia before. Upon an arm-length haft of dark metal, the inscription *Traitor's Bane* was written in High Gothic.

He treasured the relic weapon, which still felt unfamiliar in his fists even after seven years. Against detritus such as these greenskins, his gladius was more than enough to suffice. He would not let the filthy blood of weakling xenos mar an honourable weapon dating back to the Great Crusade.

The first of the creatures, alert now, came around the corner. In its fists was a collection of scrap that evidently served the greenskin as a firearm. Argo surged to his feet, superhuman reflexes enhanced even further by his armour, and before the ork could utter a sound, it was falling backwards with the hilt of the Chaplain's gladius protruding from its eye socket.

Argo rounded the corner to meet the others head-on and his bolter barked, spitting detonating shells into green flesh. Eleven of them. Each hulking figure was momentarily outlined by a flicker of light in his helm's vision, cycling through target locks. But eleven was too many, even for an Astartes. In a flashing moment of anger, Argo cursed himself for not listening carefully to their breathing and trying to discern their numbers. It was his failing, he knew. He'd acted in rage, and now it was going to kill him.

The brutish creatures ran at him even as they took fire, massive fists gripping jagged axes that were pieced together from vehicle parts and industrial machinery. Argo's bolter cut down three orks as his targeting reticule flitted between weak points in the greenskins' piecemeal armour.

'You dare exist in mankind's galaxy!' Argo's bolter spat its last shell which destroyed an ork from the jaw up. He clamped the weapon to his thigh with its magnetic seal and threw his fist forward, shattering the forehead of the first greenskin to come in range. 'Die! Die knowing the Crimson Fists will cleanse the stars of your taint!'

Axes slashed towards him, which Argo weaved to avoid. A step back took him within reach of the first ork he'd felled, and he snatched up his gladius from the wretch's skull. Rivulets of dark blood slid along the silver blade, and the Astartes grinned behind his death's head mask.

'Come, alien filth. I am Argo, son of Rogal Dorn, and I am your death.' The mob of orks ran in and Argo met them, the primarch's name on his lips.

'Break left.'

The voice crackled over the vox and Argo obeyed instantly, throwing himself into a roll that scattered a dust cloud in the ruins of the building. He came up, blade in hand, just as the speaker joined him in the fight.

The midday sun flashed from Toma's iron shoulder guard as he hammered the greenskins from behind. His bolter disgorged a stream of shells that exploded on impact in bursts of clear, hissing liquid. As he fired one-handed, he plunged his gladius into the throat of the closest greenskin, giving it a savage twist to half-sever the creature's head. Four of the orks fell back, the horrendously potent acid from Toma's prized bolt rounds overriding even the orkish resilience to pain as it ate through their flesh like holy fire.

All of this happened before Argo's two hearts had time to beat twice.

The last two orks leapt at the Fists to die in futility. Toma impaled the first through the chest, shattered its face with a brutal headbutt, and fired a single bolt at point-blank range into the alien's temple. The skull gave way in a shower of gore as the explosive shell performed its sacred function. Gobbets of flesh and bone hissed as they span away, eaten by the mutagenic acid in Toma's Inquisition-sanctioned ammunition.

Argo grappled with the second ork, his gauntlets wrapped around the thing's throat as it broke its thick nails scrabbling at his armour. He bore the howling greenskin to the ground, his weighty armour crushing the life from its chest as he strangled it in trembling fists.

'Die...'

The ork's answer was to roar voicelessly, its red eyes burning with rage. The Astartes grinned in mimicry of his helm and leaned close to the thing's face. His voice was a whisper through his vox-speakers.

'I *hate* you.'

Toma stood to the side, reloading his bolter and scanning the ruins for more foes. Argo's skulled face pressed against the choking ork's forehead. Orkish sweat left dark smears against his bone-cream faceplate.

'This is the Emperor's galaxy.' With a final surge of effort, he squeezed with all his strength. Vertebrae popped and cracked under the pressure. 'Mankind's galaxy. *Our* galaxy. Know that, as your worthless life ends.'

'Brother-Chaplain...' Toma said.

Argo barely heard. He let the creature fall dead and rose to his feet, savouring the taste of copper, bitter and hot, on his tongue. His rage had not killed him, after all. The enemy lay dead in great numbers.

'Brother-Chaplain,' Toma repeated.

'What?' Argo unclasped his bolter, reloading it now with the proper litany to the machine-spirit within.

There was a moment when Argo was sure Toma would say something; chide him for letting his fury get the better of him and lead him into reckless combat. Despite the break with tradition and authority, Argo would have accepted the criticism from a warrior like Toma.

Toma said nothing, but the silence passing between the two Astartes was laden with meaning.

'Report,' Argo said to break the quiet.

'Imrich and Vayne report their section is clear now. Brother-Sergeant Demetrian reports the same.'

'Resistance?'

'Vayne and Demetrian described it as savage.'

'And Imrich?'

'He described it as thrilling.'

Argo nodded. He was running low on ammunition, and knew the others must be as well.

'Prepare for a withdrawal.'

As Toma voxed Argo's orders to the others, the young Chaplain looked out across the ruined city. Small by Imperial standards – large settlements were rare on an agri-world – yet the focus of so much destruction.

On the other side of Southspire, the new warlord waited with the bulk of his horde. And in the heart of the city, the broken remains of the Cantorial Palace: the Fists' true goal, surrounded by foes.

Argo's blood boiled as he spat a curse behind his mask. He wanted to press on. The palace was no more than a handful of hours away, but resistance from the roaming warbands was intense. With another squad of Astartes, just five more men, he'd have taken the chance. But alone, it was suicide.

'What's that noise?' Toma said.

Argo levelled his bolter. He'd heard it, too. Drums. The music of primitives, echoing across the city like the pounding heartbeat of an angry god.

'It's a warning.'

The Imperial Guard advanced that night, and the weather turned bitter as if the heavens recognised the humans' intent.

Basilisks softened up the way ahead with relentless bombardments each hour. Ulviran was content to endure this halting advance, frequently cutting forward progress to establish another artillery barrage that took an age to set up. He pored over maps and holo-displays in his Baneblade's command room as Imperial guns pounded their own city into dust.

The big push consisted of the surviving elements of the Radimir Third Rifles, Seventh Irregulars and Ninth Armoured. These were the so-called 'Revenants,' named for the many times Radimir had replaced entire regiments due to losses against the greenskins in Segmentum Tempestus. Rebirth at the precipice of extinction was a blessing familiar to the Crimson Fists, and the Chapter had fought well with the soldiers of Radimir countless times across the centuries.

Hundreds of Guardsmen clad in the gunmetal grey of the Radimir Revenants marched alongside rattling Sentinels in the vanguard of the assault, flanked by Leman Russ battle tanks in half a dozen variants. Radimir was close to being a forge world in terms of its armoured exports. No Revenant regiment ever went to war short of armour support.

The bulk of Ulviran's forces followed the vanguard: six thousand men including a detachment of storm troopers serving as his ceremonial guard, riding alongside his Baneblade in eight black-painted Chimeras.

At the rear of this main force came the artillery: Griffons and Basilisks, their punishing guns stowed and locked until the next time Ulviran brought the column to a halt and ordered them to set up a shelling storm kilometres ahead.

Last of all came the rearguard, made of the lord general's veteran Guard squads interspersed with auxiliary units, medical transports and supply trucks.

The Fists' Thunderhawk gunship remained back at the abandoned base camp at the city's edge, ready to be summoned. For a short while, until Argo scattered them, Squad Demetrian marched in the vanguard of the force, forming the vicious tip of the Imperium's conquering blade. In scything rain and howling winds, as the elements battered down upon the miserable Imperial advance, the war to retake Southspire began. The Fists soon bled away into the night, leaving Argo alone.

Major Dace, who had been present in the Baneblade's command room when Argo reported the Fists' scouting run, couldn't resist voxing the Chaplain now. Argo's suit insulated him from the noise of the rain slashing against his ceramite armour, and he tensed his throat to activate his vox-bead as it chimed.

'Brother-Chaplain Argo. Speak.'

'This is Major Dace of the Revenants.' Argo smiled as he heard the voice. The ritual processes that had moulded his body like clay, forming him into an Astartes, had given him a memory close to eidetic. It was known by most Imperial commanders who worked with Astartes that Space Marines possessed preternatural capacities for instant recollection.

'Have we met?' Argo asked with his half-smile in place. He didn't let his amusement leak into his voice. It had the desired effect; Dace's feathers were ruffled.

'I don't see your foretold resistance, Brother-Chaplain. All is quiet on the advance, is it not?'

'I can still hear the drums,' Argo noted. And he could, setting a distant rhythmic percussion to the thunder grinding across the sky.

'I can't,' Dace said.

'You are comfortably hidden in a tank, major.' Argo closed the link and added, 'And you are only human.'

The Fists had been killing greenskins their entire unnaturally long lives. Ulviran, no stranger to the orkish hordes himself, trusted Argo's belief that the drums pounded as a challenge to the Imperials. The new warlord, a curse upon his black heart, knew they were coming, and the drums of war beat to show he welcomed the coming bloodshed. The storm swallowed their noise now. Only the Astartes could make it out, and it was dimmed even to their senses.

'Ulviran to all units,' crackled the lord general's hourly message. 'Dig in for bombardment. Shelling to commence in thirty minutes.'

Argo bit back a curse. Too slow, much too slow. His thoughts were plagued by the Thunderhawk full of digging equipment back at the base.

'Brother-Chaplain?'

The communication rune that flashed on his reddish lens display was, thankfully, not Dace. Imrich's vital signs registered as almost a kilometre ahead.

'How goes the scouting, Brother Imrich?'

'Lord,' Imrich responded, speaking quietly and clearly. 'I've found the kine.'

'So have I, sir.' This was Vayne, a kilometre to the west.

'Contact,' voxed Demetrian. His readouts pinned him in the south.

Argo looked over his shoulder, at the procession of ocean-grey tanks with rain sluicing off their hulls.

'Numbers?' he asked them all over the squad's shared channel. The weather was banishing vox integrity, masking all the words in a haze of crackles and hisses.

'I count over a thousand, easily,' Vayne said. 'Perhaps two.'

'Same,' added Demetrian.

'I've got more. I've got lots more.' Imrich sounded overjoyed. But then, knowing Imrich, he probably was. 'Twice that number, I'm sure of it. If we hear from Toma,' Imrich added, 'we're in a world of trouble.'

The Deathwatch specialist had been sent to the south, stalking a good distance behind the rearguard.

The vox clicked live again. 'Brother-Chaplain, come in.' said Toma. The rest of his message was cut off by Imrich's delighted laughter.

With a cold feeling of metallic-tasting finality in his throat, Argo voxed the lord general.

Ulviran listened without hesitation. He ignored Dace's complaints and pulled the column into a still-advancing defensive spread that, admirably, took less than half an hour to form. No small feat for that many soldiers and vehicles. The organisational aspects of war were where Ulviran most prided himself. An orderly army was a victorious one. The faster orders were obeyed, the more men survived. It was a simple mathematic he liked, and had a talent for putting it into practice.

'The shelling,' Argo voxed to him, 'is doing nothing. The warlord has put significant force into the city against us, and the horde ahead is falling back to draw us in.'

Ulviran glared down at the hololithic display of the city projected onto the large table. His Baneblade rumbled as it rolled on.

'We're surrounded.'

'If we stop now, lord general, we will be. The pincers will close around us the moment we halt. If we push on at speed, we can make it to the Cantorial Palace and engage the forward elements before the rest of the noose can close around our throats.'

Ulviran liked that. Turn the ambush into an attack.

'Strike first, strike hard, and prepare to repel the rest of the attackers once the main force is crushed.' It sounded good. It sounded right. But...

'I am going purely on your word for this, Brother-Chaplain.'

'Good,' the Astartes replied, and ended the link.

'The Cantorial Palace?' voxed Demetrian.

'Yes. Squad, form up. We're taking the prize.'

The Cantorial Palace had been the seat of the planetary governor, and a masterpiece of gothic design; as skeletally, broodingly Imperial as would be expected.

All that remained was a series of shattered walls and a small mountain of rubble, where once battlements and ridged towers had risen around a central bastion. The previous greenskin warlord had claimed it as his lair, until the Crimson Fists had dissuaded him of the notion four months ago. Refuting his claim of ownership involved razing the building to the ground with infiltrating sappers, and even then, the gigantic xenos clad in its primitive power armour had survived to claw itself free from the smoking rubble.

Imrich had battled the warlord in the stone wreckage, finally taking its head after a long and bloody duel. He wore Warlord Golgorrad's skull on his bandolier, giving it pride of place on his chest.

The ork forces of this nameless new warlord evidently favoured the former site of battle. It was to be the anvil upon which the Imperial forces would be crushed by the flanking hordes.

Ulviran's army did not march sedately to a doom surrounded by foes. Time was of the essence, and the Revenants powered on to meet the larger force ahead. Men held to the side of speeding tanks and rode atop vehicle roofs. Within the hour, the Guard spilled with overwhelming force into the great plaza district where the Cantorial Palace's bones jutted from the ground.

The armoured fist of the Revenant advance crashed into the scattered greenskin lines. Rubble rained down as tanks unleashed the fury of their cannons, and a staccato chorus of heavy bolter fire filled the air between the thunder of main guns. Lacking entrenchments, the orks counter-charged the armoured column, finding walls of Imperial Guard coming to meet them. Las-fire sliced across the night, illuminating the battlefield like some hellish pre-dawn in scarlet sunlight.

The rain lashed down on troopers in cold-weather gear as they fired in disciplined ranks, and the orks still came on in a roaring wave that drowned out the sound of thunder above.

Imperial records came to know this battle as the Night of the Axe, when the Radimir regiments on Syral were decimated by the hordes of xenos creatures they faced. Losses stood at forty-six per cent, utterly damning Lord General Ulviran's planned big push to face the new warlord that still lay in wait on the other side of the city. The Guard was bloody and beaten, and although thousands survived the assault, it was nowhere near enough to storm the warlord's position with any hope of success. The Radimir's one slim hope of survival on the kine-infested world – to strike the warlord down and cast the hordes into disarray – was gone. In turning the ambush into an attack of their own, the Guard had delayed their destruction but not avoided it.

However, for the purposes of the Crimson Fists, the Night of the Axe was neither the most critical juncture in the war for Syral, nor was it even recorded in their rolls of honour despite the harvest of lives reaped by Squad Demetrian of the Fifth Company.

The Fists, in true Astartes autonomy, had a sacred duty of their own to perform. This came to light the following morning, as the broken Guard made to move on from the scene of slaughter.

* * *

The sector was a mess of bloodshed and battle fallout. The corpses of thousands of orks and humans lay scattered over a square kilometre of annihilated urban terrain. The air thrummed with the growl of engines, frequently split by the cries of wounded men ringing out as they were tended by medics or died in agony, unfound among the charnel chaos that littered the ground.

Argo walked among the dead, gladius plunging down to end the lives of any greenskins that still drew breath. He listened to the general vox-channel as he performed his bloody work, making a mental note of casualties suffered by the Guard. He knew they were sure to be destroyed if they pressed on to face the warlord, just as surely as they'd be destroyed when the warlord's armies came hunting for them. He felt a moment of pity for the Guard. The Revenants were brave souls who'd always stood their ground in the face of the enemy. It was a shame to see them expire like this, in utter futility.

But the Fists would be long gone by then.

As he approached the edge of the colossal vista of rubble that made up the bones of the Cantorial Palace, he activated his vox and sent the signal he'd ached to send since his arrival. A single acknowledgement blip was the only answer he received, and the only answer he required.

Squad Demetrian stood a short distance from the lord general's Baneblade, honouring their wargear through daily prayer and muttered rituals. There they remained, ignoring the Guard all around, until thrusters shrieked in the sky above.

'What in the name of hell is that doing here?' Lord General Ulviran asked Major Dace as they looked up at the dark shape coming in to land with a howl of engines. The two officers left the cooling shadows of the command tank and approached the Astartes. Behind the warriors, throwing up a blizzard of dust, their Thunderhawk kissed the rubble-strewn ground and settled on its clawed stanchion feet.

'Are you leaving?' Ulviran demanded of Argo, aghast as he shouted above the cycling-down engines.

'No.'

'Then what–'

'Move aside, lord general,' the Chaplain said. 'We need room for our equipment. And if you would be so kind as to move your Baneblade, it would be appreciated.'

Dace, a short and rotund example of Radimir manhood, drew himself up to his unimpressive full height. 'We move out within the hour! You can't do… whatever it is you're doing.'

'Yes,' Argo said, 'I can.' His skullish helm glared down at the fat man. 'And if you try to stop me, I will kill you.'

To his credit, Dace did a fine job at appearing unmoved by the vox-growled threat.

'We have orders from Segmentum Command, and the Crimson Fists must abide by them.'

'That's an amusing fiction,' Argo smiled, knowing the humans couldn't see his expression. 'Feel free to entertain that fantasy as you get out of our way.'

Ulviran looked stricken, like he'd just taken a gut wound. He watched in mute sickness as servitors and robed serfs unloaded portable industrial equipment down the Thunderhawk's ramp.

'If you do not move aside,' Argo said with false patience in his voice, 'the Thunderhawk lander coming from orbit with more equipment will be forced to destroy your Baneblade to make room to land.'

'Equipment?' Dace was indignant. 'For what?'

It was Ulviran who answered. He'd seen the drills and clawed scoops on the machinery being unloaded.

'Digging...' The lord general's face was wrinkled in thought.

Argo favoured the officers with a bow. 'Yes. Digging. Now move aside, if you please.'

Defeated and confused, the two men backed away. Dace was red-faced and scowling, Ulviran subdued and voxing orders to make room for further Astartes landings.

When the Guard left just under an hour later, three Thunderhawks were nested in the ruins of the Cantorial Palace, each one freed of its cargo of servitors, serfs and machinery.

'They're heading west,' Imrich nodded towards the rolling Guard column.

'Then they'll die well,' the Chaplain snapped, and his hand cut through the air in a gesture to the work crews.

Drills ground into stone, scoops clawed piles of rubble aside, and the slaves of the Crimson Fists Chapter began to dig.

It took three days to make the first discovery.

By this time, the Guard was nearing the edge of Southspire, mere hours from their final encounter with the greenskin warlord. The Fists remained at the Cantorial Palace, silently admiring the Revenants' decision to die on the offensive, rather than retreat and die in their makeshift fort-camp.

Three days had passed since the Guard rolled out.

Three days of random sieges and petty assaults punctuating the sunlit hours and the long nights. Although the orks had been crushed in the area, wandering bands of savages still attacked the Crimson Fists' position. Each of the attempts made by the snorting, roaring mobs were met with torrents of heavy bolter fire from the grounded Thunderhawks and the seasoned killing prowess of Squad Demetrian as they maintained a perimeter vigil day and night, never resting, never sleeping.

On the evening of the third day, as the dull sun fell below the horizon, one of the serfs cried out. He'd found something, and the Astartes came running.

The first boy was dead.

His Scout's armour was largely intact, as was his body. Vayne was the one to lift the corpse from its rubble grave, treating it with all due honour as he laid it out on the ground by the first Thunderhawk. Argo came over once the examinations were complete to intone the Rite of Blessed Release. He knelt by the body, pressing his slit palm to the slain boy's forehead and leaving a smear of blood that mixed with the dirt on the child's dusty face.

'Novice Frael,' Vayne consulted his narthecium, tapping at the keypad as he examined the readout. 'Age thirteen, initial stages of implantation.'

'There's very little decay,' Argo observed in a soft voice.

'No. Blood and tissue samples indicate he died three or four days ago. My guess would be the day before we arrived.'

'Four months,' Argo whispered, looking back over the rubble. 'He was under there for *four months*, and we were three days too late. That...'

'What?' Vayne closed his narthecium and reset the data display. Surgical cutting tools snicked back into his bracer.

'That isn't... fair,' Argo finished. He knew how foolish the words sounded.

'If he'd been fully human,' Vayne said, 'he'd have died in the first two weeks. Thirst. Starvation. Trauma. It was a miracle his initial implantations even allowed him to survive this long. Almost sixteen weeks, Argo. That's worthy of the rolls of honour itself.'

They'd avoided discussing the odds up until now. It was a mission none of the squad expected to fulfil with anything approaching glory.

'Sixteen weeks.' Argo closed his eyes, though his helm stared at Vayne, its gaze unbroken.

'Even without the sus-an membrane,' Vayne was tapping keys on his narthecium bracer, 'our physiology will allow the slowing of the metabolism and the near-cessation of many bio-functions. It is still within the edge of prospective boundaries that an Astartes from the gene-seed of Rogal Dorn could survive the duration.'

Argo nodded. Full Astartes could survive, could *potentially* survive. That, however, wasn't the true issue. The Chaplain looked over his shoulder, where the corpse of the young novice lay.

'Kine,' snapped the vox. 'Kine at the south perimeter.'

Argo and Vayne were already running. 'That's penance for you, Imrich.'

'Yes, Brother-Chaplain. I'll do it right after we kill these whoreson aliens who've taken such umbrage at my trophies.'

The second body was discovered fifty metres away, two hours later. It was a dry husk, deep in waterless decay, and it took Vayne several minutes to identify the corpse as Novice Amadon, age fifteen, at the secondary stage of Astartes implantation.

'He's been dead for months,' Vayne said, without needing to point out the crushed ribcage and severed right leg. Scraps of Scout armour still clung to the dry fleshy remnants. 'He was killed when the palace fell.'

The Chaplain was conducting the funerary rite on Novice Amadon when the first survivor was found.

'Argo,' the vox crackled live with Vayne's excited voice. 'Blood of the primarch, Argo, come over here now.'

Argo clenched his teeth. 'A moment, please.' He pressed his cut palm to the ruined corpse's skull.

'Argo, *now*.'

The Chaplain forced his twin hearts to slow in their beat as he suppressed his eagerness and finished the rite. Such things were a matter of tradition.

Such things mattered, and the dead must be respected for their sacrifice. After what seemed an age, he rose to his feet and moved over to where Vayne and Demetrian were helping the survivor from the rubble.

His targeting reticule outlined the figure in a flash, indicating a failed lock-on. A runic symbol flashed onto his retinas. Gene-seed failsafe. Target denied.

The figure was bone-thin, on shaking legs. Argo's lens display conceded to a passive lock on the emaciated wraith, and at first all he saw was the digital displays of low-pulsing life signs under the figure's name. He couldn't believe anyone, even an Astartes, could be that weak and still live.

The name registered at last, a moment before Vayne and Demetrian brought the figure close enough to recognise. Hollow-cheeked, sunken-eyed and looking more dead than alive, the older Astartes grinned when he saw Argo. The Chaplain didn't miss the resemblance between the survivor's wasted face and his own skull helm.

'Who have you found?' Imrich voxed, sounding annoyed to be missing the discovery.

Argo tried to speak but couldn't form the words. It was Vayne who answered.

'Nochlitan. We found Scout-sergeant Nochlitan.'

The skeletal figure, the sergeant responsible for training both Argo and Vayne in the same squad, kept grinning as he took in the hulking form of Argo's black battle armour.

'Hello, my boy,' Nochlitan said, and his voice was strong despite a scratchy edge and the veteran's shivering limbs. 'You took your damn time.'

'We... We didn't know...'

'I can see why they made you a Chaplain with oratory like that.' The sergeant paused to cough, a dry rasp of a sound that brought blood to his lips. 'Now stop standing around slack-jawed and save the rest of my boys.'

Three of them had survived. Three of the ten.

It was enough to justify the mission – far more than enough. A single Fist novice would have justified the risk. For four months they had survived in the rubble, and they each emerged as wasted husks, life-signs barely flickering on Vayne's narthecium. Nochlitan was the only one with the power of speech remaining to him. The two novices, in their ruined armour, were little more than tangles of withered limbs, barely breathing, drifting in and out of silent delirium.

The squad had been entombed since the Cantorial Palace had fallen. Nochlitan's Scout squad were embattled in the undercroft as the explosives ticked towards detonation, and had been unable to escape the blast area.

Seven dead. Three alive. A small but blessed victory, torn from the jaws of catastrophe.

As the servitors stored the digging equipment and the serfs readied the Thunderhawks for orbital flight, Argo sat with Nochlitan in the modest apothecarion. Vayne tended to the two novices, neither one older than sixteen.

'Dorn's holy hand,' Nochlitan said, fixing the Chaplain with his grey eyes. 'What happened to Vayne?'

'A daemon.'

'Is it dead?'

'Of course it's dead.'

'Yes, of course. You see that one there?' Nochlitan waved a weak hand in the direction of the stretcher next to him. 'That's Novice Zefaray.'

Zefaray wheezed into a rebreather mask that covered half of his face. Lines of angry tissue marked his temples and neck, where veins stood out like lightning streaks.

Argo watched the boy's laboured breathing. Zefaray was the Scout squad's Epistolary candidate, marked by the Chapter Librarium for the power of his psychic gift.

'He will be greatly honoured by Chapter Master Kantor for this,' the Chaplain said.

'Damn right he will. Almost killed him, you know. Day and night, screaming into the warp and hoping one of the Librarium would hear. We were trapped close to one another. He would whisper and mutter, speaking of how he was riding a hundred minds to reach one we could trust so many systems away.'

Argo didn't know what to say. It was a psychic feat of incredible strength. When one of the Chapter's Epistolaries had reported the weak yet crazed contact, it had been all the incentive the Chapter's highest echelons had needed. A recovery operation was mounted immediately.

'Great things ahead for him,' Nochlitan grinned. 'Did you find my bolter, boy?'

They hadn't. It showed on Argo's face.

'Ah, well.' Nochlitan lay back on the stretcher, plugged into an array of tubes and wires. 'I'll miss that weapon, without a doubt. It was a fine gun. A fine gun. I killed a genestealer patriarch genus with that bolter. Tore its head clean off.'

'We'll be taking off in a few minutes. The *Vigil* waits in orbit. Once aboard, we make haste to Rynn's World as soon as we break away from Syral.'

Nochlitan sat up again, trembling and overtaxing his remaining strength as his glare speared Argo's eyes.

'You told me the Radimir were still here. Still advancing on this new warlord.'

'They are. They'll engage the enemy's main force this afternoon, if initial projections were correct.'

'You'd abandon the Revenants? Boy, what's wrong with you?'

'Please don't call me "boy", sir. Chapter Master Kantor–'

'Pedro Kantor, blessings upon my old friend, isn't here, my boy. You are. And by Dorn's holy hand, you want to face the Emperor one day knowing you ran from this fight?'

'The odds are... beyond overwhelming. Everything we came to achieve would be void if we die in this battle.'

Nochlitan grasped at Argo's bracer, clenching the smooth black ceramite in a thin-fingered claw that shook as if palsied.

'You are the future of this Chapter.' His grey eyes were the colour of summer storms. 'You shape the path these novices will one day walk.'

Argo rose to his feet, letting his mentor's hand slip from his arm, and left the room without a word.

The Thunderhawk screamed across the night sky, its downward thrusters kicking in as it hovered four hundred metres high. Its wing-mounted bolters aimed at the ground, barking in an unremitting stream. The servitors slaved to the weapons didn't even need to aim. They couldn't miss the horde below: a sea of green skin and chattering weapons, ringing a diminished cluster of grey.

The Revenants' last stand.

The guns cut out after a minute, autoloaders cycling but not opening fire again. On the ground, the armoured divisions of the Radimir kept up their onslaught against the ork host in the city's ruins, and Ulviran watched the Crimson Fist gunship as it stayed aloft, out of enemy fire range.

'It's the Fists,' Dace said, and Ulviran smiled to himself at the man's painfully obvious statement. *Good old Dace. No better man to die with.*

'We did well, Dace. Almost reached that bastard warlord, eh?'

'We did fine, sir.' The major was still looking up at the sky, ignoring the war hammering around him.

'So what are the Fists doing, exactly?' the lord general asked. 'My eyes aren't what they once were.'

'They're...'

Argo's lens displays registered the altitude as he fell. The ground soared up fast in his red-tinted vision, and he clutched his sword and bolter tightly, blink-clicking the propulsion icon at the edge of his sight. The weighty jump pack on his back fired in a roaring kick, slowing his descent, but he still landed with jarring force ahead of the others.

He hit the ground running and his weapons sang. Left and right, he slashed his gladius into flesh and fired a relentless stream from his bolter, clearing a space around him in the thick of the churning orkish tide.

Toma was next, thudding to the ground and repeating Argo's lethal sprint. Then Demetrian, then Vayne. Imrich was last, much to his gall. The others, whirling and killing, heard his curses as they started without him.

Twenty metres ahead of them through the ocean of writhing orkish flesh, unmistakeable in salvaged armour that swelled his form to the size of an Astartes Dreadnought, was the greenskin warlord.

Imrich landed and opened up his bolter, running for the brute.

'He's mine!' he voxed to the others. 'That skull is mine!'

In two gauntleted fists, one red, one black, the ancient weapon *Traitor's*

Bane was wreathed in coruscating waves of sparking force. The relic mace smashed aside three orks in a single swing, sending their broken forms to the ground still twitching with energy.

'No.' Argo stopped screaming the Litanies of Hate, drawing breath to reply to Imrich and the squad behind him.

'The kine lord is *mine*.'

ABOUT THE AUTHORS

Dan Abnett has written over fifty novels, including the acclaimed Gaunt's Ghosts series and the Ravenor, Eisenhorn and Bequin books. His work for the Horus Heresy includes the first book in the series, *Horus Rising,* and the three-volume-long conclusion, *The End and the Death.* He also wrote several novels in between: *Legion, The Unremembered Empire, Know No Fear, Prospero Burns* and *Saturnine.* He scripted *Macragge's Honour,* the first Horus Heresy graphic novel, as well as numerous Black Library audio dramas. He recently penned the Warhammer 40,000 novel *HIVE,* as well as *Interceptor City,* the eagerly awaited sequel to fan-favourite *Double Eagle.* Dan lives and works in Maidstone, Kent.

Aaron Dembski-Bowden is the *New York Times* bestselling author of the Horus Heresy novels *Echoes of Eternity, The Master of Mankind, Betrayer* and *The First Heretic,* as well as the novellas *Aurelian* and *Prince of Crows* and the audio drama *Butcher's Nails,* for the same series. He has also written the Warhammer 40,000 novels *Spear of the Emperor* and *Ragnar Blackmane,* the popular Night Lords series, the Space Marine Battles book *Armageddon,* the novels *The Talon of Horus* and *Black Legion,* the Grey Knights novel *The Emperor's Gift* and numerous short stories. He lives and works in Northern Ireland.

Sandy Mitchell is the author of a long-running series of Warhammer 40,000 novels, short stories and audio dramas about the Hero of the Imperium, Commissar Ciaphas Cain. His other stories include 'A Good Man,' included in the *Sabbat Worlds* anthology, and several novels set in the Warhammer World. He lives and works in Cambridge.

MORE FROM BLACK LIBRARY

BRUTAL KUNNIN
by Mike Brooks

When Ufthak and his orks attack the forge world of Hephaesto, the last thing they want is to share the spoils with the notorious Kaptin Badrukk. But with armies to defeat and loot to seize, Ufthak's boyz might just need Badrukk's help – though that doesn't mean they can trust him…

An extract from
Brutal Kunnin
by Mike Brooks

It had been a weird trip through the warp.

Ufthak Blackhawk knew full well that there wasn't such a thing as a normal trip through the warp, because Gork and Mork had their own senses of humour and liked to mess with the boyz every now and then. He still remembered that time he'd ended up seeing out of his own kneecaps for a while. Then there were all the interesting things you might encounter on a space hulk, like those bugeye wotsits with different numbers of arms that moved like a cyboar on nitrous. That was the great thing about space hulks – never a dull moment. Even when you thought you'd killed everything on board, you'd probably still missed a bit. And even if you hadn't, odds were you'd still have some ladz with you to have a punch-up with if everything got too boring.

This journey, though, hadn't been on a space hulk; it had been on a humie vessel, one that Ufthak and his boyz had boarded and taken, and on which Da Boffin had installed and then activated a device he'd called Da Warp Dekapitator. This had caused a katastroffic warp implosion – which was apparently a good thing, although Ufthak thought that 'catastrophic' sounded like something that should be happening to someone else – and it had dragged not only the humie ship but also all the ork ships around it into the warp and along the path of its last jump, to arrive back where it had come from.

(There was also the part where most of the bodies of the dead humie crew had merged together into a reanimated mass of flesh and steel that hungered for ork blood, and also the screaming humie faces that ran around on varying numbers of insectoid legs and spat poison, but the boyz had needed something to keep their spirits up on the way.)

Now they'd reached their destination, and had emerged from the warp again with nothing more than the sudden but quickly fading sensation that Ufthak's skeleton wasn't where it was supposed to be. And what a destination it was.

'Dat planet,' Mogrot Redtoof said, looking out of a viewport, 'is made of metal.'

Ufthak nodded sagely. Back before they'd boarded the humie ship, he and Mogrot had been rivals – two warriors jockeying for position under the command of Badgit Snazzhammer. Thanks to a series of events involving a large robot, several fatalities and a head transplant courtesy of Dok Drozfang, Ufthak's undamaged head had ended up on the decapitated Snazzhammer's undamaged and significantly larger body. After a brief meeting of the minds via a headbutt, Mogrot had settled back into a role as Ufthak's right-hand ork. That didn't mean that Ufthak trusted him, of course, but at least he was fairly certain Mogrot wouldn't try to shank him unless he was already wounded.

'Looks like a humie mekboy place,' Ufthak said. 'Humie mekboy ship, coming from a humie mekboy planet. Makes sense to me.'

'Why do dey do dat, anyway?' Mogrot asked. 'Make dere planets all shiny so ya know dey've got flashy stuff ya might want, and den when ya go to get it, dey get all annoyed an' try to kill ya?'

'Dat's da problem wiv humies,' Ufthak opined knowingly. 'Dey ain't logickal.'

'Boss!'

The shout came from the other side of the bridge, where Ufthak and his ladz had taken up residence after they'd tossed out the corpses of the crew formerly stationed there. Ufthak clumped across the deck, absent-mindedly twirling the Snazzhammer as he went. It had been Badgit's weapon, a two-handed affair as tall as a humie with its legs still attached, with an electrified hammer on one side of the head and a choppa blade on the other. He was starting to get used to the feel of it now, and couldn't wait to krump a few more enemies with it.

'Wot?' he demanded, coming up alongside Deffrow. The other ork pointed with the few fingers that remained on his right hand, having blown most of them off by hitting a humie with a stikkbomb.

'Look at dat, boss! Dat ain't one of ours!'

Ufthak sucked his breath in through his teef as a jagged piece of darkness eclipsed the stars. The ships that made up the Waaagh! fleet of Da Meklord – Da Biggest Big Mek, and a warboss in his own right – were many and varied, but Ufthak was familiar with them, and Deffrow was correct: that wasn't one of theirs. Impressive though Da Meklord's flotilla was, none of them looked quite that... killy.

'Dat's *Da Blacktoof*,' Ufthak said in something close to wonder, as the shape of it became clear. It was a monstrous kill kroozer, bristling with guns and ordnance. And there, leering down at them from under the prow, was a single, huge glyph: a monstrous, one-eyed ork skull, with crossed bones behind it. 'Dat's Kaptin Badrukk's ship.'

The rest of his mob made suitably impressed noises. Badrukk was a legend across the galaxy, a freebooter of infamy and renown, and his presence here surely meant that Da Meklord's own star was in the ascendancy.

Assuming, of course, that Badrukk was here because Da Meklord had arranged for him to be. If not...

'Message from da boss!' Da Boffin shouted, bursting into the bridge in a gust of fumes. At some point in the past, Da Meklord's favourite spanner had, either due to injury or simple curiosity, replaced his legs with a gyro-stabilised monowheel, and as a result he was now both much faster than a normal boy, and spectacularly poor at navigating stairs. 'All nobs are to get over to *Mork's Hammer* right now!'

Mork's Hammer was Da Meklord's flagship, and Da Meklord only called his nobs and bosses together if he had something very important to say... or, alternatively, if he wanted to yell at them all. As a new nob, Ufthak had never attended one of these Waaagh! meets before. His chest swelled with new-found pride, and he slung the Snazzhammer over his shoulder as he turned on the spot.

'Right den!' He frowned, as a thought struck him. 'Wait a minute. Do da 'Ullbreakers go backwards?' He and his mob had arrived via boarding pods, which were still locked into the side of the humie ship after they'd broken through its ferrous hide.

Da Boffin shook his head. 'Nah. Dey got just one gear – go.'

'So how're we s'posed to get back over dere, den?' Ufthak demanded. What was the good in being a nob if you couldn't go listen to your boss telling you what he wanted you to go and stomp?

Da Boffin shrugged. 'Da humies have shuttles on dis fing. We'll nick one.'

Ufthak frowned at him suspiciously. 'You know how to fly one?'

'Can't be hard,' Da Boffin grinned. 'After all, humies can do it.'

The Waaagh! room of *Mork's Hammer* was crowded with orks mashed in shoulder to shoulder. Ufthak saw many faces he recognised and many more that he didn't, because every single ork of any authority under Da Meklord's command was here. Surly, black-clad Goffs glowered at camouflaged Blood Axes and blue-painted Deathskulls, while the stench of fuel from the Evil Sunz was almost overpowered, but instead just sickeningly offset, by the smell of squig dung that accompanied the Snakebites. However, most numerous by far were the yellow and black colours of the Bad Moons, which wasn't only Ufthak's clan, but also that of Da Meklord himself. They were smartest, the richest and the flashest clan of all, and the reason why the Tekwaaagh! had risen so quickly and so unstoppably. Sure, the Evil Sunz might drive a bit faster, and the Blood Axes might be a bit sneakier, but if you wanted the ladz with the best guns, you wanted Bad Moons.

This many orks in such close proximity was a pretty good recipe for a massive fight, especially given the egos involved. Ufthak could see the huge, horned helm and multiple back banners of Drak Bigfang, the Goff warboss; the collection of junk and scavenged armour plates under which was Gurnak Six-Gunz, the self-proclaimed SupaLoota of the Deathskulls; and the fur-clad bulk of Da Viper, the Snakebite Overboss, whose gargantuan squiggoth was so large it allegedly had a hold all to itself in his kroozer. Any of these orks were capable of leading a Waaagh! in their own right, but no one was starting any trouble worse than jostling their neighbour a bit. No one wanted to end up like Oldfang Krumpthunda, who'd taken Da Meklord on one on one and had been... Well, no one was quite sure *what* he had been, other than it involved getting hit with Da Meklord's shokkhammer and then ending up in lots of very small pieces in very different places. Some of the boyz said they were still finding bits of him in the stew, now and then.

Horns blared, a brassy note of challenge and conquest, and everyone shut their gobs and snapped their heads around to look at the dais built at the far end. Part of the wall behind it had been turned into a massive effigy of the face of Mork – or possibly Gork, but Ufthak reckoned it was Mork – and this was now yawning wider and wider as the mighty lower jaw dropped away. Steam and smoke gushed forth, obscuring the dais but accentuating the piercing red glare of the eyes lurking near the ceiling.

Then, first as a looming shadow in the murk, and then as a mighty figure resplendent in his yellow-and-black mega armour, Da Meklord emerged from the mouth of a god.

He was a titanic figure, and that wasn't just down to the size of his armour. Ufthak's new body was large enough that he was a head taller than most of the mob under his command, but Da Meklord would have towered over him had they stood next to each other. He made ordinary orks look like grots. His mega armour made him nearly as wide as he was tall, and the bosspole rising up above his head and carrying his personal glyphs and banners added another dimension of awe to his appearance. Half of the overlarge skull that housed his enormous brain was plated in metal; in his left hand he held the shokkhammer, and his right hand disappeared somewhere into the gigantic mess of barrels, ammo feeds and coolant pipes that formed his kustom supa-shoota.

'ALRIGHT, LISSEN UP!'

The assembled nobs quietened down a bit more, each one intimidated into silence by his stentorian bellow. Ufthak stood as straight and tall as he could, to try and make sure his face was visible, even though he was standing quite far back and there were other, bigger orks with more impressive weapons and armour between him and his warboss. There was something intangible about Da Meklord that grabbed a lad by the throat, focused his attention and drove it home to him that this ork, *this* ork, was one who knew where he was going, and on whom glory and renown would be showered.

'Da humies call dis world "Hephaesto",' Da Meklord rumbled. 'Dere's a lot of 'em down dere. Da red-robe types, da ones what look like Evil Sunz, but squishier.'

A bubble of laughter ran through the assembled nobs, save for the Evil Sunz present, who were doing their best to look like they weren't glowering.

'Dey've prob'ly got a lot of interestin' tek, cos dose humies tend to,' Da Meklord continued. 'An' normally, I'd be sendin' all you down dere to get it, and kill 'em all. But dere's a little snag.'

Ufthak glanced sideways, and saw his own confusion mirrored on the other green-skinned faces around him. What could possibly be a snag to a Waaagh! as mighty as this one? Unless...

'See, some uvver gitz got 'ere first,' Da Meklord said. 'An' we could fight dem too, dat could be a good larf, but while we woz doing dat, da humies might get away, an' dat would just be a *waste*.'

Heads nodded. Humies weren't exactly a scarce resource, but you couldn't always rely on some being about when you wanted a scrap, so it made sense to use the ones that were here.

'I talked to–'

The temperature in the Waaagh! room plummeted. Ufthak could see his breath in front of his face, and faint tendrils of frost began to creep along the walls. Orks readied their weapons, unsure what was going on but ready to fight it, or, if no better options presented themselves, each other.

The air pressure increased rapidly, from unnoticeable to the point where Ufthak felt like something was pressing in on his eardrums. He shook his head and growled, trying to clear the sensation, but it persisted until–

Vorp!

A bubble of energy washed out from the other end of the dais to where Da Meklord was standing, sending the smoke of his entrance billowing, and incidentally knocking the fumes aside to give every ork in the room a clear view of...

Kaptin Badrukk.

The mightiest freebooter kaptin who'd ever lived. The hero of the War of Dakka, the Breaker of the Grand Guard, and the Plunderer of Tanhotep. He stood resplendent in his lead-lined greatcoat, his bald head crowned by his mighty bicorn, which was as tall as a well-fed grot and dripping with medals taken from the corpses of humie commanders. He was leaning casually on his longblade choppa, and had Da Rippa, a gun so radioactive its simple presence in a room practically constituted an aggressive act, tucked under his arm. He was flanked by three more Flash Gitz, each one imitating him so far as possible in their mode of dress and armament, but not coming close to rivalling his sheer ostentatiousness and utter gaudy magnificence. Lurking behind them all was an ork that had to be Badmek Mogrok, another Bad Moons big mek, who fought under Badrukk's banner and was undoubtedly the source of his teknologickal advances.

For the first time in his life, Ufthak Blackhawk laid eyes on an ork who might just be as impressive as Da Meklord.

'Ta-daaa!' Badrukk bellowed, as though he hadn't just tellyported into the middle of his rival's command structure, on his rival's warship. The sheer guts of the git was jaw-dropping.

Da Meklord turned towards Badrukk with a clank of metal and a hiss of pistons. He looked thoroughly unimpressed, but he hadn't powered up his supa-shoota or sent the triple heads of his shokkhammer whirling around each other, so violence wasn't imminent.

'Kaptin,' Da Meklord growled. 'I woz just telling da ladz about how we woz going to be havin'... a friendly kompetition.'

'Dat's right!' Badrukk beamed, showing more teef than it should have been possible to fit into one gob. 'Plenty of loot to go round down dere, I reckon. Of course, my ladz've had a bit of a head start, but dat should just help ya out! Cleared a few obstacles out da way, dat sort of fing.'

'So we're all gonna stomp da humies, an' take dere tek,' Da Meklord said. 'An' your boyz ain't gonna be shootin' mine in da back, right?'

'So long as yours don't shoot mine first,' Badrukk leered back at him. 'Dat would be a shame, when dere's so many humies to go round.'

'My forts exactly,' Da Meklord agreed. 'So we got a deal, den?'

'We got a deal,' Kaptin Badrukk said, nodding. 'Last one to da gubbinz mucks out da squiggoffs!' He clicked his fingers, and Mogrok did something.

A moment later the temperature dropped again, crackling energy surrounded the freebooterz for a second, and then they were gone once more, as abruptly as they'd arrived.

Da Meklord turned towards his assembled nobs.

'Get down dere, and wotever ya do, don't let dat git's boyz get to da good stuff before ya!' His face broke into a grin every bit as toofy and menacing as the one that had graced the freebooter kaptin's. 'I fink dere's gonna be a few "accidents" before we're done 'ere, so make sure yer aiming at Badrukk's ladz whenever ya fink yer gun might go off by mistake, like when dey'z between you and da best loot. Got it?'

Ufthak joined his voice to the others in a roar of assent to assure their warboss that they had indeed got it.

'Good!' Da Meklord drew himself up to his full, magnificent height, and filled his lungs.

'*Now get down dere, an' get fightin'!*'